PHARAOH

Eloise Jarvis McGraw

Coward-McCann, Inc.   New York

c. 4

© 1958 by Eloise Jarvis McGraw

Library of Congress Catalog
Card Number: 58-7007

MANUFACTURED IN THE UNITED STATES OF AMERICA

For my husband, William Corbin McGraw,
with my love and thanks

FOREWORD

THE germ of this story is a strange sequence of events which took place between 1510 and 1456 B.C.—nearly 3500 years ago. The trouble with events so distant is that all we have left of them is a skimpy residue of clues. We have evidence of happenings, but no records of them, and we can only guess at the human motives behind them. We have hints, sometimes provocative, sometimes baffling; but we have no facts.

Egyptologists have for years been piecing together such hints and clues in an attempt to arrive at a solution of the mystery of the Thutmosid succession, but each scholar's explanation differs from all the others. This book is not an attempt on my part to give yet another answer; if any Egyptologists are listening I beg them not to accuse me of rushing in where they themselves so warily tread. I am not saying, "This is how it happened." I am not even saying, "This is how it might have happened"—though for all anyone knows, it might. I am only saying, *"What if* it had happened this way?"

For the sequence of the succession, I have hewn to the line laid down by Winlock, Wilson, and Edgerton, who more or less agree in their interpretations of the clues, and whose research is not only authoritative but the most recent done on the subject. In building characters who would of their own accord behave in the curious manner in which the historical figures did, I have been in the position of an anthropologist trying to reconstruct a likeness of prehistoric man from the evidence of one lower left molar. Inevitably, I have had to rely largely upon imagination.

History, therefore, has served only as a springboard for a work of fiction. I cannot claim to have written truth; in fact, I wish to make very clear that I do not claim it. But within the limits of this novel and these characters, I hope I have written truly.

E. J. McG.

PART I

The First Day

THE river Nile had wrought its annual miracle in the land of Egypt. Urged by the prayers and incense of the people, cajoled by the incantations of the priests, the dead god Osiris had risen once more to bring life and the black mud of fertility to the land of his worshipers. Quietly but powerfully, through the burning summer, the waters had swelled and grown, spreading across the marshlands first a shining net, then an unbroken sheet of silver tarnished by the undulations of drowned grasses; the parched fields beyond had been engulfed, the great cracks covered and healed by the beneficent flood. Fish had played where next year's corn would sprout, villages had become islands, and the rats had gathered, homeless, on the dikes.

Now the cool north breeze of fall had come, and the waters were shrinking in their ancient rhythm. But a new flood had supplanted the old in the minds of the people—a wave of shock, of awe, of fear and deep uneasiness had broken over the land this twenty-fifth flood season of the reign of the Good God Thutmose the First. The very day the waters were at their height, there had been a hunting accident far off in the desert, and the broken body of Pharaoh's son—Amenmose the strong, the valiant, Prince of Egypt and chosen Successor to the throne—had been carried lifeless back to Thebes in the arms of his companions.

For days Egypt and the palace had lain stunned and silent under the catastrophe. Then the people, terrified for their own safety, had begun to murmur. The Successor was dead. Another must be named at once, for the gods were angry. Why did Pharaoh not speak, why did he not act? For long he had held Egypt's welfare like a jewel in his hand, guarding and protecting it with his divinity. Surely he would not abandon it now, surely he would not deliver his people into the hands of the angry gods! Let the great Horus cease weeping for his perished son, the people whispered. Let him name us another Successor!

He was growing old, the Good God in the palace. After twenty-five years on the throne of the Black Land the tie that bound him to the gods, the mysterious oneness which enabled him to breathe with their breath, think with their wisdom, endow Egypt with their plenty, was growing weak. There had been obvious indications of it, even before this last and most terrible occurrence. Had not the harvest last year been scant? Aye, and the wine imperfect, and the cattle thin and prone to lose their calves. Virtue had gone out of Pharaoh or these things would not have happened. His strength was leaving him too, if one believed a terrible rumor that had somehow escaped from the silence of the palace. It was said that when the Good God saw the body of his son borne in by the weeping nobles, he himself had turned pale as death, had clutched at his collarbone, and fallen forward into the royal steward's arms. Om, most terrible of omens! Men had been known to die, clutching their collarbones like that—

If Pharaoh died before naming a Successor . . . they dared not even think of it. None could mount the throne, then, until the Good God lay in his tomb. And he could not be carried to his tomb until his body had acquired immortality from seventy days in the vats of the embalmers. Seventy days it must float in the natron and spices, that it might never perish—but would not Egypt perish in the meanwhile, leaderless and unprotected, with no Strong Bull on the throne to order the winds and the sprouting of the grain, to propitiate the gods and breathe the Divine Fragrance into the nostrils of his people, that they might live?

Name us a Successor! prayed the people as their fear redoubled. Let Pharaoh name another Strong Bull, another Horus-in-the-Nest in place of the dead Amenmose, that we may not be left alone and desperate, at the mercy of demons! Let him name a new Successor!

At last the silence of the palace was broken, and a pronouncement came forth. Pharaoh had decreed that his Festival of Eternity, the rarely enacted Mystery of the Heb-Sed, would coincide with the coming New Year's rituals.

Heb-Sed! The people's fear was overlaid now with intense excitement. The market places and crooked streets of Thebes, the stalls of fishmongers and the villas of nobles hummed with talk of nothing else. Old men reminisced; children questioned shrilly. Word spread up and down the length of the Nile, from the Delta to the southernmost cataracts, drawing the people of Egypt together in a web of curiosity and awe. Many had never witnessed the Heb-Sed in their lifetimes. But all were agreed that there was hope now. Pharaoh was not abandoning his multitudes, he meant to weave anew the torn fabric of his divinity by enacting the most potent mysteries known to man. By means of the Heb-Sed he would half entice, half force the gods to make him one of them again. All was well, or at least all soon would be well—for at the end of the five days of the Heb-Sed he would surely name the new Successor.

Who would the Successor be? Their fear alleviated somewhat, they had time to think of that now, the merchants and barbers in the market places, the nobles in their villas. Their thoughts caused them to look doubtfully at one another from their painted eyes. Who could be the Successor, with Amenmose dead? Four children had the Great Royal Wife Aahmes borne to Pharaoh, and three of these, the infant prince Wadjmose, a daughter, Nefrubity, and now the valiant Amenmose, were in their tombs. There remained only a sixteen-year-old princess, Hatshepsut, and a maid could never wear the crown.

True, Pharaoh had a son by a lesser wife, the prince called Nenni—

Here they nervously avoided each other's eyes.

This Prince Nenni, objected the barber to the basketmaker, clearing his throat, this Tired One—in truth, one should say Prince Thutmose, as he had been named after his father the Strong Bull, but it was hard to remember, since he was called only Nenni, the Tired One—

If the barber would please to call him something, and get on with it, put in the potter.

The barber would be only too happy to get on with it, returned the other coldly, if the potter would refrain from further interruptions. As the barber was saying—was in truth remarking to the *basketmaker,* and no other—this Prince Nenni was not truly a royal prince. His mother was the Honorable Lady Mutnofret who was, if the barber knew his royalty, and he believed he did, probably better than some other people he could name—this Lady Mutnofret was merely the younger sister of Aahmes the Divine Consort, and in Aahmes' veins alone ran the ancient and holy blood of Re, the sun-god. Therefore this Prince Nenni, or as one really should call him, Prince Thutmose—

Would never have been chosen successor had Amenmose lived, rapped out the potter. Which everyone knew already.

However, put in the basketmaker delicately, it was most interesting to have it pointed out again, clarified in one's mind, so to speak, did not the potter agree?

The potter supposed he did. But it would be even more interesting to feel clarified on just what Pharaoh proposed to do about it. The prince was *not* truly royal—

True, true enough. The basketmaker nodded judiciously while his fingers flew in and out among his reeds, fashioning yet another piece of merchandise. Still, was that really a hindrance? This prince could be married to his royal half-sister Hatshepsut, who *had* inherited the ancient blood, and all would be in order. It was the obvious way out of the difficulty, the traditional way, the way that had been followed since ancient times whenever the rightful heir to the Double Crown had turned out to be a maid.

Quite so, wheezed the one-eyed onion seller, leaning from his stall. Had not the present Pharaoh, the Good God Thutmose I, mounted the throne in exactly the same manner? He had been merely a warrior-noble, raised to the status of king and god by his marriage to the royal Aahmes.

And, added the basketmaker, Thutmose had flourished like the palm, and conquered half the world for Egypt, and the land had prospered under his vigorous hand. Was it not so?

Aye, it was so, it was all so.

But this—this Prince Nenni, this Tired One whom one kept forgetting to call by his proper name though it certainly did not imply lack of respect, for the barber hoped that he was as pious as the next man and showed perhaps more respect toward royalty than most, knowing a bit more about the subject—

The potter hoped that Amon and all the other gods would

preserve him from long-winded talkers in the future! What in the name of Great Mother Nile was the barber trying to say?

That the gods and Great Mother Nile alike must frown on this prince, this Tired One, returned the barber, turning red in the face and growing more heated than was comfortable in Egypt at full noonday. Had they not struck him with fever and weakness from his childhood? The barber wished to appeal to the intelligence of his friends—which was to say, the basketmaker and the onion seller—and ask if they did not agree with what he was saying, if indeed they could hear what he was saying for the constant interruptions of less well-informed individuals who persisted in entering the conversation! He, the barber, must confess that he had grave doubts concerning this Nenni, quite aside from the matter of his inferior blood. Now, if the royal Hatshepsut had been a prince—

Ah, now the barber had said something—at last! If the princess had been a prince, they would almost have Amenmose back again. The potter had heard she was a regular whirlwind of a maid, her father's daughter in every way. It would be a strange marriage, to link the Tired One and that maiden. A wedding of the tortoise to the gazelle, the desert to the Nile.

Yet all royal marriages were strange, mused the onion seller, blinking his one eye. They married their sisters, the royal ones did, to keep the blood pure and the children truly royal. He was glad he was not royalty, was the onion seller. *His* sister had a wart on her nose and thighs like the hippopotamus.

Oh, well, if they were going to discuss thighs instead of blood strains, said the potter through the burst of laughter, that tavern maid at the Red Duck—

The conversation did not return to the subject of the Successor. The gods would decide it all anyway, the Good God in the palace would find a way. What did barbers and sellers of onions know of such matters? Be of good cheer, they bade each other as they parted, for the Heb-Sed approached and there would be feasting in the streets. . . .

But their eyes remained uneasy. Nenni, the Tired One. In the language of Egypt, "to be tired" meant also "to be dead."

There were uneasy eyes also among those who did know of such matters, and who had better reason than the barber to be concerned with royalty. At almost the same moment the potter was wishing he knew what Pharaoh proposed to do about Egypt's dilemma, three noblemen lunching together in the roof-pavilion of a rich villa in western Thebes were musing over a similar remark, just voiced by the host, Ineny, Chief Architect and Overseer of All the Works of the King.

"It is the uncertainty that plagues one," Ineny went on moodily, pushing the remains of his cake about on his plate as if he were angry at it. "Naturally we can guess what the Good God means to do—what he *must* do, if one faces facts. But I would give forty slaves to hear it from his own lips. It is unnatural, this —this reticence. . . . Has he said anything to you, Nehsi?"

The Royal Steward, Vizier of Egypt, called Nehsi, "the Negro," a grave, handsome black giant wearing a magnificent collar of silver and turquoises, shook his head slowly.

"Nor to me," sighed Thutiy, Royal Treasurer and Guardian of the Crowns. He scratched irritably under his elaborately curled wig, knocking it a little askew, then threw out both skinny hands in a gesture of despair. "The Heb-Sed he has discussed with me to the smallest and last detail. The building of the House of Reeds, the ordering of the shrines, the appointments, the offerings, the expenditures for incense and cattle—on these matters he speaks fully and precisely, as always. But of the Successor he has said not one word."

"It would be painful to him," said Nehsi softly.

"Aye, of course, painful to all of us." Ineny beckoned a slave to pour more wine, then waved him out of hearing. "Still, one word—it would so relieve the tension—"

"Pharaoh is Pharaoh," said the big black man. "He does as he wills. It is not for us to question."

A thoughtful silence fell upoon all three. Ineny, still pushing absently at the cake upon his plate, spoke at last. "Has the prince's child been born yet?"

"Child?" echoed Thutiy. "Oh, the babe of the harem woman. I have heard no tidings."

"It still delays," Nehsi told them.

Ineny shrugged and rose from his chair, strolling to the roof's edge to lean on the rail and stare down at the lawns and flower beds spread out below.

"You are thinking of the royal line, the future of the dynasty?" Nehsi asked him.

"Can one help it, when one thinks of Prince Nenni? I'll wager this child will be as the other one, a few years back. Do you remember? A little maid, sickly from birth, dead before it reached its sixth month—and its mother with it."

"The mother of this babe is said to be an exceptionally healthy young woman."

"So is the royal Hatshepsut. But even wed to her, could this prince produce sons for Egypt? Would they not be as that other child, sickly and—"

"It is not good to pry into the intentions of the gods," Thutiy interrupted. He pushed his chair back with a clatter and began to pace nervously about the pavilion. "Let us not search the future. Let us look no further than the great miracle of the Heb-Sed. It will restore the Good God to us in all his strength—"

"If it comes in time," Ineny said.

Thutiy halted his pacing; Ineny turned his back upon the beauty of his flower beds. Both eyed the royal steward, sitting so quiet and massive at the table where they had left him.

"Friend Nehsi," Thutiy began hesitantly. "Concerning that—that unfortunate occurrence at the time of Amenmose's death . . . or rather, at the moment when first his body was brought before Pharaoh's eyes—"

Nehsi looked up, guarded, grave.

Thutiy and Ineny exchanged an uncomfortable glance, and Ineny, moving to the table, leaned over it earnestly. "The royal treasurer and I—we are not motivated by idle curiosity, Excellency. We have never sought to pry into the affairs of the royal family. But when the Strong Bull of Egypt is stricken like any mortal before our eyes . . ."

"What is it you wish to know?" Nehsi asked quietly.

"If this seizure has been repeated since."

Nehsi turned his wine goblet slowly, fitting it into one and then another of the thin circles of moisture it had left on the table. "Aye," he said at last. "It has been repeated since."

"Great Amon be merciful!" Thutiy whispered.

"We have nothing to fear," Nehsi's deep, soft voice went on. "As you yourself said, the miracle of the Heb-Sed will restore the Strong Bull to the fullness of his strength and power, as in the days of his youth, when he led Egypt against the Hyksos. After the Heb-Sed all will be well, whoever the Successor."

A breeze stirred through the pavilion, ruffling the petals of the lotuses in their big bronze jar and causing the awning to flap briskly.

"Ah gods, may Amon hasten the day of Heb-Sed!" Ineny whispered.

As the day of the Great Jubilee slowly drew nearer, preparations on a vast scale were taking place throughout the length and breadth of Egypt. The great Temple of Amon, in Thebes, rang with the sound of hammers and hurried commands from dawn till dark as swarms of workmen transformed its huge courtyard into the mystic Court of the Festival. A hundred slaves toiled like busy ants, drawing the sledges that carried loads of mud-brick for the House of Reeds, the temporary palace where Pharaoh and the royal family would live for the five days of the festival. Gangs of basketmakers worked furiously constructing the archaic woven shrines, used only at the time of Heb-Sed, which would house the gods during their stay in Thebes. And in every city—in holy Abydos, where the head of the god Osiris was buried, in Elephant Island to the south and Menfe in the cool north, the priests were readying their gods for the long river journey.

All Egypt thought of nothing else—rumors were rife, chatter was unceasing, fear was strong. The stars were searched for omens, no fires were kindled before sundown, every man watched his actions lest ill luck strike. It was a time of great uneasiness. One terrifying day—the tenth before the Heb-Sed was to begin, when many of the barges of the gods had already started the hazardous journey to Thebes—black clouds covered over the bark of the sun-god, and the Nile fell from the skies, accompanied by a noise as of a thousand drums. The people moaned in terror and burned more incense; by morning the clouds were gone, but not their fear.

On the ninth day an old scribe in a village in the Delta, seeking a text to read that his young pupils might copy it out fair on their stucco-covered boards, opened by chance the scroll containing the Prophecies of Neferrohu, an ancient sage. Thoughtlessly he read it out:

"Up, my heart, and bewail this land whence thou art sprung. Behold, that which men dreaded now exists. Foes are in the east, and Asiatics descend into Egypt, and no protector hears. I show thee the land upside down; men shall make arrows of copper; they crave for the bread of blood, they laugh with the laughter of pain, there is none that weepeth for death; a man's heart careth only for himself, he sitteth in the corner careless while one man slayeth another—"

The old scribe broke off, trembling, and hoarsely ordered the staring little boys to wash clean their boards. Hastily he gave them another papyrus to copy, and leaning in the doorway of his school stared out at the swollen river, praying he had not invoked an evil omen.

Should Pharaoh die before the Successor is named, he told himself fearfully, Egypt would be so again, just as the Ancient One described it, for men would know nothing but panic and despair. . . .

The ninth day before the Heb-Sed passed, the eighth passed also, and the seventh. Many barges were on the river now, hung with golden cloth about the shrines of the gods they bore, moving slowly past villages and fields and ancient ruined temples while their priests chanted and perfumed the air with incense. Fishermen in their reed boats watched wonderingly, their nets dangling from their hands, their catch forgotten, as the Holy Ones passed by. Little boys ran shrieking along the banks until some bend in the river hid the glory from view.

In a papyrus cutter's hut in Buto, in the Delta, the family cat died, on the afternoon of the seventh day. At once the papyrus cutter was fetched from the marshes; amid wailing and prayers to Bast, the great cat-goddess, he shaved off his eyebrows and those of his wife and children, placed the cat in a box and hurried to the river, where he leaped into his little boat and paddled out furiously to hail the steersman of a passing cargo ship. "Stay a moment, comrade! I have a holy errand for you, if you be sailing southward."

The steersman peered down from his perch beside the great stern sweep, saw the fresh-shaved eyebrows, and frowned in alarm. "Your cat has died?" he shouted.

"Aye, and she must be buried in Bubastis, the Great Cat's city —will you not stop and take her?"

"Friend, what good would that do—now? The Great Cat journeys to Thebes for the Heb-Sed!"

"Bast is not in her temple?" cried the papyrus cutter.

"Her barge left the dock of Bubastis four days ago, I saw it with my own eyes. Amon have mercy on you in your misfortune, friend! Bury your cat where you found her lying, and burn incense—that is all I know to do."

Slowly the cargo ship pulled away upriver, leaving the small boat rocking in its wash, and the papyrus cutter sitting stunned and frightened, staring after it. Bast was not in her temple, but had journeyed far, far southward because of a great mystery called the Heb-Sed. The world was upside down.

The gods were not the only voyagers to Thebes. In the carpet-hung pavilions of their barks rich merchants and noblemen from the provinces sailed to the festival in luxury, towing slaves and cooks in the kitchen boats behind. Poor scribes and watchers of the stars bought passage on the Nile boats out of a burning desire for knowledge; artisans and carpenters out of a desire to share the feasting in the streets. And from all directions toward the City of God flowed the gifts with which Pharaoh would buy the favor of the gods—herds of cattle plodded southward from the king's vast estates in middle Egypt, lines of heavy-laden slaves toiled westward from the desert gold mines, boats rowed northward bearing jasper and turquoise from the quarries in the south.

On the fifth day before the festival, an old goldsmith knelt beside the basket-shaped furnace in his workshop in western Thebes, putting the finishing touches on a shining golden headdress shaped like the enfolding wings of the royal falcon. His pupils and apprentices stood in an awed semicircle around him, watching silently as the master worked, listening as he instructed them in his slow, old man's voice.

". . . and it must turn a dull red, not more—that is proper annealing. See it now, as I hold it in the flames . . . there! That is the color, you must learn that color well; you will never work your metal properly without annealing. Now then, to the stake with it, we must shape the falcon's wing a little more perfectly so that it will curve gently over the cheek of the royal Aahmes." The old man hobbled to his workbench, the pupils rearranging themselves about him and jockeying fiercely but in silence for position. Slipping the headdress over the shaping-stake he had used to form it, the goldsmith carefully selected a hammer from

18

the rack. "I choose the straight-faced hammer, but you should use the round, for it takes skill to strike with this one and not mar the gold." He struck a light blow on the wing's edge, and a dull *pang* sounded through the workshop. The old man glanced over his shoulder slyly. "Well, is that right? Have I done it well?"

"Nay, Master," the pupils murmured.

"Nay, I have done it ill. Now—" The smith lifted his elbow high, struck the helmet a sharp, true blow and the stake rang like music. *"That* is right. The ear must be alert, as well as the eye, and the hammer held just so. It must ring like the harpist's finest chord. . . . And now, fetch the golden serpent that I fashioned yesterday, and prepare the solder, for Aahmes the Queen will wear this headdress in the Procession of the Heb-Sed and the royal cobra must curve proudly above her brow."

In the barren valley behind the hills west of the city, three artists worked side by side in the underground chambers of Pharaoh's tomb, which had been building for years. The flickering light of the torches brought to glowing life the scene of the funeral procession which was nearing completion under their skillful brushes.

"The princess Hatshepsut," said one to the other, lovingly blacking in the hair of a graceful female figure, "I have heard she is the most beautiful of living women. I have been told that her hair is blacker than the night sky, her lips the color of scarlet sage, the flesh of her body pure gold."

"You had best stop mooning over the princess and attend to your painting," retorted the other. "Princesses are not for the likes of you."

"Is it a crime, then, merely to think of her? Men may think of goddesses. I will think of the princess."

"For my part, I would rather not think of one so far beyond my grasp," put in the third artist, gloomily putting the finishing touches on an eye. "Not that she is beautiful. I have it on good authority that she is plain as my own wife."

"May Amon throttle your homely wife, who has warts and a vicious tongue, and is not fit to be mentioned in the same breath as—"

"Silence, silence!" rang out the master's voice from the next chamber. He appeared in the doorway, scowling, glancing critically about the walls. Suddenly he turned ashen. "What have you done, you fools!" he cried hoarsely. "You have completed the paintings . . . not a hand but what is colored in, not an inch of the royal sarcophagus but what is gilded! Ah gods, may Osiris have mercy on us all!"

The artists stared about them, terrified, then dropped their pallets and fell upon their knees, while the master staggered out of the chamber and up the inky stairs to the daylight and across the valley to find a priest who would explain somehow to the gods that it was all a terrible mistake that they had finished Pharaoh's tomb, that it did not mean the Good God was to die yet . . . not yet, ah gods, not yet!

So passed the fourth day before the Heb-Sed, and the third day, and the second, while the barges of the gods docked every hour at the temple quays and the tension in the land mounted until it seemed all Egypt held its breath.

On the sun-drenched morning of the last day before the Day of Beginning, the suspense achieved its climax and ultimate symbol, not in the curious crowds on the water front, or the hustling officials at the palace, not in the pennant-decked temples of waiting Thebes, but in the solitary figure of a runner who crouched motionless and tense upon the western bank of the Nile some distance from the city, straining his eyes upriver, to the south. Only one of the strange but inexpressibly holy reed shrines in the temple courtyard was still empty. The barge of Nekhbet, the vulture-goddess of the south, had not yet arrived, and it grew late—ominously late.

The runner had taken up his post at dawn. Now the sun stood high above him and still he waited. His bare feet were planted in the new mud, his white kilt stirred against his bronzed and sinewy legs. About him were life and movement—frogs croaked, kites flapped, screaming, across the vivid sky, a fish leaped. The water lapped with a steady, whispering sound against the papyrus stalks. Sometimes a high-prowed fishing boat, decked with garlands and loaded with peasants and their shouting children, would ride the current past him, headed for Thebes and the morrow's festivities. The runner never moved. His painted eyes, mirroring his trembling expectation, were fixed on the farthest bend of the river, and watered so from staring too long into the sunlit glitter that at first he did not distinguish the glint of real gold he had been awaiting.

Then suddenly it was solid and real in the distance—a tall-prowed barge shining with glory and with gold, rounding the curve of the riverbank, the standard of Nekhbet clear upon its staff.

The runner wheeled and bounded for the nearest dike, while the marsh birds scattered in fright before him. Once upon the broad, dry surface of the dike, he ran with all the pent-up energies of the morning while his noonday shadow, a fluid black puddle beneath his feet, sped with him. To the west, as he ran, the desert hills of Libya curved riverward and began to sharpen into the cliffs of Thebes. To the east, across the Nile, white-walled villages gave way to the palm groves, fields and houses of the city's outskirts, and the southernmost quays came into view.

Traffic thickened on the dike. Donkeys jostled and holiday-clad peasants shouted after the panting runner, who paid no heed. Boats of every size bobbed now on the swollen river, skimming back and forth between the two shores of the City of Amon. On the east shore, beyond the square, embroidered sails, rose wharfs and buildings; whitewashed walls and thick-crowded roofs stretched on and on in the midday sun. This was Thebes, No-Amon, the City of God—gilt-splashed, brushed with azure and jade and plum and cinnamon and ochre in a brilliance of friezes and designs. On its northernmost edge the runner could make out the pennants flapping over the sprawling Temple of Amon.

At the royal landing the runner swerved westward on the broad avenue leading inland from the Nile. Straight ahead of him rose the high white walls of *per nefer neter,* House of the Good God, palace of Pharaoh Ah-kheper-ke-Re Djehuty-mes-iren-Amon, Thutmose the First.

2.

The palace lay in the grip of an unnatural calm. In the Great Court were scattered the remnants of the procession which had formed at midmorning to escort the royal family to meet the Vulture's barge. Long since, priests and nobles had sought the coolness of the palace, leaving the litters crisscross on the pavements with their bearers sprawled beside them and the gossamer-clad dancers yawning behind their tambourines. Now and then a chamberlain's uneasy eye strayed to a door of silvery wood at one side of the Great Court.

Behind that door, in a small walled garden—a garden brilliant with flowering vines, set with a pool in which reeds rustled and lotuses opened great waxed cups under the shade of a big tamarisk tree—in this garden the royal family was gathered. For two full hours now they had been waiting for the runner to arrive. And Pharaoh did not like to wait.

He sat—the god Horus, Lord of the Two Lands, Falcon of Gold, King of Upper and Lower Egypt, Son of the Sun Ahkheper-ka-Re Djehuty-mes-iren-Amon, called Thutmose, the first Pharaoh of that name—in the exact center of a slender-columned pavilion at one end of the garden, on a chair of gold and cedar raised a step above the pavilion's floor. He sat frontally, Pharaonically, from long habit—sandaled feet planted square, war-scarred legs rising sturdy as pillars to make a right angle at the knees, as in some granite statue of himself. His footstool was decorated with a frieze of Asiatic captives bound back to back, so that he might forever tread on them. Both hands gripped the chair arms, which were carved to represent the enfolding falcon wings of the great god Horus; his own nose was like a falcon's beak, and his head thrust forward a little, falconlike, under the weight of Egypt's towering crown. His thighs were wrapped in a stiffly starched white apron with a pleated front and, flashing above in a sunburst of glory, a broad collar of gold and winking garnets half covered his weathered chest.

Absolute master of an empire, worshiped by hundreds of thousands as a god, he was the most powerful figure in his world—a world his conquering armies had enlarged by half again during his energetic reign. But under the fierce brows his eyes were those of an old and weary man, and his mouth was stubborn.

He had no intention of naming his son, Prince Nenni, Successor to the throne of Egypt. He had no intention of naming any Successor at all. And he was the only person in Egypt who knew it.

He was staring fixedly at the door in the garden wall. The

22

barge will come soon, he was telling himself for the hundredth time. It must come soon. I command that it come soon!

Once the barge came, once this tedious indecisiveness was ended, he could wait the last remaining hours until tomorrow. That much he knew he could endure—though for weeks he had leaned toward the day of Heb-Sed as a chained captive leans toward his homeland, dragging the minutes with him, inch by stubborn inch. To wait longer than tomorrow—to go on expectant, idle, uncertain—he would prefer to know at once that the barge had capsized in the Nile.

Suppose it has? he reflected. Suppose the runner were to come in a moment and bring the news. Gods! Everything would have to be postponed, messengers would have to be dispatched here and there, proclamations issued. . . .

For just an instant Thutmose found himself almost welcoming the prospect, which at least offered action instead of more sitting. Crises held no fears for him. Like wars, they were something a man could set his teeth into.

Wars. . . . Pharaoh's mind slipped gratefully into its favorite path. King and god he had been for twenty-five years, but at bottom he was a warrior. Action was his natural climate, the dust of battle was the incense sweetest to his nostrils. The long river of his memory flowed back through innumerable battles and campaigns, each more distant in time and, strangely, more vivid in recollection. Now, in his aging years, the ones growing bright as yesterday were the oldest battles, those he had fought in his youth in the armies of his predecessor, King Ahmose, to drive the hated Hyksos out of the Black Land.

Tyrants, oppressors, destroyers of temples—the cursed Hyksos. Their very name could still make Pharaoh's flesh crawl and his muscles tighten. Where had they come from? The answer was lost in the mists of long ago; but come they had, in those ancient days, somewhere out of the empty reaches of Asia—a terrible, swift horde in their horse-drawn chariots—and poured like an evil inundation over an Egypt which had never before known an invader, and which had never seen a horse.

That much they did for us, Thutmose reflected grimly. They brought the horse. Aye, for two long centuries Egypt was a land of slaves; but when the slaves rose at last, they matched the tyrants chariot for chariot, and drove the fleetest horses in the world. . . .

Pharaoh's old eyes deepened with memory. Once more he was a young commander with King Ahmose, pursuing the enemy through the Delta and across the border. Once more he was living the early years of his own kingship—years he had spent, with the horror of occupation still vivid in his mind, pursuing the scattering hordes farther and ever farther, in a desperate resolve to make the Black Land safe forever. He had led his armies northward through Syria and even Mitanni, southward through wretched Kush; he had pushed the borders of Egypt outward until when he marched home at last he was master of half the world.

And so I shall remain, he thought. Three thousand palace troops, twenty thousand more ready to call up, and Amenmose to lead them—

His thoughts shattered against the cruel rock of reality. Amenmose was no more. Amenmose was dead. Yesterday was gone, this was today, the waiting, tedious, uncertain present.

Wearily, his eyes focused once more upon the garden door.

A ripple of laughter sounded across the pavilion. The two queens of Egypt, Mutnofret the Lesser Wife, and Aahmes the Great Royal Consort, were playing at hounds-and-jackals in a shady corner, on a game board balanced between them on their knees. They looked much alike, the sisters, tall in their narrow linen dresses, with fine aquiline noses and delicate double chins —a handsome though aging queen and her imperfect reflection in a mirror, outwardly duplicates save that the royal cobra curved over Aahmes' tranquil forehead, merely a fresh lotus bloom over Mutnofret's furrowed one. Near them knelt a lute player whose soft notes mingled with the clicking of the ivory counters on the board. Beyond the musician, Prince Nenni lounged on the sun-dappled steps, his long, emaciated fingers clasping a bony knee. Down by the pool, the sixteen-year-old princess, Hatshepsut, walked in the brilliant sunshine with the royal steward, Nehsi.

"Your move, my sister," Aahmes said. "Come—attend to the game."

"Aye . . . nay . . . I cannot," Mutnofret said absently,

24

glancing over her shoulder toward the gate. "This strange delay . . ."

"It is a time of delays," came the brooding voice of Prince Nenni from the steps.

"You have heard no tidings from the House of Women yet?" Mutnofret asked him softly.

"Not a word, my lady mother. Already the babe is twelve days overdue. They say they have done all they could for her, but still she waits, suffering, miserable, I've no doubt—" He broke off abruptly as Pharaoh shifted in his chair. "Of course," Nenni muttered, "it is of no importance to any save myself . . ." His words trailed off.

Pharaoh's jaw set a trifle harder, but he made no comment. Twenty years old—the son of a god and warrior—and Nenni had never known the hunt or lifted a sword. The sole surviving prince of Egypt—and at this moment of tension when all the Black Land trembled to hear the name of the Successor, what filled his mind? The plight of some concubine named Iset, whose expected babe was overlong in coming.

I must have patience, patience, Pharaoh told himself. Nenni can never be Amenmose—that wretched fever—I must make allowances.

He drew a long breath. Wrenching his thoughts from Nenni and his eyes from the garden door, he fixed both on his daughter Hatshepsut, standing with Nehsi at the pool's edge. She looked slight as a reed beside the giant black man; she was slim-hipped as a boy. She was tossing bread pellets to the fish with the casual expertness of a boy, too—but a boy she was not. Below the froth of lilies she wore for a necklace her bare young breasts swelled sweet and round. She was a maid of sixteen, Pharaoh reminded himself reluctantly—and overdue for marriage. He thought of Nenni again and frowned, shifting uneasily in his chair.

Mutnofret had seen the frown. She moved a counter nervously, again glancing toward the gate. "I cannot think," she fretted, "what could so long delay that runner!"

"Patience, my sister. The runner will come."

"Aye, he will come, when the barge comes. But what delays the barge?"

"Perhaps an adverse current," Prince Nenni said absently.

25

"Or," Mutnofret quavered, "an adverse god—"

"Nonsense," Aahmes said crisply. "The gods are all in Thebes —all save the Divine Vulture. Their very gathering proves their favor. Who among them do you think adverse to our exalted husband?"

Mutnofret was silent, and Nenni smiled. "To my lord father, none. To me, perhaps many. Is that not what you meant, my lady mother?"

"My dear Nenni, you do nothing to seek their favor," Aahmes reproved him.

"Nay, I suppose I do not. I am not protesting, my lady Aahmes. I am as I am, and I accept it. However, if it is the gods who made me so, I believe even they grew displeased with their handiwork. No doubt gods blunder as well as men."

"My son!"

"I do not blame them for that," Nenni went on quickly. "But it scarce seems just, since they are gods and should see clearly in these matters, that they should vent their annoyance not on me alone, but also on those helpless ones whose lives link with mine. It almost seems they punish without reason—not only men but helpless women and their unborn babes—"

Pharaoh shut his ears in despair. How could any prince expect favor of the gods when he persisted in speaking of them so? Doubtless Nenni did not mean these heresies—but one never knew what he meant. It was impossible to understand him, impossible to catch more than a glimpse into that strange, oblique mind. Baffled, Thutmose studied his son's profile—his high, pale forehead with its hollow temples, his unreadable eyes, his over-sensitive lips with their drooping, threadlike corners.

He is ill, Pharaoh reminded himself. Never in his life has he known vigor and health. Perhaps he cannot help talking as he does—I must be more patient with him.

"However, I can scarce believe they would punish all Egypt," Nenni was saying. "The barge is merely late. Perhaps some disaster has befallen it."

"Oh, Amon forbid!" Mutnofret wailed.

Aahmes' voice cut in like a cool silver knife. "Amon will forbid it, you may be certain of that. Pray move your hound."

"If we could be certain, my sister! But the ways of the gods—"

26

"Are perhaps not unknown to the wedded spouse of the greatest of them," Aahmes reminded her serenely. "Come, move, move."

Pharaoh's fingers began to drum on the arms of his chair. Aahmes had, indeed, been wedded to the god Amon in a ceremony directly following her marriage to himself; such was the ritual in Egypt. But she had accepted that mystic marriage with a literal ardor which Thutmose had for twenty-five years found difficult to endure. He had never gone to her couch in all their life together without the maddening feeling that there was a third presence in their bed—and the reminder of it did little to soothe his temper now. Nor did a glimpse of his daughter Hatshepsut and the fresh thought of *her* marriage—nor did another fruitless glance at the garden door—nor did the sudden decisive clicking as a counter jumped from place to place on the board, accompanied by the sound of Aahmes' cool, delighted laughter, signifying that she had won still another game.

"My dear Mutnofret, you should attend, or else you should not play. I fear I have trounced you severely. . . . Ah, wine. Here, pour the first cup for his Highness the Prince, he seems paler than usual—"

Pharaoh slammed both hands down hard on the arms of his chair and spoke for the first time in an hour. "Talk, talk, talk, talk! In Amon's name, *where* is that thrice-cursed runner?"

With his first word, the indolent activity in the garden ceased abruptly. The lute player's fingers froze upon the strings, Mutnofret's hand paused, trembling, in its sorting of the counters, the slave's in its filling of a goblet. Down by the pool, Nehsi turned sharply, then started for the pavilion.

But Aahmes, composed, imperturbable, gracing an inlaid chair whose elegance she surpassed, in a pose which for all her aging joints could have been transferred to stone on a temple wall without the rearrangement of a line, only smiled tranquilly.

"Patience, Exalted Husband."

"Patience! May the Great Judge be merciful! How long have we sat here, idle? Two hours, three—"

"My lord father," Nenni put in, rising, "pray allow me to go in person and investigate this delay. If I could set the mind of my lord at ease—"

"My mind is quite at ease!" Thutmose said testily.

"The ease of the god's mind is perfect, as always," the prince muttered, sinking back again.

"Quite at ease. I am merely bored. I am merely . . . Eh? What is it, what is it?"

The physician was at his side, vials in hand, smiling a soothing, benevolent smile that raised Pharaoh's temper to the boiling point. "If the Good God will take just a swallow of this potion—"

"I want none of your potions! There is nothing wrong with me. I merely wish to know why I must sit here enduring tedium for half a day! Be off with your vials and bottles, I've had enough of your bitter messes. Here—you with the wine jug! Fill me a cup."

"Wine, my lord?" cried Mutnofret in frightened tones.

"Exalted Husband," Aahmes remonstrated, "the physician says—"

"I care nothing for what he says. *I* have said 'Fill me a cup'!"

The two queens subsided; the physician retreated agitatedly into his corner and the slave hurried forward with a brimming jug, spilling a little on his bare feet in his haste.

Thutmose took the cup and settled back, feeling a perverse satisfaction at all the eyes fixed nervously on him as he drank a long, defiant draught. Physicians and potions be damned, he thought. I am still Pharaoh. And I trust I have proved it, he could not help adding to himself with acid humor, by thus bullying two women, an invalid and a string of underlings. . . .

Still, the cool, sharp tang of the date wine was good as it set up its familiar tingling in his throat. It was the first wine he had allowed himself in weeks.

"Possibly," he said in milder tones, "the delay seems longer than it really is."

An almost audible sigh of relief went around the pavilion. Tactfully, the lutanist touched his strings, and since no one stopped him, resumed his playing in soft, clear chords.

As Thutmose lowered his cup, he caught sight of the royal steward, Nehsi, standing with one foot on the bottom step of the pavilion, looking thoughtfully up at him.

"I stand ready," Nehsi murmured, "to issue any commands Your Majesty desires to give."

"Why, there will be none," Pharaoh said drily. "The intentions of Great Lord Amon are as an open scroll to my lady Aahmes, did you not hear for yourself?"

Nehsi bowed and started to turn away, then hesitated. "Your Majesty," he said softly, "I am acquainted with the Governor of the South, who commands the Vulture's barge. A cautious man —one who holds crocodiles in great veneration. I have heard he stops at every sandbank to propitiate Sobk the Scaly One, therefore is often late at his destination." Nehsi paused, then went on carefully. "In the face of such admirable piety, one could almost consider it a good omen, not a bad one, that he is late today. Not, of course, that the Good God's mind is troubled by any thought of omens."

"Of course not," Pharaoh said, more drily than before.

A grim smile touched his lips as his vizier turned away into the garden. How well Nehsi understood him! He gazed with affection after the tall black man, so grave of countenance, so handsome in his white kilt and headcloth and the great collar of turquoises that glowed against his dusky chest. No one knew much of Nehsi's history before his rapid rise to prominence a few years ago. Some said his grandmother was a Nubian slave; Thutmose himself neither knew nor cared. Nehsi was a loyal and able minister, even a gifted one, and the winds of occasional palace intrigue beat unavailing against his solid strength. No Pharaoh could ask more. Nor, Thutmose reflected, could any man ask a firmer friend in time of trial. . . . Once again he was remembering the arrow of pain shooting through his chest, the incredible moment of falling into those strong, supporting arms. His face darkened, and so did his thoughts.

Behind him, Nehsi's remarks had started a low-toned discussion of omens, with Prince Nenni arguing, as he always did, that omens might be mere accidents, for all any man could prove.

"Nine days ago the Nile fell from the sky, with a noise as of many drums, and the people were terrified. Yet I have heard that in other lands this happens often and there they welcome the downpour, which is their strange way of watering their crops. Then why should we in Egypt fear it? Merely because it happens seldom in our land? But it also happens seldom that our vines produce twice their usual yield of grapes—and we scarce call that an evil omen."

"But grapes are not frightening, my son, whereas the storm —the drums—the great flashes in the sky—" Mutnofret shuddered and turned pale. "Aye, it was an omen, and a fearful one! Only the prayers of the priests averted the danger of which it warned."

"What of the dangers which come unheralded by omens? The priests are powerless to avert them. If omens are truly the warnings of the gods, then the gods are sometimes unjust and cruel, for sometimes they withhold their warnings."

"Nenni, do not say such things! Always there are omens . . ." Mutnofret faltered. "Perhaps we do not always see them. Please, my son, let us talk of . . ."

Nenni was not to be turned from his obsession. "And what of the good omens whose promise is never fulfilled? Twice, just before my other child was born, I dreamed of a snow-white cow with twin calves lying in the grass. Yet my little daughter died. And twice this very week I have seen the face of Great Mother Nuit among the stars, yet in actuality she had turned her face from my poor Iset, refused to call the babe forth—"

"Amon be merciful!" Pharaoh exploded. "Can you think of nothing besides this woman and her babe?"

"My lord father—the babe is mine, also."

"Aye, and it will be born in its hour, which no man can hasten!"

Nenni was silent, accepting the rebuke—and Thutmose was instantly contrite. For a moment he scowled straight ahead of him, drumming his fingers on the chair arms; then he turned back to Nenni, his eyes weary. "My son, I spoke hastily. What is it you wish? To go yourself and inquire after this woman at the Mansion of Beauty?"

"Aye, my lord father." Nenni flushed, then rose and crossed the pavilion to his side. "I do not know if I can trust them. They may be lying to me. Perhaps she is dead—or perhaps the babe is, and they fear to tell me. In my—folly—I wish to question them myself."

Pharaoh sighed, accepting a mind he could not understand. "Go then. I will not prevent you."

Nenni bowed, left the pavilion, and walked quickly down the red-graveled path toward the gate.

"A strange youth your son, Mutnofret," Aahmes remarked.

Her glance traveled to the lily pool and her own child, and her face cleared. She motioned to the slave who stood behind her chair. "Run quickly and hold a shade over the princess Hatshepsut . . . Nay, rather fetch her here. She has been too long in the sun, do you not agree, Exalted Husband? Her complexion will darken."

Pharaoh was not attending. Over the brim of his wine goblet his eyes were fixed on the frail retreating back of his only living son. He tried once more, and once more failed, to picture the tall Double Crown of Egypt atop that stoop-shouldered, languid figure—a figure which made no effort to straighten itself, to appear more princely.

He will not try, Thutmose thought. Perhaps he cannot. No matter. Thanks to the Heb-Sed I myself will rule for many years yet, strong and in my prime again, as free of strange pains and poundings in my chest as in those other days when I fought the Hyksos. . . .

He found himself staring down at his hands, which rested on the chair arms at either side. They were blue-veined and leathery, with fingers like claws. He was an old man.

He was not aware of Hatshepsut's presence until she leaned over him, peering with unaccustomed gravity into his face. He straightened at once. "Eh? . . . you have come out of the sun, I see," he muttered, not knowing what he said.

She whispered, "All will come right, my dear lord father." Turning away quickly, she moved on to the game board. "I want an ibis for this garden," she announced to her mother.

"An ibis? My lotus, what an odd notion!" Aahmes' laugh tinkled.

"I see nothing odd about it. An ibis on a golden perch. Lovely!" Hatshepsut wandered back to the steps. "Can you not visualize his white plumage against those blossoms yonder?"

"Little one, curb your fancy. This garden is far too small for a great bird like that . . . Shesu, I pray you, do not go out again into the sun!"

"But I love the sun! So warm, so bright." Hatshepsut grasped one of the beribboned columns that supported the pavilion's roof and swung herself outward into full sunlight, turning her face directly into the rays.

"Your complexion will be as leather!" the queen protested.

"Nay, not mine!" Regaining her balance on the steps, the princess slid a glance toward Thutmose. "The beams of my father the Shining One would never harm his child."

Pharaoh absorbed the sly teasing in silence. Daughter of the Sun, the princess of the realm was always styled. And Aahmes, ever literal—or perhaps only dutiful to that shadowy presence in her bed—always claimed that Amon and no other had fathered her youngest child. How she explained the princess' strong resemblance to her earthly father, in both feature and personality, Thutmose had never bothered to inquire—nor was he certain just what Hatshepsut believed about the matter. Certainly she was not averse to reminding Nenni of her purer blood, whenever it suited her purpose—and no doubt it would suit her well indeed when the two of them were married. An ill-assorted couple they would make! She all headstrong energy, Nenni spent and tired and ill, without the strength to deal with even one of her willful ideas. . . .

Aahmes, Thutmose perceived, was being called upon to deal with one of them now.

"The garden is large enough for twenty ibises," Hatshepsut was insisting. "I desire only one, with a chain of silver and a golden perch. It is exactly the adornment these lawns require, do you not agree, Lady Mutnofret? The perch could be there, beside the pool—"

"But the creature would eat the fish!"

"Certainly he would eat the fish! Cannot more fish be brought daily from the Nile, if need be? He will look beautiful, my ibis, poking his long beak among the lotus pads."

"My child, please! You cannot of course be serious, but—" Aahmes laughed again, uneasily, and moved an ivory counter on the board.

Her daughter snatched it back. "Not that one! Can you not see the jackal will be after your little dog in an instant? Move this one instead."

She was right, Thutmose observed after a quick glance at the board. He was deriving a good deal of amusement from this little exchange. There was only one person in Egypt who could ruffle Aahmes' composure, and that was Hatshepsut.

"And I am quite serious about the ibis," she added flatly.

"My treasured child." Aahmes' voice, too, now held an edge.

"I myself ordered the arrangement of this garden and I am quite content with it. Your exalted father and I"—his paternity was acknowledged readily enough at times like this, Pharaoh noted—"do not wish a great, untidy bird—"

"Untidy? With his glossy wings, his beautiful long neck, his—"

"There would be a continual clutter of feathers and fishbones underfoot! You will put this notion out of your mind at once."

Hatshepsut's straight back stiffened in a manner Thutmose knew altogether too well. "I shall not put it out of my mind. I shall send a slave at once to capture the largest, whitest, most elegant—"

"You will not."

"I will!"

Pharaoh turned his head at last. "Hatshepsut!" he thundered. "There will be no ibis!"

A sudden silence descended on the pavilion, broken only by Mutnofret's cautious clearing of her throat. Aahmes, rather too red in the face for queenly dignity, feigned interest in her bracelets. Pharaoh, trying hard to restrain a smile, pretended to study a distant clump of palms showing over the garden wall, but he watched Hatshepsut from the corner of his eye. One never knew when even a Pharaonic pronouncement would cease to have its effect on her. Amon's daughter indeed! he thought with pride. She was his child in every trait and feature, and most of all in that stubborn will of hers which delighted him even while he loudly deplored it. The maid had spirit—look at her standing there, erect and mutinous, her hands clenched at her sides. Some thought her plain of feature; he thought her near to beauty, with her wide black eyes, her proudly arched nose so like his own, her small but obstinate chin. In addition, the gods had given her a quick intelligence more appropriate to a boy, coupled with enough headstrong notions to keep a palaceful of slaves busy and Pharaoh himself uncertain of his authority.

However, one more time she was accepting it. The hands unclenched, the stormy dark eyes developed a gleam of amusement, and the slim shoulders moved in a faint shrug. She turned, and after a reflective moment, marched down the steps and out into the garden, into sun so strong it struck blue lights off her swaying, inky hair.

Aahmes gave a little sigh but made no protest; and Pharaoh hid a smile. The maid knew as well as a general how to turn defeat into victory, backhanded though it might be. Some day, he was quite certain, there would be an ibis on a golden perch yonder by the lily pool. Ah, had she been a man, there would be no question about the Successor! No question at all! But as matters stood . . .

The smile faded, even from his mind, leaving only a heaviness. An instant later there was a sound of footsteps in the Great Court, and a chamberlain appeared in the garden gateway. Nehsi strode toward him at once, conferred a moment, then turned with a bow toward the pavilion.

"The barge has been sighted, Your Majesty."

Action, even the turgid action of yet another procession, came as an exquisite relief. Thutmose heaved himself out of the golden chair, the movement drawing the ladies to their feet as if on strings, and flinging the slaves onto their faces.

"Fetch Prince Nenni," he commanded. "We shall leave at once."

Slowly, heavily, under his tall white crown, he walked down the steps and out into the sunshine.

3.

As Prince Nenni walked slowly down the corridor leading to the Women's Quarters, he was thinking of the expression on his father's face when they parted a moment ago in the pavilion. He had been only too aware that Pharaoh's eyes—bewildered, exasperated, bleak—had followed him as he left the garden. Ever since he could remember, he had evoked in the Good God that same mixture of irritability and despair, the same desire to understand and inability to do so, that had marked their latest attempt at conversation. From the moment of Prince Amenmose's death, when the matter of the Succession had arisen, the differences in their natures had assumed a nightmare quality for both of them. Obviously Pharaoh questioned the gods—*why? why? why?*—whenever he looked at his son.

I cannot blame him, Nenni reflected. Yet it is foolish to blame myself. A man is what he is, he can be no other; he must accept himself, even if chance forces the crown upon his head.

34

Can the crown alone make a man a king? . . . What is a king? My father? But I can never be my father—is there no other answer to the question, no other *kind* of king? Does anyone know, I wonder?

Nenni stopped before the tall door inscribed with the names of Pharaoh, looking down at the broad bent back of the eunuch beside it, who had fallen to his knees. "Arise," Nenni said drily, thinking, To whom does he kneel? Not to Nenni the Tired One, though if questioned that is what he would say. Nay, he kneels to the power of my father, and to his own helpless faith that some of the Divine Fragrance which is Pharaoh's must also have rubbed off on me. In fact, the man is a poet and a seer, for he kneels to a hope. Yet do we not do the same, we others who bow the neck and stretch out our hands to the Golden Bull in the temple? It is not the bull itself we worship, nor the priests who cause the great head to move and the nostrils to snort fire. It is not even the spirit of Amon the Hidden One within the golden shell, but only our own hope that he truly dwells there and hears our cries.

A nervous movement from the eunuch reminded Nenni that he had again committed the impropriety of allowing his glance to linger on a person of no consequence.

Poor fellow, he thought, hastily turning away his eyes. He imagines he has aroused my wrath in some way, or I would never notice him. Can the world be rightly ordered when even one man craves to be as a chair or a table before his prince, instead of a man? Yet in Egypt thousands so crave.

"Open the door," he said.

The eunuch sprang forward, rapped smartly on the carved panels with his staff, and flung them wide. Nenni stepped across the threshold into the great Salon of the Mansion of Beauty, the palace harem.

A spacious, richly furnished room, the Salon was windowless, but its roof perched on graceful pillars extending above the top of the walls, allowing ample entrance for light and air as well as adorning the room with a band of the deep blue Egyptian sky. The walls were exquisitely painted with scenes showing Pharaoh surrounded by the ladies of the harem—playing at games with them, accepting fruit or a long-stemmed lotus from one, caressing another. Reality failed to bear out this amiable fiction; the

35

dozen or more bejeweled and bored beauties in the room, long neglected by the aging Pharaoh, were chattering listlessly, yawning over their game tables and refreshment trays, or quarreling peevishly among themselves. Even the advent of a stray hornet would have been a welcome diversion in this company; Nenni's arrival caused a stir of major proportions.

The prince again! It is the third time he has come in person to inquire after her. . . . The words were almost distinguishable in the murmur that passed through the room as Nenni walked its shining length, trying to ignore the glances turned on him over satiny shoulders, the curiosity brightening jewel-like eyes. He was quite aware that his actions were again ill-suited to royalty, and his concern for the woman Iset probably unique in the annals of Egypt's princes. But it was his child who was involved in this disquieting delay, and he could not be indifferent to it; could not, as usual, he reflected, behave like the son of Pharaoh.

He stopped between two massive columns at the far end of the Salon and beckoned an old slave from her post at the door beyond. "Well, Heqet? Have you news for me? How does she fare?"

"Nothing has changed, Master. She grows so great her couch can scarce hold her, yet the pains have not begun."

"Is there nothing else you can do to hasten the affair?" he asked impatiently. "Surely you and the other Old Ones hereabouts, after a lifetime of tending the women and aiding babes into the world—"

"My lord master, we have done all we know." Heqet raised a wrinkled brown hand and began to count on her fingers. "We have brought her sleep with the potion of crushed poppy pods, we have soaked her in warm baths and massaged her with oils— this morning we gave her a wine glass of the oil of the castor bean, in which was dissolved a scrap of papyrus inscribed with a powerful incantation—"

"In Amon's name! And still the babe delays?" Nenni stared over the old woman's head to the doors beyond. "Take me to her," he commanded.

The slave gaped up at him in dumb astonishment.

"Go, I say! Make haste."

"But Master—" Heqet protested.

He started past her and at last she roused herself, hurried to open the door for him, and shuffled ahead of him down the corridor. Behind him he could hear the wave of scandalized delight that rippled through the Salon at this latest, this unheard-of eccentricity. To *visit* the lovely Iset at this juncture, while she was yet great with her burden and looked like a fat Syrian in her rumpled garments? She would scarce thank him for it!

Even these chattering women, thought Nenni bitterly, can make me feel as a creature of some other world, neither beast nor fowl but the solitary monster of his kind. Have they never known anxiety, that they can so ill comprehend mine? Can they—and Pharaoh—not allow me even one moment of compassion for this woman, of fear for my own seed?

"This way, Exalted Prince," puffed Heqet nervously.

They had gone down a long hall, past the great stone-floored bath and numerous storerooms, and came now into a transverse corridor lined with the doors of bedchambers and dressing rooms. At the last doorway Heqet stopped, clasping and unclasping her gnarled hands.

"She is here, Master. But I pray you, give me leave to announce your exalted coming, that her maids may dress her hair and fetch jewels to—"

Nenni walked past her and opened the door. On a couch occupying an alcove at the far end of the room a woman half raised herself, pushing away the slave who had been tinting her fingernails.

"My lord Nenni!"

Her voice was shrill with shock, and the little black slave stumbled, spilling her tray of salves and implements. Nenni closed the door behind him and leaned against it.

"Is my presence so unwelcome, even to you, sweet Iset? There was a time when you greeted my coming with the wine of gladness, and bade your maids fetch garlands for my neck."

"My lord prince is always welcome," muttered Iset. "I could wish, however, that my lord had chosen a different moment for his exalted visit. These days I can scarce carry my own weight—much less appear beautiful for my lord when he comes."

"Nonsense, Iset." She resents me, Nenni thought, and in spite of his concern a wave of anger passed over him. "What matter if you are not always jeweled and scented like some lap dog? You are a woman, not a plaything. I have come to talk with you."

Even as he spoke, moving across the room to her bedside, he had difficulty concealing his dismay at her appearance. Her body was swollen beyond recognition, her face unnaturally flushed, with its pretty roundness blurred and coarsened by puffy flesh. Her eyes, those laughing, provocative eyes whose gaiety had once so enticed him, were dull and sulky, and her hair lay lank over the cushions as if all life had gone out of it.

"Iset!" he exclaimed in pity, sinking into a chair beside her. He took her hand and pressed it to his forehead.

She freed her fingers petulantly. "To talk to me? To talk of what?"

"Why, of our child, what else?"

"The child! I only wish I could forget it! Hateful burden that it is—"

"Hush! How can you speak so of your own babe?"

Her eyes filled with tears of self-pity. "It is easy for you to wonder! You have not to bear it! You know not what it is, to look down upon a great swollen belly, to know all your beauty is gone and nothing ahead but pain and suffering!"

"Nay, I do not know this. I spoke hastily. It is of course a burden to you now." Nenni patted her hand. She could not really feel so, it was only the long delay. His own anxieties came to the fore again. "Iset, I—have been greatly troubled, I confess. The babe tarries so long, far past its appointed time. I know not what to think. Is"—he had to force himself to go on—"is it possible the child is dead?"

"Dead?" She laughed bitterly. "My lord prince, he leaps within me from morning till night! I can neither rest nor sleep."

"Ahhh. Then nothing is too far amiss as yet! Soon, surely, it will be born, and this weary stalemate ended. You will forget all this then, with your babe in your arms."

She looked at him, her mouth pulling down at the corners. "Aye, first in my arms, then dragging at my skirts all day, wanting me to feed it, dress it, bathe it—while I grow fat and old and nagging, like others I have seen, with my breasts like empty wine sacks!" Suddenly Iset burst into helpless tears. "*Aii,* I am but seventeen, and I was beautiful, was I not? Did you not find me so? Aye, you did. You could not sleep for want of me, but must come each night to my couch. And now who will want me? Not you. You will wed your royal princess, and lie in *her* arms each night—"

"Be silent!" exclaimed Nenni, standing up quickly.

She fell back on the pillows, wailing, and he watched with a repugnance he could no longer disguise. Any sympathy he had felt for her was wiped out by the alarm her last words had produced in him. Surely she would dare say no more about that—a matter upon which he felt such quivering sensitivity that he guarded it like a raw wound, even from himself.

"You are overwrought," he said rapidly. "And your fears are imagined ones. I will give you slaves for yourself, if you like, and others for your child. Is it not my child too? I would scarce turn away my face, or neglect its welfare! I had hoped—" How could he tell her what he had hoped of her—companionship, laughter, the deepening ties of affection and interest in their child. "No matter," he muttered. "But be assured my son will have every care, whether—"

Iset struggled to one elbow, clutching at him. "Son? How do you know it will be a son?"

"I do not know," said Nenni impatiently. "It is only another hope of mine—perhaps to be disappointed also."

She took his hand and moved it slowly over her cheek, looking up at him with a gaze which once would have melted all his anger and set him trembling with desire.

"My lord," she whispered. "If it is a son, you could make me happy again. You could make me a great lady—the mother of a king."

"Iset! In Amon's name!"

"You could! You must, you will be Pharaoh, you can do what you will then. Only name him Prince and Heir, your firstborn— you would not set him aside for the children the princess will bear you? Name my son Successor, aye, while he is yet in his cradle! Promise me, my love, my prince, promise—"

He jerked his hand away. Amon pity her! Was ever a man-child born in the Mansion of Beauty that its mother did not scheme to make it Pharaoh? Once in a while it happened so, but never to this babe—child of Nenni the Tired One, the Despised of Pharaoh, and a charioteer's daughter! "You do not know what you are saying," he told her. "I will return some other time."

"Nay, wait! Stay with me, my lord. I did not intend—forgive your slave, I beg—"

But Nenni was already at the door. He flung it open to find old Heqet about to knock. "Exalted Highness," she said hurriedly, "Pharaoh has sent a messenger—the barge—your presence is desired."

Gladly Nenni fled.

Emerging into the crowded hubbub of the Great Court five minutes later, he felt the familiar weakness in his legs, the aching of bone and muscle and the queer stiff feeling in his jaw that presaged a bout of fever. With gratitude he stepped into his litter and dropped into its hard but elegant chair. He leaned back and closed his eyes, trying at the same time to close his ears to the shouted orders, the footsteps running past him, the whole wearing process of getting a procession under way.

Presently he found himself staring under half-closed lids at the princess Hatshepsut, who was leaning out of her litter scolding a slave girl for some blunder. Her hair fell thick and shining from under the gold diadem, and lay upon the curves and hollows of her shoulders like a pool of black water. A beautiful maiden— at least to his eyes. He had worshiped her—in secret—since the days when they were children together. A blithe and merry child she had been, with an unexpected will—uncontested ruler of the palace nursery, forever coaxing her brothers and sisters into mischief and causing the gray hairs to sprout daily in the head of her old nurse, Yen.

Yet old Yen doted on her, Nenni mused, and does so yet. Aye, and Lady Aahmes pampered her, and Pharaoh indulged her, and all loved her—and none thought to discipline her. Now none dares to, save Pharaoh himself. What must it be like to have such vigor, and ideas crowding thick as fish in the Nile? She let me share in them once, but now she thinks me a poor creature indeed, tired and dull. . . .

Nenni turned away quickly, feeling a flush of shame rise into his cheeks. To be wed to a bride who scorned him—such was the final humiliation the gods had in store for him.

Suddenly there was a shout, a barked command. The clamor in the Great Court died away as Pharaoh's four Nubians stepped out, bearing his golden litter upon their stalwart shoulders. Dancers, priests, fan bearers fell in behind it; runners darted off ahead. Nenni felt himself lifted now, and moving forward. Attendants and gold-hung nobles appeared beside his litter, four great fans of ostrich plumes rose above it. Sistrums began to jangle, drums to sound their hollow, intermittent notes, and the chanting of the priests rose on the air to mingle with the first clouds of incense. One after another the litters of Aahmes, Hatshepsut, and Mutnofret joined the train, swaying above their attendant groups of noblemen like golden moons appearing among stars. The procession was under way at last, and winding like some glittering serpent down the Avenue of Rams to the palace gates, outside which a strange humming, as of a swarm of bees, grew ever louder.

The gates were flung open; the humming became a many-throated roar as the waiting populace, yelling its jubilation at the sight of Pharaoh, swirled back before the staves of the runners. The noise assailed the eardrums like repeated blows. Nenni, gripping the arms of his chair, quailed inwardly before it.

The multitudes of Egypt—here they were, on every side of him, many-faced, many-voiced. Flung to their faces by the passage of Pharaoh's litter, they were scrambling to their feet by the time his own, preceded by its complement of priests and dancers, approached. The effect was that of a rippling sea of motion stilled, as he passed, into a frieze of burnished brown bodies, white garments, and black heads shining immobile in the sun.

Struck motionless, he thought. The phrase kept repeating itself in his mind as the odd illusion repeated itself down the winding avenue. Struck dumb, too; for though the cries of praise and prayer beat like waves against the litter of Pharaoh, just ahead of his, and against the Divine Consort's, just behind, there was a hush as he went by. On every face turned up to him, in every pair of eyes that searched his own, he found the same expression of speculation, anxiety and doubt.

Suddenly remembering the eunuch, Nenni turned his eyes away from them, stiffened his shoulders and for their sakes stared austerely straight ahead. So it was they expected royalty to sit—erect and godlike in a golden chair, immobilized in grandeur, eyes fixed on nothingness. Or was it into the reaches of eternity he was supposed to gaze? So sat the Good God his father, up ahead there, so sat Aahmes and, he was sure, so sat proud Hatshepsut, who had once been little Shesu, and who was ever aware of her ancient forebear the sun. He alone could not resist studying the faces of the people on either side.

Nenni stirred restively against the bosses of the carved ram's head, feeling hot and weak with the beginning of fever. He had never cared for Amenmose, but no one in Egypt had mourned his death more desperately, or been more burdened by his loss. The thought of the Double Crown's weight pressing down upon his own brow was almost unbearably oppressive.

If the crown weighed too heavily on the deep-lined forehead of Pharaoh Djehuty-mes-iren-Amon, however, he gave no sign of it. A true god and sun in his golden litter, from which the rays of that other sun high above his head struck blindingly, he moved down the avenue to the Nile as a god should move, and the hearts of the people rejoiced as they swarmed riverward with him, shading their eyes from his glory. At the landing, which was beribboned, gilded, and strewn with flowers for his coming, the Royal Barge swayed at its moorings. Down the steps and onto its broad decks wound the procession, litters and all, with the fan-bearing slaves scrambling like cats along precarious footing in order that the great white plumes might hover without interruption over the heads of the royal ones. Those of the retinue who could not crowd onto the Royal Barge boarded another drawn up behind; both embarked amid a glitter of spray and rhythmically dipping oars for the temple on the opposite side of the river, half a league to the north.

Within half an hour the procession had regrouped itself on the broad docks of the House of Amon, the gilded barge of Nekhbet with its accompanying train of southern officials and priests had arrived in full glory at its destination, and Pharaoh had received the hawser of the goddess's floating shrine into his own hand. The ceremonies of welcome were brief; the Governor of the Residence of the South, resplendent in a golden headcloth and jeweled necklaces too numerous to count, praised Pharaoh's majesty, goodness, and likeness to the sun with phrases so rich in wordplay and double, triple, even quadruple allusion that their complexity aroused the admiration of all who listened, and made almost no sense at all. Pharaoh replied with praises of the ines-

42

timable splendor of the vulture-goddess and of the governor's admirable care of her through her journey. After which the goddess and her train started for the Hall of the Great Ones in the temple, while Pharaoh and his retinue re-embarked for the western bank of the Nile.

The Great Ones were all assembled at last. The Heb-Sed could begin.

4.

The procession wound slowly up the avenue from the river, and at last into the Great Court of the palace. Within her gold-trimmed sandals the delicately henna-tinted toes of the princess Hatshepsut were wriggling with furious impatience by the time her litter was set gently down.

She was out of it in an instant. Heedless of convention, she pulled off her diadem with a little explosive sound of relief and tossed it to a slave.

The others were alighting too; the two queens fastidiously shaking out their fluted sleeves and adjusting the transparent folds of their cloaks, Pharaoh straightening himself with an effort, apparently stiff as well as tired from long sitting in the rigid pose of godhood. But Nenni, in the litter directly behind Pharaoh's, was having to be assisted by two of his bearers even to step out onto the pavement. He looked exhausted, and pale as death.

Thutmose's brows flew together as he caught sight of the prince. "My son! Are you ill?" He beckoned sharply to a slave. "The prince must rest at once. Attend him to his apartments."

"I pray the Good God be not troubled," answered Nenni faintly. "I have foolishly overtaxed myself. It will pass . . ."

Hatshepsut watched with her usual mingling of contempt and pity as he moved away between two burly slaves. Then she turned away impatiently. She found her mother at her side.

"My lotus," said Aahmes, "refresh yourself, then go at once to the Southern Garden. The ladies of the court will join us there for luncheon. I have ordered a scribe to read poetry, and later we will chat, embroider a bit perhaps, and play at draughts."

Gods of Egypt! thought Hatshepsut. "I pray to be excused today, Honored Mother," she murmured. "A little headache . . . I will lunch in my chambers."

"As you will." Aahmes shrugged and strolled away with Mutnofret at her heels.

Hatshepsut started swiftly toward the palace. Might Amon deliver her from that garden full of gabbling peahens with their embroidery and their lotus-sniffing and their gossip! She wanted to *do* something—something active, dangerous, reckless—anything to forget her restlessness for a little while and ease the tension of this interminable day. As she crossed the wide, paved vestibule of the palace she caught sight of Pharaoh, surrounded by attendants in the Circle of Respect, walking slowly in the direction of his private apartments. Her tension increased on the instant until she felt taut as a lute string. He looked old, old— nothing like the god of strength and power she had worshiped all her life. He was failing. Since Amenmose died he had changed before her eyes into a frail old man.

Lord Amon, make him whole again, she prayed as she ran up the stairs at a pace that had her slave girl puffing to keep at her heels. Let the Heb-Sed make him as he was, let tomorrow come quickly, and the magic begin! I'll give gold and silver, incense, thousands of everything, I'll marry Nenni without a word, may wild horses drag me if I complain!

Suddenly she knew what she wanted to do.

She stopped at the head of the stairway so abruptly that her slave narrowly escaped colliding with her. "Baba, make haste to the stables. Bid that a groom—you know the one—"

"Aye, my princess, I understand. At what hour?"

"At once. And tell someone to bring luncheon to my rooms. Hasten now, and if you breathe a word of it—"

"Never, Mistress! I would never dream of—"

"Go, then."

The girl turned back down the stairs, and Hatshepsut hurried on to her own apartments. "Yen!" she called, before she was well in the door. "Yen, come at once. Undress me."

"Now then, what is it now, in Mut's sweet name!" Yen came trotting into the room from the wardrobe, fresh-ironed garments still trailing from her arms. She was a sturdy, thick-waisted woman with the face of an aging mare.

"I want other clothes—the ones you brought from the servants' room."

Yen stopped. "Now, my lady! What mischief is it this time? Your exalted mother expects you in the Southern Garden—"

"Nay, she does not. I could not have endured it, not today, not now! I must get out, Yen, or I shall burst! Go quickly, find the clothes! Are they not still somewhere in my chests?"

"Nay, they are in mine," grumbled Yen, scowling as she folded away the clean garments she held. "How would it look, should anyone find that coarse linen among a princess' finery? I'll fetch them, but I do not approve, my lady, I do not approve!"

"Disapprove all you like, my old one, so long as you love me as always!" Hatshepsut gave her a quick hug, then pushed her, resisting, toward the door. "Hasten now, it will do you no good to cluck and fret over me—have you not learned that in all these years?"

Half an hour later a cloaked maiden with a hood half covering her lowered face emerged from one of the servants' entrances of the palace and walked briskly toward the stables at the rear of the grounds just inside the high outer walls. A gate used only by tradesmen and workers pierced the walls here, and near it the groom was waiting, with two fidgeting black stallions in plain military harness hitched to a light chariot from which all adornment had been stripped. Hatshepsut stepped in beside him and they were off at once, wheeling down the drive and through the gates in a spatter of gravel.

They bore west through streets lined with the high walls of noblemen's villas, then emerged into the thriving manufacturing district called the City of the Dead—a vast spread of shops and workshops, built of mud-brick and thatched with palm, housing the potters, the goldsmiths, the embalmers, coffin makers, stone-cutters, sculptors and carpenters who labored incessantly at the rich industry of furnishing Egypt's tombs. Angling across the southwest portion of this district, the chariot was soon free of the dusty, rutted streets and speeding across barren desert on a road that led westward to the sharp bluffs of the Libyan hills.

"Now!" Hatshepsut cried over the noise of hoofs and wheels. "Give me the reins!"

With some difficulty, owing to the rough bouncing of the chariot, she changed places with the groom.

45

"I pray Your Exalted Highness," he quavered, "keep the beasts at a moderate pace. Your Highness is not yet skilled in driving, and Wings of Night, on the left hand, is as fiery of disposition as—"

"Then he is swift! Let us see how swift he is!" Hatshepsut laughed aloud.

The dry desert wind streamed against her face and whipped her cloak into a banner behind her as the horses sped along the half-obliterated road. Ahead, the golden cliffs, with the ruins of the ancient Temple of Neb-hepet-Re nestled at their base, loomed ever closer. Hatshepsut, reveling in speed and the beauty of the flying black manes before her, felt a rebellious disinclination to rein in for the end of the road and turn tamely back to the city, as she had always done before. Why must the road be followed so slavishly? A hasty glance showed her no reason why the wheels would not roll equally well over the raw desert on either side. And there, paralleling the cliffs, was a world of unbroken space to drive in—the whole broad strip between the cliffs and the outer margins of the City of the Dead, many cubits wide and stretching nearly half a league in length before the hills curved toward the river to obstruct it.

Unhesitatingly Hatshepsut pulled the right-hand reins, swinging the horses to the north.

"Amon's bones and breath!" gulped the groom as the chariot pitched wildly crossing a pebble-strewn declivity. "Slow them, Highness, if you mean to drive them over this!"

"Do the war chariots slow when they carry the archers into b-battle?" retorted Hatshepsut jerkily. But in truth, the desert was far rougher than it looked. The ground was uneven, a continual series of irregular lumps and depressions invisible until one was upon them, and the pebbles were often rocks and sometimes small boulders half hidden by tufts of stringy grass. The chariot jolted alarmingly, almost lifting her wide-braced feet from the floorboards, and causing the rail against which she was leaning to gouge painfully into her middle. The horses flew even faster, perhaps frightened by the uncertain footing or the flapping of the reins. Hatshepsut pulled in hard, but it was impossible to maintain pressure on the bits when one was being flung here and there like a buffeted feather.

46

"Take care!" yelled the groom. "Ahead there!"

She had seen the boulder at the instant of his warning. With all her might she dragged at the left rein, and the groom's hand shot around her and seized the leather too. The horses swerved, but not in time for the near wheel to clear the boulder. There was a grinding jar, a splintering, and Hatshepsut found herself flung through the air as the chariot overturned and went banging and bumping away on its side in the wake of the terrified horses. She landed rolling, coming to rest face down in a sandy hillock.

It was astonishing to be so suddenly intimate with dirt and sand. It felt harsher against the flesh than she would ever have dreamed, and scorching hot. Pebbles loomed like boulders before her blinking eyes, and not three inches from her nose a beetle stumbled hastily through a patch of coarse, sun-gilded grass which seemed as large and detailed and complex as a full-sized marsh. A rock was digging into her thigh, her palms burned with scratches, and—Ptah's Beard!—she had lost control of the horses.

She sat up and glared at the groom, who was struggling to his feet beside her, daring him to criticize by so much as an accusing glance. But he was far too accustomed to the ways of royalty and his own station in life.

"I crave Your Highness' forgiveness for my clumsiness," he sighed, staggering a little and clutching one of his knees. "I earnestly pray Your Highness is not injured—"

"Nay, only bruised and very dirty. Give me your hand."

He stretched out a callused palm and helped her to her feet, then stood awkwardly by, obviously uncertain whether or not to assist her in brushing at the dirt on her person. Hatshepsut, torn between fury and amusement at the poor figure she had cut as a driver, noticed that he was gingerly working one knee back and forth.

"Are you hurt?" she asked sharply.

"I think not, Exalted One. It is only—I seem to have twisted it—pray do not trouble yourself—"

"What of the horses?"

Both turned to stare northward, where the horses could still be seen running in a little cloud of dust. The groom sighed again.

"There is little left of the chariot now, Royal Mistress. When the last of it has broken away they will lose their fear and stop to graze. I will go after them."

"You can walk?"

He tried it and ventured a smile. "Aye, well enough."

She looked at him standing there in the glaring sunlight, scratched and smudged, with his *shenti* twisted sideways and his eyes resigned. She fought to restrain a grin. "Possibly I should pay more heed to your warnings, Neb-iry."

"If Your Highness sees fit," replied the man cautiously. "But my lady's courage is as a lion's."

"Aye, and a pretty pass it has brought us to! Go then, find those beautiful brutes, ride to the palace and fetch another chariot to me. I will walk back to the chapel yonder and await you."

"Aye, Mistress. I will make haste."

He limped away northward, and Hatshepsut, her torn and dirty cloak over her arm, started across the hot sands toward the little mud-brick chapel of Amenhotep I, which stood near Neb-hepet-Re's columned ruins at the foot of the cliffs. She was laughing openly now.

5.

In the smoke-darkened confines of a little wineshop in the City of the Dead, a young man sat over the remains of his midday meal which, to judge from the amount of food still left on the platter, he had neglected in favor of the nearly empty wine jug before him. He was a tall man, somewhere in his late twenties, not handsome but arresting in appearance, with straight, heavy eyebrows and deep furrows like scars running from nose to mouth. His angular shoulders and the overlarge, corded hand clasped around his cup gave an impression of rude power, and his eyes were very black, very lively, as if he enjoyed a secret, derisive joke. He wore a silver headcloth which shone like a star in his dingy surroundings, quite blinding the eye to the fact that his *shenti* was the commonest of linen, his collar and armbands gilt instead of gold. He was alone in the shop save for the fat proprietor, who washed cups in a corner and watched his customer curiously.

48

The door of the shop opened, jingling a little bell. The thick-set man who entered, carrying a scribe's pallet and inkpots, walked straight to the proprietor.

"Someone here sent for Senmen the Scribe?"

The proprietor pointed a dripping finger toward the young man's corner and went back to his cup washing. Brows lifting a little at sight of the opulent silver headcloth, the scribe crossed the room to the low table behind which the young man knelt in the usual manner, one knee up and the other doubled under him, on the coarse reed mat which was the only seat the establishment offered. The scribe frowned with sudden intentness at the customer, then said uncertainly, "You desire my services?"

The customer did not answer at once but gazed at the scribe expectantly, black eyes brimming with amusement. Presently he began to laugh under his breath.

"Come, Senmen!" he said at last. His voice was deep and resonant but oddly harsh, like a bell with a flaw in it. "Do you not know your own brother?"

"Senmut!" Quickly the scribe shoved aside the littered platter to make room for his writing equipment, and dropped cross-legged at the other side of the table. "By Amon! I knew not whether to trust my eyes, in this dim light. It has been five years—nay, six or more. . . . You wore no cloth of silver when you left Thebes, by all the gods!" He flashed an envious glance at the headcloth, to the other's evident amusement, then leaned forward on his elbows. "What brings you from Hermonthis?"

"The Heb-Sed, of course."

"The Heb-Sed!"

"Aye, certainly. The god Montu is not as great, perhaps, as others one could name, but he could scarce sulk in his temple while the rest gather here for the Festival. He journeyed downriver yesterday, with a suitable escort."

"And since when is a temple scribe allowed to be part of that escort?"

Senmut grinned. "I am no longer a temple scribe, my suspicious one. I am Montu's Chief Prophet in Hermonthis."

"And I am Steward of Amon," jeered Senmen, "with forty slaves of my own and total power over all the estates of Amon, and over his storehouses and fields and gardens and cattle and his great temple across the river—"

49

"The Steward of Amon has many more than forty slaves," put in Senmut. "Your imagination is a paltry thing, brother Senmen."

"I speak as much sense as you do," growled the other.

"But I do speak sense. Better than that, I speak truth. I have been Chief Prophet of Montu since last harvest time."

Senmen scratched his chin, not omitting another look at the headcloth. "Indeed, it is obvious you have come up in the world," he admitted grudgingly.

"The headcloth is a tribulation to you, isn't it, my honest and hard-working brother? It is hard to endure, seeing such elegance on the youngest and most worthless of our worthless family, the rascal you last saw clad in rags and smudges on the water front, bullying you out of a few deben for passage north because the soldiers were on his heels."

"You owe me five deben still," Senmen grunted.

He had not finished speaking before the coppers were rolling across the table toward him. Senmut laughed silently. "You see, I am ready for you. I felt sure that was the first topic we would discuss—after the headcloth. My thanks for the loan. I owe you thanks, also, for your many later inquiries after me, your brotherly solicitude for my welfare."

Senmen swept the coppers into his sash. "You seem to have struggled on well enough without it," he grunted. "I had worries of my own. Amenemhet learned you were in Hermonthis, a scribe in the temple—having landed on your feet as usual. I saw no reason to be concerned about you."

"You have seen no reason to be concerned about me since I was a child of five."

"Nor have you needed anyone's concern since you were a child of five," retorted the other. "I would scarce have called you a helpless innocent, even then."

Senmut laughed and signaled the proprietor to bring more wine. "The date, not this sour grape swill," he ordered the perspiring fat man. "And clear this food away before it sickens me. Bring two cups, and hasten!"

He grinned in secret delight as the man waddled hastily away, his hands full of dishes.

"What are you laughing at?" asked Senmen.

"I am thinking of the dirty urchin this same fat shopkeeper

used to cuff and bellow at for stealing a fish from his barrel—the urchin who now sits at ease at the swine's best table, ordering him about."

"Did he recognize you?"

"Even you did not, dear brother. I have left the muck of the water front behind me—forever, I trust." He accepted the wine the proprietor brought, poured two cups full, and after tasting it contemptuously, waved the fellow away. "Now," he said, pushing a cup toward Senmen and leaning toward him, "tell me of the others. What of our honored parents, His Stinking Excellency Remose of the fish stalls, and Hat-nufer the Hyena-voiced, a mother patterned after the divine Mut herself?"

Senmen looked into his pleasantly smiling face. "By the breasts of Hathor!" he muttered. "Brother, beside you granite is soft."

"Come, answer my questions. Do our parents still live?"

"Our mother lives, after a fashion, on what few coppers she can filch from the unwary or badger her sons into giving her. I think she sells a few baskets in the market place at times. Father is dead these two years. A nobleman's horse trampled him one night as he lay drunk in the street beside his stalls. His boat and nets we sold for enough to bury him."

"And his whip? Did you sell that too, or keep it to lash your own sons?"

"We never found his whip; possibly he traded it for wine. I have no sons."

"A wife?"

Senmen shook his head, holding out his cup to be refilled. Senmut filled both cups, drained his own at a draught and poured it full again. "And what of our brothers? When I last heard, Amenemhet was a priest on the Divine Bark of Amon."

"He is still. It was on temple business that he sailed to Hermonthis and learned of your whereabouts. Pa-iry left the temple to become cattle overseer on some estate to the north. He felt it offered him a better future."

"Pa-iry is a fool," remarked Senmut. "There is no future for any poor man's son in Egypt save in the temple. You are a fool too, Senmen! A public scribe—at every man's beck and call. Can you not better yourself?"

"Perhaps you can instruct me," retorted Senmen, flashing another resentful glance at the headcloth. "You were a scribe yourself when last we met. Pray tell me your methods for rising in the world—if they can bear discussion!"

Senmut grinned delightedly. "Can you be envious of the head-cloth, my dear Senmen? Your eyes keep returning to it, and your voice, usually so beguiling, takes on an edge . . ."

"Come, how did you do it? A rogue like you, always two jumps ahead of the soldiers, not a copper to your name—"

"Merit, brother. Sheer merit and diligence. And it also helps to know the name of the high priest's lady love."

"And the lady herself, no doubt."

"Aye, and the lady herself. An exquisite creature, obliging to a degree."

"In Amon's name, I might have known!"

The curved lines around Senmut's mouth bit deeper as he leaned forward, dropping his bantering tone. "For a time I was diligent, believe me! First, in learning the scribe's arts from you, my brother, before quitting Thebes six years ago."

"A clumsy enough pupil you were then!"

"I improved, since I had to. There was no other way to earn my bread in Hermonthis. Then I found an architect who needed my services, and I persuaded him to attach me to his staff. I learned much from him, too—more than I intended. Indeed, more than I could forget." Senmut broke off, his eyes thoughtful. "I found it hard to leave him when my chance came at the temple."

"Why did you then, you fool? You might have become an architect yourself!"

"And so I shall, some day," Senmut returned. "But not to build his paltry warehouses and mud-brick dwellings. I have bigger plans. And I must climb higher before I can begin to fulfill them."

"You lack nothing of confidence, whatever else your faults," Senmen commented drily. "I suppose you mean to be High Priest of Montu before you're done!"

Senmut met the jeer with a burst of his silent laughter. "My beloved brother," he said, leaning over the table, "again your imagination fails you. Within ten years I mean to be Steward of Amon."

Senmen gave him a sour grin. "Aye, certainly! And you will be Pharaoh after that."

52

"Wait, and you will see if I jest or not. You did not think I intended to exile myself from Thebes forever?"

"The gods alone know what you intend, my slippery one! But you will end yet with your head in a noose."

"Perhaps I will." Senmut shrugged and drained his cup, glancing at the empty jug. "I have had enough of this airless den. But before we part I have a commission for you." He dug into his sash and produced a handful of coppers. "Take this to the priest at the Necropolis tomorrow. Bid him place beer in our father's tomb each week, as long as that will buy it."

Senmen stared, then gave a bark of laughter. "In the tomb of our 'honored parent, His Stinking Excellency'—"

"I want no thirsty *khefts* calling down curses on all my plans. Let him have his beer." Senmut rose and walked around the table. "Now I will bargain with you. Pay for the wine, and when I am Steward of Amon you shall be First Scribe."

"Pay for the wine?" Senmen exclaimed. He got to his feet, glaring. "You are the high and mighty one in cloth of silver! Pay for it yourself."

"Alas, I cannot." Senmut shrugged and turned his sash inside out to show it empty. "I joined a game of odd-and-even in the temple courtyard this morning, with unfortunate results."

"Why, you swindling devil! By Amon, you'll not get past me with your tricky ways!" Senmen swept up the pile of coins still lying on the table and shook them furiously at his brother. "You'll pay! I'll take the price from this!"

"You would rob the dead?" exclaimed Senmut in a shocked voice.

Senmen looked at him, and began to curse steadily under his breath. Stuffing the coins into his sash, he fished out instead the five coppers Senmut had repaid him for his loan of six years back. Muttering savagely, he scooped up his scribe's equipment, paid the fat proprietor for the wine, and stalked out of the shop without another word.

Senmut, laughing silently, followed at his leisure.

Outside the shop he paused a moment, squinting in the glare of sunshine. The wine had gone agreeably to his head, and his reunion with Senmen had furnished him a great deal of amusement, particularly the bit about the silver headcloth. He reached up to assure himself that its badly worn edges were still safely

53

tucked under, then started down the street, noting with inward mirth the respectful or envious glances turned on it by everyone who passed. He had yet to find the man shrewd or wise enough to look below it, to his worthless necklace and his coarse-woven kilt. Since he had acquired it, as a calculated gamble, two years ago, he had passed everywhere for a man of wealth. He had even been lent money on the strength of it.

A pretty young basket weaver smiled at him from her stall, and he bowed elaborately. He found that he was in excellent spirits—even, he decided judiciously, a trifle drunk. But not too much so for what he intended to do with the long, inviting afternoon that stretched before him.

Turning westward into another street, he emerged presently from the last cluster of metalworking shops into the road that led out into the desert. Keeping his eyes on the ground, he started briskly toward the sunlit cliffs half a mile away. At the base of the cliffs, though he would not let himself look at it yet, lay the ancient Temple of Neb-hepet-Re, first Theban Pharaoh of the Black Land. It had been badly damaged—like all the other old temples up and down the Nile—during the two black centuries when the cursed Hyksos had ruled Egypt; but its ruins were still magnificent. They had been strangely fascinating, even to his street-urchin's eyes. Now he had returned to look at them again —this time with the eyes of an architect.

After a few minutes of rapid walking he paused for breath and, shading his eyes, allowed himself to discover the temple as if he saw it for the first time. There it stood against the cliffs, lovely as ever—perhaps even lovelier than he had remembered—two long terraces rising from the desert floor like broad, low stairsteps, fronted with colonnaded porches.

He covered the remaining stretch of desert and walked slowly around two sides of the temple, pacing off its measurements. Scratching in the sand with a fragment of limestone, he worked out the ratio of width to length, squinted up to estimate its height, then shrugged and flung away his scrap of stone. Its proportions were admirable, but not unusual; it was not in proportions alone that the temple's peculiar beauty lay. The architect who had designed this old Pharaoh's offering to Hathor had known some other secret—something that made this building different from every other in Egypt.

Perhaps, thought Senmut, strolling along the sun-and-shadow-striped lower porch, it was all the doing of the gods, and the architect himself knew not what he did to build so well.

Senmut did not believe it. There was an answer, somewhere, if he could only discover it. And if he could discover it, not even his skimpy training could prevent him from becoming a master architect—provided, of course, that he could make good his boasts to Senmen and climb first to eminence in other ways. He smiled, and the lines bit deep around his mouth. He was not in the least afraid of that provision, men being the fools and knaves they were. The complex organization of the temple hierarchy offered a thousand shortcuts to a man who did not mind treading on a few toes as he climbed.

Reaching the northern end of the colonnade, he looked back along its airy length, then stepped out once more into the sands. The wine was buzzing in his head, its effect in no way diminished by his walk in the midday heat. A few cubits away stood a small mud-brick chapel erected by some long-dead Pharaoh for his funerary offerings. Its deep-roofed interior, walled on three sides and open on the fourth, offered a cool respite from the sun.

When Senmut stepped into it, blinking a little at the sudden transition from the glare outside, he realized that he was not alone. A girl—very young and very dirty—was sitting with one leg doubled under her on the stone bench built out from one of the side walls. She was watching him with startled interest.

He gave her a slow grin, a mocking bow. "By my *ka!*" he drawled. "It's Hathor herself! Where did you come from, pretty one?"

"Are you addressing me?" she said.

He looked around elaborately, then shrugged. "I see no one else to bear the burden of my attentions." He made himself comfortable on the bench beside her. She was not as pretty as that little basket weaver, nor could she compare at all with the high priest's lady. Still—his eyes roved appreciatively down the sweet curve of throat and bare young breasts, and the wine in him buzzed interestingly—she was in no wise unattractive. "Suppose you tell me your name," he suggested. "It will avoid confusion."

To his surprise she burst out laughing. "The name you have chosen already will do well enough."

"Hathor? It suits you well, though I never saw a goddess quite so dirty. Did your sacred cattle trample you, Divinity?"

"Something of that nature."

He leaned back, looking at her with amusement. "You are not very informative. Could it be you are trying to discourage this conversation?"

"Perhaps it is time I asked the questions," she answered drily.

"By all means. Where shall we begin?"

"With your curious actions of the past half hour. I have been watching you. You seem very interested in the temple yonder."

"I am, indeed," he admitted.

"Why so?"

"I am something of an architect. That temple holds a secret which could be of great value to me. I mean to discover it."

"By pacing off measurements and scratching in the sand?"

She had indeed been watching him. "It is something to do with proportions, this secret," he explained. "You would not understand, little one. It is architect's talk."

"Perhaps I would. My father did some building once, and I watched his architects at work on their plans."

"Your father is a man of wealth?" he asked in surprise. He had guessed her a shopkeeper's daughter, from her clothing—perhaps a maidservant.

She studied her hands demurely. "It was only an addition to a building. But I found the work interesting."

"And I'll wager the architects found you interesting also," he remarked with a grin. He was becoming more and more attracted to her. Her nose had a fine, almost arrogant arch, well set off by the delicacy of jaw-line and nostril, and her whole face, which he had first thought plain, was lent an elusive charm by her swift-changing expressions. Perhaps it was only her tricks of gesture that fascinated—the way she turned her head or flung back her hair, or glanced at him coolly from those wide, dark eyes with their curiously beautiful lids. Whatever it was, it was causing the little basket weaver's flashy prettiness to recede into the background.

"If they found me interesting they did not mention it," she said. "In truth, I believe they accounted me a nuisance. But I watched them nonetheless. I know quite well what you mean by 'proportions.' Now explain the secret you are after."

56

"If I could do that, it would be no secret. That is precisely what I cannot do—explain why Neb-hepet-Re's temple is the most beautiful in Egypt."

"You consider it so?" she asked in surprise.

"I do indeed."

"More beautiful than Amon's great temple in Thebes?"

"Aye, infinitely!"

She rose and walked to the chapel's wide entrance, moving with a lithe, bold grace that captured his attention anew. Leaning against the bricks with folded arms, she studied the temple.

"You will not see what I speak of from there," Senmut told her. "Rather close your eyes and picture the temple as it looks to one approaching across the desert—low and long, with columns white as ivory against the cliffs."

She flashed him an interested glance, then did as he bade her while he admired the sweep of her lashes against her cheek.

"White against their own shadows, rather," she said suddenly.

"Pardon?"

"The columns show forth against the shadow of the porches behind them, not against the cliffs. Backed by that rough yellow stone their effect would be quite lost. It is the deep shade which displays their form so clearly."

"Aye, true. It was only a manner of speaking, to say 'against the cliffs.' Naturally, the shadow backs them . . ." He hesitated, rubbing his chin thoughtfully. Her comment had suggested something new to him, but he could not quite capture it. Shadows, columns . . .

"I think I know your secret," she said, returning to the bench. "It lies in simplicity. The eye sees the temple's form, rather than its ornament. Even those great statues of Hathor let into the front wall are so simple of line and bulk that they do nothing to detract."

"You are clever, little one!" He was astonished at her quick and effortless grasp of such an essential. "It is true that the ornamentation is well subordinated, but this is so in other temples also, yet they remain massive, earth-bound structures. Take the pylons forming the south gates of the Temple of Amon, for example."

"Aye, that is so," she said thoughtfully. "Amon's temple has none of this one's airy grace . . . and yet would such be fitting for the mansion of the Strong Bull?"

Her point was well taken. Stimulated, Senmut plunged deeper into argument, almost forgetting she was not another architect. "True, but is there no other way to acknowledge his grandeur than to multiply size and weight and height and giant columns until men feel as ants before the might of god? I see no reason why Amon as well as the lovely Hathor could not be honored with temples of poise and balance."

"Poise, balance, grace, simplicity," mused the girl. "Doubtless your secret is the sum of these."

He shook his head, turning a baffled scrutiny on the temple. "How simple it looks, indeed! Like the house a child builds of blocks. Horizontal terraces, vertical columns—in two strokes the effect is achieved, and how admirably it echoes the structure of the cliffs behind! There lies part of the temple's charm, without a doubt. But many temples are thus wedded to their backgrounds. That is not the secret. Nay, and it is not your sum. It is something apart from all. . . . Consider the lotus, little one. Its form, its color, its texture—all are beautiful. But it would not be the lotus without its fragrance, which can neither be seen nor touched. It is a fragrance I am seeking."

He turned to her, laughing. Her eyes were no longer cool, but warmly interested. "You please me, Architect," she announced surprisingly. "You may make yourself known to me if you like."

His heavy eyebrows flew up. By Amon, where had the little wench learned such regal airs? He rose and swept her a mocking bow. "Senmut of Hermonthis, Chief Prophet of Montu, Your Loveliness. I crave my lady's pardon for not begging permission to introduce myself."

She accepted the apology as calmly as a countess, and he sat down again, enormously amused. She was bluffing, but her dignity was marvelous and quite undisturbed by such trifles as tangled hair and a smudge on her cheek. Possibly she was maidservant to some great lady—and an apt student of highborn manners and graces.

"Chief Prophet of Montu," she repeated. "Then you are in Thebes for the Heb-Sed."

"I am. I shall stand before the Double Thrones themselves on the Day of Offerings to tender Montu's gifts, and shall see Pharaoh with my own eyes. However," he added, "it is the Successor I would have a glimpse of, if I can manage it."

"Why so? It will be some years before he sits alone upon the throne. The Heb-Sed will make Pharaoh strong and powerful again, a god among gods, as in his prime— Why do you shake your head? Do you not believe it?"

Senmut shrugged. "Little one, Pharaoh is full of years. I have heard that age has sent his feet so far along the Western Path that not even the Heb-Sed can turn him back again. It is the Tired One that Egypt must look to now, I fear. A dismal prospect, if one listens to what they are saying on the streets of Thebes."

"And what are they saying on the streets of Thebes?"

"They are saying that the prince is as weak in spirit as he is in body. Have you not heard it yourself? The talk is rife. Now if only the princess were a prince, they say, then all would be well, for she is a personable maiden indeed and Pharaoh's own child in every way. Some even think Pharaoh might break all precedent and name her Successor instead of the Tired One. I believe there are actually wagers on the matter— Is something amiss, little one?"

She was looking at him with startled eyes; for a moment he wondered if she had heard his question, and he was about to repeat it when she turned away swiftly.

"And you?" she said. "Do you think this—this strange thing will happen, that Pharaoh will name Hatshepsut?"

He laughed, throwing back his head. "My lovely Hathor, do I look to be an innocent? Pharaoh will name his son to succeed him, you may be assured of it. It has never happened otherwise."

"Perhaps there has never before been such a princess!" she retorted with such heat that he laughed the harder.

"Can it be that you too have placed a wager? Alas for your hopes! Be the royal Hatshepsut ever so charming a princess, she could scarce rule Egypt."

"She might do so better than her sickly brother! How can you prove otherwise? Are you acquainted with Her Highness?"

"No more than you," chuckled Senmut, but he was delighted with the impression his silver headcloth seemed to have produced this time. The maid was elevating his rank indeed, to ask such a question! No doubt she was flattered to be conversing with so great a noble as she imagined him to be, and would look with favor on even warmer attentions.

Aye, she might indeed. The idea was in no way unattractive to him. A little dalliance in the shade of this secluded spot—it appealed with sudden urgency as his eye once more ran over the round golden breasts, the lithe curves of hip and thigh beneath the smudged white skirt. She was a fascinating creature, with her alert mind, her slowly realized beauty, and those hips and legs as slim as a boy's, yet fashioned in a manner that set his blood on fire. He must certainly quench that fire, he decided, moving a little closer to her. He could resume his study of the temple later.

"Of course," he remarked, "one may make wagers without setting eyes upon the princess, if one has had experience with women. Now if Her Highness were such a maid as you—"

"Aye, if she were?"

He noted—and misinterpreted—the quick interest in her eyes, and smiled with satisfaction. "Then she will rule Egypt in truth, though not as Pharaoh."

"I do not understand you, Architect. Who can be Horus without the crown?"

He laughed softly, stretching his arm casually along the back of the bench. "You can ask that, who must have twisted innumerable young men about your pretty fingers? She will rule through the weakling, Prince Nenni, who will certainly be her husband. By my *ka,* how I envy him, if she is anything like you."

A chariot appeared in the distance, speeding along the desert road toward them, and he cursed it inwardly before he realized that it had not distracted her attention. She was gazing straight at him, eyes wide and lips a trifle parted.

"Rule—through the Tired One?"

"Of course. Could he refuse her anything if she were like you —with the wit of a man, and a body that must be Hathor's own?"

His hand lifted, ran swiftly and lightly over her bare shoulder and down her arm, while he leaned even closer. In a flash she was on her feet, slapping him back and forth across the face with a speed and force that left him gaping.

"How dare you touch me?" she spat at him.

Incredulity, then anger gathered in him, only inflaming his desire. He sprang up, flung her against the wall, and penned her with his outstretched arms. "You carry a bluff too far, little High-and-Mighty!" he informed her.

The sudden violence of his action seemed to have struck her speechless. Deliberately he let his gaze move over her parted lips, her wide and dilated eyes, the hair in tumbled disarray about her cheeks, and wondered how he could ever have thought her plain. The blood was roaring in his ears as he pulled her to him and kissed her roughly and thoroughly.

It required more time and considerably more force than he expected to master her struggling and transform it into blind but unmistakable response. By then he was shaking with his own passion. Without releasing her, he drew his lips from hers and moved them over her cheeks and throat.

"By all the gods!" he whispered. "I must have you, little one. Never have I touched so smooth a cheek or so fair a breast— Do not push me away from you, your heart is beating too, and your breath comes as fast as mine. Come, lie against me."

Instead of obeying, she tried to pull away from him, giving him a look he never forgot—a look so wild with fear and confusion, as well as the passion he was already well aware of, that he was startled into wondering if he was the first man ever to touch her. The noise of the chariot rattling along the road sounded loud and near as they stared at each other. Then she spoke, in an intense but shaking voice.

"Loose me, Architect. I warn you. Loose me."

Something in her tone made him obey her instantly, without thinking. Next minute he was cursing himself and snatching after her as she ran out of the chapel and across the sunlit desert toward the approaching chariot. To his surprise it stopped as if its driver were expecting her. She sprang in beside him, and he turned the horses at once—great black stallions they were, magnificent beasts—and started them at a full gallop back toward Thebes without ever coming closer to the temple.

Breathing raggedly still, and furiously chagrined, Senmut leaned in the doorway waiting for the fire inside him to burn itself out as best it could. At length he ran a hand over his face, and with a last sardonic glance at the cloud of dust in the middle distance which was all he could see of the chariot, he walked across the sands toward the temple.

An hour later, feeling like a man who has spent his afternoon pursuing phantoms, he started back across the desert. His mood was far from pretty by this time. He was tired and dusty, the wine had long ago worn off, he had not found his secret, and he could not get that slim-hipped maiden off his mind.

Turning, he scowled back at the temple. There it lay, serenely beautiful, still taunting him. It was from this angle that its peculiar beauty was most apparent, therefore it must have something to do with the graceful pattern of its columns, so white against the cliffs. Or rather, as she had pointed out, white against the shadowed porch behind them. That part of their conversation had been one of those moments when a new idea had stirred, when discovery had seemed close. Shadows, columns . . . repeated white verticals against blue-gray ones . . .

Suddenly he realized what he was doing. He was looking at the spaces between the columns, as well as the columns themselves. Those blue-gray verticals were indispensable to the pattern, yet they were not part of the building at all, they were mere space, intangible air. The shadows had been planned to fall just there, in measured proportion. Old Neb-hepet-Re's architect had counted that cubic measure of nothingness between the columns as important as the columns themselves. He had built with space as if it were stone; with light and air and shadow as if they were precious metals to adorn his structure.

Senmut's heart was beating fast again; he had found his secret.

The haughty little baggage of the afternoon came back to his mind, and his smile turned grim. By Hathor's breasts! he thought as he wheeled and started again toward Thebes. I'll have you, too, for all your airs! And that as soon as I can find you.

Then he realized, with a return of his chagrin, that he did not even know her name.

6.

"You may remove the goddess," Pharaoh said.

The several slaves and wardrobe attendants gathered in the sitting room of the King's Apartments at once prostrated themselves full length upon the floor. Thutiy, Royal Treasurer and Guardian of the Crowns, stepped forward, bowed to Pharaoh, made a second, deeper obeisance to the fiery cobra-goddess Wadjet, whose gold-and-enameled body curved out from the base of the crown to project over the king's forehead. Then with skinny hands uplifted in the gesture of adoration—palms out, to shield his eyes from the sunlike radiance of the king—he walked to Thutmose and reverently lifted the Crown of Egypt from his head.

As he turned, an assistant stepped to his side and threw a veil of snowy linen over the sacred object. Both vanished through a doorway to bear the repository of Pharaoh's divine power to the heavily guarded closet which was its solitary habitation. Thutmose, freed for a while of his divinity, relaxed in his chair and rubbed his shaven, old-man's head with both hands.

The tension in the room relaxed as well. Servants bent to loosen the stiff golden sandals from the royal feet. One slave placed a tray of fruit at Pharaoh's elbow, another poured wine, others removed the flashing collar and armbands and the rigidly starched kilt, substituting a dressing robe and soft leather sandals. Thutmose, at last comfortable in body if not in mind, waved them out and was alone.

The room was his favorite, small but gracefully proportioned. Its polished clay floor was strewn with rugs, and its walls, tinted a delicate yellow, were decorated with swarms of golden bees. Adjoining it was his bedchamber, with an alcove for the lion-headed bed; a garden opened off the bedchamber. The chair in which he sat—comfortable, deep, upholstered in well-worn scarlet leather—was also his favorite. But today he derived no pleasure from either his chair or his room; and the wine standing invitingly on the low table beside him merely reminded him that he should not drink it.

Thutiy's face had been a mask of anxious inquiry, though he had not spoken. He did not need to. The Kinsmen's thoughts were plain these days. Pharaoh must order his daughter's marriage some time—why not at once? He must name his son Successor—why not admit it, and set all anxious minds at ease?

Aye, why not, why not? Pharaoh thought. They would never understand, they are not warriors. Only another warrior would understand. . . .

Presently he sighed, stood up, walked into his bedchamber and stretched full length upon his couch.

He did not sleep. An hour later, he still lay wide-eyed upon his ivory headrest, staring at the ceiling of the alcove, which was painted a deep blue and decorated in gold with a map of the heavens. His glance traveled over the delicate lines, each one, after twenty-odd years, as well known to him as the lines in his own face. Directly over his head shone the great bullheaded constellation Mes-khetiu, which he had always thought looked more like a big water dipper than anything else. Opposite, in southern skies, starry Isis chased, endlessly pleading, after her elusive Osiris, who just as endlessly averted his face. . . .

As I avert mine, perhaps, thought Pharaoh, from ugly truth?

He lay quiet a few more minutes, until he could endure his own thoughts no longer. Then he stretched out his hand and struck a savage note on a little brass gong that stood beside his bed. When the door opened he said, "Fetch Ahmose-pen-Nekhbet to me."

The servant cleared his throat nervously. "The Exalted One means Ahmose-en-Nefer, the Chief of Gardeners?"

"Nay, Ahmose-pen-Nekhbet, Commander of the Navies under my predecessor Ahmose, for whom he was named." Thutmose turned his head on its curved support and looked at the young man. "Ah," he sighed, turning back, "you are new in my service. You do not remember. Listen, then. This Ahmose-pen-Nekhbet is an old, a very old man, who was both old and wise when we fought together for the glory of Egypt in the first days of my kingship. You will find him somewhere about the Southern Barracks of the bodyguard, napping or dreaming in the sun. Fetch him to me."

When the servant had left, Thutmose stared unblinking at his golden star-map, and his mind roved among the battles and homecomings of his youth, and farther back, beyond his own youth and into the much-told tales of Ahmose's, when Ahmose was the tallest sailor on the ship *Wild Bull* and spent his nights in a hammock of net. So he always said it— "I spent my nights in a hammock of net . . ." A magic the old man made, somehow, telling his tales, until you could feel the very sway of that hammock under you and know the slap of the water against the ship's side, and the sound of voices long-dead when you were born.

64

He seemed old even when he told the tales, Thutmose mused, though perhaps he was after all no older than Thutiy is now, and I think of Thutiy as almost young. . . . Aye, well, we are both old now, Ahmose-pen-Nekhbet and I.

The door opened. Thutmose turned his head on the headrest and saw a tall, spare figure in a leather headcloth—a figure a little stooped, much scarred—attempting to get down on his knees.

"Nay, Ahmose," said Pharaoh, swinging his legs over the side of the couch. "Your joints are too creaky for such greetings. Let us meet as soldiers, as in other days."

The old man righted himself and walked slowly across the room to where Thutmose waited for him. They gripped right hands, each with his left on the other's shoulder. Ahmose's palm felt large and horny and reassuring; his shoulder was still hard under its linen drape, and his face, no less leathern than his helmet, was like the map of a familiar battleground. The old scythe-shaped scar curved as always up his cheek and caused the tip of his eyebrow to tilt rakishly; his slow grin was unchanged save for the loss of another tooth.

"My old friend," said Thutmose, feeling obscurely comforted already. "How fares the world with you? It is long since I gave my eyes pleasure by the sight of you, yet you are unchanged."

"I am older by a year since last Pharaoh sent for me," remarked Ahmose. His voice was high and rusty; his eyes, still bright amid their network of wrinkles, were taking careful stock of Thutmose. "But I continue hale and well, hale and well. One need not ask, of course, how fares the Horus in his palace, since the days of the Good God follow one another in their perfection like beads on a string."

Their glances met, and Pharaoh nodded, accepting the offer of their old fiction—that there was nothing amiss with the empire or ever would be. He knew Ahmose was well aware that something was amiss or he would not have been sent for—something Pharaoh was unwilling or unable to speak of to his Kinsmen, but might mention obliquely to an obscure old warrior who knew how to hold his tongue. Still, the fiction soothed them both and made it easier to speak freely.

Thutmose waved his visitor to a chair as if it were the usual thing for a subject to sit in the presence of the king—for how could a man talk to his friend if they behaved like god and mortal?—and sank into another one himself. Clasping his hands, he gazed out the open doors into his little bedroom garden.

"Ahmose," he said, "how many Heb-Seds have you witnessed in your lifetime?"

"Two, my lord. Tomorrow's will be my third."

"Eh, you grow too old to be worth anything—I am a stripling beside you! I have seen but one other, long as I have adorned this earth."

Ahmose chuckled and nodded. "True, true, you were yet in your mother's womb when Pharaoh Ahmose, your predecessor, for whom I was named, celebrated his first Jubilee. It was long ago in the middle of his reign. *Aii,* those were the good days, the dangerous days, when men were fighters and none thought of anything but Egypt and her freedom. I was but a stripling then myself—a lad of fourteen—but I was a fighter too! Aye, the tallest sailor on the ship *Wild Bull.* I ate my bread and onion atop the mast, watching for the enemy, and I spent my nights in a hammock of net."

Thutmose smiled, but it was not the time for listening to well-loved tales. "I know of that hammock of yours, Old One. But there is something I do not know. Why did your warring Pharaoh declare Heb-Sed in the prime of his life?"

"Because those were dangerous days, as I have said. He was preparing to drive the cursed Hyksos from their cursed capital, Avaris in the Delta. He needed the strength of the gods behind him as he never needed it again."

"And his second festival—the one he ordered in my own youth, when he married me to his daughter the royal Aahmes and named me Successor? What were his reasons then?"

Ahmose hesitated an instant. Then he said bluntly, "He was an old man. He felt death's breath upon him."

Thutmose stood up suddenly and walked to the open doors. "Aye, and this is the commonest cause for declaring Heb-Sed, this awareness of—" He found himself unable to speak death's name, not out of cowardice but out of a certain sensitive reserve, the same which restrains a man from mentioning intimate matters even to his friends. He took refuge in the scholarly terms of the priesthood. "This awareness of a growing desire to rejoin the sun," he went on stiffly. "As a king grows old, he feels a yearning to rest from life, to become Osiris and rule the land of

66

the shadows, and let another Horus mount the throne of living Egypt. As everyone knows, the magic of the Heb-Sed arrests this—this—yearning of aging Pharaohs. As the festival proceeds we become as youths again, in the full power of our kingship."

"Aye. Such is the mystery and the miracle."

"And yet," Thutmose added, "does it not seem strange? It is ever at Heb-Sed that we name the Successor. It is almost as if we did not believe that we would be restored."

There was a short silence. Thutmose turned slowly to watch the old man's face.

"My king and lord," said Ahmose, "does a man put away grain in his storehouses because he does not believe the Nile will rise again? Nay, only because he has more than he needs, and because he is provident and wise. Thus there comes a time when Pharaoh points his finger at the Horus-in-the-Nest, that his people may be doubly assured of their security. Then, even should he depart our land for that darker one, there would still remain the Fledgling to be ruler over Egypt, and—"

"Careful words," grunted Thutmose. "Shrewd and cautious words, such as old women speak as they sit hemming their shrouds about the fire while telling each other the gods will never let them die." He leaned toward Ahmose. "What if one Pharaoh believed the miracle, Ahmose? Believed and was bold enough to trust the gods? What if *he* meant to be that ruler over Egypt, when the Heb-Sed had renewed him—not cautiously with a princeling by his side, but—alone?"

The old man stared at him, blankly at first, then with growing consternation. "That Pharaoh is yourself, my lord? You do not plan to name your son Successor?"

"I do not. I shall not name anyone at all."

Slowly Ahmose rose, still studying his monarch's face. "Then you have regained your youth already, my old friend, for you have taken leave of wisdom."

There was a strange little sound as the breath departed in a rush from Thutmose's lungs. "Say, rather, that you have taken leave of courage! You—a warrior—would you have me an old woman sewing on my shroud? If I believe in the gods and their miracle, what need have I of a Successor?"

"There is too much danger! You risk too much."

"And have you never heard of danger, you who fought with me across the plains of Syria? When you captained your ship *Wild Bull* did you never risk her safety, and the lives of all the men who sailed her, if the need arose? Have you never stood desperate, with your sword broken and your comrades falling by the tens around you, ambushed, caught, outnumbered—and still hurling challenges, fighting with bare hands—"

"My lord, you cannot fight the gods. You cannot hurl challenges at the ways of heaven."

"*You* cannot, perhaps! I can—and will!"

The two old men stood gazing at each other, Ahmose grave, Thutmose glaring, his jaw outthrust.

"What do you want of me, my lord?" said Ahmose softly. "Lies, after all these years? Is this why you sent for me, that I might support you in this madness, agree with you, allay your own uncertainty—"

"I have no uncertainty! I am Pharaoh, I have made my decision. I am sure!"

"You are lord of all the earth. But if you were sure, you would not be angry."

Pharaoh's face changed. He swung away to the garden door, turning his back on Ahmose. After a moment he growled, "And you are an obstinate old man!"

"Aye," admitted Ahmose. "I have always been so. In my folly I thought it was part of my value in my lord's eyes."

"That you are stubborn, opinionated, overcautious?"

"That I speak my mind in the presence of Pharaoh, which no other dares to do."

Thutmose made no answer, and presently Ahmose walked over to stand behind him. "My lord, we have fought many battles side by side. Surely we need not do battle with each other now—simply because Pharaoh wars within himself."

Thutmose turned weary and desperate eyes upon his friend. "My decision is made. I will trust the gods. They have left me nothing else to do." Walking past Ahmose, he sank heavily into his chair. "They have taken my strong son and left me an invalid and a maid. Egypt wants a god upon her throne. But what she needs is a strong man! You know that, Ahmose, as well as I. And I have none to give her—save myself."

"Are you not forgetting the future? The royal line—"

"Forgetting it? It is the center of all my thinking on this sorry matter! If I saw any hope of sturdy grandsons—one weakling Pharaoh might not ruin Egypt. But two in a row, perhaps three? It is unthinkable. Nubia would revolt— Ah gods, Ahmose, the Hyksos might come back! Nay, I must rule!"

"My lord, that is not an answer, but only a postponement. The gods allow no man to live forever."

"They will allow me to live long enough to safeguard Egypt! To"—Thutmose's eyes flashed an arrogant warning—"to father another son! Aye, I said it—I mean it! Youth will return to me during the Heb-Sed, will it not? It will, it must! By the blood of Osiris, the gods cannot take my gifts and yet withhold theirs— and they will take mine—aye, they will take them. Did you ever see the Mighty Ones refuse gold or cattle? Thousands of everything will I give them, and they cannot deny me!"

"I see," said Ahmose quietly. "Then you will not even order the royal marriage?"

Thutmose settled back uneasily. "That I will have to do. My daughter must be wed. But I have no faith in the marriage, Ahmose, or in its issue."

"Or in your daughter? Such a child as the princess must surely be fruitful, and have many sons."

"Wed to another, perhaps. But—wed to Nenni?" Thutmose made a gesture of despair. "What but weaklings can spring from the seed of one whose very name means 'dead'?"

The old warrior was silent for a time. Out in the garden the lawns were blue with shadows, and the cool air of evening had begun to drift in through the open door. Two servants appeared through the garden gate, bearing trays and a table, and began to lay Pharaoh's evening meal beside the pool. Far away, from the direction of the western desert, the scream of a kite sounded faintly, like a distant, seven-noted bell.

Ahmose turned his scarred face to Thutmose. "Let Pharaoh not lose hope," he said softly. "There is another, if he but think on it, whose very name means 'dead.' "

Thutmose bit absently at the knuckles of his clasped hands and thought about it. Ahmose's allusion was clear enough—he referred to Osiris, Egypt's best-loved god, the tragic hero of antiquity.

"Old One," he said presently with an impatient sigh, "it is

69

Osiris whose very name means 'dead,' but what has this to do with me and my son?"

"Is not the prince at this moment awaiting the arrival of his second child?"

"Aye, a child begotten of a harem woman—but consider his firstborn! A frail little maid who was carried to her tomb before she knew a year of life. Your meaning is not clear—and your wisdom wearies me. It is not a time for the wisdom of old men, it is a time to fight, and to believe!" For an instant he glared fiercely at his friend, then the fire departed from his eyes, though his craggy features did not soften. "Go, Ahmose," he said. "I cannot believe when you are here. This time, I should not have summoned you."

After the door closed behind the old warrior, Thutmose sat for some time staring straight ahead, battling a misery that threatened to engulf him. He had not realized how much he craved Ahmose's agreement and support until they were denied him. Why had Ahmose not understood—he of all men? He too had been a fighter, and a strategist—aye, but he had never been Pharaoh. There lay the difference. He did not know the burdens of a god; he was a man.

A stubborn old man, thought Pharaoh, hardening his heart against his friend. A stubborn, obstinate old man!

At last he noticed the two servants kneeling silently in the garden doorway, and roused himself. Rising with a sigh, he walked out the door and down the graveled path to his solitary dinner.

The meal was finished, the table had been removed, and Thutmose still sat scowling beside the pool at moonrise when the garden gate opened quietly. He peered at the slim, dim shape which appeared.

"Hatshepsut? Come in, child."

She closed the gate and sped up the path to drop upon the stone bench at his side. "My lord father—I would speak with you of something—"

"Aye—what is it?" He frowned down at her uneasily. She was disturbed, very disturbed. Her hands clasped each other tensely in her lap, her profile was white and strained in the dim half-light, and she did not look at him.

Send her away! urged a voice inside him. You cannot cope with anything else tonight. . . .

But he was already bracing himself to accept her burden, whatever it might be. "What is it, little one? Here, I'll order torches brought."

"Nay, nay—please! I—like the moonlight."

She does not want me to observe her closely, he thought. She does not even want to say this thing she came to say, now that she is here. Or rather, she wants to say it but does not know how. . . .

He stopped watching her, forcing aside his own tension, and began to speak calmly of the Festival's beginning, the moon's rising, the new confection he had been served at dinner. "Sweetened with honey and stuffed with dates. Very good, I thought, though old Ahmet, who made the pastries when you were a little maid, used to invent much better. Aye, a veritable Pharaoh of a pastry cook he was, old Ahmet—"

"Father," Hatshepsut said suddenly.

"Speak, my dear." He kept his voice easy, his crossed leg swinging idly.

"Name me Successor—instead of Nenni."

The foot halted. He sat frozen with surprise, staring at her. She began to talk rapidly. "It would solve everything—everything! I am strong, and well. My blood is royal and would make a god of any man I wed, and royal princes of our sons. I could wed some nobleman—"

"Hatshepsut!" His voice was stern. "What you are asking is impossible."

She turned to him passionately. "Why, why is it impossible? *You* were not royal-born. You wed my mother and became the Good God, and there was never a mightier warrior, a greater Pharaoh—"

"But it was I who was named Successor, not your mother! And I only because there was no prince to name."

"There is none now!" she burst out. "Only a spiritless creature, always ailing, solemn, with his face turned toward his tomb. Am I not more a prince than he? I am! He fears the crown, he shrinks from it! Ptah's Beard! What a Pharaoh *he* will make, swayed by—"

"Be silent!" he gasped.

"Nay, hear me! If I were a prince instead of a princess, would you not choose me without a thought, without a question? You know you would! My father, forget my maiden's body, I would be your son, I would be an Amenmose to you and Egypt, a prince, a king to follow after you—"

"Silence!" he cried out, hardly aware of what he was saying. "Silence! Silence! Silence!" He shoved to his feet and started blindly away from her. The old, suffocating pounding in his chest halted him before he had taken three steps. He groped for support, found nothing, and turned desperately back. In an instant she was beside him, eyes wide with alarm.

"Father! Oh, Amon have mercy! Here, sit, the bench is here —I will fetch slaves, the physician—"

She moved to dart away, but he clutched her arm and held on, forming the word "wait" with his lips though he could bring forth no sound.

She stood a moment, trembling, tensed to jerk away, studying his face with frightened eyes. At last she sank down beside him on the bench. Seizing his hand, she raised it to her lips, buried her face against it. Silently she began to cry. "Tomorrow," she whispered. "Only one more night. The Heb-Sed . . . the gods will make you whole. Strong and young . . . forever. . . ."

She did not believe it. It was obvious, from all she had just been saying, from the ruthlessness with which she had spread those terrible truths in front of him.

He sat very still, waiting out the storm inside him, trying to calm himself.

All she had said was true, of course, though her solution was the wrong one. It was the very truth, unpleasant though it was to hear, which had forced him to *his* solution—which was the right one, and remained unchanged. There was no reason to be disturbed, since he believed in the mystery of the Heb-Sed. He must believe.

He had soothed the pounding to a murmur now. It was going to be all right, he would feel no arrow through his collarbone this time. It was only the suddenness with which she spoke, he thought firmly. I foolishly became excited. I must talk quietly now, as of any other matter. Explain to her.

"My daughter," he began.

"I know what you will say," she whispered. "A woman cannot

72

be Pharaoh, such has never been nor ever will be, I am your daughter and not your son. I am a princess, and cannot be a prince."

He stroked her bent head gently. "I would that you could be, my Shesu," he said in a low voice. She looked up quickly, and he nodded. "Aye, you are right. All you said is true. But you must cease weeping for what cannot be. If you would truly ease my heart—"

"I would wed Nenni and bear sons for the glory of Egypt and our line, and be the woman I was born. I know. I will do anything you ask. My lord father, forgive me, I did not mean to make you ill. . . . I will do it, I will do it all!"

"Aye, aye." He settled back on the bench with a sigh.

"You are better?"

He nodded. For a time they sat in silence, then he half turned on the bench and searched her face gravely. "Now, my little one," he said, "let us talk of why you came to me with this tonight."

She threw him a startled look. "Why, I—I don't know, it has been long in my mind—"

"Nay, it has not. It has been in your mind no longer than the afternoon just past. What put it there?"

"Nothing, I tell you." Hatshepsut rose and walked nervously along the edge of the pool. "It is only that I think of you, and my *ka* is troubled by your need of a son. *Aii,* may Amon curse me that I was not born a man!"

"You must not talk so!"

She whirled on him. "I will! It is this maiden's body that is all our trouble, yours and mine too! I hate it, I hate it!" She pushed her hands angrily down her breasts as if stripping off a garment. "It is not even mine to bestow. I must wed merely to bear royal sons, wed my brother . . . gods, what a dreary thing! No prince ever seeks his sister out of real desire, as he might seek another maid. I was taught to believe so, but it is not true, it cannot be! We wed indifferently, merely from duty, and never know the delights of love as do other folk—"

"My child, princes have more to think of," Pharaoh cut in uncomfortably. "You know as well as I that a prince must wed a royal princess, in whose veins alone runs the blood of the Sun. Otherwise his children—"

"I know, I know." Irritably she turned away. "But what of

73

the princess, denied what her lowest slave girl may rejoice in freely? No brother's touch could bring the trembling, the weakness, the—"

She broke off suddenly. Pharaoh stared at her profile, his brows furrowed and his eyes suspicious. "Your speech is at odds with itself," he grunted. "Very curiously so! One moment you long to be a prince, the next you dream of love like any other maiden. Weakness—trembling—what do you know of this, you who have never known any man's touch? It is time you were married, that is certain," he went on, half to himself. Then, as she swung around to protest, he gave a short laugh. "Aye, that is what troubles you—not me and my need for a son, not the Succession or Egypt, but marriage to Nenni. Come, admit it."

"Aye, that is part of it."

"The great part."

Her lips opened to speak, then closed again. Suddenly she dropped her face into her hands. *"Aii,* I do not want to marry Nenni, please do not wed me to him . . ." The rest was lost in tears.

Thutmose sighed deeply, and reaching for her hand, pulled her gently to the bench beside him. When she was quieter, he said, "I have no choice, my Shesu." He looked down at her. "You know that. Only a few moments past you gave your promise that you would do it willingly."

The crown of moonlight on her black hair rippled as she nodded.

"And you renew your promise?"

"Aye."

"It is not what I would do, my Shesu, but what I must. I have already postponed it too long . . . but always for reasons of my own, not because you pled to stay a maid. Never before did you protest. Even this morning in the garden—it was not marriage to a brother that troubled you then, only the matter of an ibis. And yet tonight . . ."

"Aii, I am confused tonight. My thoughts will not come straight and clear as they did in the garden, when I had only one desire."

"And whence came the other, so suddenly, between then and now? That is what I would know."

"Oh, cease questioning me!" she cried. "I do not know myself. It comes to all maids, sooner or later, does it not? What is the use to speak of it, when it cannot be gratified, now or ever . . ." Her voice trailed off. Presently she rose. "Do not be troubled. I will do all I should, and none but you shall know I questioned it."

"I too have questioned," muttered Pharaoh. She looked small and somehow desolate, standing there beside the dark pool. He longed to comfort her. "Even now, perhaps there is no need for haste. It is possible I might—find another way."

She turned quickly, studying his face, waiting.

I have said too much, he thought. I should have held my tongue. By all the gods, I cannot hold my tongue today!

"The Heb-Sed," he went on, trying to keep his voice casual. "It will give time to—consider. I will still be Pharaoh for a while yet. We know that."

"Aye, we know it!" she said eagerly.

Now he could find no trace of doubt in her tone, her hopeful face. She does believe, he thought. One other besides myself believes! Then I will tell her—

He turned away hastily, not daring to risk it. He could not have borne to see another face he loved suddenly cloud with horrified surprise. "Ah well, we shall see, we shall see," he muttered hastily. "Go, my daughter, I am weary."

"May Nuit guard your sleep," she whispered.

He heard her footsteps moving quickly down the path, and a moment later the gate clicked. He sat on, thinking. Then he pushed himself carefully to his feet and stood a moment, trying his strength. His legs felt tired, but not too weak to carry him. Very slowly he walked across the garden, into the dimly golden lamplight of his bedchamber, and on into the alcove where his couch stood. There, in a wall niche lighted by the flame of a tiny brazier, stood a small image of the god Amon, wrought in solid, brilliant gold. Perfect of limb and body was the god; he stood squarely, frontally, one foot slightly in advance of the other, his arms at his sides. The ceremonial beard of divinity curled stiffly from the point of his chin; from his golden brow rose a straight-walled crown topped by two broad and lofty feathers.

Thutmose lowered himself to his knees upon a small stool before the niche, and gazed intently into the shining face. It was a countenance of impassive serenity. Its sculptured planes were austere in the dancing light, its obsidian eyes were fixed on a distant nothingness.

"I believe," whispered Thutmose.

The golden face did not change its aspect. In the silence the words echoed again in Thutmose's ears. They sounded frail and tentative, even to himself. He cleared his throat.

"I believe!" he said strongly.

The god gazed serenely straight ahead. Hastily Thutmose threw a pellet of incense into the brazier and rose, turning his back on the cloud of fragrant smoke that enveloped the image.

He moved to the little gong on his bedside table. As he was about to strike the note that would summon his slave, he noticed an object resting on the far side of the table, just beyond the lamplight. Frowning, he held the lamp closer. It was a small, lidless wooden box shaped like a coffin, within which lay a roughly human figure molded of mud. Out of the figure, from head to foot, thrust the tiny green shoots of new-sprouted grain.

He recognized it at once. It was an Osiris image, such as the common folk fashioned for the Osiris festivals to signify the recurring cycle of fertility. Egypt was full of them at this time of year. In every hovel such green shoots were pushing up. Living grain sprouting from buried seed. . . . Pharaoh's weary brain, groping for the significance of that, for the reason this image should be here on his bedside table, traveled back to the hour of sunset, and to Ahmose-pen-Nekhbet's cryptic remark: "There is another whose very name means 'dead.' " Ahmose had sent this little image—to say those words again. What did he mean?

Thutmose ran over the story of Osiris in his mind—a story that was told to children in Egypt before they could toddle. In the beginning of the world, Osiris had been king and ruled the Black Land, and in that time all men and gods were good—save for one, Osiris' brother, Set. This brother had schemed against Osiris, had murdered him, torn his body into fourteen pieces and thrown them into the Nile, in order to usurp Egypt's throne. Isis, Osiris' sister-wife, had found the pieces and with the help of the god Anubis prepared the body for burial. She had then transformed herself into a falcon, and fluttering over the bier of her god-husband, she had conceived a son. This son, Horus, grown to manhood, had avenged his father's murder, taking the evil

76

Set captive and mounting the throne of Egypt; at that moment the dead Osiris became king forever of the netherworld.

So ran the legends, Pharaoh mused, invented to express the inexpressible—the mysterious many-sided nature of Osiris the Mangled One, the Beloved of the masses. Amon was great and holy, but Osiris was the people's own, as near and real to them as their daily bread. The endless symbolism of his life permeated all their thoughts. He was all things which die and are reborn —the moon, waxing and waning; the life-giving Nile, ever menaced by Set the burning desert yet ever making fertile the rich soil, Isis, which received his waters. Each spring when the river shrank to a red-brown trickle, the people mourned his death afresh: each fall he was jubilantly "found" in the swirling floodwaters, just as Isis had found him on that ancient day. He was life following death, good triumphant over evil, he was hope itself.

Moreover, he was each succeeding dead king of Egypt; every Pharaoh, known as Horus while he lived, became Osiris when he died, and went to rule the netherworld, while a new Horus mounted Egypt's throne. In this aspect the throne itself was Isis, who "bore" her son Horus again and again in everlasting cycle, as each died and became Osirus in his turn.

Thutmose spread these manifold concepts—all woven into the texture of his thought since infancy—before his mind's eye and searched in the rich network of implications for the meaning of Ahmose's remark. Perhaps he had only intended to comfort his Pharaoh by calling up a host of reassuring images, old and stable as Egypt itself. Perhaps he meant to point out that the choice of Successor did not matter, since each Pharaoh, whether powerful or weak, was but another wave upon an endless Nile of Horuses and Osirises, upon the strong and enduring river of Egypt's kingship.

Yet what of the cursed Hyksos, who had dammed that enduring river for two long centuries and ruled Egypt themselves? Set a weak king upon the throne and it might happen again— unless he had strong sons to follow him.

Suddenly Thutmose's mind was full of the Isis-falcon fluttering over Osiris' bier—receiving from the loins of death itself the seed of life—and he understood at last. He looked back at the little wooden coffin on his table. With this crudely molded mud image Ahmose was reminding him that even grain must be buried before it could sprout, that life ever sprang from death—that just so had begun the never-ending rhythm of Osiris the dead father, Horus the living son. Therefore—so whispered the tactful thought of Ahmose from the sprouting mud—might not even Nenni the Tired One, the Dead One, beget a vigorous future Pharaoh upon a royal bride?

Thutmose smiled and then sighed, setting down the lamp. It was a thought of subtlety and wisdom, and he was grateful to Ahmose for his effort to bring comfort. However, his decision must stand; his opinion was unchanged—as was Ahmose's also. They were a pair of obstinate old men.

He rang the gong for his slave. A few minutes later he was stretching his aching body full length upon his couch. His eyes traced once more, wearily, the golden star-map above him, then moved to the niche where the last faint smoke of the incense was still curling about the shining countenance of Amon.

"I believe," whispered Thutmose.

The god gazed on, unmoved.

7.

In the gray half-light just before daybreak the following morning —a morning weighted with portent, being the first day of the first month of the Season of Coming-Forth—seven white-cloaked trumpeters climbed to the top of the great pylon which formed the entrance to the Temple of Amon. They carried long, slender, brazen horns from which red and white pennants drooped. In silence they spaced themselves across the top of the massive gateway and waited.

Before them lay the sleeping city of Thebes, No-Amon, a spreading jumble of roofs and thrusting palms still wrapped in obscurity. The wharves were quiet, the forest of masts at the anchorage wove a gently moving black pattern on the gray sky as the ships rocked with the current. Behind the ships the Nile flowed strong and dark, swollen with floodwaters from which the familiar shapes of little islands and sand bars had not yet emerged to give the river features their usual cast. It was an

78

awesome stranger this time of year, the mighty Nile, bearing mud and promise and all good, but frightening in its power to alter the very face of Egypt. The eyes of the trumpeters lingered on the transformed river, moved across its dark breadth to the wavelets lapping the top steps of high landing docks on the other shore, to half-seen dikes and watery fields, and beyond, to the low roofs of the Necropolis stretching away dimly to the desert cliffs.

Gradually, along the topmost rim of these western cliffs, appeared a flush of light, as if a golden crayon had traced their rugged outlines against the sky. At once the trumpeters' heads swung to the east. Waves of brightness had begun to wash upward into the cloudless vault, brighter, brighter. Presently, over the farthest edge of the Asian desert, a rim of living fire appeared.

At the signal the seven trumpeters raised their horns, the pennants dropped crisp and straight. Then the silence of Thebes was shattered into a million fragments as a torrent of wild, unearthly, primitive sound poured from the slim brass tubes and flaring bells. The voices of the trumpets held something of the bull's bellow, something of a woman's high-pitched wail, much of the liquid frenzy of a battle cry. As the last notes died away the sun burst over the horizon, and the tall doors in the pylon were flung wide. Through the great gateway, atop which stood the trumpeters, a glittering procession filed down the Avenue of Rams into the brilliance of the morning. The Heb-Sed had begun.

The city had wakened at the first strident notes of the fanfare; wakened, listened, flung itself from bed. Under thrice ten thousand roofs the people of Thebes snatched their holiday garments, decked themselves with flowers, and hurried into the streets.

"Hark you—it comes, it comes! I hear the sistrums!"

"Hasten, little one! Finish your bread and beer, that we may go forth to see the great procession. . . ."

"*Heset-en-Amon!* Glory to the Great Ones in their litters. . . ."

"Heb-Sed! Heb-Sed!"

All over the city doors burst open, more and more people streamed from their houses into streets already filling with a brown tide of humanity. Dust rose in clouds from hurrying feet, shoulder thrust against bare shoulder, black heads bobbed like ripples in the current as the jubilant flood swept toward the Avenue of Rams, draining every alleyway as it went. Urchins took to the flat rooftops, leaping nimbly from one house to the next; litters carried high eddied like floating sticks upon the tide. It was dammed at last by the multitudes lining the great Avenue solidly from the temple to the river. They choked the cross streets, jammed the rooftops, perched upon the great stone rams, scrambled into trees. Close-packed in the brilliant morning sunlight, they swayed and jostled, craning their necks to peer in the direction from which glory, hope embodied, joy unbearable would come, and from their straining bodies the odors of sweat and ointment and crushed lilies rose to mingle with the drifting dust.

Far up the street the sun glanced blindingly off something gold; gradually a glittering, many-colored, many-footed creature like a monster centipede wound into view, accompanied by a distant murmuring which swelled into a roar as the procession drew near enough to resolve itself into chariots and litters and swaying shrines, banners, plumes, golden standards, delegations of priests and laymen, costumed masquers, dancing priestesses, musicians. Soldiers with lances ran ahead, beating back the populace, thrusting and shoving and stemming the brown tide trying to overflow into the street. Close behind the soldiers came Pharaoh in a chariot of solid gold, harder to look upon in the flashing sunlight than the sun itself. Squinting through this glory with watering eyes, the people could discern the Good God. The red-and-white Double Crown was on his head—red for Lower Egypt, white for Upper—and the strange, short, archaic mantle he wore only in the Heb-Sed fell stiffly from his shoulders to his hips. He himself drove the two dancing stallions, his old hands strong upon the reins.

At the four corners of his sunlike chariot trotted men bearing tall poles topped with the Royal Standards, under whose constant protection the king would live and move for the five days of the festival. The people gazed up at them in fear and worship, these mighty ones slanted against the sky—the Falcon, the Ibis, the Wolf, and the mysterious ovoid object which was the holiest of all, the Royal Placenta. In some strange but certain way which the people did not entirely understand, all their lives and health and prosperity were bound up in this golden object. For it symbolized—or contained—or was itself (this they did not understand either) the *ka* of Pharaoh, and the *ka* of Pharaoh was in some equally mysterious but potent fashion none other than the sun-god Re. *"Ka"* meant many things, and this multiplicity of meanings they had always understood without the slightest need to put the concept into words. A man's *ka* was himself, as even his body was not; it was the deep, inner, vital force which was the very mainspring of his being. No man could exist without his *ka;* but no man's *ka* could exist without Pharaoh's, nor could Pharaoh's exist without the nourishing strength and power which flowed into it from the divinity of this golden god-thing on the slanting pole, the embodiment of Re.

The crowd surged and moaned as the terrible glory moved past. Hands lifted, palms out, in adoration, ecstasy glittered in painted eyes, women offered bare breasts in frenzied gestures to the god-standards, to Pharaoh, to the sun; every throat pulsed with cries.

"Heb-Sed! Heb-Sed!"

"Let our lives be renewed, let our *kas* be strong like Re!"

"Hail to Pharaoh, Horus, Sacred Son! Hail to the Strong Bull!"

"Heb-Sed! Heb-Sed!"

Almost the people could feel in their own tense and trembling bodies the currents of life renewed, of power returned, of vigor restored, as the gods of Egypt swayed past in golden litters, one by one—Thoth the Scribe with his ibis beak, the ram-headed potter, Khnum, slant-eyed Bast and beautiful Hathor with her crown of cow's horns enclosing the disk of the sun, Horus, Amon, Mut, fierce Sekhmet the lion—all of them. The deep chanting of the priests rose on the bright air, accompanied by the jangle of sistrums. As the sound swelled in volume, hope ran like flame along the streets, joy spread like the waters of the Nile. It was true, it was real, the gods were here, in Thebes, for every man to gaze upon! Pharaoh would grow strong from them, and the people would grow strong from Pharaoh. Prosperity undreamed-of was at hand, each cow would bear twins, each field produce double, the lowliest porter would have bread and beer forever. Hail Amon! Glory to Horus of Gold, the Strong Bull! Heb-Sed! Heb-Sed!

In his litter, which directly followed the king's chariot through the tumult of the streets, Prince Nenni sat with half-closed eyes. He felt queerly detached from the yelling throngs around him, from the hysteria that beat with almost physical force against his palanquin. It was as if a great bubble enclosed him from head to foot, a tough, transparent sheath through whose shining walls sounds came only dimly, and reality not at all. It was not a new sensation, this feeling of isolation from the rest of mankind and even from life itself. He knew it well, and he had learned to know its name. It was one of the many guises of his old enemy, Fever.

His first sight, early that morning, of the temple courtyard decked for its new role of Festival Court of the Great Ones had marked the beginning of his peculiar feeling of unreality. How strange it had looked in the gray light, with the queer, archaic shrines of plaited reeds lining its walls and the temporary palace filling the whole western end, thus quite changing its familiar shape. At the opposite end, wide doors opened into a wing of the temple proper; there a large columned chamber, now called the Hall of the Festival, held the great twin thrones. In the gloom of early morning the whole place seemed eerily transformed.

Then had come the torches for the ritual of the Lighting of the Flame, bobbing like golden fireflies through the murk. Led by Pharaoh's, they wove from shrine to shrine, swept light carefully up and down the Royal Standards, filed into the Festival Hall, around the thrones, and out again, illuminating and thus casting out the last vestige of evil or unknown hostile presence that might be lingering there.

For Nenni, shivering in the pre-dawn darkness, it was easy to forget the men who held the torches, to forget their purpose in running to and fro. To his fever-distorted vision the smoking blobs of fire seemed to be moving of themselves, assembling, dispersing, dipping and bobbing in the patterns of some strange and enigmatic dance. Already the bubble had formed around him; he floated remote in time and space, looking down upon a scene the meaning of which had escaped him. At such moments there came to him, unbidden and unwelcomed, a crystalline clarity of mind coupled with the strangest of fancies. He saw that Egypt was the darkness, and the whole knowledge of mankind these tiny moving sparks which were as pinpricks in the immensity of the night.

Appalled, he had watched the sparks waver on their final

82

round, then vanish. When he climbed into his litter in the gray dawn, his heart felt frozen within him.

Now, an hour later, as the procession wound through the streets in the full brilliance of morning, the sunlight was bathing every object in radiance, and the multitudes leaped and yelled with joy. To Nenni they mouthed and gesticulated in a night more silent than the tomb.

Nay, thought Nenni. Surely a few torches light our paths—the knowledge of the physicians, the magic of our learned men . . .

He found himself studying with speculative eyes the new amulet the physician had tied around his wrist last night. It was a cord made of seven sprigs of flax twisted by two sisters who were mothers, and it was knotted seven times. From its center, directly over the spot where his exposed pulse beat, dangled a golden cross with a looped top—the *ankh,* the hieroglyph signifying "life"— binding his own life to his body. It was potent magic, this new amulet; yet, so had the old one been, and it had failed. Should this fail too, there would be many explanations. A *kheft* had untied the knots. The two mothers were only half-sisters.

But what if there were another explanation, a very simple one —that amulets had no power?

Nenni shivered a little in spite of the hot sunlight. It was folly to think such things. But slowly his gaze traveled to the Royal Standards ahead of him, shining bright against the sky. Sparks of light in the darkness? Or only a deepening of the gloom?

I do not know! thought Nenni. No man can know. Even these multitudes who cry out in fear and joy, and kiss the ground before the faces of the gods—they do not *know.* They can only believe, and hope. All their days they hope, laboring for Pharaoh, whose strength is their strength, whose command makes the floods come in season—enduring all things for the sake of that better life beyond the tomb. But suppose there is no better life, no life at all save this sore one in Egypt? Would not Pharaoh then be better occupied in lightening their toil than in performing endless rituals for the ordering of the universe? Suppose the Nile would rise and the grain sprout just the same, without him? Suppose he is a mere man like other men, with no more power to command the flood than that urchin running beside my palanquin? Suppose—suppose—

Nenni's litter passed. In the carrying chair following it rode Queen Aahmes—a profile etched serene against the tumultuous crowd, brow placid under the jutting beak and eye of her golden hawk headdress, nose curved and proud, one jewel-encrusted hand drooping from the arm of her chair as if overweighted by its treasure. A glimpse of perfection for the masses—a carving on a temple wall, made flesh.

Hatshepsut, in the next litter, fixed her eyes upon the back of the golden hawk wings and strove also to appear as a carving on a temple wall. The impact of the babbling, worshiping, shifting crowds through which she passed was like repeated blows, jarring her senses with an excitement she never felt within the palace walls. Being here, in the very midst of the people, was like living in a new element, breathing a new air which was charged beyond endurance with their massed emotion. Even her litter seemed less to be borne on the shoulders of its bearers than swept forward on a giant current, as a chip is swept onward by the Nile.

The people, the people of Egypt, she kept thinking. Thousands of them—all with brains and hearts and feelings, like ourselves. And they yearned that I should rule them, I, not Nenni! They laid wagers in the streets, they hoped, they are still hoping! He said it, did he not? That—that Senmut.

The procession curved, and far ahead she caught the glitter of her father's chariot. At once her throat constricted with anxiety. He will not die, she thought. There is time, anything may happen! He will not make me wed just yet, he said himself there was no need for haste, that there might even be another way. . . . Later, if I must. Aye, I will, I would not trouble him further, or make him ill as I did last night. Great Amon! How terrible that was! . . . What if I had told him of that other, in the desert yesterday? He questioned me enough, he came near to guessing. I should have told him. I know I should have told him. . . . It was insupportable, how did I endure it? To be touched so by a commoner, an architect, whatever he calls himself! Those hands of his—like talons on my shoulders! And his hard mouth—

A ripple of pure delight ran over her. Hastily she lowered her

eyelids, lifted her chin a trifle and smiled vaguely into nothingness, emulating the excellent example of her mother.

Stop thinking about him, she ordered herself. You will never
see the man again.

Then another thought shattered her. Never see him again? He
was here, in Thebes, confined for the five days of the Heb-Sed to
the Court and buildings of the temple, just as she was. Suppose
she met him face to face?

Hatshepsut's hands gripped the chair arms as a violent and
extraordinary emotion passed through her. What is it? she
thought. What am I feeling? Is it anger, outrage? Or is it shame,
that he will see me, know me, know what he has done—then
realize I have let him live, in spite of it? Why have I let him
live? I should have had him seized that very hour. . . . Perhaps he will not know me, though. Those rags, the dirt—how I
must have looked! Nay, he certainly will not know me. . . .

Chin lifted, the stilted faint smile upon her lips, and her eyelids half closed in the serene gaze of divinity, the Daughter of the
Sun swayed onward in her litter between the rows of great stone
rams.

At noon the litters and chariots filed back into the Temple of
Amon, the massive gates swung shut, and the multitude saw no
more of the Heb-Sed mysteries. But they were only beginning.
For the next three days the huge courtyard of the temple was
alive with color and sound and motion as Pharaoh moved here
and there, back and forth, in the complex rites of Assuming the
Protection of the Two Lands. Against the burning blue of the
sky ostrich plumes waved, golden standards glittered. White
smoke billowed from a hundred brazen censers and dust from
a thousand shuffling feet. Voices rose and fell in traditional
phrases, accompanied by the jangle of the sistrums: "An offering which the king gives . . ." "Take it, take it, take it, take
it . . ." White-clad processions came and went, priesthoods in
scarlet robes or leopard skins gathered about beast-headed gods.
Singers shrilled in trembling falsetto, beating upon their brown
and sweating chests. The very air was thick with magic, and
Pharaoh an awesome divinity with his strange, stiff mantle and
his burning eyes. Every move he made was heavy with symbo-

lism, imbued with overpowering significance. As the ritual slowly unfolded, he began renewing the torn fabric of Egypt's welfare, and cast the first spell of prosperity over the land.

8.

On the fourth afternoon of the solemn festivities, the Chief Prophet of Montu Senmut, a tall and striking figure in his scarlet robe, emerged from the reed shrine of the deity he served and set off across the crowded, busy courtyard in the direction of the temple storerooms.

Montu's visit to the Twin Thrones that morning had been a brief one indeed, permitting his Chief Prophet only time to present the bag of greenstones to the Good God, snatch an awed but shrewdly appraising look at the weary, stern old countenance beneath the White Crown, and bow himself and his hawk-headed deity and his priesthood out of the Great Hall of the Festival.

So it had happened that before the Festival had well begun, Senmut's part in it was finished. Except for tending Montu's shrine and overseeing the routine duties of the priests, he was free to launch upon a matter which seemed far more pressing to him—the furtherance of his career. Upon this delicate and interesting affair he had been busy indeed the past three days.

He had been impatient for some time to end his self-imposed exile in Hermonthis and return to Thebes, preferably in one of the widely coveted positions at the Temple of Amon. His first glimpse of the temple's interior (in his urchin's boyhood he had never penetrated farther than the outermost court) had been enough to fan into hot intensity the flames of his ambition. During the days of the Heb-Sed the visiting priesthoods were encouraged—even covertly prodded—to wander through the vast complex of corridors and halls and chapels and storerooms of Amon's House, that they might go home marveling and humbled before his grandeur. Senmut wandered, and he marveled, but he was not humbled. He was only more and more determined that the High Prophet of Montu should soon become a servant of this infinitely more powerful deity and be in a position to hum-

86

ble other priesthoods in his turn. What point was there in rising to the highest post in your world if beyond that lay another world, incomparably greater, in which you had not even gained a foothold? Senmut recognized no ceiling to his ambition. Thebes was the center of creation, and Amon's temple was the center of Thebes—with the palace shimmering just beyond. Obviously he was wasting his time in Hermonthis with the inconsequential Montu.

With this conclusion impressed firmly on his mind, he had begun to see what he could do about it. Discreet inquiries, arranged coincidences, pleasant snatches of conversation in the priests' hall during evening meals, had resulted in several highly interesting bits of information and a budding acquaintance with one Hapuseneb, the first-ranking *sem* priest in Amon's service. Senmut was on his way, that fourth afternoon as he edged his wide shoulders through the crowd in the Great Court, to foster this acquaintance and explore the possibilities of a bit of gossip he had just heard—that the High Priest of Amon, Akhem, was not a popular man with many of his subordinates.

He found Hapuseneb, as he had expected, in the service room off the western storerooms, completing arrangements for the next morning's offering to the god. The priest nodded to him, not too condescendingly, and when he had finished issuing his instructions to half a dozen underlings, strolled up to Senmut.

"Rejoice, Prophet of Montu," he greeted him, casually omitting the "Chief" from Senmut's title, whether from carelessness or intent Montu's servant could not decide.

"And to the First *Sem* Priest of great Amon, all honor," responded Senmut amiably, omitting nothing.

"Honor? That is bestowed not by men but by the gods," the priest remarked. His shrewd and intelligent eyes scrutinized his visitor. Let us understand each other, their expression said. Being human, I enjoy mention of my enviable rank and also your respectful tone. But you will get nothing from me by flattery, I'm a great deal too smart.

Senmut bowed amused acknowledgment of the unspoken warning, which tallied perfectly with his own estimate of the man, and answered the spoken one. "Of course, honor is a gift of the gods. But worldly honors are showered by men and gods alike upon the man bold enough to reach for them."

"Perhaps you will take a cup of wine with me," Hapuseneb said, after a moment's silence in which he digested this.

The two men left the room and walked down the long hall past the storerooms. Several of the doors were open, and through them Senmut caught glimpses of long, narrow chambers tiered with shelves and bins holding linens, incense, wines, gold, beeswax, natron, precious stones, food, and the innumerable rich garments of the god. Scribes were busily checking-in new offerings, or listing old ones, vestment priests inspecting their stocks, functionaries sweeping the beaten clay floors.

"A career worthy of a man's whole devotion, having charge over all that," murmured Senmut, waving a hand toward the endless line of doors.

"You are interested in management?" Hapuseneb inquired as he led the way into his private apartments. "I thought you were a priest."

"So I am," Senmut replied. "But as Chief Prophet I have found the administration of the temple revenues the portion of my duties most congenial to me."

Hapuseneb took a silver jug from a table and poured date wine into two bell-like goblets. "Then you have attained the pinnacle of your chosen field. Fortunate man!"

"On the contrary, Honorable One. I have only started."

"But at the Temple of Montu there exists no higher administrative post than Chief Prophet. The possibilities have come to an end."

"Aye—at the Temple of Montu. But at the Temple of Amon the possibilities are unlimited."

Senmut smiled and raised his goblet to his lips. When he set it down it was empty. The priest, who was regarding him blandly, refilled it and waved him to a chair.

"Sit down."

Senmut did so, allowing his eyes to rove appreciatively about the room. "You do very well for yourselves, you priests of the Great One," he said bluntly.

"The god is not ungrateful for our services. However—" Hapuseneb stopped.

"However, he could be far more grateful than he is, were it not that his favors flow too freely in certain special channels,

88

leaving but a trickle for all the rest. Is that not what you were about to say?"

"You seem very well informed," grunted Hapuseneb.

Senmut shrugged and drained his goblet once again. "It is common knowledge, this scandal. The high priest Akham diverts the stream of Amon's beneficence to himself and a few favorites, while you others—I have often wondered why you endure it."

"Because there is nothing else to do."

"My esteemed friend!" Senmut threw him a glance of amused reproach. "Surely you do not ask me to believe that."

Hapuseneb reached to refill his guest's goblet, eying him placidly. "The high priest is the high priest."

"He is, so long as he can keep peace in the temple. But a restive priesthood—"

"Akhem has the ear of Pharaoh, Prophet."

"And Pharaoh is old. He has one foot in his tomb already. Have you seen his face?"

"He is old, it is true. And of late, infirm. But the Heb-Sed—"

"Is merely Egypt's way of naming the Successor."

Hapuseneb leaned back in his chair, stretched out his sandaled feet and subjected Senmut to a thorough scrutiny—so thorough that Montu's prophet, attempting to read those astute, impassive eyes, felt a sudden tremor deep inside him. Had he misjudged his man? He thought not, but his estimate was based on very limited knowledge, and he was gambling heavily.

"What do you want, my friend?" asked Hapuseneb.

"I want to assist you to become High Priest of Amon in Akhem's place."

Hapuseneb absorbed this announcement imperturbably. Presently he said, "And your reward?"

"A post—however minor—in this temple. Merely the chance to climb."

"The reward, then, must precede the 'assistance.' Is, in fact, a preliminary condition of it."

"Aye." Senmut leaned forward. "You are thinking—quite naturally—that I might take my reward and conveniently forget the rest of the bargain. I will not do that, my friend. If I did, you could always relieve me of my post, so I am in no position to cheat you."

Hapuseneb twirled his silver goblet. His placid demeanor had not changed, he seemed unhurried without giving the least impression of playing for time. Senmut, unable to emulate such nervelessness, controlled with difficulty an urge to wriggle in his chair and drum his fingers upon its arm.

"Just what do you propose to do?" Hapuseneb inquired.

"I think that had best be left to me. Much depends upon the opportunities that present themselves. I can promise you, however, that in a few years' time the solid earth upon which Akhem stands will have become as quicksand."

"And he will call on Pharaoh to deliver him! Then what, my plotter?"

Senmut's smile carved the lines deep around his mouth. "And who will be Pharaoh, when Akhem calls? Not our Good God. He will be in his tomb by then. Think you the Tired One will have the force and experience to cope with chaos? Nothing is more unlikely."

Hapuseneb eased his shoulders back into the cushions, and thoughtfully sipped his wine. "What makes you think I desire to don the high priest's robes?" he said after a moment.

Senmut merely smiled again.

For the first time, an answering gleam of amusement appeared in the priest's eyes. He did not press the question, but remarked, "It is easy to talk, my reckless one. But I have my vows to think of—my position. As First *Sem* Priest I could scarcely go about stirring up the priesthood against my holy superior."

"Exactly. But I could. As—shall we say, Second Scribe?—no such niceties would restrain me. Nor would they later, as First Scribe—or Master of Storehouses. The higher I climb, the better able I will be to advance your welfare."

"Do you ask me to believe you are truly interested in my welfare?"

"Of course not," Senmut said. "But if you accept my offer, your welfare will become identical with my own, and in my own I have a consuming interest."

"You are most persuasive," murmured Hapuseneb.

Senmut drew a long breath and leaned back in his chair. Finding his goblet in his hand, he drained it—in a gulp or two, as he had drained the others. The priest's eyebrows rose. He remarked drily, "It appears that I must either terminate this interview or send for another jug of wine."

"I possess a truly godlike thirst," admitted Senmut with a grin.

"Also a godlike confidence in yourself. What assurance have I that you can perform the wonders you have been describing?"

Senmut shrugged. "You might care to muse upon the fact that four years ago I had just gained a post as Third Scribe of the Storerooms in the Temple of Montu. I am now Chief Prophet."

Hapuseneb gave him a quick glance, which resolved into one of his long, impassive scrutinies. "My friend," he said, "I perceive you are a scoundrel."

"Nonsense. Men are men. Most of them are either sheep or pompous fools. One has only to understand this fact to be able to manipulate them as one chooses—and only another fool would hesitate to do so." Senmut stood up. "Now I must take leave of you. I beg you, give your attention to this matter before we meet again. Tomorrow, shall we say? My thanks for the wine, for your receptive ear, for—"

"A moment, please." Hapuseneb, who had not moved from his chair, was still studying him. "What is it you really want? Your final goal?"

Senmut hesitated, assuming the air of one who gives thoughtful attention to a new idea. "Final goal, my friend? I suppose I have none. When I achieve one aim, there will be another before me. Is it not ever so?"

The priest rose impatiently. "Your price, man. Air me no more of your philosophy. I want your price."

"I have told you. Only the privilege of assisting—"

"Have done with that! I am no fool, and I do not buy a thing without knowing what it costs, in scruples or in gold. You wish to climb. Without a doubt you wish me to help you do so. How?"

"Only in small ways. You will agree to them gladly when the time comes, because it will be to your interest to do so—and I promise you, my interests will never conflict with yours." Senmut started toward the door. "That is, if you accept my offer," he added carelessly.

"Ah, now we come to it," breathed Hapuseneb. Setting his

goblet on the table, he walked slowly across the room to Senmut's side. "And if I refuse?"

"My esteemed friend," Senmut protested. "Must we envisage a situation so distressing?"

"I believe we must—just for the moment."

Senmut yielded with a regretful shrug. "Very well, then. If you refuse, at once my interests would not only conflict with yours, they would coincide with those of your enemy, the high priest Akhem."

The priest looked at Senmut without expression for a moment, then swung the door open. "I will give the matter my attention," he said in a voice as dry as a stretch of desert. "Farewell until we meet."

"May the Honorable One live forever," returned Senmut affably. He bowed himself out and started down the corridor. Behind him the door closed, with just a trifle too much force. Laughing silently, Senmut turned in the direction of the Great Court.

When he emerged, the sun had already slipped below the temple walls. Obliquely across the courtyard stretched a line of litters; the royal family was retiring to its quarters. Senmut joined a group of other priests and gods' attendants who had gathered at a respectful distance to watch. Next him, as he leaned idly against a giant column, he discovered a first scribe of the Theban Temple of Hathor with whom he had struck up an acquaintance the previous evening.

"The final ceremony for today?" he inquired of his neighbor.

"Aye, the last. I for one am not sorry. It has been a strenuous day for the servants of Hathor. And as for the Good God yonder"—the scribe bobbed his head toward Pharaoh, who was descending from his litter at the House of Reeds—"it is fortunate indeed he is not a poor mortal like the rest of us, or his strength would be sorely taxed."

"Tomorrow will be more strenuous yet for him."

"Aye, but he has the strength of the god to sustain him. As for me . . ."

The fellow murmured on, but Senmut's attention was on the scene before him. Pharaoh, attended by the Standard of the Royal Placenta, by a choirmaster, a fan bearer, and a priest bearing a golden door hinge, was being received at the door of the House of Reeds by two courtiers of the rank of Royal Friend. They were washing his feet with water poured from a vase shaped like the hieroglyph meaning "union," while representatives from Lower and Upper Egypt kissed the ground before him.

Senmut found his self-assurance ebbing as he stared at the indomitable old back, severely erect in its short stiff mantle. Pharaoh himself was there, within thirty paces—the crown upon his head, supreme authority in every gesture. The Good God was the Good God, and in his presence no man could think beyond that. Perhaps the Heb-Sed was in truth renewing him by its miracle. Though the back of his neck was crisscrossed with the seams of age, he gave no impression of infirmity, only a compelling sense of the might of Pharaoh. It cast a spell of awe upon the crowd. As he walked slowly across the pillared porch on his battle-scarred old legs to vanish within the House of Reeds, Senmut's hands shielded his eyes in worship with a thousand others.

The remaining litters moved up; the two queens and a tall, emaciated youth in a dazzling neckpiece stepped out. At sight of him the spell was broken, though the worshipful hands remained dutifully extended. Attached to his headcloth the Tired One wore the traditional youth-lock, a bejeweled replica of the dangling clump of hair on the shaven heads of Egyptian boys. It was the only thing that marked him as a prince. His thin shoulders stooped, his gestures were awkward and uncertain. He glanced nervously at the kneeling attendants around him and almost hurried into the building.

So that is the Successor! thought Senmut. It was what he had been led to expect, but reality had more force than rumor, and under his contemptuous smile he felt a deep unease as he turned away—an unease he saw reflected in faces around him.

The two queens had also disappeared, and the crowd was breaking up. Senmut started across the courtyard toward Montu's shrine, and the scribe of Hathor, whose destination lay in the same quarter, fell in beside him. Around them the participants in the last ritual were dispersing—the Royal Placenta was being carried in the direction of the Dual Shrines, the two Royal Friends walked together, arguing, toward the gates, the door-hinge bearer hurried past Senmut, stumbled, and cursed softly under his breath. Temple servants appeared with long reed brooms and began to smooth the trampled dust in the Great Court.

Suddenly the scribe caught Senmut's sleeve and drew him back a pace, jerking his head significantly. A last litter, approaching rapidly from the Hall of the Festival, was almost upon them. Senmut glanced at its occupant, then stood still and stared. The scribe, who was hastily getting to his knees in the dust, jerked at his sleeve again.

"For the love of Amon, man, don't stand there gawking!"

"Who is she?" gasped Senmut.

"The princess Hatshepsut! On your knees, you fool!"

Propelled by another violent tug upon his sleeve, Senmut fell into the proper attitude. Of his own volition he could have done nothing in that paralyzing instant. The princess Hatshepsut? It was the maid he had kissed in the desert chapel five days ago.

His jaw agape, he stared straight at her, in violation of every precedent in Egypt. The nearer she drew, the more illogically certain he became. Who could forget that triangular face, the slope from its wide cheekbones to its sensitive, obstinate chin, the oddly beautiful eyelids? Who could mistake that body for any other in the world?

Yet I am wrong, I must be, thought Senmut, aghast. He grasped at arguments that might prove him so. The coarse, smudged dress of that other maid—and this one's fluted cobwebs. This sleek, proud head, gold-diademed—the other's tangled mop. Lord Amon! This was no servant girl, this was the Daughter of the Sun, with gold and silver half-covering her breasts. Yet by the Mangled Body of Osiris they were the same breasts, the same smooth shoulders, that he had laid covetous hands on—none too gently—five afternoons ago!

"Cast down your eyes, you imbecile!" hissed the Hathor scribe frantically.

Senmut was deaf—and numb to peril. The litter was passing within a cubit of him; he could have reached out and touched the slim hand that dangled over its side. Almost as if he had done so, the princess turned, incuriously, and looked full into his eyes. For the fraction of an instant her face was illumined with panic. In a flash it was gone, leaving every feature rigid. Without haste her eyes moved past him, touched his companion and indifferently resumed their contemplation of the area ahead. Save for a delicate but unmistakable flush that spread slowly up the column of her neck and into her cheeks, it was a profile like a mask that vanished a moment later from the view of the two men kneeling in the dust.

The scribe waited until the litter was safely inside the gates of the House of Reeds before he scrambled to his feet. "Great gods of Egypt!" he said hoarsely, staring at Senmut as he might have stared at a dangerous madman. "Are you weary of life, my friend? You would have been relieved of the burden soon enough had the Radiant One been attended by other than her carriers! Gawking at her face! Lord Amon! I want no more of such a companion!"

Shaken, he hurried off across the courtyard. Senmut rose from his knees and stood uncertainly, his eyes fixed on the gate through which the litter had passed. He too was shaken, as never in all his life—a life which he marveled he had not been relieved of some days ago. He had kissed Pharaoh's daughter. He had kissed her as unceremoniously as if she were a tavern wench. And he was still alive. It was past believing.

Yet in was true. He had made love to a maid in a deserted chapel; today he had looked upon Pharaoh's daughter; and they were one and the same. It was incredible, but true.

Very well. A man must face these things. He leaned against the wall of Montu's shrine and went back to the unanswerable question he had asked himself in the first place: Why was he still alive?

He stood a long time there by Montu's dwelling, looking out over the deserted courtyard as it grew shadowy with evening. The rows of shrines were shuttered now; the geese squawked faintly from their distant pens, and a lamb bleated in the distance. From the brooms of the sweepers, who were finishing their task at the farthest end of the great Court, a few white feathers swirled lazily upward. Senmut watched them, pondering his riddle. And because no riddle is truly unanswerable for long, he found an answer, the only possible answer. He found it in the princess Hatshepsut's panic, and her flush, and in the memory of the bewildered passion he had forced from her in the chapel five days ago, which had made him wonder if he were the first man ever to touch her.

Indeed he had been. The back of his neck prickled as he realized it. The very first, without a doubt. And if memory served, the experience had been far from revolting to her, though it had frightened her. Perhaps, reflected Senmut cautiously, this incredible blunder he had committed was not altogether a misfortune. Possibly—just possibly—it was the most fortunate single thing that would ever happen to him in his life. What, after all, was the royal princess Hatshepsut, Daughter of the Sun? A demigoddess? A royal symbol? A mere collection of attitudes and titles? No, she was a woman.

And he was a man, of whom she was now vividly aware.

A smile was touching the corners of Senmut's mouth as he turned slowly to open the shutters of Montu's shrine for his evening inspection. The smile was tentative, but it was there. He was thinking of the Tired One—and the hot-blooded maiden who would wed him—and the astonishing circumstance that he himself was still alive. All together, they were beginning to suggest a train of thought that dazzled even him.

9.

Pharaoh opened his eyes reluctantly and with dread to the gray dawn of the Heb-Sed's fifth and final day. As yet no miracle of rejuvenation had taken place in his age-worn body, and his awareness of this shed a light drearier than the dawn's over all his thoughts. As he sat on the edge of his couch, rubbing his weary head, Thutmose felt as old as Egypt. Two last ceremonies lay before him—the Dedication of the Field this morning, and later, the Proclamation of His Triumphant Majesty to the four corners of the earth. The miracle—if it came at all—must come before nightfall of this day.

Thutmose stood up, waited with a patience he had lately learned for the sudden pounding in his chest to quiet, and walked to the little image of Amon, which in the House of Reeds, too, occupied a niche at the foot of his bed. Mechanically he knelt and burned a pellet of incense, looking into the golden face.

"For a few hours yet," he whispered, "I will believe."

He got to his feet with an effort, and summoned his slave to dress him.

The sun was high long before the daily ceremonies of purification were ended and the preliminaries of the Dedication ritual under way. It beat down mercilessly on the slow-moving processions, on the king and priests alike as they performed their stately, endless duties. At last the Rites of the Field began. Thutmose, holding the Crook and Flail, and sweating under the stiff, heavy mantle, stood before the entrance to the House of Reeds listening to a lector priest recite the sacred history of the Contendings of Horus and Set. The Great Court had been swept clean; in its center, the Field, an area forty cubits square, had been marked off with stakes. Around its edges were gathered all the participants of the Mysteries—priests, chanters, delegates, bearers, scribes.

"And behold, Osiris and Set were the sons of Geb the earth," droned the voice of the lector priest. He launched into the familiar tale of the murder of Osiris, his avenging by Horus his son, the contending of Horus and Set over the rulership of Egypt, Set's stealing of Horus' right eye. The voices of the singers rose in their high-pitched vibrato as two men armed with staves ran to the center of the Field and engaged in mock battle. Presently a gold-aproned priest symbolizing Geb, who carried the two crowns of Egypt, advanced on the contenders and stepped between them.

Thutmose watched them through a haze of weariness. Preoccupied with his punished and heat-enervated body, he heard only a few phrases of the long chant. ". . . and Geb made Set king in Upper Egypt, in Su where he was born . . ." ". . . Horus king in Lower Egypt, in the place where his father was drowned . . . And the Eye of Horus was restored to him and his power returned . . ."

A sudden roar from the crowd startled him. "Behold the Eye! Behold the power of the Sacred Son!" The jubilation beat like drums in Thutmose's ears as Geb in the golden apron gave the crowns to the two combatants, who turned toward Pharaoh and lifted them high. Again his attention wandered as the chanting droned on, more pantomime was enacted. Suddenly he realized the tale was drawing to its close:

97

"But it suited Geb's heart ill that the portion of Horus was like that of Set, and so Geb gave the heritage wholly to Horus, the son of his son Osiris, his firstborn, his opener-of-the-body . . ."

The men with the crowns were running swiftly toward Pharaoh, holding the crowns aloft.

"Now, Your Majesty," whispered the lector priest.

Thutmose roused himself with an effort, crossed the Crook and Flail upon his chest and started toward the shrine of Upwaut, the "Opener-of-the-Ways," just as the two men darted past him on right and left and vanished into the House of Reeds. The crowd murmured with excitement, pressing back to let him through.

The shrine was close and hot, and smelled stalely of the dried rushes of which it was constructed. Hapuseneb the *sem* priest was waiting inside, holding the Upwaut standard, and a jar of costly ointment lay open on a little stand. Thutmose dipped into the jar and anointed the standard in the ritual manner, using only the middle fingers of each hand. At once the fragrance of myrrh enveloped him so powerfully that he felt half suffocated. His legs were trembling from the long hours of standing.

"Is anything amiss with Your Majesty? If I can give assistance—"

"Nay, nothing. . . . There seemed . . . no air . . . in the shrine. Pray tell them to fetch me a little water."

The priest sent a slave scurrying toward the kitchens, then with an anxious obeisance hurried off toward an anteroom to put on other garments for the next ceremony. Thutmose found himself leaning on the strong black arm of Nehsi, who had appeared from nowhere, waved aside the formal guard of priest-attendants, and himself escorted Pharaoh to his chambers.

"It is nothing," mumbled Thutmose. "I must change my attire for the Dedication." But he was near despair. Oh Amon, he thought, I am too old to stand so long in the sun. I am too old—too old for any miracle save death. . . .

"There is time to rest, Exalted One," rumbled Nehsi's deep and comforting voice. "Here, sit. Let them take off that heavy mantle. Now, sip the water."

Thutmose lay back in his chair and closed his eyes, while his heart pounded like a drum. He was aware that someone was

98

sponging his body with cool cloths, that water passed between his lips, but his thoughts lingered on the standard of Upwaut, whose bright glitter had moved before him like a beacon in the pressing confusion of the courtyard and guided his footsteps to this haven. Upwaut the wolf—the Great Protector—standing proud and slender on his standard, with the *shedshed,* that mysterious round protuberance so significantly similar to the Royal Placenta, held firm between his forepaws. The image came home to Thutmose with an urgency, an intimacy, it had never held before. He, Pharaoh, was Horus—and the wolf too was Horus, in his aspect of Eldest Son, Opener-of-the-Body. They were bound close, he and Upwaut, they were mysteriously identical, like a man and his *ka.* More than that—Upwaut was guardian of the *shedshed,* and it was upon the *shedshed* that Pharaohs journeyed to the underworld when they died, there to enter again into the womb of Mut the Earth-Mother and be reborn into a better, kindlier life. . . .

"Upwaut, lead me," whispered Thutmose. "Prepare the way. I think it will not be long."

"Your Majesty spoke to me?" said Nehsi anxiously.

Thutmose opened his eyes. Nehsi was bending over him, and beyond clustered the priest-attendants. One glimpse of their frightened faces caused Thutmose to force himself back to the present. If Pharaoh faltered, Egypt and every soul who dwelt there faltered with him. He disciplined his features into their usual composed mask.

"Nay, I did not speak," he said in a calm voice. "I am much refreshed. Pray help me to rise, Count Nehsi."

The strong black arm was instantly about him, and he realized with deep gratitude that it was not going to leave him until he was able to stand firm upon his feet. As he rose, he saw tension fade to relief in the faces of the priests about him. Carefully and inconspicuously the supporting arm withdrew.

"Bring the garments for the Dedication," ordered Thutmose.

Silently he fought to stiffen his shaky legs as the attendants dressed him. They thought him strong again. He must be strong, he told himself—but it required will not to quail at the thought of the ritual before him. Two separate times he must traverse the length and breadth of the Field out yonder—and at a swift running walk. Would his legs hold out, even for one circuit?

He realized that his kilt was secure about him, the collar cold on his chest, the ceremonial bull's tail dangling against the back of his legs. The ministering hands had withdrawn; it was time. He turned and walked out of the room and down the corridor where Hapuseneb, garbed in a tunic of skins, waited with the Upwaut standard. Pharaoh's eyes went swiftly to the wolf and clung there. Mechanically he accepted the royal Flail, felt his other hand close upon the roll of papyrus called the Secret of the Two Partners, which was the Will of Geb and symbolized his right to dedicate the Field of Egypt to the goddess of the crown.

"Lead me, Upwaut," Pharaoh whispered.

Reverent hands placed the White Crown of Upper Egypt on his head. With his eyes fixed on the slender figure of the wolf-god, he followed Hapuseneb through the door of the House of Reeds and out into the Great Court. A burst of sunshine and the roar of the crowd hit him like twin blows. Then he was moving with the swift and leaping stride of the ritual down the long, burning Field. The standard bobbed like a will-o'-the-wisp before him; far at the other end, at what seemed an interminable distance, a priestess enacting the role of the goddess Mert, the Land, clapped her hands in rhythm to his steps and chanted, "Come—come—bring it! Bring it!" His eyes watered from the sun's brilliance; for a moment the golden standard blurred and wavered; then it shone clear again and he had reached the end of the Field, only to have the Mert-priestess elude him and reappear on the western boundary. The standard swerved and he followed, trying to force order into the confusion of his thoughts. As he crossed the Field's width the voice of the lector priest came dimly to his ears:

"The Good God runs around fast holding the Will. He runs, crossing the ocean and the four sides of Heaven, going as far as the rays of the sun disk, passing over the earth, giving the Field to its Mistress . . ."

He staggered as he reached the western boundary at last and, bracing his feet wide, dragged the air into his lungs in deep, painful gulps. The priestess moved away from him again. Why? He looked in bewilderment to the standard for guidance. Then he felt the white crown lifted from his head and the weight of the red one descend, and he remembered. He must do it all once more.

Upwaut was moving . . . Thutmose straightened slowly, forcing himself erect under the burden of the crown, though fatigue played like flames through his neck and shoulders. He took one step and then another after the retreating standard, demanding of himself the little vigorous leap, the appearance of strength and youth. Down the glaring desert of the Field, along its edge, and back to the third stake on the east. The ominous pounding had started in his chest, and the sweat lay cold on his brow and upper lip. The sound of his breathing seemed loud enough to drown out the chanting of the priest. Still he forced one foot ahead of the other as the standard led him on. He dared not take his eyes from it, though by now he could distinguish only that one dwindling point of gold in a flashing chaos.

"Come—come—bring it—bring it!" The words grew more distinct, the clapping louder; then suddenly they ceased. Dimly he grasped that the standard was motionless, that he too had reached the final goal. His arm seemed no longer a part of him, but he willed it to move, and slowly it lifted the sacred document above his head.

"I have run," he gasped, "holding the Secret—of the Two Partners"—he paused, fighting to control his voice—"which my father has given me before Geb. I have—passed through the land and—touched its four sides; I run through it as I desire."

His hand dropped. The Dedication was finished—the joyful shouting of the crowd told him that—and he was still on his feet, still regally erect.

He turned, walked jerkily to the House of Reeds and through its entrance into a swimming blackness. Aided only by memory and will he found his way down the corridor to his room, crossed its threshold, closed its door behind him. Then the fiery arrow stabbed deep beneath his collarbone. Nehsi's arms were around him as he fell.

He became aware that he was half reclining, propped high on pillows. A large, capable hand tightly clasped his own. He opened his eyes.

The light in the room had none of the sharp brilliance of mid-day. How long had he lain here, with Nehsi like a great watch-dog beside him, while outside the hours wore away? There was one more ritual. . . .

"Nehsi," he said. He was appalled by the sound of his voice. It was a stranger's.

"I am here, Majesty. Rest. Do not talk."

"Nay, the Ceremony of the—Proclamation—"

Nehsi's big hand tightened on his. "There is time, much time yet. Sleep."

I cannot, Thutmose tried to say. I must gather my strength, I must find out if I can stand. . . . But the words would not come, the effort was too great, he had not the will to force them. He gazed into the dusky face leaning over him and felt infinitely remote from it—from everything.

After a while he moved his head on the pillow until he was looking at the image of Amon in its niche at the foot of his couch. The placid golden features aroused in him a stubbornness that amounted to something like a return of strength. Around the spark of his rebellion a resolve slowly began to burn. He would not be jerked unceremoniously from life, leaving the multitudes in panic and Egypt betrayed. He would yet complete the Heb-Sed—the Great Mystery which was to have made him young and strong again, but which had destroyed him instead.

His very anger revived him. "Nehsi!" he muttered, and the voice sounded almost like his own.

"Majesty, do not tax yourself—"

"Raise me."

"But Exalted One—"

"Raise me!"

Nehsi wet his lips, then reluctantly bent down and lifted Thutmose to a sitting position, holding him with both arms.

"The chair," ordered Pharaoh.

Nehsi did not argue any more. Propping the king with pillows, he fetched the chair from the other side of the room and helped Thutmose into it.

I have succeeded, thought Pharaoh, clinging fast to the arms of the chair. The first step is taken.

"Fetch the standard of Upwaut," he whispered to Nehsi.

When the golden figure was again before him, leaning against the wall opposite his chair, he dropped his head against the cushions and closed his eyes.

When he woke some time later his first consciousness was of the wolf's clean and slender lines, the strange allurement of the *shedshed*. Then he became aware of the voices which had roused him. Turning, he saw the broad back of Nehsi blocking the doorway.

"Who comes?" said Thutmose.

Nehsi looked around swiftly. "It is Prince Nenni, Your Majesty. He—he has received a message. He craves your permission to return to the other palace, only for an hour—"

Something in Nehsi's face halted the indifferent consent on Pharaoh's lips. "A message?" he repeated.

"I feared to startle you, Exalted One," said Nehsi gently. "But it is good tidings. The woman Iset has borne her babe at last. It is a son."

"A son! When did this happen?"

"But an hour since, Majesty."

"A—son?"

"Aye, a strong and lusty boy. His Highness is much pleased, even though the child's mother is—in a somewhat weakened condition." Nehsi waved that away and smiled. "In truth, the prince can scarce contain his joy. He wishes to look upon the face of his child before the sun sets."

Strong and lusty, thought Pharaoh incredulously. Into his mind leaped the little Osiris image, with the green shoots sprouting through the mud. So old Ahmose had been right; even from the loins of death could come new and vigorous life. His line would not die out, princes would be born, Egypt was safe.

He experienced a relief so exquisite that for a moment it unmanned him. With horror he realized that his eyes were wet, his lips shaking. Amon's body and blood! he thought. Savagely he blinked the tears back.

"Prince Nenni may not leave," he said, more harshly than he intended the words to sound. "He must take part in the Proclamation ceremony." He cleared his throat and shifted in his chair, not willing to trust his voice further as yet. After a moment he added, in carefully controlled tones, "However, you may send—in haste—to have the babe fetched here. I, too, would look upon this child."

"At once, Your Majesty," murmured Nehsi. He vanished into the corridor, closing the door behind him. Through it Thutmose could hear the sudden stir, voices murmuring, footsteps hastily receding. A moment later Nehsi reappeared. He stood just inside the doorway, watching his monarch with alert, expectant eyes.

Thutmose hesitated only one final moment before he stated quietly what his royal steward was waiting to hear.

"Aye, Nehsi. Tomorrow you will begin arrangements with all speed for the marriage of Prince Nenni and my daughter Hatshepsut. I desire that the wedding take place in three days' time. You may announce this throughout the household—at once—so that all may know I have commanded it."

"At once, Your Majesty," murmured Nehsi again. This time the formal phrase was so like a sigh of relief that a wry smile softened the corners of Pharaoh's mouth. It had been a strain on everyone, this long indecision.

He sat quietly, gathering his strength, while the indecision was being ended officially and forever. When Nehsi returned at last from his long-awaited duty, Pharaoh turned slowly to search his face.

"The Princess Hatshepsut hears and obeys her lord's command," said the big black man. He paused, then added quietly, "Your Majesty need not be troubled. The princess is a princess, and the daughter of her father. I, who watched her as she heard the tidings, say this."

Thutmose sighed deeply, then nodded. After a moment he grasped the arms of his chair and pulled himself slowly to his feet, rejecting Nehsi's help. He stood erect at last, his legs passably steady under him and his shoulders once more straight and firm.

"Call them," he ordered Nehsi, "to robe me for the Ceremony of the Proclamation. It nears the mark of four."

At the mark of four on this final day of the Heb-Sed, suspense gripped the city of No-Amon like a mighty hand. Within the secret confines of the temple great mysteries had been going on for four days past, and the people knew the final hour was approaching toward which all the others had been leading. Since noon they had been gathering outside the walls of the Great

Court, singly, in pairs and groups, and finally by the hundreds, as though pulled by some gigantic magnet. They stood close-packed and waiting, clinging absently to their fretting children, speaking in low, tense voices which blended into one vast hum. Their eyes never left the wall.

The boom of a drum sounded from within, followed by a skirl of trumpets. A flurry of excitement passed over the crowd and was quickly suppressed into strained listening. Faintly they could hear the shuffle of feet, the quavering, high voices of the singers floating over the hollow drumbeats. The last procession was winding its way across the Court of the Festival toward the shrine of Horus. First as king of Lower Egypt, in a box-shaped litter, next as king of Upper Egypt in a litter formed like a basket, Pharaoh would be carried on the shoulders of high-ranking nobles to the shrine of the Sacred Son. At some point in the proceedings the god Horus would give him the *was* scepter, symbolically shaped like the hieroglyph meaning "welfare," and two officials called the Chiefs of Pe would chant his glory in an antiphonal hymn of praise, repeating their litanies until each had spoken toward the four points of the compass. Later Pharaoh himself would receive a bow and arrows from the hand of the god and would shoot toward east, west, south and north, proclaiming his might to the four corners of the earth. This much the people knew from the tales of the old ones among them, who remembered other Heb-Seds. And then, so said the old ones, would come the final moment, on which the future of Egypt hung. Pharaoh would lift up the head of his Successor and make room for him upon the throne.

The crowd pushed nervously closer, straining their ears.

The sound of the footsteps had stopped now, the singers' voices died away. Presently a single distant call floated over the walls.

"Silence—silence—silence—silence—"

A pause. Then a voice began, "Great is thy power and thy might, O Horus of Gold, King of the Two Lands!"

A second voice took up the litany. "Thy members are the twin children of Atum . . ."

"O imperishable one!"

"Thy *Ka* does not perish!"

"Thou art Ka . . ."

The Proclamation of Power went on, repeated, reaffirmed,

reinforced four separate times, interspersed with the ritual command of "Silence—silence—silence—silence—" until all fear was driven from the people's minds and their hearts sang with the promise of security.

"All will be well, my lotus," whispered the women to their children. "Pharaoh is great, the gods will smile on Egypt. Heb-Sed! Praise the Heb-Sed and the mighty god in the palace."

Dust rose in filmy veils above the walls as the procession moved once more, and for a time the happenings within were obscure to the waiting masses. They could hear fragments of singing, the occasional boom of a drum, they could watch the slowly drifting dust, and that was all.

Then, almost without warning, came the long-awaited flight of arrows. The crowd along the eastern walls abruptly changed into a frenzied mob, shrieking their joy and trampling one another as they scrambled after the sacred arrow. An uproar on the west followed immediately, then on the north. The arrow shot to the south was lost upon some temple roof, but the crowd was too maddened with jubilation to notice or care. The Heb-Sed was finished, Egypt was safe, everlasting prosperity lay before them—and Pharaoh was omnipotent. Soon—any moment now —they would see the Successor, and life would be complete.

The gates of the pylon burst open, and the procession emerged and started toward the river. Runners, horses, chariots, guards —and then two litters, side by side. In one rode Pharaoh, motionless as if carved in stone—the rigid image of a god. In the litter beside him, joined to his by golden ribbons and the invisible ties of succession, rode the new Horus-in-the-Nest, future ruler of Egypt and the Empire—Prince Nenni, the second Thutmose of the line.

The crowd screamed in wild hysteria; a hundred thousand hands shielded dazzled eyes in adoration as the procession passed down the Avenue of Rams, filed onto the royal barges, and crossed the river to the palace. The Heb-Sed was over.

As Hatshepsut's litter was set down in the palace courtyard, she realized she had been clenching the arms of her chair so tightly that her fingers were numb. Stiffly she uncurled them, forcing them to lie quiet in her lap a moment before she stepped down and walked jerkily across the court and through the great bronze door. In the wide corridor she hesitated, then turned quickly in the direction of the Mansion of Beauty. Ignoring the flurry she caused among the ladies of the Salon, she demanded to see the prince's child.

"It is—it is with its mother, Highness," faltered old Heqet.

"Then take me there."

In the three hours since Hatshepsut had first heard about the child, she had not once thought of its mother. The moment she crossed the theshold of Iset's chamber she became disconcertingly aware of her. The woman lay on a couch at the far side of the room, a haggard beauty with enormous, burning eyes. The princess stopped, startled by the almost physical impact of their hostility.

"You are Iset?" she demanded.

"Aye, Highness."

"I wish to see your child."

Iset made a grudging gesture with one shoulder; only then did Hatshepsut perceive that the babe lay in her arms. Walking to the couch, she looked for the first time into the face of Nenni's newborn son, third man-child of her kin to bear the name of Thutmose.

He was small but sturdy, with strong, fat legs and a well-shaped head set with a nose which already showed a hint of the jutting Thutmosid curve. The flesh of his wriggling little body was firm and glowing with health; his elbows were mere dimples and his wrists deep-creased. He clutched with demanding fingers at the swelling breast his mother offered him, found the nipple and drank lustily. Every move he made was arrogantly male.

Male. A feeling of helplessness crept over Hatshepsut as she stared at his tiny, naked body. Had he been a daughter, he would have been shuffled into oblivion in the palace nurseries, emerging in fifteen years or so to be wed to some count or soldier. But he was not a daughter, he was a man-child. Already his coming had changed the course of a royal princess' life.

The babe means nothing, she told herself, forcing a calm she did not feel. He means less than nothing, for all his maleness. I too will have sons, many sons, and in their veins will flow the blood of the Sun. I have nothing to fear, nothing to fear . . .

"Is he not beautiful, my little Thoth?" whispered Iset.

Hatshepsut raised her head and found herself staring into

Iset's eyes. They were the eyes of an enemy, and they burned with triumph.

That night, near the hour of midnight, slaves burst from the royal apartments and rushed to every quarter of the palace, rousing all who slept. In their wake rose the sound of wailing, which grew, as voice after voice was added to it, until the corridors echoed to the sound. The great bronze gates of the palace were slowly shut and sealed, courtiers and queens sat head on knees, the lowliest kitchen boy grieved.

A few minutes before, attended only by Nehsi and Ahmose-pen-Nekhbet, the old Pharaoh had laid aside his heavy crown forever and started his long journey on the *shedshed* to rule another, darker land.

PART II

The Garden

I.

IT WAS a beautiful boat, longer than the little boy's arm, and fashioned most perfectly from fine-grained acacia wood. And it was quite different from the boats one saw daily on the Nile. Its lines were not broad and spacious like the barks of noblemen, but rakishly slim. Its prow, instead of sweeping upward, graceful as an ibis's neck, to end in a delicately carved lotus flower, was low and fierce, thrusting out into a snarling lion's head capable of ramming an enemy vessel and tearing a crippling hole in its side. This was no elegant temple craft or royal barge, but a *mensh,* a war galley. It carried twenty sweeps—as many as old Ahmose-pen-Nekhbet's clever fingers had been able to fit into its sides—and a square, horizontally rigged sail painted scarlet. It was filled with wooden soldiers armed with tiny bows and swords; a steersman manned the great rudder sweep from his high platform in the stern, and in the crow's-nest atop the mast perched a lookout ready with sling and stone.

Truly, it was a perfect gift for a little prince's fifth birthday. Old Ahmose had forgotten nothing. He had even fashioned a tiny Eye-of-Horus talisman out of copper wire to set in each side of the slender hull, and traced a name in gilt just behind the lion's head—THE WILD BULL.

The child looked up with shining eyes at the old man as they squatted together at the edge of the garden pool. "Was it just like this one, Ahmose?"

"Aye, just like it," creaked the old general's rusty voice.

109

"Many a long watch I spent on that mast-top, when I was a lad, as we rowed down to the Delta, down to cursed Avaris, to drive the Shepherds out. I remember the crocodiles sliding off the sandbanks, and the sun like fire on my back when I stood at the oars. We had only fish and bread-cakes, and little of either, but we dreamed of vengeance. And I had no soft couch like yours, little one. I spent my nights in a hammock of net." He smiled into the child's upturned face and added softly, "And when I grew up I captained a flagship. That was in the reign of Pharaoh your grandsire."

"The one I was named for?"

"Aye. The same."

"And he was a very great Pharaoh, wasn't he?"

"A very great one. And a mighty warrior. We fought the Hyksos together, he and I, and drove them out of Egypt and over the edge of the world."

"And you got that scar?"

"Aye."

The child gazed up seriously into Ahmose's seamed old face, tracing the scythe-shaped scar with his eyes. "Did it hurt?" he asked softly.

In the pavilion, Nenni turned to exchange a smile with Hatshepsut and found her looking with distaste at the little boat.

"War, always war and fighting!" she said. "Why could he not have made the child a pretty bark, or a fishing punt?"

"You expect too much. A man can be only what he is, and Ahmose is a warrior."

"Nonsense. A man can be what he sets himself to be—strong, weak, rich, poor. *You* do not expect enough."

"Of myself, you mean," said Nenni.

She flung him an irritated glance. "Must you take to heart everything I say? I spoke in generalities only." After a moment she got up and walked restlessly to the edge of the pavilion. "Oh Amon, how dull the afternoons are!"

Nenni sighed and turned back to watch the two at the pool's brink. The sunshine gleamed on the boy's sturdy, nearly naked little body, and his head, close-shaven except for the youth-lock dangling over the right ear, was bent to Ahmose's shiny bald one in perfect companionship.

"I caught a snake, Ahmose," the child was saying, his brown hands busy rearranging the soldiers in the boat.

"Did you? When?"

"Today. It was only a little one. He wiggled in my hands. It felt so queer." He grinned at Ahmose, wrinkling his nose, then returned to the boat. "Where shall I put the captain?"

"Here, amidships. He is this one, see, with the little head-cloth."

"Aye. There now. Ahmose?" The boy sat back on his sandaled heels.

"I am here."

"Did they call him Thoth, like me?"

"Your grandsire? Nay, they called him by his whole name, Thutmose, 'Born of Thoth.' He was a man, you see, a great king. Perhaps when he was a little lad, they called him Thoth."

There was a pause, as old man and child studied each other gravely. "Where is he, Ahmose? Why can't I see him?"

"He journeyed to the West the day you were born, lad. He is Osiris now, and wears the Crown of the Dead, and rules the Dark Land just as your father the Pharaoh rules Egypt. Yet you might see him, if your eyes could bear it, for each day he travels in glory across the sky in the golden bark of Re."

Thoth raised wondering eyes to the bright disk of the sun, high above in the sky's limitless blue arch. Its brilliance made him blink and turn away, digging his small fists into his eyes. He caught sight of the boat again, and reached for it eagerly.

"I want to sail it, Ahmose!"

"You're the captain, little one!" Chuckling, the old general lifted the galley into the pond. "Up anchor! Make sail, my mates! Ho! May Amon send the wind."

The little vessel slid bravely out over the dancing water, while Thoth jumped up and down, shrieking his delight.

There was a stir at the gate as her nurse brought little Princess Neferure into the garden. She was three years old, a pale, thin child, rather tall for her age. She ran at once to the pavilion and flung herself into her mother's waiting arms.

"There, now, my lotus!" exclaimed Hatshepsut. "Did you have a lovely sleep? How nicely Rama has dressed your hair! Come, let us walk out to the pool. You must see Thoth's beautiful new boat."

"Where is the boat—Thoth has a boat—" chanted the little princess. Clinging to her mother's hand she danced across the grass toward the pool, then suddenly stopped and pointed. "Oh! There it is! It's going fast!"

The wind had caught the miniature sails, and the galley was speeding perilously toward the far end of the pool, which was choked with rushes. Thoth shouted his alarm.

"Ahmose! She's going to run aground!"

"Aye, she's headed for shipwreck. Run save her, little one." Old Ahmose, chuckling, hobbled toward the danger spot, while Thoth darted past him. The galley plunged into the rushes and caught there, her sails fluttering.

"I can get her! I'll get her!" the boy sang out.

He arrived at the end of the pool, squatted and reached, but his arm was not long enough. He ran around to the opposite side, hesitated, then retraced his steps. The boat was out of reach. He kicked off his sandals and plunged into waist-deep water, pushing his way slowly through the thick growth of rushes toward the imprisoned galley.

The mud was velvet-soft under his feet, and squished up delightfully around his toes. He could see faint brown clouds rising through the water each time he stepped—slow, dreamily moving clouds of watery dust. He stopped and dipped his face into the water, opening his eyes wide beneath the surface to watch the water-dust move. He was entranced with the new world he saw, a greenish, dim world with slow, changing clouds of brownness weaving in and out among a forest of swaying reeds. There were his feet, looking very far away and unnaturally white, and vague in shape—not like the feet he was used to at all. And there—there was a goldfish! It was hanging as if in mid-air behind a reed stem, motionless except for a gently pulsating fin. Thoth stared at it with deep, astonished pleasure, holding very still so as not to frighten it. He wondered if it was asleep.

His absorbed gaze moved in search of other fish, traveled up a further clump of reeds and came to rest on a wavering bluish shape that seemed vaguely familiar. He realized suddenly it was the prow of his galley, seen from underneath. He jerked his head from the water, caught his breath, and slinging the drops from his face and eyes hastened forward again, stumbling a little as the reeds caught at his ankles. How beautiful, how warlike the little vessel looked, shining so bravely in the sun! She wasn't hurt in the least. Lovingly he disengaged her from the binding stalks and waded on, pushing her before him, to the edge of the reed-growth.

"Shall I lower her sails, Ahmose?" he called, squinting toward the old man on the bank.

"Aye, you'd best do that. She'll be going downstream now."

Thoth loosened the little cords carefully, and the scarlet sail slid down the mast like a collapsing fin and rested on the deck.

"Lift oars! Pull, men—pull, men—" commanded Thoth under his breath. He gave the vessel a long, even shove. "Find the Hyksos! Drive them out of Egypt!" he whispered.

The little Neferure, darting ahead of her mother, had reached the edge of the pool. "It's coming to me! It's coming to me!" she screamed.

It was, indeed, wavering toward the bank straight for her eager hands. Thoth frowned and opened his mouth to shout, but he was not quick enough. The clutching little hands seized his vessel awkwardly, hauled it bumping and scraping over the lip of the pool and dragged it onto the grass where it overturned, snapping a mast and spilling all the soldiers.

"Nefer! Let go my boat!" Thoth splashed frantically for the pool's edge, flung himself recklessly over the rim, was up in an instant and running toward her, streaming water.

"I want the dollies!" Nefer was crying joyously.

"They're *not* dolls! They're my soldiers! Give me them!"

Thoth seized the boat in rage; Nefer clung to it, shrilling protest. For an instant they tugged it back and forth, but Nefer's frail arms were no match for Thoth's sturdy strength. He jerked the prize from her and both staggered backward, he shouting, she bursting into outraged tears. In the same instant Hatshepsut arrived.

"Thoth, let be! For shame! Nefer—Nefer, hush, my lotus . . . Ptah's Beard, such an uproar! I can scarce make head or tail . . . You should know better, Thoth, jerking it from her like that! Nefer, cease wailing, little one, be quiet, quiet."

Thoth was already quiet. His shouts had ceased abruptly as soon as Hatshepsut had appeared. He stood looking up at her, his side-lock dripping water upon his shoulder, the boat forgotten in his hands. She was angry with him—Lady Shesu. Oh, how beautiful she was, standing there in the sunlight! She told wonderful, funny tales, too, and laughed in a way that made him feel bursting with happiness, and he would have given her his new boat unhesitatingly and with all his heart had she asked for it. But it was very hard to know what was going to make her angry. She was often angry with him—seldom with Nefer, only with him. And never did he know beforehand what was going to make her so.

Nefer's howls had quieted to spasmodic sobs and snifflings. Hatshepsut, holding her close with one arm, turned exasperatedly to Thoth. "Whatever made you act so? She wished to play with you. She would not have harmed your precious boat!"

Something was squeezing Thoth inside, squeezing hard and painfully. She was angry with him, very angry.

"Well? Can you not answer when I speak to you?"

Thoth tried, but could not. Mutely he held out the boat, with its mainmast dangling.

Lady Shesu's face changed as she looked at it, and her voice changed too. "Oh, the mast—I see." She raised her eyes to his and he felt the thing inside him begin to loosen. "It is too bad, Thoth. Ahmose will fix it for you. But Nefer meant no harm. You must remember—she is only a little maid yet, and you a great boy of five. You must treat her gently."

"I will," whispered Thoth.

Suddenly Nefer turned in her mother's embrace and slapped vindictively at him before Hatshepsut could catch her hand. Thoth dodged, nearly colliding with Ahmose, who had hastened as rapidly as his old legs would permit him to the scene of the quarrel.

"Your Highness, I regret exceedingly—Thoth is sorry, are you not, my boy? I will carve some dolls for her little ladyship . . ."

But as Ahmose was saying this, his hands closed reassuringly over Thoth's shoulders, and he pulled the boy against him.

"It is no matter," Hatshepsut told him rather irritably. "Neither was blameless, as usual. Come, my Nefer, you had best sit in the pavilion with me. Would you like a story?"

Thoth watched the two retreat across the grass, wishing Lady Shesu were his mother instead of Nefer's. Even Ahmose was not wholly his—Ahmose was Nefer's Father-Tutor, and only

Thoth's friend. But such a good friend! He turned to the old man, sure of understanding.

"Ahmose, she broke the mast!" he whispered indignantly.

"Aye, let me see it, lad. I think we can mend it, aye, we can indeed. I'll whittle a new mast. Your galley has been in battle, little one, and she's a bit the worse for it. But she won gloriously."

The old man grinned down at Thoth, displaying the wide gap in his upper row of teeth which Thoth thought almost as interesting as the scythe-shaped scar. He gazed at it, fascinated. It was not often he got to see it.

"And now," continued Ahmose, starting slowly for a stone bench, "she must put in to home port for repairs. Fetch her along, while I find where I left my knife."

For a few minutes Thoth stood beside the bench watching Ahmose work, shivering occasionally as a cold drop fell from his side-lock onto his sun-warmed flesh. He could not resist glancing often toward the pavilion, where Nefer was settled cosily on a cushioned stool, leaning against her mother's knee and listening to a story which was no doubt twice as wonderful as Lady Shesu had ever told before.

Presently, though he really did not mean to leave Ahmose, who had understood so comfortingly and who was carving the new mast for him, Thoth's feet began to move of themselves across the grass, between the bright flower beds, and slowly, kicking and scuffing at bits of rock, up the graveled path. At the foot of the pavilion steps he hesitated, fingering the tendril of a vine that twined around the gilded column, and glancing from one to another of the faces beyond. His father was sitting still and hunched, as always, gazing over Thoth's head. Nefer was laughing and squirming against her mother's knee, prattling about the story just finished—and it *had* been a new one, and he had not heard it!—and Lady Shesu was laughing with her. Then she glanced up and saw Thoth.

"Well, child, don't stand there gawking, come up if you like. Do you wish to hear a story too?"

"Aye!" breathed Thoth, darting up the steps to her side.

"Will you not speak to your father, my son?" came Nenni's voice.

Thoth swung around guiltily and went to him, dropping self-consciously to one knee. "Good afternoon, my lord father."

"Is it? I suppose it is. Do you like your boat?"

Thoth rose, answered him, and stood awkwardly while he put a few more questions. His father was always kind to him, and always smiled when he looked at him. But the voice which asked the questions was so tired, and the smile so tired too, that Thoth felt shy and uneasy before them. As the questions trailed off, he edged a little to one side. His father's eyes remained absently fixed on the place where he had been.

Relieved, he ran to stand by Lady Shesu's shoulder.

"Nay, you are still wet, child, don't lean against my dress. There, that's better. Now listen, and I'll tell you a tale my old nurse used to tell me when I was a little girl. Far away, far to the east of Egypt, there is a land where the gods live . . ."

Thoth listened eagerly, his eyes tracing the well-known line of her cheek, the little tilting curve at the end of her eyelid. He was soon lost in the tale of Godsland, the beautiful, far-off country with fragrant incense trees, and gardens terraced down to the sea. But he was careful not to lean against Lady Shesu's dress. After a time, very gently, so that she might not notice, he raised one hand and touched her hair.

Then the garden gate opened and everything was spoiled. A chamberlain in a golden headcloth strode up the path, dropped to one knee, and began to talk to Pharaoh. Thoth felt himself and the story go out of Lady Shesu's mind as if they had never been there.

"What is it, Nenni?" she said as the chamberlain went away.

"A priest, craving audience."

"The third in a week! You had best see this one."

"Why? It will be nothing of importance. Priests never say anything of importance."

"How can you tell, if you refuse to see them? Ptah's Beard! Suppose some crisis—" The sharp voice broke off abruptly. "Children, run now and amuse yourselves. Nefer, bid a slave fetch your dollies for you. And Thoth—your mother comes to fetch you. See, in the gateway. It is time for you to rest."

"Nay, it is too early, can I not stay with you a little longer? I am not sleepy—"

"Hush, you must go now. Hasten."

Propelled by a gentle shove, Thoth went reluctantly down the steps—reluctantly, yet hastening a little too, for his mother was approaching nearer every minute. He did not like his mother and Lady Shesu to be together. He ran toward the familiar frail figure and intercepted her halfway up the path. "I am coming, my mother—but wait—I must tell Ahmose something."

He ran across the grass, leaping the smallest flower beds, and halted breathless at Ahmose's bench. The new mast was almost finished. "Ahmose," he puffed, "I have to take my nap."

"May Amon send you a good sleep, little one."

"And Ahmose—"

"I am here."

"May we play with the boat again afterward?"

The old fingers kept steadily at their placid work. "Till midnight if you like. You had best run now."

Jubilant, Thoth ran, remembering to snatch his sandals from where he had dropped them at the end of the pool before he hurried to join his mother. She took his hand and as he walked beside her down the path he threw a last glance over his shoulder toward the pavilion. Lady Shesu was leaning toward his father, saying something he could not hear. He could tell she was angry, by her frown and the movements of her hands.

She is not angry with *me,* he told himself quickly so that the squeezing would not start up again inside him.

"Come along, come along," said his mother, pulling him around so that he faced front again.

They were at the gate; in another moment it was clicking shut behind them and they were crossing the Great Court in the direction of the Mansion of Beauty.

They did not speak as they walked the long way across the flagstones (hot under Thoth's bare feet, so that he danced a little) between the tall painted columns (the ones with pictures and words running right around the column so that the lady and the calf and the royal falcon were always cut in half, and he could never see the rest of them as he was hurried by) through the tall doors where the sentries stood (one stiff and haughty like a wooden image, the other a nice one, who always slyly winked at him) and down the long, shiny-walled, cool-floored corridor to his mother's chambers.

"Come, let us take that wet *shenti* off you," Iset said, closing

117

the door behind them. "Your feet must be washed also. I do not see why you cannot play without muddying yourself from head to foot! Now tell me, did Ahbi say the formula over you this morning when you woke?"

"Nay, Mother."

"*Ast!* That girl! It does seem that Pharaoh could find me a trustworthy slave . . ."

Thoth's eyes moved to the shelf of toys in one corner of the room, where his jointed crocodile on a string, the one that snapped its jaws open and shut as he pulled it along, was grinning at him. Thoth grinned back at it.

". . . I shall say the formula before your nap. One cannot be too careful, as Sata the magician was telling me only today. I bought you a birthday gift from him, you shall have it presently. You did not look into a fire this morning?"

"Nay, Mother."

"Ah, that is fortunate! Today is the seventh day of Tybi, had you ventured near a fire you would have felt an evil aura and been sickly all your life. . . ."

Iset's frail, complaining voice droned on in the familiar talk of magicians and talismans and potions as she knelt beside Thoth, working with the wet and obstinate knots of the scrap of linen which was his only garment. He half listened, having no comprehension of the mysterious matters which filled her mind, and knowing she would expect nothing of him except an occasional "Aye" or "Nay." At length the stubborn knots gave way and she flung the *shenti* aside.

"There—run now into the bathchamber and bid Ahbi cleanse your feet. Ah, me, I am weary, I must rest a moment."

Thoth scampered away, naked, to the bathchamber, shouting for Ahbi as he ran. She appeared suddenly and silently, as she always did—a large, black woman with eyebrows that joined over her nose, and big, pink-palmed hands. Without a word she fetched the water jar and washed his feet, while he renewed acquaintance with the faint stain on the bathchamber wall which looked exactly like a jackal with very large ears and a wavering, vague tail. He did not speak of it to Ahbi, however. There was no use talking to Ahbi, she never answered.

When she had dried his feet he went back down the corridor,

more slowly this time, pretending the wavy lines painted on the pounded clay floor were truly water, and he a frog who must jump from lotus pad to painted lotus pad without once falling in. A last prodigious jump landed him on all fours in the room where his mother waited for him. She sighed and raised her head from the chair back.

"Well, and has your birthday been a pleasant one?"

"Aye, Mother. Ahmose—" Thoth hesitated, then burst out, "Ahmose carved me a boat!"

"Indeed. What sort of boat?"

Thoth opened his mouth to let the wonder of it spill out, but something chilled the words on his tongue. "Oh, just a boat," he said. He did not really want to tell her about the boat.

She did not even notice that he had evaded her question. She had risen and walked toward the clothes chest. "And now," she remarked, "I suppose I shall have no peace until I give you my gift."

"What is it, Mother?" asked Thoth hastily. He followed her to the chest, feeling guilty that he had forgotten about her gift.

"Something far more valuable than any foolish little toy," she said severely.

He smiled uncomfortably, glad he had not told her about the boat. "May I see it now?"

"Aye, you may. There—green for strength, the Eye for health." She had unwound the linen, exposing a length of flaxen cord with an Eye-of-Horus carved delicately from a thin green-stone lying among its coils. She bound the amulet around his wrist so that the Eye dangled over the place where a vein showed faintly. "There. Do you not feel its strength already, flowing into you?"

"Aye, Mother," said Thoth dutifully. He tried to sound more enthusiastic. "Thank you, Mother. I—I like it very much."

"No doubt you would have preferred some silly plaything." Iset shrugged and gave him a little push toward his couch.

Thoth climbed into bed, stealing a glance at the marsh reeds painted on the wall beside his couch, then hastily looking away because it was not time for that game yet. His mother arranged the little curved headrest to fit comfortably under his neck, and he studied her face, bent close above him. Her lips turned down at the corners, not up like Lady Shesu's, and her eyes were set in darkened hollows. He wished he wanted to tell her about his wonderful boat.

She loosened the new amulet on his wrist, knotted the string once and, closing her dark-circled eyes, murmured rapidly, "Thou arisest, O god Shou; thou arisest, O god Re! If thou see-est the *kheft*-woman coming against Thoth, born of Iset, do not permit her to take the child in her arms. I will not give you, my child, I will not give you to the thief from Hell, but the Eye is a charm for you . . ."

The formula finished, she bound the amulet tight again and turned away. "Call Ahbi when you wake, but take care not to disturb me."

The door closed behind her. Almost at once Thoth's un-comfortable feeling was gone, as if she had taken it out of the room with her. He wriggled luxuriously on the soft mat of his couch, then turned his head with a little thrill of anticipation and allowed his eyes to rove as they would over the painted papyrus marsh that decorated the wall beside him. He had dis-covered long ago that if he squinted just a little and shut out the memory of the rest of the room, he could imagine himself right into the marsh, wandering among the tall, waving stalks of papyrus, visiting one by one the painted birds which nested among them or hovered above—the fluttering quail, the fat, pompous duck, the graceful hoopoe. The quail was his favor-ite. She had three tiny nestlings in her little woven house. He knocked at her door, waving politely to the spotted bug that crawled up the reed beside him, and was invited in to call on the baby quails. He was telling them Lady Shesu's story of far-off Godsland, where the myrrh trees grew, when he fell asleep.

2.

The fresh breeze of early morning poured gently over the hovels and workshops and villas of western Thebes, along with a radi-ance of light. In a bedchamber in the women's wing of the royal palace, on a superbly fashioned golden couch, the King's Daugh-ter, Divine Consort, Great Royal Wife and Mistress of the Two Lands Khnemit-Amon-Hatshepsut stirred restlessly, moved one hand in a vague groping gesture, then suddenly kicked off her coverlet and scratched industriously at her naked thigh. Her eyes still closed, she eased the motion of her fingers to a gentle rubbing, smiling with sleepy satisfaction. For a time her hand lay at rest on the spot of pinkened flesh it had been abusing. Presently it began to move slowly and lightly up her body, into the satiny hollow of her stomach, over the firm swell of breasts, across a sleep-flushed cheek. Disentangling the other hand from her tumbled hair she drew both high above her head, yawning prodigiously and twisting her whole body in a voluptuous and catlike stretch. Then, at last, she opened her eyes and blinked expectantly at the day.

Blue lotuses swayed from the bowl on her bedside table. Beyond, the familiar painted geese winged across an expanse of pale gray wall; on the littered dressing table below them silver-mounted vials and pomade pots caught the light like stars. Hatshepsut's gaze wandered drowsily over carven clothes chests, a robe of gossamer-sheer linen spilling like a drift of smoke off one of the chairs, scarlet sandals flung atop each other on the polished floor. Then her eyes lifted again to the strip of morning sky, broken only by slender columns, which ran across the top of one whole wall of the room. Silhouetted against the limitless blue of space, a hawk wheeled slowly.

A little shiver of delight ran through her. Drawing up her knees, she hugged them against her breast. If only something exciting would happen today—something altogether new.

For a time she lay motionless, still clutching her knees as if she could also hold fast the freshness of the moment of awakening. Then gradually her fingers loosened, and with a sigh she let her legs go slack upon the coverlet.

Something might happen . . . aye, it might, but nothing ever did. Not when one was Great Royal Wife and Queen of Egypt. Things used to happen, but that was before Amenmose died— before Nenni meant anything to her but a shy, thin boy who was always being led away to rest or drink more goat's milk . . .

Goat's milk—perhaps that would help put some weight on little Nefer's bones. Surely something could be found to fatten the child a little! She was so thin. Of course, she was growing rapidly . . .

A bee sailed in suddenly through the clerestory and began to buzz with noisy preoccupation about the lotus flowers. How clumsy he is, bumbling about so, thought Hatshepsut. Thoth would like to see that.

She adjusted the ivory headrest more comfortably, smiling as she remembered the boy's excitement over his little galley yesterday. His image formed in her mind—the sensitive, eager face, the youth-lock always dripping from some plunge into the pond, the scrap of a *shenti* always muddled or askew on his sturdy, active little body. Strange, he looked enough like her to be her own son, resembling his grandfather as he did. Of course he was not her son, she had no sons . . . Hatshepsut's smile vanished. It is Nenni's fault, she thought bitterly. Nenni's fault I have no child but a frail little maid, I who am strong and full of vigor. Never have I known illness in my life! It is Nenni's fault she is sickly, not mine but Nenni's. Nenni's!

Suddenly she jerked the headrest out from under her neck and flung it across the room. All that vigor—and nothing to expend it on! Oh, if Amenmose had lived! Everything would have been different, he knew how to laugh, to enjoy himself. There were always parties and river trips then. While now . . . Solemn, rigidly polite conferences with the Chief Cook, the Overseer of Wines, the Master of the Gardens—to all of whom Aahmes had already given their orders. Hours of sitting beside Nenni in the Audience Chamber, saying not a word. The Weekly Reception for the court ladies—the important and elderly ones, with their elderly manners, their throaty chatter about nothing whatsoever, and their suffocating heliotrope perfume.

Ptah's Beard! If I were Pharaoh I would ban them all from the palace! thought Hatshepsut. If I were Pharaoh I would make things happen, I would order a festival, plan a great feast, perhaps build a grand monument to myself for all the people to wonder and gape at as they sailed up and down the Nile. . . . Aye, but first of all I would call in artists to redecorate the Hall of Columns, for those tiresome water-rushes have been adorning the walls there since the day Atum first stood on the Primeval Hill and spat forth the gods from his mouth! Nothing is ever, ever changed. . . .

In truth, were it not that the river rose and fell, that the fields showed flood and then waving grain and then deep-cracked mud as the seasons passed, she might believe that time had ceased to move. The same faces, the same voices were around her always, even the same stilted greetings . . . they were only conventions, those greetings, phrases mummified through a thousand years into a never-varying formula for greeting the queen, but their wording never failed to grate on her. She quoted them under her breath, with savage mimicry: "May the Great Royal Wife be fruitful. May Your Radiance have many sons. May you be Mother of the King . . ." Little whips, flicking across her most sensitive spot. Five years of it!

Five years. They stretched behind her like a wasteland, and the few events of any importance rose like lonely hillocks. The marriage and the coronation—they were the first hillock. The death of Mutnofret was the second. Then came that memorable day of rebellion when she had run away to drive the horses as she used to do—and the sudden miscarriage that followed. Recriminations, remorse; the end of escapades forever. Later, after long and cautious months, little Nefer's birth, and life had leveled into monotony. That was all, since the day she had become queen of Egypt.

Queen? Hatshepsut's eyes followed the bee's blundering course as, heavy with pollen, he sought the clerestory again and at last sailed out into the blue. She had heard that bees had queens, whom they kept prisoner in the hive to bear their young. Was she not the same? Mistress of the Two Lands . . . she was not even mistress over her own household. Aahmes ordered the meals and instructed the gardeners and directed all affairs. When Nenni rode out, Aahmes' litter was second in procession. When he held a levee, Aahmes stood beside him on the Balcony of Royal Appearances and threw down the gold of favor on whom he wished to reward. And at the Weekly Receptions there were only Aahmes' guests, with their gently sagging chins and their sharp glances at the Divine Consort's waistline. . . .

Oh, Amon! Today was Reception Day.

Hatshepsut sat up in bed and clutched at her temples. *May the Great Royal Wife be fruitful . . . May you be Mother of the King . . . And how is the little princess today, a dear child, so like her father . . .*

Was something wrong with herself, she wondered, or were people truly as tedious as she thought them? Perhaps it was only the highborn, the elegant and noble. The lower classes were not

123

dull—think of the grooms and the kitchen maids jesting with one another as they worked, and the rivermen singing on the Nile, flinging taunts and laughter from boat to boat. Think of that architect, the one called Senmut—

Rolling over on her stomach, the Great Royal Wife plucked a lotus out of the bowl beside her bed and waved it absently under her nose. Propped up on one elbow, she caught a glimpse of herself in the copper mirror above the dressing table—a slim golden body glowing against the chalk-white coverlet and ink-black hair, with the lotus a spot of burning blue. Unconsciously she moved the arm that concealed her left breast, adjusted the position of one leg a trifle. For a moment she gazed with deep interest at the image in the mirror, raising an arm languidly and letting it fall in abandon, drawing a hand slowly down the curve of hip and thigh. Presently her eyes wandered away, stared wistfully a while at nothing, then closed tight as she flung herself onto her back, stretching her arms wide to enfold empty air. She lay quite still and tense for a time, then with a sigh, relaxed.

Why should I even trouble myself to get out of bed? she thought. There is really no sense to it. I can be as idle here as elsewhere, and perhaps less bored.

Still . . . She raised on her elbow and struck a note on the gong beside her couch. Lying back and clasping her hands beneath her head, she propped one leg upon the other and began to swing her foot back and forth.

I must try the goat's milk for little Nefer, she thought.

A tap sounded at the door.

"Come in, come in," she called irritably. "You need not tap when I have summoned you. Put the tray—" She broke off abruptly. It was Nenni who stood leaning against the closed door, looking down at her.

"You are late arising," he said. There was a note of constraint in his voice she knew well.

"Is there anything to get up for?" she retorted, deliberately starting the lazy swinging of her foot again.

He did not answer, but his face grew even more masklike as his eyes moved from the swinging bare foot up the length of her body. Prompted by a perverse impulse, she drew her hands from under her head, raised them high, and twisted in a slow and provocative stretch.

Tearing his eyes away, he walked to the other side of the room, flinging her the filmy robe from the chair as he passed. "Have you summoned your slave yet?"

"Aye, I have summoned her," she murmured. Why does he not come and take me, then, if he wants me so much? she thought contemptuously. Nay, he waits always for my leave, never commands my favors but requests them, no matter how badly I behave. By the gods, he would take them by force if he called himself a man!

Once more she was remembering the rough, strong hands of a commoner named Senmut.

Abruptly she sat up, reaching for the robe. "The slave will be here presently. I thought you were she when you came tapping a moment ago. I believe there will be ripe grapes today—do you care to Perfume the Mouth with me?"

"Nay, I wish nothing," he muttered.

She rose, wrapping the sheer linen about her and flinging him an impatient glance. "Well, sit down, sit down." As he sank into a chair, she moved to the dressing table and began to comb her heavy hair. "What brings you here at this hour? Surely Nehsi is not late for the morning conference?"

"He was early. I have seen him already."

Something in his tone made her glance at him sharply in the mirror. "Is anything amiss?"

"There is apparently some disorder in the temple. I know not what it is—perhaps nothing serious."

"You should have spoken to that priest yesterday. Or one of those who came before."

"They came merely to arrange an audience for Akhem, the high priest, so Nehsi tells me. Why should I see the man? I know little of temple affairs save my own duties there. I depend on Akhem to keep order among the ranks of the priesthood. Yet I am told some priestess is causing a furor with her visions and prophecies, creating dissension, turmoil, open resentment and disobedience of orders—"

"Merciful Osiris! In the Temple of Amon?" Hatshepsut dropped the comb and swung around to face him. "But that is serious, Nenni!"

"Perhaps, perhaps!" He flung out his bony hands in a gesture of impatience. "If so, it is the affair of the high priest and

125

the Steward of Amon. I have demands enough upon my time and strength. The rule of all Egypt is on my shoulders."

On Nehsi's, rather! thought Hatshepsut. On old Thutiy's, and the other ministers who ask for guidance and receive none, who await decisions until they can wait no more and must make them themselves. Thank Amon theirs are broad shoulders, and that my lord father instructed them so well! Oh gods, had *I* been born the prince. . . .

She rose from the dressing table and walked to Nenni's chair, looking down with growing exasperation at his thin, stooped neck, his strained face framed in its striped headcloth, the proud cobra of Egypt jutting over his sunken, averted eyes.

"Nenni—you cannot refuse to see the High Priest of Amon!"

"I will see him. Nehsi suggests I give him audience at the temple this morning. It is the Day of Offering, I shall be there in any case. I cannot imagine what good will come of it, but Nehsi urges—"

"Oh, in Mut's sweet name! 'Nehsi suggests,' 'Nehsi urges'— *you* are Pharaoh! Why do you not stiffen your neck just once, give orders, behave like a god and king? You have only to command, and all Egypt will obey you. You cannot sit forever avoiding this affair and that one, you must act!"

"And if my action be unjust?"

"You are worrying about that again?"

"Aye, again. Still. Always!" He rose and stood looking at her with an expression of such bitterness that she was silenced. "You are plagued by no such worry, are you, my lovely Shesu?" he said drily. "You do not ask yourself 'Is this just or unjust?' but only, 'How do I desire this to be?' It is better so. Far better, believe me. You are fortunate."

"Indeed!" retorted Hatshepsut. She felt the reply was inadequate, but she could think of no other. What does he mean? she thought indignantly. Naturally she inquired of herself only how she desired things to be—if she desired them so, then they were just. Was she not the Daughter of the Sun? She never knew how to handle Nenni in these moods. He became an enigma. "I see no need for such questions," she said coldly. "If the priests are in disorder, they must be punished—or else united under a new high priest."

"True. But which?"

126

"That is for you to say."

"And I would it were not so! Who am I to judge men, to decide their fate?"

"You are Pharaoh, you are a god!"

He started to answer. Then an expression of utter weariness crossed his face. He turned away without speaking.

To Hatshepsut's relief, the slave girl came into the room with a salver of fruit and cheese. She stopped short at sight of Pharaoh, and her face brightened with interest. "May the Great Royal Wife rejoice," she murmured, darting excited glances at Nenni as she set the tray on a low table.

"Tell Yen to prepare my bath," muttered Hatshepsut.

"At once, Radiant One. May the Divine Consort bear many sons."

The girl departed, followed by the Divine Consort's glare.

Sinking into a chair, Hatshepsut selected a fig from the salver with an annoyed look at Nenni's back. Everything had gone wrong, as usual. They were quarreling again. She had half intended to mention the redecoration of the Hall of Columns, or even the abolition of the Weekly Reception, but this was scarcely the moment. Still, she might avoid the countesses this one day—

"Nenni," she said suddenly. "Let me go with you this morning to the temple."

"Of course, if you wish." There was a pause. Then he turned to her with a faint, ironic smile. "Is it possible you desire my company?"

She glanced at him and forgot the careless answer on her lips. Ah gods, how lonely he is, she thought. After a moment she said, "I would desire it oftener, Nenni, were you not so gloomy! Come, sit with me, and let us talk of something besides the temple! Could we not be gay for once? We did not use to snap at each other like cat and dog at every opportunity—"

"Until we became man and wife."

"Must that make all the difference, then? Can we not live amicably as sister and brother, if not as wife and husband? Surely there is more to marriage than—" She stopped, knowing she should not have said it.

"Than the bridal couch?" he finished with a forced lightness. "You could so easily forget it, could you not, my Shesu? It becomes important only to the rejected."

"Nenni," she said in a low voice. "I do not reject you."

"Nay, not with words." He looked away, speaking rapidly. "I blame you for nothing, lovely one. You are as you are, you can be no different, nor can anyone. You are commendably—dutiful. Let us speak of something else—something gay, if you like."

She groped hastily, as anxious to change the subject as he, then was struck by the ridiculousness of her search. "Nenni," she said gently, "you make a labor even of enjoyment! To say earnestly 'let us speak of something gay' is to slam the door on any chance of gaiety. Come, look outside yourself for once, think of something else. Could we not plan a fete, do something new—perhaps go on a river journey! . . . Nay, never mind, I know quite well you cannot leave. But you do not even want to! You prefer to sit and brood!"

"Nay, I do not prefer, it is only . . . I do not have your gift of health, my Shesu."

"I know."

She sighed, leaning her head against the cushion. For a moment they regarded each other in silence. If only, if only, she was thinking, but she did not know quite what it was she longed for, or why she felt it lost to her forever.

"You are very beautiful," whispered Nenni.

Her mood underwent a rapid change. She sat up, hastily drawing the thin robe about her. "Nonsense. I must look like the wife of Set himself. My hair is not even dressed."

"You would be beautiful were it snarled like a peasant girl's."

It cost him to speak so, she knew that. He must tear down his ironic defenses, leave himself vulnerable. Yet he could not seem to help it. One word of softness from her and he held out his wrists for chains. . . . She selected a second fig with busy, prosaic motions, not looking at him. His sandals moved on the polished floor, and she felt him standing close beside her chair. Suddenly he was alien, repellent, a stranger whose fumbling hands and hoarse panting in the night filled her with loathing. The Hall of Columns, she thought cynically. A little wheedling, a caress or two . . . Nay, let the water-rushes stay there forever! It is not worth it.

"Nenni, I pray you sit down," she said rapidly. "Share my fruit with me."

"Nay, I must go now." He hesitated, then added with an attempt at casualness, though the words seemed wrung from him, "However, I would gladly sup with you tonight—if *you* would care to. . . ."

Oh gods, and after they had supped he would be constrained, self-conscious, with desire plain in his eyes, but still waiting silently for some sign that she desired him, too. And she would not desire him—she never did, she never would—and he would know, with a humiliation he would try, and fail, to hide, but it would not rouse anger in him, only a deeper and more hopeless longing. Ptah's Beard! The marriage ritual had given him her body, why could he not take it, as any other man would, and be satisfied? No, he must have more; he must hope, he must wait. . . . Let him wait, then, and go on waiting! she thought angrily.

But of course that was folly. She must have sons, for Egypt.

"As you wish," she murmured.

There was a silence. Then he turned abruptly away from her. "Nay, we will wait until you wish it also." The sandals moved across the floor, the tight voice said, "We will depart for the temple at eleven, pray join me in the courtyard." The door closed behind him.

Hatshepsut sat motionless, the two halves of the fig still in her hands. Suddenly she flung them back into the salver. Now it was her fault, was it? Now she must feel herself a monster, take all the blame—

Her anger collapsed as abruptly as it had come. Ah gods, she thought, poor Nenni, poor Nenni, he cannot help it, and now I have hurt him again—and I cannot help that either.

Her body sagged back against the cushions; reaching with a listless hand, she sank her teeth into a fig.

There was a quick tap, and the door opened again. Old Yen, grayer and stouter than in former years, as befitted the dignity of one titled Childhood Nurse of the Divine Consort and Great Royal Wife, bustled into the room.

"May the *ka* of the Radiant One rejoice," she remarked, casting a pleased, inquisitive look at her royal mistress. "Imagine my confusion—walking along the corridor as on any other morning, and whom should I meet face to face but Pharaoh himself, coming from my lady's—"

"He was here only a few moments," Hatshepsut informed her tartly.

"Oh," said Yen, deflated.

"We spoke of the temple."

"I'm sure it is none of my affair what my lady spoke of with His Majesty." With an air of immense dignity the old nurse turned and began taking garments from a clothes chest.

"Nay, it is *not* your affair, my beloved Old One—yet it is far more yours than it is the concern of the Chief Chamberlain, or the Head Gardener, or three dozen aged countesses or five dozen slaves and underlings of this household—all of whom would take up residence in that corridor if they dared, in order to chronicle every visit Pharaoh pays me! Gods of Egypt! How I wish they would all cease staring at my middle!"

"Now come, come, my lady, it is only natural; after all, Your Radiance is a very important person, on whose—eh, middle, as Your Radiance is pleased to call it—depends the future of your royal line. . . . Still, my Shesu, I do understand."

Smiling at the dumpy, devoted little figure standing with her arms full of starched linen, her wig a bit askew, as always, and her face puckered in a sympathetic frown, Hatshepsut pushed the fruit away and sprang up to envelop her in a hug. "You always understand, do you not, Old Nobody, Old Come-Come-My-Lady—"

"Blessed Isis save us, watch what you're about, you're crushing this lovely fluting!" Staggering free of her impulsive mistress, Yen cast one glance at the garment she had been holding, then flung it on the bed. "*Aii* well, that must be ironed again, but then *I* need not do it, thanks be to my lady, who is ever sending another slave or two to help old Yen with her work . . . and if ever I see one of *those* worthless ones staring at my lady's middle—! Ahh, feel the cool breath of the north wind floating in to us, it is like a blessing, is it not? Come, into the bathchamber, this is Reception Morning, we had best scrub some manners into you. . . ."

At least, Hatshepsut reflected as Yen released her from the rubbing-table half an hour later, I shall spend only a few moments in the countesses' company today; we leave at eleven for the temple.

130

She knew there was little excitement to be expected there; the familiar journey by litter and royal barge, the solemn greetings from the priests, a period of standing piously behind Nenni as the incense burned. . . . Still, by contrast with her usual morning occupations, it seemed a round of giddy pleasure.

Hatshepsut stifled a sigh, walked back into her bedchamber, and bade the slave girl dress her hair.

3.

Following Nenni in slow procession out of the incense-drenched Holy-of-Holies, Hatshepsut wondered irritably why she had chosen to come to the temple this morning instead of staying out the last tedious hour of the Weekly Reception. The audience with the High Priest still lay ahead, and Amon alone knew how long Nenni would linger here, debating, worrying. . . .

At the door she glanced back at the great golden image in the torchlit niche, across which a priest was slowly drawing a crimson curtain. Awesome and magnificent, more beautiful than any mortal—Amon, her father.

Truly my father, she thought with a strange, deep thrill. He came to my lady mother in the guise of Pharaoh and lay with her all of one long night— Ah gods, if only he would come to me so!

She moved on across the jasper pavements, through the carven door and into an antechamber a little larger and a little lighter than the tomb-dark Holy-of-Holies, out of that and on into a chamber still larger and lighter, with six tall pillars; that opened at last into a lofty and spacious hall in which a forest of cedar columns, clustered as thick as tree trunks on the hills of Lebanon from which they came, rose up and up through the dim reaches to pierce the shafts of sunlight pouring in from the clerestory high above.

She loved this hall, which her father Thutmose had built long ago to the glory of Egypt and the god Amon; she felt close to him here. His handiwork was all around her, made visible and tangible through the skill of his architect, Ineny. A great king he had been—this was only one among the many buildings he had caused to rise from the black earth of his kingdom to mark his long and energetic reign. In the five years since Mutnofret's son had worn the crown not one stone had been set atop another, not one monument had been started or even planned.

At the high priest's door Akhem, a stout, chilly-eyed little man, came forward with the Steward of Amon and the Overseer of Fields and Works to usher the royal couple into his rooms. Solemnly the unctuous ritual of bowing, stretching out the hands, praising Pharaoh and wishing the Great Royal Wife many sons was mechanically performed.

It is like a slow and stately dance, thought Hatshepsut. Not one gesture different this time from the time before, or a thousand years ago. . . .

She looked without interest from Nakht, the Overseer of Works —a bony, sullen-looking individual who kept suspicious eyes on Akhem—to Sekhwed, the Steward of Amon, whom she remembered well from his regular monthly visits to the palace. He was a doddering, amiable old man, very dignified and sleepy, who had, she felt privately, outlived his usefulness some years ago.

"I pray it will be pleasing to Your Majesties to accept my unworthy hospitality," Akhem was saying as he beckoned slaves and fan-wavers. "If Your Majesties will deign to be seated . . . I fear I may offer you nothing but honey-and water. As Your Majesties realize, we priests live dedicated and frugal lives and enjoy none of the luxuries to which Your Majesties are accustomed. . . ."

Hatshepsut cast an ironic glance at the little man's paunch, his sleek and oily flesh and the exquisite linen in which it was clothed, but refrained from comment.

Nenni touched the insipid drink to his lips politely. He was paler than usual, sitting with his neck rigid beneath the crown's weight. "You may address My Majesty concerning your grievance," he said.

"My thanks, Great Horus. I scarcely know how to begin. It is a matter of great delicacy."

"It concerns the statements of a certain priestess?"

"Aye, in part, Your Sublimity—"

"That is *all* it concerns," Nakht put in with sudden vehemence.

Hatshepsut, glancing at him, saw that he was watching Akhem as a cat might watch a particularly dangerous rat.

The high priest ignored the interruption. "There is in the

temple a priestess of the rank of Divine Handmaiden, one Nofret-Hor, a woman who in the past has exhibited extraordinary powers of vision and divination but who has now, I fear, gone quite mad—"

"Perhaps. Perhaps not," Nakht snapped.

Akhem shot an icy glance at him. "If the overseer will be good enough to refrain from interruptions—"

Nenni cleared his throat. "What is the prophecy that so disturbs you?"

"She says . . . of course Your Majesty understands that this cannot be called a prophecy, if the Strong Bull will forgive this unworthy one for correcting his divine words. It is a lie, the mere raving of a disordered mind . . ." Akhem continued in this vein for several minutes, his smooth, reasonable voice unchanged but his upper lip betraying a hint of moisture, which he blotted with a kerchief of cobweb-thin linen.

"But what does the woman *say?*" Nenni interrupted him at last.

Unexpectedly, the old steward spoke up in a voice as innocently cheerful as a child's. "She says the high priest is unworthy of his office."

"Indeed!" murmured Pharaoh.

Hatshepsut examined her rings, bubbling with sudden inner mirth as the high priest's kerchief came inconspicuously into play again. Of course, he was explaining carelessly, the woman was mad; her infamous statement—which she claimed to be the word of Amon, sent to her in a vision—need not be considered save as an illustration of that madness. Akhem deplored the necessity for even mentioning it to Pharaoh; but he was sure Pharaoh would now agree that something must be done at once to remove the woman from the temple.

"Is this so impossible?" Nenni said. "Dismiss the woman. Turn her over to a magician, that he may drive the *kheft* out. Surely you do not need Pharaoh's assistance."

"Your Majesty does not fully comprehend the situation," Nakht said in a tone which indicated that he now intended to have his say. With a venomous glance at Akhem he placed himself squarely in front of Pharaoh. "Nofret-Hor is the wife of the Master of Storerooms, an excellent man, indispensable to the administration of the temple! I am sure the high priest will agree. Had it not been for the Master of Storerooms, the records of the treasure chambers would long ago have reached a state of chaos. I think I do not exaggerate, Honored Akhem?"

His smile was malicious; Akhem's shrug was just a little too casual. "He has been useful, aye. I think we need not burden the Good God with these petty details—"

"A few are not petty," Nakht interrupted. "For instance, the errors he found in the treasury records . . ."

"Aye, some enemy had falsified the records," Akhem explained. His manner was now so casual that his words slurred together. "Made it appear that I—that some of the richest offerings were entering my own coffers, that—"

"Plots—enemies—*Apparently,*" said Nakht, watching Akhem, "the temple is shot through with them. If Your Majesty can believe it, certain of the priests—men whom the high priest trusted implicitly, in fact his favorites—were actually accepting honorariums from the wealthier worshipers. Indeed, not only accepting but demanding rich personal gifts for setting an offering before the god—"

Akhem raised his voice and drowned the other out. "Naturally, when the Master of Storerooms called the matter to my attention, the men were scourged from the temple. That is all over and done with, Overseer."

And, thought Hatshepsut, he still looks a bit annoyed about the end of that little game, in which I have no doubt he shared handsomely!

It seemed to her that this Master of Storerooms was entering the conversation with interesting frequency. While the high priest was talking to Nenni again about the prophetess' madness, she murmured to Nakht, "Did I understand you to say that this Nofret-Hor is the wife of the Master of Storerooms?"

"Aye, Your Radiance."

"Indeed! An unfortunate coincidence."

"Aye, unfortunate, monstrously unfortunate!" The overseer's eyes grew frightened; there was something very like panic in them. "Therein lies the problem—for if she is dismissed, the laws of the temple demand that *he* be dismissed."

"And you consider this man indispensable?" she said.

Nenni heard the question and turned to listen to the answer.

"Your Radiance, I scarce know how I could perform the many

duties of my office without him! Why, at this moment I do not even know where . . ." Nakht stumbled a little. "That is, I mean to say he is not only indispensable, he is irreplaceable. Adept at figures—superb at organization—aye, and able to shoulder responsibility when necessary; a most important point when one remembers how frequently I must be absent on temple affairs, journeying each month to Abydos and Menfe—"

Again Akhem's voice overpowered the other's. "No underling is indispensable. It is true that this one has made himself extremely useful; I fear the overseer depends on him almost too heavily. However, the madness of his wife has made it quite impossible to keep him in the temple any longer. Your Majesty, her poison has spread through all the priesthood! It is impossible to describe the havoc she is creating with these lies."

"If they *are* lies," Nakht said distinctly. "That is the question for His Majesty to decide."

Nenni sighed, looked at the two men a moment, then turned to the old steward, who was blinking contentedly, enjoying the breeze from one of the great plumed fans. "How is it, Sekhwed, that in your reports to me each month you have said nothing of these falsified records, this spreading poison?"

"Eh? Have I said nothing?" inquired the steward, turning.

"Do you not know what you write in your own reports?"

"Your Majesty, I am approaching my seventieth year of wisdom," the steward pointed out in gentle reproof. "It is impossible for me to be as active as in the days of my youth. Naturally, I direct in person the larger affairs of the temple; but the Master of Storerooms, a man of most unusual qualities, has long relieved me of such details of my duties as the writing of reports. . . ."

To Hatshepsut, the unusual qualities of this Master of Storerooms were becoming more obvious every minute. Why, the scoundrel, he had the whole Temple of Amon in the palm of his hand, and now he was squeezing. Probably he wanted to be high priest himself.

Ptah's Beard! What a rogue he is, she thought. But what a clever rogue!

Moreover, he was going to get clean away with his roguery, she realized a moment later, unless she did something about it. Nenni's questions had returned to the prophetess; he was speaking of justice and injustice, and listening anxiously to Akhem and

Nakht, whose hatred of each other was scarcely concealed now beneath their surface smoothness. Two jackals, trapped and snarling—and Pharaoh, earnestly weighing and reweighing the evidence against the prophetess, was so absorbed in examining the bait for poison that he did not even see who had set the snare.

Merciful Osiris, we shall be here till sundown! Hatshepsut thought. Five minutes with this precious Master of Storerooms and I could settle the entire affair. . . .

Why not? It would be amusing to confront him, calmly lay bare his schemes, and teach him once and for all that the Daughter of the Sun was not to be hoodwinked by a common schemer. Yes, by all means she must see this man before he was thrown to the dogs for his iniquities. Rogue he might be, but he could not possibly be a bore.

She rose, patting away a yawn as the three dignitaries stiffened hastily to attention. "My lord husband, I weary of sitting. Pray give me leave to stroll about the temple and await your coming."

"As you wish, my lady . . ."

She was out the door and hurrying down the corridor before anyone could think to offer her an escort. There was a little chapel, if memory served, just off the columned Hall of Praise. Seeing a temple servant plying his broom in one of the priest's chambers, she beckoned him to her.

"Send the Master of Storerooms to me at once, in the chapel yonder."

Smiling at the man's goggle-eyed awe as he made off down the corridor, tripping on his broom, she found the chapel, chose the first of its small antechambers as well suited to her purpose and strolled to its farther end, absently fingering one of a pair of tall alabaster vases while she planned what she would say. She was still engrossed in her mischievous thoughts when a step sounded behind her in the doorway, and a throat was cleared.

"Your Radiance sent for me?" said the voice of Senmut of Hermonthis.

She stood frozen, her fingers rigid on the vase's lip, feeling a curious lifting of the hairs on the back of her neck. It could not be, of course. She was mistaken.

She forced her hand to move casually about the rim of the vase, forced herself to say, "I did. Pray enter."

"As the Divine Consort wishes."

There was no mistake. Impossible to forget that harsh deep voice, impossible to mistake the note of suppressed excitement in it. It was the same man. Her mind flashed to that day of the Heb-Sed when her litter passed him and she had seen shocked recognition staring from his eyes.

Oh Amon, he knew very well who I was! she thought. How can I face him? He knew it was I. He knows he kissed the Daughter of the Sun!

Then all at once her agitation dissolved before a rush of inner laughter, mingled with wild delight. Somewhere, deep inside her, she was not even surprised.

Slowly she turned and faced him.

4.

It was time, Nenni knew, to rise from his couch and dress for the evening meal. The sun's last rays were slanting in through the garden doors, creating a pool of soft color on one of the rugs. Soon the bedchamber would be in shadow, as the alcove where he lay already was.

Yet he continued to delay, moving his head on its ebony rest so that his eyes were again directed toward the star-map on the alcove ceiling. His morning at the temple had left him distraught and edgy, as he had known it would. How in heaven's name did one decide whether a priestess's visions were true or false, prophecy or politics? How would his father have decided it?

It was a familiar question, that last. The only trouble was that he could never find the answer to it. He had not, he reflected ironically, enjoyed his father's confidence. Their minds had traveled paths as different as those of the sun and the stars up yonder, so guessing was impossible. Hatshepsut would be able to guess, and guess correctly. However, it would never occur to her to try. What did it matter to her what her father would have done? What she chose to do was sufficient. It was the way she was most like him. Amenmose had been the same. . . . Ah, if Amenmose were Pharaoh!

But Amenmose was not Pharaoh.

True or false, true or false? One thing struck the mind immediately—that these particular visions seemed oddly direct to be the authentic word of heaven. Usually prophecies were mysterious sayings, full of ambiguities and irrelevancies which required much study and complex interpretation by councils of learned priests. Indeed, were it not that the priests were so learned, so solemn—and so ingenious—about interpreting them, one would scarcely take them seriously. It was very strange that the gods, whose thoughts were perfect and whose tongues could not be confused, should choose to send down their messages in so garbled a form.

This message, therefore, was suspect because of its very clarity. "The high priest is unworthy of his office." It had all the blunt directness of a man-made statement, none of the lofty confusion of a god's. Very likely the vision was man-made too. Even so, it did not necessarily follow that the priestess was lying, except in claiming her statement to be the word of Amon. Nenni was inclined to believe that the statement itself might be entirely true. This morning, as on other occasions, Akhem had struck him as lacking in intelligence and overburdened with a love of luxury and himself. Still . . . Akhem had been high priest under the first Thutmose. Instinctively Nenni shrank from altering any arrangement of his father's that it was possible to keep. Suppose Akhem was not a perfect high priest? Did he know a better? No, nor did he care to invite worse trouble by attempting to discover one. Let things run on as they were. After all, did it really matter?

Ah, there was the great difficulty—he could not convince himself it mattered. To him it was like watching the frantic scurrying of ants whose hill had been stirred—he felt no emotion concerning it, except a sense of weariness because he knew he must descend into it. There was no question but that he must descend, must exert his best and most conscientious effort to solve the problem with justice. For to Akhem it did matter, and to the priestess, and to those others who were embroiled in it. Even Nehsi had been gravely disturbed about it, Shesu almost alarmed. Without a doubt, all Egypt—except himself—felt that it mattered enormously who served the god Amon as his highest priest. But suppose Amon himself did not exist? Then a monkey could wear the robes and light the incense; it would be all the same. . . .

I am losing touch with Egypt, Nenni reflected. More every day. I am no longer frightened by these fancies of mine, no longer even shocked by them.

He turned his head slightly to look at the golden statuette of Amon, now a little blurred with the dusk fast gathering in the wall niche. Once his heart would have swelled in worship at sight of it—once long, long ago. Amon, the Hidden One, who lived in the wind, who spoke from the wind, who perhaps, quite simply, *was* the wind in the beginning, when the world was new and the people's minds as children's. Amon, who in another form was the Great Bull, possessed of terrifying horns and vast genitals of awe-inspiring potency—and in still another form was this beautiful young man with the face of inscrutable peace. (Inscrutable? Or only blank?) Amon—a miraculous and therefore singularly unconvincing figure. . . . When logic became so strained one began to doubt the premise. Which did one bow down to, the Great Bull, the man-image, or the invisible wind? What did men mean when they said "Mighty Amon"?

Nay, thought Nenni, that is my defect and my stumbling block. When men say "Mighty Amon" they mean them all. One must not seek reason in worship. Does my servant balk when he must think of Isis not only as Divine Mother of Horus but also as the Dog-Star, the fertile soil of Egypt, and the royal throne? Is he confused when he considers that Thoth the Moon, the Scribe of the Gods, is at times an ibis and at others a baboon, or that Wadjet is at once the Crown, the cobra on the crown, the goddess dwelling in the south and a mysterious tongue of flame? Nay, he is not at all confused; on the contrary, each aspect adds another meaning to his concept of the god, and he is not troubled by a lack of logic, for he does not think—he feels. I do not feel, I think—therefore I balk. It is a defect in myself.

Yet Nenni, examining his thoughts, wondered if the gods were in truth invalid simply because they were redundant. Perhaps the premise of Egypt's worship, traced back far enough through all its multitudinous gods and forms of gods, through heaped-up imagery and epithets each of which mysteriously re-enforced while seeming to contradict the other—perhaps this premise had in the end its own miraculous logic and triunal unity. Creation, procreation, resurrection—they were all. What else existed in the mind of man? A god which represented that all-inclusive trinity could be capable of infinite division and variety, and yet be One.

In the person of Amon one could find all three. As the Hidden

One, the Breath of Life, he was the Creator. He was the Pro-creator when he was called the Strong Bull. He was the Resur-rector when he was called the *Kamutef,* Bull-of-His-Mother. In this aspect he had the power to beget himself over and over again upon her who bore him, and was thus changeless and immortal. Amon was the begetter of himself, it was his supreme quality. And he was also, Nenni mused, the father of a son, the enigmatic child-god Khonsu, who wore the youth-lock and carried the blue lotus and was clothed in the wrappings of the dead—and had no other qualities or history, being none other than the personified form of the Royal Placenta, the stillborn twin of Pharaoh. There-fore—by the elliptical but inspired logic of the worshiping human heart—Khonsu, twin of Pharaoh, was also the moon, that pallid, ghostly twin of the royal sun. It did not matter that Thoth was the moon as well.

So it was with all the gods—hundreds of them, each with mul-tiple aspects which intermingled and overlapped and encroached on the provinces of other gods—yet perhaps all were at bottom One. Creation, procreation, resurrection: life. Men worshiped life.

Nenni's thoughts halted with a shock of pleasure, clustering around his discovery like travelers clustering in a surprised group around an object of strange beauty and meaning found in the desert sands. Then, being Nenni's thoughts, one of them must poke the object doubtingly.

Men worshiped life? Nay, not quite. They possessed life, and they knew not where it came from, therefore they fell down in awe before it. . . . It was not life they worshiped, but the un-known.

Another poke—this time a jab of contemptuous recognition.

Men worshiped the unknown, and for no better reason than that it was unknowable.

Of course, thought Nenni sardonically. And being unknowable, the mystery is by nature inexpressible. Man cannot tolerate the inexpressible, which shows him his own terrifying inadequacy, therefore he must set out at once to express it. Amon the Hidden One becomes first the Spirit, then the Breath of Life, then—even more tangibly—the Wind, then a presence in the wind. The Pres-ence becomes the Procreator and the *Kamutef,* then, far more understandably, the Strong Bull and the Man-image with the beautiful, inscrutable face, and then finally and miserably, the bellowing, mortal bull in the temple stable, with horns and hair —and a small golden statue in a niche. Thus man has enlarged himself as he reduced his god, and is content to worship the bloody flesh of a placenta and forget the terrible glimpse into the abyss of truth.

Poke—jab—poke. The beautiful, meaningful object in the desert was now a heap of rubble—as no doubt it had been all along. Nenni sighed and closed his eyes.

When he opened them a few minutes later they wandered back to the shadowed traceries on the ceiling above him and came to rest on the starry image of Isis, forever pursuing Osiris across the heavens. As always, the slender, active form of the goddess brought Hatshepsut to his mind.

The figures should be reversed, he thought. It is she who flees, she who is ever elusive, and I who grasp fruitlessly after her. Nay, not always . . . the irony faded from his mind. Often, he mused, she reaches out to me, seeks in her own way to rend the veil between us, seeks to touch me and draw me into that bright world she knows, as if she were life itself stretching out her hand to me. . . . Aye, there lies the meaning in the figures, if one must find a meaning—life beckoning after one who bears the seed of death and who therefore cannot turn back from the path his feet must follow, even though he might wish to. And do I wish to? Perhaps not. Perhaps she is right, I prefer to sit and brood. I have lost touch with Egypt, with life itself. But for her I would turn back, if I could. Her touch I would answer if I knew how. . . .

He was barely able to see the lines of the star-map, the light had grown so dim. Reluctantly he swung his feet over the edge of the couch and sat up. He did not want to put on his diadem and go back to being Pharaoh, but it was stupidity to struggle against imprisonment. Who was free?

He clapped, and a slave came in silently from the antechamber and lighted the lamps. Nenni sat blinking in the sudden light. The shadows departed; the room swung into prosaic focus. At once the scurrying problems of the anthill took renewed possession of his mind. The visions—the priestess—he must decide.

He stood up wearily. "Tell them to prepare my bath." He stopped, as a tap sounded on the door.

"Nenni." It was Hatshepsut's voice.

"Open it," Nenni ordered quickly.

The slave swung the door wide to reveal Hatshepsut standing like a lovely apparition in the opening. She was clad in a fluted robe through which the pale bronze of her body showed warm and clear. Her hair flowed loose and she wore no ornament except a collar of fresh-plucked lotuses whose fragrance filled the room.

Nenni murmured a dismissal to the slave. His heart was beating rapidly with his own private form of worship.

She stepped through the doorway and hesitated, rather nervously, he thought. "Nenni—I want to talk to you."

"Of course, my dear." He walked to her quickly and led her into the room. "How cold your hand is!" he added in surprise.

"Nay, nay, I'm not at all cold . . ."

She freed her hand and went past him to the garden door, talking rapidly as she gazed out into the clear dusk.

"It is only that I want to talk to you, and I do not know if you will listen to me. You *should* listen, Nenni. You must listen!"

"Naturally I will listen," he said gently. "What is it, my Shesu?"

"It is—about this morning, the trouble at the temple. I think the prophetess is right. I think Akhem should be removed from office. He is a corrupt, paltry little man who for years has been lining his own nest at the expense of the greatest god in Egypt, my own father Amon. He is a disgrace to the temple, to Egypt, to you, Nenni! Could you not see that for yourself this morning? One needs no prophetess, only one's own eyes."

"Aye, aye, I agree with you." Nenni sighed. So this was all she had come for. "The problem is to choose someone to replace him. Someone who would not be worse than Akhem."

"That is no problem at all," she announced surprisingly. "I know the very man—Hapuseneb of Thebes, First Prophet of the temple. He is a man of dignity and character—my lord father knew him and thought well of him when he was but a *sem* priest. He could assume office tomorrow and within a month have all the confusion disentangled, the trouble quieted, everything flowing smoothly. . . ."

"Then by all means, let him do so!" murmured Nenni.

He had spoken half to himself, but she whirled, her face lighting. "Do you mean it, Nenni? Oh, you are right, you are right to decide so! Have you decided, in truth? Was it as easy as that?"

Gods, I would decide anything to make you look at me so, thought Nenni. He, too, reflected wonderingly: Is it as easy as that?

"Aye, I have decided," he said slowly. "I will give the orders tomorrow. I remember Hapuseneb, he took part in the Heb-Sed. But I would never have thought of him. It is curious that you chanced to do so. What called him to your mind?"

"I saw him—for just a moment, this morning after I left Akhem's chambers to stroll and await you." She hesitated, as if she, too, were trying to make a decision. Abruptly she said, "I saw the Master of Storerooms, also."

"Ah yes, the Master of Storerooms, the Indispensable One, the Remarkable One."

"He is as remarkable as Akhem and the others think him," she said slowly. Turning away toward the dusky garden again, she added, "Hapuseneb deems him so—and it was my own impression, also. In fact, Nenni, I would not be surprised to see him become Steward of Amon before long."

"Indeed?" Nenni had a strange, sudden feeling of uneasiness for which he could find no reason except that the forced casualness of her tone, on a subject concerning which her casualness might more logically have been real, revealed to him that he knew nothing of what was going on in her mind. "At least the choosing of the steward need not be my decision," he remarked with relief. "Hapuseneb may have that problem, and I wish him joy of it."

"I think Hapuseneb will not find it a problem," she said with an amusement he understood no better than he had her tension of a moment before. Turning toward him again, she gave him a smile of such unexpected warmth and friendliness that everything else vanished from his mind. "Nenni, you make problems where there are none. I could help you—where there are decisions like this—where I see the answer and you do not. I never thought you would listen to me. But I could help you." Suddenly she crossed the room and sank down in a whirl of fluted, filmy draperies upon the stool beside his chair. "I do not want to dress and go into that great formal hall tonight! May we not dine here together, as you said this morning—perhaps in the garden, by the edge of the pool?"

Nenni remembered the morning, and the knots of self-consciousness snapped tight within him. He knew he should refuse her request and save what little pride remained to him. He also knew that pride meant less than nothing to him if he must choose between it and an hour in her company.

For a moment he wished with all his heart that his love was blind, as well as overwhelming. But he heard himself saying, "Nothing would please me more. If you—truly wish it."

"I do, I wish it. You misunderstood me this morning. I do wish it, Nenni."

Shamed by his joy, he rose, summoned his slave, and sent him hastening in the direction of the kitchens. When he turned back, Hatshepsut was standing in the garden doorway, watching the moon rise through a fringe of palms. Crossing the room, he paused behind her, longing to take those warm golden shoulders in his hands and pull her back against him, dreading to feel the familiar slight stiffening of her body if he should do so. As long as he did not touch her, he could almost believe this moment of silence was a moment of closeness, that she had come to him for no other reason than a desire to be with him and share his bed, his love, his life, just as other men's wives came to them. Perhaps she wanted to reach out to him, and did not know how.

"Shesu," he said, forcing his voice to keep steady. "You will —stay with me, tonight?"

"Of course."

He hesitated, then asked it, very low: "Why?"

"Why? Because you wish it—and I said I would. Besides . . ." She hesitated too, and he held his breath. Then she spoke in a hard, intense voice he had never heard. "Besides, I wish it too. I must have a son, Nenni. I must. I must!"

"I see," he whispered. No matter, he told himself. She wants your son. That is almost the same. Almost the same as wanting you.

It was not the same, but he did not let himself think how very different it could be. He raised his hands and let them close at last on her smooth, warm shoulders. And he felt her body stiffen, just slightly, in every nerve.

144

Almost roughly he pulled her back against him and buried his face in her hair.

5.

"If the Good God please," murmured a respectful voice.

Nenni, smiling as he watched Thoth and Nefer playing with their painted eggs, turned reluctantly to find a chamberlain bowing.

It was the morning of the Festival of Un, the Great Hare. At daybreak the streets of Thebes had swarmed with people dancing, drinking wine, celebrating with unleashed passion the fertility of the sprouting fields and of their own bodies. As Un's great Eye, the moon, faded slowly before the dawn, many a youth and maiden just turned thirteen had known the delights of love for the first time—and grasped, for the first time, the meaning of the gaily colored eggs they had received on the Great Hare's day since they were babes. Now it was midmorning. The farmers were already back in the fields tending the delicate green shoots which showed everywhere through the black mud; the royal family, like many a common one throughout the city, had gathered in the garden to watch the little ones playing with their eggs.

Nenni acknowledged the chamberlain's presence grudgingly. "Oh, yes, the Council. Is it time?"

"Nay, Your Majesty, there still remains half an hour before the Royal Kinsmen's Council, but His Excellency Senmut, Overseer of the Fields and Works of Amon, is hopeful of five minutes audience before then. . . ."

Hatshepsut looked up quickly from the children's games. "I'll see him, Nenni. I know what he wants."

There was a tiny sound as the dowager Aahmes, on the other side of the pavilion, shifted in her chair. She said not a word, but Nenni was as conscious of her instant disapproval as if it were a palpable substance let loose upon the air. He sighed. Here was another of those situations.

"Take His Excellence to the Southern Garden," he told the chamberlain.

He watched the man stride off down the path. Then his eyes moved to Hatshepsut. She was already rising from the pavilion

145

steps, shaking out her draperies, smoothing her hair, busily not looking at him. She smiled at the children.

"Be good little hares now, and do not quarrel over your eggs."

"Are you going? Oh, please do not go!" Thoth cried, scrambling to his feet.

"I must. Take care, you will knock over your basket!"

Thoth sidestepped hastily, glancing down in alarm at his painted eggs, then moved the basket to safety under the steps. Nefer had flung her arms about Hatshepsut's knees, chanting, "Don't go, don't go, don't go."

"My darling, I must. Here, loose me, little clinging-bur, and I'll hold you for a moment . . . Ohhhhh, what a big heavy girl you're becoming!" Hatshepsut hoisted her up, smiling and frowning a little, then set her down and started up the steps.

"Lady Shesu," came Thoth's soft voice, "you never stay with us as you used to."

"I have not the leisure I used to have, that is why! I am busy, very busy, all day, every day. I do very important things."

Thoth's mouth was smiling in response to her mock-stern tone, but his great black eyes were yearning. "I wish you could tell us stories again. You haven't told us a story since—a long time. Since my birthday, when I had my boat."

"Twenty little days—that is not so long. I'll tell you another one day, but I've no time now. Run back and play with your eggs."

Thoth turned reluctantly down the steps, and Hatshepsut mounted the last of them to meet Nenni's eyes at last. "You have no objection, of course?" she said casually.

"To your seeing this Senmut? Not the least. Since you know his errand and I do not—"

"I'm sure I do not understand *that*," put in Aahmes crisply.

"It is not necessary that you understand it, my lady mother," retorted Hatshepsut. "However, if you desire to, I can make it quite clear in an instant. Nenni was ill yesterday. Also the day before. Also the day before that and the day before that. A matter arose in the temple that demanded someone's attention immediately. I took care of it." She turned to Nenni. "He merely wishes the Royal Seal on the document. There is no need for you to disturb yourself. I will be finished in time to join you at the Council."

146

"Very well," murmured Nenni.

Aahmes could not keep silent any longer. "The Council? Again?" She rose with a gallant attempt at her old indulgent smile. "My beloved child, there is no possible need for you to concern yourself with all these affairs. Indeed, it is hardly seemly that you should do so. Your sacred gift to Egypt is the blood of the sun-god which flows only in your veins; your sacred duty is to bear children for the crown. Aside from accompanying Pharaoh occasionally to the temple, or riding forth in procession on feast days, you need bear no other burdens. In truth, my lotus, there is something—well, not quite ladylike—in your mingling with the Kinsmen and all those others, and asking questions about the rule of the Two Lands. I fear I must remind you that your place is with the ladies at the Weekly Reception, not with the ministers at their council."

"Oh Amon, deliver me! I loathe the Weekly Reception!"

"Nevertheless, I shall expect you there in half an hour, my treasure. You have failed to attend for two weeks now, and the countesses are whispering among themselves—"

"What can that possibly matter?" said Hatshepsut coldly. To Nenni she said, "I will join you at the Council, as I planned."

She turned abruptly, descended the steps in a whirl of fluted linen, and made off down the path with her lithe, swift walk, the sun shining blue-black on her defiantly swinging hair and the cobra glittering on her brow.

Nenni's eyes moved in compassion to the dowager queen, standing motionless where Hatshepsut had left her. Aahmes' aging but exquisitely boned face presented its usual mask of queenly serenity and her head was poised at its old angle on her withered stem of a neck; but her authority had departed. There was no doubt she knew it; if she did not, she was the last person in the palace to find it out. It is hard, my lady, Nenni wanted to say to her. Still, all authority crumbles, with age and time. It is as mortal as ourselves. The young and strong must always be ruthless toward the old and weak. . . . He did not say it. Aahmes would scorn to take comfort from Mutnofret's son. He was silent, and presently she moved down the steps with trembling dignity and vanished in the direction of the Great Hall and the Weekly Reception.

Nenni turned back to the children; he found Thoth standing on the bottom step, watching the dowager just as he had done.

"Was Lady Aahmes very angry, my lord father?"

Startled but amused, Nenni answered, "Aye, Lady Aahmes was angry, I fear. Her composure was badly damaged. But never fear, she will repair it somehow. She must. It is her shield against life."

Thoth came slowly up the steps. He was obviously struggling with the big words, but he grasped the meaning of the last phrase, at least, and it seemed to interest him. "What is your shield, my lord father?"

"Indifference, perhaps," said Nenni drily after a moment. "Or a thing called 'fever.' Those are my shields. They are not very good ones."

"And what is mine?"

Nenni smiled at him, feeling a tug at his heart. "You have none yet, my little one."

"Oh. Then what is Lady Shesu's?"

"Ah, Lady Shesu needs none. She has the gods with her."

His irony escaped Thoth, who said seriously, "Do you not have the gods with you, too?"

How was Pharaoh to answer his son when he asked a question like that? With the truth, how else? said a voice inside Nenni instantly. He turned and looked directly into the boy's eyes. "I do not know, Thoth," he said. "And I will tell you something. Whatever you ask me about the gods, I will give you the same answer. 'I do not know.'"

Thoth searched his face a moment with grave, interested eyes, then said in an experimenting sort of tone, "Are the gods truly there, above us and below us?"

"I do not know," Nenni said with a smile.

"You did answer like you said," mused Thoth softly. He became rather solemn. "Ahmose knows."

"Aye, many people know. I envy them. But I do not know."

There was a silence. Thoth leaned against his father's knee, gazing out across the garden, and Nenni wondered what was going on in that groping little mind, and whether he had been kind or cruel to plant the seeds of doubt there.

Cruel, perhaps, he thought. The truth is always cruel, like a harsh light shining in the eyes. But at least it is a light, for all its painfulness—a light and not more darkness. What matter if it shows an empty wasteland where we thought there were trees and comfortable dwellings and a purpose to things? Truth remains truth, whether men are blind to it or not. And if truth shows us emptiness, the dwellings were lies and deceptions in the first place. Is it not better to see the wasteland clearly, once for all, than to search and grope in the darkness, year after wistful year, for what was never even there? Aye, it is better. It hurts but it is better.

He looked down at the boy's fresh young profile, unformed as yet, though the nose had always shown a hint of the jutting Thutmosid strength. As yet he was untouched, unhurt; he had all the darkness and deceptions still to stumble through. In twenty years the effort would have pared away the childish curve of the cheek against which the youth-lock dangled, carved the soft lips into planes of vigor or weakness, harshness or cruelty or resignation—molded the whole boy, flesh and spirit alike, into the unknown shape of the man his life would make him. Nenni's hand reached out gently to touch the curling youth-lock—for once not dripping from the pool, since its small owner had been preoccupied this morning with colored eggs. That would mold him too, that little clump of hair that marked him "prince," perhaps more brutally than everything else combined. Nenni sighed and dropped his hand. He longed helplessly to shield Thoth. But not even Pharaoh could do that for his son. Thoth must make his own shield, somehow, out of courage or despair.

Nenni's eyes focused, and he found the boy's wide dark ones fixed self-consciously on his face.

"Did you speak to me, my son?" he asked in embarrassment.

"Nay."

"What are you thinking, then?"

"I was thinking that I do not know you very well," said the boy shyly.

"Nor I you, little one. It is too bad. But then no man ever knows another."

"Not ever?"

"Nay, we are mysteries to each other, we live alone, each in his separate box. We cannot seem to get out of them. It is strange, is it not?"

"Aye," said Thoth uncertainly. He pressed closer against Nenni's knee. "Boxes—like my toy boxes?"

"Nay, those have lids that open freely; these do not." Nenni smiled and went on absently with his metaphor. "These are sealed for eternity—aye, coffins, they are, in truth—shaped like a man, and with a golden mask set in where the head should be. None can ever know with certainty what dwells behind another's mask, and none can burst his own sheath; though he batter with all his might it is still there, hard and wooden and impassible . . . We reach out to one another but touch only the wood, the gold. We stare until our eyes ache but can see only the outlines of the shape inside. We cannot guess its true form and color though we try hard—sometimes we try very hard indeed." Nenni's eyes had returned wearily to the path. He had again forgotten his son leaning against his knee. Thoth's soft, confiding voice penetrated only the edges of his consciousness.

"You *are* lonesome sometimes, aren't you?"

"Aye, my son. I am a man. To be a man—that is to be lonely."

"Ahmose said—to be a king is loneliest."

Nenni turned slowly, fully attentive now. The child did not know what he was saying, he was parroting, he was merely struggling to fit together the puzzle of scattered grown-up remarks. Ah, but Ahmose had known what he was saying! How could he know? He had never been a king.

But he knew a king, thought Nenni. He knew my father—perhaps as well as any man may ever know another.

He stared down at the boy, strangely moved. A few words from a child's unknowing lips, and that most impenetrable mask of all, his father's, had slipped a little, giving him a glimpse of a soul as solitary as his own.

"Ahmose is a wise old man," he murmured. "And he is right, quite right. . . ."

He was still thinking of what Thoth—and Ahmose—had said as he walked through the corridors a few minutes later on his way to the Kinsmen's Council. Look at the attendants, walking at a careful distance before, behind, beside him, in the Circle of Respect. The Circle of Loneliness, rather. They would not come close to him, as they did to their fellows; they dared not. The thought grew terrible when he realized he dared not come close to

150

them, either. What was that strange space that separated him from all mankind? Royalty? Fear? Fearful royalty, perhaps. His mind flashed to his own metaphor of the coffins with golden masks, and he saw the tomb of his father on the day of his burial —the torchlit procession descending endless rocky stairs to the last chamber hidden deep in the earth, the priests in their leopard skins, the glittering dignitaries, the queens weeping with stylized dignity—and old Ahmose, in the background, weeping truly. Hatshepsut's lovely face had never been more a mask, though it was a mask of grief and rebellion. And his own? No doubt a mask as well. . . . Aye, and priests and all had kept the Circle of Respect about the great sarcophagus. And within the sarcophagus, thought Nenni, torturing himself, was a coffin of inlaid wood, and within that a coffin of ebony, man-shaped, with a golden mask, and within that still another, of solid gold—and within that, wrappings and natron and amulets widening the terrible Circle even in death, until his father was lost, lost within it all and more solitary than he had ever been in life.

Ah gods, Nenni thought, how fortunate are those too poor to dig a tomb, who are merely laid in shallow desert graves to merge gradually and acceptingly with the empty sands—

"Behold, the Good God comes!" the chamberlain intoned.

Nenni came back to himself with a start, realized that he was opposite the entrance to the Council Chamber, that without the chamberlain's reminder he might have walked right past. Embarrassed by his lapse and glad no one else knew of it, he entered the chamber. There was a scuffling of sandals, a dipping of snowy headcloths and ink-black wigs, a murmur of ceremonious greetings.

"May the Strong Bull live forever."

"May the Great Horus rejoice."

"May Your Majesty's ka be strong like Re."

At the far end of the room, Nehsi straightened and moved away from Hatshepsut's chair, greeting Pharaoh in his deep, soft voice.

"May the ka of my lord husband be living," remarked Hatshepsut, rising and waving away a scribe.

So she and Nehsi between them had again been arranging the order of business. There was a slight tension in the air; his ministers thought he did not know what had been happening, gradually but very surely, since the Divine Consort had begun attending Council meetings. They were wrong. He knew very well.

Nenni crossed the room and sat down awkwardly in his beautiful armchair, with his back to the great golden shield that hung on the wall.

"May the *kas* of the Kinsmen rejoice, Horus is among you," he murmured. "You may address My Majesty."

Uah, Superintendent of the Armory, stepped forward with his scribe and the drone of business began. Nenni was not surprised that the accounting of arms and soldiers came first of all; these first few reports would be the ones in which the Divine Consort had no interest. Later, when they progressed to palace affairs, river trade, the output of the stone quarries far to the south and the gold mines to the east, harvest forecasts drawn up by mathematicians who studied the river's rise, next year's taxation computed on the forecasts—ah, when they came to those matters she would lift her head and begin to listen, interrupting with a question here, a shrewd comment there, ending with a suggestion so entirely practical and to the point that he would let her have her way. Then he would realize he had been rushed into a decision on which he was still undecided and to which he should have given more thought, and when the next point arose he would set himself stubbornly against her, whether she was wrong or right. And *that* would strike him as so lacking in intelligence that he would begin weakening again. . . .

Aye, he would end by letting her have her way in everything, conscious always of the ministers' averted eyes and enigmatic faces.

As the Council progressed just as he had pictured it, Nenni studied those faces, trying to discern what each man was making of the Divine Consort's increasing intrusions into the government of the Two Lands, and his own inability to control them. Nehsi, handsome and grave and ebony black against the pale golden hangings that lined the room, would keep his thoughts to himself until they ripened to maturity in the quiet caverns of his mind; but Nenni did not believe Nehsi wholly deplored the situation. Thutiy the Royal Treasurer, spare and brown and quick-moving as a desert lizard, with a brain as full of sudden dartings and stoppings, was patently uneasy. His skinny hands, through which passed the golden stream of Egypt's wealth, drummed

152

restlessly on the top of the carved chest against which he leaned, suddenly desisted to plunge into his sash, just as suddenly popped out to begin drumming again.

But in the end, reflected Nenni, Thutiy will think as Nehsi thinks.

And Ineny? Hope was plain in Ineny's eyes. He stood—the only one who looked directly at Hatshepsut—between Uah and the Royal Sealer Khenuka, both of whom were glaring in disapproval at a point just above the golden cobra on her diadem. Ineny was a head shorter than either of them, a slim, quiet man whose childlike candor of countenance middle age had been unable to destroy. He looked like one of the soft-eyed fowlers of whom the poets like to sing—or like the poet himself. But he was Overseer of Overseers of All the Works of the King, and had built monuments and temples for the first Thutmose and finally his tomb.

And for the second Thutmose—nothing, thought Nenni with a faint smile. Small wonder he looks to her, with five years of discontent showing in his eyes.

No matter—Ineny would have to go on being discontented. There were some things in which even a weakling could be strong; some beliefs a man must stubbornly cling to—even though it were only a belief that one should believe in nothing. There would be no raising of temples under the second Thutmose.

Nehsi asked some question, and Nenni with difficulty pulled his mind back to the discussion in progress around him. He was really becoming very absent-minded—also, his head had begun to ache; whether from Hatshepsut's energetic voice, his own weariness, or the onset of fever, he did not know. He wondered fleetingly what would happen if he simply got up and left the room. He doubted if they would even miss him.

He shifted uneasily in his chair, sat up straighter, and made a determined effort to fix his mind on what was being said.

6.

The delicate green that had covered the black fields at the time of the Festival of Un had ripened into thick gold on a spring afternoon four months later, when Pharaoh's three chief Kinsmen, Nehsi, Thutiy and the poet-eyed Ineny, were gathered in a little chamber on the first floor of the palace, hearing the first of the season's harvest reports. The beer they were sipping had hung in its earthen jug in a well all morning; slaves stationed here and there about the room waved huge plumy fans. Far above, on the roof of the palace, great air scoops trapped what breeze there was and sent it flowing through cleverly designed conduits to the rooms below, including this one. Despite air scoops, beer, and fans the day was hot; so hot that Nehsi's broad black torso gleamed with sweat, and all three men had put aside their jeweled collars, which lay in an opulent heap on the table beside them.

The scribe's voice droned to a halt at last. He rolled up his sheet of papyrus and looked inquiringly at Nehsi.

"All in order. And better than I expected, in truth. . . . Leave the document on the table here, I will try to get Pharaoh's seal on it before nightfall."

Nehsi took another swallow of beer, and the scribe departed in haste to do the same. Thutiy poured his own goblet full. "Do you really hope to seal that document by nightfall? Pharaoh is still ill."

"I thought to ask the Divine Consort . . ."

"Again?"

The two men exchanged a glance, but Nehsi said nothing.

Thutiy settled back, drumming his bony fingers restlessly on the chair arm. Ineny's great brown eyes dwelt on him.

"It is mere routine, Excellence. A matter of expediency."

"Aye." But Thutiy shook his head and scowled. "I do not like it, I do not like it!" he grumbled. "It is all very well for her to affix the Seal to a few reports when the Good God is indisposed, and even to take some interest in the proceedings of the Council. But matters have gone beyond that, there's no overlooking it any longer! Ever since the appointment of Hapuseneb as high priest . . ." He stopped, staring reflectively ahead of him. "Aye, it began precisely then, now I think of it. A bare four months ago. In the space of four short months, my friends, we have come to feel it almost natural to consult Her Radiance instead of Pharaoh on matters great and small—"

"You exaggerate, Excellence," murmured Ineny. "There has been no decision of real importance—"

154

"Do you call the choosing of a new Steward of Amon last week of no importance?"

"That decision was Pharaoh's, or Hapuseneb's," said Ineny.

Thutiy looked into the architect's limpid eyes a moment, then said flatly, "That decision was the queen's." Receiving no answer, he rested both thin hands upon the table and leaned toward the silent Nehsi, lowering his voice still more. "Who is this Senmut, in Amon's name? No one ever heard of him until he was suddenly lifted out of nowhere to become Overseer of Fields when Nakht was ousted. Now, a mere four months later, he holds the highest administrative post in all the temple, with a power equal to the high priest's—nearly equal to our own! Hapuseneb I know of old. I approved that appointment, as did all of us. But this newcomer, this upstart—"

"An upstart of great ability," put in Ineny's soft voice again. "A newcomer who is also a gifted administrator. It was Hapuseneb who urged his appointment on Pharaoh—and Hapuseneb does not give praise lightly. He is a sober man, conservative, he weighs every opinion."

"There still may be a thumb upon the scale, my friend," snapped Thutiy.

Ineny shrugged and walked over to stand directly in the sluggish breeze from one of the fans. Nehsi, who had been making a careful chain of interlocking circles on the table with his sweating cup, spoke softly, without raising his eyes.

"Remember, no one had ever heard of me, either, when Pharaoh first lifted up my head."

"That is different!" exploded Thutiy. "It was the Great Thutmose who chose to uplift you, and no choice of his was ever wrong."

"But this new choice may not be wrong either. Look beyond the chooser for a moment and consider the man chosen. Reflect a moment upon his recent reorganization of the Estates of Amon. It is clear already that he will be excellent, even brilliant, as Amon's Steward. Have we really any reason to distrust him?"

"Ah!" Thutiy jabbed a long, thin forefinger at him. "You said the word, friend, not I. Distrust. You feel it too, reason or not. Amit it."

"I admit it," said Nehsi slowly. "I distrust him. Yet also I

155

distrust my distrust. Perhaps it is based on no more than resentment of an unknown. Perhaps I see him through the narrowed eye of jealousy."

"The question is not how you see him, but how the queen does! I swear before Ma'at the Truthful, I believe she sees him through an eye utterly blind to his faults. Never have I watched a man rise to such smiling favor in so short a time, or had one's opinions quoted to me so frequently! The week is unusual which does not find him at the palace twice, three times, sometimes more than that—always in conference with the queen! And if it is she, not Pharaoh, who is to order the affairs of the Two Lands—"

Nehsi looked at him a moment, then leaned forward, folding his hands on the table. "My friend, let us be realists. She *must* order them. The fever dwells in Pharaoh with increasing persistence—far oftener than in other years. He is not one whom the gods will burden with a long life, you know that as well as I."

"Aye, all know that."

"Well, then? Someone must rule Egypt in these periods when he must keep to his couch—and also after he has gone to the gods. Should it be you and I?"

"Nay, but the royal children—"

"May still be children when Horus becomes Osiris. Her Radiance would then be regent, whether she is prepared to be or not. Would we not be wise to face this squarely, as I believe she has done—help her prepare for it now, guide her, lead her to depend on *us,* whom she can surely trust? With care and thought, we might forestall another calamity to Egypt."

Thutiy rubbed his chin uneasily. For a moment nothing was to be heard in the room except the monotonous creaking of the fans. Ineny strolled to the table, watching Thutiy's face. "Nehsi is right, friend," he murmured.

"Aye, he is right," sighed Thutiy at last. "It is a wise plan—if it works."

"If it works?" said the Negro.

"If Her Radiance will allow herself to be guided—and by *us.*"

"She will listen to old friends."

"She will listen to the voice that offers her power, Nehsi."

Ineny leaned forward. "Then let that voice be ours! She has the royal blood, the royal manner . . ."

Nehsi smiled. Then said drily, "It is already out of our hands.

156

She will do as she likes—with our support or in spite of us. Is it not so, my friends?" The words were rueful, but as he stood up, his face warmed with interest and with hope. "She is very like her father," he remarked.

"Aye, she is," said Thutiy. Gradually his wrinkled, anxious face relaxed into more peaceful lines. "She is indeed," he repeated hopefully.

A few moments later the three ministers emerged from the palace just as a handsome litter bearing the insignia of the temple was set down in the great court. Out of it stepped the new Steward of Amon, Senmut, bearing a cloth-wrapped bundle under one arm. His angular, powerful body was arrayed in exquisite linen, and a headcloth of woven gold set off his dark, sardonic features with striking effect. He greeted the ministers cordially, received a polite murmur in reply, and striding to the door of the small garden where the Divine Consort liked to spend her afternoons, let himself in and closed the gate behind him.

Nehsi cleared his throat. "Possibly some urgent temple business which could not wait for Pharaoh's recovery." He glanced down at the rolled document he held, then slapped it absently against his thigh once or twice. "No matter. I will present it later for the Seal," he said.

Avoiding each other's eyes, the three men turned back into the palace.

Senmut permitted himself a private grin as the gate clicked shut on the gaze of three speculative pairs of eyes. Let them stare, the Great Ones. They were going to know him long and well.

He walked eagerly up the path toward the pavilion, which was so covered over with green vines now, that he had reached the steps before he realized it was empty. Halting, he looked around. Across the emerald lawns the two royal children were playing together by the pool's edge, splashing a great deal of water on themselves and on the grass, where it clung in glittering droplets, like a new kind of jewel. Their voices rose high and shrill on the quiet air. Apparently there was no one in the garden but himself and them; Hatshepsut had not yet arrived.

Depositing his bundle in a corner of the pavilion, Senmut strolled across the grass to wait. Pausing on the slope above the pool, he stood a moment watching the children at their play.

157

There was a striped kitten scampering about between them on the grass; the little princess kept trying to catch it and put it in a basket. In appearance she bore an unfortunate resemblance to her father. Senmut's glance lingered briefly on her spindly legs and sharp-drawn, nervous features—then flicked to Thoth's bronzed and glowing little body, every inch of which bespoke the constitution of a young bull. Bull? As well say stallion or even goat, thought Senmut, annoyed with himself for thinking first of an image so inseparably connected with royalty. The boy was *not* truly royal—that was the one fact of incalculable importance about him, on which no telling how many futures hinged. His only claim to divinity was his startling resemblance to the Divine Hatshepsut—and by the Blood of the Mangled One, thought Senmut, he looks enough like her to be her own son.

Her face took shape in his mind; it was now almost as familiar to him as his own. He had found, in the early weeks of his stewardship, when he was reorganizing the sprawling temple estates, that the quickest way to gain royal approval for his plans was to bring them to Hatshepsut. Choosing his moment carefully, he would present himself in the little garden pavilion, glance respectfully toward the cedar-and-gold chair standing empty in the corner, then gesture, with assumed regret, toward the documents he held.

"Since the Good God is indisposed today, I fear I must trouble Your Radiance once more with temple matters."

"What is it this time?"

In spite of her bored tone, her face would liven with interest; she liked nothing better, he was sure, than to usurp Pharaoh's prerogatives. He would unroll his documents and explain his plan, enjoying her quick grasp of what he was trying to do and the shrewd intelligence of her questions. Afterwards, he would linger over his cup of wine and often the conversation would turn far away from business.

Senmut stood thoughtful in the sunshine, running over those many conversations in his mind. With every one, their pretense that this was official business had grown a little weaker, and he himself had become a little bolder. When one considered the tone of those earliest conversations . . . The picture of one formed clearly in his mind.

". . . a remarkable plan, Architect," she was saying as she

158

tossed a last document on the table. "Well proportioned, spacious, simple in design. It is"—she smiled a little—"it is architectural. I approve it. That is," she amended hastily, "I will present it for Pharaoh's approval. Shall I have Akhi refill your cup?"

Senmut picked up his documents and with a sigh began rolling them together. "Aye, if Your Radiance pleases—one cup to stave off the heat into which I must plunge in a moment. This garden is delightfully cool. I would I could stay all afternoon in the light of my lady's countenance—undimmed, today, by any cloud." His glance flicked to Pharaoh's empty chair.

She ignored his implication, as he had guessed she would. Had she admitted its existence she would have been compelled to order his head cut off. "You cannot stay?" she repeated.

He dropped the documents on the table at once. "Aye, forever, if it is my lady's wish!"

"Excellence, *I* have no wish in the matter, one way or another! I merely wondered—"

"What prevents me from staying?" he supplied glibly. "I am overwhelmed by Your Radiance's interest in my affairs."

She set her goblet down and looked at him. "My interest in your affairs is almost nonexistent, Steward! Will you cease reading meanings into every word I say?"

He grinned. "As Your Radiance pleases. I will henceforth consider all your remarks meaningless, and your interest void. But then will it not seem strange for you to address me as 'Excellence' and 'Steward,' since it was surely Your Radiance's interest that made me such?"

For an instant he thought he had gone too far, for a dangerous gleam came into her eyes. But it melted into a gleam of amusement, and she motioned her slave to fill his cup. "I shall address you as 'Insolence' instead," she told him drily.

She liked his insolence; he was sure of it. He left her that day with a jauntiness in his bearing that caused Hapuseneb's eyebrows to raise when they met later at the temple.

"The Divine Consort did not disappoint you?" the high priest said drily.

Senmut flung the documents triumphantly on the table and helped himself to Hapuseneb's wine. "The plan is approved. Next week I will see what she thinks of doubling the size of Amon's herds. Cattle bring far more gold than grain."

"I advise you to let the ink dry on these documents first, my impetuous friend. You will overstep."

Senmut grinned and drank his wine. Already he was beginning to suspect that it was impossible to overstep with the Divine Consort. . . .

The picture faded. Smiling to himself at the memory, Senmut summoned up another to compare it with—this a conversation that had taken place only a week ago. This time she was not sitting, erect and formal, in a chair, but half reclining on her cushion-piled couch. . . .

"Well, Senmut! You seem to be making good your boasts. The revenues have doubled in the last two months. Amon grows rich—and your fame is growing every day." She lay back against her cushions, looking up at him. "Your wife, the prophetess, must be very proud of you."

"My wife is more inclined to jealousy," Senmut returned. "She has never had much confidence in me since the day I left off being Master of Storerooms. I cannot explain it; it is simply one of her failings."

"But not one of yours," Hatshepsut observed.

"Nay, not one of mine." He studied her a moment, and dropped his banter. "Why should I be humble? It is given to some to know in their hearts they are destined for great things. You, of all people, must know that feeling—it is impossible you do not."

"And if I said I did not?"

"I would not believe you." Senmut leaned toward her, lowering his voice. "Why else do you so confidently assume Pharaoh's burdens when he is ill?"

She neither answered nor changed expression. Senmut leaned closer.

"Shall I tell you? You are quite capable of ruling Egypt yourself—and you know it."

This time her nostrils flared with a quick intake of breath. She turned away. He did not know whether he had pleased her or angered her, but a faint flush was staining the ivory above her cheekbones. Fascinated, he watched it spread down the slope of a smooth cheek only inches from his own. It struck him suddenly that he was very close to her—and she had made no move to repulse him. Deliberately he let his gaze wander from the up-tilted corner of her eyelid, down the outline of her profile and the sweep of her throat, to the round breasts thrusting up through her collar of lotus blossoms. He forgot all caution in a stab of sharp desire. He sat down beside her on the couch. Instantly alarms sounded wildly in his brain; he paid no heed to them.

"Senmut," she said.

His eyes flew to hers; heat rushed into his cheeks and through his body.

"I think you had best arise," she said.

Breathless, reluctant, he obeyed. She was watching him with dark and mocking eyes, but he noticed that the lotus blossoms were rapidly rising and falling on her breast.

She rose abruptly. "Let us walk down to the pool. . . ."

The picture faded, and Senmut drew a long, uneven breath. Her Radiance liked to play with fire. Well, so did he.

"Fool! She will ruin you when it suits her!" Nofret-Hor had screamed at him yesterday during one of their frequent quarrels about the matter. "You'll end with your head in a noose. Amon help me, I'll put it there myself, I swear before the gods I will!"

Senmut had only laughed at her yesterday; and today, standing on the grassy slope above the pool watching the royal children, he smiled again. Everyone was so busy warning him of what he stood to lose that no one realized what he stood to gain.

His smile faded into slit-eyed thoughtfulness as he studied the boy beside the pool—the one dark cloud on the horizon of the Daughter of the Sun. He was picturing the brilliance of a future without that cloud—a future with the Tired One in his tomb, Hatshepsut on the throne with her only rival a little girl entirely under her sway . . . and, of course, Senmut of Hermonthis standing at the queen's right hand.

With another long, intoxicated breath he turned away.

He was about to stroll on when he heard his name called, in a high, rusty old voice. "Will you share my bench, Excellency? It is shady here."

It was Ahmose-pen-Nekhbet, Father-Tutor to the little princess, beckoning from his hidden seat beneath a big tamarisk tree. At sight of him Senmut's mood soured at once. He cursed himself for not having guessed that Ahmose would be here somewhere, and not taking care to avoid an encounter with him. He had found only one person at court able to ruffle his composure, and that was none of the highborn aristocrats as he had expected, but this gnarled old man. Why it should be, Senmut could not imagine, but there was something about Ahmose's rheumy old eyes that made him as acutely uncomfortable as if the stench of the fish stalls still clung about his garments. He could never forget that Ahmose had been a lifelong intimate of the Great Thutmose—had touched him, talked to him, fought at his side and been his friend. He felt a tinge of awe in Ahmose's presence, and in spite of his angry efforts to resist it, he felt inferior.

He glanced impatiently at the gate, then with very poor grace sauntered toward the bench. He was miserly with his bow, bending not a hair lower than convention demanded.

"A pleasant day, but an uncommon hot one," Ahmose remarked, hospitably making room for Senmut beside him.

"It is so, Honored One."

"The children do not mind, though." The old man waved his stick toward the pool, chuckling. "In and out of the water all day, what do they care for a little heat? Though the little princess frets about it sometimes."

"But not the boy?" prompted Senmut, mechanically making conversation.

"Nay, not he. He is too busy with his games and his imaginings. Ah, what a quick, bright mind he has! You might jerk the whole world out from under him—he would create a better one for himself tomorrow."

How fortunate, thought Senmut. He may need to. He smiled and flicked a glance at the old man. "You seem very fond of him," he remarked pointedly.

"Aye," Ahmose agreed. "As fond as if he were my own! There is none like Thoth."

"That is an interesting opinion. Actually, it is the little princess who has been entrusted to your charge, is it not?"

Ahmose turned without haste and looked at him. "Aye, Excellence," he said. "And I am fond of her as well. Far too fond to neglect her in any way—or to need reminders on the subject of my loyalties."

Senmut forced the negligent smile to remain on his face, but as Ahmose turned away he became infuriatingly aware of having been put very efficiently in his place. Again they watched the

162

children—the old man unruffled, Senmut stiff-jawed with resentment.

However, not even the Steward of Amon could afford to insult the Guardian of the Royal Child. When Ahmose began presently to comment on the harvest returns, Senmut prodded himself into suitably polite, if chilly, replies.

A few minutes later Hatshepsut appeared at last in the gate. Barely remembering to take leave of Ahmose, Senmut leaped from the bench and strode across the grass toward her, raking her with his eyes as he would not dare to do at closer range.

Their greetings, exchanged on the sunny walk in full sight of Ahmose, the children, and the handmaidens who were still bowing themselves out, were formal and even a little stilted. Their conversation, begun the moment they reached the privacy of the vine-hung pavilion, dismissed formality altogether.

"Did you bring it?" Hatshepsut demanded at once.

"Aye, as I promised. But it was a rash promise," he added with a grin. "I barely finished it in time, and in truth, it needs many more hours spent on it yet."

"No matter, let me see it!"

He was more than willing. Fetching the bundle, he unwound the linen wrappings and set on the table a small wooden model of Neb-hepet-Re's desert temple, built to scale and differing from the real one only in that the ruined columns and porches were restored to what he felt must have been their original lines. He had coated it with thin white plaster and carefully indicated its decorations, even to tiny replicas of the statues of Hathor which adorned the upper terrace.

Her face was completely satisfying; astonishment, delight, and intense interest lighted it. "*Ast!* How beautiful!" she breathed. "Now explain again, as you said you would. All that about using space as stone—perhaps I can understand it better with this before me."

Carefully, and with his usual growing absorption, he explained the subtle and exquisite balance he had discovered in the proportions of this temple. She listened attentively, with the quick intelligence that never failed to delight him. Now and then she interrupted to ask a question which indicated how perfectly she was following his reasoning.

She stood back at last, nodding. "So that is the secret. A fragrance, you called it once—aye, it is almost that subtle. But what happens when the shadows change?" she added suddenly. "There is a difference between morning and evening, the light will fall differently on those columns—"

"Quite right. I have planned for it. I played a long time with this little model, held it this way and that beneath a torch—"

"A torch is not sunlight. You should have carried it to the desert, where the sands would throw their reflection."

"I did that, too." He shot her an admiring glance. "You should have been the architect, my lady."

She looked up at him, smiling absently, but he saw quick discontent in her eyes. "You may be sure I would keep every architect in Egypt busy if I had my way!" She turned and gazed out over the garden. "Nenni feels differently. Senmut—I do not understand him, as Amon lives, I cannot! Did you know he has not even ordered Ineny to build him a tomb?"

Sacred Mother of the gods! thought Senmut. Her statement shocked him more than he let her see. It was inconceivable that any man able to build and furnish a habitation for his Three Thousand Years in the other life would not do so. "Will he not listen to you, my lady?" he said in a low voice.

"Nay, not in that matter. In others he seems entirely indifferent. He delays, neglects—. Oh, no matter, let us not talk of it! Ptah's Beard, how hot it is today! I suppose you had refreshment while you waited for me?" Sinking into a chair, she gestured toward a moisture-beaded jug of beer that waited on the table, along with two blue goblets.

"Nay, only a dry conversation."

"Then you must be parched by now—a man of your thirst! Pour for us both, quickly." As he moved to obey, she flashed a glance around the garden. "With whom did you have this dry conversation? I see no one but the children."

"With the Honorable Ahmose."

"Oh. You say that as if you disliked him very much. Do you?"

"Nay, nay, he is nothing to me one way or the other," said Senmut. Smiling, he handed her a goblet, then added casually, "However, I find his attitude toward the little lady Nefer very curious. I should think you would be jealous for her."

"Jealous? Why?"

"Because he is so obviously partial to the boy."

"To Thoth? He is devoted to both!" But she glanced sharply at the children, who had brought the kitten up on the path and were making it chase a feather. A slight frown puckered Hatshepsut's slanting brows. "You are wrong, Senmut. I am sure he is equally fond of both."

"Perhaps. Yet even that seems odd to me—that he could be as fond of the son of Iset as of a princess of the blood." Senmut finished off his beer, watching her, then he set his goblet down and moved closer to her chair. "Did it ever occur to you that the boy is a threat to your future? The only threat?"

She glanced up at him, then away. "I do not understand," she said.

He was sure she knew quite well what he meant, but he came out with it bluntly. "I mean, if Pharaoh should die during one of these attacks of fever, who would succeed him? That child—who is not even your own flesh and blood. Is that what you really want?"

"Of course not, but there is no danger of that, Senmut."

"There is every danger!" He leaned over her chair. "You think to be regent, of course—for your royal daughter. But how long would that last? If she could marry a noble of your choice—some pliable, weak-willed youngster like Count Imhotep's son—ah, then all would be well. But tradition will wed her to her half-brother, and that boy is no pliable, wellborn nobody, he is a prince—or the nearest thing Egypt has to one. He'll claim full royalty, I warn you, and he'll listen to no woman for long, not even the Daughter of the Sun. In Amon's name, my lady, *you* should rule Egypt, not the son of a harem woman! Without him, the regency could go on as long as you chose, you could do as you liked, you could build, you could wear the Two Lands like a necklace! And nothing's preventing it but that child—"

A piercing scream from the path brought Senmut upright in alarm. Next instant he was cursing silently at the ill-timed interruption. It was nothing but the children quarreling over the kitten, which was mewing piteously as they tugged it this way and that between them. But it was Nefer who had shrieked, and Hatshepsut was already out of her chair and hurrying down the steps, deaf to anything else for the moment. There was nothing for Senmut to do but follow.

"Thoth! Take care! The poor creature, you'll kill it! What-

165

ever is the matter, Nefer?" Hatshepsut said angrily. Thoth wrested the kitten from Nefer's grasp, and with set jaw whirled half away from her, holding it against his cheek. "It's *not* hers, it's mine, Lady Shesu! It's mine!"

"Just so," Senmut whispered to Hatshepsut. "He'll snatch Egypt from her too."

Hatshepsut flushed and her jaw set harder than the boy's. "Thoth, give the kitten to Nefer this minute."

Thoth looked up at her, wide-eyed, then dropped the kitten as if it had burned him. Hatshepsut turned to quiet her daugh-and the boy's eyes moved to Senmut's and stayed there. Senmut met them coldly. Amon curse him, he thought—aye, and Pharaoh for begetting him! he added to himself, too reckless to fear whatever gods might hear his thoughts. This one small scrap of humanity was all that kept his dream of building the world's most beautiful temple still nothing but a dream. . . .

The boy wheeled suddenly and ran off across the grass toward the big tamarisk tree, the placated little princess following more slowly in contented possession of the kitten. Senmut swung to face Hatshepsut, beyond being cautious of what words he chose.

"Send the boy away!" he said roughly. "To Babylonia, the Islands, anywhere, so long as he is far away from Egypt! Can't you see—"

"Senmut, be silent!" Her tone halted the arguments on the tip of his tongue. He searched her face uneasily, while she studied his. "Babylonia—in Amon's name!" she said under her breath. "I don't even know where it is. How can you be so ruthless?"

"Where your interests are concerned—" he muttered.

"They are not concerned here." Her eyes flickered and swung away from him, fixing on empty space for a moment. When she turned back it was with an air of decision. "Senmut, I am going to tell you something," she said. "Thoth will never be Pharaoh. He cannot—because my own son will supercede him."

"Your *own* son?"

"Aye. I have been pregnant for some weeks."

The words dried up in Senmut's throat. He felt the blood rush to his head and pound there, but he could not believe the bottom was dropping out of everything like this, without warning, without logic. For his purposes, a true heir was as bad as a false one —worse, in fact. It was as if with a single gesture she had left him empty-handed and in rags again. For an instant he wanted to seize her with rough and furious hands and shake her until she told him it was not true.

"Senmut—in Amon's name, have you seen a *kheft?* Say something."

"My felicitations," he ground out in a voice that did not sound much like his own.

She smiled, but continued to look at him oddly. He felt as if he were floundering in a morass and could not get his feet under him.

"When do you expect this child?" he jerked out.

"At the next High Nile— Do not say 'child.' It will be a boy." One foot touched solid ground at last. "And if it is a girl?"

"It will not be a girl, Senmut! It will be my son, for whom I have waited all these years—the son of the god my father, Amon."

There was a slight but distinct emphasis on the last words. Was she trying to convince herself that it really would be a son? Or had the stress been unconscious, born of a wish to repudiate Pharaoh and all his claim in her child? Whichever it was, it, too, steadied Senmut's footing. He drew a long breath and gained control of himself.

"May Nuit the Great Mother guard you in your hour," he said in a fair imitation of his normal tones.

The conventional remark put a convenient end to the subject, and they did not return to it. They strolled a few moments longer, speaking of other things, but Senmut took his leave of her as soon as he could manage it. He felt an urgent need to be by himself, where he could go over the whole situation again and if possible, reorganize his thoughts into a more reassuring pattern. He had never felt more vividly that man was the plaything of the gods.

Thoth watched him go, from the safe retreat of Ahmose's knobby but comforting old knees. With his hands still soft from the feel of the kitten's fur, and his heart still empty from its loss, he followed the tall man with his eyes, down the path and through the gate until he could see him no longer. Then he turned away, feeling strange and desolate, partly because of the kitten and partly because of the man's cold black eyes and the oddness of his

167

smile. It was the man's fault, Thoth knew, that he had lost the kitten. The man had said something and Lady Shesu had grown angry, very angry—not with the man but with himself.

Thoth looked down at Ahmose's knees, against which he was leaning, and fingered a fold of the coarse linen that covered them. "Ahmose," he said softly.

"I am here."

Like an easing of his hurt, he felt the old man's hands pat against his backbone, but he went on anyhow. "Ahmose, I do not like that man."

"Do you not, little one?"

"Nay."

Ahmose cleared his throat, looking away over the pool. "Many people are not as they seem when you have spoken with them only once."

"He took my kitten. It was not Nefer's, it was mine. Count Nehsi gave it to me, all for my own, and that man took it from me. I am going to tell Lady Shesu."

"I would not tell Lady Shesu," Ahmose said quickly.

Thoth raised his eyes and searched the old man's seamed, beloved face.

"Does Lady Shesu like him?" Thoth questioned softly.

"He is a very clever man," Ahmose said. "He has become very important in the temple."

Thoth watched him a moment longer. Then he said, "Ahmose, I do not like him anyhow."

At last the old eyes came down and met his own, squarely and gravely, as they had always done before. "Nor do I, little one," said Ahmose. "Nor do I."

Hatshepsut watched Senmut go, and for some time afterward sat alone in the pavilion, staring into the thick green curtain of vines, as unconscious of their gently shifting patterns as she was of the sun dropping into the hills beyond the City of the Dead. As always after she had been with Senmut, her mind was speeding twice as fast as usual and her emotions were behaving like strangers.

Her eyes moved to the table, where his superb little replica of the old temple still stood beside the forgotten beer jug and goblets. It was easily the most beautiful object in the pavilion.

But—gods! That about Babylonia. . . .

She got up restlessly and started down the steps. It was time to dress for the evening meal; already Iset was standing in the gate, calling to Thoth. Nefer's nurse had borne her off some time before. Nenni would be waiting, he was better tonight, well enough to dine with her in the garden off his bedchamber.

She walked down the path slowly, roused from her thoughts by the sight of Thoth crossing the grass toward her, his eyes anxiously on her face.

"Come here, little one," she said.

He ran to her eagerly, and she laughed in spite of herself. "*Ast!* What a sorry state you get your clean *shentis* into by the end of a day." She shook her head over the pool-bedraggled scrap of a garment clinging about his sturdy little thighs, then on an impulse bent over him and caught him into her arms. He responded with a passion of love that warmed her heart.

"You're not angry any more, Lady Shesu?" he whispered.

"Nay, of course not. I was not angry—"

Just so will my own little son cling to me, she thought as she smiled into the boy's worshiping eyes.

"Go now and be a good child."

She watched Thoth scamper away toward the waiting figure by the gate, taking pleasure in the radiance of his face, meeting Iset's brooding, hostile glance with one of tolerant indifference. For the first time since she had seen the little newborn man-child clutching at his mother's breast, her affection for him was unmixed with resentment.

Babylonia . . . there was a river in that land which flowed in the wrong direction; her father had spoken of it sometimes. His pursuit of the Hyksos had brought him to its brink—but everyone knew he had chased the Hyksos clean off the face of the earth. She was not sure whether there really was such a land; perhaps it was only a way of saying "the end of the world."

She followed Thoth and his mother through the gate and across the courtyard, glad that Senmut's terrible plan need not even be considered.

The spring wore on in Egypt. Slowly the river shrank between its banks and the heat grew more intense. The Khamseen winds began their fifty days of blowing—dry and hot and harsh, they filled the air with swirls of sand, stinging necks and faces and squinted eyelids. The last of the harvest had long been gathered; now the fields lay parched and lifeless, and great cracks spread crazily in all directions, wide enough to trap a man's leg, deep enough to hide a ten-foot pole. Fifty days the winds blew, and then a burning stillness settled over the land and tension mounted in the hearts of the people as they watched the Nile. Day by day the waters dwindled, day by day the islands rose higher like the backs of surfacing beasts. At last all navigation ceased; wharfs and landing-steps rose tall and stark from curling mud, and the mighty river was no more than a red-brown trickle —the last blood flowing slowly from the mangled body of the god. Osiris was dead.

Egypt bowed under the oppressive burden of his absence. Women cut their hair in grief and mourning, boats lay useless, nothing could be done. The fishermen came down to the docks and stood aimless, talking loudly with each other and casting glances at the waste of mud. Each year Osiris died, and their memories told them that each year he rose again in virile and triumphant flood to impregnate the waiting earth; but memory faded and grew uncertain in the face of the reality that now met their eyes each morning. They wished the time of waiting were over; they wished the god would begin to rise.

In the market places squabbling arose more shrilly than was usual. Quarrels sprang up in wineshops and in the crooked streets, flaming in an instant from the embers of uneasiness deep in every breast. The uneasiness was caused, in part, by the rumors drifting out of the palace—unsettling rumors that all was not as it should be with the Good God. It was said the heat had been very hard on him this year; it was said the fever held him to his couch for days together; it was said, in low and troubled voices, that even between the attacks of fever he behaved in a strange, detached manner which no one could understand.

Would the river rise, if the *ka* of Pharaoh sickened within him? Would the lands be watered, and the crops grow? They were desperately afraid.

Then, one day, everything began to change. It started with royal couriers driving out of the palace gates and through the streets to make the first public announcement of the Great Royal Wife's pregnancy. The proclamation was like a cooling hand laid on a feverish cheek. Rumor subsided in Thebes within an hour; nothing was too amiss with Pharaoh if he could beget a child. The people turned calmer eyes upon the shrunken river; possibly they had given way to panic, they told one another judiciously. They must wait patiently for Osiris to come forth from his tomb. Perhaps he tarried longer than in other years. Did that mean he would not return? Of course not. Nothing of the sort.

Shortly after this reassuring occurrence, their minds were further distracted by another one. A perfect Apis bull—successor to the sacred animal that had recently died in Menfe—was discovered, with some well-timed assistance from Senmut the Steward of Amon, in a small herd near Thebes. The announcement was received with jubilant pride by every Theban; the owner of the favored herd became a great man overnight and was looked upon with reverent respect. For a week after the new divinity was led off toward Menfe by a ring in his mouth, the whole city feasted in the streets. It was while the people's faces were turned in joyful preoccupation to their brimming cups that the river began to rise.

From then onward, all was well. Later, looking back on their time of fear, the people felt that a deeper change had taken place then than they had first supposed. Certainly once it had begun, the river had risen and was still rising more rapidly this year than last; and surely there was a new briskness in the atmosphere, a new vigor in the air. Something was different. Something was more as it had been when the great Thutmose had worn the crown. They could not name it, but they could feel it, as a man riding blindfold in a chariot can feel a different hand upon the reins.

In the palace, they felt it too—but there was by now no minister, courtier, chamberlain or even slave who could not have named it. They knew that there was a different hand upon the reins; it was the hand of the Great Royal Wife. It was a situation without precedent in Egypt, but they had seen it begin, and grow, and at last become necessity with the strange transformation which had taken place in the Tired One during the months of the shrinking of the Nile.

Hatshepsut had been the first to become aware of the change in Nenni. In the beginning, near the end of spring, it had seemed no more than an exaggeration of those qualities in him which she had always found difficult. Time and again she had tried to interest him in building of some sort, without the slightest sign of success.

"You have done nothing with your power, Nenni!" she said one evening as they sat together in the little moonlit garden opening off his bedchamber. "Is that how you want Egypt to remember you, as the Pharaoh who raised not even one monument to himself?"

"My lovely Shesu, only a strong man or a fool raises monuments to himself, and I am neither."

"Then raise monuments to the gods! That much, at least, is your clear duty. Think of the temples up and down the Nile that have lain in ruins since the days of the Hyksos—and more are crumbling! Why do you not rebuild them?"

"It seems to me more fitting that they should lie in ruins," said Nenni obscurely.

"Oh, how exasperating you are!" She sprang from her chair and walked angrily to the edge of the pool. "Those temples are a disgrace to Egypt. Do not speak to me of what is fitting!"

Nenni leaned his head against the back of his chair and looked wearily into her face. "Then let me speak to you of facts—with which you have only slight acquaintance, my Shesu, despite all your efforts. Building requires gold—much gold. Where is it to come from? Egypt's treasury? Aye, that would restore one temple, perhaps two, perhaps three if there were no other demands upon it meanwhile. But after that?"

"Is not the treasury replenished year after year?" Hatshepsut asked in surprise.

"Aye, and year after year it is diminished by the normal expenditures of a great kingdom. The building of temples is not a normal expenditure, it is an abnormal one. The people would have to be taxed—"

172

"Then tax them!"

"They are burdened already with taxes. Would you have me bow their backs until they are no longer men but only laboring beasts? As well build your temples with their flesh and blood, instead of stone. Aye, and it is they who must do the building. Laborers do not grow like reeds in the marshes, they must leave their fields and families to toil for Pharaoh—"

"I will not listen to more of this! What do I care for a rabble of laborers, they do not concern me—or you either! You are Pharaoh, you should restore the temples. That is the only fact here."

Nenni smiled at her and shook his head. "You may close your eyes, but nothing is changed thereby. Even Pharaoh cannot bring great things to pass merely by raising his scepter."

"You are wrong," she said distinctly, leaning close and glaring into his face. "That is precisely how these things are accomplished. If you would once raise your scepter, you would see."

She whirled and walked angrily out of the garden.

She had not really expected a different answer. Though it seemed more pronounced these days, such obstinacy was his nature.

Callous indifference, however, was not. Yet as the spring heat increased in Egypt, so did this unnatural trait in Nenni. Routine had always bored him; but where once he had dealt with it, wearily but patiently, now he turned his back on it entirely. As a result the always sluggish flow of minor affairs through the weekly Audiences was dammed completely, and the Scribe's List choked with petitions that must be heard again and yet again. Hatshepsut found herself cajoling and then prodding.

"Nenni, will you not make some decision as to those two merchants from the south? You have said 'tomorrow, tomorrow' for a month now!"

"My Shesu, I cannot believe it matters one whit whether they settle their little wrangle one way or the other. What is at stake? A few sacks of grain and a poor donkey both men have done their best to work into his tomb."

"Donkey? Sacks of grain? Ptah's Beard, Nenni! Their plea concerns a great fortune and a fleet of cargo vessels each manned by forty slaves!"

"It is the same, in the end," said Nenni, shrugging.

And that, thought Hatshepsut, is all the answer I will get. Very well. I will deal with the matter myself.

She had begun to deal with many matters herself, coming to his bedside in the early morning with a list of petitions on which she had already formed an opinion, and then rushing him through them one by one. It was possible to accomplish a great deal this way, and the ministers did not protest, for it had become harder and harder to get any answer at all from Pharaoh. The more insistently one pinned him down, the more oblique his responses became, until one felt he was speaking of some entirely different matter, thinking from a totally different point of view.

For instance, there was the scandal that broke over Thebes one week along with the summer winds, concerning the robbery of several royal tombs. Mysteriously, ancient golden cups and boxes kept turning up in certain Theban shops. By the time the mystery was unraveled, and the robbers exposed, three guards of the Necropolis, a priest of Hathor, two weavers and a prominent judge had been implicated in the crime.

"It is imperative, therefore," Thutiy argued earnestly as he explained the matter to Pharaoh at the Minister's Council, "not only that the punishment of these men be immediate and severe, but that it be public. Hapuseneb has doubled the guards at the Necropolis; but since the guards themselves were traitors in this case—"

"Three guards, a priest, two fine artisans and a judge," murmured Pharaoh. "Ah gods, and the poor men got nothing but gold for their terrible ordeal."

At the other end of the room Nehsi shifted his weight, glanced uneasily at Ineny, who was staring at the floor, then fell to examining his fingernails. Thutiy's eyes swept round the circle of puzzled faces, his brown skinny hands flapping a rolled document against his thigh. He turned back to Pharaoh.

"Your Majesty, they *wanted* nothing but gold. That is not the question. The question concerns their punishment."

"I should think it would be punishment enough, to come forth from hell with nothing but gold in their hands."

"Nenni, in Amon's name!" cried Hatshepsut. "You do agree that such criminals must be punished, do you not?"

Pharaoh turned slowly and looked at her. "You think their death would give them back their souls?"

"I—that is not what I said. I had not thought of death, I thought—perhaps a public beating, that is usual in such cases—a hundred strokes of the whip on the soles of their feet."

"Ah, yes. The compromise." Pharaoh smiled faintly. "The solution which solves everything but the problem."

"Then do you think they should be put to death?"

Nenni did not answer; his gaze had wandered from her face to a vague area just beyond her right ear.

"Nenni! Will you not speak?"

He muttered thoughtfully, whether in response to her question or to some reflection of his own she could not tell, "Aye, why not? Their lives are meaningless now. No doubt all lives are meaningless."

There was a little silence. Hatshepsut turned her gaze from him at last and rose, clasping her hands tightly together and looking at no one. "His Majesty has sentenced the men to death," she said.

No one contradicted her. If he had given any answer, as nearly as they could calculate, that was it.

Hatshepsut became ever more decisive in her role as Nenni's interpreter and mouthpiece. She was the Daughter of Amon, after all, and she bore the future within her. Her rights were unquestionable and her duty clear. She became expert at knowing precisely when to approach Nenni on this type of question or that. Sometimes he was more easily handled when he was racked by fever than when he was free of it; she made realistic use of this fact when she thought the matter important enough.

She discovered, quite by chance, a magic key that opened to her many of the locked doors of Nenni's obstinacy. She happened one day to use the phrase, "It is what my lord father would have done." The words had caused Nenni to fall silent and look at her with a strange expression, like blind relief. When he spoke again it was to agree without argument to what she was proposing. The incident startled her, then made her thoughtful. With her discovery of that phrase the reins of Egypt's government quietly changed hands.

Then one day of rising waters, the morning after the gates

of the canals had been thrown open to let the Nile reach glittering fingers through the fields, Pharaoh emerged from his chambers for the first time in twenty days—gaunt, weak, but fully clothed and free of fever, with tired, sane eyes—and went directly to his queen's apartments.

Hatshepsut, sitting by her tray of fruit and cheese with her hair still loose about her shoulders and the delicious fresh breeze of morning sliding over her swollen body, looked up in utter astonishment as he entered.

"Nenni! Are you well enough to be walking about like this? . . . Aye, I see you are. You are much better, aren't you?"

With only a brief nod, he closed the door behind him and motioned Yen and a little slave girl out of the room. When they had vanished he walked over and dropped into a chair near Hatshepsut's.

"Shesu—I want to talk to you."

"Very well," she said cautiously. He did not go on, and his eyes made her uneasy. "Will you Perfume the Mouth with me? Here are figs and peaches, I will send for fresh cheese—"

He broke in as if she had not spoken. "Shesu, I have been very ill. For a week or more, I think—the time runs together."

"You have been ill all summer, Nenni."

He gave her a strange, expressionless glance, then turned quickly away. "Aye, all summer, I meant to say. Off and on. But most particularly this week past, and I shall no doubt be ill again."

She watched him, not answering.

"This is an uneasiness for the people of Egypt. I do not think I shall die soon—perhaps not for years. But if I should, it would leave none but you to rule. . . ."

And who do you think has been ruling, these past long months? she thought.

"I have been pondering all this. It is not fair to the people," he said. He stood up suddenly and walked across the room. "I wish to arrange a ceremony immediately to name my son Successor and co-ruler, and set him on the throne beside me, that they may be reassured."

"Your son?" echoed Hatshepsut. "Do you mean Thoth?"

"Aye, Thoth—is he not the only son I have?"

For a moment she stared at his stooped back in openmouthed silence, feeling incredulity and then fury gather in her. "Are you mad?" she burst out. "Are you blind, that you do not see *my* son is to be born within a month? What are you thinking of? What are you scheming and plotting against me, you and that charioteer's daughter—"

"Shesu! In Amon's name!" Nenni hurried to her and took her hand, pushing her back onto the cushions. "What makes you say such a thing? There is no plotting—I have not seen Iset in months, perhaps years—"

"Then what is this mad talk about *her* son, when *mine* is on the way!"

"My lotus," he said very gently, "if your child is a son naturally another ceremony will be arranged at once, to cancel out the first. There is no thought in my mind of raising Thoth above him. But he is not yet born—if a son it is—and meantime—"

"You're talking nonsense as usual!" she cried. "Oh, curse you! Why did you have to mention this, nothing could be so unlucky, such a dreadful omen!" She flung her hands over her face and burst into frightened tears. To herself she repeated wildly, It *shall* be a boy, it *shall* be a boy, I will not *let* it be otherwise, may the gods strike him down for saying such things!

"Surely you cannot believe this will make any difference?" he exclaimed. "My beloved, I pray you, calm yourself! If your child is a man-child he is so already, and nothing can change it. Merely to suggest that Thoth be enthroned with me temporarily—"

"Be silent, do not say it again, I will not listen!" She glared at him, clutching the arms of her chair with shaking hands. "Perhaps your words will leave no mark. But to place the cobra on another child's head would be to fly in the faces of the gods, to bring down evil upon us. . . . Aye, *you* do not believe it, you believe in nothing! But I *know*."

There was silence for a moment. Nenni straightened slowly, looking down at her with a strange expression, as if he looked into an abyss. "May Amon forbid that I deepen Egypt's night," he said. "You may rest easy, my Shesu, the plan is forgotten."

He turned and left the room.

On the last day of the month of Paophi, fifteen days after the Festival of the High Nile, Hatshepsut's child was born. The birth went well, but it was not easy, nor was it quick. Drugged almost to insensibility by the merciful poppy, the Great Royal Wife lay exhausted for some time after old Yen and the other women had borne her gently to a clean bed and left her to rest. The darkness had fallen and a lamp flickered in one corner of the room by the time she stirred, turned her head on its ivory headrest, and opened heavy-lidded eyes.

"Yen—"

"Here I am, my lady."

Yen hastened to the couch from her vigil beside the tiny golden cradle and smiled into her mistress' face. Hatshepsut smiled back at her, and her eyes opened wider.

"Let me see my son," she whispered.

"My Shesu, it is a little daughter, the most beautiful little girl that ever I saw, save only one, and that was you, when you were — My lady! What is it?"

"Yen, let me see my *son!*" came a hoarse, unnatural voice.

"Lie back, my darling! The babe is a little daughter, do you not understand? As beautiful as the day . . . she is the image of you. Now, you never saw yourself as a babe, but you saw little Thoth. This little girl looks like Thoth. . . . My lady, in Amon's name, what ails you? Oh, Hathor help us! Baba! Nyweyre! Get yourselves in here, hasten, the queen is ill! Fetch that cloth there, bring wine and water, one of you— My Shesu, tell me what ails you, will you not speak to me?"

There was no sound from the couch. The three worked over the queen, sponging, offering wine, making futile motions.

"She cannot have fainted," whispered one of the little servants. "Her eyes are open."

"Fetch the babe, that will comfort her. Let her hold her babe."

Yen waddled hastily across the room, caught up the tiny, naked princess and put her in Hatshepsut's arms. That indeed produced a reaction. The queen recoiled as if a snake had been put in bed with her.

"Take her away," she whispered.

"But it is your own babe, it is the dear little princess—"

"Take her away, I said!" screamed Hatshepsut. "I do not want to see her, do you understand? Not now, not ever!"

Yen snatched the baby and held it close against her as if to protect it from the shocking suddenness of the outcry. Turning so that her square dumpy body hid it from the couch, she carried it again to its cradle. It began to whimper, then to cry in a small but lusty voice.

"Poor darling, poor darling," whispered Yen. She beckoned fiercely to the two servant girls, who still stood staring dumbly. "Come hither, stupid ones! Take the cradle, one at each end—carry it to my chamber. Find a wet nurse at once, ask around in the slaves' quarters. Hasten now, get the babe out of here, the queen is not herself as yet, this will all be over in the morning. . . ."

As the door closed behind the wailing little princess, Yen peered anxiously toward the couch. There was no sound, no movement, but Hatshepsut was not asleep. She was lying with her eyes wide open in a calm but rigid face, staring straight ahead.

It was not over in the morning, or the next day, or the next. One by one the courtiers, summoned by Pharaoh according to tradition, filed by the cradle to bring gifts and do homage to the new scrap of royalty. Yen received them distractedly, unsupported and alone. The elder princess, Nefer, was led in by old Ahmose, took an indifferent glance at the baby and went out petulantly demanding her kitten. Thoth tiptoed in with the impassive Ahbi, peered long into the cradle and lifted a face so radiant with awe and tenderness that Yen hugged him and burst into grateful tears.

The Queen-Mother Aahmes did not appear, nor did she protest her daughter's strange behavior. Shattered at last by the constant shattering of precedent, she had ceased to protest about anything; but she no longer emerged from the Apartments of the Queen no matter what the occasion. Serenely and beautifully, as she had always done everything, she had quietly turned her back on a reality that was no longer bearable to her.

All this time Hatshepsut lay on her own couch, silent and unnaturally composed, enduring the pain of her milk-swollen breasts without complaint or comment, steadfastly refusing to allow the little princess in the room. She refused to see Pharaoh, who finally ceased to press the matter. She was told that he had named the little girl Meryet-Re-Hatshepsut—Beloved-of-the-Sun, Foremost-Among-Noblewomen; she was timidly informed that the child lived in Yen's chamber, that a wet nurse had been found for it, that it flourished. She evidenced no interest in any of these matters. She seemed to be thinking, continuously and calmly, and she seemed to be waiting for something.

When she was able to be up and around in her room, she began to inquire each morning after the health of Pharaoh. "He is well," she would be told. "The fever dwells elsewhere and his *ka* rejoices." She would nod and drop the subject, but the next day she would ask again.

Then one morning, twelve days after the birth of Meryet-Re, she was told, "The fever dwells in him again."

She sat silent for a moment, looking at her hands clasped tightly in her lap. Then she stood up.

"I wish to speak with him. Dress me and arrange my hair."

"But my lady," objected Yen, "did you not hear me? He is ill today. You would do better to wait until—"

"I said I wished to speak to him! Fetch my garments."

A few minutes later she went alone into Pharaoh's chambers, and closed the door behind her.

8.

The words were faint and infinitely far away at first, gradually growing closer and louder.

". . . all praise to Amon the Mighty One, King of Gods who is like to the rising sun and like to the setting sun. . . ."

Nenni felt his spirit whirling back through the dark spaces, over and over like a flashing, two-spoked wheel, and experienced the familiar tiny shock of dizziness as it united once more with his body. Then he was blinking, opening his eyes—though he instantly questioned that they had really been shut—and there was a heavy fragrance about him and a vast presence before him, gleaming fitfully through a moving cloud of vapor. He watched it, waiting patiently to understand, and presently his vision cleared and he saw a white plume of smoke curling upward from between the forefeet of the great golden bull, whose vast shoulders and head towered and gleamed above him. At the same moment he became aware of the renewed drone of the voice that had summoned him back, of the rattle of a sistrum and the enclosure of ivory-studded walls.

He was in the Holy-of-Holies in the temple, making the weekly offering.

Quickly and secretly he took stock of his person; he felt pressure on the soles of his feet and knew he was standing, found his hands to be crossed on his breast, each holding something. Moving one finger exploringly over smoothness and rough, curling design, he recognized with a little flash of reassurance the enamel-and-gold handle of the Flail. The other hand, then, held the Crook. All was well, the priests moved at either side of him and the incense was burning. No one had noticed his absence. He wondered how long he had been gone. It was very curious; he was always aware of the return of his *ka* to his body, but never of its departure.

He heard the rustle of starched linen close beside him and Hapuseneb's slightly rasping breathing, then felt the subtle touch of oil on the backs of his hands. The High Priest stepped back, and Nenni turned, moving easily and naturally, and crossed the stretch of jasper pavement to the door. It swung open before him and he went out, hearing behind him the soft swish of drapery as a priest drew the curtains over the niche that held the Golden Bull.

Sensations continued to strike him with a succession of stimulating little shocks as he walked through the three ever-larger, ever-lighter anterooms to the high, cedar-columned Hall of Praise. Everything seemed extraordinarily vivid; he smelled the piercing-sweet perfume of lotuses as if for the first time, he noticed details of carvings on the columns, colors in the rug, which he had never seen before. At the same time he felt capable of a nimbleness of mind which allowed him to respond to these impressions, even while standing coolly off from himself to remark upon them and to contrast their reality with the strange absence of mind from body he had just passed through.

It must be true, he reflected as he paused in the Hall of Praise, that the *ka* is a separate spirit, independent of the body and able to depart from it at will. All men's *kas* fly away at night, what else is sleep? As for my own, it has a greater love of liberty than many others, or else my grasp on it is weak, for it does not wait for a time of sleep to depart from me.

He glanced down at the intricately knotted flaxen cords that bound the golden *ankh*-sign to his wrist and purported to leash his fluttering *ka* to his body. Obviously amulets were useless; he had always thought so. Or was it somewhere else the *ka* had escaped, at whatever hour this morning it had taken flight? Perhaps it could escape through the nostrils or some other part, all unknown to the magicians who knotted the cords so solemnly.

Nenni realized the high priest was speaking to him, and turned his attention to the formalities of taking leave. Afterward he walked out of the temple into the courtyard where his litter waited, noting the beauty of the early light on the paving stones and the clear deep blue shadows still lingering in the angles of the wall. In an hour the court would be filled with dust and heat and harsh yellow sun and the strident voices of hawkers selling lotuses and fowl for offering, oil and consecrated bread. It was empty now, except for the silent litter bearers and the little cluster of attendants who surrounded and moved with him at three paces' distance, in the hollow Circle of Respect. The Circle had a gap on its western side, through which Nenni's long morning shadow projected. The attendants in that quarter kept their eyes anxiously on the ground and were careful not to step on it.

For an instant, fresh awareness of the Circle and the shadow grated against the spot in Nenni's mind already long rubbed raw by the contact, and he went rigid, uneasy, taut within him, in the old, weary way.

Nay, I will not think of that, he told himself. Why can I not simply accept it as a custom, a fact, why must I constantly feel the ambiguity of its meaning?

It has no meaning, he told himself, and pushed the awareness of the Circle out of his mind.

He stepped into his litter quickly, hoping to preserve the simply observed beauty of the morning, and tried not to think at all as he was carried under the giant pylon and out into the dawn-washed streets of Thebes. Across the river, the first sunlight was touching the western cliffs; the air was clear and pure, the palms rustled lightly. The street was almost as bare as the courtyard had been, but here and there Nenni could see a few peasants hurrying toward the market places with baskets of produce on their heads. Occasionally a door would open or a woman emerge from an alley; there were signs of awakening life all about him.

What dark journeys have their *kas* made, through the night? thought Nenni, forgetting that he was not going to think. How do they call them back so swiftly and firmly merely by waking, while mine lingers incontinently in those other places? Why have I no knowledge of its going or its sojourn, not even the memory of a dream?

His brows puckered together as he tried to remember, to recollect anything at all of the darkness from which he had just felt his spirit come whirling back. There was nothing except that sensation of revolving end over end and the impression of flashing spokes, as in a wheel, then the small dizziness and the feeling of being right side up and located in time and space, and then the gradual consciousness of his body and senses. Was the *ka*, then, shaped like a wheel, when through all these thousand years men had pictured it as shaped in a man-image, the shadowy duplicate of themselves? Or was it the man-image after all, distorted by its rapid spinning into a semblance of spokes, and tracing a rim that was nothing but pure speed? If so, what was its substance, what was it that flashed?

Nay, that was nonsense, that was only a fancy of his own, that it flashed. It was his way of picturing the mysterious process of returning consciousness, which happened more slowly with himself than with other men, therefore with more observable sensations—other men might visualize it in quite a different way, might not visualize it at all, in fact. With them the return of the *ka* was merely the opening of their eyes. . . . Aye, but that was sleep, or fainting; his own eyes could be already open, he could move, talk, behave in an outwardly normal fashion. (It must be so. Had he not been standing there quietly in the Holy-of-Holies, holding the right things, facing the right direction? The priests had noticed nothing.) He could, apparently, perform all the gestures of a wakeful human being, without his *ka* being present in him at all. Was drunkenness something like that? Aye, something, but not quite.

Was madness?

Nonsense, he thought quickly. It is the fever that causes it, the fever is what sets me apart from other men, only the fever, and thinking too much, and being Pharaoh . . .

The thought of the Circle touched against that raw spot in his mind, and he winced away from it and tried, tensely and anxiously, to perceive the beauty of the morning again, fastening his eyes on a blowing palm, a stone ram beside the avenue, a rooftop pinkened by sun. But his eyes were not really seeing now. Thought came between them and their object, and though he could tell himself, growing even tenser, that he saw the roof, and that it was pink with the sun on it, all the time he was not really thinking of the roof, he was thinking of his eye and wondering what had risen up to obscure it.

Was it his *ka?* The *ka* was said to be visible in a man's eye, standing straight and small, a little man-image in the pupil. Remember the little Eye-of-Horus talismans that were made that way—the wide, black-and-white enameled eye with the extended lid-line curved up to join with the eyebrow in a decorative little curl, and within the pupil, the tiny, inscrutable figure, standing stiff and quiet. Inscrutable, like the face of Amon. Must all things be inscrutable? thought Nenni in sudden desperation.

Hush, hush, he thought. Look at that flagstaff, flashing in the sun. . . . What was it that flashed? What was the *ka's* substance? Nay, the *ka* had no substance, not like wood or metal or stone. It was real, though, perhaps just as real as any of those things, for it certainly could be present and just as certainly be absent, and it was true that it looked at one out of a man's eyes. Not, perhaps, in the form of the little image, though if one looked closely enough—

The litter tilted and for a moment bales of hides and the mud-bricks of a warehouse moved past with sudden, sharp reality. The smell of the Nile was all around and the water slapped with a bright morning sound against the sides of the royal bark. Nenni crawled out of the litter, conscious of a stiff, tingling exhaustion in his legs, and walked slowly to the shaded pavilion amidships, with bearers and boatmen bowing on either side at a distance of three paces, and the captain waiting with right hand on left shoulder. Nenni stopped before this man, speculating. The captain's head was bent—a nuisance—it was always so hard to find out anything.

Bending too, Nenni peered up into the man's eyes, peered closely and earnestly; no matter how he sharpened his vision to see only the pupil, only the black space within the circle of the pupil, he could make out no man-image standing there tinily. All the same, men's *kas* looked out of their eyes, gay, sad, confident,

184

fearful, ashamed . . . and sometimes inscrutable. However, to recognize it one had to view the whole eye, not just the pupil; perhaps even the whole face, for the mouth expressed much too, without ever speaking. It need only harden, or curl a trifle, or twitch and shake like this one—

With a shock Nenni saw the captain's face whole. The man was terrified, bewildered, desperate. Gods of Egypt, no wonder, Nenni thought. Here he stands innocent as a man can be and Pharaoh stops and bends and actually glares into his face.

"It is nothing, I mean no harm to you, you do your duties well, excellently, I was merely—"

No use. How could one make amends for this terrible notice, when all they wanted was to remain unnoticed? He was only making it worse. Breaking off in mid-sentence, Nenni turned and entered the pavilion, and the Circle of Respect formed silently around him, each man three paces from the pavilion, careful about the shadow in case any portion of it should project outside onto the deck.

Nenni's head had begun to throb a little, and all the matters he had forbidden himself to think about were pushing in. Why must they exclude him like this—from themselves, from the world outside their circle, from life itself? Or were they excluding him? Suppose they were enclosing him instead? Sometimes the Circle seemed an enclosing, a wordless, inexorable pressing in about him; the men did not move but the empty space crept closer, widening itself in *his* direction, not theirs, encroaching, nibbling inconspicuously at his outlines as if it would finally consume his interfering presence and leave only itself, a ritual circle of empty space. Would they not be as happy, these millions in Egypt who formed the Circle about him, to have the Circle empty? They could put an image in it; they could put the crown or the cobra in it; it would be all the same. They resisted fiercely his tendency to be a man. They did not want a man—*they* were men. You are not allowed, they said. You are a god, you are Pharaoh. Stay in your circle, where you belong, where we can keep you safely caged; protect us by being divine but do not bother us by looking in our faces or behaving like a man. You are not a man, you are not really alive, you are merely one of our beliefs. Keep away —three paces away from our lives, in your circle of nothingness. We will tell you when we want you, then—still in your circle—

you may make the gestures we have taught you and perform your proper functions. After that be still and look remote and inscutable as a god should look until we want you again. . . .

Enclosing or excluding, it was all the same. Either way they destroyed him with loneliness, they built a bubble around him far tougher and more impossible to break than ever his fever had built. They drove him inward to the cage of his own thoughts and left him to go mad or die. And he could not die. He had tried many times. Perhaps the gods had not finished their gaming with him. No doubt the gods were devils, rather than myths as he had supposed. Aye, they must be. Devils, gathered in a circle, poking in turn, with gusts of laughter, at the tiny writhing figure in the cage of Nothingness. . . .

Nay, nay, there was not that much purpose to any of it. If the gods squatted in a circle, poking, they probably did so as meaninglessly as small boys poking at a toad, really thinking of something else, having no particular wish to hurt the toad and yet no particular wish not to hurt it.

"Majesty, will you enter your litter to disembark?"

How long, in Amon's name, had the boat been rocking at anchorage, had the litter been standing there before the pavilion, had the unnerved captain waited in silent agitation for Pharaoh to make some move, some sign that he meant to do something besides sit and stare all day?

Nenni rose, stiff-lipped with apprehension, aware of a curious sensation in his head, as if a metal band encircled it just above the eyebrows. Had his *ka* escaped again? Nay, for he had not felt it return, and surely it was with him now, he could see the litter, could he not, and feel himself walking toward it, and know that the boards of the deck were beneath his feet? Yet he glimpsed those strange expressions on the faces of the men as they glanced at each other—the expressions he knew so well, that told him he had done something queer. Was his *ka* with him or was it not, this minute, as he climbed into the litter? Perhaps in a while he would feel it come whirling back, flashing, and then he would remember none of this—not the litter, not the captain, not the warehouses. . . . Then when had it left him? Nay, surely it was with him still. *"Blood of the Mangled One!"* Nenni whispered. It was this fuzzy uncertainty that

186

tortured! The not knowing, the not being able to determine. . . .

It had been so that other morning (Had it been morning, and he had waked from sleep? Or was it some other hour and he had merely waked from absence, waked from fever?), that terrible morning he could not remember, when she had come in, beautiful with her hair freshly dressed and her waistline slim again, but not yet as slim as before, since the birth was so recent and the babe so new. Her breasts were still swelled with the milk, and he had been distractedly aware of his sweat-drenched bed and the tumbled sheets and the smell of sickness in the room. Perhaps that was why he had not listened, could not remember. . . .

The metal band drew tighter around Nenni's forehead and his hands were clutching the arms of his litter but he could not help it now. He had held it off as long as he could and he was again floundering in the quicksand memory of that morning, trying to remember.

She had sat down beside his couch. That was clear, as clear as her shining hair, the swollen look of her breasts. She had talked. Her voice had been smooth and calm. Though he could not remember her face, he could remember her voice. But—*Name of God*—he could not remember what it said.

Only one phrase: "It is what my lord father would have done." That phrase had soothed him. It penetrated the haze of the fever and the further confusion of the fact that he could not see her clearly and did not know precisely what she was saying—but to that phrase he had answered "Aye." That he remembered.

He did not remember when she left. The fever had engulfed him for a time—hours perhaps, more likely days. He never knew about that and it always shamed him to ask, for it revealed that his *ka* had been absent and he had not known it. Then one day he had wakened, with his *ka* whirling back.

He was standing in a little room he had never been in before and old Yen was standing near him, and he was bending over a cradle in which his tiny daughter was lying. He saw her clearly and beautifully, with her small, curled toes, and joy had run through him at the sight of her. He had straightened and smiled at Yen, who looked older and tireder than he remembered her, and he had gone at once to the garden off the great court, eager

187

to see Thoth because today he could see him clearly and could talk to him and listen to what he said, and such moments were rare and precious.

Thoth had not been in the garden. Old Ahmose was there, keeping watch over little Nefer, but he did not see Thoth anywhere. He had started toward Ahmose to ask where Thoth was, and suddenly he had stopped.

From that moment, ever after, for two months now—sixty agonizing days—he had not been able to ask where Thoth was.

He had tried. Very cleverly, very obliquely, he had brought Thoth's name up in the presence of Nehsi, of Thutiy, of various chamberlains; they had only looked at him with that strange expression he dreaded, and he had been forced to change the subject quickly. Then he had tried to find Ahmose again, belatedly—but Ahmose had vanished. Senmut, the Steward of Amon, was guardian to Princess Nefer now. At last one day he had forced himself to pronounce Thoth's name to Hatshepsut, trying to keep his voice under control and his hands from shaking. She, too, had turned that look upon him.

"*You* know where Thoth is, Nenni," she had said. "It was your command."

Nenni lay back on the cushions of the litter, exhausted. It was over, he had gone through it again and it was over for a while now, he could keep it at bay for a few days.

The litter had come to rest in the Great Court of the palace. Nenni slowly emerged from it, stood a moment with the Circle forming about him, and tried to see the green palm growing beside the great columns of the palace entrance. It was a beautiful tree, with a curve as tender as a woman bending over her child.

His eye saw it; but it was not real to him, his mind had moved on. He walked into the palace and paused in the wide transverse hall. "Leave me," he said to the Circle.

The attendants faded away.

He had never tried that before. He was Pharaoh, after all. He need not endure the Circle and its ambiguity. He could dispel it with a word, and be free.

He looked around him at the empty hall, the columns. He was still alone. The Circle had only widened, its emptiness was just as empty, just as encroaching, just as destroying.

188

He started, almost aimlessly, across the corridor, into the vast Hall of State, which echoed his footsteps in its emptiness. He thought of Hatshepsut. She must feel it too, she too was royal and unapproachable, she had no one but himself—whatever their differences, their distance from each other, she could penetrate his circle and he hers. They were bound together, no matter how negatively, by untouchableness and divinity. . . .

His steps took on purpose and direction. The Southern Garden, perhaps she would be there. Or in the anteroom off the Audience Chamber, listening to Nehsi's morning report. Burdens had fallen upon her with his illness, he was aware of that— all the intolerable monotony and loneliness of ruling, with only Nehsi and the ministers and the Steward of Amon to advise and guide through all the mazes.

The Steward of Amon.

I have no reason to dislike the man, Nenni told himself. He is an excellent Steward; if he seems much in evidence it is only by contrast with the old Steward, who was of course not half so much in evidence as he should have been and would have been had he been discharging his duties competently. So Nehsi says. And Nehsi, who always discharges his own duties competently, is a far better judge of such matters than I, who never do. . . . Nay, there is nothing of the looter, the predator about this Senmut. That is an unreasonable notion of my own based on no more than a certain cast of his features which may be purely accidental. Remember the old sentry, when we were children— the one always by the garden gate at nap time—a very Devourer of cruelty he looked, and he was the kindest man alive. It was nothing but an old scar which twisted his mouth like that. He could help it no more than I can help my twisting thoughts. . . . There is nothing wrong with Senmut's hands, either. Aye, they are large, they are corded with strength. Why should they not be? There is no reason whatever to be repelled by them, as if they concealed some sort of threat. A threat to whom, toward what? It is nonsense. To put it finer, it is envy. Do I not envy all vigorous men their strength, I with my strengthless claws, suitable only for empty gestures. . . .

Nenni glanced down at his hands, then stopped, and raised them, and looked at them. That one morning, had they made a gesture that had not been empty?

Minutes later he found himself standing in the same spot, sagged against a column, still staring at them—bony and pallid and long, he knew every contour of them, the familiar shape of the nails and that blue prominent vein like a twisted rope—but they were like strangers, secretive, inscrutable, perhaps terrible.

What did I say to her that morning? What did I command?

The hands were beginning to shake uncontrollably. He dropped them, pressed them flat against his thighs, and after a moment walked hastily out of the Hall of State into the brilliant sunshine of the morning, feeling the metal band squeeze tighter around his forehead. She would be in the Southern Garden, perhaps, or was it too early? He could not think what hour it was. No matter, he would find her. It would be better when she was beside him.

Nenni reached the square-arched entrance to the Southern Garden, but he went no farther. Hatshepsut was there, standing by the shimmering waters of the pool, with the sun bright upon her hair, and an expression on her face he had never looked upon in his life. Beside her stood the Steward of Amon, in the act of raising one of her wrists to his lips.

The band drew tighter, crushing at last all sensation, all emotion.

True, she gently freed her hand from Senmut's. But she did not summon the guards, order him forever from her presence, or even move away. Instead she laughed under her breath and made some remark in a tone as unintended for other ears as her expression was unintended for other eyes. And there he stood, this Senmut, with his smiling, deep-grooved face, his terrible hands, looking down at her.

I am Pharaoh, thought Nenni. I could summon the guards. I could destroy his smile, his hands, his body and life. I have only to command.

He did nothing. He stood silent in the archway, wondering that they did not see him. It was as if he were invisible. And of course—the knowledge came, and he could not stay it—of course he was invisible. He had wanted to die, but he had not realized that he was dead in the minds of those around him, and had been perhaps for months. Now he could feel his invisibility drawing around him like a curtain as he watched the two in the garden and asked himself what it had to do with Thoth, and knew quite well what it had to do with everything.

She was not alone—ah no, never. What a mistake that had been. Senmut was with her. She would not feel the stealthy, nibbling pressure of the Circle; she would never be lonely, and drawn in her loneliness to himself.

I could destroy Senmut, he thought again.

And what would that be? The invisible gesture of a weightless arm. Every gesture of his life had been invisible—even that one he had so feared. His hands were after all not strangers, they had never deviated from the prescribed round of solemn and meaningless gesticulations.

He stood a moment thinking about it, feeling the Circle encroach swiftly and surely now and swallow him up without pausing, as if it had only been waiting and the time had come at last. He saw now, from his shining emptiness, that another circle had already formed about the two in the garden—had perhaps been there all along. But there were two in that one. Two.

Possibly it was better this way. He had never wanted to rule Egypt or be a god. He wanted only some answer, some partial affirmative, some hint of meaning out of the strange spectacle of life. It was too bad that he wanted that, it was really too bad, for it was the one thing no man could have. The spectacle was quite devoid of meaning.

Nenni turned aside, pressing his hand against a sudden pain that shot fiercely through his head. He divested that of meaning too, and it slowly faded. Without glancing back into the garden he returned to the palace, walked down the long corridors, and found his own apartments.

Briefly, but without agony now because he was past that, he wondered what they had done with his son.

9.

Between the donkey's ears the land spread out gray and vast and undulating before Thoth, like the waves of a motionless sandy sea. Far, far away to the left, as far away as the edge of the world, was a tiny something that might be a clump of palm trees. He had been watching it all morning, whenever the undulating dunes did not rise and blot it out—not because he was going there, but because it was something to watch, the only feature in a featureless world. While he was looking at it he could almost imagine that he was walking in under those palms, and that it was a different place altogether, green like Egypt, with black, cool mud and a Nile. The moment it vanished behind the gray, heat-baked curve of a dune the imagining vanished too and he could not be anywhere but here, swaying monotonously with the donkey, with the faint *ting, ting, ting* of its little bell in his ears, and the dust in his nostrils and in his eyes and swirling all around; and beside and behind him, dimly visible through the dust, the shapes of the other donkeys and their humped and silent riders. Then he could not make Egypt real, he could not bring it back.

Home. Ahmose, he said to himself now, trying. "Ahmose," he said aloud, under his breath. A face with tears came up before him, but that was wrong. Ahmose had not cried, he had been smiling as the ship moved away from the dock that day, but the smile had made Thoth feel queer, as if it were really tears. Now he could not bring Ahmose's face up clear, only a face with tears.

"Ahmose," he said more loudly.

The man riding nearest turned his head, and from the slit in the cloth that covered his face two black, vaguely curious eyes looked at Thoth. Thoth looked back, shrinking, wishing he had not spoken aloud. The man would not hurt him. Thoth knew that by now. He would do nothing but look, and then turn away. This was the one with the red cloth over his head and face, and the little scar beside his eye. He had a vast, curly beard beneath that cloth—thicker and curlier than any of the others. Thoth was becoming almost used to beards now, though every night when the men unwound the cloths from their faces he was frightened all over again for a minute.

The man leaned out of his saddle and said something quick and sibilant, with a questioning lift at the end. Thoth shrank farther back and shook his head, wanting nothing but for the man to turn away again. The eyes studied him a moment longer, moved rapidly over the saddle, the saddle bags, the bridle, the donkey's feet, then turned away.

The tight little squeezing inside Thoth slowly relaxed and after it came the queer disappointment. He wanted nothing but for the men to turn away again, yet when they did, he was lonelier than before.

He looked to the left, searching for the tiny something that might be palm trees, but he saw only vast, rippled dunes. It was hidden now, he would have to wait for the little green memory of Egypt.

It had been different at first, long, long ago when he had still been on the ship and the waves around him had been real water, high and terrifying after the smooth Nile and different, so different from everything he had ever known, with the beards everywhere and his mother screaming and moaning in her hammock, pushing him away when he knelt beside her in fear and tried to bury his face in her neck—everything had been strange and terrible then, too, but he could remember Egypt. He had remembered it all the time then. He could close his eyes against the tossing water and the beards and his mother's terrified face, and at once the calm, green fields and black mud and the little garden with the pool and Ahmose and Nefer and Lady Shesu would come up before him real and close, so that he ached intolerably with the sweetness of it and the longing.

He did not know when he had stopped being able to remember. Perhaps the night on the ship when Ahbi, silent and expressionless as always, had waked him in his tossing hammock and taken his hand in her large, pink-palmed one and led him along the swaying, wet deck with a torch to where his mother lay, wrapped in a piece of sail, not wailing now but still and white and unrecognizable. The men had looked at him and then at Ahbi. She nodded, and they wrapped the sail over the strange white face and lifted the bundle and slid it overboard. He had not quite understood it was his mother until morning, when he went to find her and instead found the empty hammock swinging back and forth.

Or perhaps it had been later, when they had touched shore in a strange land, in a town full of curiously dressed people with swarthy skin and strange, fat bodies, and beards—and Ahbi had been holding his hand one minute and the next she was gone, vanished up a crowded street and out of his life forever.

Thoth sighed and shifted his position on the donkey, looking again for the far-off palm trees and again not finding them. He wondered where Ahbi had gone, how she could have left him. But it was only out of habit that he wondered. She had been gone so long now, and he could not even remember his terror very well any more, or the agony of trying to tell the men, or the desperate loneliness of knowing that there was no one who could understand what he said. He knew he had cried, huddled in his first tent and frightened of it looming above him as he was frightened of everything—he could remember, a little, choking on his own sobs and finally comforting himself because there was no one else to do it. He had done it by thinking of Lady Shesu, who would surely send someone to fetch him when she knew he had been abandoned to the Hyksos. He was sure they were the Hyksos. Ahmose had always told him the Hyksos wore beards.

On the ship his mother, wailing in her hammock, had often screamed that all that was happening was Lady Shesu's fault, but that was not true. Lady Shesu had not even known about it, she had not been at the wharf when they left Thebes. Only Ahmose had been there, with Thoth's little boat under his arm, wrapped carefully in a cloth—

Thoth sat upright with a jerk, twisted hastily in the saddle and felt over the bumpy surface of the right-hand saddle bag—yes, the boat was safe, it was safe, it was there. His heart beat fast as he settled back.

"Ahmose," he whispered, but very softly, so the man with the red headcloth would not hear him.

The beloved face did not come. He would try again tonight, holding the boat against him in the dark of the tent, running his fingers over the little oars and the carved faces of the tiny men. He could sometimes remember very well at night. After the confusion of halting and unloading and tethering and putting up the tents and cooking the black meat was over, after the smell of food and dung had spread over the camp and after the nightly agony of yearning to be noticed and fearing he would be and listening in silent loneliness to the sound of the foreign tongue— after those things were all over, and he lay at last in the darkness, alone with the boat, he could often see Ahmose clearly, and hear his rusty voice saying "I am here."

He was not really here, though. No one was here that Thoth had ever, ever known.

Thoth's eyes lifted longingly to the sun. Ahmose had said once that if he looked closely enough, he might see his grandfather, who was once Pharaoh and now was Osiris, riding in the bark of Re. Did Re drive the bark of the sun here, too, as he did in Egypt? Or was it some other god up there now? For this was not Egypt. He did not know what land it was, but it was not Egypt. That he knew with all his lonely, homesick soul. His eyes watered from the glaring cruel brightness of the sun and he had to rub them. Probably that was not even Re up there. The gods must be different in a land where the men wore beards and there was no Nile. His grandfather was not up there. No one was there but a strange, burning god he did not know.

Tears welled up hot into Thoth's eyes and the terrible tightness came into his throat. He felt his mouth straining downward at the corners and he could not help it, could not help the desolation that rose and engulfed him.

"Ahmose!" he sobbed. *"Ahmose—"*

The man in the red headcloth turned quickly and looked at him. He said something, but Thoth could not understand.

"Where are we going?" Thoth cried to the man. He knew it was no use, the man would not understand him, but he sobbed it out again, trying desperately to say it with his eyes, too. "Where are we going?"

The man's eyes looked at his a moment, black and faintly curious, then moved rapidly to the saddle, the saddle bags, the bridle and the donkey's hoofs. Finding nothing wrong, they came back to Thoth's another moment, and then turned away.

Thoth turned away too, resolutely pushing back the sobs because it was no use to cry, no use at all. He looked for the palm trees again, and again he did not find them. Perhaps they were gone for good now, and he would never see them again. Still he searched beyond the dunes at the left, while the old, weary, lonesome question echoed over and over in his heart. Where are we going? Oh, please, please, where are we going?

The donkey plodded on, its head bobbing monotonously, and its little bell tinkling, and the dust swirling around it and around the other donkeys with their silent, swaddled riders. The caravan wound slowly over the rise of a dune and into the hollow of the next one, following the ancient road to Babylon.

PART III

Expulsion

I.

OVER the mountain-ringed saucer of the earth, Amu, Lord Sky, arched like a vast dish cover, a high dark dome. Against the glassy vault, stars coursed in intricate slow patterns, each one heavy with meaning to certain watchers far below in Babylon. To the uninitiated the stars might seem no more than a swarm of jeweled bees flying across the face of night; to the *baru* they were the finger of God slowly writing the answers to all riddles.

Silent in their pallid light, Babylon lay sleeping upon its vast expanse of plains—a flat, sprawling city from whose heart one massive seven-tiered tower thrust up, stage on lofty stage, like a man-made mountain, to dominate the canal-crossed land for miles.

Around the tower lapped an angular sea of rooftops, softened here and there by clumps of palms, edged on the west by the broad, steel-gray band of the Euphrates, a river half friend to man, half enemy—unpredictable, tricky, brooding and unfathomable as its creator Enki, Lord of Earth and Water. A few fine, straight avenues bisecting each other at sharp angles divided the city into clean-cut, well-planned areas fit for the dwelling place of gods. But mortals dwelt there; long since, the areas had divided themselves again into a helter-skelter maze of crooked, comfortably untidy alleyways, narrow enough for the women to call back and forth to each other as they worked at their weaving or grain-grinding on the flat roofs, crowded enough with houses and shops and struggling humanity to afford some measure of comfort to the lonely human heart. Even now, with the roofs empty in the starlight and the alleys deserted, the houses seemed to huddle together through the long, uncertain night, shouldering and pressing inward against one another until the inmost leaned against the high walls of the Temple Enclosure itself.

The Enclosure lay in the city's heart, between the river and the broad Processional Way. Here, serene within the sturdy walls which firmly excluded importunate humanity while providing it with a bulwark to lean against, a long and spacious area had been set aside for the service of the gods. In the southern courtyard, which occupied a rough third of the Enclosure, Esagila, the Temple of Marduk, stood alone. To the north of it, storerooms and outbuildings with low, clean lines and saw-toothed tops ranged around an immense forecourt. At the far end rose the temple-mountain, the ziggurat, whose name in Babylon was Etemenanki, Foundation of Heaven and Earth. A vast hulk of darkness in the waning night, it reared its gigantic stair-stepped shape against the sky, dwarfing men and walls alike. The eye had only to lift, from any spot in Babylon or the surrounding plains, to see Etemenanki and be reassured that amid the perils, uncertainties and ceaseless change of life on earth, one thing, at least, endured.

To be sure, that which endured was in a way the very symbol of awe and dread. Etemenanki might be the Foundation of Heaven and Earth on ordinary days, but on the twelve most important days of the year, the days in the spring month of Nisan when the Akitu, the New Year's Festival, was enacted, it became none other than the Mountain of the Netherworld, and its door the gate to death. It was there, in a chamber tunneled into its solid mass of brick, that the god Marduk was imprisoned for a time each year by the terrible Tiamat, the goddess who was Chaos. It was a fearful, a painful thing to know—that mighty Lord Marduk was become a *lillu,* a "weak one," caught and bound in the dark mountain, with dust in his nostrils and blinded eyes—but one had only to look about at the barren fields, the blowing dust, the pastureless flocks, to know it. One had only to see the driverless chariot of Marduk careening down the road on the first of Nisan to the Bit Akitu, the Festival Building out-

198

side the city, to know that the Lord of Babylon had vanished once again.

Then many perilous things must be done to release him—each year the same things, for they had been known to work before and they might work again. One named The Enchanter told the news to Marduk's sister, the goddess Beltis, and she wandered, dazed, to Etemenanki, wailing, "O, my brother! O, my brother!" and the people hastened after her frantically, saying "Where is he held captive?" The king, like Marduk, was deprived of his crown and scepter, and struck twice in the face, and confessed his sins, and the gods gathered in anxiety and Nabu the son of Marduk hurried to the temple, and there was disturbance in the streets. Finally Beltis his sister found him—in the dark, dread chamber of Etemenanki—and Nabu released him that he might fight and conquer once again the forces of Chaos, as he had done in the beginning of the world.

Then, while the days of the Festival proceeded in the Bit Akitu, and the rejoicing gods banqueted and planned the destiny of all living things for the year to come, Etemenanki again changed its character. It was a symbol of hope as well as fear, and above the dread door in its base long flights of steps climbed from one stage to the next, slanting up and up across its face, dwindling into high distance at its summit. There, far above the earth and all mortal doings, stood a golden sanctuary, the *gigunu,* within which was a great rich bed, a golden table, and nothing else. One night each year—the last night of the Akitu Festival—a woman chosen from all her kind by the god himself was taken up with songs and waving branches to Marduk's bed; no other human ever entered. There, the people knew, the god came to her like a rumbling storm, and took her into his black arms; there the sacred marriage was consummated and the fertility of the god once more awakened. Then the sweet spring rains and green vegetation returned to Babylon. Such was the night of Etemenanki's glory.

But that night was not tonight. Tonight no procession climbed the slanting stairs; the high, windy shoulder of Etemenanki was deserted except for one old man who stood alone in the darkness of the sixth tier, watching the stars. He was tall and spare, clad in a flowing garment. Hands fragile as paper rested on the balus-

199

trade before him; his head was tilted upward, his body motionless except for the sparse white beard that moved gently in the breeze.

His eyes were tired; he had been at his post many hours, and the night was almost done. The Finger wrote slowly, and what it wrote he must read, and what he read would guide the king and the great city called the Gate of God. Muttering at times to himself, or nodding a little as if in acceptance of a message, he watched until the stars began to fade, until they vanished one by one and the glassy dome above became colorless and then transparent. When at last he blinked his star-wearied eyes, stiffly lowered his head and began to rub the back of his neck, the outlines of tower and balustrade were already visible in the gray of dawn.

A cock crowed from somewhere outside the city walls. As if at a signal the tiny figure of a scribe, carrying an orange-flamed lamp, a slab of moist clay and a stylus, emerged from a door in the tower's base, far below, and started toiling up the vast face of the ziggurat toward his master. The stargazer started his slow descent to earth.

They met on the second stage. The scribe hastened forward, seated himself on one of the benches placed as rest stations on the long climb, set his lamp beside him and poised his stylus. Standing at the balustrade, the astronomer dictated his report.

"To the king my lord, your servant Belasi: Greetings to the king my lord. May Nabu and Marduk bless the king my lord. As to what the king wrote, 'Something is happening in the skies, have you noticed?'—I say, 'What phenomenon have I failed to see or failed to report to the king?' For whom does the king my lord fear misfortune? I have no information whatsoever. Let the king rejoice. The signs are good. As to that eclipse of the sun, of which the king spoke . . ."

The scribe scratched away at his clay tablet. When the report was finished he gathered his materials and with a respectful bow departed down the long, slanting stairway.

The astronomer sighed and leaned forward on the balustrade, waiting to see bright Shamash, Lord Sun, come up over Babylon, and wondering who was behind these sudden vague uneasinesses of the king. *Something is happening in the skies, have you noticed?* Nay, he had not noticed, since there was nothing to notice. The king did not even know what he was alarmed about, for he was never specific. Of course—that was natural. The astronomer knew that. Alarm, anxiety, despair—that was the climate of a king's mind. In Egypt, the astronomer had heard, the king was a god, advised and supported by other gods, and privy to all their plans. Marvelous, the old man reflected dubiously, if true. In Babylon, the king was but a poor wretched mortal like the rest of mankind, differing from them only in that he must bear a more-than-mortal burden. Small wonder he was prey to unreasoning alarms. . . .

He was prey to an uncommon number of them lately, the astronomer could not help reflecting. Someone was putting these ideas into his head—and the king believed each time, sent panic-stricken messages to the royal astronomer, and could only be told the truth, that nothing was amiss and the signs were good. How long would it be before he ceased to believe the truth, and cast his astronomer down in anger? Only as long as it took for some small misfortune to occur which the astronomer had failed to predict.

A shiver went through the old man's body, as if chill fingers had touched the back of his neck. Small misfortunes happened all the time, unpredicted and unpredictable. No man could read every intention of the gods, though he put his eyes out staring at the stars. The gods did as they pleased; men, whether astronomers or kings, could only try to read their riddles.

And if I fail? thought the stargazer.

Those whom the king cast out in anger were sentenced to death without burial; and the shades of the unburied roamed without rest forever, preying on every living thing. But what would the king care for that, or the gods either? What would anyone care save the miserable ghost of an old man who had tried all his years to live obediently and avoid such fate?

The astronomer's shoulders went slack and he sighed, leaning heavily on the balustrade. Man might strive as he liked, but what was his portion? Not heaven, that was reserved for gods. Earth, with its floods and disasters and swarming demons and treacheries from mortals and gods alike—that was man's lot while he lived. When he died, the wailing gloom of the underworld, a garment of feathers, dust to eat and mud to drink, with demons of pestilence and disease as guardians. In the end, astronomer and king alike descended to murky ruin.

". . . for mere man, his days are numbered, whatever he may do he is but wind . . ."

The stargazer nodded slowly as the familiar words came to mind. Thus the great hero, Gilgamesh, had spoken long ago—and every mortal found the same thought shaping in his heart before life had done with him, whether he be prince or slave.

The old man straightened. Below and far forward from where he stood on the tower's second stage, figures were moving across the forecourt toward the altar before Etemenanki's base. A priest was hurrying to make offering for some anxious mortal and read the omens from an animal's liver. The astronomer could see the ewe now, borne struggling between two attendants. With all his heart, he wished the offerer good omens and a surcease, however brief, from the despair which was their common lot.

Raising his glance briefly to the one lone planet which still hung in the pink-stained sky, he continued his long descent to earth.

Below, in the forecourt, the priest had placed a brazier before the altar, casting alert glances toward the ever-brightening east as he did so. Hurrying, he motioned for a table to be placed behind the brazier, and on it four pots of sesame wine, three dozen cakes, a dish containing a mixture of butter and honey, another of salt. Beside him the offerer stood shivering with nervousness, his eyes, too, fixed on the fiery glory of the sky where any second now Lord Shamash would appear. Quickly the attendants placed a few sticks in the brazier, set a torch to them, and then stepped back. There was an instant's wait, while all stared eastward.

The sun burst over the horizon.

With a sweep of his arm the priest scattered salt over the brazier and grasped the trembling offerer by the hand. "May thy servant at morning's hour offer sacrifice before thy august majesty!" he cried in a high, clear voice.

The ewe, bleating and struggling, was dragged forth to the altar; the knife plunged, she jerked once and lay still. The offerer, a merchant, fell to his knees, not daring to address the god but babbling soundless promises of gifts to the temple if the omens should be favorable. The smell of blood rose strong on the air to mingle as the priest and his attendants worked in silence, butchering the ewe. The carcass was borne away, dripping, toward the temple kitchens, leaving only the liver upon the altar. This the priest now examined carefully, occasionally comparing it with a clay model which was marked into fifty sections and inscribed. At last he turned to the merchant.

"The signs are favorable, on the whole," he stated, observing the other's trembling with disdainful eyes. "However, you have done something to offend the god. I see a death in your household before the moon is full."

Wiping his blood-smeared hands upon a cloth, he turned and started across the forecourt. The staring merchant gave a cry and followed, seizing his arm.

"A death? Whose death? Not my little daughter's? She has been sickly of late, it's true, but she is better now, my wife swore to me that she is better—"

The priest jerked free and walked quickly to the base of the tower, where he disappeared into one of the many shrines. The merchant stood gazing after him, his face contorted with grief, until a touch on his shoulder made him jerk around. A second priest stood there, recognizable from his robe as an *abkallu,* one who read the will of the gods in a drop of oil on water.

"Take heart," he said gently. "Perhaps only a slave will die. Who is the god of your fathers and your hearth?"

"The divine lady Gula, *abkallu,*" whispered the merchant.

"Ah, she who binds the wounds the gods inflict. So much the better. Go home, make offering to her, call in a scribe to write a letter, which she will surely notice though she may not hear your voice. When you have done this, return to me here. You must bring five shekels for the king, one for the vizier, and one for me. I will then drop oil upon water and tell you at once, from the mysteries known to me, whether your child will live."

Quivering with hope, the merchant hurried off across the forecourt. "Five shekels for the king, one for the vizier, one for the *abkallu.* Five shekels for the king, one for the vizier . . ."

He emerged from the Temple Enclosure into a Babylon already astir in the bright, early beams of Shamash, who would later glare down on it with cruel heat. Slaves were ambling toward the river, balancing huge water jars on their heads, farmers led donkeys burdened with produce toward the market place, scribes were gathering outside the temple gates to await the coming throng who would wish documents written, agreements witnessed, bargains sealed, boundaries made legal, quarrels settled. As the merchant vanished down one twisting street, bakers and sweetmeat vendors emerged from others, calling their fragrant wares. Barbers took up their usual posts in the shade of buildings, women appeared on their rooftops with spindles and wool, calling greetings to each other, and from a thousand vents the smoke of morning cookfires curled up against the brilliant sky.

In the Street of the Golden Bees, a boy of eleven emerged from the red-painted door of the house of Ibhi-Adad, the potter, and started on his way to school. He was short for his age, but stockily and strongly built, with a chest that would one day be powerful. A bold, arching nose and a shy mouth marked a face which was at once intense and thoughtful; any Babylonian would have noticed his ears, whose size gave sure proof of intelligence above the ordinary. He wore a short, vividly embroidered tunic which exposed legs and arms glowing bronze with health; under his soot-black hair, which was bound with a thong about his forehead and fell straight to his shoulders, his eyes were dark, and as long as an Egyptian's.

He turned into the Avenue of Enlil and headed toward the great ziggurat, walking with long and springy strides, pausing occasionally to scoop a clod of hard clay crumbled from the pavement and hurl it at a door post or a straggly palm. His aim was excellent, which seemed to satisfy but not surprise him. A short distance down the avenue he paused before a doorway, hurled one last clod which chipped whitewash from the lintel and set a dog to barking furiously within, and shouted, "Kalba!"

Nothing happened, beyond a renewed outburst from the dog. The boy walked on, squinting upward at the sun at first casually and then with an expression of thoughtfulness settling over his face and the look of old, half-glimpsed memory in his curiously un-Babylonian eyes.

A moment later the door behind him burst open, there was a hail, "Ho, Thoth! I'm coming!" and a fat boy of the same age but twice the other's girth catapulted into the street, waving one half of a chunk of honeyed bread while his cheek bulged with the other.

"Make haste, then! We're late. Old Dog-Face will give us greeting with his stick unless we hurry."

"A man must eat," puffed Kalba indignantly, catching up. "And can I make more haste than I have already?"

"Nay, but we'll try you. I'll wager a whack on the head I can touch yonder archway before you."

"Agreed!"

Both boys darted off down the avenue which, despite its width, was beginning to be crowded by early morning traffic streaming toward the city's heart. Kalba reached the archway a poor second, accepted Thoth's shout of laughter and a thump on the head with equal cheerfulness and instantly challenged the victor to a broad jump. This time length of legs counted for more than girth and Thoth earned a whack of his own, wailed mock despair and proposed another race. Accepted at once, he made off through the crowd with Kalba at his heels. Rounding a corner in too great haste, he joggled the elbow of a surgeon busy incising the Inalienable Mark upon the right hand of a slave. The slave groaned, the surgeon bellowed his annoyance. As Thoth whirled to stammer apologies Kalba passed him by. He was away in an instant, leaving the surgeon muttering imprecations and the slave's master, a wealthy winegrower, holding his belly with laughter as he watched the two boys—alternately running and leaping and whacking, yelling taunts at each other over the heads of gloomier folk—disappear on their erratic way toward Etemenanki.

"Cursed young ones," grumbled the surgeon, whipping out a bandage. "They've made me botch the task."

"High spirits, that's all," the winegrower said tolerantly. "All right, you," he added to the slave. "Get along to my house, and fetch those bundles with you. What fee, surgeon?"

"Twenty shekels of silver."

"Robber!" screeched the winegrower. "By Marduk's ears, do you take me for a madman?"

"Fifteen, then," said the surgeon, shrugging. "Though I rob myself by the price, while it is no more than a hair of a bushy beard to one as rich as your honor."

"And how think you I became so rich?" retorted the wine-grower, though he gave a mollified chuckle and combed his fingers through his beard. "Not by paying bandit's prices. I'll give you five, and that's the end of it."

The silver was weighed out—with the surgeon's thumb upon the scales—and the winegrower took himself off. Across the street, a woman in the yellow-bordered robes of the *harimate*, lowest class of sacred prostitutes, stepped from a doorway into his path. As the winegrower stood, grinning down at her, she moved her hand slowly up his arm and into his beard, tilting her unveiled head up to whisper in his ear. He laughed and beckoned her to follow him.

The surgeon snorted; an old song-seller sitting in an archway nearby beat on his little copper drum and in his thin, high voice made free gift of wisdom:

"Marry thou not a harimatu, *whose husbands are innumerable;
In thy misfortune she will not succour thee . . ."*

"Save your effort, friend," remarked the surgeon as the two vanished in the crowd. "She will extract the hairs of his fine beard one by one, and his shekels with them. Ah, well, there is no fool like a rich one. . . ."

Humming under his breath, he cleaned the slave's blood from his sharp little knives and settled himself to wait for the day's next customer.

Over the crowded street bright Shamash mounted higher and ever hotter, as the morning wore slowly on toward noon.

2.

In the School for Scribes which nestled in Etemenanki's shadow, close against the Temple Enclosure's walls, Thoth bent over his work, his tongue clenched firmly between his teeth and his fingers tight about his reed stylus.

From the street outside, a light, hot wind drifted over the courtyard walls, stirring the dried palm fronds that shaded and sketchily roofed the portion of the court that served as school-room, and bringing with it a medley of familiar sounds and odors to the dozen-odd restless boys who sat on the rows of mud-brick benches, working over their slabs of moistened clay. The smell of dust and refuse, of fish drying in the sun, of rank canal water and fresh, earthy clay all mingled in the sleepy noonday heat of Babylon. Thoth, absorbed in his work, noticed none of it.

He was writing, *Pay heed to the word of thy mother as to the word of thy god.* The face of Nanai, his foster mother, flashed through his mind as he wrote the words, and the ironic tone of her voice. He wrote, *Revere thy older brother. Anger not the heart of thy older sister,* and other faces appeared—the supercilious one of his brother Egibi, the blinking, sleepy one of his married sister Ili-imdi—both wearing appropriately smug expressions and shaking a finger at him. He made a preoccupied mouth at them and went on with his work. These admonitions to obedience were far from new to him; he had heard them so many times from every member of his foster family that he could have reeled off a dozen more like them without stopping to take breath. But the task of putting them into writing was still new enough to require his closest attention, and he chewed his tongue in his anxiety to do it well.

Finishing the third sentence, he straightened with a sigh and shook his cramped hand while he compared the little wedge-shaped marks on his side of the clay tablet with the far more perfect ones his teacher had made on the left-hand side for him to copy. His looked a little straggly, but he had formed them correctly this time . . . no, there in *brother* he had left out one of the little wedges in the last syllable. Scraping the place smooth with the edge of his stylus, he started to correct the word, then stopped and frowned at the tip of his reed. Taking his knife from his wide belt, he carefully reshaped the end of the stylus into a sharper triangle, then tried it again on the clay. Ah, better! The wedges were clear and perfect now, almost as good as Scribe Inatsil's sample. Encouraged, Thoth bent over his tablet again.

Workmen without a foreman are waters without a canal inspector. . . . Be thou obedient to those who instruct thee, and abide by their decisions.

A shadow fell across his tablet and he looked up to find the scribe Inatsil leaning over him.

"Very good," the teacher approved, nodding, and Thoth flushed with pleasure. "Your wedges are a trifle crowded here"— a long forefinger touched the clay—"and you have written the sign for 'utterances' incorrectly, it should have three oblique wedges, not two . . . but on the whole you have done very well. If you were a bit older, I would say you were ready for the story of Gilgamesh, but it is difficult."

"I am old enough, Master," Thoth said eagerly. "I am eleven."

"Eleven?" Inatsil raised his busy eyebrows in surprise and stared at Thoth. "You look nearer nine."

The pleasure dimmed; Thoth made his face expressionless. He knew an excellent way of replying to such remarks, but unfortunately one could not rub one's schoolmaster's nose in the dust as one did one's schoolmates'. However, the scribe evidently realized he had trod on a sensitive toe. He said hastily, "No matter, we may try you on Gilgamesh tomorrow in any case. Long legs have nothing to do with long wits, and I see your ears are of excellent size. What was your name again, boy? Tot? Doth?"

"Thoth," said Thoth automatically. The master could never remember any of the boys' names, no matter how often he was reminded.

"Ah, yes. You are the son of the potter Ibhi-Adad, are you not?"

"Aye, Master." As usual Thoth found himself adding, "His adopted son," and wondering, also as usual, why he alone in all of Babylon should feel there was something shameful in knowing neither mother nor father of his own.

Inatsil's eyebrows had flown up again. "Adopted? Yet you study to be a scribe, and not a potter?"

"Mine was not an apprentice-adoption, Master," explained Thoth, who had expected the question and salvaged some pride in answering it.

At least I have that, he thought as the scribe nodded and moved on, leaving him to his work. Adoptions were common in Babylon; most were aimed at acquiring workmen for the foster-father's trade. Thoth's had been quite another sort, as his foster-mother Nanai had made clear to him. Long ago, when caravan men had brought him to the potter's house, they had also brought a sum in silver as fair exchange for the inheritance portion he would henceforth be entitled to as Ibhi-Adad's legally adopted son.

"You were sent to me by Lord Ea the Wise One," the potter always told him, and Thoth was fairly well convinced by now that it was true, for everything fitted like the pieces of a puzzle. Before he had appeared, Ibhi-Adad had been deeply in debt. In despair, he had written a letter to his personal goddess, Nibada, begging her to go to the great god Marduk, who for her sake might go to his even greater father, Ea the Remote and Wise. And behold, only five days later had come the caravan men with Thoth and the silver, which had been sufficient to pay all Ibhi-Adad's debts. Obviously, it was the goddess Nibada's answer to his plea for help.

"You can see," the potter often told Thoth, "how wise is the man who is ever a good and obedient servant to his god, for when trouble strikes, that man has a protector."

It was true, Thoth could see it plainly. He also saw plainly that he himself was neither more nor less than the instrument of great Ea's mercy. There was no other way to explain any of it—especially the part about the silver. Thoth knew *he* had never owned so great a sum of silver—yet when the men offered him to Ibhi-Adad for adoption, they had offered the silver too, as if it had belonged to him. Obviously the silver was the crux of Ea's plan. No doubt he had leaned down from heaven and plucked it from under the nose of some puzzled treasure-house guard, just as he had leaned down to pluck Thoth from under the noses of those dim, beloved figures of another life—Ahmose, Lady Shesu—and send him on his long journey across the desert. Thoth's few memories of that journey were confused and broken, like snatches of a nightmare, but sometimes a chance sound or smell could bring them suddenly back to him. When a caravan wound into Babylon, the *ting, ting, ting* of the donkey's bridle bells was enough to turn him cold inside and make him hurry out of earshot. It seemed to him the loneliest sound in the world, that little tinging; it filled his mind with the echo of an old, weary question— *Where are we going? Please, please, where are we going?*

Well, he knew now where he had been going—here, to the City of God on the banks of the Euphrates, sent by Ea the Wise One that Ibhi-Adad might pay his debts. The plucking of a child from Egypt and of silver from a treasure house, the terrible journey —all this had happened for the sake of a humble potter of Babylon.

Thoth chewed the tip of his stylus, and his eyes clouded with thought. That was the thing he did not understand—that all had

209

been done for Ibhi-Adad. Why was the comfort of Ibhi-Adad so much more important than that of the child who had been stolen, or the unknown parents who had lost him? Surely his Egyptian father and mother must have grieved sorely for him, just as he grieved for them sometimes even now, though he no longer had the faintest recollection of who they were. When he first came to Babylon he had had some childish notion that his real father was a king, and that he had once played in the garden of a beautiful palace and eaten off dishes of gold. He flushed to remember it. How quickly—and rudely—he had been disembarrassed of that idea by the jeering laughter that had greeted it on every side. Now, of course, he could see what a ridiculous notion it had been, but at first he had believed it honestly and the laughter had hurt like knives thrusting into him. Months later, when he had more fully mastered the strange hissings and mutterings of the Babylonian tongue, Nanai, who at first had added her tinkling laughter to the rest, explained his mistake to him gently.

"It was only natural you should think some such thing, little one," she said, with her odd, twisted smile. "To the happy child, his father is always a king and his mother a queen, and even the poorest house a palace. No doubt your parents were good and gentle people, obedient to the law and respectful to the god of their fireside. And that is almost as fine as being a high priest or a king."

Then why, he had asked her, if his parents had been so good, so obedient, had their little son been torn from them in order that a stranger in a foreign land called Ibhi-Adad might pay his debt? It did not seem fair.

Nanai's ironic laugh had tinkled out again. "You expect life to be fair? Goodness to be rewarded? *Hai,* there speaks the know-nothing child! Sad it is that we cannot all be children, believing the world a bright place and our fathers kings! When I become an *edimmu* I'll try not to haunt you for those words, my Thoth!"

Laughing harder than ever, she had gone away quickly to her chamber, leaving Thoth conscience-stricken and downcast to think he had clumsily reminded her of her trouble. Life had dealt cruelly with Nanai, and death would deal more cruelly yet—all through no fault of hers. She was wise, kind and good—but she was barren, so when death claimed her she would unfailingly become one of the malevolent *edimme,* to spend all eternity working evil on mankind and haunting them day and night.

There was but one small comfort. She had owned her own slave woman when she married Ibhi-Adad, and this woman, Ahata, had borne the potter two children in her mistress' place, saving Nanai the disgrace of being cast out or superceded by another wife. Legally Egibi and Ili-imdi were regarded as Nanai's children, not Ahata's. But it was not the same, not to Nanai; Thoth could see that in her every glance and gesture, hear it in her too-frequent laughter and the very tones of her voice. Moreover, the legal solution of the problem could not change the doom death held for her, which was the thing she dreaded most and therefore laughed at oftenest.

Thoth sighed as he nibbled his stylus. Now that he was older he knew that Nanai was only one of many whose lives were harsh and cruel through no fault of their own. Think of the floods and the whirling winds that swept away people, crops, houses, and even whole towns in one terrible hour; think of the thousand ways a man might bring disaster on himself or his children by some unknowing offense against the gods—even though he had spent his whole life earnestly avoiding the thousand offenses he did know about.

It was hard, very hard, to understand the ways of the gods. Perhaps it all seemed fair to them, as Ibhi-Adad said, but Thoth could not grasp it, and neither could Ibhi-Adad, for that matter. He had admitted as much. The words of Gilgamesh were true, man was a paltry thing, his days were numbered and whatever he might do he was as wind—

The schoolmaster's low chuckling brought Thoth back to the present and a guilty knowledge that he had missed something that was said to him.

"I crave pardon, Master—I—I did not hear—"

"Small wonder." Inatsil waved a long-fingered hand, still laughing a little. "Such powers of concentration are sure to make you a good scribe, my boy—if applied to the proper lesson. What were you thinking of so hard?"

"Oh—I—many things," mumbled Thoth, conscious of his schoolmates' giggles. "Of the tale of Gilgamesh I am to copy tomorrow."

Inatsil glanced at a set of tablets stacked against a wall, then at Thoth again with a gleam of curiosity in his eyes. "So you have taken the hero's words to heart? 'Man is as wind—' You are young to pay heed to such despairing wisdom—yet it is wisdom all the same, one may as well accept it soon as late. 'He who lives today dies before tomorrow'—harsh but true. Well, my young philosopher, will it please you to set it down on clay? If so, make ready for dictation."

That was the order he had not heard; he saw now that the others had put away their copying tablets and were awaiting the master's signal. Hastily Thoth scraped his side of the clay slab smooth, leaving the teacher's sample for someone else to copy tomorrow, and rose with the rest to file toward the supply bench in the shadiest corner of the little courtyard. The boys stacked their tablets, one on another, between folds of damp cloth which would keep the writing surface moist, and each dug a handful of fresh clay out of the bin. Thoth took a good big handful and kneaded it well as he walked back to his seat.

"Wait for me afterwards. We'll walk home together," Kalba whispered as they passed each other.

Thoth nodded, and grasping his lump of clay firmly in his left hand, he thumped it on his bench until one side was flat and smooth. Then he picked up his stylus again. Only a little dictation, and school would be over for the day.

"We will write proverbs," Inatsil announced, raising his voice in order to be heard over the clamor of thumpings. "Ready with your reeds, we are going quickly today. First proverb! 'He who is alive today dies before tomorrow.' Next! 'A man must wholeheartedly obey the command of his god.' . . . Here! You on the first bench—you have written 'obey' incorrectly. *Two* diagonal wedges, mind you remember. All of you, do you hear? 'Obey,' 'obedience'—those are the most important words in the tongue of man . . ."

The teacher's voice droned on in his usual rambling mixture of instruction, dictation, admonition and soliloquy. Half an hour later he clapped his hands in dismissal and the boys, released at last, hurried past the clay bin and out the courtyard gate into the street. Thoth was about to fling his wad of clay into the bin after the others when Inatsil stopped him.

"Stay—let me see yours."

Dropping out of line, Thoth handed over his lump, the flattened side of which was now covered with the incised wedges of Babylonian writing. The scribe studied it and nodded. "Eleven, you say? It is very good. You may copy the tale of Gilgamesh tomorrow, boy— What was your name again?"

Thoth told him automatically, casting a longing glance toward the courtyard gate, through which the last of his fellow pupils was bounding to freedom. He hoped Kalba would wait for him; his stomach was growling with hunger, and Kalba always had bread or date cakes secreted somewhere about his pudgy person.

"Ah, yes. Thoth. An odd name."

"It is Egyptian, Master."

"Is it, indeed!" The scribe's bushy eyebrows flew up; he seized Thoth's shoulder and peered eagerly into his face. "Are you Egyptian, then?"

"Aye."

"By Marduk's ears! Think of that! How came you here, boy? No matter, no matter, tell me one thing only! Can you write the Egyptian tongue?"

"Nay, I—I cannot," Thoth faltered, startled by the other's excitement. "I never learned the signs—I was very young. It was very long ago."

"Aye, of course." Inatsil sighed, settling back against the clay-bin and folding his arms resignedly. "It is always so. Ah, would that Great Lord Marduk might someday see fit to send me an Egyptian scribe—just one, just a stupid one, I do not ask a scholar. A mere schoolboy would do so long as he could teach me to write and read the little pictures— That is the way Egyptians write, you know, in rows of charming little pictures on scrolls and stones."

Unexpectedly, the words flashed light into Thoth's mind and illumined a memory, small and clear and perfect. There was a sunlit column with rows of little pictures carved around it; three of them—a lady and a calf and a falcon—seemed always cut in half by the column's curving. Where had that column been? He had known it well, once, long ago . . . there was a man always standing by it, wearing strange garb but holding a spear straight up beside him as did the sentries at the gates of the king's palace here in Babylon.

"Aye, I remember the pictures," he said slowly. "Though I remember very little. I doubt I could even speak the tongue now, it has been so long. . . . Why do you wish to read the picture-writing, Master?"

"Why, because I do not know how!" answered Inatsil as if it were the most obvious reason in the world. "Because the pictures speak and I cannot hear. For him who can read, all doors swing open. I do not like to have one closed to me."

"Aye, I understand," Thoth said softly. He was deciding that he liked his schoolmaster very much indeed. He wished he knew just a few of the little pictures to teach Inatsil. Then in a sudden flash, he knew he did. "Master!" he blurted. "I think I can show you some of the pictures—just one little phrase."

"You can? Then show me, show me—here, take clay and stylus!"

Thoth obeyed, suddenly self-conscious because he was not entirely sure he could do it. The reed, with its triangular tip, would make nothing but wedges; he had to sharpen it to a fine point before he could trace the fluid curves of Egyptian hiero-glyphs, and when he held out his work a moment later he was ashamed of its crudity. It looked little enough like the delicate tracings on the prow of his little galley—tracings he had seen there and caressed, with both fingers and eyes, a thousand times without realizing until now that they spelled the galley's name.

"I think—I am sure—that says 'ka suwy,' which means 'the wild bull,' " he said.

"The wild bull!" the scribe echoed in tones of pure delight. "Now think of that! Where did you learn it? How did you happen to remember?"

"Well, I—I just . . ." Inatsil was not listening, he was digging in the bin for a lump of clay to practice on. Relieved, Thoth let his answer trail away. He liked Inatsil very much, very much indeed. But there were some things a person could not share with anyone, and the little galley was such a thing. Only when he was alone at bedtime, after closing his door tight, did he take it out, raise and lower its little sails, and fondle its wooden sailors one by one as he yearned for an Egypt he did not even remember. Then he hid it away safe again in his clothes chest, where it lived beneath his tunics and shirts, and only then unlocked his door. The thought that Egibi might stray in some night and see it was a thought not to be borne.

He did not mind giving Inatsil the words "ka suwy," so long

as he did not have to explain how he came to know them. That was the galley's name, *The Wild Bull*—so much Thoth would never, never forget, for Ahmose had told him. Ahmose had been captain of a ship just like it when he was young.

Seeing that Inatsil had quite forgotten him—the scribe was hunched over his table copying the pictures, his bearded face absorbed and happy as a child's—Thoth moved quietly toward the gate. He wished he could remember more about Egypt, about a beautiful garden he had known once, about Ahmose and Lady Shesu, and who they were. Sometimes he wondered if they could have been his parents, but he did not think so, for Ahmose was an old, old man, and Lady Shesu beautiful and young, the loveliest lady in the world. He was almost sure she wore a diadem, too, like a queen or a princess . . . There was that ridiculous idea of his again! Something was always swimming up from the depths of his mind that seemed to substantiate it—like that column with its sentry he had recalled a few minutes ago. Surely only palaces had sentries, only queens wore crowns? It was very aggravating, not being able to remember. Egibi could easily remember things that had happened when he was five or six years old, and so could Kalba and the others. Thoth could muster only scraps and flashes from those years before he crossed the desert into Babylon; even the faces of the caravan men were lost in confused recollections of loneliness and fright. It was as if that long and terrible journey had torn a great rent in the fabric of his life, one that could never be mended, one that separated him from those early years as if they had never been. He had only the galley to prove he had not lived all his life in Babylon.

Emerging from the courtyard into the brassy glare of the street, Thoth saw Kalba still waiting for him.

"At last!" exclaimed the fat boy, shoving his ample figure away from the wall and coming toward Thoth. "I thought you meant to chatter all day with Old Dog-Face."

"I thought *he* meant to," said Thoth, adding thoughtfully, "We shouldn't call him Old Dog-Face, though. He is not so bad—in truth, I think I like him very much."

"All right, but the name fits him, all the same. Here, have a date cake—er, what was your name again, boy? Tot? Doth?"

Kalba's mimicry was at once so cheerful and so accurate that

Thoth could not help laughing. He bit gratefully into the cake, which was a bit squashed from nestling in Kalba's straining sash all morning, but good nonetheless.

"My thanks, friend. Let's be off."

Dodging a squealing donkey cart with the agility of long practice, the two boys started along beside the high wall of the Temple Enclosure toward home. After the filtered light of the courtyard, the sun was mercilessly brilliant, beating down on whitewashed walls and the clouds of ever-present dust and the vivid garments of slaves and beggars and donkey drovers and canal men among whom they threaded their way. Two streets off, the Euphrates flashed blindingly through a gap in the buildings. Ahead, Etemenanki's seven gigantic stairsteps—the first painted white, the next scarlet, then black, white, flame, silver and gold —climbed in a crescendo of color to the sky. Thoth shot a sundazzled glance toward the lofty pinnacle, where he could just glimpse the golden shrine that crowned it, and marveled as he always did that men could build such a wonderful thing with their hands and their puny little tools. Why, that shrine far above there had its roof in heaven itself, or so near it that the gods sometimes came down and walked about the porches. Imagine —if one should climb all those ramps and tilting runways to hide at the very top, one might see Ea and Enlil and Anu, and silvery Sin, the moon, with his children Shamash the sun and Ishtar the lovely lady of the star, all strolling about and holding counsel together—

A figure stepped out of a doorway, and Thoth jolted back to the present as he fetched up with a bump against his sixteen-year-old brother, Egibi.

"Where have you been all this time?" Egibi demanded crossly, pushing Thoth away. "The other pupils came by long ago."

"I couldn't help it, Inatsil kept me."

"He kept you? Why? Have you been disgracing my father with poor work?"

Thoth bit back an angry retort, remembering in time that one must revere one's older brother. "Nay," he said gently. "The scribe praised my work—and commented on the size of my ears."

Egibi, who had very small ears indeed, flushed crimson. "So say you," he jeered.

"It's true, I was there and heard him," put in Kalba.

Egibi stared loftily at him and decided to change the subject. "Be that as it may. I have an errand for you." Fishing in his sash, he drew forth an earring. "Here. My mother bids you take this to Murashu to have it mended. The jewel needs replacing."

Nanai is more my mother than yours, slave's son! said Thoth in his mind. Aloud, he muttered, "I'll wager she bade you take it yourself."

"And I bid *you*. I have other things to do."

"I, also! I've been in school all day, and my stomach is emptier than an apprentice's head."

"I can't help that. Here, take it and be gone."

Tossing the trinket so casually that Thoth had to scramble to catch it, Egibi made off down the street, leaving his young brother muttering his exasperation to empty air.

"Brothers are a scourge of the gods," remarked Kalba sympathetically.

Thoth shrugged, looking at the earring, which he had often seen swinging against Nanai's smooth cheek, and led the way into the dusty, shop-crowded thoroughfare that edged the river. The fiery countenance of Shamash shone blindingly on the water. Shading his eyes, Thoth squinted up into the sky, remembering the curious idea he used to have that if he looked hard enough into that brilliant orb he would see his grandfather. His grandfather! In Ea's name, where had he picked up such a notion? It was the strangest of all the strange ones he had brought from Egypt. He was glad he had never mentioned it to anyone; folk would have thought he was trying to claim kinship with the gods themselves as well as with royalty! Not even royalty could claim that. The gods were the gods; men were only men, poor wretches. They were reminded of it every minute of every day.

"Yonder is the smith's quarter," remarked Kalba. "Murashu must be somewhere nearby."

Bringing his mind back to the business at hand, Thoth glanced around him. They had already passed through the Market of the Weavers and Embroiderers; the solid line of booths hung with the magnificent fabrics of Babylon had now given way to a series of river wharfs, beyond which lay the next market and the workshops of the smiths. At the nearest dock the boys stopped to watch the unloading of two slabs of stone—a rare commodity in Babylon. An escort of twelve Kassite soldiers was forming around the hauling cart to conduct the precious blocks to their destination.

Thoth looked curiously at the soldiers' Elam-styled tunics with their long tight sleeves and many-colored shawls, so different from the fringed Babylonian garments. Kassites had ruled Babylon for two hundred years or more, but in everything except dress, the "foreigners" had by this time become more Babylonian than the Babylonians.

All the same, reflected Thoth, it is a shameful thing for a land to be ruled by outsiders. Then he wondered how he was so sure of that. Perhaps Ahmose had told him? Or perhaps that other, even dimmer figure from the past, whose weary voice he heard in his ears sometimes but whose face he never saw—the one he always thought of as the Lonesome Man.

Turning away from the soldiers and the high-wheeled cart, he looked around for Kalba. In a moment he spotted the fat boy pushing hastily toward him through the crowd, which was beginning to drift back to its sundry occupations.

"Ho, Thoth! Do you know what someone yonder was saying a minute ago? There were Egyptians here yesterday."

"Egyptians? Where?"

"Here, in the market place! A great throng of them, a score or more, so that man yonder in the yellow sash was saying—and not traders, either, but men of importance, with great jeweled collars and haughty ways, and soldiers with them . . . only a few soldiers, like a guard—and other men carrying a wonderful little chest made of wood and ivory, so beautiful no one had ever seen its like, and other things done up in wrappings of linen . . . a long string of these porters, each bearing something, as if they were bringing gifts to the king. There was a huge black man walking at the head of all, carrying a staff made of pure gold with a golden falcon at the top."

Thoth was already peering frantically around him, wild to have a glimpse of real Egyptians.

"Did they all go away, Kalba? Where were they marching, toward the king's palace?"

"Doubtless. The man did not say which way they went or whence they came, only that they were here."

"Let us find Murashu. Perhaps he saw them."

Thoth darted away like a mosquito, Kalba puffing along behind him. A few minutes later they burst into Murashu's tiny workshop, babbling questions.

"Hold, hold, Master Thoth, your words are like bees, swarming all together . . . Ah, the Egyptians? Aye, I saw them." Murashu put aside his work, smiling at another spate of eager questions. "Aye, I saw them plainly—if Egyptians they were," he went on in his deep, quiet voice. "And I think they could have been no other, for they were beardless and their eyes were painted. There were many of them—thirty, perhaps forty. And their jewels—*Aii!* We know naught of jewelry-making here. We are as infants, we are as the clumsiest of apprentices! The great Negro in the lead—he wore a necklace of silver and greenstones, each link of which was a masterpiece, both of craft and design. . . . And there were bracelets of gold, shaped like serpents, shaped like coils of rope—"

"Which way did they go?" interrupted Thoth impatiently. "Where are they now?"

"Who knows?" said Murashu with a shrug and another smile. "They went toward the king's palace, I think. Perhaps they are still there."

"What could they be doing there?" said Kalba.

Thoth was staring in the direction of the palace. Perhaps if he went there and hung about before the gates, he might see them coming out. But Nanai would be wanting him at home— Suddenly he remembered the earring and dug it out of his sash.

"My mother wishes this jewel replaced, Murashu. Can you do it now, or—"

"Let me see it." The slave took the trinket in his big, deft hand and examined it with maddening deliberation.

"I could come back for it," Thoth offered eagerly, thinking, If I ran *very* fast to the palace, and *very* fast back again . . .

But Murashu had already picked up his little pliers. "No need. It will take but a few moments."

He set to work in his deliberate, placid way, every movement effective. Giving up all hope of seeing the Egyptians, Thoth wandered disconsolately into the back of the workshop.

Presently he beckoned Kalba to a little metal barrel pierced lengthwise with a rod, to one end of which was affixed a handle roped to a treadle.

"You see, Murashu can pull it up beside him and turn it while he works," Thoth said, putting his foot on the treadle and setting the barrel to revolving briskly. A muffled clattering noise resulted.

"But what is it for? What's rattling inside?"

"The gems."

Thoth halted the barrel and opened a little door in it. Reaching inside, he drew out a handful of the semiprecious stones used most commonly in jewelry, with a few rubies and bits of coral mixed with them. Some were of irregular shapes, with sharp edges, just as they had come out of the quarries; but the ones which had been longest in the barrel had been rounded and polished by the continual friction against each other until they shone smooth and lustrous in Thoth's palm.

"Ohhh!" said Kalba in admiration. "By the god of my fireside, they look good enough to eat!"

Murashu's soft voice cut through Thoth's laughter. "I am ready to set the gem, Thoth. Find me a greenstone to match that in the other earring."

Thoth reached into the barrel again, picked out several turquoises, and squinting in an effort to remember the exact coloring of the earring's mate, finally chose a round bluish stone. A few moments later the mended earring was safe in his belt and the two boys were on their belated way home.

Thoth bade farewell to Kalba at the latter's house and walked swiftly to the next corner and around it into his own street. It was narrower than Kalba's, with its long row of dwellings set so close together that their blank front walls, pierced only by doors, gave the street the appearance of a whitewashed canyon.

The eighth door was Ibhi-Adad's. Its frame was painted red, as were most of the others, to keep out devils, but in addition it boasted some little designs in green and blue, and the picture of a jug as a sign of the potter's trade. Thoth opened the door, walked through the dim gloom of the passage and emerged into the courtyard around which the house was built. Ibhi-Adad's old dog, Kiag, struggled up from the cool spot beside the water jar and padded forward to meet him, his tongue hanging out with the heat but his big mastiff face wrinkled into what Thoth always insisted was a smile.

"*Aii,* they judged right when they named you Faithful, old

one," Thoth said to him, rumpling his ears affectionately. "Go back to your napping, you have done your duty now."

"Is it you, Thoth?" called Nanai's voice from somewhere in the upper story.

"Aye, my mother. I have your earring that Murashu mended."

Thoth rummaged in his sash, his eyes searching the balcony which ran all around the four sides of the courtyard. Nanai appeared presently from one of the upper rooms which opened off it, and stood leaning on the railing, looking down at him.

"*You* have the earring? But I bade Egibi take it."

"Aye, and he bade me." Thoth found the trinket and held it up. "Shall I bring it to you?"

"Nay, I am coming down. That boy!" added Nanai angrily as she walked with her light, quick steps along the balcony and down the staircase at the corner of the courtyard. "You should have had your bread and cheese an hour since—I'll wager the front of your sash is rubbing against your backbone by this time!"

"Nay, I was with Kalba," Thoth explained with a grin, handing her the earring and moving to the great water jars half sunk in the hard earthen floor of the courtyard to get himself a drink. Nanai's laughter rippled after him.

"Ah, then you were saved! This Kalba, where does he carry so much food? It is well his sash is a broad one— Aye, that is very neatly mended, a good match for the other. Murashu is a fine workman. Ahata! Ahata! Come and make bread for the youngest son, he is home from his school. . . . Go now and greet your father, little one, then come back for your food. I will sit with you while you eat it."

"I will, but first I must tell you something! We heard in the market place, Kalba and I, that there is a great troop of Egyptians in Babylon. Murashu himself saw them yesterday as they walked among the shops—"

"Egyptians! A troop? Soldiers, do you mean?" exclaimed Nanai.

"Nay, nay, *amamu*, there were only a few soldiers with them, like a guard; they were peaceful men, and at their head was a giant black man in a wonderful necklace . . ."

Thoth rushed on, excitement growing in him again as he told about it, making the words tumble over each other. When he had described all he knew, Nanai stood bemused, one slim hand supporting the other elbow, a forefinger thoughtfully toying with her lower lip. How beautiful her eyes were, Thoth was thinking —light-brown, like honey—but always with the shadow of her trouble in them.

"Not soldiers, you say? Nor traders, either? Now why could they have come here?" she said.

"No one knows."

Pleased with the effect of his news, and eager to startle someone else with it as well, Thoth took a last hasty gulp from the long-handled terra-cotta dipper, returned it to its peg on the other side of the water jug, and darted off across the courtyard. Passing through the common room with its little altar for Nibada, he emerged through a door at its far side into the second part of the double house. This part was only one story high and was devoted entirely to Ibhi-Adad's trade. His kilns ranged along one end; new clay jugs and jars and platters and bowls and mugs stood everywhere, drying in the sun. In the center of all sat Ibhi-Adad at his wheel, his heavy, brooding, bearded face with its despairing but kindly eyes bent patiently over the new bowl which was spinning and taking form under his clay-smeared fingers.

"May Nibada guard your health, my father," Thoth said with the shyness he could never quite lose around this reserved, unsmiling man.

"And yours, Gift-of-Ea," returned the potter gravely. He raised his head and gave Thoth his usual scrutiny. "You were obedient in school today?"

"Aye, my father. Inatsil praised my work."

"That is good, my boy. But praise can be a demon's trap for the light-minded. See that it does not make you less diligent tomorrow."

"Nay, my father." Squirming inwardly with impatience, Thoth waited until Ibhi-Adad had completed the daily ritual of questioning him about his schoolwork. Then, eagerly, he told his news.

Ibhi-Adad's reaction was his habitual one of foreboding. His bushy brows drew closer and closer together over his somber eyes as Thoth talked, and at last he rose, cleansed his hands and started for the common room where the little altar stood.

"Go, eat your food, little one," he told Thoth. "I will mak

222

a small offering to Nibada to make sure no harm comes to our household from these Egyptians."

Leaving him still murmuring gravely to himself as he prepared his offering, Thoth returned to the other courtyard and Nanai, who had brought her embroidery to a chair beside the mat she had spread for him.

"Ahata, he is here," she called.

Thoth dropped down upon the mat and waited without speaking while Ahata set before him one of the short-legged tables upon which were cheese, onions, and the little thick pats of bread made by sticking pieces of dough to the inside of the hot oven. Thoth greatly preferred his bread in the flat, thin cakes, and he knew Ahata knew it, but he did not comment. It was only one of her ways of showing that she resented him and his presence in this house where her children had been sole heirs before his coming.

"Will you not eat, my son?" said Nanai. He turned to find her watching him with her twisted half-smile. "You do not like your bread cooked so, do you?" she added.

"Nay."

Her eyes flicked to Ahata's receding figure, then she shrugged and gave the shallow, careless laugh. "Eat it anyway, little one. It is better than the dust you will eat and the mud you will drink in that other place—the Land of No Return—" She straightened her slim shoulders abruptly and, turning back to her embroidery, began to work at it very fast, laughing again with determined gaiety. "Ah, well, this life is good sometimes, though the other one is not. Where can that Egibi have got to? It is time he collected the jugs for tomorrow's market. How came you to meet him? He did not go to your school?"

"Nay, he was waiting near Etemenanki. . . ." Between bites Thoth told her of their meeting, and why he had been late coming from school, and what Inatsil had said about his work, and everything else he could think of to keep the chatter going and help her flee once more from the dread that forever pursued her.

He was halfway through his meal when Egibi burst into the house, full of the news that Egyptians were in the city.

"I have told all about them," said Thoth imperturbably, enjoying the expression of chagrin on his foster-brother's face.

"You knew already?" Egibi cried.

"An hour ago. I heard about them in the market place."

"You *heard* about them! Ha! I *saw* them!"

"Saw them? Where? When?" Thoth leaped to his feet, the food forgotten.

"Only a moment ago! They are marching down the Avenue of Enlil, a great line of them, two by two, carrying a curious box and leading a white donkey all draped with golden cloth."

It was the first Thoth had heard about the donkey. The Avenue of Enlil—that was where Kalba lived, only two streets away!

Ibhi-Adad appeared in the courtyard, disapprovingly asking the reason for such loud voices. Leaving Egibi to explain, Thoth whirled to Nanai.

"*Amamu*—please—I could run there in only a moment and see them pass!"

"Aye, go, little one, of course you must go!"

He had no need of her affectionate shove to send his feet across the courtyard and into the passage as fast as they would carry him. In an instant he was in the street, running headlong toward the Avenue of Enlil. He had not covered a quarter of the distance before he saw the familiar pudgy form of Kalba, running equally fast toward him. They came together, breathless, each seizing the other to tug in opposite directions.

"Nay, this way, this!" panted Thoth. "The Egyptians—they are marching down the avenue—"

"That is why I ran! They have turned into this street now! Look behind me—can you see—I thought on your rooftop—"

Thoth stared in wild excitement. It was true, far down the street behind the puffing Kalba he could see figures in white, and something glittering in the afternoon sun.

"Quick, then! The roof is best, from the roof we will see everything!"

Back down the street they fled, into the house again and, panting out the new tidings as they ran, crossed the courtyard and scrambled up the ladderlike steps two at a time. Nanai and Egibi hurried after them, and Ibhi-Adad followed more slowly, muttering uneasily under his breath. "Now could this be an omen, their passing down our street? Surely not a bad one; Egyptians are good luck to our house, our little Thoth was the gift of Ea himself. Perhaps more good fortune will waft to our doorway as they pass by."

They did not pass by. Thoth, hanging precariously over the railing that edged the flat rooftop, saw the white-clad double line move closer and closer up the street, until he could pick out the gold necklaces and bracelets glittering on the first group, and the white donkey plodding in the midst of the second, and the wonderful box carried at the forefront of the third. There was the great black giant with his silver-and-greenstone necklace, walking alone at the head of all, with seven soldiers flanking him at either side. Outside the procession and yet apparently part of it, walked a single Babylonian—a man Thoth had seen sometimes in the potters' quarter of the markets along the wharf.

"It is Lugaldurdug!" exclaimed Egibi, lifting his voice over the excited chatter buzzing from every rooftop on the street.

The big Negro glanced casually upward toward the sound of the shout, and Thoth, who had just opened his mouth to cry out his own discovery of the crockery merchant, felt the words die on his lips. He had only a glimpse of the Negro's face, for the big man turned his head at once to glance up at another rooftop. But one glimpse was enough to make Thoth stare, transfixed.

Kalba, swinging around from the railing to point out some new excitement, stopped and peered curiously at him. "What happened to you? Did you see a demon?"

Thoth did not move, and for a moment could not answer. The stillness in him seemed to reach clear to his toes. "That man," he whispered. "I think—I knew him once."

"I know him too! It is Lugaldurdug, the—"

"Nay, I mean the Negro. The big man in the lead."

Kalba gaped from Thoth back to the black man, and suddenly went as still as Thoth. The talk ceased abruptly over the whole rooftop and those of the neighbors. The procession had reached a point opposite Ibhi-Adad's door—and stopped.

In the silence, Lugaldurdug's footsteps echoed on the dusty street, and his knock on the door sounded like a drum.

"My husband," Nanai whispered, shrinking back from the railing.

Ibhi-Adad had already started down the narrow stairs. The boys clustered about Nanai, who returned their looks of wild inquiry with one of her own.

"Let us go down to the balcony, *amamu!*" Thoth whispered.

"Aye!" Kalba urged. "We can hear from there—"

225

"And see just a little—"

"My mother and I will go," Egibi interrupted, pushing between Nanai and the younger boys.

"Nay, Thoth shall go if he likes!" Nanai said. "They are his countrymen, strangers or not. . . . Ah gods, I pray it has nothing to do with him!"

Thoth scarcely heard her, and was only dimly aware that she held him close before starting down the stairs. He followed in a turmoil of excitement, Kalba treading on his heels and breathing hard upon his neck.

"*Where* did you know him?" whispered the fat boy.

"I don't know—perhaps I will remember more—"

"*Hsst!* Be still!" Nanai said. "Come this way."

The slave woman, Ahata, had answered the knock; she fled out of the passageway just as Thoth reached the balcony above it, her eyes not downcast for once but bulging with astonishment. After her came Lugaldurdug, a bony, nervous little man. He paused jerkily to glance behind him, then hurried to Ibhi-Adad, who stood motionless in the center of the courtyard. There was an exchange of whispers; then Lugaldurdug drew aside, and Ibhi-Adad turned to face the doorway, bearded, somber, stained with clay, but with a dignity that made Thoth suddenly feel proud and glad.

The courtyard began to fill. First the big Negro, then one by one the men in the wide golden collars and gleaming armbands, after them the men with the wonderful box. Thoth forgot caution and hung over the balcony railing, staring. How curious they looked, without a beard among them!—like a crowd of boys, until one saw the furrows on this one's brow, the skinniness of this one's shanks. Their painted eyes shone like enamel and darted curiously this way and that as they filed into the courtyard, though their heads stayed arrogantly still. How black their hair was! Black as ebony, every shining head . . . or was it wigs they wore? Aye, it was! He could see the separate strands now, sewn down the part and cropped off sharp and neat across the brow and dipping low around the back of the neck . . . they must be hot things to wear! There was no denying they made the men look wonderfully trim and elegant, very different from the Babylonians with their tangled beards and shoulder-length

226

hair, whose elaborately fringed and colored draperies seemed suddenly a little tawdry beside the visitors' crisp white garb.

"Now who is that one, do you suppose?" Kalba whispered as a man carrying a strangely shaped little board came forward to a place beside the Negro.

Thoth shook his head dumbly. He watched the newcomer sit down cross-legged on the floor, swiftly remove lids from two little paint pots on the board, snatch a pointed reed from behind his ear and produce a roll of thin leather—and suddenly he understood.

"A scribe, Kalba!"

"Why, it cannot be! Where is his clay?"

"They do not use clay, and their writing is different, it is all little pictures—"

"*Hsst!* Be still, boys!" hissed Nanai.

They would have fallen silent without her warning, for apparently all who were intended to come into the house had now come in. Thoth realized, with disappointment, that both the soldiers and the donkey were to wait outside in the street; then he forgot all about them as the big Negro stepped forward to Ibhi-Adad, inclined his glossy wig in a bow of great dignity and spoke the first words of his harsh and guttural tongue.

The sounds fell on Thoth's ears like fragments of a long-forgotten song—confused and strange as yet, but drawing responsive echoes from some far, dim corner of his memory, long disused. Tears sprang to his eyes; he found himself trembling with the same sense of almost-grasped recognition he had felt when he saw the Negro's face.

"I do not understand your lordship," said Ibhi-Adad in a voice which quavered with anxiety though his face was as grave and dignified as ever. "But I trust you will do me the honor of accepting refreshment—Nanai, make haste."

Obviously the potter was grasping at any familiar thread which might guide him through the mazes of an unfamiliar situation. Whatever these foreigners might want, and however he might eventually be made to understand their wants, it could not be amiss to serve them wine.

Poor father! thought the boy, suddenly feeling so fierce and warm a loyalty that the Egyptians seemed almost enemies.

227

Apparently they had come prepared for the situation. Even as Nanai was hurrying down the stairs in response to her husband's summons, the scribe tucked his reed behind his ear again and rose to bow toward Ibhi-Adad.

"I offer my services as interpreter," he said in heavily accented Babylonian. "Your guests come from the City of God in the land of Egypt, being emissaries of the Great Horus who rules upon the throne of the Two Lands, to whom be life, stability, and welfare forever. He for whom I will be a mouth for you"—he bowed again, toward the Negro—"is Hereditary Prince, Count, Wearer of the Royal Seal, Sole Companion, Favorite of Horus, Lord of the Palace, the Royal Steward Nehsi, the revered—who says to you, May your house prosper."

He sat down cross-legged again, amid deep silence. For an instant no one moved. Then Nanai, transfixed on the stairs by the black man's reverberating list of titles, recovered the use of her limbs and hurried on; Ibhi-Adad, swallowing, recovered enough use of his voice to mutter "My house is honored," and Kalba and Thoth turned to stare at each other with wide eyes.

"You *knew* that great noble?" Kalba whispered incredulously.

"I must be mistaken," gasped Thoth. Again he turned to peer down at the top of the Egyptian's head—all he could see of him with any clarity. *Nehsi, Nehsi,* he repeated to himself. Is that his name? Only "The Negro"? Then he realized with a start that he had known the meaning of an Egyptian word. He began to listen to what Count Nehsi was saying, and before the interpreter had a chance to speak he had partially grasped the sense of it— something about joy and wine and house . . .

"My lord wishes me to inform you," interpreted the scribe to Ibhi-Adad, "that it gives him joy to accept the wine and hospitality of your house."

"I am beginning to understand!" Thoth whispered excitedly to Kalba. "Quick, let us creep down the stairs a way. I must be closer."

The two boys stole halfway down the ladderlike stairs and crouched there as inconspicuously as possible, staring at the copper-hued shoulders and shining wigs now almost within reach. Thoth's eyes were moving about eagerly, his ears straining to hear fragments of murmured conversation. He caught a whiff of an odor, faint and fresh, tantalizingly familiar, which he could not name.

More words were beginning to come back. He found one here, two there, suddenly clear and intelligible, and felt the gutturals form in a remembered way in his throat as he whispered them over to himself. "Sour stuff," he heard one man mutter to another, and with a shock of indignation he realized they were disparaging the wine. *And is your own so superior, Lord Arrogance?* he thought with sudden belligerence. He glared about him, listening suspiciously now, trying to watch all of them at once and follow the direction of every glance. Were they all making derisive remarks about Ibhi-Adad's wine, and maybe about his house and his clothes—oh, even about beloved, troubled Nanai, who looked pale and nervous as she filled their cups? They did not understand about her . . . cursed foreigners! Their manners did not match their jewels! Let them go away, then, out of Babylon, away, far away, back to their own land!

Thoth caught himself, dismayed. It was his land, too—or had been once. Aye, once. But he had been someone different then. It was his land no more; they were foreigners. They were sneering at his family and his home, and suddenly he hated them. He wished they had never come.

He turned blindly to Kalba. "Let us go up again—let us go—"

"Nay, why? I want to hear . . . *hsst!* It is too late now."

He was right. The ritual of the wine was finished; the Negro began to speak to Ibhi-Adad through the mouth of the scribe and the courtyard grew quiet. With what now seemed to Thoth the rankest hypocrisy, Ibhi-Adad was thanked for his hospitality, his excellent wine, his gracious welcome, and begged to accept a few tokens of Count Nehsi's and the Great Horus' appreciation, after which Count Nehsi prayed to ask the excellent potter a question or two. . . .

While the interpreter was still speaking, the bearers hurried forward and flung open the lid of the wonderful box before Ibhi-Adad. The Babylonians gazed openmouthed, the Egyptians with slit-eyed satisfaction, at the treasures within. There were three exquisite alabaster vases, a golden bowl, one of the broad collars of gold and carnelians, six vials of a heavy-scented ointment, and a bolt of linen so sheer one could see one's hand through it.

"Great Enlil's fingernails!" said Kalba in a choked whisper. "It is a fortune they bring your father!"

Thoth kept defiant silence. He was staring, too, he could not help it; surely no one had ever seen such things before save these rich and arrogant and condescending ones. He hated them nonetheless—the very richness of their gifts was a sneer thinly veiled, for these things so outshone Ibhi-Adad's possessions and his house that their effect could only be to humble and overawe him.

And they had done so; Thoth saw the look of a servant in the eyes Ibhi-Adad slowly lifted to the Negro's face.

"And the questions?" asked the potter almost inaudibly.

Count Nehsi watched him for a moment. Then he said through the interpreter, "Some years ago a boy was brought to you, whom you adopted to be your son. Is that boy still here?"

"Aye," answered Ibhi-Adad more softly still.

"I ask you to summon him."

Ibhi-Adad's eyes moved confusedly about the courtyard, raked the balcony, and found the two boys on the stairs. Every head turned to follow his gaze; Thoth, huddled against Kalba on the narrow steps, suddenly found himself the focus of a dozen pairs of painted eyes, sharp and piercing as so many arrows.

"Come hither, Thoth," the potter said gently.

At first Thoth felt that he could not swallow, then that he could not move. But somehow he found his knees straightening and his foot searching for the step below him.

Then a terrifying thing happened. Every Egyptian in the room, including the grand Count Nehsi, bent in slow, profound obeisance—to *him*. He stood paralyzed, looking wildly to Ibhi-Adad for guidance, which he did not find. The potter seemed to have turned to stone, and stood staring with bulging eyes at the rows of bent brown backs. The last thing he had said had been "Come hither." In the absence of a second command, one obeyed the first, no matter if the sky fell in the meantime. Somehow Thoth moved down the remaining stairs, between the sleek black wigs and across what seemed a hundred leagues of courtyard, hearing the slight rustle of linen as the men straightened up behind him, aware of their eyes following him and acutely, overwhelmingly aware of his own dusty feet and rumpled garments and tangled hair, uncombed since morning. Reaching the haven of Ibhi-Adad's side at last, he turned to see Count Nehsi straightening from his bow. For a long moment the two scrutinized each other in silence, while Thoth wished desperately that he were taller. There was no expression whatsoever on the big Negro's handsome countenance, nor in his voice when he spoke.

"Do you understand my speech?"

"A—little," Thoth whispered, but in Babylonian.

Nehsi waited for the interpreter, then said, "Do you remember me?"

Thoth swallowed. Another memory was stirring as he stared at the Egyptian's face. It seemed so foolish that he was ashamed to speak of it, but it was all he could think of, and he ended by blurting it out. "Did you give me a kitten once?"

For some reason the question seemed to disconcert Count Nehsi. He exchanged a swift, odd glance with one of the nobles standing nearby, and shifted on his feet. "I may have. I believe I did. You remember your early life, then? You know who you are?"

Thoth slowly shook his head.

"I see," Nehsi said heavily.

Nor does he want to tell me who I am, thought the boy suddenly. He does not like me. He does not like to be here, talking to me. Well, I do not like him either! He may go away, back across the desert, to where he came from! I'll ask him nothing, not a word.

But so many questions had clamored in his mind, these many years—and this was his only chance to have them answered.

"Was there—a garden?" he asked, very low.

"Do you remember a garden?"

"Aye—with a pool, and lilies, and shady trees. I think I played there."

"I am sure you did. I do not know which garden you remember, but there are many in the palace."

"The—palace?"

"The palace of your father, His Majesty the Strong Bull, the Horus of Gold, Ahk-kheper-en-Re Thutmose, Lord of the Two Lands, King and Pharaoh."

There was a ringing silence, in which the interpreter's rolling syllables seemed to echo on and on.

"My father—is a king?" Thoth whispered.

"Aye. You are His Highness Men-kheper-Re Thutmose,

Prince of Egypt." Count Nehsi drew a long breath and cleared his throat while the scribe changed the words to Babylonian.

Thoth wished just one thing would begin to seem real to him, so he would know he was not dreaming. He felt he should say something, Nehsi was waiting, looking at him—everyone was looking at him.

"At first," he said, in a strange, quavery voice that sounded nothing like his own, "when I first came here—long ago—I remembered my father was a king."

He felt himself flush as soon as the words were out—first because his voice sounded so queer, next because it seemed a silly thing to say. While the interpreter was translating he became aware of a curious tension that passed like a ripple over the nearest Egyptians. Because of something he had said? He was instantly wary again; his eyes flashed back to the Negro, to find his features more expressionless than ever.

"Do you know how you came here?" Nehsi murmured.

"Aye. The caravan men brought me." In truth, Ea had brought him, Thoth knew that very well. He had no intention of saying so to these foreigners who might not even know who Ea was.

Nehsi nodded as the interpreter spoke, and the tension in the courtyard subtly relaxed. "Your Highness was stolen out of Egypt by—unknown enemies," said the Negro rapidly. "Many searches were made, to no avail. These years have brought changes to Egypt; your father Pharaoh lies ill, very ill. He has commanded me to search once more, to find Your Highness and bring you back to Egypt. Now by the aid of Amon the Hidden One all shall be as His Majesty has commanded." Nehsi paused, waited impassively for his words to be translated, then clapped his hands together. Four men dressed in plain linen came from the back of the courtyard and knelt before Thoth. "These are your slaves, which His Majesty your father has sent to you. If there is anything you wish to take from this land, bid them fetch it. We must depart as soon as Your Highness is ready."

"I am—to leave Babylon?" Thoth said in strangled tones.

"Of course. At once."

"But—I do not—want to leave."

For a moment the interpreter stared at him as if he could not bring himself to translate. When he did so at last, every painted

232

eye in the courtyard widened incredulously, and there was a buzz of muttered indignation which Nehsi had to lift his hand to quiet. He was staring at Thoth coldly.

"Pharaoh has commanded it," he said.

Thoth clenched his teeth a little more tightly together. This was an enemy, this Nehsi; to give way to tears or fright or bewilderment or anger before him could not be thought of. But there was one thing he knew he wanted; from the swimming chaos which seemed to have taken the place of his brain only one way to get it emerged with any clarity—a way too unbelievable to accept without making very sure he was not dreaming.

He took a long breath and plunged. "I am . . . a prince, you say?"

"You are."

"Am I . . . *your* prince? Must you obey me?"

There was another stir. Thoth did not heed it, but kept his eyes firmly on the Negro's face. It remained impassive save for a faint smile.

"Unless you ask me to disobey my Pharaoh's orders. Has Your Highness some command?"

There was a trace of irony in the words, and hidden anger; Thoth heard it but did not care. He gathered all his courage and tried to speak with equal calm. "Aye, I have." To his dismay his voice broke into a squeak on the last word. Furiously he shouted, "I wish you to go outside—all of you—and wait until I call!"

They won't do it, he thought. I've made myself ridiculous, they'll never do it. . . .

After a moment's hesitation Nehsi bowed and started for the door. The others followed. They did not want to, that was entirely clear. But they did it.

In a moment the courtyard around Thoth was empty, save for Kalba, still huddled on the stair, Egibi, transfixed above him on the balcony, Ahata and Nanai standing like statues near the sunken water jars, and Ibhi-Adad, equally motionless before his treasure-heaped box.

Thoth whirled to him, eyes stinging with the tears he would not allow himself to shed. "My father—must I go?"

For a moment the potter did not answer, but stood staring at Thoth as if he had not understood his words. At last he whispered, "Your father has commanded it . . . Your Highness."

Nothing could have cut Thoth adrift more cleanly and surely than to hear his father say "your father"—and call him by the strange title he himself had heard only today. The words made him a trespasser in the familiar courtyard. He turned slowly to Nanai, whose lips smiled a jerky attempt at comfort denied by her stricken eyes.

It was final, then. It did not matter whom he thought of as his father—both fathers had commanded the same thing. He must obey.

Numbly he set his feet in motion—across the courtyard, up the stairs. Kalba gazed at him respectfully as he passed, Egibi with open awe. Even if he stayed, nothing would be the same; he would be a stranger to them all forever, and they to him. He walked along the balcony longing for yesterday as for a lost and beautiful dream—the school, the dusty street and Kalba jesting with him, handing him a date cake, scuffling and racing and laughing, Inatsil droning out proverbs and forgetting names—it all seemed good now, even Egibi ordering him loftily on errands and Ahata cooking his bread wrong out of spite, and oh, Nanai, Nanai. . . .

He ran into his room, closed the door behind him, and stood miserable and alone against it. Never again would Ibhi-Adad turn slowly from his work, wiping clay-smeared hands, and question him concerning his studies and his deportment as a pupil, never again would he sit and chatter to Nanai until he saw the trouble clearing from her lovely eyes. . . .

Thoth straightened and crossed the room to his clothes chest. Burrowing beneath the clean garments he found the galley, and drew it out carefully. There it stood, on his two palms, rakish and beautiful as always, with its wonderful little carved men, and its masts and sails, and the pictures on its hull which spelled THE WILD BULL. With the sight of it the old dream returned, and the dim, beloved features of Ahmose, smiling at him.

I am a fool! he thought. What ails me, that I should feel this way? I am going back to Egypt, I shall see Ahmose, and Lady Shesu, and the garden . . . I am a prince, my father is a king, just as I told them!

Sudden joy rose and engulfed him. I shall see Ahmose! he thought. I shall see my father! I am going home!

234

Then, from below in the courtyard, he heard the strangled, heartbroken sound of Nanai's weeping, and Ibhi-Adad's deep voice as he tried to comfort her.

This was home.

Thoth pressed his forehead against the wooden hull of the little galley and let the tears he had withheld so long burst out at last. He did not know which was home, or where he belonged, or whom he loved the best. He knew only that he was being torn in two.

3.

It was the tenth day of the third month of the Season of Coming-Forth, by Egypt's reckoning—Thoth had lost track of time by Babylon's reckoning uncounted weeks before—when the *Star of the Two Lands* cast off her nightly mooring ropes for the last time and headed south upon the dawn-pinkened waters of the Nile. Today they would reach Thebes; by noon, the captain said. Thoth could scarcely believe it.

He had stationed himself as usual at the highest point of the poop deck, near the great stern sweep, to watch the sail climb slowly up the mast. Rib by rib it rose, like a gigantic fin, like a great white wing unfolding in the morning light. The cluster of straining brown bodies on the deck below seemed to have nothing to do with its majestic spreading. As it caught the southward-blowing breeze which had filled it day in, day out, all the way from the sea called the Great Green, the *Star* leaped forward with a creak of timbers.

Thoth spun around swiftly to watch the other sails rise. Trailing the *Star* across a stretch of glittering water came the *Golden Falcon*, after it the *North Wind,* and last of all, far back, the kitchen tender. One by one the square sails spread and filled, one by one the ships glided into midstream to align themselves in the familiar pattern which during the last weeks had become for Thoth the one unchanging thing in an ever-changing landscape, a fixed and steady image by which to orient the rest of the world.

Of course nothing was really fixed, nothing remained steady forever, as he used to believe—not even the ziggurat, which he had seen every hour of every day for years, towering above the roofs of Babylon, until he could not imagine the world without it. Wherever one went, whatever one did, there always were Etemenanki's seven mighty steps against the sky, the very shape and form of permanence. Yet Etemenanki had vanished now, out of his life; the sky was empty. By noon today this other permanence would dissolve too, the pattern of three white sails would vanish just as the ziggurat had vanished, just as the desert dunes had vanished, just as long ago the face of Ahmose had shatteringly vanished, leaving the world a chaos.

". . . The depth of a reed—and four cubits! . . . The depth of a reed—and five cubits! . . ."

With the melodic cries of the lookout taking soundings in the bow, the familiar music of a ship under sail started up around Thoth. Planks creaked, taut ropes sang, water hissed softly past the hull. At his elbow the great rudder sweep screeched rhythmically in its gunwale socket; high overhead and a little forward, where the sweep's tall-slanting shaft met the top of the rudder post, its lashings creaked in echo as they rubbed across the cow's horn which supported them. At the base of the post the steersman squatted beside the tiller with his back to Thoth and whistled softly to himself.

It was the last lap of a long, strange journey; one which had seemed so certainly endless that to think of its ending was the strangest part of all. It was hard to remember they had not been traveling always. The white donkey on which he had ridden out of Babylon now seemed to Thoth a creature in a distant dream. Surely it was years ago instead of months that he had looked out between those twitching white ears upon the unchanging wastes of the desert, where each day's landscape was that of the day before—dunes, rocks, sky and blowing sand—where the old, dim memories of fear and bearded riders came back with terrifying vividness sometimes with the sight of an outcrop or a distant palm. Yet the desert had finally ended in mountains, and the mountains in a city called Kadesh beside the river Orontes; suddenly there had been carts and people and houses, and women in strange tiered skirts, with little capes about their shoulders and their hair hanging down their backs in shining ropes.

Kadesh was a possession of Egypt, Nehsi had informed him. Long ago the Great Thutmose, Thoth's grandfather, had conquered these people. They had felt the might of Pharaoh and ever after had bent their necks, praising the glory of the Black Land and rejoicing in their good fortune to be the Strong Bull's vassals.

Thoth saw no bent necks and heard no rejoicing. He saw only inscrutable, hooded eyes and felt glances exchanged behind him as he passed. It was very uncomfortable.

However, he did not discuss this—or anything else—with Nehsi. Once, early in the journey, he had nervously gathered his still-fragmentary knowledge of Egyptian and asked Nehsi the question that was filling his heart and mind—"Do you know Ahmose?"

At first Nehsi could remember nothing of him—or said he could not. An old man, Thoth told him anxiously; very old—a warrior.

"Ah, *that* Ahmose," Nehsi said then. "He was once Father-Tutor to the princess, in her infancy. Count Senmut holds that post now. I have not seen old Ahmose for years."

"But—he still lives?" Thoth faltered.

"I really could not say, Your Highness," returned Nehsi distantly.

Thoth stared at him in silence, wondering if he were lying, feeling a new and terrible chasm beginning to open at his feet. He whirled away from the polite, closed faces of the nobles and went into his tent. Since then he had not asked them anything.

After Kadesh there were more mountains to climb—high, rugged places where the road sloped and twisted and led them through silent forests of cedar and up breathless heights and down into plunging, rocky valleys with cold little streams running through the bottom. At last the land leveled and they traveled across a broad brown plain and came upon Arvad in the land of the Dahi, on the shore of the Great Green.

In Arvad a strange thing happened to Thoth. Following Nehsi through the teeming market place he had seen a jumble of donkeys and baggage clustered about a group of hooded desert men, as a caravan made ready to depart. Suddenly a memory had come back clear and whole, the memory of a tall, silent black woman dropping his hand from her large, pink-palmed one and walking swiftly away from him, through a swarm of men and merchants and donkeys, and out of sight, leaving him crying and

237

alone. Ahbi, her name was; he remembered it at once, with hatred.

But in all his traveling across the desert and the mountains and the plains, retracing the steps of that different, younger Thoth, he found no other of the multiple threads of memory he had dropped there so long ago. The skeins were scattered, rotted away, lost forever. Apparently the great rent in the fabric of his life was not to be mended.

They stayed a restless week in Arvad, waiting for a ship to be made ready. When at last they walked down to the docks one morning Thoth was filled with admiration at sight of the huge, goose-necked galley which was to carry them across the sea from the Phoenician coast to the Delta. He climbed aboard eagerly, curious to explore every cranny of the decks and hold, impatient to set sail.

That the Egyptians felt differently was clear at once. Their gloom puzzled Thoth. Surely the spray, the salt breeze, the snapping of canvas, were a refreshing change from the dusty monotony of the caravan? As for the choppy waters all around, while they were obviously perilous they held no novel terrors for one who had grown up beside the treacherous Euphrates.

For the Nile dwellers, conditioned by a river whose astonishingly regular and beneficent habits sounded incredible to Thoth, the sea voyage was the most dreaded portion of the journey. They embarked with long faces and dark foreboding, each one clinging to his most potent amulet and muttering prayers and promises to Amon. The vessel was scarcely out of sight of land before most of them grew seasick. The nobles vanished into makeshift pavilions, leaving the slaves and bearers to huddle miserably nearby, retching and unstrung. The soldiers of the escorting guard, hardier but no less apprehensive, squatted here and there about the deck, continually burning little pellets of incense to the gods and straining their eyes for the first sight of land. Thoth was left to himself, with time on his hands and nothing to do except stay out of the crew's way and make a closer inspection of his fellow passengers.

It was his first chance to observe the soldiers, who had always marched some distance behind or ahead of him on the overland journey, and he studied them carefully, intrigued by their weapons—most of which he recognized from the miniatures in his

238

little galley—and puzzled by the fact that they all seemed to be calling on the same gods. In Babylon every man had his own god. Did these soldiers have only one or two to share among so many? He watched them with growing curiosity, wishing he dared ask.

There was one young soldier to whom his gaze kept returning —a handsome boy, not much older than Thoth himself, with alert dark eyes and a wide, extravagantly curved mouth. He seemed less terrified than the others; like them he burned incense and mumbled supplications, but the glances he shot at the fearful sea contained a good deal of lively interest. On the second morning, when Thoth's curiosity finally overcame his shyness, he approached this young soldier and attempted to strike up a conversation in his halting Egyptian.

At first he failed; the boy merely scrambled to his feet, looking startled at being addressed, and glanced uncertainly past Thoth's shoulder in the direction of the nobles' pavilions.

Speaking coldly to cover his embarrassment, Thoth asked, "Can you not understand my speech?"

"Aye, Your Highness, I understand it."

"Then why not answer? We might talk a bit—to pass the time."

The soldier hesitated, moistened his lips and colored to the roots of his hair.

"Oh, no matter, if you do not want to," Thoth said stiffly, and started to turn away.

The encounter might have ended right there, in a muddle of wounded pride and misunderstanding, had he not turned to see Nehsi almost at his elbow—a somewhat altered Nehsi, looking drawn, and leaning on an equally pallid slave, but no less formidable with authority all the same. He paused beside Thoth with a slight, formal inclination of his head.

"If Your Highness desires companionship, I shall be glad to summon one of the younger nobles. I believe Lord Wenamon is feeling somewhat better today—"

"I do not want Lord Wenamon," Thoth muttered.

"As you wish." Nehsi's voice was rigidly polite. He cleared his throat, and his eyes flicked to the young soldier and back again. "However," he added, "I must remind Your Highness of your position—to which you have not yet become accustomed, perhaps—and advise you against speaking with underlings, even in abnormal circumstances. On this wretched ship or off it, Your Highness is a prince, this fellow but an archer of the guard."

Thoth had been growing angrier by the moment, more on the defensive because he had again done the wrong thing, more humiliated by Nehsi's condescending tone. Scowling furiously because he was near to tears, he almost shouted, "If I am a prince, then I can speak to anybody I choose!"

"That is true, of course," Nehsi said coldly.

He hesitated an instant, then shrugged and proceeded along the deck without glancing at either boy again. Surprised and a little confused by his sudden victory, Thoth turned back to the soldier. "*Do* you want to talk to me?" he said bluntly.

"Aye," breathed the boy. He appeared surprised too, and his eyes were respectful, even admiring, as he studied Thoth. Slowly the corners of his mouth curled up in a shy, engaging grin. "I would like very much to talk with Your Highness."

Thoth's scowl faded into an answering smile, but as he led the way back to his favorite bench in the vessel's stern, he found himself shyer than the other. He had won his victory, but now he did not know what to do with it, and a self-conscious silence descended on the two. Thoth broke it finally by blurting, "Let me see your bow."

The boy handed it over with alacrity, offering an arrow as well. After a moment he ventured a few remarks on its construction and the best technique of aiming the shaft; before long Thoth was testing his own strength on it and wanting to examine the dagger as well. Gradually their awkwardness wore off, and the young soldier turned out to be a lively and garrulous companion. His name was Amenemheb, he told Thoth, but he was called Tjah, "The Fledgling," because he was the youngest soldier in the regiment. He was fifteen, son of a minor Theban judge, and on fire to be a captain of archers and win a great name for himself in battle.

"It is the only career I would choose," he confided, "though my father wished me to become a scribe. He says this is no time to be a soldier, if I wish to make anything of myself. No doubt he's right—there's small chance to win a hero's fame nowadays, with a woman ruling Egypt. The army rots in the barracks, week in, week out, without so much as one campaign these thirteen years to shake the kinks from their legs. Sometimes I wish I had drawn my lot for Nubia. They've had a few uprisings down there at any rate, and old Turo is commander. There's a hero for you! He served under the Great Thutmose, and saw action in as many campaigns as I have fingers. . . ."

"A woman rules Egypt?" Thoth repeated, not certain enough of his Egyptian to be sure he had heard aright. "I thought my father was Pharaoh."

Tjah spoke quickly. "Aye, he is, he is, Your Highness! Pharaoh and Lord of the Two Lands, great Horus himself. I—my tongue wags, I meant no—"

"You said a woman ruled Egypt," Thoth insisted.

"Aye, well, in a way—that is, in effect, she—" Tjah swallowed and nervously started over. "Your Highness' father, His Majesty the Strong Bull, is—is ill. The Divine Consort Hatshepsut makes his will known in the Two Lands."

"Oh," Thoth said vaguely. It was not at all clear to him yet, but he did not like to admit it for fear of sounding stupid. "Tell me her name again," he said. "The woman. The queen."

"Her name is Ma-ke-Re Hatshepsut, Daughter of the King, Sister of the King, Wife of the King, Mistress of the Two Lands, may-she-be-living-forever."

Hatshepsut. Thoth whispered it to himself. Could that be the one he had known as Lady Shesu? "Is she—a beautiful lady?" he asked Tjah.

"As beautiful as Hathor's self, some say. I have never seen her, Your Highness, save from a distance."

It was she, it must be. Fragments of dim, sweet memory rushed through Thoth's mind—laughter and sunshine, and water dripping on his sun-warmed shoulders and a beautiful lady picking up a little girl and swinging her high. . . . Perhaps he had a sister?

Thoth was suddenly self-conscious again. "I—do not remember much about Egypt. But there was a garden—Nehsi told me it was in my father's palace. And there was a little girl I used to play with, I think . . ."

"Perhaps that was Your Highness' cousin, the princess Neferu-Re, elder daughter of the Divine Consort."

Nefer! Thoth experienced a flash of recognition. I called her

Nefer—and she used to slap me. She was not my sister, but my cousin. . . .

Something else struck him suddenly. If Lady Shesu was Nefer's mother, and Nefer his cousin, Lady Shesu was clearly his aunt. Then who was his mother? Rather reluctantly, Tjah enlightened him on that, too. His mother was apparently dead. They had expected to find her with Thoth, in Babylon, but no one had heard of her there. She had been one Iset, a woman of the Mansion of Beauty.

"Then—I am only half a prince," Thoth said confusedly.

"Nay, not so, Your Highness!" Tjah exclaimed in a shocked voice. "Your Highness is the son of Pharaoh, sole prince of Egypt. The Divine Consort has two daughters, it is true, but that makes no difference to the Succession, since a woman cannot . . ." He paused, suddenly appeared to be a little bewildered himself, then started over carefully. "Your Highness is Pharaoh's only son. When Pharaoh is gathered to the gods, Your Highness will unfailingly become Pharaoh in his place."

"*I* will be Pharaoh?" gasped Thoth.

"Aye, when His Majesty—may-he-live-forever—departs for the Land of the West."

For a moment Thoth could only stare, with mouth agape. It was hard enough to believe his father was a king. That he might be one himself some day had never occurred to him in the wildest of his dreams. It was a thing he needed to think about alone—some other time. He closed his mouth and turned quickly to look out over the sea, instinctively making his face a mask.

"The Land of the West," he repeated. "You mean when he dies?"

"If Your Highness cares to put it so," said Tjah, sounding shocked again.

"How else can I put it? Do not all men die?"

"Aye, but—one would scarce call Pharaoh a man!"

"What is he, then?"

"Why, he is Horus! He is—Pharaoh!"

Thoth turned curiously to scrutinize his friend. Obviously here was something else he did not yet understand. Tjah understood it, that was clear enough, but he seemed unable to explain, and something about Thoth's questions was making him very nervous.

Thoth tactfully dropped the subject and gazed at the sea again as he prepared to open another one, of far, far deeper importance to him. "There is—someone else I have—wondered about. I once knew an old man—a warrior. His name was . . ." Thoth swallowed and then finished breathlessly, "Ahmose."

"Aye, Ahmose-pen-Nekhbet!" Tjah exclaimed at once.

"Then you know him?" Thoth cried.

"Nay, *I* do not. I told Your Highness I am but the youngest archer in my regiment, how would I know *him?* But all the barracks knows his name, and the glory he won in the old, old days. Three Pharaohs he has served, that old one—never was there such a warrior! Why, he helped drive the Hyksos out of Egypt, he stormed cursed Avaris and fought shoulder to shoulder with the great Horus who was Your Highness' grandfather, and sailed across this very sea to give chase to those wicked ones. He drove them clean over the edge of the world, they say—"

"But does he live still?" Thoth whispered.

Tjah blinked and considered. "No doubt he does, for I have not heard of his death, and surely there would have been a day of mourning in the Two Lands. Still, I do not know. I have never seen him."

"Nehsi did not know either. I asked him once. He did not even know at first what Ahmose I meant—or said he did not. Do you not think that is queer?

He turned a troubled gaze on Tjah, who met his eyes in equally troubled silence. Finally Tjah spoke in a lowered voice. "Many things are queer these days—so my father says. But no warrior will ever forget Ahmose-pen-Nekhbet."

Nehsi had forgotten him, though—or wanted to forget him—and so had the other nobles. Even when they remembered, they said nothing of his glory or his great exploits, they spoke of him only as former guardian of the princess, whom some noble called Senmut had replaced years ago.

"Who is Count Senmut?" Thoth asked resentfully.

"Steward of Amon, Overseer of the Fields and Works of Amon, guardian of the princess, Nearest Friend of the Queen."

Thoth felt a soothing warmth steal through him. Without even looking at Tjah he could tell that his new friend disliked this Senmut as much as he did—and perhaps Tjah had never seen him either. It was nice to know somebody was on your side, even though you did not know why.

"Come," he said suddenly. "Let's climb the mast yonder and see what we can see."

That was the first of many hours the two boys spent together, in talk, in roughhouse play so noisy that the crew turned to watch and the nobles thrust pale, disapproving faces from their pavilions, in the cautious exploring of each other's foreign personalities and alien homelands. As the days passed and the great galley dipped and bounded across the choppy sea Thoth found a clearer picture of Egypt forming in his mind—a long green land with cities and temples and people, where the great Nile rose and flooded and deposited its gift of fertility and withdrew and died only to rise and flood again, with magnificent and ordered regularity.

As for the Egyptians themselves, if Tjah were to be believed, they must be the most favored of men. Even after death their souls, far from eating dust and drinking mud in gloomy Hell, roamed the Field of Reeds in the Land of the West, living in fine houses with every luxury of meat and drink and amusement forever at their disposal. To be assured of this future paradise a man had only to live a passably just and righteous life, so that when he stood before the forty judges after death, watching Osiris weigh his heart against the Feather of Truth, the scales would balance and he would be welcomed into the company of the gods.

To Thoth, this sounded like purest fantasy, though it was obvious Tjah believed all he was saying. In many ways, however, Thoth found the young soldier as bluntly realistic as himself. Tjah, too, had noticed in the city of Kadesh a signal lack of the bent necks and rejoicing proper to vassals of mighty Pharaoh.

"Rebellious ones!" Tjah said moodily. "They show disrespect now; next there will be uprisings and trouble."

"Then you should tell my father!" exclaimed Thoth. "Surely my father does not know! *I* will tell him!"

Tjah glanced at him quickly, then away. "Your Highness' father is ill. He does not interest himself in conquest."

There was an odd gentleness in his tone, as if he spoke to a small child. It made Thoth feel suddenly alone again, uncertain of himself. This new father, of whom he knew little save that he was ill—Tjah always looked strange when he spoke of him. Perhaps he was very ill indeed. Perhaps he would not even want to see his son and welcome him.

Lady Shesu will welcome me, Thoth assured himself. And Ahmose—oh, Ahmose will welcome me, if only I can find him. . . .

The water was very rough that day, the last of the sea voyage. The seasick groans from the pavilions had grown loud again, the soldiers' incense filled the air.

Seeing that Tjah, too, was clinging to his amulet and muttering under his breath, Thoth asked, "Who is it you pray to?"

"To Amon the Hidden One," Tjah said. "Also to Isis and Ptah and whoever else I can think of. It does no harm to have all the great ones on your side at a time like this."

"You pray direct to your great ones? You call on their names yourself?"

"Of course," said Tjah, looking puzzled at the question.

"But—do they hear you?"

The other shrugged and made a gesture that included pavilions, his fellows of the guard, and the whole bounding, rolling ship. "They must. Have we not come a long way in safety?" He watched Thoth's face curiously a moment, then said, "Does Your Highness not call on the gods too?"

"I *did*, in Babylon, but now—" Thoth thought of Nibada and the familiar little altar in Ibhi-Adad's house, both far behind him now, cut off from him by a thousand alien leagues of desert, mountains, sea. With a terrible sinking sensation, he said, "I have no god now."

"No god!" Tjah burst out. "Why, name of Amon, Your Highness' own father is a god! He is Horus, he is Upwaut, too, the Opener-of-the-Ways. You will be a god yourself, when you are king!"

"*I* will be? Why, I cannot! That is—that is absurd, it is—" It is dangerous, Thoth thought with a shiver, to talk that way! "Men are men. The gods are—the gods!"

"Pharaoh is a god too," Tjah said firmly. "And so will you be, when the Two Feathers are bound upon your head. Your own grandsire is Osiris himself. Look yonder in the sky—if our eyes could bear the glory we should see his face this very instant."

"My *grandsire?* But that is Shamash, Lord Sun," whispered Thoth.

"I know not Shamash. That is Re in his golden bark, and Osiris sails with him day and night, over the earth and under it through the Land of the West where he is king."

Thoth was staring up at the sun, with blinded watering eyes and a strange agitation tingling through him. That was Shamash, and he knew it. But long ago he had been possessed of this same incredible notion—that if he looked hard enough at the sun he might see his grandfather there. He had learned to laugh at it. Still, he had also learned to laugh at the old notion that his father was a king, and *that* had proved quite true.

Tjah was still talking, but Thoth had lost the trend of what he was saying. Something about the years to come, when Thoth would be Horus, and his father, Osiris, would—"

"I thought my *grandfather* was Osiris," Thoth interrupted in bewilderment.

"He is now," Tjah explained patiently. "And your father is Horus. But Horus becomes Osiris when he is gathered to the gods. Then a new Horus rules in Egypt, and Osiris mounts to the bark of Re and sails over the sky—"

"Stay a moment! My father will be this Osiris you speak of now? Then what will my grandfather become?"

Tjah answered with irritating vagueness. "The Royal Ancestors are the Souls of Pe and Nekhen, Followers of Horus. They are very great, very holy."

"But are they all Osirises?"

"There is only one Osiris!" Tjah exclaimed in a shocked tone.

"Then who *is* he?" Thoth burst out, exasperated.

"Why, he is—Osiris." Tjah's eyes were very serious; they shone with a curious, gentle awe, and his voice was hushed. "Osiris the Beloved, who dies each spring and rises again to life in floodtime, that you and I may live."

Thoth's head was aching. He escaped from Tjah and spread his mat on the pitching deck, as near to the ship's center as he could get it, and lay on his back dizzily watching the mast trace great circles against the brilliant sky. Some other time, when the ship was not tossing so, he would think it all out.

By nightfall the waves had lessened; at dawn on the seventh day of the voyage the Phoenician galley glided under oars into the wide, marshy Delta of the Nile, and an hour later swayed at its hawser beside the wharfs of a bustling harbor town. The Egyptians poured down the gangplank praising Amon, falling to their knees to kiss the black mud of home, filling their cups with the water of the Nile. Nehsi and the other dignitaries, once more fully in command of themselves and the situation, summoned the harbor officials to arrange for food, rest, and Egyptian vessels to transport them up the Nile.

The first news to greet them was that Pharaoh had died two months before.

Dazed and only partially comprehending, cut off from Tjah and surrounded by a blurred confusion of changed plans and hurried orders, Thoth stood silent and trembling on the unfamiliar docks until he was hustled away to wait in a tiny room in the harbor offices. There, acutely conscious of the urchins and passers-by who stared in through the open door at his shoulder-length hair and Babylonian clothes, he nibbled at alien food, sipped strange-tasting wine, and tried to understand that his father was lost to him forever.

Now, twenty days later, Thoth stood beside the *Star*'s stern sweep while for the last time the pattern of the three sails in the wake etched itself upon his memory. Today when they reached Thebes his father's entombment would already be a thing of the past, even beginning to be obscured, perhaps, in the press of more recent happenings. He would never know him now, he was gone forever, he was dead. Thoth wondered if all his life he would feel this strange loneliness for a man he never knew.

He thought of what Tjah had said and his heart began a sick thudding that was half excitement and half dread. Were they really waiting there in Thebes to hail him as their new Pharaoh, to bear him off to the palace and place the crown of Egypt on his head, and transform him, somehow, into a god? Nehsi had said nothing about it, nothing at all.

Perhaps Tjah was wrong; Thoth did not know whether to hope he was or not. It would be very grand to be a king of course —in Babylon, where he knew how kings acted and how the people felt about things. But to be a *god-king*—Thoth searched his heart and found he simply could not believe that he could ever become a god, no matter what the magic or the spells. Besides, to be a king of any kind of this big, strange land where everything was new and unfamiliar, where his simplest remark caused people to stare at him in such astonishment that he had grown afraid to say anything at all—that was a different matter altogether. He would not feel grand. He would only feel awkward and all wrong. He felt that way already, had felt so all the long journey up the river, where every fisherman, every goosegirl or crowd of villagers had gaped at him as if he were a curiosity, not their prince.

Thoth turned from the gunwale, fingering the neck of his tunic.

It is my clothes and my hair, he thought miserably. If I had Egyptian clothes to put on— But Nehsi had not offered any.

Nay, and I would die before I asked! he thought belligerently. There is nothing wrong with these garments anyway. It is my best tunic, with three rows of fringe, too, and all made by Nanai's hand. . . .

Egyptians did not seem to judge the fineness of a garment by the number of its rows of fringe. Fringe meant nothing to them, they thought it outlandish—Thoth could see it in their eyes. It was just one more way in which everything was different.

Thoth swallowed a big lump of homesickness in his throat and once more turned his back on the sparkling highway to the south. If it were not for Ahmose and Lady Shesu, he would not even want to reach Thebes.

By the time the hot sun of noon poured down upon their decks, the four ships were entering the northern outskirts of Thebes. On either side, green farmlands gave way to flower fields and boat landings and ever-larger clusters of houses; traffic on the river increased until the sparkling expanse of water was alive with craft. Huge barges, linked together and piled with blocks of granite, floated ponderously downstream; past them skimmed the delicate boats of noblemen—high, curled prows shining with gilt, oars flashing swift as the legs of a water beetle, princely owner sitting arrogant and impassive in a pavilion amidships, eyes forward, hands motionless and formal on his knees. A temple bark with a purple sail overtook the *Star* and scudded easily ahead; ferries crossed her path, patched and lumbering cargo boats made way for her, tiny fishing punts that were scarcely more than bundles of papyrus reeds darted in and out among them all like water-borne mosquitoes. And on both sides of the Nile's pulsing artery rose No-Amon, the City of God—the vast metropolis of Thebes.

The advance messenger Nehsi had dispatched from the Delta had arrived at the palace the previous evening. By the time the ships sailed slowly into view just north of the sprawling Temple of Amon, every wharf and landing dock was crowded with Thebans craning their necks for a first glimpse of the child who was said to be their prince.

Just who this prince was and where he had come from so suddenly, when they had never heard of him before, no one seemed able to explain. Many openly doubted there was such a child; and when the *Star*'s closer approach plainly showed a boy standing beside the great sweep in the stern, they expressed even more positive doubts that he was a prince.

"Look at him," said a young sailmaker to his father, as many other onlookers were at that moment saying to those standing nearest. "That is no royal prince, that lad! Why, he is not even Egyptian! Can you see him, old one? Royal prince indeed, whoever told you that had his foot in his mouth! That is some young barbarian the great excellency has brought back to amuse the queen. . . ."

Others put a more sinister interpretation on the matter. One sharp-tongued fellow, a potter, walking back to his stall in the market place with a few of his comrades, put forth the theory that the child was no living child at all but a *kheft,* sent by the brooding spirit of the late Pharaoh—whom everyone knew had been possessed by devils—to harass the Divine Hatshepsut as Pharaoh had harassed her while he lived.

Come, there was no use looking shocked, Pharaoh had flown up to the gods now and one could face facts. For five full years Her Radiance and no other had caused the flood to rise in its season, the grain to sprout, the lives of men to go on as usual. She had saved Egypt from ruin at the Tired One's hands.

So stated the potter, in unequivocal tones, and his hearers were compelled to agree with him—at least in the matter of the queen's divinity and Pharaoh's devils, of which all had seen conclusive proof. However, concerning this theory that the child was actually a *kheft* . . . well, in the basketmaker's opinion that statement was perhaps a trifle strong. The child was plainly a child—no doubt some barbarian, but nothing so fearful as a *kheft.* For one thing, *khefts* did not look like children, they looked more like large bats—aye, and sometimes like women with their heads set on backwards—but never, that the basket-maker had ever heard of, like half-grown boys.

There followed several moments of intense discussion on the varying forms in which *khefts* had been seen to appear, until the onion seller brought the talk back to its original subject by asserting that *he* thought the child a real child—and perhaps, since everyone was saying so, even some sort of prince.

The argument went on, and theories as to the identity of the boy in the *Star* sprang up all over the market place. On one thing only all agreed: if the child was a threat to the Divine Hatshepsut's beneficent hold on Egypt's welfare, they wanted none of him. They had had enough of peculiar kings.

The subject of all their discussion had meanwhile disembarked, and stood now beside Nehsi on the beribboned royal landing, listening to a stilted speech of greeting delivered by the Steward of Amon, Chief Guardian of the royal princess, Count Senmut. Behind this saturnine, heavy-browed excellency stood an official delegation of courtiers arrayed in all their jewels. Beyond these, the long avenue leading from wharf to palace was lined with silent watchers—artisans, housewives, goldsmiths, tomb-priests, sculptors, servants of the wealthy; and on slave-borne palanquins and carrying chairs which seemed, appropriately enough, to float at shoulder height above these cruder folk, were nobles and their ladies, glittering with gold, silent and watchful too.

These palanquin-borne great ones knew with perfect clarity who Nehsi's young charge was and whence he came. It was true they had never known why Pharaoh, his father, had suddenly dispatched him to the end of the earth six years ago. The thing they did understand, emphatically, was that once dispatched to the world's end, the child should have stayed there; it was folly to bring him back. They had felt this strongly even when Nehsi set out for the Great Green months before; now, as the young prince climbed into a waiting litter and was carried past them up the great avenue to the palace, their first clear look at him confirmed all their forebodings.

A royal scion of Egypt should have sat upon that litter. Instead, they saw a barbaric-looking little foreigner, square-built and stocky, like some peasant's son, with a wild mop of hair beneath which enormous, shy dark eyes peered out dazedly. His tunic was of outlandish cut, dyed and embroidered all over in gaudy scarlets, saffrons, greens—and further decorated by diagonal rows of fringe. Yet they might have forgiven his appearance—hair could be cut, clothes changed, tastes civilized—if his manner had displayed the stamp of royalty. They looked for it in vain, feeling their doubts slowly harden into certainty. Even the princes of barbarians bore themselves with a certain savage arrogance; this child shrank back in his chair, clinging to its carved arms with both hands as he stared about him at the watching crowds. Obviously he was rigid with self-consciousness, unsure of himself, overwhelmed by everything he saw.

To the disenchanted nobles it came as an affront, a discovery of impertinent presumption, to discern rising from his plebeian features the unmistakable strong, arched nose of the Thutmosid line.

4.

Hatshepsut had slept late that morning. Even before she was fully awake she had been aware of the sun streaming directly onto her closed eyelids. She turned her head on the ivory headrest in a vague effort to escape it, wondering why Yen did not close the lattices. Then she remembered—Yen was not there. For nearly six years Yen had not been there.

It is ridiculous, the queen reflected with sleepy irritation, that every morning I should still expect her.

Perhaps she had been hasty, to banish Yen from her presence just because of that little period of strain between them after the princess Meryet was born?

It was Yen's fault! she thought, as she always did. Not mine, not mine at all. Yen was obsessed by that baby. I could not have her around when she kept looking at me so—as if I had hurt her somehow, or mistreated the infant! What nonsense. I bear the child no ill will. It is just that I do not care to look upon her face.

No one cared to gaze day in, day out, upon the evidence of a god's rebuke—and that was precisely what Meryet was. Long ago Hatshepsut had realized that she had misinterpreted Amon's will by determining to bear a son. He had decreed that she should have no son—because from the very first he had intended that *she* be his son in Egypt—she and no other.

The familiar morning sounds from the world beyond her closed eyelids began to penetrate Hatshepsut's consciousness— the murmurs of the doves that always clustered on the eaves, the call of a hoopoe interrupting them, the immemorial creaking of the water-lifts far away beyond the palace walls. Her thoughts faded before their reality; stretching luxuriously, she opened her eyes and blinked at the day.

Suddenly she sat up, sick with awareness of the runner and his news. This was the day. Today the ships would arrive from Babylon; today the two blessed months of freedom since Nenni's death would come to an end. Everything was coming to an end.

For a moment she could not bear the knowledge. Flinging herself back upon her couch, she lay with eyes tight shut, hoping to escape again into unconsciousness. Sleep was far away now; every nerve and muscle in her body was tense with wakefulness. Her mind fought and struggled like a trapped thing, going over the same unyielding problem for the hundredth time in search of one flaw, one weakness, one chink through which she could force her way out. For the hundredth time she found none.

She could not avert this thing. Incredibly, it was all going to happen exactly as Nenni had willed it. Thoth had actually been located in far-off Babylon, alive and well. The ships had actually made their way back with him to Egypt, escaping every one of the innumerable perils that must beset such a journey. It was real, like a nightmare coming true. Doubtless Senmut was already organizing an official cortege to meet the ships—in a few hours she must come face to face with the child she had thought never to see again.

Unsummoned, Thoth's face rose up before her, hideously clear —the fresh, innocent face of a five-year-old, set with great dark eyes which searched her own with questioning sadness.

She jerked upright in the bed, opening her own eyes wide to prevent the old dizzy sinking into the morass of memory. Surely she was not going to begin that again—first seeing his face, and his childish, sturdy legs running toward her, then counting the

eagues upon leagues to unknown Babylon. She must *not* begin
again! She had conquered all that once and for all when she removed old Ahmose from the garden and her sight.

I am too sensitive, Senmut is right, I am far too sensitive! she
thought. There is no need at all to torture myself over someone
else's affair, take another's guilt upon myself! I should not do it,
t is a fault in me. It was not my command that sent Thoth into
exile, it was Nenni's, Nenni's, Nenni's!

And it was Nenni's command that was bringing him back
today. What malevolent irony that was! Nenni who had never
wanted his power, who had always obstinately refused to use it.
. . "Who am I to judge men, to decide their fate?" . . . "Nay,
I will not gesture, I am tired of amusing the gods."

For a moment Hatshepsut's fists beat a tattoo of impotent
rage against the coverlets. Weeks, months, years of that she had
endured, and the Kinsmen with her. Then, when Nenni had been
confined to his couch so long that no one dreamed he would ever
leave it again, when at last, at last, she was unhampered by his
interference and Egypt's tangled affairs were beginning to
straighten out under her careful hand—then had come that morning three months ago in the Council Chamber.

She could not comprehend it yet, though its every detail
was as vivid in her mind as if it were still taking place. She remembered even the feel of the thin leather documents she had
been holding, the Kinsmen's frozen faces all turned toward
the doorway, the eerie shock it was to see Nenni standing there
after all those weeks in which no one had seen his face. It was
incredible—as if he had risen from the dead. Yet there he stood,
corpse-thin and haggard, but with a terrible, dogged purpose
in his eyes. Looking neither right nor left, he walked slowly
across the room and stopped in front of her. In a voice which
sounded as if it had not been used for months, he whispered,
"Where is my son?"

She had found herself on her feet without knowledge of how
she had moved; her legs seemed turned to water, and she could
not get her breath, but she began talking rapidly. "Nenni, you
are ill. You should not be walking about like this, let me call your
slave, you are trembling . . . Chamberlain! Assist His Majesty
to his chambers, His Majesty is—not himself."

With one movement of his arm Nenni swept the chamberlain

into oblivion, never taking his eyes from her face. He was shaking violently, alarmingly. "Where is my son?" he repeated

"Your son? Do you mean—Thoth? Why, he is long gone Nenni—you sent him away yourself— You are ill, you have forgotten. It was years ago. Come, I pray you—"

"Where is he, Shesu?

Her own breath was strangling her. He was terrifying standing there with his terrible, fixed eyes, like a *kheft,* and shuddering in every limb. He is truly mad this time, she thought with a spurt of fear. She fell back a step; when he followed, she gasped out the answer. "Babylon!"

For an instant there was silence; his lips formed the word silently several times, as if tasting a strange and evil fruit. Gradually his trembling ceased, and his eyes lost their stare and regarded her merely with a weary curiosity. Some of her terror began to leave her. This was Nenni, after all, surely she could control him, she always had. Anger stiffened her courage as she suddenly became aware again of the presence of the Kinsmen Nehsi, Thutiy, Ineny—even her detractors Uah and Khenuka those conservative fools whose prejudice hampered her every move—they had all seen it, they had heard Nenni as good as accusing her, pretending she had committed some crime—

"Well?" she cried. "Why do you look at me so? Yours is the blame!"

"I did not know how great your fear was, my Shesu. Babylon *Babylon.* He was so small—to send so far."

"I tell you I sent him nowhere! It was your command, yours your whim, your will, I had nothing to do with it—"

He was not listening to her. Slowly, as if she were not there his preoccupied eyes turned from her, moved carefully around the circle of faces and came to rest on Nehsi's. "You," he said. "Find my son and bring him back to me."

Her breath deserted her so suddenly that for a moment she was incapable of speaking or even stirring. It was the sight of Nehsi's stunned but accepting face which goaded her into action

"Nenni, that is impossible!" she burst out. She sprang forward, clutching furiously at his arm. "Did you not hear what I said to you? Thoth is in Babylon—at the end of the world!"

"If he sails the Dark River itself, he must be found—and

brought to me. Make haste. Find ships. Depart before sundown of this day. Bring back my son."

"Aye, Majesty," Nehsi whispered.

"Nenni, in Amon's name!" she shouted. With a wrench at his arm she pulled him toward her, glaring up into his eyes. "You cannot do this! No one can bring him back, not now—you do not know what you are saying! He is half the world away, if he is not dead—"

"Be silent. I am talking now—for once." He started to turn away from her, then hesitated and turned back, a curious faint smile on his lips. "I have found that there is something in the Circle after all," he added softly. "It is a crown. They must obey that, do you see? It is their own invention."

"Oh gods, you are ill! You're mad!"

"I am Pharaoh," he said. He shrugged off her clutching hand and looked about the room, his head thrust forward under the crown's weight so that the golden cobra curling over his brow seemed to reach out and threaten them all. "I am Pharaoh," he repeated slowly and distinctly.

She could see their faces change, become wary, then prudent, then strangely relieved. Their eyes lifted to the cobra and became blind to all else. Nehsi walked through the door and vanished.

"Not Nehsi," she whispered. "Not *Nehsi!* Nenni, you cannot take Nehsi, he is needed here. I pray you, if you insist upon this folly, send one of the others—send Senmut, he is loyal—"

"Nehsi shall go. *He* is incorruptible."

Suddenly all her strength deserted her. She sank down limply in her chair, her face in her hands.

"I want a scribe," said Nenni.

In an evil haze she heard the scribe come, heard the hurried scratching of his pen as he wrote the words Nenni spoke slowly, doggedly, in his rusty, unused voice. ". . . and My Majesty does command that my son Men-kheper-Re Thutmose, my son of my body, shall dawn upon the horizon of the Two Lands as Horus after me, and shall be Pharaoh in my place . . . and that this My Majesty's decree shall be sealed by my hand this day and shall be placed in the House of Gold in the place of the Archives of the Two Lands."

When the scribe had gone she raised her head and looked at

255

Nenni. "Can you not see you are mad?" she said in a low, bitter voice with all her hatred in it. "You cannot simply wave your hand and expect—"

"My Shesu, did you not tell me once yourself that only so are great things accomplished? If I would once raise my scepter, you said, then I would see. Very well, I have raised it. Now we shall see."

His eyes escaped her again. He looked about the room, his body shaking, his face completely calm. With a long breath he sat down slowly in his golden chair and addressed the ministers of the crown.

"Proceed with your reports. Horus is among you—and will remain among you. I shall not go back to my couch today."

He did not go back to his couch save to sleep, then or for two weeks afterward. Day by day she watched him, hating him, waiting for him to collapse so that she could send swift runners downriver to overtake Nehsi's ships and bring them back to Thebes. Day by day Nenni appeared at the Kinsmen's Council, at the audiences, with the family at the Southern Garden. He spoke rarely and took no part in anything that was going on, but he was inescapably *there,* shuddering and impassive, the heavy crown always on his head, his eyes already dwelling in some other world. For two weeks the palace was haunted and oppressed by his presence, and she herself reduced to such a state of frustration and nerves that she could neither eat nor sleep.

Then, one morning, he did not rise from his couch. By evening he was dead.

Hatshepsut, tossing with helpless defeat now on her own couch, pressed her hands hard over her eyes. Two weeks—twenty little days. Oh, if only he had sent Senmut! Or Ineny, or even Thutiy—once out of sight of the cobra they would have come to their senses, they would have found some reason to delay, to linger at the borders of Egypt awaiting the call from her that must surely come. But Nehsi—the incorruptible—was far out upon the waters of the Great Green by the time her runners reached the Delta.

Now he was returning with his unwelcome passenger.

Again, before she could stop it, the childish face with the sad and questioning eyes rose up and blotted out the room. She sprang from her couch and struck a clashing note on the gong that stood upon the bedside table. A maidservant scratched tim-idly on the door and entered. A mere slave girl—a stranger—not Yen.

Hatshepsut glared at her hopelessly a moment, then snapped, "My bath."

Three hours later she emerged from the Council of the Kins-men, white with suppressed rage, and crossed the passage to the Apartments of the King.

Fools, she thought. Fools, fools! All of them!

"We fear we cannot agree with Your Radiance's suggestion. Pharaoh's will was plain, it is inscribed in his own words, sealed by his hand—we cannot tamper with it. . . ."

Had she asked them to tamper with it? No. She had made the simplest, the most reasonable, the wisest of requests—merely that the child's accession be postponed a few months . . . until they could discover what he was like, until a suitable feast day could be chosen, until—until—

"We fear we cannot agree, Your Radiance."

"Then you must disagree, and accept the consequences," she had said acidly. "I only hope they will not be too unpleasant."

"Unpleasant, Your Radiance?"

"I fear they will be extremely unpleasant—for yourselves, and even for me. I shall hate to see the nobles of Egypt, my lord father's own trusted and honored servants—like yourself, Lord Uah—ordered about like peasants by a strutting, ignorant little boy, the son of a harem woman. It would be less painful if he were of royal blood himself, but—"

"Your Radiance forgets that he will be wed at once to Her Highness the princess Neferu-Re! With that union, his blood will become as royal as—"

"There will be no union with my daughter, my lord Khenuka, until I consent to it. I assure you, that will not be 'at once.' "

"But, Your Radiance—"

"It is out of the question. I cannot possibly subject the prin-cess to marriage with some crude stranger without allowing her a few months to adjust to the idea. She is sensitive and high-strung . . . and as you know, she is not . . . robust." Even in her fury, even in her desperate need to sway them, the admission had stuck in her throat. The princess is not . . . robust. The

257

princess is like her father. "Name the boy Successor if you like," she had flung at them. "Name him so tomorrow—and crown him next week! Without the marriage his claim to the throne will be a travesty of everything Egypt has revered since the time of Re."

"That is true," Thutiy had said nervously.

But Lord Uah had said, "The will of Pharaoh is plain, it is sealed by his own hand."

Five minutes later she left the room. She had accomplished nothing, they had stiffened themselves against her wishes, against all her arguments, against wisdom itself. Even Thutiy, who had begun to see reason when she had conferred with him earlier this morning—even Ineny, her devoted partisan—still hesitated and vacillated, so influenced by the thought of that cursed document lying in the archives that they could not listen to common sense. Of course Uah and Khenuka, blindest of traditionalists, were obsessed by the cobra on a dead king's crown.

They must obey that, do you see, my Shesu? It is their own invention. . . . What had he meant? Invention! The crown was no invention, it was the holiest of mysteries.

But the king who had worn it was dead, dead, dead!

Tears of helpless rage stung Hatshepsut's eyelids as she gained the privacy of the Apartments of the King. Closing the door behind her, she leaned against it and stood a moment, looking around the familiar sitting room. It was her father's room again —there was nothing of Nenni left in it. He had never changed the pale lemon-tinted walls with their swarms of golden bees, or moved his father's worn scarlet chair from its place beside the low table. He had even been buried in his father's tomb, having obstinately refused to build one of his own. It was as if he had seen himself an interloper, a stranger in the world.

Shrugging, Hatshepsut moved with swift and decisive steps across the room, through the wardrobe chamber adjoining it and into the bedroom beyond. What had that futile, defeated soul to do with her? Not for her, Nenni's ephemeral life and traceless vanishing. She intended to leave so large a mark upon the face of Egypt that no man, woman or child for thousands of years would be able to forget that she had lived, that she had been Hatshepsut.

But always some man stood in the way of her intention.

She paused in the bedroom, looking into the sleeping alcove with its ceiling of golden stars, beneath which stood the lion-headed couch in which two Pharaohs had died and a false one would soon be sleeping, if the Kinsmen had their way. How could Amon let it happen? Her eyes moved in desperate questioning to the niche in the alcove's corner, where the golden statuette of Amon gazed enigmatically into space. She was his child—his son—she knew it. Why had he not created her male? Then everyone else would have known it too. How strange, how desperately strange and troublesome, that he should have placed the heart and *ka* of a prince in a woman's body!

My Shesu, gods blunder as well as men. . . .

Nonsense, she thought with sudden fear.

Moving to the golden image, she dropped to her knees and hastily set a pellet of myrrh alight in the brazier. Amon did not—could not—blunder. He *could* not mean for her to be merely a woman, merely a queen. It was impossible, it was unthinkable . . .

But she was suddenly imprisoned by the thought of it. As the gray smoke curled upward from the brazier her mind filled with pictures of her mother. Elegant, serene, unquestioning, Aahmes had moved with gestures of stilted grace through a life as planned and ordered as a temple dance and, still unquestioning, into her tomb. Her every move had been a maxim: When Pharaoh makes offering, stand behind him, when he throws gold to a favorite, smile from your place behind his left shoulder, when he commands, obey, when he crooks his finger, come, when he makes love, bear him sons . . . never mind the Kinsmen, the treasury, the taxes, they are his affair—your place is with the countesses at the Weekly Reception, breathing heliotrope and eating cakes—keep your chin high, your eyelids down, a faint gracious smile upon your face—move, act, speak, think, like a sculpture on a temple wall. Then the Kinsmen will never oppose you. They will not need to; you will be of no importance whatsoever.

With a violence that scattered the gray curl of smoke, Hatshepsut was on her feet. She was *not* her mother, as those fools of Kinsmen would soon find out. The Daughter of the Sun need not bargain, argue, reason with Egypt's ministers or any other mortal. She need only act.

As she moved swiftly through the garden toward the Queen's

Apartments her mind was already working with its accustomed swift precision, uncluttered by other people's opinions and foolish doubts. The moment she reached her own bedroom she struck a resounding note upon the gong, and ordered the chamberlain who appeared to fetch the High Priest of Amon to her private sitting room.

"Stay—have the ships been sighted yet?" she added.

"They warp into the dock this moment, Your Radiance, according to my lord Ineny, who—"

"Then you must hurry. Find Hapuseneb—he is in the Great Hall somewhere. Make haste! I must talk to him at once!"

That boy, she thought, will soon find he has no mere weakling of a woman to deal with!

On a sudden impulse she walked to her dressing table and sat down before it, gazing into the polished silver mirror. Her own eyes, wide, dark and luminous, stared back at her as she examined the reflected face. It was no longer the face of the young and blooming maiden who had watched Thoth's ship set sail for the north six years ago. She was twenty-seven years old, honed thin by the long struggle with Nenni. Her hair, falling black and helmet-like to her shoulders, outlined her face with a starkness it had not had in earlier years; and in the face itself every soft curve had sloped into a plane. Her cheekbones were sharper, her small chin harder, her mouth flatter and firmer. It was as if some sculptor-magician had changed an image of tenderly modeled wax into an ivory carving.

She drew back from the mirror, satisfied. She had found no flaw in the reflection of the Daughter of the Sun. Thoth would see at once that she was Amon's living child, and that he must obey her.

A discreet cough sounded from her sitting room. She walked in to find Hapuseneb waiting in the corridor doorway, looking as unruffled as ever despite the haste with which he had been summoned.

"Excellency, rejoice," she said.

He bowed with his accustomed dignity. "May the Divine Consort live forever."

"Come in. Close the door behind you. I have something to say, and it is for your ears alone." When he stood beside her she looked appraisingly into his face a moment, not certain whether to be reassured or otherwise by the man's unshakable calm. "Excellence," she began slowly, "I wish to give you a problem to solve. You are a man of piety and intelligence. I think you can solve it—if you choose."

"My poor powers are at your command, Radiant One."

"This problem concerns the Tired One's son, the child who is arriving at the palace wharf this moment. He comes from Babylon, Excellence. He has lived from the age of five to the age of eleven, the formative years of his life, in a country which knows not Re."

The high priest watched her closely for a moment, then said, "It is fortunate for the prince—and for Egypt—that he will have Your Radiance as regent during his first—"

"It is fortunate indeed, though he will not deem it so. But I alone can scarcely be expected to provide the training he will lack appallingly, in both sacred and state affairs."

"Oh, as to that, Your Radiance may rely completely upon myself and my staff to guide him in his sacred duties. I understand your meaning. Pray let me assure you that whatever mistakes he may make at first in such rituals as the Weekly Offering, they will never come to the notice of anyone save myself and a few trusted assistants. Believe me, I understand you perfectly."

"Excellence, you understand me very imperfectly indeed," Hatshepsut informed him tartly. "In my judgment a child who has been reared by barbarians will need far more than a little discreet guidance before he is fit to mount the throne of Horus. In my judgment he needs a thorough schooling from both scribes and priests—plus the sobering influence of a strict and pious life—the sort of education he can gain only in the temple. And he needs it before, not after, his anointment as Successor."

"Do I understand Your Radiance—perhaps again imperfectly —to mean the anointment will be delayed some months?"

"Some years," Hatshepsut said distinctly.

No change took place in the priest's impassive features, but his shrewd dark eyes moved carefully over her face. "I see," he murmured. "Forgive my curiosity, but have the Kinsmen agreed to that? I believe I heard Lord Khenuka saying—"

"Excellence, Lord Khenuka is the crux of our problem. He possesses a great office—and a small intelligence. An intelligent man does not oppose the judgment of the Daughter of the Sun.

An intelligent man—such as yourself, Hapuseneb—does not act in flagrant disregard of his own future, but has the wit to make such decisions now as will benefit him later."

"I understand," Hapuseneb said drily. "Now—the problem itself?"

"The problem is how to relieve me of this child's interference —so that I may take Lord Khenuka's offices and titles and add them to your own."

Hapuseneb looked at her with thoughtful, weary eyes a moment, then gave a faint smile. "This has a familiar ring," he commented. "It seems to me I solved a similar problem, years ago."

"If you choose to solve this one, it will work to your advantage years hence."

"If I choose?" mused the priest. "I think a man chooses once, for good and all. He is not really allowed a second chance, though it may seem so." He smiled again, and shrugged. "I repeat—my small powers are at Your Radiance's disposal."

"You will do as I ask?"

"Of course. There was never any question of it, was there?"

Before she could answer, a tap came at the door, and the chamberlain's muffled voice sounded from the corridor.

"They have arrived, Your Radiance. I am sent to ask where you will receive them."

"Them? Nay, I wish first to see the boy alone!" Hatshepsut moved swiftly to the door and opened it. "They are here already? In the palace?"

"In the Great Court, Radiance."

"Then show the prince into that little garden. I will go there at once. Count Nehsi and Count Senmut may await me here."

As she closed the door, Hapuseneb faced her. "What do you want me to do?"

"Refuse to anoint a barbarian as Successor."

"And after that?"

"After that I will send him to the temple to begin his education. Enter him in the ranks of novices like any other lad who desires to become a priest. He will belong to the temple then, and not the palace. *Keep him there.*"

Five minutes later she closed the gate of the King's Garden behind her, walked eastward on the path that ran close along the south side of the palace, and across a stretch of open lawn to the

262

little garden off the Great Court. Without giving herself a chance to hesitate, she opened the gate and stepped inside. There she stopped.

She had entered the side gate. A graveled walk, running at right angles to the path she stood on, led through the center of the garden to the pavilion from the courtyard entrance. In the middle of this walk stood a boy who must be Thoth—must be, since it could be no one else. She stared at him in disbelief, while the word "Babylon" slowly took on a dismaying and formidable reality.

She had spoken glibly of barbarians to Hapuseneb, but unconsciously she had expected to confront a stripling in immaculate linen, with the royal side-lock dangling over his cheek and defiant arrogance in his scowl. Now her shocked eyes moved incredulously over a strange, uncivilized little figure she could not have imagined had she tried. There was nothing of Egypt in him, nothing of the prince—except his nose. He stood slowly looking about him, without arrogance, without a scowl, but with an expression of such bewilderment that her heart went out to him as it would have to any lost and frightened waif. She could almost have believed he was merely that, a waif strayed in somehow from a merchant vessel—had it not been for his nose.

I must speak to him, she thought dazedly. He does not see me. I must speak, go forward, say what I planned to say, briefly, formally . . .

This was not the child she had pictured when she planned all that. She had not thought he would touch her heart this way . . . nothing was as she had pictured it, nothing at all. In a voice as strange as her own mixed-up emotions, she faltered, "Thoth?"

He whirled and saw her. Awed recognition dawned in his face, slowly transfiguring it. "Lady Shesu!" he whispered.

The sound of his old name for her, spoken in his strange new accent, made her throat tighten as if a hand had closed over it. Poor child, poor child! she thought. Why, he loves me just as he always did. . . . Of their own accord her hands stretched out to him.

He started toward her, his bare feet spattering on the gravel and then pounding silently across the grass. In another instant he was in her arms, clinging to her with his rough, loving boy's

263

arms as no child but he had ever clung, and as no girl-child ever would. The silent, passionate reality of his love completely unnerved her. Tears sprang scalding into her eyes, she felt her face twist and her throat constrict intolerably.

Gods, I must get hold of myself, she thought, what is the matter with me, I must not weep. . . .

She grasped his firm, hard little shoulders and pushed him away from her, wrenching her mouth into a smile. His eyes were full of tears too, but he was smiling radiantly.

"Well—Thoth," she managed to say.

"Oh, I am so glad you are here, I am so glad!" he breathed.

"And—glad to be—in Egypt?"

"Aye! I am, *now*."

It was still a child's voice. He was not half so grown up as she had imagined, nor half so tall; indeed, he was no taller than Nefer, who was only nine—but these were far from being Nefer's frail shoulders under her hands.

"What a—strong boy you've grown," she went on, scarcely knowing what she was saying. "You have changed a great deal since I last saw you. You were but a little lad then—"

"I do not remember very much about—then."

"But you remembered me?"

"Oh, I remembered you always!" He hesitated, then added softly, "You have changed a little bit, too."

"Have I? How?"

"I don't—know."

She realized that his eyes were searching her face—the same dark, questioning child's eyes that had so often haunted her. She straightened swiftly, and to distract herself began running one hand through the untidy fringe of hair that hung over his brows, pushing it to one side, then stroking it back, talking rapidly.

"Well, I know how you have changed! You have grown up —why, you are eleven now, are you not? That is a great age. And you look quite unlike yourself. This hair, for one thing—we must summon a barber to shave it in the Egyptian manner, you will find it far cooler, far cleaner—"

She stopped, catching her breath, and her hand froze where it was, holding the fringe of hair straight back. Seen this way, with the broad forehead fully revealed above the arching nose, the proportions of his face were abruptly altered. The effect was

264

uncanny. Except that the marks of sixty years' hard living were absent from these smooth cheeks, it was the face of her own father that looked up at her.

"What is wrong, Lady Shesu?" the boy faltered.

"Nothing. Nothing," she said quickly, jerking her hand away. "Come, let us walk up to the pavilion, there is much we must talk about."

"The pavilion. I remember the pavilion! Lady Shesu, is this the garden I used to play in?"

"Aye, I suppose it is."

"I am sure it is." He halted where the two paths joined and looked slowly around again, as if groping after something that eluded him. "But—is it—changed, somehow?"

"Nay, I think not. Does it seem different to you?"

"Not exactly . . ." His voice trailed off uncertainly. He hesitated, then raised puzzled eyes to hers. "It is just a *little* garden. I thought it was very large."

"Well, you were very small when you played here. I expect everything looked large to you then." His accent was beginning to disturb her badly—every word was a tiny, nagging reproach. She could not help adding, "You must say 'garden,' not 'garlen.'"

He looked at her quickly, then away. "I am sorry," he said in a low tone, taking great care with the words.

Now I have hurt him, she thought. He is like his father—too easily hurt. "Come," she said, thinking, I must say what I have to say! But she did not know how to begin, and they walked in silence up the steps of the pavilion.

"I guess nothing is ever *quite* the same," he said softly as he followed her. At the top of the steps he paused again, his eyes on the empty gold-and-cedar chair upon the dais. "My father used to sit there," he said suddenly.

"Aye." She did *not* want to talk about Nenni. As she sank into her own chair, she added with a smile, "And I used to sit here, and tell you stories. Do you remember them?"

"I remember about Godsland," he said shyly. He turned again toward his father's chair. "Lady Shesu—"

"And do you remember playing in the pool down there?" she said quickly. "And sailing your boat? You had a boat once—"

"I have it still!" he exclaimed.

"You—have it still? You carried it all the way to Babylon, kept it all these years?"

"Aye. The men did not take it from me—the men with beards, you know. I think they were the Hyksos, Lady Shesu."

"Oh, Thoth, the Hyksos are gone forever. My lord father drove them over the edge of the world many years ago."

"Nay—I think he drove them only as far as a place called Kadesh. Lady Shesu—" The boy came over to her and peered earnestly into her face. "The men of Kadesh are not as you think they are. Nehsi says they bend their necks and praise the glory of the Black Land, but they do not! I did not see even one do such a thing. They scowl and stare at Egyptians, and whisper behind their hands. Tjah says if they are disrespectful now, next they will be rebelling! He says if warriors were sent there at once, only a few warriors—"

"Nonsense, there is no need to send warriors anywhere. You are as full of imaginings as ever."

"Nay, it is true! It was not only I who saw it—"

"Thoth, cease arguing with me!" she said sharply. As quick anxiety flooded his face, her own apprehension receded. He was not going to be hard to handle, she had only to be firm with him. In a calmer tone she went on, "You will do well to leave such matters to older and wiser minds. Children should not meddle in affairs of which they know nothing."

He gazed at her mutely for a moment, then turned and walked to the pavilion steps, where he stood looking out in the direction of the pool and its big tamarisk tree. "I am sorry," he said in a low voice. "But it is so, what I told you. Ahmose would know." Suddenly he swung around to her with an expression of such anguish that she was startled. "Lady Shesu," he said. "Please—will you tell me where Ahmose is?"

"Ahmose-pen-Nekhbet? Why, he is—I do not know, exactly, he—"

"You do not know either?" the boy cried.

"He always lived somewhere about the Southern Barracks of the bodyguard, and he may be there still. I have not set eyes on him for years. He grew . . . too old . . . to be useful. When I relieved him of his post I offered him a house and lands upriver in Nekheb where he was born—or even here in Thebes—slaves to care for him, physicians . . . it was obvious he needed them.

266

But he would have none of it. He had slept all his life, he said, in a warrior's hammock of net, and preferred to die in one. An obstinate old man. I believe someone told me he was ill—and now, here he is without physicians."

"But—oh, he is not dead, is he?"

"Nay, I would have heard of that."

Thoth drew a long, quavering breath and moistened his lips. "May I see him? Please, may I go to him very soon?"

"Today, if you like." Her fingers were beginning to drum a little on the arm of her chair. Every time she glanced at the boy he seemed to look more like her father. Besides, she did not want to talk about Ahmose, either. More to change the subject than anything else, she corrected his accent again. "You mean 'soon,' not 'shoon,' Thoth. I cannot understand why you should have forgotten so entirely! Did your mother not speak Egyptian to you?"

"My mother? Do you mean Nanai?"

"Nanai? Who is that?"

"She is my—mother. My Babylonian mother."

She stared at him in consternation. "I mean your *mother*. Iset. Was she not with you? Did she not—care for you, in Babylon?"

"Nay," he faltered. "I do not know her."

"But surely you had someone! I sent—I—you had a slave-woman, a Nubian—"

"Aye. I remembered *her,* on the journey back." The boy's voice had suddenly grown hard and resentful. "In Arvad. She was tall and never answered me. She let go my hand—in the place where the caravans make ready. Then she walked away and left me."

"She *left* you? But—did she not come back?"

"Nay."

A deep shiver ran through Hatshepsut, and all her assurance crumbled away again just as it had when she first saw him standing on the path. Iset gone—dead, no doubt, on the sea voyage—the slave-woman faithless, and a five-year-old boy alone among bearded strangers, thousands of leagues from everything he knew. . . .

I do not want to know about this, she thought swiftly. I will not ask him anything else.

But she heard herself saying in a strange, strained voice, "Where did you live, then—in Babylon? With this—Nanai? With *Sand-dwellers?*"

"They are not Sand-dwellers in Babylon," he corrected her. "It is a great city, with a river—though not like this one—and a tower called Etemenanki, where the gods walk about sometimes on the highest stage— The—the *other* gods, you know—"

"Thoth! There are no other gods save ours of Egypt—no *real* gods!"

"Aye, Ea is a god. He must be. It was he who took me away from you and Ahmose, and brought me to Babylon that Ibhi-Adad might pay his debts."

"Ibhi-Adad?" she repeated faintly, stumbling over the unfamiliar syllables.

"The potter who was my—who adopted me. He was very kind to me, they were all kind. Nanai . . ." He drew a deep breath and went on hastily. "I studied at the School for Scribes, by the temple walls."

"Thoth, listen to me! You must forget what these barbarians have taught you. Amon-Re is god, do you hear me? Not this Ea—" She almost choked on the word.

Gravely, reluctantly, with his dark eyes troubled, he shook his head. "Ea is a god too," he said softly. "Or else neither is a god at all."

It was so much like something Nenni would have said that she felt the little hairs rise on the back of her neck.

"Do not talk so!" she cried. "You sound like your father—" She stopped abruptly, but already his eyes had moved with quick interest back to the big gold-and-cedar chair.

"My father sat there, didn't he?" he mused.

"He did indeed," she muttered. "For hours together—days together—brooding and staring straight through one."

"Aye, I *remember* that!" Thoth breathed. His face was suddenly alight with some inner discovery. "Why, I know who he was—he was the Lonesome Man."

"Nonsense," began Hatshepsut.

"He *told* me he was lonely," the boy insisted. "I remember it. He said all kings are lonely."

"That is absurd! Your father was full of absurd ideas. Kings are not lonely, how could they be? My lord father was the greatest of kings, and I am certain *he* was never lonely. That is really *his* chair, your grandfather's. Did you know that? This is his garden —his palace—his wine cup on the table there, brought from the treasure house of a king of the Nine-Bows whom he conquered. He was greater than all kings together, my lord father. . . . You were born the day he flew up to the gods. How well I remember *that*."

"Where was *my* father's palace?" asked the boy softly.

"Oh—this is the royal dwelling. Your father occupied it too, of course—for a time."

Thoth watched her for a moment in silence, then said, "Lady Shesu, please tell me about him. I remember so little, not even what he looked like. Is there not something here—like the chair, like the wine cup—that belonged to *him?*"

"Nay, nothing. I would scarcely know what to tell you of him, Thoth. He was a very strange person." She paused, then finished abruptly, "He was ill, ill for years—and now he is dead. There is little else to say about him."

"I thought—someone told me Pharaohs do not die."

"He has—flown up to the gods," Hatshepsut amended rigidly.

"But he was a great king too, like my grandfather?"

"He was king, yes."

She stood up suddenly and began to walk about the pavilion. I cannot bear any more of this, she thought. I must say what I have to say—at once—very briefly—merely tell him what he is to do, then leave, get away from him!

She swung to face him, and was stricken again by the sight of him standing there in his gaudy, touching finery, and by the haunting quality of his eyes.

"Lady Shesu," he said in a low voice, "will I be king too?"

Now, she thought. *Now,* quickly. "We must talk of that, Thoth," she answered. "And soon, too. I cannot be with you much longer, Nehsi and many other affairs are waiting for me. We had best speak of it now."

"Aye," he whispered. She saw his throat move convulsively as he swallowed. Suddenly he burst out, "Lady Shesu, they do not like having me here, all those people on the riverbank, and at the landing, when we docked. They do not like *me.* I could tell by the way they looked at me—they do not want me for their prince! Please, must I be king now, right away, I mean, at once? I do not know how to be a king! I do not even know how to be a prince yet."

She had been listening in stunned astonishment. "You do not—want to be king?"

"Not yet! I cannot!"

"You—are—quite—right," she breathed, reaching blindly for a chair. The king's chair was nearest and she sank into it.

"I am—right?" he repeated uneasily, watching her.

"Aye. Aye, indeed you are! Entirely right. We are quite in accord. I am—very glad you are so sensible about it, and understand so well." Her confidence was returning with a rush as she realized how miraculously well everything was beginning to work out.

"Oh, I understand. I must learn to be a prince."

"Before that, you must learn to be an Egyptian," she said pointedly—too pointedly; she had not meant to bring the painful color into his cheeks. She rushed on. "You have much to learn—more than ordinary boys, naturally, so an ordinary scribe's school would never do. You will enter the temple, that will give you the proper training."

"The temple? The big one across the river, that we sailed past this morning?"

"Aye, that is the Temple of Amon. There are many learned men there to instruct you in all you should know. You will absorb their teachings best if you enter one of the lower orders, like any other boy desiring to be a priest."

"But I do not want to be a *priest,* do I?" he asked in bewilderment.

"In the beginning, aye, of course you do! To prepare yourself for—whatever may come later, you must be taught a priest's duties, as well as a scribe's skills and a statesman's wisdom." She smiled, feeling that she had put it very well, and leaned back with her hands on the golden falcon heads that decorated the arms of the chair. "Time enough after that to taste a prince's amusements and a king's responsibilities. Do you not see that?"

"Aye," he faltered. As if to make up for his uncertain tone, he nodded rapidly, but his eyes showed both confusion and dismay. "I am to live at the temple? But—I will see you sometimes, won't I?"

"Oh, you must not worry about that! Your first duty is to

270

study very hard. You must learn our gods and our ways again, that is the most important."

He nodded again, this time with reluctant obedience; but he was still frowning slightly. "Who will be king, though—while I am learning?"

"That need not trouble you. I am the living daughter of Amon. He gave Egypt into my keeping some years ago; he has told me already that my duty is not yet finished. I will know when it is time for you to—to rule, Thoth. You must trust me."

He said slowly, "I—do." But his eyes searched her face so questioningly that she waited a moment for him to speak before she realized he was not going to.

Nervously she rose. "I must go now. If you like I will summon someone to take you to Ahmose. Do you wish me to do that?"

"Aye!" Obviously he wished it so much it almost hurt him.

"Very well." She clapped her hands; a slave appeared at once in the gateway opening onto the Great Court. "Merely tell him where you wish to go . . ."

Thoth had already turned away from her and was running headlong down the path.

Well! she thought. He has no manners, that is certain. Not even a farewell, for all he seemed so glad to see me. . . . She sat down again abruptly in her father's chair and for a few moments sat motionless, staring toward the gate through which Thoth had disappeared, gripping the golden falcon heads with hands that she presently realized were stiff and icy. Irritably she rubbed them together, reflecting, Whatever the child does, he manages to upset me.

5.

"*This* house?" whispered Thoth.

"Aye, Master. This is where the captain said he lived. Will I open the door for you, Master?"

Thoth swallowed but did not answer for a moment. Now that he actually stood here, separated from Ahmose only by a wooden door, he felt a strange reluctance to go in. It did not seem the sort of place where Ahmose would live—this tiny house at the farthest edge of the parade ground west of the Southern Barracks, a mere hut built of crumbling mud-brick and half smothered by palmettos and weeds, with no sign of a garden or any care. No wonder Tjah had not known of it. The slave had questioned one officer after another before succeeding at last in guiding him here; no one would give this place a second glance unless he was searching for it. It even looked empty.

The slave moved a tentative hand toward the latch, and Thoth's mouth went dry. He realized suddenly why it was he did not want to go in. Everything, everyone he had seen so far had been changed, somehow. Even Lady Shesu. He had borne that; but if Ahmose were not as he remembered, he knew he could not bear it.

"Master—will I open the door?"

"Nay, wait! Let us knock, first."

The slave obeyed with such vigor that Thoth seized his arm. "Hush! I think he is ill—"

The door opened. Thoth found himself staring up into the yawning face of a Nubian boy little older than himself, though twice as tall. His lanky black body seemed to stretch up and up forever, and his eyes blinked sleepily, then in astonishment, at Thoth and his companion.

"Cease your gaping!" the latter snapped out. "This is your prince, brought here by order of Her Radiance to find Ahmose-pen-Nekhbet. Is he inside?"

"Aye," croaked the boy.

"Then stand away, you fool." To Thoth, the older slave added with a bow, "Will I wait for you, Master?"

Thoth shook his head, swallowing again, and stepped into the hut.

After the brilliant sunshine outside, it was like stepping into a cave. For a moment Thoth could see nothing at all; then gradually, as his eyes adjusted to the greenish light filtering through the palm fronds that choked the small, high openings on one wall, he made out a single room with a few sticks of crude furniture and an earthen floor. His eye hurried in distaste over an encrusted cooking pot, a heap of unidentifiable litter in one corner, the film of dust over everything—then fixed on a dim alcove in the far wall, where hung a ship's hammock bulky with the outlines of a man.

In an instant Thoth was beside it, looking down on the mo-

272

tionless figure of his old friend. His legs gave way; he sank to his knees beside the hammock, whispering "Ahmose." The old man lay sleeping, his gnarled hands at his sides, his gaunt profile pointing up at the ceiling. Recognition flooded back to Thoth; every line of Ahmose's face, every feature, was as familiar as if he had never been away. The skin of the face had become as fragile as paper, but the scythe-shaped scar still traced its pattern across one cheek.

Thoth's gaze followed it lovingly as he repeated, "Ahmose." Still the beloved, scarred face did not turn to him, the sunken eyes did not open. "Ahmose!" Thoth said, louder. Then, in sudden panic, "Ahmose! *Ahmose!*" Leaping to his feet, he whirled toward the gaping slave boy, crying, "He is dead!"

"Nay, he is not dead, Master. He is sleeping."

"Then why does he not hear me? I cannot wake him! Ahmose!"

Falling to his knees again, Thoth grasped both the wide, bony old shoulders in his hands and tried frantically to rouse the old man. Behind him, the Nubian boy added, "No use to do that, Master. This old one sleeps all day—all night, sometimes."

"But will he not wake?" cried Thoth.

The boy did not answer at once. Thoth, half-blind with tears, turned to glare up at him, and found him peering intently down into the hammock.

"I think he is waking now, Master."

Thoth whirled back just in time to see the wrinkled eyelids flutter almost imperceptibly. He watched, not daring to breathe. Presently they fluttered again, then slowly lifted. Feeling a relief so exquisite it was almost pain, he flung his arms around as much of Ahmose as he could reach. He felt a tremor go through the old man's frame, and the sagging cheek jerk against his own. I have startled him, he thought in remorse, quickly lifting his head. He does not even know I am here.

"Ahmose," he whispered very softly.

An expression of unutterable longing crept over Ahmose's face; his eyes still gazed straight ahead, but they slowly filled with tears.

"Ahmose! Look at me—it is I, Thoth!"

"Little Thoth," muttered the old man yearningly.

"I am truly here, Ahmose! Look! Please look at me!"

Ahmose gave a faint, comforting smile and whispered, "I am looking, little one."

But he was not; he still thought it all a dream. In despair Thoth reached out and with one hand on each wrinkled cheek gently turned Ahmose's head toward him.

"*Now* can you see me? Oh, please, please see me!"

The old man's eyes finally focused on Thoth—at first in mild surprise, then with growing intentness. Suddenly his whole face quivered; tears sprang to his eyes as he groped for the boy with one hand, trying to raise himself upon his elbow. Thoth seized the hand and hugged it to him hard, torn between joy and terrible anxiety. Ahmose was so old, so frail—but he had not changed. He never would.

"Thoth?" quavered the rusty old voice, tremulous now with eagerness, but still uncertain.

"I am here, Ahmose. It is truly I. Did you think you were dreaming?"

Ahmose nodded in silence, his mouth working, his hand moving tremblingly over Thoth's face and shoulders as if to convince himself they were real.

"I came back only today. I look different, I know. I have been in Babylon. But you knew me, didn't you?"

"Aye. I have been waiting."

The voice was so weak that Thoth's heart suddenly overflowed with pity and terror. "Ahmose—you are ill. And no one has taken care of you! Let me get physicians, someone to move you out of this place!"

"Nay . . . do not fret, little one. I am content now."

"They have potions and magic—they could cure you—"

"There is no cure—for what ails me." A hint of the familiar grin crept over Ahmose's face, twisting his scar in the old way and giving Thoth just a glimpse of the gap between two front teeth. "I am too old, little one—that is all. Too old to live. Too stubborn to—die. I was—waiting for you."

"Oh, Ahmose . . . I missed you . . ." Thoth's throat tightened convulsively and he swallowed twice in an angry effort to control his voice. "Ahmose, do you remember the little galley you carved for me? I have it still, I kept it all the years I was in Babylon."

Ahmose gave the ghost of his old chuckle and slowly winked

274

one eye. *"Aii,* we fought some—mighty battles in her, didn't we
—little one? Mighty—battles. But all my wars—are won now."
A note of dim surprise came into his voice; he added, as if to
himself, "I have won. I waited—and now you are here."

"Aye, I am here. I won't leave you again, Ahmose. Not ever."

"I knew—they would have to bring you back. I knew. I—
waited. Stubborn." Again a faint smile flickered over his lips,
then his face changed. "Thoth—" he whispered. "I must tell you
—something—"

"What is it, Ahmose? Wait—lie still!"

But suddenly the old man was trembling, trying to sit up. His
eyes sought Thoth's with desperate urgency, his lips moved;
when he could bring forth no sound he redoubled his efforts to
raise himself on his elbow, though the struggle drained all color
from his face.

"Ahmose, wait! You are not strong, you must not tire yourself! Tell me later—rest now, you must rest, you might—"

"Nay. Nay. It is why I waited!"

"Oh, Ahmose, lie still, please! Lie still and tell me. I can hear
you. See, I will come very close, like this, you can just whisper
it—"

The old man fell back, his eyes still urgently holding Thoth's.
In his haste to relieve their anxiety Thoth put his arms around
Ahmose before he had finished scrambling up from his knees.
The hammock swerved a little under his weight, and to catch his
balance he put an instant's pressure on the hand resting on Ahmose's chest. To his horror the old man gasped and closed his
eyes, whispering in a breathy sigh, *"Aii*—little one, you hurt me."

"Oh, I am sorry, I am so sorry, I didn't mean to—Ahmose, is
it all right now? Ahmose—*Ahmose!"*

In terror Thoth stared down at the still face, the closed eyes.
Hastily he moved his hand over the old man's chest, felt it still
rising and falling, though so gently he could barely be sure of it.
It was all right, he was alive, perhaps he had fainted. I must
do something, the boy thought desperately. Help him some
way. . . .

Quickly but very carefully he disengaged his other hand and
began to rub one of the old man's between both of his. It felt so
lifeless it frightened him; he dropped it and began stroking the
domelike old forehead, glancing frantically about in search of

275

something, someone who might help. His eye encountered the lanky figure of the Nubian boy, who still stood in the center of the room gazing vacantly at his master.

"You! Fetch help, do something! Can't you see he's—he's ill? Make haste!"

"No use, Master. He's asleep now."

"But he was awake only a moment ago! Something is wrong!"

The boy shook his head. "It's the same as always. He will sleep a long time now."

"But he said I hurt him! Has anything like that ever happened before?"

"Aye."

Partially reassured but still uneasy, Thoth turned back to look at Ahmose again. It was true he seemed only to be sleeping; his chest still rose and fell peacefully, and a little color had returned to his face, which a moment ago had looked pale as a Libyan's. Perhaps he was all right—only exhausted from the effort he had made to sit up. Perhaps when one was as old as that, one could not stave off sleep when it was needed, or interrupt it before its needful time was up.

"How long will he sleep?" he asked the Nubian.

"A long time. Till sundown—maybe till night."

"Oh." Thoth's heart sank with disappointment. It was hours until sundown. If only Ahmose had not tried to get up—if only there had been a better way to calm him. He had grown too anxious, too excited. What had he wanted to say?

For a moment Thoth stood disconsolately, gazing down at the beloved, silent face. Then he sighed and turned away, walking to the door to stare out at the empty parade ground, returning to stand irresolute by the hammock. Suddenly the squalor of the room became unendurable. He turned on the stupid-faced slave boy, angrier than he had ever been in his life.

"Well, why do you stand there gaping? Do something! Clean this room—get that litter of food off the table, those rags out of the corner! What have you ever done to make him more comfortable, you small-eared *edimmu,* you despised one of all fireside gods, you washer of *harimates'* linen!" In his fury Thoth had lapsed into Babylonian, and the Nubian turned ashen at the flow of terrible-sounding foreign curses. Half in tears from anxiety and rage, Thoth picked up a broom leaning against one wall and flung it at him with all his might. "Move, I tell you! You *shall* take care of him, I'll *make* you! Sweep this room clean, do you hear me? And after that get a knife and chop off those branches out yonder so that some light and air can come in here for once! And after that make him something good to eat, and fetch him beer in the best goblet you can find, and get him a clean coverlet for his bed! I'll—I'll kill you if you don't take care of him after this!"

Already the Nubian had fallen to work so frantically that curling food, litter and dust seemed to be melting before his hands by magic. Thoth watched a moment, drawing great, shaky breaths and trying to gain control of his emotions. Finally he knelt by the hammock, satisfied himself once more that Ahmose was sleeping deeply, then left the hut.

Outside, he stood a moment blinking in the glare of early afternoon. Ahead of him the dusty expanse of parade ground lay deserted in the sunshine, edged on its far side by the low line of mud-brick barracks. Behind the barracks the palms of the grove near the palace stirred gently against a brilliant, empty sky. Nothing else moved. In the stillness he could plainly hear the faint crunching of his sandals in the dust as he started walking aimlessly, restlessly, toward the palms. There was not another sound except the distant creaking of a water-lift—two flutelike notes monotonously repeated—and occasionally, from far off in another direction, a desert lark's lonely, echoing song. The whole world seemed to have withdrawn from him into the mystery of sleep.

He found himself walking faster, uneasy at the sound of his own footsteps; soon he was running, with his head down and his elbows clamped against his sides, as if to make himself as small an intrusion as possible in this still, sunny wasteland. I remember the way, he told himself nervously. I need only skirt the barracks to the left there, go through a bit of the grove and down that walk between the vineyards and the tall hedge, and that will lead past the storehouses and the place where I saw the scribes working, back to the Great Court.

A few moments later he arrived, breathless, at his goal. The Great Court was empty too, now—except for the sentries standing motionless beside the great carved columns of the palace porch—and silent, with the sunlight filling it as golden wine fills a cup. He crossed it quickly, quietly, to the door in its wall that led into the little garden. There he paused, his hand on the latch and his forehead pressed against the smooth-worn wood. It is the first time, he told himself firmly. I will pretend I was not here earlier.

He raised his head and looked at the silvery wood of the gate, and knew precisely what lay beyond. It could not really have changed, it had only seemed so because he was upset and tense, afraid of what Lady Shesu would think of him. Now he would go in as if for the first time, and there it would be, just as he remembered it—spacious, green and cool, with its red graveled paths and brilliant flowers, and the tamarisk tree throwing a long, pointed shadow across the water.

He opened the gate, walked quickly a little way down the graveled path and stopped, looking carefully around him. It still seemed small—much, much too small to be quite like the garden he had always pictured. That was because he had grown; he would have to get used to that. For the rest, there was the pavilion ahead of him, dressed in its lacy vines; there were the lawns and flower beds, the deep shade under the acacias beside the wall. The air still smelled of grass and flowers and sun-baked brick. He drew a long, trembling breath of the old, remembered fragrance and slowly turned. There was the pool—again, smaller than he expected—but still the same, with its reeds waving gently at one end and the sun dancing on the water. And there was the tamarisk tree beside it.

Thoth's feet moved of their own accord off the path and across the grass toward the sheltered spot beneath the tree, where Ahmose had always sat. The stone bench was still there, but it was empty—naturally, since Ahmose lay sleeping in his dim little house far across the parade ground. Probably Ahmose had not been in the garden for years. No matter, Thoth told himself, kicking restlessly at the turf. Lady Shesu still comes here, often —and she has not changed. Anyhow, she has not changed *much*. I'm sure she hasn't. Not really.

His eyes returned to the bench, drawn back by a still irresistible feeling that Ahmose must be sitting there, his twisted fingers busy with a knife and a whittled mast, the fascinating gap in his teeth showing with his smile. To make the bench seem less desolately empty, Thoth sat down on it himself.

278

Sitting there, with the stone cool and gritty under his thighs and palms, he heard a door slam in some distant courtyard, and a faint burst of laughter. The sound seemed to release something in him; now, as if his ears had been unstopped, he began to hear the garden itself. Birds were talking softly among themselves with little flutelike noises; the breeze had one voice when it sighed through the tamarisk branches, quite another when it rattled through the reeds in the pool. He remembered both. A fish plopped with a neat, tiny noise and drew Thoth's eyes to a set of widening circles beside a lotus pad. At the same time he was again aware of the old fragrance filling his nostrils. This time even the fish seemed to be in it, and the way his hair used to smell when it was wet from the pool. It was as if the garden had waited until he was alone, then had risen up like a comforting presence all about him.

For one brief moment he came near to capturing the old magic, as bright and fresh as it had been in his dreams. Sitting bolt upright on the bench, his hands gripping the stone seat, he strained after the one obscure detail that still seemed to be missing. What was it? In an effort to hurry its coming, he whispered, "I used to play right there, in that pool. I used to sit on this very bench with Ahmose. Maybe right there, on the grass, is where I stood when he gave me my galley."

Used to—used to—was that the trouble? The words brought a wave of homesickness washing through him.

That is foolish, he thought, how can I be homesick for the garden now, when I am right in it? I cannot be.

But the secret presence of the garden had withdrawn from him a little; he was not as close to it as he had been a moment before. "I sat on this very bench," he whispered urgently. "Played in that very pool—"

He stopped at once. He was only making it worse.

He stood up and walked slowly toward the pool, dragging his hand over the heavy trunk of the tree as he passed it, and feeling the bark rough and serrated under his fingers. That was odd, too; he knew the feel of that rough bark, his hand remembered it. But never before had he thought of the tamarisk tree as having bark at all—bark and foliage and branches, like just any tree. It had been The Place Where Ahmose Sat. As for the pool—before his unwilling eyes it divided itself into a thousand small objective

279

details: water, lilies, sunlight, smooth mud, reeds—commonplace things he might see in any pool. There had been nothing commonplace in the magic sea beneath his galley.

As he turned away, a new noise struck his ear—a large, fluttering sound, quite unfamiliar. He searched for it, and discovered at the other end of the pool a tall golden perch half hidden by the papyrus stalks that rimmed the water's edge. A great white bird with a bare black head and neck sat on the perch, chained to it by a silver chain. Thoth walked toward it, frowning uneasily. As he watched, the bird raised one snowy wing and industriously pecked and groomed underneath it with its long curved bill, making its head dart in and out as swiftly as a snake's; then suddenly it raised its head and both wings together, settled its plumage with the fluttering sound Thoth had heard before, and lapsed into sleek passivity, gazing around it with a stupidly indignant expression.

Thoth stared back at it resentfully. An ibis. What was it doing here? It was no part of his memory of the garden.

For some reason the ibis' presence deepened his depression. Turning his back on it, he walked slowly up the slope and along the path, scuffling his sandals through the fine red gravel and struggling with a sense of foreboding he could neither define nor understand. He had almost reached the pavilion before he became aware of the small figure sitting very still on the topmost step, surveying him with grave and interested eyes.

He stopped short. It was a little girl, no more than four or five years old to judge by her size, and she was quite alone. Like other children her age she was naked, except for a necklace made of tiny golden stars and a pair of diminutive scarlet sandals. She sat with both hands clasped about her knees in a pose of unconscious grace and childish dignity, her silken hair just touching her shoulders and framing a delicate, pointed, intelligent little face.

"I—I didn't see you," Thoth said at last.

"I saw *you*," she answered seriously. "I've been watching you a *long time*."

"Oh." Thoth smiled in spite of himself at her solemn, vehement way of talking. Unexpectedly, she smiled back, then leaned toward him with a confidential air.

"You don't like the ibis, do you?" she whispered.

"Nay."

"Nor do I! He flaps his old wings at me. Once he chased me. But we can't get rid of him, it's no use your trying. Yen says my lady mother wants him here."

"Who is your lady mother?" asked Thoth, who had been puzzling over a nagging familiarity about her features.

"My mother is the queen. But you mustn't talk about me to her."

"The queen! Lady Shesu is your mother? Then are you Nefer?"

"Nefer? Of *course* not!" exclaimed the child in a tone of such utter scorn that he smiled again.

"Who are you, then?"

"I am Meryet."

The name was unknown to Thoth. He repeated it after her, stumbling a little on the unfamiliar Egyptian way of joining "r" and "y." Instantly the little girl went into a gale of flutelike laughter, pressing both hands over her mouth and gazing up at him with dancing eyes.

"Not 'Mayet'!" she said between giggles.

He realized his Babylonian accent had turned her name into the Egyptian word for "cat." To cover his embarrassment, he said quickly, "Aye, Mayet! That should be your name. You look like a little kitten."

She sat perfectly still for a moment, looking up at him with her eyes growing round with shy pleasure. In a moment she recovered her quaint, adult poise and said graciously, as if giving him a present, "I am six years old. What is *your* name?"

"Thoth. I am eleven." She was very small for six, he reflected, but he did not say it, in case she hated such remarks as much as he did. She did look like a kitten, with her pointed chin and her wide, slightly tilted eyes. She looked like Lady Shesu, too.

"Why must I not mention you to your mother?" he asked.

"Because she doesn't like me."

"Why, she must!"

"Nay, she doesn't," insisted the child solemnly. "Because Amon sent me and not a boy, Yen says."

"Who is Yen?"

"My nurse. *She* likes me. But none of the others do—they mustn't. Yen told me."

"What others?"

"You know. Count Senmut and Count Nehsi and Count Thu tiy and Count Ineny and Lord Hapuseneb and—you know."

"Oh." Thoth smiled faintly. "If it's they you mean—then no body likes me either."

"Nay," she agreed, but she looked a little puzzled.

"Who *do* they like?" he asked with some bitterness.

To his surprise, Mayet answered, "Nefer."

Thoth studied her a moment, trying to remember her olde sister. He could recall only a thin, pale child who used to sla him—nothing at all like this little maid. "Do you like Nefer?" h asked.

"Nay." She shrugged her small shoulders, again with tha quaint, grownup air. "But I don't play with Nefer."

"Who do you play with?"

"Myself. And Yen, when she isn't busy." She hesitated, gazing up at him intently, then added, "Are you going to live here now?"

"I don't—know." Thoth turned and looked out over the emer ald lawns, the bees drunken over the flower beds, the little pool "I *used* to live here," he said longingly. "I used to play in thi garden, all day, every day. It was so wonderful. . . ."

"Why didn't I see you?"

"Because I went away, a long time ago. I only came back t the garden today."

"And now it isn't wonderful any more?" she said softly.

He glanced around to see her whole small face mirroring hi own sadness.

"Nay," he faltered. "That is—it is still beautiful, but somehow it is different." Suddenly he could not look at her any longer could not bear to watch her face reflecting everything in his mind "I must go now," he muttered, turning away hastily.

"Oh, why?" she cried.

"I have to—see someone—right away."

He was already hurrying down the path, possessed by such need to move, to act, to burst through the mysterious pall of de pression which had settled over him, that he felt as if ants wer stinging him all over. Sundown? Why had he believed that stupid Nubian? Ahmose might wake much sooner—he might be awake now. I must get back! he thought. I must be there when he wakes I must *make* him wake! He has something to tell me. . . .

282

He ran headlong across the Great Court, struggled for a furious instant with the heavy gate on the opposite side, and finally wrenched it open to plunge into the walled North Walk by which he had come. Down the narrow canyon of sunlight he sped, past the open gates of the Scribe's Court, past the House of Weights and the thick, secret walls of the Treasury, past sentries who stared after him and palace servants who dodged out of his way, through the hedged walk flanking the vineyard, across the corner of the grove and out at last upon the great dusty desert of the parade ground. Panting hard now, he stumbled across its endless expanse on legs that pumped slower and slower until they seemed about to rebel altogether. At last he flung himself through the litter of fresh-cut palm fronds now scattered about the little house and, catching sight of the Nubian, cried out, "Has he waked yet?"

"Nay, Master!" The Nubian dropped branch and knife and hurried after him as Thoth forced his legs to carry him the remaining few paces to the door. "I cleaned everything very good, Master! I swept and let in the light and made everything like for the queen, don't kill me, Master, I'll take care of him very good now, I brought beer and made food—"

Thoth jerked open the door and stumbled at last into the room. For a moment he could do nothing but stand there, struggling for breath, while the frightened slave chattered at his side. Plainly, he had been busy—all signs of trash and dust had vanished, fresh air and sun poured down into a room that was a model of cleanliness and order. A moisture-beaded goblet of beer stood on the table, beside a covered dish. But there was something wrong about the figure in the hammock, something terribly wrong.

"Hush!" gasped Thoth, waving an imperative hand toward the slave.

Instantly the room was still—too still, like the hammock itself.

Thoth flung himself across the clean-swept floor and fell heavily on his knees, which refused to support him any longer. Ahmose lay exactly as he had left him, sunken eyes peacefully closed in their bony cavities, gnarled hands by his sides—but the fresh coverlet over his chest was no longer rising and falling, even very gently.

6.

The boy in front of Thoth hung up the towel and moved away
sandaled feet shuffled all along the line as Thoth stepped into his
place and scooped a dollop of natron-and-clay from the big copper bowl.

As he began methodically scrubbing his arms and hands, he
wondered how many times he had washed himself during the
thirteen months he had been at the temple. Many more than in
all his years at Babylon, that was certain—in two weeks here
one washed more than they did there in a year. To begin with,
one washed all over twice each day and once at night. Then there
were these washings before and after meals, as well as the washings and mouth rinsings before preparing offerings for the god or
filling the lamps for chapel ceremonies or mixing the wines for
libations. Besides that, one washed whenever the priests told one
to, and on feast days they seemed to be telling one to continually.

Not that I mind, really, he reflected, holding his arms over
the basin while the fat little priest-servant poured water over
them.

Being clean was like having your head shaved—once you got
used to the feel of it, you rather liked it. The little itchy creatures
which used to plague him in Babylon found no place to hide in
the curling, gold-wrapped side-lock which was all that remained
of his shock of hair. And he liked the thin linen *shentis*—a fresh
one every morning—which felt cool and pleasantly crisp against
his thighs. In plain truth, he felt better, clean. There was no doubt
he smelled better.

He raised one wrist and sniffed at it. I smell like an Egyptian,
he thought.

He smiled faintly, remembering the half-alien, half-familiar
mingling of scents which had risen from the crowd of Egyptians
in Ibhi-Adad's courtyard that day. One especially had teased his
memory—a faint, pungent smell he knew but could not identify,
though he had searched his recollection for it like a woman rummaging in a drawer. He knew it well now—it was clay-and-natron. Myrrh and beer and clay-and-natron, that was the smell of
an Egyptian. Crisp white linen and oiled brown flesh, that was

284

the look of one. He could not really say he missed the heavy embroideries and dirty fringes and sweaty armpits and scratching his head.

All the same, it grew deadly monotonous, washing all the time. Everything about temple life was monotonous.

It is the temple I mind, he thought. Not just the washings. The temple—day after day of it. Trying to be a priest. Why does she not let me be a *prince?* Why does she—oh, if I could talk to Ahmose!

The familiar ache stole through him as the old man's image filled his mind, and the old questions rose up—still there, still tormenting him, still unanswered. He had learned to live with them; but at first, when the wound was raw and fresh, he had gone to bed each night in dread, squeezing his eyes tight shut to keep that terrible picture from appearing. It always appeared, just the same. Out of the red-green blackness behind his eyelids the interior of Ahmose's little hut would slowly take shape, with himself kneeling beside the hammock. Then he would see the hammock swerve as he rose, see with agonizing clarity his own hand press for an instant on Ahmose's chest. *"Aii, little one, you hurt me."*

In anguish he would fling himself over in bed, every nerve and muscle rigid with the effort to change the picture, to imagine the hand not even touching Ahmose—grasping a chair instead, or a projection of the wall, or grasping nothing at all and letting himself fall flat. Oh, why had he not fallen, thrown himself down, *anything* except touch Ahmose. . . .

But he had touched Ahmose. The picture would not change. Down came the hand, inexorably, irrevocably. *"Little one, you hurt me."* Little one, you killed me.

Then he would leap out of bed and stumble about in the dark room, while the picture gave way to the questions. Ahmose—what did you want to tell me? Oh, if I had not leaned on you—? Would you be alive now if—? You wanted to say something, what was it, what was it?

It had been the worst at night, but in the daytime it was bad enough. How he had longed, those first weeks, to escape from all the strangers and the sound of their voices, to run away back to Babylon and some kind of life that was familiar.

Instead, three days after Ahmose's death he had found himself

285

stepping out of a litter in the temple courtyard—a stranger even to himself, with his shaven head and different clothes—to plunge straight into a life of such bewildering unfamiliarity that for weeks he moved through its mazes like one in a nightmare.

It was a life that held no privacy at all. Every minute of his day was regulated and prescribed, from the moment he rose in the low, barracks-like dormitory he shared with a dozen other boys, to the moment he returned at night, exhausted, to fall asleep once more upon the jackal skin which was his bed. He ate his meals at a long wooden table in the priests' common room with the same chattering crowd of boys—not whenever he was hungry, as people ate in Babylon, but at specified hours marked on the sun-stick in the courtyard. Even the food was regulated; its quantity was carefully measured to preclude any possibility of impious overindulgence, and its variety was strictly curtailed. No pulse, peas, beans, lentils, mutton, swine's flesh, onions, garlic, leeks or fish appeared on a priest's table, and during the days of certain festivals even salt disappeared. Kalba, Thoth reflected sadly, would have starved here—and he was in no danger of growing fat himself. Sometimes he craved a good salted fish so mightily that the very thought brought the saliva flooding into his mouth.

When he was not eating or sleeping—or washing—he was busy with lessons from the scribes in reading, writing and figuring, with instruction from the *sem* priests in the ways of Egypt's gods, with endless duties in the storerooms and offering chapels, with monotonous, solemn trips up and down the Nile on the sacred barges and across the river to the City of the Dead. He never saw Lady Shesu except from a distance when she walked through the Hall of Praise, remote as a star, to make the Weekly Offering. He did not know how to see her, and he had no time to find out. He was too busy learning to be a priest.

But he did not *want* to be a priest. . . .

Thoth sighed and reached for the towel. *Be obedient, give heed to those in authority, abide by their decisions.*

"Wait, young Highness!" The attendant priest sprang forward, wreathed in smiles, and snatched the towel from his hand. "Not that one! This. I saved a fresh one for you—as always."

Flushing, Thoth mumbled thanks and self-consciously used the clean towel, not looking at the priest. He knew well enough what Rehotep looked like—a little fat man, always short of breath, beaming, teetering obsequiously back and forth on his toes and heels—doubtless only trying to be nice. But there was something odd about his eyes. They were shrewd, prying; they didn't smile when he did.

"No trouble, young Highness?" he whispered on a forward teeter. "I thought I heard you sigh."

"I didn't sigh."

"Small wonder if you did, to be sure. This is a dull life for a young prince . . ."

"I didn't sigh," Thoth repeated, frowning. He left the room quickly and walked down the long corridor to start the day's lessons, wishing Rehotep would keep his clean towels and his solicitude to himself. What was he trying to do, make him more dissatisfied than he was already? Make it harder than it already was to be obedient, to trust Lady Shesu, to keep patiently at his tedious priestly tasks? There were several of the priests who were always at him like that—Khwed, that tall thin one, Chief Bearer of the Bark of the God, and a couple of his subordinates, and that long-chinned Sata from the storerooms—always wanting to know if he was bored, if he wouldn't be happier at the palace where he could associate with nobles' sons instead of these common boys; handing him a clean towel, giving him the easiest task, pushing the other novices out of the way to make room for him. No wonder the boys didn't like him. No wonder they never felt at ease with him, or tried to talk to him, or wanted him around.

Of course, there are more reasons than one for that, he reflected wearily.

He pulled open the tall door at the end of the corridor. It is because I am the prince, he thought. Then I wish I were not the prince! Or that I might *be* the prince, in fact as well as name. . . . Nay, it is something else. They just don't like me. There is something wrong with me.

He knew very well what it was. Though in appearance he was now thoroughly Egyptian, and his accent was fast vanishing, they still thought of him as a foreigner. Everyone did, whether they teetered and beamed at him or not. Perhaps they were right. Sometimes he thought he would never understand the thoughts of these Egyptians.

Outside, in the big forecourt of the temple, his spirits rose a little. There was nothing depressing about sun and mornin[g] breeze and crystalline air. The palms beyond the high wal[l] waved their heavy heads languidly, each leaf a cut jewel agains[t] the brilliant sky. From the direction of the Nile the shouting [of] rivermen and the slapping of sails sounded, faint but clear; fro[m] round about the court rose the usual morning clatter of beggar[s] and peddlers setting up shop for the day. Folding stools rattle[d] open, covered baskets filled with squawking sacrificial fowl wer[e] shoved and dragged into position, everywhere white *shentis* flut[t]ered, brown arms reached and flexed, gleaming backs ben[t.] Along the wall old men spread out mats and arranged thei[r] wares, their corded hands moving among the onions and offer[-] ing-bread to an accompaniment of gossip and bursts of cacklin[g] laughter. A piece of the sky had fallen in the flower sellers' shad[y] corner; it was a great sheaf of lotuses, Thoth saw—blue one[s] fragrant as the presence of a god, still dripping water from th[e] long, tubelike stems. A ragged urchin of nine or ten was arrang[-] ing them, vigorously scolding a naked little girl who stood besid[e] him sucking her finger and gazing around with enormous, solem[n] eyes. For just an instant the little girl at the palace flashe[d] through Thoth's mind—the one who looked like a kitten. Th[e] one Lady Shesu wanted to forget.

One would think she wanted to forget me, too, he thought.

He walked slowly across the huge court, the sun warming hi[s] bare shoulders. As always, his impulse was to swerve, mak[e] one glorious dash through the tall gates and lose himself in th[e] swarming streets of Thebes. *This is a dull life for a young prince* . . . He entered the east wing of the temple instead, passe[d] through the chilly, incense-freighted gloom of another columne[d] hall, and emerged into the staider sunlight of the Scribe's Court[-] yard beyond. He had his education to finish.

Khwed, Chief Bearer of the Bark of the God, leaned his tal[l] thin body far out of the storeroom doorway in order to watc[h] the young prince disappear into the east wing. Then he straight[-] ened and turned to the storeroom priest Sata and Rehotep, th[e] plump little attendant of the washroom, who stood beside him.

"I think it is almost time," he murmured. "Did you see hi[m] hesitate and glance out the gates yonder as he passed?"

"He did so yesterday also," said Sata. "And the day before that."

"And he sighs as he cleanses his hands," added Rehotep, teetering happily and hugging a stack of clean towels to his ample middle. "He denies it, but it is so, it is so, I see him do it."

"He still denies it?" asked Khwed, frowning. "Perhaps it is still a little early."

Sata rubbed his long, bony chin and nodded. "It will not do to be hasty," he muttered. "The affair is dangerous enough in any case. Senmut—"

"What more can he do to us?" demanded Rehotep. "Do you think to be a *sem* priest again some day, as we were under Akhem? The days of Akhem are over forever, the damage is done, our careers will end in the washroom and the storeroom. Nothing is left to us but this revenge, and why we should hesitate to take it, why dilly-dally and perhaps let it slip through our fingers, is more than I—"

"Patience, friend," Khwed soothed him.

Sata was still gazing thoughtfully in the direction the young prince had gone. "Dangerous," he repeated. "A dangerous business, stirring hornets' nests."

"Dangerous for Senmut!" Rehotep told him.

"For Senmut, for ourselves—and perhaps for all Egypt, too. Have you thought of that?"

"Did *he* think of it, when he stirred *his* hornets' nest?" demanded Rehotep.

"Peace, peace, we must keep cool heads." Khwed put a hand on his two friends' shoulders and guided them away from the doorway. "Our plans are made, and we will abide by them. We must choose our moment, that is all. I think I will talk to the prophetess once more."

One of the assistant high priests appeared in the passageway, headed for the Great Court. Unobtrusively the three separated, Sata vanishing into the nearest storeroom, Khwed starting briskly toward the Hall of Praise, and Rehotep, his plump jowls quivering with his usual beaming smile as he nodded to the passing priest, pattering breathlessly back to the washroom with his stack of towels.

"Aye, that is better, Highness, your accent is improving. Now the next proverb—keep the gutturals deep in your throat—"

" 'Let thy mind be deep, and thy speech scanty,' " read Thoth, reflecting wryly that nowadays he had small chance to do anything else. " 'Silence is more valuable than the *teftef* plant. Speak only when thou knowest thou canst resolve the—the question.' "

"The 'doubt,' " corrected old Neferneb. "Very good, very good. Now make me a fair copy of Ptah-hotep's wisdom, all that we have read this morning. Mind you fashion the ducks properly. . . ."

Folding his hands across his sagging belly, he leaned back against the acacia tree and went to sleep.

Thoth, cross-legged on a woven mat, spread out his writing materials. He could scarcely have imagined anything more unlike Inatsil's school in Babylon if he had tried. Instead of clay and stylus he had a vial of water, a rectangular pallet—slotted to hold reed pens and hollowed for two ink-cakes—and a smooth-plastered writing board which could be washed clean at the end of each lesson. One did not even hold a pen as one held a stylus, between palm and thumb, but gripped it with all the fingers bunched together—very awkward until one got used to it. Thoth had to admit, though, that drawing birds and animals was more interesting than poking wedge-shaped marks in clay. *"Rows of charming little pictures."*

But the things he found himself writing, in those charming little pictures! The more he studied the Egyptian sages, the more he marveled. Nowhere in the wisdom of these ancient ones had he found so much as a hint that life was sometimes cruel and the gods unjust. "Great is righteousness," Ptah-hotep had written. "It hath not been put to confusion since the days of Osiris." Staggering statement! Thoth thought of Gilgamesh and shook his head. He wondered what Nanai would say if she could read Ptah-hotep's "wisdom." He could almost hear her mocking laughter. "You expect life to be fair? Goodness to be rewarded?" *She* knew.

However, he copied diligently on, trying to believe the scrolls were right and he was wrong. Lady Shesu had said he must learn to be Egyptian.

Later, though, when old Neferneb had waddled back into the temple archives and stern-faced Wenamon had taken his place for the hour of mathematics, Thoth became stubbornly Babylonian again. Inatsil had taught him square roots, cube roots, compound interest, algebra—Egypt was ignorant of these matters. Wenamon's "algebra" was simple geometry; he had never even heard of a quadratic equation, and could no more have determined the area of a regular polygon than he could have sprouted wings. As for fractions—in Egypt if one wanted to express the double of one-fifth, one had to write "one-fifteenth-and-one-third." Today, when Wenamon handed him a long list of these "natural fractions of fractions" and ordered him to memorize them, Thoth could not restrain a protest.

"But teacher, I can work any problem you like in a much easier way! In Babylon—"

"You are no longer in Babylon, Your Highness," Wenamon interrupted, giving an irritable shake to his parchment. "You are in Egypt, which is a civilized land and performs all tasks in a civilized way. Your Highness will please work all problems in the Egyptian manner. Shall we proceed?"

"Aye, teacher," muttered Thoth, resigning himself to obedience and the memorizing of the list. Privately, he concluded that the Egyptians' "natural fractions of fractions" were the most unnatural mathematical device he had ever encountered in his life.

Still, if his days had consisted of nothing but lessons, he would have been reasonably content. Instead, after luncheon each day he joined the other novices for the boring round of temple duties under the guidance of various minor priests. Why, why? he asked himself. What a prince should know was how to aim a spear and draw a bow. Surely Pharaohs led armies as often as temple processions. He himself might be called upon to lead one soon—remember Kadesh!

Hatshepsut watched the door of her sitting room close behind Lord Uah and his two companions, and for a moment remained motionless, her hands clasped tightly before her and her body tingling with the strange tautness that had grown so familiar of late. Her brain was whirling, but underneath the tangle of thoughts and angry emotions one part of her was standing off curiously and studying the other.

It is as if my nerves were harpstrings, reflected this detached part of her mind. Stretched to the breaking point, jangling, giving off discords instead of music. . . . Look at me, standing here with my fingernails digging into my palms, actually hurting myself . . . that is not like me, not like me at all, what is happening to me lately?

She drew a long breath and spread her palms out flat against her sides. A wave of fatigue washed over her; her legs ached as if from violent exercise as she walked slowly through her bedroom and out into the little garden.

Uah—it was Uah who had twisted the harpstrings tight. Uah with his eternal nagging about that document, his eternal scolding about the army's needs. He always sapped her energy, wore her out with hatred— Aye, she hated the man, why not admit it? Superintendent of the Armory—she even hated his title and his function. It made one wild to see gold forever pouring out of the treasury and into Uah's hands, spent on feeding a rabble of soldiers who could be put to far better use as laborers—quarry laborers, building laborers.

Ptah's Beard, I must do something about it! she thought. There is so much I want to do—that *needs* doing. If I were a man, if I were free to move. . . .

She was no freer than in Nenni's day; at every turn that hated document in the archives bound her hands. She dared not destroy it, and she could not forget it—not with Uah always there to remind her. Could she rid herself of *him* somehow? she wondered. Nay, his father was Prince of Nekheb, one did not offend the heirs of Nekheb. They were all but independent monarchs as it was, and their vast holdings in the south were Egypt's sole buffer against the quarrelsome Nine Bows. Act too hastily against Lord Uah and she might really need his cursed army. . . .

She sighed and leaned her head against the back of the bench, closing her eyes. How dared he presume to remind her of her "duty"—how dared he mention Thoth's name! Until he did that she had been calm enough.

There was a slight noise at the gate; she whirled and found herself staring into Senmut's inquiring face.

"What's amiss, my lady? It is only I." He latched the gate and

292

came toward her slowly up the path. "Is anything amiss?" he repeated.

"Nay. You startled me, I suppose. Senmut—" Glancing up, she found him at her elbow, frowning down at her thoughtfully. "Send for wine. I am so weary."

He spoke to the slave posted inside the door of her apartments, then returned to her side. "Something has upset you," he said.

She nodded, then suddenly flung both hands over her face and drew a long, shuddering breath. "Senmut, I cannot bear this Uah any longer, something must be done about him—or about the boy, one or the other. The way Thoth looks at me, when I go to the temple to make the offering—never takes his eyes from me—I cannot bear that any longer either! I hate to go there. *I hate to go there!* To the temple of my beloved father—" The shrillness of her own voice shocked her. When Senmut reached out to her she moved quickly into his arms, glad to feel the warm, hard vigor of his body against her. "He wants to talk to me—each time he pleads with his eyes, and I never stop. Poor child!" The words came with a wrench. "Senmut, I have been cruel to him."

"Cruel? You have been merciful almost to a fault. And Nehsi, to the point of folly! The boy should never have left Babylon alive."

An unpleasant flash of heat rippled through her. "Senmut, what are you saying!" She pulled away from him, feeling as if she had said it herself. "Nehsi is no murderer—nor am I. Violence is abhorrent to me, I have told you that time and again."

"I'll say no more, my lady. But sometimes I think you are forgetting your own destiny in your concern for this waif."

"Waif? Thoth is my own nephew—almost my son!"

Senmut's arm drew tight and hard around her; with his other hand he turned her face to him and studied it. "Thoth is nothing, nobody," he said. "He is the son of a charioteer's daughter—the Tired One's bastard. That is all."

It was true. Her own father, Thutmose, had borrowed his divinity from the royal Aahmes—Mutnofret's children could not partake of it. The two lines were separate and distinct, scarcely even kin. For an instant she saw them clearly in her mind, as two lotus plants growing side by side from intertwining roots—one incandescent with the golden blood of Re, the other common greenery. Senmut was right, Thoth was nobody, nothing.

"Poor child!" she said again, but this time the words came more easily, with an obscure feeling of relief. She relaxed against the bench; a sense of peace stole over her.

Senmut leaned close, taking her hand in one of his big, corded ones. "I beg you, do not expose yourself to these difficult scenes again. Let me handle them for you. When Uah asks to see you— send for me."

"I will. I will."

There was a little silence, close and comforting, between them. Then he raised her hand, and his lips moved, warm and sensuous, against the inside of her wrist. Desire stirred in her; she moved her head against the back of the bench until she was looking into his eyes. After a moment he bent and set his mouth on hers; then he slid onto the bench beside her.

For a while she forgot how much she longed to be a man.

They sprang apart as the slave appeared in the doorway with the wine. Senmut took the tray and dismissed the man. Pouring a chilled and fragrant cup, he handed it to her, a slow smile carving the lines deep into his cheeks. She smiled back, her eyes and thoughts lingering on his strong, sensual mouth as she watched him over the rim of her cup.

They began to talk of other things; presently she found herself laughing at one of his disrespectful remarks about some pompous excellency and realized that she felt quite herself again.

Senmut is always good for me, she thought.

Thoth, once more newly purified by hand scrubbing and mouthrinsing, was in the Holy-of-Holies, finishing his usual after-luncheon task of fanning dust from the Sacred Bark of the God with a duck's-wing fan. He was breathless from the stuffiness of the sanctuary and from scrambling about over and under the bark to reach the last speck of dust. Irritably muttering "natural fraction" tables to himself, he tried to hasten his task. The novices were to witness a "Nodding of the God" at the mark of two—if they completed their assigned tasks in time—and Thoth did not want to miss it, for it was a type of oracle he had never seen.

As he straightened, puffing, from a particularly inaccessible spot under the right-hand carrying pole, he heard the faint note of a gong. That was the signal for the oracle, and he was not yet finished. Disgusted, he flung down his duck's wing.

"I do not blame you," said a voice behind him. "These menial tasks—and you a prince. Why do you not rebel?"

Thoth turned to see the cadaverous Khwed, Chief Bearer of the Bark, standing in the doorway. *"Rebel?"* he echoed.

"Aye. Demand your rights of Her Radiance. If you were to create a great trouble about it—"

"Nay, I could not!" Thoth was aghast. All the familiar warnings rushed into his mind: *Be thou obedient to those in authority . . . obey . . . rebel . . . obey.*

In the distance a second gong sounded.

"Leave the task, Your Highness. It is done well enough."

"Well—if you really think—"

An instant later Thoth was darting down the corridor toward the rear of the temple, trying to outrun his thoughts.

The oracle of the Nodding of the God always took place in the courtyard fronting the temple stables. The other oracles Thoth had seen—the ones called The Heaviness of Amon's Splendor—had occurred in the sanctuary's first antechamber. If a merchant, for instance, wished to discover whether a certain journey would be profitable, he gave gold or grain or fine linen into the hand of the officiating priest. Then the Bearers of the Sacred Bark, headed by Khwed, carried the golden image of Amon out of the Holy-of-Holies and three times around the antechamber. If good fortune was to befall the merchant, the bark grew heavy each time it passed him, so that the bearers staggered and could barely support it. Thoth had seen this with his own eyes and marveled at the weight of the hand of Amon, which could push bark, heavy golden image, and eight strong men about like toys. He wondered if the Nodding would be anything like that. He was eager to see it, that he might marvel again.

By the time he reached the stable courtyard a priest was already burning incense, three rich gifts were arranged on a table, and the first petitioner, a river captain, was standing beside it, with folded arms. As the priest put aside his censer, the riverman knelt in the dust, stretched out his hands toward the stable door, and droned his question—something about a voyage to Heliopolis.

There was a muffled thumping from the stable. Thoth, craning around the other novices, saw the door swing open, a glossy black head with flower-decked horns appear. Then the Apis himself plodded out of his sumptuous stall between two priests of the rank of Servant of the Bull, who held gilded lead ropes attached to a ring in the sacred mouth. He stopped directly in front of the petitioner and stood motionless except for a twitching of his tail. Then the lead ropes grew taut, pulling downward on his mouth. He lowered his head. The ropes became slack; he raised it up again. A cry of joy and praise burst from the kneeling river captain. The Apis turned, and escorted by his servants, plodded back into his stall.

The god had nodded.

Thoth, staring at the door through which the bull had vanished, tried hard to marvel but could not. Surely there was nothing marvelous about a bull lowering its head if its ropes were pulled downward. A glance around him showed only the novices' interested faces, the priest's impassive one, the captain's joyous one as he gave the next petitioner his place.

I must have been mistaken, Thoth reflected. I will watch more closely next time.

Four petitioners and four varying decisions later, he was still puzzled and in grave doubt. He knew the god Amon inhabited the shining black body of the Apis as well as the golden image in the sanctuary. He knew also that the Apis made no sign until the priests pulled on its ropes, or prodded it to make it shake its head. Did the same Amon who pushed the bark about so easily need *help* from the priests to make a bull's head move?

After the courtyard cleared, he asked Benat, Chief Servant of the Bull, about the matter.

"Aye," Benat admitted readily enough. "We help the Honorable Apis to make his signal. We are the instruments of Amon's will."

"But how do you know whether Amon wishes you to make the sign for aye or the sign for nay?"

"Oh, that is simple, Highness. We have only to look at the offering. The gods favor him who has given a rich gift."

Thoth's eyebrows rose. The statement had a familiar ring to it; there was a bitter Babylonian proverb which ran, "A royal gift guarantees a favorable prophecy." Babylonians, though, knew that even the most favorable prophecy could not guarantee the divine favor of which it was the promise. In Egypt, if one might judge by the expressions of the petitioners who had received an "aye," the gods were bound by the gift to fulfill their promises.

"Then can one buy the favor of the gods like onions in the market place?" he asked the priest.

"Nay, Highness!" Benat's voice was shocked. "One must also lead an upright life. Surely you have seen the texts of the Declaration of Innocence? Each man's *ka* must repeat those words before the scales of Osiris after death."

Thoth nodded thoughtfully and started back across the courtyard. He had seen the texts, many times, written in the new-made coffins stacked for sale in the carpenters' shops. *I have committed no wrong against people. I caused no one to weep, I did not murder, I did not load the weight of the balance, I caused no man misery. . . .*

All this, and much more, inscribed inside those unsold coffins which might be bought by anyone—even men who were at that very moment committing every variety of crime listed in the spell. Would Osiris believe a pack of lies, then? If the gods could be bought with gold or fooled with words, which was more powerful, the gold, the god, or the words? Which could one depend on? Thoth found he did not know.

He stopped suddenly in the middle of the courtyard. A sentence had sprung into his mind—an echo from the past. "Whenever you ask me about the gods, I will give you the same answer —I do not know." Someone had said that to him once; the voice in his memory was that of the Lonesome Man.

My father, he thought with an uneasy little thrill. My father told me that. *He* did not know, either.

Slowly he walked on across the courtyard and into the temple, feeling small and chilled by where his thoughts had led him.

Despite the fact that he had momentarily soothed Hatshepsut's anxiety, Senmut rode back to his villa in the Avenue of Mut in a very thoughtful frame of mind. She was worrying about Thoth far too often lately. Something must be done.

He dismissed his litter and bearers in the courtyard and walked slowly into the house. His brother Senmen, who had for some time now been his personal assistant as well as First Scribe of the Temple of Amon, as Senmut had promised him years ago, was waiting for him in the sitting room off his bedchamber.

"By Khnum's right ear!" growled Senmen, leaping thankfully from his chair. "I thought you were never coming. Now perhaps I can rid myself of that string of merchants and favor seekers in the kitchen courtyard. The traders from Kush arrived this morning—if you will see them first—"

"Send them away," Senmut said, clapping his hands for a slave.

"Send them away? But you wanted ebony and ivory—"

"I want nothing but solitude just now. I need to think." To the slave who appeared, Senmut added, "Bring wine to the garden. And my luncheon." He walked into the bathchamber adjoining, Senmen at his heels.

"You'd best see the goldsmith, at least," the latter insisted as his brother stripped off his headcloth and plunged his face into a bowl of water. "He says he cannot finish your new collar before the Festival of the Sun next week without a fitting."

"Send him away," Senmut repeated through the folds of a towel. "He can come back tomorrow."

"But he says there will not be time—"

"I said send him away!" roared Senmut, flinging the towel into a corner and striding out of the room.

Senmen glared at the empty doorway, whispered, "*Yes*, Your Excellency!" and headed for the kitchen courtyard, cursing under his breath.

Senmut ate slowly and abstractedly, gazing into space. When he had finished, he sat for a while over his wine, then rose and crossed the garden to his little study. In a cupboard set into its shelves was his little model of the temple of Neb-hepet-Re. He took it out tenderly and set it on a table, sinking into a chair beside it. It had changed in the years since he first built it to show Hatshepsut—it had grown a bit larger, and become considerably more detailed. It was, in fact, no longer Neb-hepet-Re's temple but his own—the one he meant to build, princeling or no princeling.

He looked at it long and silently, with something near to worship in his eyes. Then gradually his expression changed, assuming the grim thoughtfulness it had shown when he left Hatshepsut, and finally grim decision. He set down his cup with a little crash, flung out of his chair and strode across the garden to his bedroom, yelling for his brother. When Senmen appeared, he was hastily replacing his golden headcloth.

"I am going to the temple to see Hapuseneb. Order my litter again."

Senmen thrust his head out the door and gave orders to a slave, then came back to study his brother's face suspiciously. "What are you hatching now?" he demanded.

Senmut's eyebrows rose. "My dear Senmen," he said mildly, "must I always be 'hatching' something? I merely wish to confer a few moments with the high priest."

"On temple business?"

Senmut reflected a moment, then nodded. "Aye, on temple business—a little service I must do the queen." He grinned mockingly at his brother and left the room.

Thoth sat stiffly in the elaborate chair, trying to arrange his feet somehow to hide his worn and shabby sandals, while his eyes traveled in astonishment over the sumptuous furnishings of Hapuseneb's private chambers. There was no sign of pious austerity in this priest's quarters; the room looked as if it belonged in the palace instead of the temple. Thoth tried to fix his mind on what Hapuseneb was saying, wondering again what it was all about. The summons itself had been startling enough, but he had gone at once, straight from his corn grinding, with flour still on his hands, and knocked on the door as he had been told to do. To his further surprise he had been ceremoniously greeted by the high priest himself, and two richly turned-out slaves had hurried forward to so embarrass him with deferential attention that within two minutes he was rigidly self-conscious, and so preoccupied with trying to conceal his flour-smeared hands and the hole in his sandal that he was unable to follow what the stately personage before him was talking about. He caught references to his exalted rank, to the unfortunate severities of temple protocol. . . .

". . . but this ambiguous state of affairs must shortly cease. The time has come for Your Highness to assume the prerogatives of your station."

What was the man saying? Thoth stared raptly at the priest,

suddenly all attention. He had seen Hapuseneb face to face only once before, on the day of his entrance into the temple. Now, as then, he decided he had never seen a countenance of such serene and massive calm—or one so hard to read.

". . . dwelt in the temple for over a year now . . . quite unnecessary for one of your rank to remain a novice any longer. If you would approve a change . . ."

A change? From temple to palace, from priestling to prince, at last?

"Aye!" exclaimed Thoth eagerly. "Aye, Excellence! I would approve—indeed, I am most anxious—"

"I have no doubt of it, and I do not blame you in the least." Hapuseneb smiled benevolently, then rose with great dignity and made a formal bow. Thoth rose too, trembling in expectation of the announcement he had so long awaited.

"In that case, Your Highness, it is my duty and honor to inform you that one week from now, on the day following the Monthly Festival of the Sun, a special ceremony will be arranged at the hour of midday in the Chapel of Anointments. At that time I myself will confirm you as a full priest, with the rank of Servant of the God's Vestments."

"Oh," Thoth faltered, stunned with disappointment.

Hupuseneb's eyebrows lifted a fraction in his impassive face. "It is a minor rank, of course, Highness. But even you can scarce expect to become a *sem* priest at once."

"I did not expect to become a *sem* priest at all!" Thoth burst out. "Or any other kind! I expected—I hoped—to go back to the palace, where I belong!"

"Oh, I fear that is unfeasible as yet, Your Highness—indeed, quite impossible. You are not ready."

You must learn to be Egyptian . . . a priest's duties, a scribe's skills, a statesman's wisdom—time enough after that to taste a prince's amusements and a king's responsibilities. . . .

Of course he was not ready. Thoth felt himself flush. He had acted like a fool—worse, he had been ill-bred and defiant, and disgraced Ibhi-Adad's training. No doubt Hapuseneb was judging him more of a barbarian than ever—even less ready than he had supposed. Catching sight of his flour-caked hands, Thoth tucked them behind him and mumbled through the formalities of taking leave.

At least, he thought as he returned to his grinding, I shall have to do *this* only one week longer. By the time next month's Festival of the Sun rolls around I shall be sleeping in another place and eating at another table and not wondering all the time why the other boys are laughing. . . . And by the time I am sixteen and have come of age, I will have left all this behind me, long, long ago. I will scarcely even remember it. . . .

But he sighed as he emptied his mortar of flour and reached for the grain sack.

The same evening, the royal steward Nehsi dined with Lord Uah, Superintendent of the Armory. Not entirely by accident, the young prince's name entered the conversation before they were fairly started on the meal, and now, midway through the duck-braised-with-lotus-root which was the main course, the subject had not been changed. As usual with those who held conversations with Nehsi, Uah was doing most of the talking.

"I realize," he was saying, shaking a drumstick under Nehsi's nose to emphasize his words, "that I have little influence these days. And no partisans, since my lord Khenuka departed for the Delta. Oh, I am very well aware of it—too well altogether. I have been reduced to the status of a gadfly, and I've no doubt Her Radiance would be pleased to rid herself once for all of my buzzing and stinging. She *would* rid herself of it, if my father were not a prince of Nekheb—I'm well aware of that too."

"Come, you exaggerate," murmured Nehsi.

"You know I do not," said Uah. He sighed, tossed the drumstick on to his plate and leaned back in his chair, gazing past Nehsi at the musicians playing softly in a corner of his columned hall. He was a thin, earnest man with a worn face shaped oddly like a hatchet's blade—broad and flat-planed seen in profile, narrow as a blade's edge seen full-front. He turned the blade's edge to Nehsi again now, and his eyes and tufted brows seemed to crowd almost together over the high bridge of his nose as he peered anxiously into the big Negro's face.

"Excellency," he said, "you know I am a man of conscience. I do my duty as I see it. Perhaps I am old-fashioned, perhaps I am even wrong. But since the day I heard the Tired One command that his son be king after him, I have conceived it my duty to fulfill that command. Now stay—I know, I know, you can tell me nothing about the Tired One. I suffered too. I feared for Egypt, but he was Pharaoh nonetheless, Excellency, and in times past, Pharaoh's will was not a thing to be tampered with. The—"

"I have not tampered with it," Nehsi interrupted him quietly. "I journeyed to Babylon, as he who was then Pharaoh had commanded me. I found the boy. I brought him home. I did not—approve. Still, it was not for me to disobey—or to pretend, however conveniently, that I had *not* found him. I would have been a liar before myself and the gods." Nehsi hesitated. "It is true I did not disguise him as an Egyptian. I felt all Egypt should understand what I was bringing. But I fulfilled my orders, just as in times past."

"I know, I know. The times past were good ones, that was my only thought about it. I admit I am conservative. I admit I am old-fashioned. But I served the first Thutmose—may his Three Thousand Years be full of joy—and in *his* day—"

"I, too, served him."

"Aye," said Uah gently after a moment. "Aye, I know that. None served him better, none was closer to him." He picked up the drumstick and twirled it thoughtfully, then flung it down again. "And for that very reason I cannot understand why you of all men countenance this inexplicable delay, this—this dangerous break with the old ways, with tradition, with the will of the first Thutmose's own son, heir to his kingship—"

"His daughter is heir to his spirit," Nehsi said softly. For the first time he raised his eyes from his plate and searched Uah's startled ones. "One almost feels one is serving him again, when one serves her."

"One may feel so," said Uah in a shocked voice, "but it is scarcely true, Excellency! She is a woman."

"Aye, she is a woman. An extraordinary one—alive in an extraordinary time."

"She will scarce give me enough gold to keep the chariotry on wheels," muttered Uah. "*He* defended Egypt, drove the Hyksos out, smote all the enemies of Amon. We would be far safer to go back to the old ways."

"Lord Uah, there are still older ways—the ways of our ancestors before the cursed Hyksos came to disturb the peace that had not been disturbed since the time of the gods. Why not go back

302

to peaceful trading, prosperity, wisdom, stability? *Those* were the ways of Egypt for two thousand years and more. We must find our way back to *them*. The Hyksos are gone now."

"And if they return?"

"They will not return," said Nehsi flatly. "My lord the Good God saw to that."

Uah sighed and motioned his servants to clear away the duck. While the plates were being changed, a tray of cakes and fruit brought in, date wine poured into goblets blue as Egypt's sky, the two men kept silence. Finally Uah waved the last servant out of earshot and leaned forward again.

"Excellency, we have somehow got off the subject. Egypt may go back to the old ways or the older ways—that is all one with me. The fact remains that the throne of Re stands empty, which is an offense against the gods. Her Radiance is not king, she cannot be. The chosen Successor is here, in Thebes—yet he has not been crowned. *That* is the urgent matter." Uah peered straight into Nehsi's eyes and emphasized each word with a bang of his goblet on the table. "Can you honestly say, my lord Nehsi, that we should ignore the will of Pharaoh any longer?"

Nehsi met his eyes reluctantly for a long moment, then he, too, sighed. "Nay," he answered. He raised his goblet, drank its contents, and set it down carefully in the ring of moisture it had made. "I will speak to her tomorrow," he said quietly.

The following afternoon Thoth was working alone in one of the smaller storerooms, tying up onions into the circular bunches proper to the offering table, when a familiar prickling sensation on the back of his neck warned him that someone's eyes were on him. He scarcely needed to glance around to know that a certain prophetess was standing in the doorway, watching him.

His first impulse was to find business elsewhere at once. His duties seldom brought him into contact with the priestesses of the temple; he saw them occasionally, dancing and rattling their sistrums before the god, but not often enough to sort them out as individuals. Of this one prophetess, however, he had been uneasily aware from his first day in the temple.

She was a tall woman, somewhat angular but arresting in appearance, with long, expressive hands and smoldering eyes. She wore her hair in a thick clump over each shoulder, with the remainder hanging down her back in an elaborate arrangement of tiny plaits so thickly twined with strands of gold beads that they tinkled faintly when she moved. This elusive chiming, added to the opiate-like perfumes she favored, gave her a hypnotic, melodramatic aura that made Thoth acutely uncomfortable. Moreover, she was always watching him. The first time he noticed her she was standing stock-still, with her sister priestesses flowing past her like a stream around a boulder, staring at him with a peculiar, fixed intensity. Each time he had seen her since, he had found her eyes upon him. Now the very sight of her made him so self-conscious that he would detour long corridors out of his way to avoid encountering her.

There was no avoiding her today; the storeroom had but one entrance and she was standing squarely in it. Even as he measured the distance between her and the doorjamb, she gave a cautious glance both ways along the passage, stepped into the room and closed the door.

"May Your Highness' *ka* be satisfied," she murmured. Her voice, low and husky, contrived to make even the conventional greeting sound heavily significant.

Thoth mumbled "Rejoice" and turned back to his onions, hoping she would simply take some item from the shelves and go away. But he heard the faint music of her hair ornaments as she moved closer.

"If Your Highness please—I would speak with you a moment. I am concerned about Your Highness' happiness. You have been in the temple twelve months and more now. May I inquire—have you found the life attractive to you?"

"It—it has been interesting," Thoth mumbled.

"Indeed." She smiled, gazed meaningfully into his eyes. "So interesting that you would be willing to spend all the other years of your life here also?"

"Nay! I do not mean to be a priest for all my life."

"Doubtless you do not. But is that not precisely what is happening?"

"Why, not at all. I—"

"Do you know my name?" she said softly.

"Nay."

"It is Nofret-Hor." She waited a moment, then smiled bitterly. "It means nothing to you? I thought not. It means nothing to anyone now—but there was a time when all Thebes knew it, from noble to beggar! They used to follow my litter along the streets, stretching out their hands to me and whispering my name to their children. A word from me—the merest word—has cast down the mighty from their places, and lifted others up."

Thoth watched her uneasily but could think of nothing at all to say. He wondered if she might be mad.

"You do not believe me," she said calmly. "It is not surprising. Perhaps you will listen when I tell you that but for my gift of prophecy his holiness Hapuseneb would still be a *sem* priest! Aye, and the great excellency Count Senmut the Steward of Amon would be unheard of—save as the husband of Nofret-Hor."

"Count Senmut is your husband?" echoed Thoth in astonishment.

"He *was* my husband. *Hai!* No more! His Loftiness has grown far too high and mighty to consort with her who lifted up his swollen head! He loves the queen now—I am merely a clod to crush beneath his sandal—and he has crushed me." She paused, fixed Thoth with her smoldering eyes and added softly, "*She* means to do the same to you."

"What—what do you mean?" stammered Thoth. Then he saw what she meant and felt the blood rush to his head in a strange and violent revulsion. "I think you are mistaken!" he said furiously.

"But you suspect I may be right," she whispered.

He turned his back on her and began snatching onions out of the basket to form another bunch. His hands felt stiff and clumsy; the onion skins slipped and skidded in his fingers with a thin, papery crackling. For a moment it was the only sound in the room. Then her little hair ornaments set up their faint tinkling, and the thick fragrance of her perfume overpowered even the smell of the onions as she moved close beside him.

"Your Highness—His Excellency Hapuseneb summoned you to his chambers only two days since, is that not true?"

"Aye."

"And did he not inform you that you were to be anointed full priest, of the Vestment rank, within a week?"

"Aye, but—"

"And did he also inform you how long you are bound to this

temple, if you take those vows? Nay—I thought not. But I will tell you. Those vows will bind you for ten years."

Thoth turned slowly, numbly, and stared at her. At last he whispered, "Not me. They will not bind *me* that long. They cannot! Why, in only *four* years I will be of age—in four years I—" He stopped, suddenly gripped by a terrible uncertainty.

"Will be king?" she finished.

"Aye! I am the prince—"

"Yet all your life here seems strangely unsuitable for a prince destined to be king. Do you not think so?"

"It is—it is the education. That is why I am here. I must learn many things—"

"You could learn many more at the palace, from better tutors."

Thoth looked at her in silence, wishing desperately that she would go away.

"Your Highness, I have had visions about you, dreams and visions. Senmut has stilled my voice but he cannot still the voice of Amon, who speaks to me in the hours of darkness. If you do not believe me, ask your friends here in the temple. They know my powers."

"I have no friends in the temple!" muttered Thoth, at the same time thinking, Does she mean the fat one who is always teetering and asking questions? Does she mean Khwed? Khwed, who told me to rebel, who said *demand your rights?*

"You do have friends! Did you not know that?"

"Nay, I did not know it!" cried Thoth, wild for her to go, to leave him alone. "I know only that I must finish this task before the evening offering—and I cannot do it while you talk to me!"

"Aye, the task. How long, in Amon's name, must you stay at tasks like this?"

"That is in the hands of the gods!"

Nofret-Hor straightened, and a slow, approving smile spread over her face. She nodded. "Just so, Highness—just so. The hand of god. Look you—next week, on the fourth of Pakhons, is the monthly Festival of the Sun. Stand alone in the northern colonnade of the Hall of Praise that day, and you will see the hand of god move."

With another enigmatic smile, she turned swiftly and left the room, leaving Thoth staring at the doorway with questions swarming thick as bees into his head. He wanted to shout

"Wait!" He wanted to run after her. But somehow he did neither. He merely stood there, an onion forgotten in one hand, listening to the mysterious little chiming of her hair ornaments recede down the passage.

7.

On the fourth of Pakhons, the appointed day of that month's Festival of the Sun, Senmut rose before daylight, had himself arrayed in his best, and started at once for the palace. He chose a carrying chair for the short trip, prudently ignoring his new chariot and the pair of highstrung stallions who had wrecked the old one and two others before that, under his insufficiently skilled hand.

"Would it not be less trouble merely to throw half a dozen chariots into the river at once, then buy some horses you can manage?" his brother Senmen had inquired caustically the day Senmut came limping home by back alleys for the third time in six months.

Senmut had merely grinned and informed him that as usual, his advice smacked of the fish wharf. "You think like a peasant, brother, that is your trouble. Does Count Nehsi buy manageable horses? Does my lord Thutiy, who is half again my age?"

"Nay, but they were learning to drive the brutes when you were still peddling fish in the—"

"And I will learn too. Come, help me to the house, I think those beautiful devils have sprained my knee."

So far, the new chariot was intact; but this was not the morning to tempt the gods. He would be too much in the public eye all day. Accepting his long jeweled staff from a slave, Senmut settled himself contentedly in the carrying chair. It was where he loved to be—in the public eye.

At the palace, the Great Court was aglow with torches, the procession beginning to take shape. Chamberlains, servants, slaves, hurried this way and that, lining up litters and chariots in strict order of precedence for their aristocratic masters, who were milling about in the Great Hall, awaiting the appearance of the queen.

In the Women's Quarters on the second floor, in the little gray-and-gold chamber which had once belonged to her mother, the ten-year-old Princess Neferu-Re was having a tantrum because the fluting of the sleeves of her new royal-linen dress did not suit her. She was a pale, thin-faced child, tall for her age, with a drooping mouth and an expression of perpetual discontent. She was generally conceded to be the image of her father, though no one mentioned the fact aloud. She had even inherited his sickly constitution—but fortunately, not his tendency to madness or even his brooding turn of mind. Where he had been stubborn, she merely nagged; where his eye had turned always inward, hers was on appearances.

At the moment, it was alternately on her own reflection in the mirror and on the agitated servingmaids who surrounded her.

"Look at that!" she screamed, plucking angrily at the delicate fluting of one cobweb-sheer sleeve. "It *puckers!* I won't wear it, I won't wear it! You will have to fix it!"

"But Your Highness," quavered her nurse, "the procession— there will not be time."

"Then the procession must wait!" shrieked Nefer, tearing the garment off and hurling it to the floor. "I am the princess and I will not wear that ugly thing! Take it away from me, take it out of my sight or my head will begin to ache!"

"Very well, Your Highness, as you wish, Your Highness."

The nurse snatched the offending garment from the floor, handed it to a maid and hastily waved her out. Amon forbid that the princess fall ill with one of her headaches—and that her mother the queen find out it was all the nursemaid's fault! Anything was preferable.

Turning to the white-faced Nefer with soothing words, she coaxed her to lie down while slave girls hurried off in search of the fluting irons.

In another wing of the palace Hatshepsut, fully dressed and diademed, with the last amulet in place and the last servant maid dismissed, paced the sitting room of the Queen's Apartments and tried to nerve herself to walk out the door and start for the temple.

The boy has been there thirteen months, she was thinking. Yet still I dread to go there—each week it grows harder instead of easier!

It was ridiculous. It was maddening. The fact that Thoth was at the temple was not *her* fault, it was the fault of the Kinsmen and their cursed precious document. *She* had done nothing but solve a dangerous problem with vigor and dispatch, exactly as her lord father would have done. Had *he* ever been influenced by some Kinsman's clouded opinion? Nay, he made his decision, then he acted.

But—in Amon's name! Ten years—

That was not my decision, she thought hastily. I had nothing to do with it, it was entirely Hapuseneb's idea to bind the boy over as a priest. I ordered no such thing, I was not even told of it until last night—

Her memory suddenly rang with her own instruction to Hapuseneb: *Keep him there.* To drown it out she walked swiftly to the door, jerked it open, and demanded of the startled guard outside, "Has Count Senmut arrived yet?"

"Nay, Your Radiance. At least, I have not seen him—"

She slammed the door and began her pacing again, twisting her hands together.

You do not need to talk to Senmut, she told herself angrily. You are the Daughter of the Sun, your actions are always right. You will not even see the boy today, calm yourself.

But what if she did see him? What if he demanded to see her? What if he made a scene?

He cannot—he must not! she thought, turning cold all over and beginning to walk faster. If he does I shall ignore him. He has no claim on me, no claim to Egypt yet. . . . Last night Nehsi was only saying what Uah urged him to say. Thoth must become a priest. Nothing else could prevent him from coming back to the palace, being right here, underfoot, around me all the time. I could not bear that! He must take the vows.

Yet—ten years of this harp-string tension—she could not bear that either.

I must burn the document! she thought frantically. I must banish all the Kinsmen, as I did Khenuka— Nay, I cannot do that, it is impossible. I will banish all but Nehsi and Thutiy and Ineny, send the rest far away to estates in the south and north— Gods, I cannot do that either! Then I will wed Nefer—quickly— to someone else, as Senmut keeps urging— But the document will still be there, not Amon himself can change that!

Again she whirled to the door, flung it open, and found herself face to face with a chamberlain who had been about to knock.

"Well? What is it, what is it?"

"I crave Your Radiance's pardon, I was sent to remind Your Radiance that the sky grows light—all are waiting in the Great Court—Count Nehsi begs to inquire if Your Radiance is ready."

"Has Count Senmut arrived yet?"

"Aye, Your Radiance, he—"

"Send him to me. At once. At once!"

She turned her back on him and slammed the door.

Ten minutes later Senmut escorted a pale but composed Hatshepsut to her litter. She was still stiff with dread, the set of her jaw told him that. No matter, he thought. She will carry it off all right, she always does, nothing will happen anyway, the boy would not dare to make a scene.

Half a league away, across the river, Thoth stepped up to the bowl of clay-and-natron and began to wash his trembling hands. He was in a fever of indecision, which had been mounting steadily for five days and was now reaching its climax.

Stand in the northern colonnade, Nofret-Hor had said. Was he going to do it, or was he not?

One torch still flickered in its wall bracket, but the darkness framed by the room's high window was beginning to look gray. He would have to decide—time was running out. This was the last hand-washing before the ceremonies would begin. When he left this room, just a moment from now, he must turn either left, to follow the other novices, or right, and slip off alone to hide himself in the northern colonnade of the Hall of Praise.

What did she mean, the hand of god will move? he thought angrily. I think she is mad anyway, probably nothing at all will happen, and then I shall feel like a fool.

But suppose something did happen—and he was not there?

"You must step along, Young Highness, the others are waiting, and time grows short."

Reluctantly Thoth moved away from the wash table, accepted a towel, and slowly, thoroughly, dried his hands. He made the rubbing with ointment last as long as possible, walked with dragging feet toward the door. At last the moment could not be put off any longer. He stood in the dim-lit corridor, his mouth dry and his heartbeat slow and heavy, looking first to the right, after the other novices, and then to the left.

He could not make up his mind.

The first streaks of red were shooting into the eastern sky as the barges carrying the royal procession bobbed their way across the Nile. A lookout stationed on the top of the pylon waved a signal, and from somewhere below began the measured pounding of a drum. In the Great Court the packed masses who had been waiting for hours, crowded together like netted fish, made patient by their hushed expectancy of what was to come, stirred like a many-headed beast beginning to waken.

Doors swung open on another side of the temple, and the priesthood of Amon—a river of white threaded with the dull gold of the *sem* priests' leopard skins, splashed with the scarlet of the prophets—poured out upon the landing to greet the barges. A thousand shaven heads caught the tint of dawn as they moved to either side of the broad stone dock. Priestesses ran to the water's edge, scattering garlands and whirling until their garments formed filmy clouds about them; singers lifted their voices in wavering falsetto above the boom of the drum. As the leading barge grated against the landing Hapuseneb and his six high priests advanced over the flower-strewn way to hand Hatshepsut from her litter and escort her, between the ranks of the god's servants, into the temple.

Senmut helped the little princess down and followed. Gold-decked dignitaries alighted in silent haste from the barges, raised intent eyes to the slowly reddening sky. None was thinking now of palace politics or even of himself; with the first hollow drumbeat that had reached their ears across the water, all lesser matters fell away. Like the chanting priests around them, like the emotion-charged crowd in the Great Court, their hands were clammy and their breathing uneven as they passed into the temple to watch the enactment of the holy mysteries on which depended, for another month, the daily rising of the sun.

In the Hall of Praise the hymns died away to be replaced by the chanting of a solitary lector-priest, whose voice rose and fell in rich antiphony to the soft, soaring ululation of the chest-beating singers. Sandals shuffled as the crowd of priests and noblemen filed to their stated places about the dawn-gray hall; and down its exact center passed Hatshepsut, bearing a cup of wine, flanked by Hapuseneb and the First *Sem* Priest, followed by the droning lector. As they vanished into the first of the antechambers leading to the Holy-of-Holies, the drumbeat ceased, the singers fell silent. In a breathless hush the hall and all its occupants waited. The voice of the lector grew fainter and yet fainter through the series of antechambers; finally it stopped.

Every ear strained as if to catch the sound of the libation being poured, the incense set smoldering, the prayers and incantations droned. There was intense silence in the hall for a few moments that seemed endless; then the rattle of sistrums was heard from the secret place of the god. The rattle grew more intense, grew louder, was joined by the jingling of tambourines. The god was emerging from his sanctuary—he was in the first antechamber now. His entrance into the second was hailed by a burst of women's voices singing his praise; his progress into the third marked by the piercing cry of flutes. Through all the columned hall now, the ineffable fragrance of his presence spread; as the first whirling dancers burst through the door to herald his appearance, drums and male singers joined the chorus of supplication, and every mortal in the great hall fell to his knees.

> *"Awake in peace, thou Cleansed One, in peace!*
> *Awake in peace, thou Eastern Horus, in peace!*
> *Awake in peace, thou Eastern soul, in peace!*
> *Awake in peace, Harakhti, in peace! . . ."*

Nobles, prophets, priests, stretched out their hands and shouted with the singers, feeling their flesh tingle and their blood pound as the god himself was borne forth in glory amid a cloud of burning myrrh. Twelve sweating bearers carried the great bark with its golden image; the fragrance of the divine presence rose from twenty smoking censers. A throng of tambourine-shaking, ecstatically swirling priestesses surrounded the cortege and moved with it toward the huge doors at the south end of the hall. At the god's approach, the doors swung open; beyond, across the shining entry, the outer portals also swung wide, admitting a flood of rosy light and the high-pitched rapture of the waiting commoners. As the divine bark passed outside into the throng of

312

worshipers, the trumpeters standing high upon the pylon lifted their long horns and blew a brazen, moaning, shrilling fanfare to the sun-disk flaring on the eastern horizon.

This was the climax, the moment of certainty, when intolerable suspense changed to wild thanksgiving. Golden Re of the sky had risen once more over Egypt, golden Amon-Re of the temple had dawned before the eyes of his adorers at the same mystic instant. For another month life and sunlight were assured. The hymns rose in joy as the bark with its radiant burden crossed the Great Court to the Festival Altar.

> *"Thou sleepest in the bark of the evening,*
> *Thou awakest in the bark of the morning,*
> *For thou art he that soareth over the gods,*
> *There is no other god that soareth over thee!*
> *Awake in peace, thou Cleansed One, in peace!*
> *Awake in peace, thou Eastern Horus, in peace! . . ."*

The nobles in the Hall of Praise, rising from their knees, found their limbs shaky, their senses extraordinarily heightened, as if by wine. They felt drunken, vigorous, virile, intensely alive, with their *kas* renewed and their strength restored by the sight of the god. While in the courtyard more libations were being poured by Hapuseneb and his *sem* priests, within the Hall palace and temple dignitaries pushed absently past each other to their new positions for The Return, every man's thoughts upon his *ka*.

Senmut guided his young princess to her place seven paces eastward from the Station of the Queen, where Hatshepsut stood waiting with exalted eyes. Involuntarily, Senmut's own eyes traveled beyond her to the Station of the King—an empty circle on the pavement where the first beams of sunshine would soon rest in golden blessing when the sun had climbed to the level of a carefully placed opening on the opposite wall. For a moment Senmut's thoughts strayed from the ceremony, as did those of many others whose gaze rested speculatively or uneasily on that empty spot. Then the drums boomed again from the Great Court, the tambourines and flutes and voices lifted, and all eyes sprang back to the returning god.

> *"Awake in peace, thou Eastern soul, in peace!*
> *Awake in peace, Harakhti, in peace! . . ."*

Senmut's ears throbbed to the chanting, and his whole soul fastened hungrily upon the golden countenance of Amon.

Serene, impassive, beautiful as his own dawning, the Great Procreator, the Breath of Life, the Hidden One swayed high over the heads and the smoking censers of his servants. In the Hall, the bark turned, moved with slow majesty across the end of the room and then started down its length. It would make a complete ritual circuit of the Hall before advancing down the center to vanish once more into the sanctuary. Slowly it passed the rows of outstretched hands, passed Nehsi, passed Thutiy, passed Senmut and the trembling princess, passed Hatshepsut. It moved on to the empty Station of the King—and stopped.

A shock that was like a physical impact rippled through the big room. The chanting broke off, the singers' voices trailed to nothing, the drumbeats ceased. For a stunned instant there was silence, as the hair rose on the back of a thousand necks and a shiver ran down every spine. Then, with a lurch, the bark began to move again, erratically, angrily, shoving its bearers this way and that until they staggered and even cried out. A moan of terror rose from every part of the Hall. Priests and nobles alike fell to their knees and stayed there, watching the god rush to and fro, this way and that, while the bearers strained and panted to do his bidding. Suddenly the bark darted toward the columns in the northern section of the Hall. The half-hundred spectators huddling there scattered in a panic, shoving and clawing each other in their haste to get out of its way. At the far end of the path thus abruptly cleared one small figure was left standing, pressing in fright against the wall. It was one of the novices—a boy ten or twelve years old, with eyes enormous and mouth agape in his startled face. The god moved straight toward him through the columns, stopped before him, and forced the bearers to their knees.

For an endless instant the silence was profound; the boy's gasp was plainly audible as he flung himself face down upon the pavement. A moment later he raised his head, as if he were listening —then slowly he rose and placed one hand on the edge of the bark. Never taking his eyes from Amon's golden face, he followed the bark as it moved backward through the crowded columns and turned toward the center of the room.

Floating serenely now, neither shoving his bearers nor press

ing down upon them, the god moved down the hushed and waiting Hall, leading the boy beside him. Every gaze was on the
bark; every eye saw the unmistakable nudge with which it
pushed the boy straight into the Station of the King, that empty
circle which was now bathed in radiance by the beams of Re.

For most of the stunned spectators, the moment the sunlight
struck the golden wrappings of his side-lock was the moment
they first recognized their half-forgotten princeling, the Tired
One's son. But they were in no doubt that Amon had named him
Pharaoh before their very eyes.

For Senmut, that moment of recognition was the moment at
which the mists of awe and fear cleared abruptly from his brain,
to be replaced by the cold, hard light of skepticism. This was a
miracle, was it? Then it was the most perfectly timed one he
had ever heard of. Tomorrow that boy was to have taken vows
that would have kept him chained fast and out of the way for
ten more years. Today, in the dramatic nick of time, he had suddenly stepped beyond the reach of vows and chains alike, into
the Station of the King. It would have been astounding even if it
had occurred in the dark secrecy which surrounded most miracles. Even more astounding—it had just happened to take place
before a cloud of witnesses.

Senmut paid grudging and silent tribute; the plan was mas-
terly, the staging perfect. Then his disenchanted gaze moved
away from the prince and started slowly about the crowd in
search of the stage manager.

He found her where he had begun to suspect he would—in the
ranks of the prophetesses. For a moment, as their eyes held, Senmut had time to reflect grimly upon the two-edged nature of the
weapon he had used for his own ends seven years before—and to
curse himself for not breaking it before carelessly tossing it away.
He could almost hear Nofret-Hor screaming at him: *"You'll
end with your head in a noose, I'll put it there myself, by all that's
sacred!"* He had never believed her. The more fool he.

His eyes moved on. He was going to find little satisfaction in
revenge now. She had already done her damage, as the briefest
study of the awed faces around him proved. One glance at
Hapuseneb's frozen countenance convinced Senmut that he had
nothing to do with the affair; for a moment he stonily memorized

315

the faces of the Bearers of the Bark, so that he could find them when he wanted them. Then, with dread, he turned his full attention to Hatshepsut.

He saw what he had feared to see. She had not moved from her place—it was obvious she could not move. She was death-pale, her wide eyes fixed; and she was staring not at the boy but at the god, with an expression that made Senmut discard his last hope of salvaging the situation. The boy was Pharaoh from this moment.

Senmut drew a long breath and with difficulty mastered the thing inside him that wanted suddenly to go berserk. No use to rage, one gambled and sometimes one lost—lost heavily. But not disastrously, if one was careful not to lose one's head as well. He must think, and he had better think fast and realistically. This was not the same world he had moved in so confidently three minutes ago.

For a moment, despite all his efforts to be calm, Senmut felt the panic of sliding down a dark shaft into oblivion. Then he caught sight of the little princess, standing transfixed beside him, and with an agile twist he mentally landed on his feet. He was still Nefer's guardian. Not even Pharaoh could change that without the queen's consent. It was a foothold.

Hatshepsut moved at last. With dreamlike finality her two hands stretched out before her to acclaim the king. The spell of silence broke; the Hall became a sea of hands, the air a roar of excitement. Senmut stretched out his hands and roared with the others, but his mind was elsewhere. Amon was great, but this was no time to dwell on it. As the god slowly and majestically turned from the small figure in the pool of light and started back to the sanctuary, Senmut was already busy exploring his altered world.

Two chaotic hours later, he left the palace and jogged wearily homeward to the Avenue of Mut. His brother was waiting for him on the broad porch of the house, his face and whole thick-set body one question.

"Senmut!" he muttered as soon as the bearers were out of earshot. "I heard—"

"Of course you heard. All Thebes has heard by now."

"Well? Is it true?"

"Quite true."

"Great Ptah have mercy!" whispered Senmen. "So Amon himself was forced to make a miracle—"

"The miracle was man-made, brother."

Senmen's eyes fastened on him sharply, then understanding spread over his face. "What will happen?"

"Exactly what you would expect to happen. The prince's accession will be solemnized tomorrow. Next week he will wed the princess Nefer—and more than likely her younger sister as well, to make everything quite certain. Then a few months hence, probably on the next New Year's Day, he will be crowned Pharaoh—with Her Radiance as his regent during the four years until he comes of age."

"Her Radiance has—consented to all this?"

"She has commanded it. She is exhausted by the long struggle with herself."

Senmen studied his brother's face—it showed signs of strain, but also a faint, sardonic smile. Senmen sighed and straightened.

"Four years from next New Year's," he repeated grimly. "Your career will be a short one, Senmut—and so will mine."

"Perhaps not."

"Aye, *perhaps* not!" echoed Senmen savagely. He glared at his brother a moment, then burst out, "By the gods, I always said you'd come to a bad end—but I never thought *I* would! Curse the day I left my honest poverty to follow you! You're the same swindling devil you always were, silver headcloth and an empty sash, all smiles and fine-sounding promises—"

"I've kept the promises! Am I not Steward of Amon, and you First Scribe? I never said it would last forever!" Senmut turned and started for the garden. "Have someone fetch wine to me. My throat's a desert."

"What are you going to do?"

"Try to guess how these sticks will fall—and then become magnificently drunken, if I can."

Senmen followed the wine to the garden and set himself down firmly in a chair opposite the one in which Senmut had wearily thrown himself. "Do your guessing aloud. I want to know where I stand, for once."

"Stand?" Senmut smiled. "I've climbed far, brother, and dragged you with me. We stand on dizzy heights."

"The greater the crash when we are hurled down from them!"

"No one will hurl me down—if I switch my devotion from Her Radiance to his majesty, use all my influence as guardian of the princess in support of the young Pharaoh instead of the queen —and forget those beckoning peaks ahead. I should be satisfied, I suppose, with a high plateau."

"Well? Will you?"

Senmut's smile deepened as he watched his brother's face. "My poor Senmen. You would love that, wouldn't you?" He drained his goblet, twirled it a moment between his fingers, and tossed it to the grass. "Alas, we differ. I find something so tedious about a plateau."

"You fool!" Senmen choked. "Then you have four years—no more. I, also."

"You may be right. But you may be wrong, brother. Hatshepsut is still Hatshepsut."

"Did you not tell me she has commanded all this?"

"Aye," Senmut admitted. He leaned forward, no longer smiling. "Senmen, I know her. I've seen her do all this before—bow to the inevitable, give up one thing after another, let rights, titles, claims, prerogatives slip through her fingers—but at the last minute, she clings. I've seen her give up everything except real power."

Senmen was shaking his head. "You're measuring your neck for that rope. You'd best begin your tomb, your life will be a short one."

He stood up angrily and stalked out of the garden.

Senmut looked after him thoughtfully a moment, contemplating, without enthusiasm, the plateau's safe green vista. Then he shrugged and turned his face to the peaks. His life might be brief, on those dizzy pinnacles, but it would be glorious while it lasted.

Groping for the wine goblet on the grass beside him, he retrieved it and poured it full. His choice was made, his wager placed. Now he could drown the memory of this day.

8.

The Oracle of the Choosing, as it began to be called—whether in tones of awe or of skepticism depended on the speaker—was ollowed shortly by the young prince's formal accession, and his marriage to the two little princesses was solemnized within a few weeks. Then, after a suitable interval had elapsed, allowing the wedding feast mood to subside and a more solemn one to take its place, Egypt embarked on the most gravely momentous, the most intricate, complex and important of all the spells of magic known to it—the coronation of its king.

It required powerful and ancient magic to imbue a mortal prince with the divinity of Pharaoh, to establish between him and the gods, then between him and his people, the mysterious ties on which Egypt's life depended. The long rites began at Thebes, on the day of highest inundation at the end of Athyr; they would end on the first of Tybi, the new year's Day of Beginning, at Menfe in the northland—that ancient City of the White Wall where in the old, old days beyond remembrance King Menes had first welded the Two Lands into one and become Pharaoh of all Egypt. Between the first ritual and the last stretched a month of ceaseless, mystic activity.

The King-Who-Will-Rule, as the young prince was known during this period of transition and transformation, traveled for weeks along the narrow green ribbon of his kingdom, living aboard the royal barge and stopping at every principal city from Nekheb in the south to Heliopolis in the Delta. At each city he performed the same forty-six scenes of the Mystery Play of the Succession, re-enacting the age-old story of Egyptian kingship. Each time he performed it another area of his country was drawn into the web of power he was weaving, and something was changed in the heavens and on the earth. But not until he enacted three final rites at Menfe—the Union of the Two Lands, the Circuit of the Walls and the Festival of the Diadem—would he become god and king.

In a city expecting the royal barge, little of a workaday nature was accomplished for weeks beforehand. There were a thousand things to do, to arrange for, to decide. When the barge arrived at last, everyone's tools were flung aside and utterly forgotten for five transcendent days. The people left their homes and flocked to the Festival Site, jamming streets and wharves, perching on rooftops and lining the decks of ships, transforming the entire area around the barge and the Festival Pavilion nearby into a sea of squirming, craning, awed humanity. In this one never-to-be-forgotten moment of his life the lowliest fisher boy, clinging perilously to a swaying mast, might see the king; the most obscure herdsman might smell the actual fragrance of the gods.

Few grasped all the complexities of purification and preparation which occupied the first two days, though a recitation-priest stood on the steps of the Pavilion explaining everything. The people, baffled by the elliptical wordings of the ancient ritual, listened instead to the drums beating their slow rhythm, to the singers who wove around it an intricate pattern of sound with thin, howling voices in an eerie key. They caught glimpses of glittering processions, of dignitaries moving here and there dressed in costumes usually seen only on old temple walls, of priests in the beast-headed masks of gods, and of the small, tense figure always in the center of all. They watched the smoke of incense curl up in gray veils against the brilliant sky, and smelled its fragrance; they heard snatches of dialogue which called up a multitude of awesome images in their minds. But they did not know precisely what was going on. Only the priests knew. The people questioned each other, strained to see, pushed into more advantageous positions.

However, the third day they ceased their wriggling and grew quiet and intent. Out of the jumble of symbolism, ceremonies, and ritual, the story of Osiris was beginning to emerge, and this they knew; this age-old, beloved drama they had always known. They had drunk it with their mothers' milk, seen it enacted every year of their lives in the ever-dying, ever-returning river and in the buried, yet sprouting, grain. In the Barley Scene, when the male animals were brought in to trample and thresh the grain, they groaned softly, for that was Osiris being beaten; later, when men boxed fiercely and some were defeated, joy burst from their lips, for that was Horus fighting Set. When the Djed-pillar was raised they watched in a breathless hush, knowing it for the triumphant, stiffly erected fertility of the dead god, a promise of resurrection to Osiris. They needed no recitation-priest now; they knew the son had avenged his murdered father and stood triumphant, ready to assume the crown and kingship which were his by inheritance.

So there were moments of joyful affirmation in the forty-six scenes of the Rites of Succession, as well as moments of anxiety;

and there was one moment of grave and critical danger. This was the moment in the fifth day when death must be conjured up and faced as reality, when in the ritual and so in sober truth Osiris actually died and made the perilous journey to the Land of the West, in order to transfer his divinity and earthly kingship to his son. The masses crowding close around the Festival Pavilion were silent as death itself in this danger-fraught moment, and every eye was on the Qeni garment—a short, sleeveless jacket of peculiar design, fastening in the back—which the high priest carefully slipped over the young king's outstretched arms. Once it enfolded him, and his arms in turn enfolded it, the people breathed again. The Qeni garment was the spirit of Osiris, and as its power flowed into the new Horus, the king's embrace protected it on its lonely journey to the Lily Lake.

Thoth was hurrying down a long and undulating road that ran endlessly through a dusty, glaring landscape. There were trees in the distance but he could not reach them; he could find no shade. He came to a field where grain had been spread out to form a threshing floor; bulls and asses were plodding around and around on it, their heads slowly bobbing. He knew the animals were Set and his wicked followers, and that the grain was Osiris; he seized a stick, crying, "Do not beat this my father!" He could see the sun shining through the dancing dust-motes and lighting the long gray ears and the glossy, horned heads still bobbing placidly in their rounds ignoring his order (because, of course, the grain must be threshed) and could feel his stick bouncing on their bony backs, raising more dust and stirring the heavy animal-scented air. The barley prickled his bare knees as he knelt and addressed Osiris in the grain—"I have beaten for thee those who have beaten thee!"

Then suddenly the field turned into the courtyard of Ibhi-Adad's house in Babylon, and the Egyptians were there, flinging Nanai's wine onto the dusty ground and swarming over Ibhi-Adad and beating him with the wonderful box. Thoth, from his perch on the stairs, was shouting, "Do not beat this my father!" but they only came crowding up the stairs to rain blows on his head, his body, on the Qeni garment he wore, striking him across the face as the Babylonian king was struck at the time of Bit

Akitu, and crying, "You are become a weak one, a *lillu!*" He folded his arms across his head, enduring the rain of blows, still sobbing, "Do not beat this my father—"

Thoth's eyes flew open. Conscious of excruciating discomfort, he stirred, groaned, and painfully extricated one arm from its cramped position under him. Working it cautiously back and forth, he blinked, for a moment uncomprehendingly, at the tiny square window through which the sun was streaming with blinding force. Then he felt the familiar rocking motion under him and knew that he was not in Babylon, but in his couch on the royal barge. No one was beating him or Ibhi-Adad. Those were only the words he spoke in the Barley Scene, which he had repeated so many times in the past few weeks that they had dug like burs into his brain. He would be saying them again today . . . no, he had said them yesterday. That part was finished for this performance.

Suddenly he sat upright. It was finished forever. This was not Abydos or Nekheb or Heliopolis, this was Menfe. It was the first of Tybi, New Year's Day. Today, when the crown was placed upon his head, it would remain there. Today he would at last perform the final ceremonies of the Union, the Circuit, and the Festival of the Diadem. Later, when the setting sun colored all the little evening clouds gold and scarlet, so that the whole sky became the feathered breast of Great Horus, the Falcon, four birds would be released to fly to the four ends of the earth with the news that Horus the Son had mounted the throne of Egypt.

Today, at sunset, he would be a god.

I will not be nervous *then,* he told himself hastily. Once it has happened it will all seem quite natural to me. I will know exactly how to act and what to say.

And besides, he thought with a little flash of relief, I will not need to know everything at once. Lady Shesu will be regent. For four whole years she will be close to guide me and teach me.

A scratching sounded at the door. Thoth sprang from bed, then remembered who and what he was and sat down again, murmuring, "Come."

One servant entered with water, ointments, clay-and-natron, a second with fruit and cheese; beyond them Thoth glimpsed color and movement on the deck—the glitter of a standard, Nehsi in the archaic dress of a Spirit-Seeker, Hapuseneb leaning over the

322

gunwale beckoning to someone on the wharf. Already the day had begun, the procession would soon be assembled and waiting for him.

He ate hurriedly, then submitted himself to the six ceremoniously garbed Priests of Isis who arrived to perform the exacting and lengthy task of bathing, perfuming, purifying and dressing him for the day's rituals. As they moved about him, now kneeling, now standing, now waving censers, now proffering sandals, he stood with his nostrils full of the fragrance of burning myrrh and his eyes traveling slowly about the little cabin which had been his only home these past few weeks.

Soon he would be sailing back to Thebes, and then he would live in the Apartments of the King. It was strange and a little awesome to think of that. He had scarcely looked twice at those chambers yet, in all the hurry and bustle and confusion of his accession and the weddings. He did remember a yellow-walled sitting room and a worn chair of scarlet leather where his father and his grandfather had sat before him—where *he* would sit now, thinking, resting, deciding momentous affairs, or perhaps only looking at his little galley and remembering Ahmose. His glance flashed over the heads of the priests to the wall above his couch, where the galley traveled with him on a special shelf he had ordered made for it, all its red sails set and every tiny man in place. He would have a shelf built for it in the palace, too, in the yellow-walled sitting room where he could see it every day. Someday he would have a real warship built exactly like it; its name would be the *Wild Bull* and he would journey in it down the Nile and across the Great Green to bend those arrogant and disrespectful necks in Kadesh.

"Wash thyself, and thy ka washes itself;
Anoint thyself, and thy ka annoints itself;
Perfume thy flesh and thy ka perfumes its flesh . . ."

"The myrrh, Your Royal Highness," murmured the chief priest through the chanting. "Dip the middle finger of your left hand—"

Thoth dipped his finger into the proffered jar, touched his forehead, chest and shoulders. "I have washed myself, I have anointed myself, I have perfumed my flesh . . ."

In the bedroom of the Apartments of the King there was an

alcove for his couch, and on the ceiling overhead were dozens of golden stars, arranged like a map of the heavens. It was the most wonderful thing Thoth had ever seen. Soon, only a few nights from now, he would be sleeping there, in the king's lion-headed bed, looking up at them just as his father must have done.

". . . now the garment, Your Royal Highness. 'I have put on the garment'—and if you will just lift your arms a moment . . ."

"I have put on the garment, and my *ka* puts on the garment," Thoth mumbled.

There was an image of Amon in the alcove, too—a small golden figure standing in its own niche for all the world like a household god of Babylon. Perhaps it was the niche which had made the little gold Amon seem so much more approachable than the huge august presence in the temple. When they had taken him to burn incense before it, on the morning of his weddings, Thoth had been almost able to believe that Amon was his own special god, just as Nibada was Ibhi-Adad's.

"Now the sandals, Your Royal Highness . . ."

Thoth squirmed his foot into a sandal, automatically reciting the proper response while his thoughts moved on, uninterrupted. It was so, Amon was his special god, he must be. Think what happened that day, the day of the Festival of the Sun. . . .

A small, secret whisper of doubt ran through Thoth's heart, as it did every time he thought of that day and the oracle. He could never remember the great bark lurching this way and that, the swirl of frightened faces, the wild disbelief with which he had watched it scatter the spectators and head directly for him, without also remembering two gilded lead ropes stealthily tightening on the mouth-ring of the Apis-Bull.

My oracle was different, he thought quickly. My oracle was the hand of god.

But it had not been the voice of god which had whispered to him as he huddled in awe before the bark: "Your Highness. Your Highness! Rise. Put your hand upon the bark—" Nay, that had been Khwed's voice.

We help the Honorable Apis to make his signal . . .

Thoth drew a long breath and glanced restlessly toward the door, wishing the long ceremony of the attiring were over so that he could move about, leave the cabin, begin on the real business of the day.

"Stay—stay—just one moment, Your Royal Highness—do not move your head . . ."

There was a snip of scissors, and the strands of Thoth's youth-lock slithered down his shoulder and fell to the floor. He could not restrain a little gasp; this was completely unexpected. Of course, he thought an instant later. The lock is the mark of a prince; before the day is over I shall be a king.

While the priest's razor moved swiftly and expertly over the small stubble of hair still left on his head, he stared down at the black strands on the floor. There lay Thoth the princeling, all that was left of him. Queer, that it had taken a miracle to accomplish that one snip of the scissors. The hand of god . . . or Khwed.

What difference whose hand it was? he thought. It showed me that Lady Shesu was only waiting for a sign, waiting for the proper time for me to rule. I was right to trust her, and that prophetess was wrong, wrong! Now I will learn how to be the king, and when I come of age four years from today . . .

Thoth felt his whole chest expand almost painfully with a great bubble of excitement and awe. He straightened his head so that the priest could bind on the pleated headcloth more quickly; he was suddenly anxious to be finished with all the rituals and ceremonies and to be back in Thebes. Most of all he longed for a long, uninterrupted talk with Lady Shesu, to tell her how fully he trusted her, how earnestly he meant to work at learning to be king.

Not about the miracle, though—the hand of Khwed. There was no need to mention that; it was over and done, it did not matter any more.

"All is ready, Your Royal Highness," came the low voice of the priest.

With another glance at the dark locks on the floor, and a swift one at his little galley, upon which he would never again look with the eyes of a mortal boy, Thoth walked eagerly out the cabin door into the morning sunlight.

PART IV

The Fruit

I.

ON a brilliant afternoon toward the end of the fourth year of the regency, the fifteen-year-old Horus—Men-kheper-Re Thutmose, King of Upper and Lower Egypt—sat enthroned upon the canopied dais that adorned one end of the Great Hall of the palace. The Double Crown was on his head, the ceremonial Beard of Royalty was affixed by golden ties to his youthful chin, and his hands held the symbols of his kingship, the Crook and Flail. He was gazing impassively over the heads of the courtiers gathered for his audience; his eyes, half veiled by sternly drooping lids, were moving—unnoticed by his courtiers—in a series of little jerks from right to left.

He was counting the lotus flowers in the painted frieze which decorated the top of the opposite wall.

On a lower level of the dais, Her Radiance Hatshepsut sat energetically erect in a golden chair, transacting the business of the Two Lands in his name. At the moment, the royal steward, Nehsi, was standing before her, holding the scrolls of the tax reports in his dusky hands. At the other side of the lower level, the Divine Consort Neferu-Re toyed placidly with the exquisite fluting of her sleeves.

There were, Thoth discovered, fifty-five lotuses in the frieze —four more than he had estimated. Storing the figure in his mind, he made a brief survey of the buds, placed a wager with himself that there were twenty-two half-open ones and thirteen closed, and started counting them, working methodically back from left to right.

Moments passed; Nehsi continued to discuss the tax situation. Presently, when the matter of Senmut's new appointment came up, Pharaoh would be required to speak—and he knew exactly what he was to say, for both Hatshepsut and Nefer had instructed him. He was to say aye. He knew very well how to do that. He had been saying aye at audiences for nearly four years now, when he said anything at all. But the time to say it today had not arrived.

There were twenty half-opened buds and fifteen shut. Thoth added the fifty-five flowers to their total and arrived at a grand total of ninety. That exhausted the possibilities of the frieze.

His left foot was beginning to go to sleep. He wriggled it, felt tingling pains shoot all the way up into his thigh, and shifted his whole body slightly in the chair. Nefer turned and shot an icy glance at him. He met it with one of cold dislike, then his eyes moved for the hundredth time to the patch of blue sky and waving, sunlit palm branches visible through the clerestory opening. Out there, in the dust and sunlight of the parade grounds, the bodyguard would be drilling, by his orders—having archery practice and javelin practice, and driving the war chariots in battle formation. He would be with them, as soon as this was over—if ever it was over.

I should not sit here wishing it were over, he thought guiltily. I should be listening. In only six weeks I shall be king, all by myself, then I will not have Lady Shesu to do all this for me. No wonder she grows more and more nervous, and says I am not ready—I will be, though. I must be.

Firmly he turned his attention to the measured voices in the Audience Hall. The tax discussion had merged into one about the current scarcity of myrrh.

"But we *must* relieve it!" Lady Shesu was saying. "The scent of myrrh is pleasing to the nostrils of my father Amon. He must not be without it. What has happened to the Sand-dwellers who have always brought it?"

Nehsi shrugged. "They have not been seen this year."

"We should not depend upon barbarians for such important trade. Our best ointments, our best incense . . . Where do the Sand-dwellers get it?"

328

"From other barbarians to the south, they say. And those trade with still others, perhaps in Punt itself."

"Punt," Hatshepsut said dreamily.

Thoth, whose thoughts had already strayed as he lovingly inspected Lady Shesu's profile, pricked up his ears. Punt? *The land of Punt, which is called Godsland, where gardens of incense trees are terraced down to the sea, and the gods walk abroad among them. . . .*

"If we could sent ships to Punt ourselves . . ." Hatshepsut mused.

"No one knows where it is, Your Radiance," Nehsi reminded her. "Far to the south and east of Egypt, the old tales say—but many think there is no such land, that it is but a memory, that the tales are but tales."

"The incense is real enough! So is the gold we pay for it. I've no doubt we pay twice or thrice its worth to those thieving savages. . . ."

The talk degenerated into a discussion of prices and trade goods, and Thoth's interest waned as the momentarily bright visions of leading an army to capture Godsland faded from his mind. Probably Lady Shesu would not let him lead an army to Godsland even if anyone did know where it was. She did not like armies; she hated all talk of war and fighting. Even the bodyguard drilled despite her wishes; she had withdrawn her opposition but Thoth knew she had never withdrawn her disapproval.

She is a woman, he thought forgivingly. She is gentle and feminine, and violence distresses her. It is only natural. I would not wish her to be any other way.

Nevertheless, Egypt must have troops—far more than the three thousand of the bodyguard. When he was really king, in six weeks, when he had transferred to his man's shoulders the burdens she had carried for him so willingly while he was yet a boy, then he would do what he knew to be right about the matter. He had a dozen plans for expanding the army—good plans. He could scarcely wait to try them out. Everything would be different when he was making the decisions himself; probably even tax scrolls and the price of myrrh would seem interesting then, and he would not have to count lotuses and fight to stay awake during these long audiences.

He wondered what Nefer did to pass the time. Admired her

329

bracelets, perhaps; enjoyed the flattering eyes upon her gown. Never mind Nefer—she was good for nothing but sitting still and being stared at. What of Rekhmi-re and Amenuser?

Thoth's eyes moved to the far left corner of the big room, where stood nine youths near his own age who would eventually be the Royal Kinsmen. His academic studies, interrupted by his sudden exit from the temple, had been resumed at the palace under the tutelage of court scribes—and in the company of these nine noblemen's sons, whose high birth entitled them by tradition to the honor of being educated with him. Thoth had found himself drawn to only two; but the more he observed these two, the better he liked them—Amenuser for his intuitive, subtle mind, Rekhmi-re for his jesting, his reckless love of escapades, and the deep warmth of nature which underlay both. On that all-important day four years ago when Thoth had discovered Tjah again in the palace barracks and immediately added a class in the arts of war to his academic schedule, it was Amenuser and Rekhmi-re who asked to join it. The friendship of the three had ripened in the informal atmosphere of the drill field, from which Thoth banished the last constraint by forbidding the title of Majesty during maneuvers. From highest officers to lowest horseboy, the soldiers called him Tjesu, "Commander"—and so did Rekhmi-re and Amenu. By this time he knew them well, so well that even before his eye found them in the group of Young Kinsmen, he had guessed what each would be doing to pass the time.

He was right—so right that he restrained a grin only with difficulty. Amenuser's long chin and longer neck were craned around intervening heads, and his eyes, narrowed to dreamy slits, were fixed on the charming figure of fourteen-year-old Countess Nofretari, standing with her mother on the other side of the hall. Rekhmi-re, beside him, was observing this devotion with an expression of resigned tolerance on his square, blue-jawed face, meanwhile stealthily working at the knot of Amenu's *shenti*. Thoth watched, fascinated. If it fell off, here in the midst of this jeweled and pompous company— No, Amenu had caught him at it, yanked the knot tight again, and moved out of reach to resume his dreaming over the little countess. Rekhmi-re's sigh was visible if not audible; his large, ink-black eyes with their coarse black lashes wandered, as Thoth's had done, to the clerestory and the patch of sky.

330

Rekhmi-re, too, was thinking of the bodyguard out yonder —three thousand men trained, drilled, already needed—and never used.

No matter, Thoth told himself, restraining an impulse to shift impatiently in his chair. Six more weeks—then I shall be Pharaoh in fact as well as name, and everything will change. I am much more ready to rule than Lady Shesu supposes—she thinks of me as a child yet, but she'll soon see that I am a man, and really more capable than she of handling such matters as that uprising in Nubia—

"Thoth! In Amon's name!"

Nefer's outraged whisper sent Thoth's daydreams scattering. With an all too familiar sensation of sinking guilt, he realized that something had been said that he had not heard. Nehsi was gone; the royal herald stood in his place, holding a parchment. Everyone was looking expectantly toward the throne.

Oh gods, Thoth thought. Why can't I listen?

It was the schoolroom in Babylon all over again—only Inatsil had always found his absent-mindedness amusing. Lady Shesu was far from amused. Her face was set and exasperated, and Thoth did not blame her.

"I—was not attending," he muttered.

"The Good God is like his father," Lady Shesu remarked— as she always did at such times. And—as it always happened when she said that—the courtiers' expressions changed to deep uneasiness, and they slid glances at one another.

"Read the petition again," Thoth ordered.

On fire with humiliation, he listened as the herald launched into a long paean praising Count Senmut's accomplishments.

"Wherefore," he wound up at last, "Amon has instructed Her Radiance, as regent for the Good God Men-kheper-Re, to heap honor upon his servant Senmut . . . wherefore my lord Senmut shall be hereafter Superintendent of the Private Apartments, of the Royal Bedroom, and of the Royal Bath, forever and ever until he does join Osiris in the Land of the West. . . ."

Thoth cleared the rustiness from his throat.

Hatshepsut turned to him coldly. *"If the Good God was attending . . . is it the will of Men-kheper-Re that his regent obey the will of her father Amon?"*

"Aye," Thoth said.

Five minutes later the elaborate etiquette of a Royal Audience had reached the point at which it was proper for him to rise and start for the Window of Royal Appearances for the concluding ceremony of the day. Stiff-jawed, he started down the center of the long room—miserable at having again provoked, and deserved, Lady Shesu's disapproval—and acutely conscious, as usual, of the humiliating fact that Nefer, who followed with Hatshepsut a pace behind him, was taller than he by half a head. He walked rigidly erect, hoping the high crown might conceal his shortness but knowing very well it did not. No doubt his courtiers, too, thought him a mere boy— What *were* they thinking? He could never tell.

Out of the long room at last, he walked quickly across the transverse hall and up the left side of the short double flight of steps leading to the Window of Royal Appearances, which pierced the exact center of the palace's façade. As the shutters opened before him, he looked out over a crowd of heads, to which were added more and more as the courtiers poured out of the palace doors to join the throng. In the center of the courtyard Senmut stood alone, with modestly lowered eyes.

Thoth mumbled, "Come forth, Senmut, Superintendent of the Private Apartments, of the Royal Bedroom, and of the Royal Bath."

"Speak louder, Thoth!" Nefer hissed. "In Mut's sweet name, no one can hear what you are saying!"

"Let them guess, then," Thoth retorted. He had no intention of speaking louder and running the risk of having his voice shoot up into a mortifying falsetto, as it still often did. "It is pleasant to the heart of My Majesty," he said, still mumbling, "to reward your diligence with the Gold of Favor."

Turning, he reached into the chest held ready by a chamberlain and began throwing golden necklaces, chains, and armbands down into the court. A cheer went up from the crowd below; Senmut caught the first bauble, then stepped deftly out of the way while his servants rushed forward to catch the rain of treasure with practiced efficiency, and pack it into the baskets they had brought.

Small wonder they are experts by now! Thoth reflected.

His eyes moved with dislike over Senmut's tall body with its easy stance, its angular, powerful shoulders, its arrogantly held head. Count Senmut, Steward of Amon, Guardian of the Princess —that was all he had been, five years ago. Now he was one of the Kinsmen themselves, and his offices were so numerous they left scarcely a one for anybody else. Superintendent of this, Overseer of that—he came near to being Overseer of the regency itself. As of today, he was also Superintendent of the Private Apartments, the Royal Bedroom, the Royal Bath.

Which meant, of course, master of Her Radiance Hatshepsut's life and bed. The secret was finally out in the open.

Not, Thoth added to himself, that there was anyone left who did not know.

He glanced from Senmut to Hatshepsut, caught the smile that passed between them, and looked away, sick with a hurt he could not analyze or even grow accustomed to. *He* had not known, until about a year ago. What a child he had been—wondering why Lady Shesu piled honors on this one man, why Senmut alone could do no wrong, why Nehsi and the others coldly deferred to him while obviously resenting his growing eminence at court. Thoth had resented him most of all, had quarreled with Nefer continuously because she defended him. He fully intended to take away most of Senmut's offices as soon as possible. Six more weeks. Let the great steward continue to rule Lady Shesu's life and share her bed, if that was what she wanted—but he should not rule Egypt.

Hatshepsut was still throwing the last necklaces when Thoth turned abruptly, paused long enough for the Circle to form around him, and started down the stairs.

Of course, he thought, I won't disgrace Senmut, he shall keep a few offices—for Lady Shesu's sake. She can't help it if she loves him. It doesn't mean she doesn't love *me*. I am not jealous, that is not what hurts. . . .

What hurt was not that she loved Senmut, but the discovery that she had never loved his father, the Tired One—had hated him, in fact. Thoth did not know when he had begun to realize this, but he knew it now, and apparently everyone except himself had always known it. It gave him a strange, hollow, painful feeling whenever he thought of it—quite illogically, he told himself. *He* was not his father, it had nothing to do with him.

I am being childish, he thought. Suppose she didn't love my father? Do I love Nefer? Nay, I can't abide her. These things just happen, it is nobody's fault.

He could not imagine how anyone could love Nefer—Nefer the angular, the pettish, always acting as if she had wed beneath herself, always just coming down with an illness or else recovering from one. She was impossible to talk to, worse to sleep with —a mere political burden he had assumed along with his crown. It did not matter, he told himself. If he craved a woman's company, he had a dozen in the Mansion of Beauty to choose from . . . But once he had satisfied desire, they were no good either. There was not one whose company he enjoyed, not one he could talk to.

I can talk only to Mayet, he reflected. He smiled briefly at the thought of little Meryet-Re's solemn, kittenlike face. It always startled him to remember that Mayet was his wife too. Some day, perhaps— However, as yet she was only a child, ten years old. She could not possibly understand the problems of a man almost sixteen.

"Your Majesty's pardon, I do not wish to intrude upon Your Majesty's reflections—but if Your Majesty would permit me to remove the goddess . . ."

Thoth discovered that he was standing in the middle of the yellow-walled sitting room, encircled by attendants still waiting to be dismissed. Old Thutiy, Guardian of the Crown, was regarding him with acid patience, disapproval in every line of his skinny body.

Thoth walked to the scarlet leather chair and sat down, scowling to offset the flush he could feel creeping up his neck and cheeks. He knew what they were thinking, all of them. *Like his father, exactly like his father.*

Suppose I am like him? he thought angrily. Make what you will of it.

At the back of his mind he was taking careful note: *my father was absent-minded, too—sometimes thinking so hard he did not hear them—and they hated him for it. Why? Perhaps only because his thoughts were not like theirs.*

It was another small insight into a nature he was beginning to know from frequently glimpsing its reflection in the mirror of himself. Each time they said, "You are like your father," the

334

image grew clearer—and it was an image with which he felt an ever-increasing bond of sympathy.

Thutiy bore away the Crown-goddess. With a sigh of relief Thoth reached up and snatched the Beard of Royalty from his chin. As the Circle filed out of the room, taking his last responsibility with it, he sprang from his chair and sent his jeweled sandals flying against the opposite wall. "Bring a common *shenti* and some tougher footwear," he ordered his wardrobe master. "And the blue Battle Helmet. Make haste, I am late at the barracks."

It was an hour later that the messenger from Nubia arrived. Thoth, rattling at full speed around the parade ground in one of the swift, strong, feather-light war chariots, with dust rising in clouds about him, the reins tied about his hips and his eyes narrowed to slits as he sighted along his arrow's shaft, was at first only vaguely conscious of some unfamiliar activity around the barracks. He let fly the arrow and watched it hit the target before he turned for a closer look. It was hard to see through the swirls of dust, but he could make out a knot of men at the door of the central barracks, with more running to join them. At the same moment he saw Tjah standing at the edge of the drill field, trying to signal to him.

Leaning hard into the reins, he turned his stallions out of the circle of speeding chariots and brought them to a halt near the stables, where an orderly and his slave were waiting. By the time he stepped to the ground Rekhmi-re had rattled up beside him.

"What is it?" called Rekhmi-re above the snorting of his horses.

"I don't know." Thoth pulled off his leather gloves, squinting toward the crowd around the barracks. "It is time to stop drilling anyway. Call a halt and then get Amenu—we'll see what has happened."

In another five minutes the crowd was parting hastily before the three of them. In its center stood one of the captains of infantry, grasping the arm of a stranger who wore the leather kilt of a border garrison.

"Who is this?" Thoth asked.

"My brother Neb-Re, from Turo's command in Nubia,

335

Tjesu," the captain answered. "There is more trouble upriver."

"Let him tell me."

It was the same story he had heard a month ago, from another messenger. General restlessness, rebellious incidents here and there, a minor uprising among the tribes far southward from the garrison. Turo was dealing with each thing as it occurred but, he begged Pharaoh to heed his words, that was not the answer. One campaign, merely the display of Pharaoh's might paraded through the southland, and all incidents might stop—if it were done soon. If that were impossible, let Pharaoh increase the strength of the regulars at the garrison. But *something* should be done. . . .

As Thoth listened, he felt the familiar gnawing restlessness, the sensation of struggling with his hands tied, that was beginning to be the usual climate of his mind. Two years ago, when a rumor had come of attacks on the garrison at Kadesh, he had burned to lead his three thousand there. Six months later he had wanted to march on Libya, to secure a shifting, sliding border. A year after that he had pleaded, almost quarreled with Lady Shesu about strengthening border garrisons. And now—two messengers from Nubia within a month.

I must go to her again, he thought. *Insist*. Make her see! She does not understand these things . . .

He wondered if he could ever make her understand them. He dreaded to try; she was so tense these days, so easily annoyed—and he had annoyed her once already today.

"Have you made a report to Her Radiance?" he asked.

"Aye, Your Majesty. She did not seem to—understand the—danger of the situation," the man said awkwardly.

"Do not say 'majesty,'" hissed his brother, nudging him. "'Tjesu,' on the drill field."

"No matter," Thoth said shortly. At times like this he wondered if either title had any meaning. He was a majesty who did not really rule, a commander who had no power to command. He looked around him at the faces of the soldiers and their officers—young Makhet with the eager eyes, Sekhwed and his half-brother Sushan, two faithful remnants of a family of warrior-nobles whose kind had almost disappeared from Egypt. None of these soldiers had treated him as a boy, but as a man among men.

336

For a moment a man's order trembled recklessly on his lips—
prepare for campaign, prepare to embark for Nubia at dawn.
. . . He clenched his jaw tight to hold back the words. Having
to withdraw them later would be more humiliating than to keep
silent now. It would do no good to say, "I will come in six weeks,"
and he could not bring himself to say, "I will come—if she will
let me." He stood silent, feeling a hot flush creep up his neck.

She must let me! he thought. She *must,* this time!

"I will talk to her myself," he said. "Wait here."

When he strode, breathless, across the little garden that
separated her suite from the King's Apartments, she was sitting
before her dressing table, gazing into the silver mirror with such
an abstracted expression that he wondered if she was even aware
of the reflected face that stared steadily back at her.

"Lady Shesu—?" he said.

She started as though he had shouted, and whirled about. Instantly she was laughing, picking up the ivory *kohl*-stick which
had flown from her hand, turning back to make busy motions
among the silver ointment pots and perfume vials. "Ptah's
Beard! You stole in so silently . . . I thought you were a *kheft.*
What are you doing here at this hour?"

"I must speak to you." Thoth moved closer, wishing she would
stop rearranging the jars and look at him. "Lady Shesu—it is
about the messenger from Nubia."

"Oh—Turo's man. You need not trouble yourself about him,
Thoth. These commanders in distant posts—they are always
begging Pharaoh for more gold, more troops—"

"But more are needed! There have been uprisings—this is the
second message Turo has sent!"

"Aye, and it is likely he will send a dozen more before he copes
with the matter himself, as he is supposed to do. Turo merely
wishes a visit from Pharaoh, to enliven the tedium of that
wretched place . . . and you, my dear child, are merely longing to march proudly at the head of your soldiers, and shout
commands, and cut a fine figure! Now come, admit it—"

She glanced at him, laughing, but Thoth could not laugh with
her. Instead he felt himself reddening with anger.

"You always think I am a child!" he said. "Perhaps I am. But
Turo is not! Turo is a seasoned commander, a veteran of thirty

337

years in that Nubian post and of half a dozen campaigns before that. Such a man knows what he is saying!"

"Oh, nonsense. Thoth, please do not argue about trifles with me now. I have other matters on my mind, far more important ones. I have no time for these foolish—"

"They are not foolish!" he shouted. "They are not trifles! I am right about this, and you are wrong, all wrong!"

"Thoth!" Hatshepsut flung the *kohl*-stick down and stood up, facing him.

Instantly he was miserable. Her voice had snapped taut again, as it had in the Audience Chamber this morning, as it seemed always to be doing lately, and on her face was the expression he dreaded most to see. Even the thought of his waiting soldiers dwindled beside the knowledge that Lady Shesu was looking at him with cold dislike.

"I am sorry," he whispered.

"No doubt," she said. She sat down again on the dressing table stool, her back toward him. Her voice, though low, had a peculiar, rigid intensity. "You would do better to think before you speak. You would do well to remember that I have been guiding Egypt since you were an infant—and guiding it well."

"I know."

"And that you are very young and inexperienced indeed."

"I know," he repeated miserably.

He had never felt more young, more inexperienced, more bungling. He had only wanted to show her the importance of Turo's message. Now, thanks to his blundering, she would refuse to give it her attention at all. There was nothing to do but leave —go back to his soldiers and tell them— Gods! What could he tell them?

He hesitated at the garden door and glanced back at her, but she was again gazing at her reflection in the mirror, lost in thought.

As he stepped out into the sunshine, someone flung open the gate and started hurriedly up the path. It was Count Senmut. At sight of his young Pharaoh he stopped short and made low obeisance—lower than necessary, considering his exalted rank. Thoth kept walking, ignoring the great royal favorite. There was always something faintly mocking about Senmut's bow, elaborate though it was—always a glint of something in his eyes

338

that was gone the moment one turned to look. Thoth did not look. He walked woodenly past Senmut and through the gate into the arbored walk that ran between the palace and the crafts-men's courtyards to the south. As the latch clicked behind him he heard Senmut's footsteps moving quickly toward the queen's apartments.

She will listen to *him,* whatever his errand is! Thoth reflected bitterly—then at once was ashamed of the thought. When had Lady Shesu ever failed to listen—kindly, if a little absently—when he came to talk things over with her in a quiet and civil way? How could he expect her to listen when he came in shout-ing abuse and defying her? Such behavior was scarcely what he had promised when he told her after the coronation how obedi-ent he meant to be, how fully he trusted her.

I do trust her, he thought. I always will.

But surely, about this one thing, he was right, *right!*

He sighed deeply, knowing he had forfeited all chance of con-vincing her of that. He glanced toward the drill field—then started slowly along the walk in the opposite direction. He would have to send someone to tell the men . . . but not yet. He could not think what to say yet; he could not bear to picture them idling expectantly around the barracks, waiting. . . .

Three thousand soldiers—and they were useless to him. Of course there should be twenty thousand more; there should be nonprofessional troops all up and down the length of Egypt, ready to conscript at any moment into a full army, of which the body-guard would form an elite core. That was the way it had been in his grandfather's time. There had been no lack of officers then. Now all the young nobles wanted posts at court, instead of in an army that did nothing but stay in Thebes and drill.

Six weeks, Thoth promised himself, trying to take comfort in the thought. Just six more weeks. Meantime, Lady Shesu is my regent and I must obey her.

Emerging from the covered walk, he crossed a grassy stretch and let himself in the side gate of the little garden off the Great Court.

Sunlight, rich and golden with late afternoon, striped the lawns and lay along the tops of deep-shadowed walls, turning the flower-ing vines there into cascades of flame. Gravel crunched under Thoth's feet as he walked slowly up the path toward the pavilion.

Suddenly a half-grown hound—more golden than the sunshine on back and flanks, creamy-white underneath, with a furrowed face and luminous, almond-shaped green eyes—emerged from the shadows beneath the tamarisk tree and bounded across the grass. It was Mayet's dog, Kiag—named by Thoth, in a nostalgic moment, after the old hound in Babylon—which he had given her some months before. Thoth stooped to greet the dog, which was twisting and squirming against his knees, uttering the queer little joyful gurgle that was the only sound its breed could make. Then he glanced about in search of Mayet. There she was, at the end of the pool among the rushes. What was she doing?

Diverted as always by Mayet's unexpectedness, he started down the grassy slope. Usually, if she was anywhere in the garden, she came running as soon as he opened the gate. Today she was sitting perfectly still among the rushes, her chin on her knees and her arms doubled around them, apparently as oblivious of his presence as a small bronze statue.

He stopped a few feet behind her, and after a moment's amused puzzling, said, "What are you doing?"

"Watching a frog," she murmured without turning.

Now that he knew what to look for, he discovered a very small frog sitting as motionless as Mayet on a lotus pad about ten inches from her toes.

"And what is *he* doing? Watching you?"

"He is having dinner. He caught a fly a few minutes ago—so *fast,* Thoth! I want to see him catch another."

"What of your own dinner?"

"This is more important."

Thoth stood watching her, smiling a little but feeling oddly piqued as well. Mayet had *always* come running when he opened the gate. Well, what of it? he thought. She is not lonely today; I should be glad of that. But he heard himself saying, "More important than talking to me?"

"Nay!" She stood up, whirling toward him so quickly that her heavy black hair whipped out like a curtain. At the sudden motion her frog disappeared with a tiny plop into the pool.

"Now! You've frightened him away," Thoth said.

Mayet was studying him intently, her wide, tilted eyes grave in her kittenlike face. "Has something bad happened?"

"Nay, nothing is wrong." Thoth smiled, ashamed of himself for having tested her, but obscurely comforted by her reaction. To this one small maid, at least, he was truly the sun and center of existence, especially since old Yen's death last year. Mayet had no one else; he was the only other person who had cared to notice her existence. She was solitary still, going quietly about her own odd little affairs, passively accepting the services of the slaves he gave her, but responding to no personality except his own.

To Mayet, at least, I am king, he reflected. But to Lady Shesu —and the rest of Egypt—

He wondered if Egypt would ever look on him as a god and sun, as they had looked upon his grandfather. It was clearer every day that no one had ever looked upon his father so. Supposing—after the six weeks were ended and he could no longer depend on Lady Shesu—he proved to be no king at all, but a blunderer, as he had been today? Supposing even his ideas about the army, which he was so sure were right, were in truth all wrong?

Depressed, he started back up the slope, as usual forgetting all about Mayet until he heard her voice calling after him.

"Stay, Thoth—I will find us another frog to watch."

"Another day, little one," he said absently, then felt a pang at the uneasiness on her face. He added, "Nothing's amiss."

The sound of the gate opening, plus another joyful outburst from Kiag, made him look around. Amenu and Rekhmi-re were coming into the garden from the Great Court. Thoth met them on the path; their questioning, eager faces changed to tactful masks as soon as they saw his expression.

"You dismissed the troops, Rekhmi-re?" Thoth said casually, avoiding their eyes.

"Aye, Tjesu."

"And then," Amenu added cheerfully, "we came in search of you—dusty, disreputable, with parching throats—hoping to be invited to share a jug of beer. May I send for some?"

"Aye, do." Thoth glanced at him and forced a wry smile. "At least I can command beer when I want it."

"You will command all Egypt soon," Amenu returned in a matter-of-fact tone. He walked off, whistling, to find a servant.

Rekhmi-re stooped to rumple the dog's ears. Suddenly he said, with apparent irrelevance, "When one thinks of it, Tjesu, six weeks is not long. There will be a full two weeks of festivities before the actual day of your coming of age—and that leaves four weeks only, and half of this one is already gone. In truth, there would not be time to get to Nubia and back—"

"Nay," Thoth said quickly. "Nay, there would not really be time."

It was the last mention of the campaign, but as they walked up the path to the pavilion Thoth's mood grew heavier, until depression sat like a stone inside him. Neither Amenu's return with the beer, nor the efforts of both his friends to turn his mind to more cheerful matters, brought any comfort.

At last he said bluntly, "How do they think of me, in truth—the nobles—all those people at the audience? They stare at me so, as if I were still that Babylonian—or in any case someone they could not trust, could not understand. *You* do not do that."

"Naturally we do not. We know you," Amenu said. He hesitated, then added, "But the Tjesu we know is someone quite different from the Majesty the courtiers see—that person walking stiff and stolid down the Great Hall—"

"It is they who make me stiff and stolid! All those eyes staring at me—I feel as if they are picking me to pieces, bit by bit. What is more, they are."

"Nay, that is in your mind," Rekhmi-re put in easily. He leaned back against one of the columns of the pavilion and crossed his dusty combat sandals in front of him. "I know that feeling. My father says it is nothing but the age we are. He says every lad of sixteen is sure the eyes of all the world are on him."

Thoth smiled half-heartedly. He envied Rekhmi-re his closeness to his father, a great, craggy man of both humor and wisdom, usually well worth listening to. But in this case his wisdom did not fit. "They really *are* on me," he said.

An uncomfortable silence attested to the truth of the statement.

"Tjesu, you do not let them know you," Amenu insisted. "In all Egypt, I'll wager, there is no one who knows you as you really are, except we two and perhaps your little wife yonder—and your soldiers."

"Aye, my soldiers!" Thoth said bitterly. "Even they must be

beginning to wonder. They drill and drill and I do nothing with them. Soon they will be staring at me too, and saying 'He is like his father,' the same as everyone else."

"Tjesu, you are not like him!" Rekhmi-re said.

"Nay, I do not think I am. But what if I were? Is there something so wrong with being like my father? I think no one knew *him,* either. I think he was entirely misunderstood. Do you know what I am doing, usually, when someone says 'The Good God is like his father?' I am merely thinking of something else—often something of far more importance, at least to me. Now tell me what is so dreadful about that?"

"*That* was not what was—" Rekhmi-re stopped.

"What was dreadful about him?" Thoth finished. "What was it? Can you say? Did you know him?"

"Nay."

"Nor did I." Thoth settled back with a sigh in the gold-and-cedar chair. "I wish I had. . . ." He fell into disconsolate silence. When he was adrift from Lady Shesu he felt as if he did not know who or what he was; everything seemed shifting and uncertain. Why did I quarrel with her? he thought. I cannot bear to quarrel with her!

He drained his goblet and thrust it at Amenu. "Here, fill this. In Amon's name, let us talk of something else!"

Amenu got up to pour more beer and at once launched into his favorite topic—the charms of the countess Nofretari. He had first met her, he had once confided to Thoth, when she was three years old, and had loved her helplessly ever since. Rekhmi-re's blue-jawed face lost its unnatural gravity as he began to tease Amenu about her. Thoth drank his beer and listened, trying to forget his depression in Rekhmi-re's nonsense, and watching the late sun gild the pool and the motionless figure of little Mayet, who had evidently found another frog.

A few moments later the side gate opened and Count Senmut entered the garden. He strode hastily to the pavilion and made obeisance on the steps.

"Your Majesty's pardon—I have come from Her Radiance. She begs Your Majesty's presence in her chambers. At once, if Your Majesty pleases. It is urgent."

There was something electric in Senmut's bearing and in his

343

eyes. Thoth stood up, peering at him closely. "What is it about?"

"About—Nubia, Your Majesty. I believe—"

Thoth was already pushing past him, his eyes alive with hope. "Wait here!" he flung back to Rekhmi-re and Amenu, and started for the gate with Senmut at his heels.

It was no more than ten minutes before the two Young Kinsmen were answering a second urgent summons, this time from Thoth. When Amenu tapped at the door of the King's Apartments, Thoth himself flung it open, seized the two and pulled them in.

"I am going!" he cried. "To Nubia, to fight the Nine Bows! I'll be off at dawn, think of it—Gods, how I misjudged her! She was listening all the time—she went at once to consult Amon. He told her I was right. I was right! Oh, I knew I was, but I am so glad *she* knows it. She is not angry, she forgave all my blundering, she understands perfectly. Now I am to go! Look you, Rekhmi-re—both of you—hurry at once to the barracks, give the order for me."

They were already jostling each other to get at the door latch. Rekhmi-re cried over his shoulder, "Will we go with you?"

"Not this time. I am to take only two platoons."

Both boys whirled to stare at him.

"It is enough," Thoth said impatiently. "Even Turo said only a show of force was needed, and I shall have his troops, too, once I reach the garrison. We will make a show, believe me! Afterwards I am to leave my soldiers with him, to strengthen his forces. . . ."

Amenuser came back from the door. He hesitated a moment, then said, "You will return from Nubia *alone,* Tjesu?"

"Of course not. I shall have a squad or two for escort—what more do I need, in my own land? What is the matter with you, Amenu?"

"Nothing, nothing. I was just thinking—"

"The festivities!" Rekhmi-re said suddenly. "The coming of age. You will never get back in time, it is only six weeks—"

"They will be postponed! Amon's blood, there is all the time in the world for *that!* Just now *this* is the important matter. Can you not see that?"

"Aye." Rekhmi-re relaxed a little. "Of course, I see."

"Then don't stand gaping at me. Go!"

344

*　　*　　*

Nine weeks later Thoth's lone ship sailed back into a strangely quiet Thebes. No crowds lined the wharves, though he had sent a runner ahead; no bejeweled company waited to greet him at the royal landing. Once inside the palace grounds he dismissed his weary escort and walked alone, with mounting bewilderment, up the curving avenue. He was full sixteen now, the veteran of one campaign. He had left Thebes a boy, burning with dreams of glory; he was returning a man of experience, richer by the half-healed mark of a Nine-Bow's war ax, an intimate knowledge of the red bluffs and scorching wastelands of upper Nubia, and a far clearer idea of what battles were all about.

It was obvious to him—now—that he should have had more men, many more, and better armed. He had come home to fetch them, secure in the knowledge that the regency was a thing of the past, that only a few formalities stood between him and the full kingship for which he had waited four long years.

But was this any way to greet a king?

There was not a soul in sight on the palace grounds. The gates of the Great Court stood open; within was sunlit emptiness, save for the usual two sentries and an old chamberlain who cowered just outside the palace door. Thoth walked up the steps and confronted him, staring. The old man looked as if he were about to faint with fright.

"Well?" Thoth demanded.

The chamberlain's mouth worked. He closed his eyes; for a moment Thoth thought he was about to fall. Instead he brought out a terrified whisper.

"His Majesty—awaits Your Highness—in the Great Hall."

"My *Highness?* His Majesty? What Majesty?"

Pushing the old man roughly out of the way, Thoth strode through the door, across the entry and into the Great Hall.

It was filled with people—courtiers, gathered as if for an audience—but not one of them turned to look at him, or made a sound. Slowly he walked down the cleared path they had left, then stopped, his eyes fixed on the dais. There were the Kinsmen, ranged as usual on its lowest step. Behind—not as usual—stood a double row of his soldiers, with javelins at the ready and faces like those of wooden statues. In the midst of all stood the throne of Egypt—his throne—and it was not empty.

345

Lady Shesu was sitting on it. She held his Crook and Flail in her two hands, she had tied his Beard of Royalty upon her chin, she wore his crown upon her head. She was dressed in *shenti* and pleated headcloth—the garments of a king, not a queen.

As he stood in the silence, stunned and unbelieving, there was a stir in the crowd to his left. Dazedly he looked around. Rekhmi-re and Amenu, with faces as tense as the soldiers', pushed through and walked toward him. Behind them he caught a glimpse of the countess Nofretari staring after Amenu with horrified eyes—of Rekhmi-re's father standing as if turned to stone. His two friends dropped to their knees before him.

He stared at them, feeling as if he had walked into some masque the meaning of which he did not understand. When he turned his eyes once more to the throne, Hatshepsut had risen. She began to speak, in a high, unnatural voice, rigidly controlled. He listened, he heard—but he did not believe the words she spoke. Egypt, Thebes, and the court, she was saying, welcomed His Highness. He would always be welcome, always revered and honored—but it was not Amon's will that he rule as yet. She had long known that Amon had fathered her to be his son in the Two Lands, to be prince and Pharaoh—while she lived no other must wear the crown. Amon's own voice had told her that four weeks ago, and had repeated it with increasing urgency until she dared not disobey. She was sure His Highness would not want her to disobey the god. Naturally, as husband of the Divine Consort Neferu-Re, he would always have an honored place in festivals and processions, and an entire wing of the palace had been set aside for him and his household . . .

Her voice went on, cleaving the silence like the thin prow of a ship, curling up a wave of treachery on either side.

It cannot be true, he thought.

The whole scene took on a fantastic unreality. Surely these were *khefts* around him, not living, breathing courtiers whose features he recognized, whose names he could have called. Those were not *his* soldiers up there. His eye traveled over their rigid faces and paused in utter incredulity at Tjah's. It could *not* be true—that Tjah had turned against him. None of this was true, it was not real. He would not believe it.

The voice stopped, and silence flowed around him—a waiting silence. *They* believed it; they were waiting for him to leave

346

Suddenly he felt suffocated. He wheeled and walked swiftly down the shining length of the room, through those rows and rows of silent *kheft*-courtiers, and out at last through the tall doors into the transverse hall. The doors closed soundlessly behind him.

It was several moments before he realized that Amenu and Rekhmi-re had followed him, and were standing at his side.

"There is some terrible mistake," he whispered.

"Tjesu," Amenu said in a strange, strained, somehow heart-breaking voice, "there is no mistake. Please—come with us."

He laid his hand on Thoth's arm and started toward the north wing. Thoth climbed stairs, walked along corridors, without realizing that he moved, without noticing where they were going. They entered a room; Rekhmi-re closed the door.

Thoth turned and stared into their faces; they looked as if they had been through some painful illness.

"She wore my crown," he whispered. "She sat on my throne."

"Tjesu," Amenu said, "she has usurped them."

The word hung evilly in the room. "Impossible," Thoth said. "Impossible! It is a mistake! Rekhmi-re—it is some incredible misunderstanding."

"Nay, it is not," Rekhmi-re said harshly.

"It must be!" Thoth was shouting now. "The campaign to Nubia—"

"A trick, to get you out of Egypt."

"Nay! Nay! She understood, agreed—Amon spoke to her—had soldiers, arms—"

"Two platoons! She kept the others here—for very good reason. You saw them today, standing there beside her. They are hers now."

"They cannot be! *I* trained them—*I*—"

"Tjesu, all is hers now. There has been a coronation in your absence."

"Coronation . . . now that, I know, cannot be true. She cannot be Pharaoh, she is a woman!" Thoth backed away from them, glaring as if they were enemies. "It is all impossible. You are wrong! You have misunderstood her—everyone has. She has some plan you do not know about. She thinks me young yet—aye, that's it! She means only to rule a while, a year perhaps. She would not steal my crown, Lady Shesu would not do that to me! Never, never!"

347

He broke off, clutched at the back of a chair to steady himself, and for the first time looked about him at a room he had never seen. It was spacious and richly furnished, pierced with doors leading to several other rooms. Through a bedchamber adjoining, he could see a balcony and a flight of outside stairs. His hands tightened on the chair back.

"What is this place? I do not know it."

"Tjesu," Amenu said in a low voice, "these are your new quarters."

With a wrench Thoth sent the chair crashing to the floor. "They are not my quarters! The King's Apartments are mine, and I am king! I am king! I'll talk to her—I'll prove it to you!"

He was already jerking the door open, flinging himself out into the corridor. If his friends called after him, he did not hear. He ran wildly down the hall, down the stairs. The broad entry was full of people now—courtiers, emerging from the Great Hall. Thoth pushed blindly through them. A moment later he flung open the door of the yellow-walled sitting room.

She was there, and Senmut was beside her. Both whirled; Hatshepsut backed away as if she had seen a *kheft*. Her face grew whiter and whiter as she stared at Thoth.

"Why are you here?" she gasped. "It is all finished, it is over, I have said all I have to say."

"Nay, you have not! You have not—" Thoth broke off, staring at Senmut with all his old dislike. Stepping clear of the door, he ordered, "Leave us."

"Senmut—stay!" Hatshepsut said. She flung a hand out; Senmut moved quickly to her side.

"I said get out!" Thoth cried. "Obey me."

"Your pardon, Highness," Senmut said carelessly. "His Majesty Ma-ke-Re has given a different command.

The insolent ease of his manner set Thoth's blood to pounding sickeningly in his temples.

"*I* am His Majesty! Obey me or I'll have your life for it!"

"Cease your threatening!" Hatshepsut straightened with an effort, and the color came rushing back into her cheeks. "What do you want?" she demanded. "Say what you wish to, and then go."

"Go? I belong here. These are my chambers! You know that." Something was squeezing Thoth tighter and tighter inside, tak-

348

ing his breath, shutting off his voice. He moved slowly to her, looked into her face. "You *know* that," he whispered.

"I know nothing of the sort. *I* am king now. Can you not understand that? *I am Pharaoh.*"

"For a year? Until I am older? Until the affair in Nubia is righted?"

"Until I die!" she cried. "I am Pharaoh, I am king, I am Horus! Amon intended it from my birth, it will be so until my death! Is that clear enough?"

He was silent. Every object in the room, including her once-beloved face, grew slowly hideous to him.

"Well?" she burst out. "Why do you stand there, staring? Why did you come questioning—you have no right to question me. No one may question me! I am Ma-ke-Re. I am the daughter of the god. What I do is done by Amon's command."

He could not answer. He could scarcely see her because of the pain inside him that was wrenching and distorting and changing the shape of all his thoughts and every aspect of the world. He could still hear her voice, though—sharp and shrill, a stranger's.

"Go, I did not summon you, I do not want you! For four years I have deferred to you. Now it is ended, by the will of Amon. I knew he would guide me. I have always known he would never let the son of a harem woman rule my land. Gods, what sacrilege it would have been!" She stopped, and suddenly whirled across the room and faced him with its breadth between them. "Go, I tell you! I forbid you to enter this room again. You have your quarters—you have my own daughters to wife, you have gold, a prince's rank, slaves to do your bidding. What more can you ask of me?"

"My crown," he whispered.

"The crown was never yours! I am the Daughter of the Sun and Horus of the Two Lands. You are nobody, nothing! I command you to leave my presence, I command it, I command it—"

Already he was moving into the corridor, retreating from the sight of her, from the sound of her voice.

There were still courtiers in the broad entry hall, standing about in little groups. Numbly he started across the shining pavement, watching the faces go tense and blank, the eyes expressionless, the heads incline to the precise angle required by the presence of minor royalty. Even the chamberlains at the door bowed no lower, though they turned pale and their eyes fixed on anything but him. At last he was past them, climbing the stairs, moving along the hall into his new apartments. He closed the door behind him.

Rekhmi-re and Amenu rose from chairs at one side of the room. At sight of them a chill went through Thoth that left him cold to his bones. For the first time he grasped what they had done when they stepped out to kneel before him in the Great Hall. They had deliberately stripped themselves of everything—of all the past had meant to them, all the future had promised; they had turned their backs on position, rank, inheritance, family—Rekhmi-re on his father, Amenu on the little countess he had loved since babyhood. They had nothing, now, but him.

He found himself walking, with an odd sensation of weightlessness, to face his two friends.

"Do not do this. I release you," he said hoarsely.

"Tjesu, we do not want to be released," Amenu said. "Please do not say any more about it."

You do not know what you are doing. I am—I am no longer king, I am—"

"You *are* king. You are Pharaoh of Egypt, god and Horus. Amon himself so named you, in the temple, and nothing can change it—not Hatshepsut, not any mortal."

Thoth looked at him in silence. The belief in his eyes was complete.

"You, Rekhmi-re?"

"I feel the same."

Thoth turned away, vowing to himself that they would be justified, that somehow, someday . . . He looked around the unfamiliar chambers and felt everything in him crystallize into a solid core of rage.

"I'll have it back!" he burst out. "I'll have it all back and I swear by Amon and Marduk I'll destroy her!" He faced them, sick with a fury he had never known existed. "All these years I loved her—now I hate her. I hate her, gods how I hate her, *how I hate her.* . . ."

He flung himself into a chair and grasped his head with both hands.

2.

The patient masses of Egypt now found themselves confronted with a theological monstrosity—a woman on the throne of Horus. To put it finer, a *female Horus.*

It was a combination of words they had never heard or dreamed they ever would hear; it was a concept they had never imagined they would have to grasp. However, it did not occur to them to protest. Conditioned by fourteen years of strange happenings in the palace, each of which had wrenched the forms of kingship a little farther from the hallowed tradition of Horus-succeeds-Osiris, they were now almost inured to shocks. This was the sharpest wrench of all, but what could they do against the powers of temple and palace? They merely blinked and tried to understand.

For weeks there had been repeated proclamations from the Golden House to aid them in their efforts. Almost daily, while the young king was safely far away in Nubia, the royal herald had issued from the palace gates, followed by a retinue of scribes who scattered throughout the city and read from long, important-looking scrolls in stentorian voices.

Ma-ke-Re Hatshepsut had been sired by Amon himself, the people were reminded. She had been suckled by goddesses and named Pharaoh in her cradle by the will of her divine father. She had also—this they learned for the first time—been intended for Successor by her earthly father Thutmose, the Strong Bull of sacred memory. He had meant that she succeed him on the throne of Re and had stated his intention to her many times. The subsequent disastrous appointment of the Tired One had been the result of confusion, error, and (it was strongly hinted) demons, whose black hands had been working havoc in Egypt ever since. Now at last, by the command of mighty Amon, the mistake was being righted. The new coronation already launched in the south, and progressing downriver with startling speed, would fulfill the will of the gods and Great Thutmose, and place the crown on Hatshepsut's head, where it belonged. Henceforth she would rule Egypt—not as regent, not as queen, but as King Ma-ke-Re. Might His Majesty be living forever!

The people listened carefully, thought it all over, and slowly nodded their belief. It was unusual, highly unusual, for Horus to be a woman. But they already knew there had never been a woman like Hatshepsut; doubtless she was born to be Horus, just as the proclamations said.

As the coronation sped toward its climax, another thought came to reassure them. The moment Hatshepsut mounted the throne of Re, her father the old king, the long-beloved Thutmose, would return to mount the throne of Osiris once more. It was a great relief to realize that they need no longer depend on the frail hand of the Tired One to guide Egypt's dealings with the gods. They began to tell each other that all was well now; all was as it should be. The coronation proved it.

By the time the young king came back from Nubia they were able to dismiss him from their minds. He had been graciously welcomed back to the palace, had he not, allowed to keep royal rank, royal wives, and royal wealth? He had no responsibilities and all the time in the world to go hunting or travel up and down the Nile in his own sumptuous bark. What more could any youth of sixteen want?

The moment the crown rested securely on King Ma-ke-Re's head, things began to happen in Egypt. His Majesty had the reins to herself at last; her first move was to crack them over Egypt's back and set off at full gallop to release the stored-up energies of sixteen years. For all that time and more no public works had been undertaken in the Two Lands; now a new era abruptly commenced. The masses had not yet ceased to nod and blink, and stumble over calling a woman "His Majesty" before they found themselves galvanized into all manner of activity. Carpenters and brickmakers all up and down the Nile were snatched from their work and sent swarming to central points to be assigned new and greater tasks; stone workers were commandeered in droves, artisans' workshops began to hum, wharfside tale-spinners and ne'er-do-wells suddenly found themselves on their way to the long-idle gold mines in the eastern desert to lead strenuous and useful lives.

In the Theban shipyards keels were laid for five grand new ships the purpose of which nobody knew; in a matter of days giant ribs began to sprout upward from every keel.

352

"Warships?" hazarded a young sailmaker, standing beside his aged father to gape at the nearest prow.

"Not those, lad," returned the other. "Warships have prows like daggers, not like lily stems." The old man gave a cackle of laughter. broke it off as suddenly as it began, and added, squinting at the great naked ribs, "This rigging is different, as well. You'll find no lower yard on a *mensh*."

"I find none on this ship yet, Old One," retorted his son. "Nor even so much as a mast or sheet. So far, not Amon himself could tell what—"

"Nay, I can tell, I can tell. She's a cargo vessel, as are those others with her. I know a *mensh* when I see one, though it be nothing but a length of keel." The old man paused, sucking ruminatively at his toothless gums. "Many a Nile has risen since I saw one, too. Aye, and I'll wager many more will rise before I see another, now a woman is Horus in the Two Lands."

"May Her Majesty's—*His* Majesty's—*ka* be joyous," said the young man quickly.

A rich harvest was gathered that year, while the ships' ribs were slowly and meticulously sheathed with sturdy planks. Soon the river began to shrink, and the spring winds to blow over the stubble fields; the sun burned down, gathering intensity, and sand stung the sweating backs and squinting eyes of gangs of bricklayers laboring in various parts of the Two Lands. In the nome of Cusae, on the cliffs of Pakht, at other points up and down the Nile, mud-brick scaffolding was slowly rising about the gaunt remains of temples which had lain in ruins since Hyksos days.

Astonished villagers streamed out of neighboring towns to watch and question; women braved the sand-laden winds and brought their children to see. The children stared with large and disappointed eyes; all their lives the old temple had been their own. They had played at housekeeping in the ruined sanctuaries, chased one another through the grass-grown halls, climbed the broken columns or lain on top of the crumbling pylons, poking at lizards and watching the kites wheel through the brilliant sky. It had been their favorite of all places, the old temple—now all was changing.

Their elders shushed their protests and bore them off home again. They should rejoice, scolded the mothers, that Beautiful

353

Lady Hathor was to have her home restored. They should beware, warned the fathers, how they coveted the dwelling of a goddess. But many a husband and wife exchanged uneasy glances, remembering the stones they had dug out of the ruins years ago and carried home to form a hearth or to bolster a foundation. They had best just chisel away that bit of inscription, they muttered to each other casually. Not that anyone would be likely to notice it, blackened as it was by so many cookfires, but . . . well, someone—the lady Hathor or the lady Horus—might misunderstand.

The winds died away at last, leaving a heat-soaked silence brooding over the dwindling river, from which wharves and idle water-lifts thrust up high and ever higher. But the tempo of life did not diminish. Count Senmut, trailed by a gang of workers with measuring sticks, was spending much time exploring a bay-shaped curve in the cliffs west of Thebes; Hapuseneb, with another, smaller group, was prowling the desolate valley behind. At the palace, in the series of sweltering small chambers in the Treasury which contained the royal archives, a group of scribes rummaged day after day through shelves of musty documents—leather scrolls which crackled with age when they were unrolled, rolls of papyrus which blistered under a drop of sweat. Slaves stood by with damp towels to mop their gleaming faces and torsos, to fan the moisture from their hurrying, searching fingers. It was not here, they knew no such record was here—no route such as that had ever existed, if indeed, the land itself really existed! A dozen times already they had tried to convince Her Majesty—*His* Majesty—of this, but she only repeated, "It is there, among the records of my forefathers. I know it is! Amon himself has told me so. Now find it. Find it! Find it!"

And at last, one day only a few weeks before the Nile was at its lowest ebb, the youngest scribe among them straightened suddenly, eyes fixed on a curling sheet of papyrus in his hands and then lifting incredulously to his colleagues.

"I have found it," he whispered. "It is all true, Amon spoke to her, he must have. There was a canal, long ago, somewhere in the eastern Delta. . . ."

Within a few hours a ship set out hastily for the north, all oars working to aid the sluggish current. At Heliopolis it swerved east; some days later, with the waters so low its shallow hull almost scraped the bottom, it arrived at the shrunken lake which was its destination. A village with a population half Egyptian and half Sand-dweller squatted beside the lake; a few leagues away the fortress city of Tharu, eastern gate of Egypt, turned its face toward Asia.

The Thebans disembarked, glanced arrogantly over the rabble of curious villagers, and bade them bring out their oldest men for questioning. Canal? Canal? quavered these ancients, peering about them with rheumy eyes as they leaned on their grandsons' shoulders. Nay, they had known of no canal. They remembered when the Great Thutmose passed through here, though, like Re himself in his flaming chariot, heading for cursed Sharuhen in pursuit of the Hyksos—

The Thebans cut short the flow of reminiscence and set out to explore the lake shore. At last, on the lip of a broad gulch leading southward from the lake, they found a weathered stela, almost covered with sand, bearing the cartouche of a Pharaoh who had ruled four hundred years before. Straightening slowly from the sand-scratched hieroglyphs, they shaded their eyes and gazed in silence to the south, where far out of sight beyond the dunes and ragged gullies lay the shores of the Red Sea. Then they went back to the village and began conscripting diggers in the name of His Majesty Ma-ke-Re.

Before the river had reached its ebb Hapuseneb, in Thebes, was conscripting diggers too—but with the utmost secrecy. One burning morning the chosen gang of workmen filed out of the City of the Dead under the escort of three foremen and an overseer. They were blindfolded at the foot of the western cliffs and led up a well-hidden path through the hills and into the lonely, barren, boulder-strewn valley behind. After an hour's walking they arrived at a point directly behind the bay whose eastern face Senmut had been exploring. Here the blindfolds were taken off. Here a great new tomb was to be dug.

The men were in complete ignorance of where they stood. They faced a rocky hillside in a landscape devoid of vegetation, of any life at all except themselves. Though they darted hasty, surreptitious looks behind them, they could see only rocks, gully-torn earth and barren rises, in endless, featureless repetition. They shrugged, unwrapped their mallets and their copper chisels, and

355

began to work. They knew their jobs; the foremen knew how large the stony chambers must be; the overseer knew the route through the valley and the way back home.

Only Hapuseneb, in whose hands the project had been placed, knew the reasons and the plan behind the tomb.

It was a masterful plan—bold, imaginatively conceived—a plan worthy of Ma-ke-Re and put into execution with the speed and vigor characteristic of her. She had decided that her father Thutmose must no longer rest in the compromising company of the Tired One, who had intruded uninvited into his tomb. When the little copper chisels had done their work, the Strong Bull would be moved to this new Precious Habitation—here to await the day when his daughter and true Successor should lie beside him in a sarcophagus the twin of his, as if no other reign had come between theirs.

Thus from the chain of Egypt's kingship one despised link, that of the second Thutmose, was to be plucked and made to vanish utterly and forever.

Through all these months a ragged Sand-dweller merchant had been moving northward with his string of donkeys. When the new keels first thrust up in the shipyards he was at Thebes, trading his curious crockery and embroideries for Egyptian linen. As the scaffolding rose about the ruined temples he was leaving Menfe, herding his animals aboard a north-bound barge. By the time the Theban engineers reached the lakeshore village in the Delta, he had finished his trading in Tharu and was starting his slow and solitary trek through the Asian desert.

Still he traveled, trading all the way—over the jagged ridge of Carmel, past a fortress called Megiddo in the great plain of Jezreel, and up the long valley of the Orontes River between the two cedar-clothed mountain ranges of Lebanon. Finally, one hot and brilliant morning, he entered the city of Kadesh. He went straight to the palace, located an old acquaintance among the guards, and spoke to him in rapid whispers.

The guard stared, then hurried into the palace. Presently a chamberlain emerged, studied the merchant suspiciously, questioned him, and at last beckoned with a jerk of his head. In the antechamber to the Royal Apartments he stopped and jerked his head again, this time in the direction of a tall carved door. The merchant disappeared within.

Half an hour later he emerged, tucking a rich gold chain into his sash, and returned to the palace courtyard. He collected his string of donkeys and went his way.

Before he was out of sight four scribes were hurrying toward the same tall carved door, moistening their ink-cakes as they came. The voice of the Chief Chamberlain inside was calling for yet more scribes, for interpreters who spoke the many tongues of Syria, for runners to carry messages to the princes of Yeraza and Naharin, to all the rulers of Zahi, to the king of great Mitanni in the north and the monarch of small but memorable Sharuhen in the south. In the midst of this uproar the vizier of the city-kingdom pushed his way through the royal chambers to the tall figure who stood beside the window, looking out.

"Your Majesty! You have heard tidings?"

"Aye," said the king of Kadesh. He turned—a tall, sinewy man with flashing black eyes and a silky, pointed beard. Flexing his fingers and powerful arms, he smiled upon his vizier. "I have heard tidings, Zohaki," he said softly. *"A woman is king in Egypt."*

3.

Once more the god Osiris died in the Black Land; the muddy river bed showed nothing but a last trickle of his blood. Once more his sister-wife Isis came weeping for him, and her tears swelled the trickle, at first almost imperceptibly, then more and more; finally with a joyous gush of swift, silt-laden water the Beloved One revived. Egypt put off its mourning and feasted in the street; fishermen launched their boats again, the canals were thrown open to admit the fertile flood.

On the swelling bosom of that flood a ship called *Lotus of Khonsu* came back from the south. It was an ordinary Nile boat, carrying a cargo of natron and fourteen oarsmen who needed to dip their paddles only occasionally, so swift was the current bearing them down to Thebes. The encumbering mast and sail had been taken down and lashed to the flat roof of the cabin which ran almost the length of the ship; on the forward end of the roof three passengers sat together, silent, watching the roofs of No-Amon move past on either side.

All three were youths: one square-faced, blue-jawed, with great black eyes framed by a thicket of wiry lashes; another beside him slit-eyed and thoughtful, resting his long chin on one propped-up knee. The youngest of the three sat a little aft, on the butt of the lowered mast—a seat which raised him above the level of his companions and made him appear at first glance much taller than he was. His face was taut and lean, as if from an illness, with its boldly arching nose belied by a young and vulnerable mouth which he held clamped tight and hard. He sat tensely, his long eyes glassy under his plain white headcloth.

Suddenly he flung himself off the mast, moved to the low railing to look out over the passing quays, then wandered to the far end of the cabin roof, where he began to walk restlessly back and forth. His companions, who had snapped alert at his first movement, were following him with their eyes; the long-chinned youth would have risen had not his friend put out a restraining hand.

"Let him be," he muttered in a low voice.

"I fear to see him start that pacing again."

"He is not pacing, merely walking about. You worry too much."

"I do not, Rekhmi-re. Look. Already he has fallen into the old pattern. Four steps this way, four steps back."

Rekhmi-re looked, and turned away uneasily. "He can do nothing else at the moment, and he must do something. Let him pace. . . . Nay, I know he is not himself yet! But at least he broke forth from those few rooms in the palace. He is fighting now, he can hope and lay plans—look at his plan concerning Turo."

"Aye, look at it."

"Well? As a *plan* there was not so much wrong with it."

"There was nothing wrong with it at all—except that it did not work."

"At least it was action! I tell you, Amenu, I feared for him at first. But that part is finished, thanks be to Amon."

Without answering, Amenu rested his chin on his doubled-up knee; both stared in silence out over the river with its bobbing, vivid traffic of sails—two motionless bronze figures on the roof of an old boat, each with his own thoughts. A great stone statue of some bygone Pharaoh slid by on the western bank to reveal the royal landing, beribboned from some recent gala occasion they knew nothing of. Behind the landing, the broad avenue wound away in the direction of the palace, where the familiar red and white pennants fluttered above walls and clustered trees.

"I wish this part were finished too," Amenuser muttered.

"What part?"

"The next few hours. Coming home empty-handed like this." Amenu's eyes moved bitterly around the sun-washed roof. "No horde of soldiers behind him, no standards glittering, not even a weapon in his hand. In Amon's name, why could old Turo not have listened to us? May Set wither his *ka* for that! When only a few weeks earlier he was fighting at Tjesu's side—"

"We did not reach Turo soon enough." Rekhmi-re shrugged. "No use to think of it. Turo serves Pharaoh, and only Pharaoh. By the time we arrived in Nubia *she* was Pharaoh—and he had learned it. Senmut saw to that."

"Senmut—or Nehsi. Nehsi! That he would support her in this—I can scarce believe it yet."

After a moment Rekhmi-re muttered, "These friends of his at the temple—I hope they are powerful."

Amenu studied his face thoughtfully, then leaned closer. "Rekhmi-re, there is something strange about that. The Khwed, this Sata—why do we know nothing of them? In all the four years we have known him he has not spoken of them. I do not see how they can be such friends of his—or how they can be powerful, with Hapuseneb in the temple—or how they can help him if they are."

"He seems certain of it." Rekhmi-re glanced uneasily toward the other end of the roof. "I know who they are; he told me. He counts them his friends because they are Senmut's enemies. He says—he says they made the Bark of God move, at the Choosing. They, not Amon."

Amenu stared at him, his eyes slits of disbelief. "*He* says that? He repudiates his proof of divine anointment—merely to count a few more friends? Rekhmi-re, you do not know what you are saying."

"I know what he said."

The ship dipped and rocked as it glided over the wake of a

passing ferry. Amenuser said slowly, "Then he is desperate—already. This changes everything. I thought this new plan, like the other, had at least nothing wrong with it as a *plan*. Gods! Even if the oracle happened as he says, can he believe Hapuseneb would keep those priests in the temple? We shall find they have vanished four years since."

"We can only try." Rekhmi-re glanced at the other's face, and burst out, "Would you have me argue with him? As far as I am concerned, he is still the king."

"Aye—he is the king."

"Though we two are his only subjects," Rekhmi-re added after a little silence. A trace of grim humor appeared in his eyes. "His subjects—and his whole Council of Kinsmen as well. Do you appreciate our importance in the Two Lands, friend? For the past nine months we have been Treasurer, Chief Steward, Overseer of the Royal Chambers, Master of the Royal Wardrobe—aye, and a whole staff of porters, guards and body-servants besides. By Hathor's horns, once off this ship I mean to buy a slave or two to share my honors!"

"And that brings up another matter." Amenu gestured toward his own broad jeweled collar and armbands. "We are wearing our entire fortunes—and so he is. The rest is gone. Had you realized you and I can get no more, Rekhmi-re? Our estates are no longer ours."

Rekhmi-re looked at him blankly. "But Tjesu—"

"What funds has he to draw from?"

"Have you lost your senses? He has the entire treasury of Egypt to draw from."

"Aye," Amenu said patiently, "providing he will take up residence in the palace, in the household of Her Highness Neferu-Re, and become what Hatshepsut wishes him to become—the husband of Hatshepsut's daughter, a man without identity."

After a silence, Rekhmi-re growled, "That is impossible."

"Yet it is also impossible," Amenu went on inexorably, "that a king live among commoners in the market place—without admitting he is not king. Nehsi would give him funds, I'm sure of it, but Tjesu will not ask him. I think Tjesu must return to the palace, soon or late."

"Not under those conditions!"

"He cannot dictate his own. We are without wealth, position, influence, friends, or even homes. We are three mortal heads battering against the entire might of Egypt—and Hatshepsut wears the crown." Amenu paused to let that sink in, then finished flatly, "It is time you and I faced facts, even if he cannot."

Both turned once more to glance at the pacing figure, to find that it had ceased its pacing. The deposed king of Egypt was standing rock-still, staring down at a passing fish-wharf crowded with his former worshipers. Every line of his body was stiff with rage.

An instant later both his companions were at his side. "What has happened, Tjesu?" Amenu asked quietly.

Thoth pointed toward the mass of fishermen and dockhands on the wharf, a few of whom were gazing up incuriously. "Look at them! They mock me!"

"Tjesu, they only go about their tasks. A few glance up, of course—they glance at every ship that passes."

"And soon one of them will seize another's arm and say, 'Look you, the great warrior returns from Kush again! Last time his beloved regent slapped his face and took away his crown, but he swore he would bring an army with him this time. Where is it? Do you see it, friend? Where is His Highness' army that he has brought to do battle with one woman? Has she taken it, too? Has she—' "

"Be silent!" Rekhmi-re exploded.

As Thoth whirled to glare at him, Amenu put in hastily, "He cannot bear to hear you speak so, Tjesu—nor can I. You torture yourself needlessly. Those clods on the wharf are thinking of fish and trade, nothing else. They know nothing else. They do not even know who you are."

"They do not know me?" Thoth echoed incredulously. "After four years they do not know the face of their king?"

"How can they? What have they seen of you, save a glimpse now and then in processions, half hidden by their fellows leaping up and down in front of them, gone before they can blink their eyes. They know the royal litter has passed—perhaps they catch sight of a profile beneath the crown. But the same profile beneath a plain white headcloth would be as a stranger's to them."

Slowly Thoth turned back to the wharf. "So even to them, I

361

am nothing without the crown," he said. "Are *they* nothing without their boats and nets, then? Do they not even wonder, sometimes, what happened to the king?" His voice thickened with anger. "Do they expect me simply to vanish, as if I were no longer flesh and blood?"

With difficulty Amenu edged between him and the rail to cut the wharf from view, while Rekhmi-re urged him in the other direction, saying carelessly, "What do you care what they think —or whether they think at all? They are peasants and cattle."

"Nay, they are people." Thoth walked with him a few steps and then dropped down on the mast. "You do not know that, Rekhmi-re, but I do—I have lived among just such as those, in Babylon." He stared thoughtfully ahead of him as the others sat down at his side, then added obscurely, "They did not believe me there, either, but it was true. Or was it?" He gave a sudden laugh which made his companions exchange nervous glances.

"No matter," Rekhmi-re growled. "Soon enough all the world will know you."

"Aye! That is true, isn't it? You believe that, both of you." Thoth's mood had changed again; he sat bolt upright, his face once more tense with determination. Suddenly he was up and pacing again, four steps forward, four steps back. "Today will change everything! You'll see. We've no traitor of a Turo to deal with this time! We shall go straight to the temple— Nay, what am I thinking of! Khwed must come to me, not I to him! We must go ashore at the next dock, wait somewhere in the city, and send a messenger. Make haste, Rekhmi-re—fetch our things from the cabin. I'll speak to the captain myself."

He sprang for the ladder and vanished onto the deck below while his two companions were still scrambling to their feet.

"Wait *where* in the city?" Rekhmi-re muttered as they started after him. "Find lodgings, does he mean? Amon's bones! Some little wharfside hostel, with a moldy mat for a bed and rats in every corner?"

"You see? Here are those facts I was talking about." Amenu paused at the top of the ladder and chewed his full underlip. "We must find something. It is up to us, Rekhmi-re, he knows no more of Thebes than—"

"Than we do," Rekhmi-re finished wryly.

They exchanged baffled glances, then Amenu shrugged. "I fear we have not had the proper training for our new way of life. But we must acquire it—and quickly."

Five minutes later, groping in the gloom of the cabin for cloaks and boxes, they were paralyzed by a sudden commotion from the deck. It was Thoth's voice, made almost unrecognizable by fury, cursing and shouting over a babble of startled protests from the captain.

"Gods be merciful! Someone has mentioned her name again," Amenu muttered, dropping the box he was carrying and heading for the door. He vanished into the glare of sunshine just as the ship grated against the wharf. Rekhmi-re, with a convulsive effort, picked up all three boxes, and clinging to their thongs with one hand while he snatched the cloaks with the other, stumbled out on deck. Thoth was struggling in the grip of a brawny oarsman, his face contorted and white, his eyes shocking.

"—and I say she is *not* 'His Majesty!'" he was shouting at the captain. "You cursed of Amon—may Set shrivel your *ka* if you speak her name to me again! *I* am His Majesty, I, I, I, I—"

"Hold him!" cried the captain hoarsely. He was scrambling away from Thoth, holding up an Eye-of-Horus talisman as protection against the evil eye. Backing into Amenu, he leaped aside, then turned and clutched him, babbling incoherently. "He is a madman—I did nothing—a *kheft* has possessed him—"

Rekhmi-re hurried past, flung the boxes to the wharf, and hurried back. Amenu was holding Thoth by both shoulders, talking quietly through the uproar. "Tjesu, come with me. Forget that fool, he is dust under your sandal. Let us go ashore, Tjesu."

"Aye, he is a fool, he is far worse than a fool—"

"And who is *he?*" bellowed the captain. "I did nothing, only wished him the favor of His Majesty Ma-ke-Re as any civil person—"

"Gods! Let me go! I'll kill him!"

Rekhmi-re pushed through the excited crew and seized the captain by the throat. "Be silent, you idiot!"

"Who is he, then?" choked the captain, struggling. "To call me—"

363

"Clean out your ears, swineherd. He *told* you who he is."

The captain stopped struggling. In the sudden lull Amenu repeated calmly, "Come with me, Tjesu, I beg of you."

Thoth turned abruptly, walked past the group of staring oarsmen and left the ship at Amenu's side.

Rekhmi-re freed the captain with a shove that sent him staggering against the side of the ship, where he stood fingering his throat and gazing with popping eyes in the direction the other two had taken. Sweeping the oarsmen with a glance that reminded them of urgent business elsewhere, Rekhmi-re followed his companions off the ship.

He found them in a nook formed by a stack of baled hides and an overturned fishing punt. Thoth was sitting motionless on a bale with Amenu before him, watching. Rekhmi-re set down the boxes and threw the cloaks on top of them, muttering, "We'd best find lodgings."

Thoth raised his head wearily. "Gods! Why do I do such things? I must get used to it! I shall hear her name often. No doubt I shall speak it myself." He paused. *"Hatshepsut. Ma-ke-Re Hatshepsut."* A spasm of revulsion twisted his face.

"Tjesu—the message to the temple."

Thoth rose mechanically. His companions collected the boxes and cloaks once more, and they walked across the busy wharf and into the nearest of the mean and crooked streets.

It was a street lined with fish stalls, slippery with refuse, crowded with noisy humanity; the air was rank with the odors of all three. The friends threaded their way through the press, stumbling over scavenging dogs or nets spread out to dry in the sun, dodging the beggars who clutched at their garments and whined after them, and the ubiquitous urchins who dashed this way and that under their feet or fought savagely in corners over bits of bread. Strings of dried fish hung everywhere, surrounded by clouds of flies which were continually dislodged by someone's passing and as continually settled back again.

"Amon's blood!" Amenu muttered. *"Hai!* Clear a path there, you *kheft*-spawn!"

Rekhmi-re, sending a couple of urchins sprawling with a contemptuous toe, motioned toward an alley. "Let us try some other street. This stench is choking me."

The street into which the alley led was only slightly wider and no less noisy, though the stench altered somewhat as fish stalls gave way to the diversified clutter of a market place. The street was alive with squabbling shoppers and lined with cubbyholes—tiny caves of shade amid the glare—in which artisans squatted at their work. The two young nobles, accustomed to ride through such rabble in a closed litter, behind runners clearing a path with staves, grew ever more arrogant and tense; but Thoth's eyes were beginning to lose their look of glazed detachment. When Amenu stopped at last, flinging down the box he was carrying and confessing savagely that he did not know how to find lodgings in such a place, Thoth suddenly took charge.

"I do," he said in a calmer tone than his friends had heard all day. He smiled faintly as they stared at him. "All cities are much alike when one stands in the market place. This is not so different from Babylon, though a different Lord Sun shines down, and different faces look up, and one never smells wet clay here. . . ." His gaze lingered curiously on a nearby cubbyhole, where a jeweler was grinding away at a bit of turquoise. "In Babylon they polish their gems by tossing them together in a little clay barrel, and the stones come from it smooth as water, each in its own shape and like no other on earth—"

"Tjesu—the lodgings."

"Find a barber," Thoth ordered. "Let him shave you and you will learn everything you want to know. I will wait in the wineshop yonder, with our boxes. And you, Rekhmi-re—you must go to the temple."

"*I* go? Nay, I'll not leave you in this rabble. We will find a messenger."

"What messenger could I trust?" Thoth's voice sharpened again. "Everything depends on this. You will know how to enter the temple unquestioned, how to inquire without attracting a dozen eyes. Find him, Rekhmi-re. Khwed, his name is—a tall, gaunt man. Make him believe you, bring him to me! However you must do it, *bring him.*" He stopped, drew a long breath, and added more quietly, "I will wait in the wineshop."

He pushed past them and vanished through a doorway set in the honeycomb of stalls that lined the street. His companions hastily followed, stumbling through a black passage and emerging a moment later into a cave of light. A fire-pan blazed in the center of an earthen-floored room; the dim shapes of wine jugs traced a pyramid against one firelit wall. Among the shadows that lay thick along the other walls, figures could be discerned, sitting, kneeling, sprawling, gesturing. There was a low hum of guttural conversation punctuated by the occasional rattle of gaming-sticks; the odor of musty reed mats crept insistently through a strong reek of smoke and wine.

A few heads turned as Rekhmi-re and Amenuser stood in the entrance, scowling distrustfully about them. Thoth was already walking toward an empty space in the shadows.

"In Hathor's sweet name, let me stay with you, Tjesu!" Amenu whispered. "There may be thieves here, cutthroats!"

"Nay, nay, stack the boxes beside me and go find lodgings. Rekhmi-re"—Thoth clutched at his friend's arm and stared into his eyes—"bring him—if not Khwed then Sata or the prophetess. Bring me but one of them and you shall be Vizier of Egypt within a month. I promise you. I swear it!"

"Tjesu, I will do my best." Rekhmi-re turned and hurried across the room. Amenu cast a last uneasy glance at the proprietor—a cadaverous, earringed individual who looked like a cutthroat himself—then followed.

It was nearing sundown when Amenu returned two hours later—minus his broad jeweled collar but now pushing his way down the narrow street with the confidence of a man who knows his way around. Most of the cubbyholes were shuttered, but the smell of cooking food drifted out of the wineshops and passers-by drifted in. Amenu followed a pair of burly rivermen through the door Thoth had chosen earlier, and stumbled through the gloom to the place where he had left his king. Thoth was still there, a wine jug and empty cup beside him on the mat, the boxes dim shapes nearby. With a sigh of relief Amenu sat down.

"You were right, Tjesu, a barber is the answerer of all questions. This street is a rabbit-warren of dwellings behind those shops; back of a wigmaker's stall lives an old woman who wants nothing on earth but a fine winding-sheet in which to go to her tomb." Amenu paused, blinking through the shadows at the unresponsive figure across from him. "In short, she was glad to exchange her poor house for my collar, and she'll also serve us . . ."

366

The words trailed off. Amenu leaned forward, staring into his friend's face, which he now saw clearly for the first time.

Thoth was very, very drunk.

"Tjesu!" Amenu exclaimed. He started up, then sank back onto the dusty mat. "I suppose you have had tidings." Thoth's eyes met his hazily for a moment, then swerved away. Amenu reached over and grasped his shoulder. "Tjesu. Tell me. Rekhmi-re has come back?"

"Nay," Thoth muttered.

"He has not? Then why—" Before the question was phrased, Amenu knew the answer. Slowly he settled back, his body sagging as he leaned on one drawn-up knee. He watched as Thoth's hand groped toward the empty wine jug, tilted it unsteadily over the equally empty cup, then dropped it. It rolled in an erratic course across the mat.

"Fetch more," Thoth said thickly.

"Nay, you need no more," the other said gently. "What did you give those thieves for it? Your gold collar?"

Thoth made no answer, but his throat was bare. They sat in silence until Rekhmi-re's broad form loomed up beside them. He dropped on his knees before Thoth.

"Tjesu, I could not find Khwed—nor the others either. They are not to be found! No one has heard their names in years—"

"*Tsst*, my friend," Amenu said softly. "He knows. He knows."

"He *knows?*" Rekhmi-re echoed.

"Look at him. I think he knew before you left—as did you and I."

Rekhmi-re frowned more closely at Thoth, then drew away. After a moment he glanced at Amenu. "You found lodgings of some sort?"

"Aye."

"Come then. We'd best get him out of here."

The wigmaker's tiny shop—closed and shuttered now, for the sky was red with sunset—was only a short distance up the street. Thoth walked unsteadily but unassisted, while the others struggled with the boxes. As Amenu led them through the dingy door into a tiny courtyard, Rekhmi-re stopped.

"Here?" he exploded.

"Aye, here!" Amenu said with a glare. "Did you expect a lotus pool and a row of slaves?"

They crossed the crumbling pavement toward the largest of their three rooms, off which two cell-like bedchambers opened. Rekhmi-re's nose wrinkled as he took in the glories of his new abode, but he made no further comment, merely rid himself of his load and began arranging a cloak over the one battered folding stool. Aside from the usual reed mats, a squat three-wicked lamp and a few shelves on the wall, it was the only furniture the room contained.

"Will you sit here, Tjesu?" Amenu muttered. "I am sorry . . . tomorrow we will buy a chair and some sort of table. Rekhmi-re, find what is keeping that old woman."

Thoth swayed out of the doorless entrance and dropped down upon the stool with scarcely a glance around him. He showed no more interest in his surroundings than he did in the beaming, timid old woman who padded in presently with a platter of boiled lotus-root, a few dried fish, and some coarse bread. But as Rekhmi-re was dragging forward one of the boxes to serve as table, he lifted his head.

"The *mensh*," he said in a low, thick voice. "Fetch the little galley." Without waiting for anyone to obey, he rose and stumbled across the room to fling open the lid of his box. After a moment's rummaging he drew out the carved wooden ship and straightened, examining it carefully and fumbling with awkward fingers at the threadlike sheets.

"A brave craft," Amenu said. "Let me hoist the sail for you."

"Nay, nay, let be. She cannot sail to war yet—or anywhere else." Brushing Amenu aside, Thoth moved unsteadily past him and set the galley on one of the shelves, then braced himself against the wall, staring up at it. "The *Wild Bull*. I taught a Babylonian to write that once. Old Inatsil. Old Dogface." He turned toward them with a faint smile. "He was a gloomy fellow—but wise. 'Man is as wind.' 'A man must obey his god.' 'Obey those in authority.' Obey, obey, obey . . . Nay, he was not so wise."

"Tjesu, here is food. Come, eat it, we will talk later."

Thoth glanced vaguely at the food but turned back to the galley. "I think none was wise but Ahmose," he said. "I killed Ahmose, did you know that? He was going to tell me something— but I killed him before he had a chance."

"*Tssst,* eat your food, Tjesu. You did not kill him."

368

"Aye. I did. I put my hand on his chest."

"Rekhmi-re—" Amenu muttered.

"Nay, nay, I will eat if you like," Thoth said irritably.

He returned to his stool and began to eat from the crockery bowl Rehkmi-re handed him. They spoke little during the meal. It was clear the wine was leaving Thoth's head; it was also clear that sobriety was bringing with it black depression. He finished before the others, flung down his bowl, and went to stand in the dark arch of the doorway, staring out. When the old woman beamed and nodded her way in and then shuffled out again with the dishes, he followed her with sardonic eyes.

"Who is that?" he demanded of Rekhmi-re.

"Our staff of servants, Tjesu. I think her name is Tiya."

"Well, send her for wine," Thoth said savagely.

"Nay, wine is for rejoicing. Let us plan first, and I will gladly outdrink you later."

Thoth turned, looking almost like himself for a moment as he studied his friend. "What a fool you were to follow me out of the Great Hall that day," he said. "You could be with your father this minute—rich, favored, untroubled—and Amenu might be wed already to his little countess. You were both fools."

"Not such fools as to talk of things that are past." Rekhmi-re turned away abruptly.

"They are not past. Look at you. You cannot even endure mention of your father. And Amenu stiffens and flushes as though I had hit him—"

"Well?" Rekhmi-re shouted. "Are you trying to wound us just for the pleasure of it?"

"Be silent! I am trying to show you your folly. Repent it and go your ways. It is not too late."

"I'll not go until you have ceased to fight," Rekhmi-re retorted, planting himself in front of Thoth. "To me you are king. I call you Tjesu because I mean to follow you into battle. Do you mean to lead me, or do we cast down our standards after only two defeats?"

"I'll not cast down my standards before a *woman* as long as Re burns in the sky! When you see the great god a cinder, then doubt me—but by Amon—"

"When you have ceased quarreling," remarked Amenu, "we can plan. And then we can send for wine."

Thoth glanced at him, then back at Rekhmi-re. After a moment he grasped the latter's arm briefly, and walking into the room again flung himself upon his stool. "Very well, I will plan. But I do not know how."

"I do," Amenu said. "We must make a long plan, and you will not like it, but if you will listen I will say something. The way to regain your crown is to father its heirs." He paused, waiting for his meaning to penetrate, then went on quickly. "Soon or late, Egypt must have a prince, a Successor, and you alone can beget him. Nay—hear me out! I know well how you feel toward Nefer. But she is the key to everything. So long as the queen and Senmut control her, they control Egypt and the council. But the moment a babe is born to Nefer, *it* is the Royal Child, and she only queen-mother. Then the future is yours, for the child is yours. The Kinsmen would have to shift their allegiance, Nehsi would compel it—"

"Nehsi!" Thoth choked.

"Aye, Nehsi! I am willing to swear it. He is blind now—I think he squeezes his eyes tight shut. A royal birth would open them. It is a slow plan, to be sure, but—"

"You have lost your wits," Thoth told him. "Blood of Osiris! Is that what you think of me? That I would creep meekly back, seek favors of—Hatshepsut's daughter—"

"Seek them, nay! Command them. Nothing would so enrage Ma-ke-Re. If you hate her—"

"Amenu, as the Devourer hates men's souls, so I hate her." Thoth paused, then stood up and walked across the room. "But I will have nothing to do with her precious daughter."

The words were final. For a time they hung heavily on the air of the little room, which was growing thick and rank with the smell of the fish oil burning in the lamp. Rekhmi-re eased his big shoulders off the doorjamb and lounged across to trim the wick, then sat down beside Amenu.

"Very well," Amenu conceded. "I ask the impossible. Then what of Mayet? You are fond of her, and she is wife to you too. Only Second Wife, but—"

"Mayet! Poor child!" Thoth turned away suddenly. "Say no more of Mayet."

"I know she is a child yet. The plan would be even longer. But at least I ask the possible now."

"Nay, you do not. By the gods, I do not like your plans! They are too slow and cautious. I will not wait so long to take back what is mine."

"So be it," Rekhmi-re said suddenly. "Now perhaps you will listen to *my* plan. Return to the palace—"

"I will not set foot in the palace!"

"Not even to claim it as your own?"

After a moment Thoth turned and looked at him more attentively.

"It is your own," Rekhmi-re went on. "Yet you are letting her exile you from it. You are letting the Kinsmen enjoy their crime in peace, without so much as your presence to accuse them. Why should they rest easy in their beds at night?"

"Aye," Thoth said slowly. "Aye, why should they? Why should *she?*"

Rekhmi-re leaned forward. "Take up residence in the north wing. You need not go near Nefer—or her mother. Seek out the Kinsmen first. Dog their footsteps. Face them one by one and demand your throne, and keep demanding until each one feels he lives in a nest of ants. They were honorable men once—I think one of them will break."

"Aye, that is a plan I could follow," Thoth said. "By the Mangled One, I will follow it! Corner them one by one, time after time—"

"Then start with Nehsi," Amenu said softly.

4.

Something was happening in the bay in the western cliffs. As the summer's heat at last receded before a northern breeze, farmers trudging along the dikes to market their baskets of produce squinted curiously at the distant spirals of dust and dark knots of working men.

It was certainly some new project of the queen's, they told each other, tracing with their eyes the long, complex system of water ditches which had been constructed for no other purpose than to fill two identical pools carefully spaced and hollowed there in the sand. Now what could she want pools for, out there in the desert? Gangs of laborers were knocking down the little mud-brick offering chapel which had stood near old Neb-hepet-Re's ruined temple since long before anybody could remember; others were digging holes here and there, seemingly at random, in the area around.

Foundation deposits? hazarded an old glassmaker to his son as they crawled about the roof of their workshop in the City of the Dead, mending the thatch with fresh palm fronds. Perhaps it was a site for a colossal statue of the queen. There was a stone-cutter's shop around the corner where just such a statue was taking shape this minute—taller than three men, carved of pure granite, representing the great queen as Osiris, which of course she would be some day. . . .

The mystery was cleared up one morning when the royal herald, trailed by his now-familiar group of scribes, issued from the palace and delivered to every street and market place in Thebes yet another royal proclamation.

Through their mouths His Majesty Ma-ke-Re, divine Horus and Daughter of the Sun, announced to her gaping subjects that she had heard the voice of her father Amon speaking to her again. This time it had instructed her to build a mansion for him by her own hand, a small but exquisite temple, lovelier than any House of Amon ever known. It would be called Djeser-Djeseru, Holy of Holies. This beautiful building would be not only a place for Amon's worship but also a memorial to the first Thutmose, as well as a monument to the queen herself and her greatness. In years to come, when she had joined the ranks of the gods and ruled as Osiris over the Dark Land, her *ka* would be eternally honored here and provided with offerings of food, sweet oils, and burning myrrh. At the hour of sunrise, on the next day but one, the ceremony of the Stretching of the Cord would take place in the bay of the western cliffs. The god himself would come forth in his bark to view the dedication.

Immediately all Thebes was obsessed with the desire to view the dedication too. Long before sunrise on the great day the wide, roped-off area at the base of the cliffs was circled by a squirming half-moon of humanity, and the desert road was blackened with the throngs still coming. Late arrivals moved about the rear of the crowd seeking a vantage point, craning their necks and jumping up and down to see over their neighbors' shoulders; those fortunate enough to be in front gazed their fill at the elaborate preparations for the dedication. Besides the brick-lined foundation pits marking the temple's outline there were tables piled with autumn fruits, tethered sacrificial bullocks lowing plaintively as they waited for slaughter, green mounds of persea branches, pyramided jars of ointment, boxes filled with the commemorative scarabs which would also go into the pits by handfuls at the proper moment. Near the pools, cages of water fowl stood ready for release at that point in the ceremony when the Beautiful God herself would hurl the throw-stick, afterward cutting papyrus into lengths for paper-making in order to dedicate the pools as well as the ground to the active service of her father Amon.

And they would see it all—they would actually look upon the face of the Radiant Ma-ke-Re. They craned their necks to peer in the direction of the palace.

Out of sight among the deserted shops of the City of the Dead, the royal procession had come to a halt ten minutes before. According to the carefully planned timing, the bark of the god should have arrived at this spot too; all up and down the line of the royal procession slaves were leaning upon idly slanting fans, bearers were setting litters down, and dignitaries were emerging from them to look down the empty street.

In the first litter Hatshepsut sat tense and anxious, while Senmut, who had been walking in the place of honor by her side, leaned into her litter and tried to soothe her.

"My beloved, there is no omen involved. Pray try to calm yourself. We were a little early, that is all. Hapuseneb will see to it the god arrives on time—did you ever know him to fail you? All will be well, compose yourself—"

"It is Thoth's fault," Hatshepsut interrupted tautly. "I knew— I knew! For a month or more he has been upsetting my ministers, forcing them to keep guards around them merely to go about their ordinary tasks—but I thought he would keep himself decently out of *my* way and sight! Then yesterday—*yesterday*— the very eve of the dedication—he dares to come pushing into the King's Apartments as if he owned them, demanding to see me!"

"I begged you never to talk to him."

"I could not avoid it! He—" Hatshepsut broke off and started again, in a less shrill voice. "I am too merciful to refuse him what he asks, Senmut. I realize I am generous to a fault

373

with him—I always have been. Even today when I dedicate my own temple, I shall throw into the pits a few scarabs inscribed with his name, that he may share the favor of the gods. And how does he repay me? By casting some evil spell over all the arrangements, calling down bad omens—"

"My lotus, no omens have appeared save good omens, this is merely a slight delay." Senmut darted an impatient look over his shoulder, only to find the street still empty.

"Good ones!" Hatshepsut was repeating furiously. "Do you call Nefer's illness a good omen, then? Merely to see Thoth upsets her—and no wonder. It upsets me too. . . ."

Senmut peered at her curiously a moment. "What did he say, when he came pushing in like that, demanding to talk to you?"

"Nothing," whispered the queen. "Nothing at all. Once he was face to face with me he seemed unable to speak. His lips parted, as if he would say something, but he was silent. He simply looked at me—Senmut, I do not like the way he looks at me! Suddenly he turned and left. . . ."

"Let *me* see him hereafter," Senmut said grimly. "I assure you I do not care how he looks at me. If you would only allow me to spare you these trying scenes—"

"I will," she said, sinking back wearily upon her cushions. "Hereafter I will, Senmut. You are right." Abruptly she straightened again. "Look! They are here! Yonder are the first priestesses."

Senmut jerked upright to glance down the intervening streets; the other dignitaries were already rushing back to their litters.

Hatshepsut's face was radiant now. "How foolish I was to let that hateful boy upset me." She smiled, then suddenly the smile vanished as she clutched his arm. "Senmut! Do you think he will come *here*—to the dedication?"

"My beloved! Be sensible. Would he deliberately shame himself before your greatness? He will be nowhere near you today."

"Nay, of course not. Of course not." Her face was clear again; she settled back, the serene half-smile of royalty on her lips, her eyes luminous with anticipation. "The procession may move on."

Senmut raised one of his big, corded hands, and the litters lifted at last.

An hour later every pit had been filled, every bullock slaugh-

374

ed, every ritual chanted. The crowds dispersed for a day of
·sting at the expense of the queen.

Hatshepsut stood a moment with Senmut beside her litter,
·r face exalted as she looked back toward the bay in the cliffs.
·ll went well—superbly well. The gods did not allow one move
·be made, one word to be spoken, to dim My Majesty's pleas-
·e in this day." Turning away at last she entered her litter,
·ining out again to fix Senmut with brilliant eyes. "It is their
·al proof to me. Everything I have done is right."

"Naturally," he said softly. "My dear, cease worrying."

Senmut was not worrying. His mind was so buoyantly clear of
·rries that he scarcely listened to what his cherished queen was
·ying. As her litter moved off, his eyes and thoughts alike re-
·rned to the newly dedicated rectangle of sand enclosed by stakes
·d cord. There in that very spot had stood the little mud-brick
·apel in which, long ago, an ambitious gutter-rat with too much
·ne inside him had recklessly kissed the Daughter of the Sun.
·ere, in that spot, would rise the earth's most beautiful temple
·designed and built by the same gutter-rat, now utterly trans-
·rmed—to commemorate for eternity that most fortunate of
·istakes.

Senmut's mind was intoxicatingly free from care. His wildest
·nbitions had been realized.

But later that day, while the streets of Thebes still rang with
·e Feast of the Stretching of the Cord, he returned alone to the
·y and strolled about a long time, pacing off the measurements
·ain, stepping back to visualize the columns rising against the
·ffs, staring thoughtfully at the cord. When he turned at last
·ward the city a dissatisfied frown had appeared between his
·avy brows.

Already the rectangle of sand enclosed by the cord had begun
·seem too small to match his vision.

Within a month after the Stretching of the Cord, the shape
·d size of the hole being excavated for Ma-ke-Re's temple bore
·most no relation to the ceremoniously placed foundation de-
··sits. The people's attention was not called to this; further
·undation deposits were made, vastly enlarging the outlines
·d shifting them so that the temple would face east instead of

southeast, but there was no further feasting or fanfare. The good will of the gods was assured anyway, Hatshepsut was Amon's favorite. As for the huge additional expense involved in the temple's enlargement, that could be taken care of quietly and simply by still another increase in taxes.

The people's attention was not called to this, either.

Through the winter the clouds of dust floating always beneath the cliffs became as familiar a sight to Thebans as the undisturbed sands had been before, and their curiosity turned to something else. This was the puzzle of the five great ships—finished now, and swaying at their moorings in all the glory of their bright new paint. What were they for? Where were they going? And why didn't they go?

Late in the winter this mystery also was solved. One day a runner with a message for the queen arrived from the party of engineers in the Delta; by the next afternoon porters were swarming about the five ships, loading them with trade goods and provisions for a long voyage. On the third day the palace scribes once more fanned out into the streets of Thebes carrying the scrolls of a royal proclamation, while in the Great Hall Senmut faced the assembled courtiers and unrolled an identical scroll.

"Silence—silence—silence—silence—"

In the market places, potters stopped their wheels, housewives left off their bargaining, jewelers stilled their little hammers.

"His Majesty Ma-ke-Re speaks through my mouth . . ."

Rekhmi-re stepped into a corridor flanking the Great Hall, found it deserted, and crossed it to put his ear against the wall. Thoth joined him reluctantly, grim and stiff-jawed, telling himself he did not want to listen, he did not care.

"A command was heard from the throne, an oracle of the god himself . . ."

Amenu, driving past a street corner in his chariot, pulled in his horses, tossed the reins to the nearest urchin, and joined the crowd around a scribe.

". . . saying that the ways of Punt should be searched out, that the highways to the myrrh-terraces should be penetrated."

Punt! All over the city a buzz of voices broke out, people eyes bulged with disbelief, as the meaning of the words began to penetrate. She was sending those ships to *Punt?*

". . . The voice of my father Amon spoke, saying—'We

376

me, my sweet daughter, my favorite! Thou art the king, Hat-
epsut. I have given to thee all lands and all countries; I have
ven to thee all Punt as well. Behold, before the day of thy glory
one trod the myrrh-terraces, and the people knew them not.
nt was known of only by hearsay—mouth to mouth from the
cestors . . .'"

In the Great Hall, Thutiy was already pale with consterna-
on. "Mouth to mouth!" he whispered agitatedly to Ineny. "Aye,
at is the only way one has ever heard of it, or ever will hear!
he whole land is but a tale. In Hathor's sweet name, she can-
t be serious about this—"

He shot a despairing glance toward the throne, where Hatshep-
t sat slim and upright, a smile of happiness on her lips and
rene assurance in her eyes.

"'The marvels brought from that far land,'" went on the myr-
d scribes, "'under thy fathers, the kings of Lower Egypt, were
ought from one to another, as a return for many pay-
ents . . .'"

Thoth turned slowly, in utter amazement, to meet Rekhmi-re's
es. He was suddenly remembering an afternoon long ago and
e voices of Nehsi and Hatshepsut discussing the myrrh short-
e. Had she conceived this whole idea then? But it was mad. It
as entirely mad.

". . . 'But I will cause thy messengers to tread them. I will
ad them on water and on land, to explore the inaccessible chan-
ls, and to reach the myrrh-terraces. It is a glorious region of
odsland; it is, indeed, my place of delight.' So spake my father
mon to My Majesty."

In the temple courtyard, the scribe paused to clear his throat,
d Hapuseneb, standing outwardly calm and imperturbable on
e steps, moistened his dry lips.

"I have built ships to sail this voyage. I have chosen His Ex-
llency Count Nehsi, Honored of the Two Lands, to command
em in their journey to the myrrh-terraces, through the channel
ly Majesty's hand has dug to the Great Red Sea. From this
ly forward His Excellency Hapuseneb, High Priest of Amon,
all serve me as Royal Steward, and shall perform all the duties
vizier in the Land of Egypt."

As the scribes finished and rolled up their papyruses, a roar
talk arose in every part of Thebes. A change of viziers—and

an expedition to Punt—both announced in the same proclamation! The tongues could not wag fast enough. Crowds gathered about the five brave new ships and stared in wonder. Were these very ships going to that fabled land? So far away, so vague . . . was it anything *more* than fable? Maybe these fine strong boats would never come back again. Maybe even Ma-ke-Re could not perform this marvel.

"No matter," said a young riverman, staring at the first vessel with burning eyes. "Where yonder craft goes, I go. *Hai!* Who will sign up with me? If we never come back, who cares? We will be in Punt, smelling myrrh all day and dining with the gods!"

He rushed along the wharf to the gangplank and disappeared among the porters and bales of trade goods. Within a few moments a dozen more had followed him.

"She tempts the Great Ones," an old judge was murmuring dubiously to a colleague as they walked back to their offices.

"She is very great herself," returned the other in an appalled whisper. "But—bones of Osiris!—to send Count Nehsi into such unknown dangers . . ."

I see Senmut's hand in this, the Steward of Amon's brother Senmen was thinking as he returned to the mansion in the Avenue of Mut. *At last he has a vizier he can control completely.*

At the palace, Thutiy had cornered the broadly smiling Senmut and was bombarding him with anxious questions. "You *knew* she meant to do this? And did not stop her? In Amon's name, man! We must dissuade her from so hazardous a—"

"But, Excellency, why?"

"Why?" For a moment Thutiy could only sputter incoherently. "My dear Senmut, after but one year on the throne, she asks the gods to perform a miracle! What if they refuse? I will look as if she has already fallen from their favor!"

"Nonsense. She is Amon's darling."

"Not even Amon can lead ships to a land that is not there! If the venture fails . . . By Hathor's breasts, do you not realize what might happen to her prestige, to—to you, to me, to all of us?"

"My gloomy one, calm yourself. And think—just for a moment—of what will happen if it succeeds. Give her but one such triumph, and Re himself will not sit more firmly on his throne."

At the moment Senmut was speaking, Amenu entered the north wing of the palace. He bounded up the stairs two at a time, ran along the corridor and burst into the apartments of the deposed king.

"Tjesu—Rekhmi-re! Did you hear?"

"Aye, we heard." Both turned from the table. They were holding wine cups. Thoth splashed another cup full and thrust it at Amenu with an exultant gesture. "For the first time we have hope, real hope! Those brave new ships—why, they'll never come back. They'll be lost, and she will too. Drink with us, Amenu! To Ma-ke-Re's voyage!"

Three days later, in the golden flood of morning, Nehsi's five ships set out for the Delta and its miraculous canal. The people crowded the wharves, lined the river banks for miles. Some wished they were going, and talked loudly of the myrrh-terraces; others predicted disaster in lowered tones. Most stood silent and watchful, waiting to see how it would all come out. Until the last bright sail had dwindled to a speck in the distance, they squinted after it, shading their eyes against the sun.

No one knew how far away Punt was, but all knew there would be a long time to wait. Harvest season came, and the people were busy; after that the winds came, and the heat, and the curling mud, and still no one glanced northward, for it was obvious the ships could not return on a summer Nile, when there was scarcely enough water to keep the fishing punts afloat.

But with the rising of the waters, a few eyes began to turn downriver, and by the time of inundation everyone was watching. Shortly after this, a rumor went around that the new vizier, Hapuseneb, had said the journey might take a year.

A year! Aii—only nine months had passed. With reluctant patience the people bent to their work and the expectant tension relaxed.

It did not relax at the palace. Among the Kinsmen tempers grew shorter with every week that passed, and faces longer. Only Senmut continued to present his bland smile to the world, masking whatever doubts he had; only Hatshepsut felt no doubts at all.

The tenth month passed, the eleventh passed; the fields were emerald with grain again and still the ships did not come.

"Now let them claim she is divine!" exclaimed Rekhmi-re as the three stood on the roof-pavilion above Thoth's apartments, watching the sun go down.

"They can claim it for another month," said Amenu. "Then the legend is finished."

"It is finished already, if they would only admit it." Rekhmi-re turned away from the railing and sank into an armchair under the awning of the loggia. After a last glance downriver, Amenu joined him.

"How do you think we should arrange matters, when the time comes?" he said thoughtfully.

"I do not think we will need to arrange them at all! The day will come, and the ships will not, and the year will be over—then everyone will know. We need only walk into the Great Hall with Tjesu between us, denounce Ma-ke-Re as the usurper she is, and claim the crown in the name of Horus and Almighty Re."

Amenu's long jaw tightened with satisfaction, but his eyes were still thoughtful slits as they wandered over the reddened sky. "It will not be that simple," he said.

"You are thinking of Ma-ke-Re. Well, I say that even she will be forced to admit—"

"Don't be a fool. She will admit nothing."

"In the face of this? Name of Amon, the gods themselves do not support her!"

"The Kinsmen will, though, and the nome governors. Their lives depend on it. If she falls, they fall. They have no choice."

Rekhmi-re's black eyes moved to his friend's face. "Let us give them a choice, then!"

"Exactly what I was thinking. Forgiveness—or at least the preservation of their honor and estates—if they will acknowledge that Tjesu is Pharaoh and always has been."

Excitement caught them up all over again. They leaned close together over the table, planning the details.

Thoth, still standing at the railing, scarcely heard the mutter of voices behind him or saw the flaming sky before him. Another day had passed, and the river was still empty—empty of those five sails, though dozens of smaller ones scudded here and there, catching the blood-colored light. Each time he saw it empty at another sunset the hard ball of excitement in him grew larger, and its pressure more intense, and his alternating hopes

380

nd fears wilder. He woke each morning sick with dread of
vhat the day might bring, went to bed each night feverish with
riumph because it had brought nothing. In between, he paced
he garden, paced his apartments, tried to lose himself in reading
ncient scribes' rolls from the palace archives, but the hours
rawled by until each sunset.

One more day gone, he told himself now, savoring the thought
f it like a man who counts his gold. One more day mine. Only a
ew more weeks and the crown will be mine too.

He leaned against the railing, remembering the final hour
f his coronation, at Menfe, when the crown had settled—
nally and forever, he had thought—over his newly shaven
kull. It had felt strange and heavy to him then, and he had
valked carefully to balance it, secretly worried because this was
he instant at which he was supposed to become a god and he felt
o different from the mortal prince of a moment ago. He had
vaited anxiously for the moment when divinity would burst upon
im. The moment had never come.

It will come now, he thought. As soon as these last weeks
ass. Let Ma-ke-Re pretend what she likes, she has overreached
erself this time. It is in the hands of Lord Nile now, and Lord
Amon, who holds the winds. Let *them* decide.

As the twelfth month slowly wore away, the eagerness of the
eople was shot through with anxiety. Hapuseneb had said the
oyage would take a year. Did he mean a year to the day, in
Amon's name? Could the ships not come a little sooner? whis-
ered the women waiting for sons or lovers or husbands who
ad sailed as crew or as soldiers of Nehsi's guard. If they came
efore the day named, no one would deem the high priest's word
ess authoritative, no one would criticize him in the least—nay,
quite the contrary, the women told each other earnestly. If any-
hing, their respect for His Holiness would become even greater,
f only those five sails should appear this minute around the
end of the river yonder . . . But no matter how hard they
tared, the sails did not appear.

They will come tomorrow, the nobles assured each other,
lancing about their gardens or their sumptuous dining halls in a
areless manner. Perhaps day after tomorrow. Or—just possibly
—next week.

Then someone gave way at last, and whispered, *What if they never come at all?*

It was as if a door had been opened, or a spigot turned. One person said it, and then a thousand were saying it, and a flood of fear poured over Thebes and overflowed in each direction. The Nile was already dwindling; would it ever rise again, if the gods had deserted Ma-ke-Re? Next spring, instead of this thick, rich grain around them, would they see only dust and yawning, evil cracks in the earth, and dying children?

The day that marked the year's end dawned, and ran its course, and passed—all without a glimpse of sails.

Next morning the temples were jammed with frantic suppliants, the market places were a turmoil. The women cut their hair, tore their garments, and went wailing into the streets, pouring dust upon their heads.

Then Hatshepsut showed herself. She drove out of the palace behind two dancing stallions, crossed the river on the royal barge, and clattered up the opposite bank in full sight of the people, who abruptly ceased their talk. The chariot was blinding gold, the horses white as linen, and Ma-ke-Re herself held the reins—a slight, erect figure wearing the beard of royalty and the Double Crown, guiding her two excited horses with the firm skill of a man. She drove slowly to the Temple of Amon, looking neither right nor left, though the streets were lined with silent throngs. Her face was radiant and calm, as a god's should be.

Slowly the panic receded. It did not subside, but it shrank to controllable proportions. The people turned silently, tensely, to the work of harvest. They would wait a little longer.

"I told you it would not be simple," Amenu remarked to Rekhmi-re.

"Well? We have a plan for this! Why not begin on it?"

"It will be easier if we let everyone become as sure as we now are. Wait until harvest is done—or nearly done. Then we will start with the northern nomes, gathering governors like ripe plums, and work back toward Thebes— Do you agree, Tjesu?"

Thoth did not answer. Even in the midst of his wild elation, Hatshepsut's action and its effect had caught on something in his mind and would not let go.

"All they had to do was look at her!" he said. "Gods, no one ever behaved so at the sight of my face! What did they see? It

382

vas not something she did, it was something she *is,* and they saw
t."

"Bah, they saw the crown," Amenu said with a laugh.

"She is a usurper, that is what she *is,*" Rekhmi-re added.

"Aye, she is." A moment longer he examined the tiny, baf-
ling question in his mind, then dismissed it. "She is!" he re-
eated. "It is proven now." The knowledge of victory swept
hrough him again, lifting him up high, high, to the dizzy peak
where he had stood all morning. He sprang from his chair and
began to walk joyously about the room. "Your plan is a good
one, Amenu. Let them look their fill at her, until they understand what they see and what she is! Then we will start north."

Three weeks later he decided to wait no longer. He ordered
his bark and crew, pushed arrogantly through the silent throngs
that had gathered about the palace, and embarked for the north
to gather the first ripe plums.

They had reached Menfe before they ran head-on into the tidings that were sweeping upriver to the queen. The ships had been
sighted in the Delta.

5.

On a burning afternoon when the heat brooded like a tangible
presence over the shrinking river, Nehsi's ships sailed into
Thebes.

They looked no more like the five ships which had departed
than the man who returns from war resembles the untried youth
who started out. The look of far places was upon them; the very
smell of other lands. Their once-brave paint was worn and
faded, their sails patched, their spars weathered. There were
baboons in the rigging, sitting like solemn-faced idols or stalk-
ing along the yards with swinging and dignified stride. Chattering monkeys scampered past them up and down the sheets; greyhounds ran from side to side of the decks to bark at the crowds
packed solidly along the river banks. The ships seemed alive with
motion and noise, and they rode low in the water with their ex-
otic cargo—myrrh-resin and the green gold of Emu, ebony, cinnamon wood, *khesyt* wood, pure ivory, skins of the southern
panther. In the fourth ship, between the bales of hides and the

383

bundles of sharp, curved tusks, a little group of Puntites huddled with their children and their fat wives. The men had aquiline noses and narrow, pointed chin-beards; their hair was arranged in short braids all around, with the ends hanging down like fringe and a thong binding it about the forehead. Nothing like them had ever been seen in Egypt.

All this was marvelous; but there was a greater marvel—one only Ma-ke-Re the divine would have thought of and ordered Nehsi to bring. That was the row of myrrh trees which rose like living miracles from the scuppers of every ship. There they stood, each tree with its careful ball of earth, triumphantly green and fresh after all those leagues of journeying. Their countless leaves blowing in the breeze turned the ships into moving gardens.

Never again would Ma-ke-Re's beloved father Amon be forced to depend entirely on wretched barbarian traders for his supply of myrrh. He would have his own incense-garden now, his own Punt in Egypt. She had fetched all the wonders of Godsland to put into his golden hand.

From the deck of his bark farther down the river, Thoth watched the five sails move slowly past the Temple of Amon toward the palace docks. A poem was repeating itself in his head, over and over—a poem he had come across some weeks ago in one of the old scribes' rolls, and now wished with all his heart he had never read.

> *Behold, my name stinks*
> *More than the odor of carrion birds*
> *On summer days when the heaven is hot.*
>
> *Behold, my name stinks*
> *More than the odor of fishermen*
> *And the shores of the pools they have fished.*
>
> *Behold, my name stinks*
> *More than that of a woman*
> *Of whom slander has been spoken concerning a man*
>
> *To whom shall I speak today?*
> *Yesterday is perished . . .*

384

The rhythmic whispering in Thoth's ears was interrupted by the sound of Rekhmi-re's footsteps crossing the blazing expanse of deck to stop at his side.

"Tjesu, come away. You've stared at them nine days now, and I say it is time to stop. Gods, we should have stayed on at Menfe until all this is over! No sense in following them home, keeping them before our eyes every minute of every hour . . ."

I should answer him, Thoth told himself. I should say something careless, and go back to the deck-pavilion with him, and drink some beer though it chokes me, and keep up the pretenses. *They* can still pretend. They can still talk of patience and say that nothing changes the truth and that great Ma'at will triumph in the end, just as if they believed it. It is even possible that they believe they do believe it. It is astonishing how they can go on pretending.

"Tjesu."

To whom should I speak today?
Yesterday is perished,
And violence is come upon all men.

To whom should I speak today?
There is no heart of man
Whereon one might lean.

To whom should I speak today?
The righteous are no more;
The land is given over to evil-doers.

To whom should I speak today?
I am heavy laden with misery,
And am without a comforter . . .

"Tjesu, I am going back, out of this sun. You'd best come, you're running with sweat. I urge you. We have food and beer in the pavilion."

The footsteps receded.

They had beer in the pavilion. Aye, and no doubt they were drinking it, too—swallowing it down, their hopes along with it, and talking of something else. Not of the ships, no, anything but that. Not of Amenu's silent agony last year over the marriage of his beloved little countess to a southern nobleman, for which the triumph of his king might partially have made up. Not of Rekhmi-re's joyful expectations, last week, of at last standing justified in his father's eyes. Not a word of what sort of king they had followed, who did nothing but fail them, who had somehow mortally offended the very gods. No, they looked like men who had been ill for months, but they drank beer and covered whatever they were feeling.

How can they feel anything but loathing? Thoth thought. The gods themselves despise me.

He stared down at his hand, where it rested on the rail. Its familiar square, blunt-fingered shape was repugnant to him, simply because it was his. His whole person was repugnant to him. He had a sudden vision of himself as others must see him, going in and out of the palace—a short, stocky figure, with his big nose and forehead overshadowing his small chin, and futile anger in his eyes. He flushed with hatred of his flesh and the creature who inhabited it. *Behold, my name stinks, more than the odor of carrion birds* . . .

"Tjesu?" Rekhmi-re said from the pavilion steps.

"Aye, I'm coming."

He started across the deck to the pavilion, wondering why these two men, alone in all Egypt, did not yet see him for what he was.

They do, underneath, he thought. They must.

He found himself wishing violently that they would say so, that they would repudiate him utterly, go back to their families and fortunes and never think of him again. The weight of all they had given up for his sake was an intolerable burden. But of course, it was too late. There was nothing left for them to go back to.

He walked under the awning of the pavilion and felt the burning heat sliced off his shoulders as if by a cool knife blade. Amenu rose from the table and placed another chair. Thoth sat down, trying to pretend, listening to the poem in his head and watching with growing revulsion the fetching of a certain goblet, the careful pouring of his beer from a fresh-opened jar, all the small ritualistic deferences to which the two had clung obstinately all these years through all their easy intimacy with him, jealously

386

preserving the belief that they were his subjects and he their king.

Pretending? he thought. We are lying to each other.

Suddenly he could endure it no longer. "In Mut's sweet name, Amenu, sit down! Cease waiting on me." In the silence he half turned away from them. "It is over. Why not face the fact and have done with it? You should live your own lives. I release you."

"We did not ask to be released," Rekhmi-re said.

"I know that! Why should you ask me anything? It is over."

Amenu said doggedly, "Nothing is over, Tjesu. Nothing's even begun."

"Nay, and nothing ever will be."

"Aye, it will! We must wait a little longer, that is all."

"Wait for what, in Amon's name? For Ma-ke-Re to die of old age? For the gods to step in and make everything right? It seems that is what they did two years ago, when I came back from Nubia. It seems they have decided this is how things should be."

"Nonsense," Amenu said. "You do not believe that yourself."

Thoth stared at him, thinking, Nay, I do not quite believe it, even yet. I am a fool, an idiot. "It makes no difference," he said, his voice bitter with scorn for himself. "Even if I did not believe it, nothing would be changed by what *I* thought the right of the matter. Your trouble is that you believe there is a right and a wrong. You expect life to be fair, goodness to be rewarded."

"Of course."

"Aye, of course, of course!"

"Why do you sneer at him?" Rekhmi-re demanded angrily. "Every man has the right to expect that!"

"So Egyptians believe," Thoth retorted. "The gods alone know why! In Babylon, any child knows better."

"Babylon!" Rekhmi-re spat out the word as if it were a mouthful of something rotten. "This is not Babylon—this is Egypt."

"Aye, so they were always telling me at the temple." Why am I quarreling with them? Thoth thought in bewilderment. Am I *trying* to anger them, trying to hurt them? He heard his own voice saying harshly, "The fact is, it does not matter. The truths I was taught in Babylon as a child, I discover for myself in Egypt

387

as a man. It would have been far better for me if I had not learned fairy tales in between."

"Fairy tales!" Amenu whispered. "In the name of Amon, Tjesu, do you call great Ma'at a fairy tale?"

The despair in his voice shook Thoth. He gazed into Amenu's face and became aware that a terrible gulf had opened between them. You believe in Ma'at, he thought, and I in Gilgamesh. Gods! We should have gone on pretending.

He said almost pleadingly, hoping by some miracle to be convinced, "Who is Ma'at? A goddess. Justice incarnate. The power of truth. Now show me justice among men and I will believe her power."

"Her power exists regardless of your belief! Does the sun cease shining because a man is blind?"

"Must a man suppose himself blind because there is no light, because he feels no warmth? I said show me Ma'at's justice—"

"Justice is but her little finger. She is more, much more!" Amenu was leaning forward with dilated eyes. "She is the Right Order of all things, which was established the first day of the world, when Ptah spoke the great word and the gods came forth from his mouth. There is one order and one only, and it has never been put to confusion since the time of Re."

"You were taught that as a child. Amon help you—you believed it!"

"Do you mean you do *not* believe that Ma'at will triumph?"

"Will? If she triumphs always, as you say, then she has triumphed already—and Ma-ke-Re belongs on the throne. That is what I mean," Thoth said savagely. "But you will not understand."

"Nay. Nay—I will not understand such words from my king." Amenu sat back in his chair, and his eyes swerved away from Thoth's. "You have had a blow," he said in a low voice. "It has driven you to say these things you cannot mean. Ma-ke-Re does not belong on the throne. You know that. She has warped Ma'at's designs, but she cannot do it forever. Ma'at *is*."

Ma'at *is*. For just an instant, Thoth saw the universe as Amenu saw it—a green and level saucer, cleft by the Nile, ringed by desert hills, with a heaven of stars cupped above and a heaven for the dead underneath—a planned and perfect creation of the gods, unchanged since the beginning, with the Right, true

Order of things inherent in its very structure. In that static, perfect universe the sun rose and sank, the moon waxed and waned, the stars wheeled, and kings succeeded one another in serene and imperishable rhythm, according to the designs of Ma'at. It could not be altered, it could not be changed, it could not be disputed; it *was*. He glimpsed it as one might suddenly remember a lost, once familiar face which now meant nothing.

"That is Ma-ke-Re's world," he said. "I knew it once. But it is not mine. I think the throne was never mine either."

"In Amon's name, Tjesu!" Rekhmi-re burst out. "*We* believe in you. Why is it so hard for you to believe in yourself?"

"What is my 'self'? What is it you believe in? I cannot find anything there!" Thoth said desperately. He got up and walked to the other side of the pavilion, thinking, Now I have said too much. Suddenly he realized what it was he was doing. He was murdering their god—toppling a king-shaped idol off its pedestal, peeling off its gold that was only gilt, laying it open with desecrating hands to show nothing but clay and shards inside. These two had given up everything for a belief, an image. Now he was destroying the image and scattering its ashes before their eyes.

"You are Men-kheper-Re," Amenu whispered.

Thoth did not answer. They were only repeating a ritual, both of them, clinging to formulas whose validity had already perished, blindly shaking the sistrums before an empty altar. Men-kheper-Re? There was no such creature, half god, half man. There never had been. There was no one here but Thoth.

And gods, who is that? he thought. Who am I—why am I— if I am not Men-kheper-Re?

They did not mention Ma'at again. In the silence that had fallen among them Rekhmi-re suddenly and wordlessly left the pavilion and walked far back to the stern, out of sight. Thoth and Amenu sat on, like strangers, looking into the gulf and trying to draw back from its edge. After a while Thoth got up, went slowly down the steps, and returned to his place by the rail.

Half an hour later he was still there, his face in his hand and the deck beneath him lifting and sinking with the movement of the river as the poem washed back and forth across his thoughts.

"I crave pardon—but if Your Highness would care to give some command—"

The captain's voice, stiff, carefully expressionless, but with an undertone of excitement that penetrated even through the whispering verses, sounded behind Thoth.

"A command?" he muttered.

"About the mooring, Highness. Unless you wish to pass through the city altogether."

Impatience danced just beneath the captain's level tones. Naturally, Thoth thought. He is beside himself to moor the bark, to have done with me and go to see the ships like everyone else in Thebes.

"Lower your sails," he said.

"Aye, Your Highness. After crossing the river, Your Highness means."

"I mean now! We will not cross the river yet."

There was a stony silence behind him; he could feel the captain's resentment as one feels the heat of a fire. Then quick hard footsteps moved away.

Behold, my name stinks more than the odor of carrion birds . . .

Thoth raised his head. The bark had passed the fishing-wharves and ferry landings, and was moving slowly by a stretch of papyrus marsh below the east bank. Directly across the river Nehsi's ships were warping into the palace docks. Both banks were black with people; some were even scrambling down into the muddy river bed to get nearer the great spectacle, and every island that thrust up from the dwindling waters had its crown of watchers and a necklace of fishing punts about its base. Other small boats encircled the five tall hulls; their crowded passengers stared and pointed upward at the waving greenery as the tiny craft bobbed up and down in the wake of the ships and got in the way of the big oars. A glittering procession, with Senmut's blue-and-gold litter at its head, was winding down the avenue toward the docks.

The bark's sail slithered down its mast, leaving the sky suddenly empty and the deck lolling this way and that. A moment later Rekhmi-re appeared from the direction of the stern, and Amenu from the pavilion.

"They have lowered the sail, Tjesu!" Rekhmi-re said.

"Aye."

There was a pause. Amenu said nothing; presently he walked to the rail and stood looking at the ships.

"You ordered them to?" Rekhmi-re said incredulously. "You mean to skulk here among the papyruses while—"

"Would you have me show myself at such a time?"

"Aye—at exactly such a time! You cannot lurk here in the background, as if you had changed your plans to suit hers! It puts you in a false position!"

"What difference does it make, Rekhmi-re?" Thoth asked wearily. "Everything I do puts me in a false position. Merely being alive puts me in a false position. Kings should be dead, or else they should still be kings."

"They should behave like kings until they *are* dead," Rekhmi-re said.

Thus bluntly and abruptly came the challenge. Was that what they had been deciding, both of them, in these last silent moments on the river? Give us our empty forms to believe in, we have nothing left but loyalty, everything else is gone. Amenu was watching him too, with strange, lusterless eyes.

"Oh, very well," Thoth said quietly. "It cannot possibly matter, whatever I do."

Rekhmi-re whirled and bellowed the order to raise sail.

They stood like three strangers as the bark crossed the river, and in silence they climbed the stairs of the royal landing. At the top Thoth paused, and in spite of himself his eyes moved to the spot just below and to his right where the first of the five ships had now moored at the next dock. With the river so low he could look right down onto its swarming deck, could see the sun gilding the hairs of the panther skins, could watch one greyhound, more excitable than its brothers, leap and bark and leap again against the leash a soldier was holding. Someone threw down a gangplank between stairs and deck. From the noisy confusion a figure extricated itself and stepped out onto the slender bridge. Nehsi was coming ashore—the same ebony-skinned giant in a turquoise collar, looking only a little older than in Babylon, moving with the same erect, grave dignity up the seven water-stained steps exposed by the depleted river. He too held a leash. On the end of it was a snarling panther cub, spotted black and gold; no doubt a personal present for the queen.

391

Nehsi seemed always to be returning from some impossible journey to the ends of the earth, holding firmly to something troublesome. Last time it had been a princeling from Babylon. That one, Thoth reflected bitterly, had turned out to be quite docile in the end. No doubt this spotted cub, too, would be tamed and disciplined, taught a few remarkably intelligent-looking tricks, and then placed prudently in a reinforced golden cage before he grew old enough to become dangerous.

"Let us go, Tjesu," Rekhmi-re muttered.

"I'm coming. Go on."

Behind them, Amenu said suddenly, "Look. Down there in Nehsi's honor guard."

Thoth glanced back and found himself looking straight into a pair of familiar, intent dark eyes. It was Tjah, standing motionless among the milling soldiers, staring up at him. For a moment ships and river faded; he could see nothing but the silent crowd in the Great Hall, and the wooden soldiers, and that face among them, gazing stiffly past him. He averted his eyes. So Tjah had been to Punt instead of Kadesh.

"Traitor!" Rekhmi-re growled.

Thoth flung him a sardonic glance. Habit, Rekhmi-re, he told him silently. Tjah's only crime was that he had no choice. Would you not be happier today if you had had none?

He turned and started up the avenue.

An hour later he walked aimlessly onto the balcony opening off his bedchamber, and stood looking out over the honeycomb of walled courtyards, stables and kitchen gardens which formed the northwest section of the palace grounds. Today all was deserted and silent; every soul in Thebes was at the docks, or lining the palace avenue, or jamming the Great Court, gaping at the treasures of Punt as they were carried in formal procession to the queen. Even here, the distant hum of many voices, punctuated by the barking of the greyhounds and occasional outbursts of excitement, came plainly to his ears. Too plainly; he was about to start back into his bedroom when a flash of gold drew his eye to a spot near the north gate. The place was not quite deserted, after all; in one courtyard off the rear avenue half a dozen poor devils were moving about—doubtless obeying some order of the queen; nothing less could prevent them from joining their fellows on this great day. . . .

The sarcasm faded from Thoth's mind and was replaced by a familiar sinking dread. What order of the queen's? None had ever boded anything but ill for him.

He stepped closer to the balcony rail, staring toward the courtyard. Across it, four carrying-chairs had been arranged in a line —it was Hatshepsut's golden one which had flashed in the sun and caught his eye. Several men were busily stacking flat-litters behind them; two others squatted in a corner, binding long splints together into bundles. At sight of these Thoth's eyes widened in surprise—then narrowed to slits as another man appeared from nowhere and approached the two, apparently to give some order.

This last man wore the robe of a Necropolis priest.

Thoth left the balcony abruptly, strode through his apartments and flung open the hall door. The servant who was supposed to be outside it was far down the corridor, leaning over the stair balustrade in an attempt to glimpse the marvels passing through the entry. Swallowing a gorge of anger, Thoth summoned him, gave him a gold band from his arm and terse instructions. He stood a moment watching the sulky figure trot off toward the rear stairs before he stepped back into his apartments and slammed the door. As he crossed the sitting room, Rekhmi-re and Amenu rose and followed him.

"What is it, Tjesu?" Amenu muttered.

"I have sent to find out." Leading the way to the balcony, Thoth nodded toward the courtyard. "What do you make of it?"

"A procession?" Amenu hazarded after a short silence.

Rekhmi-re grunted dubiously. "A monstrous short one, with only four carrying-chairs."

"And a monstrous strange one," Thoth said, "which must be formed in secret behind a bolted courtyard gate, which is under the direction of a Necropolis priest, and which will go forth in the dark."

"In the dark?"

Thoth pointed to the long bundles of splints.

"Torches!" Rekhmi-re exclaimed. He leaned forward on the rail, staring. "Why the flat-litters?"

"Aye, why? And given the flat-litters, why nothing to load

393

upon them?" Thoth struggled in vain with a growing, nameless sense of dread. "Their load will be picked up elsewhere—and carried somewhere else."

"But where?"

"I do not know! Where does that road lead?"

Three pairs of eyes moved to the graveled drive, along which Thoth's servant could be seen running. It led past the courtyard, through the north gate in the palace walls, and into a street which meandered across a rich section of western Thebes, skirted the City of the Dead, and became the road which crossed the stretch of desert to the western cliffs. Thoth shivered and took a restless turn up and down the balcony. Would she go—at night—into the barren valley behind those cliffs?

"It may have nothing to do with you, Tjesu," Amenu said.

"All she does has something to do with me!" He returned to the rail. In the distance the servant was pounding on the courtyard gate. "We'll soon find out," he added.

"With such secrecy, they may not answer that fellow's questions," Rekhmi-re told him.

Thoth laughed shortly. "They'll answer. There's a priest among them—and I sent a bribe."

"A bribe?" Rekhmi-re turned. "Some possession of your own? Suppose they recognize it?"

"Suppose they do?"

"Then they will know that you have sent to question!"

Thoth looked from one to the other of their dismayed faces. "I see," he said. "You think a king should not behave so—that I should hold myself above such action, that I should scorn even to find out what next evil she plans against me. Is that it?"

"Tjesu, we merely think this cannot concern you," Amenu said. "A few carrying-chairs in a courtyard—doubtless she means to convey some treasure to her temple. Aye, at night, in secrecy —it is logical enough."

"With a priest of the dead to show the way! And to a temple that is scarce more than flooring and a few half-raised walls!"

"Well, to some tomb, then! In any case—"

"Let be, Rekhmi-re," Thoth said wearily. "What I have done I have done."

He turned and went into his bedchamber, stared an instant at he little galley on its shelf, and moved on into the sitting room, unable to stay still. *To whom should I speak today? Yesterday is perished, perished. . . .*

He was still pacing restlessly about the room, trying to escape the poem and his own pressing sense of dread, when a tap sounded on the door. The servant entered and stood eying him, neglecting even to make obeisance. Thoth's jaws clamped; he walked slowly to the man and stared until the other bobbed his head.

"Well?" Thoth said.

"It is a reburial, Master."

"A *what?*"

"A reburial." The man's eyes were insolent; he looked straight at Thoth. "By the order of His Majesty Ma-ke-Re, the body of her father the first Thutmose—may his Three Thousand Years be full of joy—will be removed at the hour before dawn tomorrow to the new tomb Her Majesty has built for him."

"A new tomb," Thoth said numbly. "What was wrong with the old one?"

The servant hesitated; but at last he said, "The Tired One lies there."

Then it was clear. The last visious slap of the triumphant hand across his face—that was what this was.

Thoth stood silent, feeling as if everything inside him were breaking up, crumbling like a rotten building. Suddenly he swept his arm in a powerful backhanded arc that sent the servant sprawling.

"Tjesu! In Mut's sweet name!"

His companions were staring, in the bedroom doorway. Thoth smiled blindly in their direction. "Well? Is that not the action of a king? The fellow was insolent enough to bring bad news. I must behave like a king, you say—until I am dead. Gods, I wish I were dead. I wish I were."

Pushing past them, he gained the balcony and stumbled down the outside stair. Gods, can she never be satisfied? he was thinking. She has my crown, my army, my humiliation before the world. She has made me into a *lillu*. In Amon's name, what more does she want? To prove I never existed? That even my father never existed? . . . Aye, that is exactly what she wants.

He heard hurried footsteps behind him. "Do not follow me!"

he said hoarsely. Without turning, he made an emphatic gesture behind him, then started along the path toward the front of the palace.

My father, my poor father, my lonely father, he thought. Stripped of everything, discredited, destroyed. . . .

Never had his father seemed so close; it was as if the Qeni garment were slipping around him again, enfolding him as he enfolded it, merging two identities into one. *The Good God is like his father* . . . it was true. They were right, all those who said that. He thought, We have been alike since the beginning. We are still alike now that everything is ending for both of us. . . .

He opened the door to the Great Court and stopped short, stunned by the throng that packed it, by the color and motion, the noise he must have been hearing all along. He had forgotten—the treasures of Punt. Above the jiggling, leaping, shouting crowd he could see myrrh trees and curving tusks moving by on the heads of bearers. Somehow he pushed through the press, past elbows and oiled brown shoulders, through the file of bearers and the jam of sweating humanity on the other side. The gate slammed behind him; he stood at last in the haven of the garden.

There were the lawns, the gently blowing acacias, the flowers and familiar paths, the smell of sun and bricks, the vine-draped pavilion. There was the pool, and the tamarisk tree.

He wandered down the slope, filled with longing, with a sense of loss as sharp as pain.

Oh, if I could go back! he thought. If I could see my father sitting yonder in his cedar chair, if I could hear his voice, talk to him. He would understand all that is happening to me. It happened to him too. Oh, gods, why must she do this? Can she not even leave his poor bones alone? What did we do, my father and I, or what did we leave undone, that the gods must punish us so? *A man must always obey the command of his god* . . . but I did not hear when the gods commanded me. I must not have heard. But that will not save me. You must hear, then you must obey. If you do not—

His thoughts scattered. Mayet was lying asleep under the tamarisk tree. She was thirteen and looked eleven; a golden-skinned child with a wealth of black hair flung out upon the grass, one bare leg drawn up and one hand tucked under her cheek, pushing the dusky semicircle of lashes askew. Her pointed face was ab-

396

sorbed, her lips parted, in the intense preoccupation of sleep. On the stone bench near her, her old musician Djedi sat playing softly, his back as curved as his harp. Neither noticed Thoth's presence, since the harper was blind, and Mayet deep in some dream no doubt as completely different from other people's dreams as she was from other people.

Thoth gazed silently for a moment at the old man on the bench. It was a bench made for old men, apparently; it looked right only when one was sitting there.

When he started to turn away, Mayet's eyes were open, fixed apprehensively on his face. She scrambled to her feet.

"Thoth—something bad has happened?"

The old harper's song broke off abruptly at the sound of her voice, and his face assumed an anxious expression. "Someone is with us," Mayet explained to him gently. His old man's smile was sweet and melancholy; his head followed the sound of her voice, like a plant turning with the sun, as she moved toward Thoth.

"Has it?" she repeated.

Thoth shrugged, then started abruptly back up the slope, wishing she had not wakened. "Something bad is always happening, isn't it?" he said.

"I don't know. Not to me. Will you tell me?"

"You must know already. The ships are home."

So the noise in the Great Court was telling earth and heaven in joyful repetition—and the garden was no protection from it after all, the walls were not thick or high enough. He walked swiftly toward the pavilion, stumbled on the steps. Mayet was beside him, still questioning.

"Thoth, that is not all."

"Nay, it is not all." He told her the rest, bluntly and without looking around.

"But why would she do that? I do not understand—"

"She wants my father to be forgotten in Egypt. She wants to make it seem as if he had never lived. As if I had never been born."

"But she cannot make *that* seem so! You are *here*. I can touch you."

He turned, smiling faintly. "And what is it you touch?"

"Thoth."

"Aye, Thoth! And who is that? Nothing. Only someone named Thoth."

Mayet sat down slowly on the top step. "I am only someone named Mayet. But I am not—*nothing*."

"Nay?" he said gently. "What are you, then, little one?"

"I am Mayet!"

Her tone was firm; there was no question in her mind. She is a child yet, he thought. She does not realize. He sat down beside her on the step. "Listen to me. You are nothing too. Do you not know that? She has done the very same to you, since the hour you were born. . . . Now she must do this to my father! He was your father, too—why do you not feel it?"

"Thoth—*he* will not feel it. He is dead."

"*I* am not dead!" he cried. "What she does to him, she does to me!" He stood up again; it was impossible to sit still. After a moment he added, "Of course he will care. She will make him lonelier than ever—feet will walk past his tomb, and over it, and no one will even know he is there. Egypt will forget he lived!"

"I do not think he will mind being forgotten. I think he would rather."

Thoth glanced down at her. She had taken a bit of clay out of a flowerpot and was working with it on the step, her chin resting on her drawn-up knees and her hair falling like a silken curtain over her profile. He could see only the tip of her nose and the lash-fringed curve of one eyelid.

"What makes you say that? Did you know him? Do you remember him?"

"Only a little. But one time I remember very well. Yen brought me here, into the garden, and he was here. I sat on his lap for a while—he trembled all the time."

"What did he say?"

"He said, 'Little Meryet-Re. Little Beloved-One-of-the-Sun. Little Forgotten-One-of-the-Gods.' He asked me questions, and I answered something, I do not know what. Then he said, 'Yen, listen to me. It is better for her that she should be as she is—forgotten. Do you understand that, Yen? Never try to make them remember her. She is better off as she is.'" Mayet's eyes flashed to Thoth's face. "That is why I think he will not care."

Thoth was silent. His whole soul had fastened onto his father's words, as if they held great meaning for him, but he could not

uite make out what it was. He groped anxiously, not daring to
eak because it seemed at any minute he might understand.
urely his father was speaking to him out of this child's mouth.
. is better that she should be forgotten. . . .

*Nothing has value, my son, nothing has meaning, let go your
own, your friends, your life; living is struggle, death is peace.
ive up.*

Was that what he meant?

Something was squeezing, squeezing inside Thoth until he
as sick all through. In his mind a picture slowly formed—it was
vast, lonely plain, with dust blowing and the wind moaning from
ne end of the earth to the other, crying, "Oh, a pity, a pity, a
ty." The plain widened and widened in his mind; it was im-
easurable, he had to expand inside to encompass it. It seemed to
im the whole world was full of pain and blowing dust and crying
ind.

Nay, never, never! cried a voice somewhere within him.

He silenced it. Yes, that was what the words meant. They were
easonable, authoritative; they had the power and ring of truth.
eath is peace, give up. Surely he had always known that?

> *. . . Gilgamesh, whicher are you wandering?*
> *Life, which you look for, you will never find.*
> *For when the gods created men,*
> *They let death be his share,*
> *And life they withheld in their own hands . . .*

There was a renewed outburst from beyond the gate. Outside
 the Great Court, the sound of some queer foreign tongue,
poken in the high-pitched voices of children, began to mingle
ith the Egyptian gutturals, with the laughter and astonished
houts. The noise grated on Thoth's raw and wounded mind like
 fingernail screeching over slate. He wanted to stop his ears, to
ide from all the pitiable people in the world, who did not know
ow pitiable they were.

Mayet straightened, holding up her clay. "Thoth, look what I
ave made. Do you see, it—"

"Oh, be silent!" he cried.

Her eyes, shocked and disbelieving, flew to his face, and the
lay dropped from her hands.

Now I have hurt her, he thought. Why did I shout like that?

399

But the pain in her eyes only drove him to lash out again. "Why do you want to sit here with me, anyway? Do you not hear all that out yonder? Go, see all the marvels, all the wonderful curiosities—apes and ivory and Puntite children—do you not want to see them?"

"Aye," she whispered.

They mattered nothing to her, he knew. All that was only another of the great happenings that continually took place on the other side of the garden wall, outside her life. What mattered to her was that she had angered him, somehow, merely by being. Her face was stricken with the knowledge of it.

His anger had collapsed, but it seemed to him that everything in him had collapsed with it. He could not bear her presence.

"Go, Mayet. Please. I cannot talk any more now."

She stood up, walked silently down the steps and across the grass toward the tamarisk tree. *I am Mayet,* she had said. Yes, she was Mayet—and she knew exactly what that was. He watched her, wondering how it was that she was impervious to the same deadly influences which were destroying him. They had shaped her life, but they had not harmed her *ka*—it remained somehow safe and free and whole in that fragile body of hers.

Only I can hurt her, he thought. That is what I am sure to do, it is what I always do. I have already begun.

He walked slowly up the steps, trying to find his own *ka* in the echoing, wind-swept reaches that seemed to have taken the place of whatever used to be inside him. He could feel it there, his *ka* —a tiny entity scurrying about, shrinking all the time. It no longer fitted his body as a hand fits comfortably in a glove; there were great empty distances between the two. Instead of looking directly out of his eyes as he had always done, he felt as if he were peering through two deep tunnels, at the faraway ends of which he could see sunlight and red flowers in a pot. He reached out slowly, and his fingers entered the distant spots of light, and he felt the soft petals. The flowers were here on the step, as close as his hand; but his *ka* was far away inside him, growing tinier every minute. It was clear that it might soon vanish altogether.

Then what will happen? he thought. What will it be like, with nothing left inside me? How can one live that way? That is not living, that is dying.

It would be better to die and have done with it. That was what his father had said; that was what the poem had been saying all day. No use pretending he had not known it.

The lines began their whispering rhythm in his ears again, and this time they filled him with longing, they soothed like balm on a wound.

> *Death is in my eyes today*
> *As when a sick man becomes whole,*
> *As the walking abroad after illness.*
>
> *Death is in my eyes today*
> *Like the scent of myrrh,*
> *Like sitting beneath the boat's sail on a breezy day.*
>
> *Death is in my eyes today*
> *Like the smell of water lilies,*
> *Like sitting on the bank of drunkenness.*
>
> *Death is in my eyes today*
> *Like a well-trodden road,*
> *As when men return home from a foreign campaign.*
>
> *Death is in my eyes today*
> *Like the unveiling of heaven,*
> *As when a man attains there to that which he knew not.*
>
> *Death is in my eyes today*
> *Like the desire of a man to see his home*
> *When he hath passed many years in captivity.*

Thoth sat down in the gold-and-cedar chair, his back turned to the garden and Mayet and the sounds of the pageant in the Great Court. They seemed infinitely remote—a thousand leagues, a thousand years away—and his father's weary spirit very near.

I will go down into his tomb and find him, he thought. Then neither of us will ever be alone again.

6.

He had slept. He knew that when he opened his eyes and found his bedchamber cool and still, and heard, outside in the dark, the slight, secret sounds he had been waiting for. He rose from his couch—in the same movement, it seemed to him, with which he had lain down on it—and found that his body had rested. His *ka* had not; there had been no break in his thoughts or in his consciousness. He did not need to remind himself that this was the morning, this the hour, those small, secret sounds the starting of the procession toward the tomb.

He walked to the open doors of his balcony. The sky was still velvety with night, the stars had not yet faded. Below them, like puny reflections, a few yellow pinpricks of light moved across the palace grounds, appearing and disappearing among clumps of trees, trailing toward the little-used north gate. The procession was almost silent; only the occasional crunch of gravel, the faint jangle of metal on metal, the splutter of a torch, carried to the balcony.

He turned back into the room, knotted a *shenti* about his lean hips, bound on a plain headcloth, groped in the gloom for his sandals. Then he stepped out onto the balcony and moved silently down the outside stair.

Half an hour later he stood on the summit of the western cliffs. Far ahead of him the torches of the procession moved down the slope like a luminous, many-legged insect, into the empty wasteland beyond.

No. *No,* whispered a voice inside him.

Hesitantly he turned and looked back over the dark, Nile-threaded valley where Egypt lay sleeping; then he plunged down the slope after the distant torches, stumbling in the darkness on the rocky, uneven footing, grasping for bushes or roots that were not there. Nothing was there, nothing grew in this western valley. It was bare of life—a glaring hell of harsh red rocks by day, a silent wilderness by night.

On the valley floor the land leveled out, making it hard to follow the torches that were his only guide. Giant boulders kept looming up to cut them from view and leave him momentarily alone in the immensity of night. At such times his steps slowed, as if an invisible cord binding him to the procession had been severed, and he found his eyes drawn irresistibly upward to the great jeweled vault above him. Purple-black, and deep as silence, it stretched over him and all around him, as far as he could see, with the stars moving across it in their mysterious patterns. Be-

402

fore its majesty he seemed to dwindle to a speck, a tiny, waiting figure in the center of the world.

What do I wait for? he thought. For instruction, for some command? From whom? In Egypt that is merely a great canopy up there, supported on four distant pillars—or merely the body of Nuit the Dark Goddess, who has no interest in me or any mortal.

He pulled his gaze away and groped on, around the boulder and down the dimly seen jagged trough of the next declivity, after the moving lights. Each time they vanished he found himself slowing again, staring upward expectantly. It grew harder and harder to think of that majesty up there as a canopy, or a woman arching her body over earth, or as the spangled belly of the Great Cow, or as anything Egyptian. He felt ever more strongly a stern and overwhelming Presence. He stopped at last, head tilted backward.

"Anu. Lord Sky," he whispered.

He waited, but still he did not know what he waited for, and he heard no command.

He stumbled forward again, felt his way around a great heat-split rock, and went on. After what seemed a very long time, a faint radiance appeared among the rocks ahead, and the torches filed into a gully which led toward the spot. Instead of following, Thoth circled cautiously along the higher ground, climbed the brow of a rise, and found the procession gathered in a sandy hollow just below him. The torches were bunched around it in glowing knots; a row of temple candles, great cones of tallow on sticks, was thrust into the ground along the base of one of the low, barren hills that rose everywhere through this silent valley, like the waves of a rocky sea. In the face of the hillside a door had been uncovered; the piles of rubble and sand lay there, on either side of it, and a group of stoneworkers stood in the background with tools, attended by a Necropolis priest.

The seals of the tomb's door had been broken. It stood open, and a torch flickered dimly within; but no one was entering. The *sem* priests with their torches and their long censers stood about uneasily; the three Kinsmen chosen for this secret pilgrimage were clustered about the royal litter, into which Hapuseneb leaned, talking. Something had gone wrong.

By moving a little closer Thoth had no difficulty finding out what it was. Hapuseneb, who with the Necropolis priest and the workmen had arrived an hour earlier to open the tomb and prepare the great king's coffin on its traveling litter, had discovered that the great stone sarcophagus in which the coffin rested was a full finger longer than the one awaiting it in the fine new tomb. After eighteen years, no one had remembered how tall the old man was. Now a troublesome predicament confronted them; the coffin was too long for the new sarcophagus, the old sarcophagus too heavy to move. The reburial would have to be postponed.

A shiver ran through Thoth as Hatshepsut's crisp voice issued from the litter. He had not heard her voice, or seen her, face to face, for months.

"Postponed? Of course not. The new one must be altered. Now. At once. Let Senmut take the workmen ahead, to the new Precious Habitation. We will follow with my beloved father."

"But Majesty—to attempt such a task in haste—"

"It must be done! My father must not remain in this place another hour."

Feeling queerly hot and cold at the sound of her voice, Thoth watched Hapuseneb turn and with obvious discomfiture give the necessary orders. The Great Royal Vizier of both Amon and Egypt had not distinguished himself for efficiency this night.

The workmen were hastily blindfolded and herded into the gully by Senmut and two of the *sem* priests. In the hollow the procession re-formed, under Nehsi's quiet direction, leaving an open path between the litter and the door; then every man fell to his knees.

Hatshepsut stepped to the ground. She stood a moment, silent, looking about the little lighted space and her kneeling servants, and finally at the open door of the tomb. Thoth found himself gripping the big rock over which he leaned, trying to quell a storm of emotions. There she was, not ten paces from him—tiny, and as vigorously erect as in his childhood, though the fluted Pharaonic headcloth, with its stiff white pleats framing her face and falling in broad, masculine flaps over her shoulders, erased the last trace of Lady Shesu from her starkly emphasized features. As she looked about her the thrusting cobra on her forehead turned this way and that, glittering, glaring.

After a moment she faced the tomb door and motioned curtly.

404

At once Hapuseneb rose and led the way inside; the *sem* priests hastily set pellets of myrrh to smoldering in their censers and fell in behind him, beginning the chant of the funerary ritual. 'O Thutmose-iren-Amon, arise, sit thou on the throne of Osiris . . ." The voices receded into the hillside chamber, and after them Hatshepsut and the Kinsmen, then the lesser priests, carrying empty baskets and the wicker flat-litters and the torches, disappeared one by one.

The night closed in on Thoth. Only the row of candles burned now, on either side of the door; the chanting sounded far away in the depths of the hill and seemed to come from nowhere, like the voices of disembodied *khefts*. He leaned heavily on the boulder and closed his eyes, exhausted.

He did not know how long he waited. He was conscious only of a powerful desire to have it over, finished. Once he looked up at the Presence above him, silently questioning it again, but he was vouchsafed no sign though he scanned the unbroken immensity in every direction. He saw only remote majesty and stars, and behind him in the east the gray beginnings of a day he would not know. Lord Anu would not answer. His father alone had promised him an answer.

The faint sounds of chanting brought his attention back to the tomb. A dawn was breaking in its doorway, too; the black rectangle grew slowly gray, then golden with torchlight. Presently Hapuseneb emerged with the first of the *sem* priests. Their voices sounded thin and reedy against the vast silence of the valley.

*"Thutmose-iren-Amon, arise, sit thou on the throne of Osiris;
Arise; thou ceasest not to be; thou perishest not . . ."*

A long flat-litter emerged from the doorway, borne by sixteen straining bearers. Upon it, shining against the night, was a huge golden coffin, over which the torchlight played in ripples of splendor. The priests around it waved their censers, chanting the litany of Ascension.

*"The head of Thutmose-iren-Amon is like that of the vulture
When he ascends and lifts himself into the sky.
The skull of Thutmose-iren-Amon is like that of divine stars
When it ascends and lifts itself into the sky . . ."*

Hatshepsut came out of the tomb with the Kinsmen behind her, entered her litter, and was borne away after the shining coffin. Behind followed the priests, their flat-litters and baskets now heaped with the great king's possessions—boxes of ebony and ivory, alabaster pots and vials, ornamental weapons fashioned of gold, of electrum, of silver; jeweled collars, golden cups, inlaid chairs and tables—all the treasure which had furnished and adorned his Precious Habitation. One by one the rich burdens glittered and blazed as they passed between the candles, then moved away, twinkling in the uneven torchlight, across the hollow and over the rise.

"The mouth of Thutmose-iren-Amon is like that of him who traverses
    the great lake,
  When he ascends and lifts himself into the sky . . ."

A single priest emerged from the tomb, carrying a bow in his outstretched arms. Thoth's eyes suddenly focused upon it. This was no jeweled facsimile like the other weapons, but a plain bow of wood and horn and gut, scarred and nicked by hard use, with a well-worn leather grip. Its gut string was eaten away by time; only a twisted scrap hung stiffly from one horn-sheathed tip. But the extraordinary length, the aura of grim power that still hung about the weapon, told Thoth more plainly than words that this was his grandfather's own bow, the one he had used to drive the Hyksos out, the one with which he had conquered and held an empire.

Thoth did not see the remaining treasures pass through the candlelight and on into the dark. His eyes followed the bow until it was swallowed by blackness and bobbing torches, and even then they remained fixed on the spot where it had vanished. For the first time in his life he had a vivid picture of his grandfather as a man and king, instead of a distant being in the sun. It was as if, when the bow was carried past him, the old king's *ka* had brushed his own.

He turned hastily back to the hollow. It was empty. The last of the torches had disappeared over the brow of the rise, and the chanting was already fading. He was alone.

A curious tingling started up all over him. There stood the door, yawning open before him, a black rectangle flanked by temple candles left to burn themselves out. For a moment it wavered

fore his eyes, growing enormous, shrinking to a pinpoint,
panding again into an ordinary door.

He pushed himself away from the rock and started toward it.
t the threshold he stopped to pluck one of the big candles from
e sand, then he stepped through the doorway into the tomb. Be-
re him were steps, leading downward. He stared at them a
oment, thinking, This cannot be happening. But it was hap-
ning. This was his hand holding the candle, his feet on the
itty floor. He need not think or feel, he had done all his reason-
g and his feeling yesterday. His father was waiting.

Slowly he began the descent.

He moved down step after step after step. The only sounds
ere the measured padding of his sandals and the tiny, silken
uttering of the candle flame. The poem began to repeat itself in
s head in time to his footsteps. *Death is in my eyes today as
hen a sick man becomes whole, as the walking abroad after
ness* . . . Death is in my eyes today, in my nostrils, in my
otsteps . . .

He found himself staring at a doorway that had appeared on
s left. He hesitated, then moved toward it. It was the entrance
a small, square room with hieroglyphs carved thick on the
alls, column after column of them. He extended his candle and
rases from the Declaration of Innocence flashed into clear re-
f: "I have committed no wrong against people. I have not done
il in the place of truth. I allowed no one to hunger. I caused no
e to weep . . ."

I caused no one to weep. Could any man say that?

He glanced hastily around the room, not wanting to think, not
anting to feel. Some of those golden treasures had dwelt here
the darkness, awaiting the pleasure of ghostly royalty. Now
ere remained only a dessicated food offering, a few splinters of
lded wood in one corner, spots of fresh tallow on the floor. His
ther was not here, there was nothing here. He returned to the
airs.

He found two more such rooms below, stripped bare, and an-
her below them. He leaned a moment in the doorway of the
ird, feeling dazed and suddenly tired. Lifting his eyes from the
anty rubbish on the floor, he caught a glimpse of painted figures
d held his candle forward. Instantly he was surrounded by viv-
ly familiar scenes—of harvesting, of hunting, of the slaughtering

of cattle and the pressing of wine—all painted in softly glowing colors, and in meticulous detail, so that the old King's *ka* might move among the fields and vineyards and lack nothing it had ever known. Thoth moved into the room and turned around slowly, gazing from wall to wall. He knew these scenes, too. He had left them only this morning, far, far above this stony room, in Egypt. Here, Egypt and life itself were only memories upon a wall.

Well? Is that not what you wanted? he asked himself. To leave them all behind? Do not think, do not think, you did that yesterday.

He wheeled and left the room, hurried down more stairs, and yet more, until his thighs ached and his arm protested the weight of the heavy candle. He leaned the stick back against his shoulder, stumbling because the light now fell behind him. It did not matter; haste possessed him and he wanted to see no more, he wanted only to reach the bottom of the steps. Then, abruptly, he was there.

He stood a moment, comprehending only gradually that he had arrived at last. The stairs had ended in a small vaulted chamber which at first glance seemed crowded with august, towering figures. It was an assemblage of the gods, painted all around the walls. They stood motionless, square-shouldered, with their tall fantastic headdresses rising from the heads of bird or beast or the pale-fleshed mummy that was Lord Osiris. Their impassive profiles were all turned toward the great scales painted on the central wall, in which the dead king's heart hung in balance against the Feather of Truth.

Thoth moved his awed gaze from it. On the floor before the scales, directly in front of him, stood a huge stone sarcophagus gaping and empty, with its ponderous lid leaning against it and its pall of sheer linen crumpled beside it on the floor. Away in the gloom of the farthest corner was a second sarcophagus—narrower, plainer, showing the chisel marks of hasty construction on the lid. It was still lashed to the framework on which it had been carried here seven years before. At one end of it, on the stone floor, a few small objects stood in a little group.

The rest of the room faded into oblivion. Thoth moved straight to the corner on his aching legs, thrust the stick of the candle into a bracket on the wall and sank down beside his father's bier

Even the soft sound of his own footfalls had ceased now; the almost inaudible sputtering of the candle only emphasized the profound, ringing silence. Thoth sat motionless, eyes fixed on the stone that still hid his father from him, waiting, longing, straining for the sense of contact, for the consciousness of a living presence that must surely come.

It did not come.

Unbelieving, he rose to his knees, pressed close to the sarcophagus, gripped it with outspread hands as if to dissolve its thickness by the power of desire alone. He sensed no response. He felt nothing; only the cold stone of the sarcophagus under his fingers.

He straightened and drew back a little, staring at the sarcophagus. It was his father's, it could be no other. But suppose it were empty? Suppose his father was not in there at all? In imagination he tore aside the heavy lid, broke frantically into the gold coffin within. . . .

Chilly moisture burst out on his forehead; he put his face in his hands and leaned forward on the stone. It was not empty, he knew that. If he could do what he had pictured—cast aside this lid it would take four men to move, somehow tear his way into the coffin—he would find his father's linen-swathed body lying inside. He would find a body, and that was all. Then he would stare at it, too, waiting vainly, thinking, Is he really in there? At last he would be impelled to tear through the linen wrappings too —through endless windings of cloth yellowing with age, stiff with dried ointments and bitumen, layered with amulets—perhaps even through the dessicated, unrecognizable substance that was now no more flesh than the mummy was a man. At the end, when he sat silent amid the destruction, would he have found what he sought?

No. He would have found nothing but a pathetic rubbish of rags and bones. His father was not here.

Then where is he? Thoth asked of the silence.

He lifted his head, looked quickly toward the small group of objects at the foot of the bier which constituted all his father's treasure. Quickly he picked up one after another. Then, slowly, he put them back. His father had cared nothing for these things; there was not one to which a flavor of personality yet clung, as it had clung to the old king's bow, not one that spoke of use and love. His father had worn these sandals, these jewels, but without

attachment, as he had worn his crown. He had worn his flesh th
same way, and loved it as little, and left it as empty of him whe
he departed. He was not here.

There was nobody here but his son.

Thoth sat motionless, staring at the flickering of candleligh
over the wall. Slowly the silence began to press in on him; he be
came eerily conscious of the room itself, as if it were making itse
known to him for the first time. Its air was chill and stale; it
odors were those of dried flowers, natron, and death, overlai
with a reek of hot tallow which did not seem to belong in th
place any more than the leaping candle flame or his living breat
which stirred it. The grainy texture of the stone grew roug
and irritating against his arms; he lifted them uneasily and dre
them away.

He was not wanted here. His very warmth was an intrusio
Yet here he was.

Now what will happen? he thought.

He got to his feet and stood gazing down at the sarcophagu
conscious of his intrusive, bated breathing, not wanting to loo
behind him. On the stone floor beside his foot was a dried brow
stain—the remains of the last libation the priests had poured fo
his father's *ka* before they left him in this tomb seven years age
Seven years ago—seven ages ago. He knew, now, what Ahmos
had wanted to tell him. What if Ahmose had succeeded? Thoth'
mind suddenly expanded to encompass the possibilities. I woul
be in Kadesh now, he thought. I would never have gone to liv
at the temple, never, never trusted a word she said— But Ahmos
had not been able to speak. The hand had come down, murdering
irrevocable, on his chest—the hand of god, of fate. Which god
Amon? All he could think of when he thought of Amon was
priest's hand pulling on a lead rope, priests' legs carrying a lurch
ing bark— In Babylon it was Marduk who ordered men's fate
But in Egypt?

Thoth forced himself to turn. Instantly he was faced with th
formidable assemblage on the wall. The room seemed filled wit
gods, with their awesome crowns, their beaked or snouted pro
files, their long, averted eyes. Osiris, stiff in his death-wrapping
sat upon his throne, the others were grouped about the scales—
Anubis the jackal, ibis-headed Thoth with his scribe's palle
beak-nosed Horus. The squatty, crocodile-mouthed Devoure

410

waited malevolently on his perch between the balance pans. In the pans, two small objects weighed delicately, tensely against each other—a heart, and a feather poised upon its tip.

The judgment of the human heart—it was on this, the figures were saying, that in the end each man's fate depends. Concept, idiom, gods, were pure Egyptian; Marduk had no place here. These were the beings into whose hands he had delivered himself. He stood dry-mouthed in the silence, waiting for some command.

Still nothing happened.

Gradually he realized that nothing was going to happen; there was nothing to give a command. Ma'at was a fairy tale, Lord Anu had refused to speak, the sarcophagus had cheated him. As for these gods upon the walls—

He stared at them, his eyes slowly widening.

—Upon the walls of a *tomb*. Why, they were dead. They were less than dead, they were only paint upon rock, the invented outlines of men's dread. He was utterly alone here.

His aloneness defined itself slowly and excruciatingly. He felt the emptiness of the valley above, the full weight and mass of the stone through which he had descended, the tininess of his figure standing here beyond the world in this lost and hidden place—utterly alone. In the end, then, a man could depend on nothing, had nothing except himself.

Thoth had the dizzy, sickening sensation of slipping into a void.

There was a sense of shock, as if he jolted awake. Suddenly, unreasoningly, everything in him began to struggle against that void. Anger flared, sprang up like a sheet of flame, ran like fire into every portion of his body. He did not know what was happening to him, he was aware only of mutiny against the dragging seduction of the void, and a sense of blind, inflexible resistance. He found himself shouting defiance that echoed eerily through the rocky chamber— *"No, no, no, no, never—"* he discovered that he was beating furiously against the painted figures. He stopped short, stared in surprise at his bruised hands and then fell to studying them in meticulous detail. Every aspect of their shape and size, down to the last callus on their palms and the last hair springing from their backs, was familiar to him. But never until this moment had he felt wonder at the heat that warmed them, the force that made them move, the mystery that made them live. It filled him now. His eye moved in awe along his right palm to the soft flesh of his wrist; a twisted blue vein pulsed there, visibly, mysteriously.

"Who is this?" he whispered.

Nothing, only someone named Thoth.

I am only someone named Mayet, but I am not—nothing.

I am not *nothing,* either, he thought. I am I.

He spread his hand, flexed it, clenched it into a fist and rubbed it with his other one. It was a mortal hand, made of flesh and bone—impermanent, destructible, soon enough to be dust—and it was all he had. So be it. Raising his head, he stared defiance at the painted scales upon the wall. Suddenly he stepped forward and struck them forcibly with his fist.

The light flared and flickered; in the instant before darkness he could have sworn he saw the balance pans jump crazily. He did hear the crash of metal, but it came from the wall above the sarcophagus—his candle had burned out and slipped through the bracket to the floor, engulfing the room in darkness.

A few moments before, he would have taken that as an omen, an answer, a command. He had another answer now; his hands had given it to him—his own two hands, the Hands of Fate. He started blindly toward the door.

He did not find it easily; he groped for some moments in the black, ringing silence before his fingers met air and his foot bumped against a step. He would have searched much longer without dismay; he would have searched tirelessly and determinedly forever. Stretching his hands to touch the wall on either side of the steps, he started up. It was a long, long way to the door at the top; but the farther he climbed the faster he went and the stronger he felt. His thighs ached with the exertion, but the strength he felt had nothing to do with them. It spread through his muscles, filled his chest, tingled in every nerve end.

Gradually the splotch of gray far above him paled, drew nearer, sharpened its edges, and defined itself as a doorway. A little light spilled in; he could see the last ten steps of the way. He bounded up them and burst out into the morning.

Fresh, living air flowed around him, washing away the chill of the tomb. Drunk with liberty, he ran across the hollow and up the gully, feeling that he had walked this way in chains an hour before, and now was free.

On the crest of a rocky eminence he stopped, panting from the limb, and looked around him. Dawn was upon the valley; in its ray light the hills and barren ravines seemed unconvincing, like things cut from paper. Overhead the stars were gone and the sky was translucent and colorless as water. He stood with his head tilted back, staring up at it, waiting skeptically for the sense of that powerful presence, Anu. To his surprise, it came, in a rich awareness of awesome majesty.

Are you still there, then? he thought. Are you god?

He got no answer, but he did not feel the oppression he had felt before, and he did not feel overwhelmed.

I do not know what you are, he told it. But you are no greater than the mystery in my wrist.

Nevertheless, he stood motionless for some time, staring upward, caught by some emotion he could not name. When he walked on thoughtfully, he felt akin to all the groping, uncertain mortals in the world—a world that was larger and more various than most of them knew. In Bayblon, in Kadesh and Punt and desert Libya and the Islands of the Sea, in all places and since the beginning of time, men had been pausing like that to lift questioning eyes to the sky. The trouble was that they misinterpreted what they saw; they feared what they felt, and ended by falling on their knees. They feared what they saw in their wrists, too, thinking only that it would not last.

And do I not fear something? he asked himself in astonishment. What happened to me, back there in the tomb, that everything seems changed?

He did not know what had happened. All he knew was that suddenly he had felt strength rising in him from nowhere, strength like a god's, when only a moment before he had been a *lillu*.

His thoughts paused, fled back to Babylon on a tide of recognition.

Nay, he thought. That is a tale men tell, a masque they enact every year. The strength I feel is not Marduk's, it is my own.

The knowledge did not diminish him. Instead it increased him until he felt tall as his own shadow stretching behind him on the slope. He was finished with depending on divinities, with trying to borrow their strength or crowd his life into their legends. But he was not finished with Anu; when he raised his eyes something he could not explain still held him. Are we separate? he

413

asked the Presence silently. If I were not here, if there were n
one here to raise his eyes to you, would you still be Majesty?

He pictured the slope empty of himself, empty of his shado
—sun-gilded and rocky like this, with a few sparse tufts of gras
a few scorpions rattling secretly among the pebbles and a kit
wheeling high and lonely—but without himself there to see. The
he pictured the green valley ahead of him empty too—the Nil
flooding and sinking unwatched, the rats scurrying mindless
for food in the shells of houses; and Babylon standing empty, n
women on the roofs, no priests in the temple, no man nor cart i
the streets, the market place deserted. He pictured the world an
its seas and its spreading plains, and trees growing unseen on it
mountains, all empty of mankind under the spreading sky—an
the picture was strange and powerful.

Aye, you would be there, he said to Anu. But you would nc
yet mean anything. You would be waiting—all your space an
power and mystery spread out above the scorpion and the rat-
waiting till _I_ came. You would be there, without me—but it is
who name you "Majesty."

A moment later the question formed, irresistible, inevitable
Then am I your creator, or are you mine?

He got no answer. Slowly he realized that he might never gc
one—that perhaps there was none. He stood a long time, absorb
ing this, accepting it.

"So be it," he whispered at last. "I will live without an answer.

Thoughtfully, but with a step that did not hesitate, he starte
down to Thebes.

7.

Five years passed over Egypt. Hatshepsut's power was absolut
her works were everywhere. Soon after the return of the ship
she had created a Garden of Punt on the grounds of Amon's ten
ple in Thebes. It was a re-creation of the land of the old tale, wit
the myrrh trees planted in terraces down to a new landing at th
river's edge, and Puntite leopards in their cages set here and ther
along walks graveled in crushed lapis-lazuli. A pavilion at the to
of this garden looked straight across to the bay in the wester
cliffs, where the queen's own temple, Djeser-Djeseru, grew slowl

414

nd beautifully, like a great flower unfolding. While the temple
workmen raised column after column to shine white against their
wn shadows, others were building a high causeway which would
weep from Djeser-Djeseru straight across desert and valley to
he river and the Puntite garden on the other side, linking the
wo temples of the god. Still other crews continued to restore
ne after another of the Hyksos-ruined temples up and down the
and.

In all this work, Senmut's hand and talents could plainly be
een. His blue-and-gold litter was a familiar sight in every city
of Egypt, as he went here and there, stretching the cord for new
works, overseeing repairs on old ones—and so was his big, angular frame and saturnine face. His jowls had become a little
heavier with advancing years and his waistline thicker, lending
him an air of dignity and seasoned maturity. He was altogether
an imposing figure, and his greatness was second only to Her
Majesty's, as she herself seemed eager to point out. In the courtyard of the Temple of Mut in Thebes, where he was building a
new pylon, she allowed him to set up a statue of himself which
et forth in clearest terms how the populace—and posterity—
were to regard him. It was an eye-catching statue, archaically
simple in design—a black granite figure of the great steward
seated on the ground, swathed in a cloak which enveloped
both his body and the child-figure of the princess Neferu-Re,
whom he clutched fast between his drawn-up knees. The simplicity of the design gave great prominence to the two heads,
Senmut's and his royal ward's, and left a vast amount of space
for the inscription, which needed it. It proclaimed to all who
could read:

*I was the greatest of the great in the whole land . . . I was one
with whose advice the Mistress of the Two Lands was satisfied, and
the heart of the Divine Consort was completely filled . . . I was one
whose steps were known in the palace, a real confidant of the ruler,
entering in love and coming forth in favor . . . one useful to the
King, faithful to the god, without blemish before the people . . .
there was nothing from the beginning of time which I did not know.*

Those who could read, did read, and nodded in awe. Those
who could not read studied the figure with its tenacious grip on
the princess—and did not need the words.

The people were content that it should be so, they were content with all their ruler did. If taxes were heavy, so were the harvest. Never had the inundations been so uniformly excellent. It was obvious the gods loved Hatshepsut; in the face of this, the rumor of foreign unrest which occasionally spread through the market places roused little interest. Let the barbarians mill about if they chose. Egypt had gone back to the old, peaceful ways of a thousand years ago, and turned her back on the rest of the world.

"*Aii*, what an awakening will come some day," Thoth said to Rekhmi-re one morning. They were standing in the Street of the Merchants, gazing thoughtfully at an empty stall. In the line of busy cluttered booths with their colorful festoons of merchandise, it gaped like a missing tooth.

"You think it portentous that the Sand-dweller did not come back this year?"

"I think it more than chance. Year after year, without fail, that old fellow has come to this same stall to sell his dyes and his donkey bells and wine—then suddenly he does not come. There is some reason. Well"—with an angry shrug Thoth turned from the stall and started back toward the river—"we'll get no news of Kadesh from him, that is certain. So much for our hopes." He shot a wry glance at his companion. "Our coarse garments, the stink of the streets—all for nothing, Rekhmi-re."

"His absence seemed not to alarm that cloth merchant you questioned."

"Nay, nay—nor any of the others! 'Aye, the Sand-dweller —doubtless misfortune overtook him—I always told him he should stay in a civilized land instead of journeying to those far off, wretched places . . . ' They do not even stop to wonder what might be happening in those far-off places that would force a man to change all his plans, abandon all his settled habits. They think only as Ma-ke-Re tells them to think, which is no farther than their noses."

The two threaded their way through the crowded streets to the dock, and boarded a waiting bark.

"Of course," Rekhmi-re said, "the old Sand-dweller might be dead."

"Aye, he might. All the same, I would give much to know what is going on in Kadesh at this moment."

416

He did not speak again; when they climbed the outer stair to his apartments he left Rekhmi-re to inform Amenu of their disappointment, and went at once to change his smudged and ragged garments. Later, when his slave Unas had gone, he joined his companions in the sitting room, still thoughtful.

"I must find some surer way of getting information," he told them. "I have been thinking. Suppose I sent a runner—"

"To *Kadesh?*" Rekhmi-re asked in astonishment.

"Nay, to Tharu in the Delta."

They considered this in silence a moment, then Rekhmi-re's heavy brows drew together. "But Tjesu—a palace runner—"

"Gods, I would not send a palace runner! Why not buy a slave —a natural gossip, all ears, all eyes, all wits, with the surface appearance of a good-natured fool."

Amenu was staring at him. "Tjesu, you are describing my old slave Nepri."

"Aye. I am." Thoth faced him. "Do you think you can buy him?"

"I can and will do anything you require, now and always."

"Then be off. See what you can do." As the door closed behind Amenu, Thoth added, "It may not work. If not, I will try something else—and something else—and something else! I must have news."

"Tjesu—I will go to Kadesh myself," Rekhmi-re said.

"Nay, nay, nay, that would be folly." Thoth took an impatient turn about the room. "It is those merchants that trouble me, Rekhmi-re—they and their fellows. They hear these rumors, too—and pay not the slightest heed to them. She reduces the bodyguard to a mere thousand men—and they are not alarmed. She adds an extra tax to what they already pay—and they rejoice that her building is winning the favor of the gods. They have forgotten that anything exists outside of Egypt and Hatshepsut!"

Rekhmi-re shrugged bitterly. "She is king. They believe all she tells them."

"Precisely. She is king. But what *makes* her king?"

"The crown."

Thoth did not answer, but he thought, Nay, it is more, much more than that.

His restless pacing slowed as he pondered his own question, long a familiar one to him. *This* question had an answer, he was sure of it—and he meant to find it.

If she is king, he thought, then who am I? What am I, that I am *not* king? What makes a king? Something my father did not have, though he wore the crown. Something I did not have, or the crown could not have been stolen from me. She has it. It was what calmed the people when she drove through the streets among them, in the days before the ships came . . . not something she did, but something she *is*. My grandfather, the Great Thutmose—he had it too; it is something that leaves no doubt in anybody's mind, that says, "Here is Pharaoh!" Something that lingers even in a decaying bow. . . . What is it? Inner certainty? Belief in the divinity of kings? Mere force of will? . . .

"Rekhmi-re," he said wryly at last, "I wish I knew more about my grandfather." He smiled at the puzzled look his friend turned on him, but did not explain. He never explained nowadays. "Leave me," he said presently. "I will summon you when Amenu comes back."

He walked into his study and stood looking at the clutter of papyrus rolls on the table. They were the Documents of the Kings, which he had brought here from the Royal Archives; he had lately been searching them, thinking that if he knew what thoughts other kings had had, he might have an answer to his question. However, he had found little of the old kings' thoughts; with only one exception they hid themselves behind official wordings and traditional attitudes, which revealed the Horus image but not the man within it.

The one exception illuminated this very secretiveness. Thoth selected a scroll and sat down to read again the instruction of Amenemhet, of the Twelfth dynasty, to his son.

"Hearken to that which I say to thee, that thou mayest be king of the earth, that thou mayest be ruler of the lands . . . Harden thyself against all subordinates. The people give heed to him who terrorizes them; approach them not alone. Fill not thy heart with a brother, know not a friend, nor make for thyself intimates . . . When thou sleepest, guard for thyself thine own heart, for a man has no people in the day of evil."

Bitter advice, Thoth mused. It had been learned from bitter experience; Amenemhet had ruled Egypt in a troubled time, protected it with strength and courage against enemies both without and within, and had been repaid by treachery from those he trusted.

"It was after the evening meal, night had come. Lying upon my couch, I relaxed; my heart began to follow slumber. Behold, weapons were flourished, council was held against me . . . I awoke to fight, utterly alone."

Kings are the loneliest . . . the old voice echoed in Thoth's ears. Perhaps, he reflected, the heart of the loneliness of kings was the king's secret knowledge that he was not divine—knowledge he could share with no one for fear of destroying those who depended on his divinity. At least it was the heart of his own loneliness . . . He turned back to the scroll.

"They who put on my fine linen looked upon me as a shadow," Amenemhet had written his son. "They who anointed themselves with my myrrh, defiled me."

Their next step had been to destroy him who had destroyed their faith by revealing himself as man, not god—because he had admitted them, as brothers, into his heart. "Behave like a king!" Rekhmi-re had said scornfully, almost five weary years ago. The next step would have been—

Thoth tossed the scroll to the table and leaned back in his chair, thinking what a terrible wreckage he had almost made of two who loved him. The danger was over; when he returned from the tomb he had found some instinct awake that had been asleep before, and since that day he had kept his thoughts, his doubts, his knowledge of his mortality locked tight in his own heart. Surely the new loneliness he had imposed on himself was part of what made a king, for his reward had been to see his friends heal, day by day, before his eyes. They were men whose *kas* had literally been restored, just as Egypt was restored in strength and hope with the rise of the Nile. They lived again because the god they had thought was dying lived.

Then is not the king truly a god, in spite of himself? Thoth mused in astonishment. I see myself as one thing, they see me as another—but their god-king image has a power over them that no man-king could ever have, for they literally live or die according to its existence. Then how can I say it does not live? How can I say those gods on the tomb wall are dead, as long as even one man believes in them? Horus, Amon, Marduk, all may be

dead to me, but alive in the minds of their believers. Even for m
Anu will not quite die.

He stood up and walked to the doors that opened onto his ba
cony, looking up at the sky and wondering if he would still fe
that sense of living majesty if he had seen *it* painted on a ton
wall. How could anyone depict that spreading vault? By a fe
stars? By a canopy on posts or the spangled belly of a cow?
would die at once, all its majesty would depart. Ah, there lay tl
death of the gods—in men attempting to express the inexpre
sible. You could paint a picture of the sky or of your wrist, b
you could not paint your awareness of the vast mystery they co
tained. You could paint men, but when you tried to paint lonel
questioning mankind . . .

A knock sounded suddenly on the sitting-room door. Tho
turned, his thoughts scattering. "Come."

The door opened to reveal a bowing chamberlain. "May Yo
Highness' *ka* rejoice. Her Majesty Ma-ke-Re desires to hon
Your Highess at the dedication of the new pylon of the Temp
of Mut tomorrow. Her Majesty graciously invites Your Hig
ness to make offering to the goddess, for the welfare of Her Ma
esty and Egypt—"

"That will do," Thoth cut him off. "I understand your me
sage. You may go."

"Your Highness wishes to make no reply?" inquired the cha
berlain with raised eyebrow.

"My Highness' absence tomorrow will be reply enough
Thoth told him curtly.

Alone again, he returned to his study and dropped down befo
the scrolls. Surely these years were the slowest, the weariest, th
he would ever know.

For Hatshepsut, the same period was one long, exhilarati
festival. There was not a soul on earth who could contest or co
trol any of her actions, or say nay to any of her desires.

It was always meant to be so, she told herself. In truth, I ha
been king for years. It was only the short-sightedness of tho
around me that prevented the fact from being recognized lo
ago.

In order that there should be no further confusion on tl
point, she issued a proclamation specifically explaining it, a

sealed the matter by commanding that the years of her reign be counted from the day of Nenni's death, as Amon had intended. Thus, it was actually in the seventh year of her reign, instead of the first, that she had stretched the cord for her temple; the eighth that the ships had set out for Punt, the ninth that they had returned with their precious cargo. She was delighted with this new scheme of reckoning; it banished all ambiguity from the past. As for the future, its possibilities were unlimited. Beyond every bright horizon lay a brighter one.

There were only three small clouds in this radiant sky. These were the annoying rumors of trouble beyond the border, a tiny persistent notion that some change had taken place in Thoth, and the continued ill-health of the Divine Consort Neferu-Re.

Admittedly, this last was distressing; it had been distressing Hatshepsut all the years of Nefer's life. But strangely enough, the more clear-cut the situation became, the easier it grew to bear. Nefer was a confirmed invalid; very well. When one faced the fact it lost much of its power to alarm—especially when one was determined not to be alarmed by it.

"After all, she has been frail from birth," Hatshepsut told Senmut one day as they emerged from a quarter hour at Nefer's bedside. "I've no doubt she will outlive us all—I could name a score or more of such frail ones who outlived the strongest men."

Senmut murmured agreeably, if somewhat noncommittally, and Hatshepsut's mind moved on, with relief, to other matters. The truth was that she found the odors of the sickroom offensive and Nefer's complaints tedious. Privately she had begun to wonder if Nefer's affliction were not simply Amon's way of nullifying Thoth's presumptuous marriage to a Daughter of the Sun —his way of saying, "Thus far the insolent Pretender may go— but no farther." For it was clear the Great Royal Wife could never bear a child; Thoth's seed would never inherit the throne of Re. What else could that be but Amon's plan? Just who the Successor would be, and where he would come from, seldom crossed Hatshepsut's mind.

What did cross her mind, far oftener than she wished, was the curious notion that Thoth was somehow different since the ships had returned. Time and again she brushed the idea aside or explained it away, only to have it come back, as tiresomely persistent as a mosquito, though she told herself it was of no more importance. She did not even know what gave her the notion;

she seldom saw Thoth and did not want to see him. But when she chanced to, she found something different in his face, his stance.

"Of course it is not important, it is merely an annoyance," she said to Senmut one evening in the little garden off the King's Apartments. "But I do not like the way he looks at me!"

"Oh, in Amon's name!" Senmut laughed, but he moved impatiently on the stone bench. "For years you have been complaining about the way he looked at you! Have you ever been harmed? Has any evil ever occurred—"

"That is not what I mean." Hatshepsut sat down beside him. "Thoth has changed some way."

"My lotus, naturally he has changed. Growing up changes a man. So does ruin."

"That is not what I mean."

Senmut leaned forward into the moonlight, dangling his empty goblet and studying her with a faint, tolerant smile. "Very well, my beloved. Then tell me what you do mean."

"Oh, nothing, nothing!" she said in exasperation. "I cannot explain. I will not think of him any more."

However, it was not until the Year 13 of her reign, five years after the return of the ships from Punt, that she discovered the way to banish him from her mind.

That day—a cool and breezy one in mid-autumn—two runners had arrived, almost in the same hour, and Hapuseneb had considered their messages important enough to send on to her at the desert temple, where she was inspecting the progress of her causeway.

On her way back to the palace, as she sat gazing out through the swaying curtains of her litter, tapping the folded messages against her teeth, she could not help reflecting how often it happened that one's moments of triumph were tempered by something irritating. Everything she had seen this morning proclaimed her glory—the temple, the land shining with inundation, and the causeway, which was impressive already and would be superb when it was lined on either side with the great sphinx-form statues of herself that were nearing completion in a hundred stoneworkers' shops. Besides, one of those runners had brought news that the reopened mines in Sinai had begun to yield gold by the grain-measure.

But the other runner had come too.

Irritably Hatshepsut spread the second message out and looked at it again. Phrases sprang at her, each one an affront, though they were couched in the most tactful and flattering language old Tuaa, commander of the frontier post of Tharu, could invent.

. . . that cursed King of Kadesh, fit only to be Your Majesty's footstool . . . stirring the city-kingdoms to revolt . . . behold, from wretched Yeraza to the Marshes of the Earth . . . all the allied countries of Zahi . . . it is rumored even Mitanni far to the east . . . insolent ones, unheedful of Your Majesty's glory . . . they should be crushed like crawling things beneath Your Majesty's sandal . . .

She rolled the note again and stuffed it angrily into her sash. For a year or more Tuaa had been sending her such tiresome messages. What did she care about the king of Kadesh and his petty neighbors? Remote barbarians, dancing about in ridiculous rages, let them dance! Tuaa should know better than to annoy her with such trivia.

I shall replace him, she decided. Perhaps with a priest, or a judge—military men are always alarmists.

Her litter was set down in the Great Court of the palace and she stepped out, to find herself suddenly face to face with Thoth.

"I wish to speak to you," he said.

It was so unexpected that for a moment she could not collect her wits. How could he be standing here, so close to her? Where was the Circle? She took a hasty step backward, then was furious with herself for doing so as she realized that the Circle was around her, just as usual—he had simply broken through it. The attendants were standing horror-stricken, obviously torn between their duty to shield her and their fear of the cobra on his brow.

"I wish to speak to you," Thoth repeated, a little more loudly.

"I cannot imagine what you would have to say to me."

"I hope to make that clear."

Her mind sought frantically for a way out, and found none. "As you wish," she said.

She felt the greatest reluctance to dismiss the Circle at the door of the yellow-walled sitting room; as she walked across the room with Thoth's footsteps sounding behind her, she was so near to

423

panic that her very fright procuded an abrupt reversal of her feelings.

What am I afraid of? she thought angrily. I am Ma-ke-Re, I am the beloved daughter of the god, I am king of all the earth.

"You may speak to My Majesty," she said coldly.

For a moment he was silent, obviously struggling to master his resentment of her tone.

"Well?" she said.

"Kadesh is in revolt," he blurted.

"So that is it! Surely you did not suppose My Majesty to be unaware of this?"

"On the contrary," he retorted. "I was sure you had been told of it. I was equally sure you would have not the slightest comprehension of its significance."

"It has no significance for Egypt."

She was growing calmer and more confident, and he more tense. She could see distinctly the gleam of sweat under his eyes and on his upper lip.

"It has no significance for Egypt," he echoed. "Would you say, then, that a fire in the garden has no significance for the house? Would you say the mace descending on an unarmed man has no significance for his skull?"

"You are being wildly fanciful. No harm could come to Egypt from that tiny, wretched village of barbarians. The garrison will put down the trouble, and banish the leaders."

"There is no garrison!" he shouted. "It is rubble and corpses, can you not understand that? There is not one Egyptian alive in the kingdom of Kadesh. All were murdered months ago! Where is the tribute from Kadesh? Have you received so much as one bolt of cloth, one jar of oil?"

"What need have I, with all the riches of Punt at my—"

"Punt! May the Destroyer swallow it! We are speaking of Kadesh! There is no tribute because the tribute has ceased. We have lost Kadesh, but that is only the beginning of it, we shall lose everything—all the kingdoms my grandfather conquered, and those he did not. I tell you, the Hyksos he scattered all those years ago are uniting again. Act now and we may save something—but if you wait, I warn you, if you wait—" Thoth broke off. He was shaking with anger.

Hatshepsut stared at him coldly. How ordinary-looking he is,

424

she thought. Common as a peasant, with his harsh voice and his face flushed with all this shouting at me. How could I ever have thought he resembled my lord father?

His eyes had lost their glare and become impenetrable, as if he had pulled a curtain over his emotions. He walked across the room and stood stiffly, with his back to her.

"I did not come to quarrel," he said in an equally stiff voice. "I came to offer my services. You cannot train an army and lead it to Syria. I can. Turn these enemies over to me and I will restore order in the Empire. That is what I came to say."

"Very well, you have said it. Now leave my presence."

The back of his neck flushed darkly, but his voice remained quiet. "You reject my offer, then?"

"Offer? You would have me put aside my great works that I make for Amon, you ask me to give you huge sums for weapons and chariots, to take thousands of men away from my holy work of buildings—all so that you may brandish a spear and shout commands. Well, you ask too much. I see quite clearly—"

"You see nothing!" he said, swinging about to face her. "Nothing at all—save what you wish to see."

"I see that all this talk of danger is so much nonsense! Let the barbarians slay each other, it is none of Egypt's affair."

"Gods, you believe that." He gazed at her a moment in silence. "As Marduk lives," he said violently, "never have I seen such powers of self-delusion!"

"Marduk!" She choked with outrage. "Marduk does not live!"

"In that you may be deluded too," he said shortly.

It was too much. She found herself beating her fists against her sides, shaking in every limb, backing away from him in horror and hatred. "Silence! Silence! Leave me!" She collided with a chair and clutched it to save herself from falling. "Leave me!" she screamed. When he did not move but merely gazed at her with that strange look of preoccupation growing on his face, she leaned forward over the chair's back in a transport of fury. "Leave me or I will call the guards to drag you out!"

"Nay, you will not do that. It would spoil your cherished fiction of how beneficently you treat me."

She stared at him, suddenly stricken by the fear that the guards might have heard her already—heard her screaming at him. Suppose they were running, this instant, toward the door. I can

425

dismiss them again, she thought swiftly. Tell them they were mistaken, that I was laughing . . .

"However," Thoth said, "there is obviously no reason for my staying longer."

He walked across the room and out the door.

After a few moments she moved unsteadily around the chair and sank into it. One thought was paramount in her mind: she must prevent this ever happening again. Thoth must *not* be free to walk into her presence, he must be restrained, restricted, thrown into chains if necessary! Nay, not chains of course, not actually restricted physically. That would look as if . . .

It would spoil your cherished fiction of how beneficently you treat me.

Nonsense, she thought angrily. But at least Senmut must always be by my side to cope with him. He should have been by my side today, he should be here this minute!

Springing from her chair, she walked to the door, jerked it open, and snapped at a startled chamberlain, "Fetch Count Senmut from the new temple. At once!"

Slamming the door, she turned back into the room. The first thing her eye encountered was the footstool by her father's scarlet chair. It was made of Kadesh cedar, and all around its base were carved the groveling figures of conquered barbarians, upon which his feet had symbolically rested. The very sight of them revived her earlier exasperation with Tuaa, with Thoth, with rumors she knew were forever circulating in the market places, perhaps disturbing her happy subjects. She turned away, then suddenly turned back and looked at the footstool again. As she stared at it, all the tight, tense feeling in her relaxed and she was conscious of a buoyant rush of triumph.

Why, of course, she thought. That is the way to deal with insolent pretenders—show forth my greatness.

When Senmut's tap sounded at the door some time later, she straightened eagerly.

"Senmut! Come here quickly and listen to me. I have new orders for you concerning the statues on the causeway. Amon has spoken to me on the matter of these rumors from the wretched lands of the east . . ."

The queen's new orders delayed the completion of the huge

426

stone sphinxes—and therefore, the causeway—for many weeks, though every sculptor in Thebes was put to work on the added decorations. At last the huge stone figures and their massive bases moved one by one toward the causeway on sledge and rollers, preceded by a fan of ropes and a hundred straining, antlike men. A few days after Thoth's twenty-second birthday, the last one was mounted on its base.

All Thebes turned out to marvel at the broad, smooth road, raised high above the inundation, sweeping straight from the river to the temple far back against the cliffs—and at the great sphinxes that lined its full length on either side. Their bodies were crouching lions, and each huge head was the smiling likeness of the queen. Beneath the sphinxes, fresh-carved on the high stone bases, was a frieze of groveling barbarians.

All could see for themselves now—there, in impressive repetition, rose Ma-ke-Re, greatest of Pharaohs, crouching in unassailable strength over all the countries of the earth. What did rumors matter? There was her powerful spell of truth, graven in unchanging stone before their eyes—and now that it was graven there, it was so.

Thoth, sitting in his carrying-chair at the edge of the causeway, stared grimly at the nearest sphinx.

Gods! he thought. So that is her answer to Kadesh—and to me.

A few weeks after the completion of the causeway, Her Majesty recalled old Tuaa and sent a noble-born young priest to replace him at the garrison of Tharu. She also disbanded the troops of the bodyguard, keeping only enough foot-soldiers at the barracks to serve as personal escort. She merely smiled at Nehsi's uneasiness. In the New Egypt, soldiers were not important—and outside of Egypt, nothing even existed.

8.

Senmut bade farewell to his last guest and stood a few moments on his columned porch, watching the torches of the departing litters wink and flutter down the palm-lined drive to the Avenue of Mut. It had been a highly successful evening—at least from

Senmut's point of view. He grinned into the darkness, as he ha
been grinning inwardly all evening at the spectacle of thirty no
blemen—the cream of Egypt's aristocracy, the scions of her proud
est and most ancient lineages—gathering to celebrate the birth o
a grubby urchin fifty years ago.

My dear old mother should have been here, he thought. Hov
proud she would have been of her boy! And how she woul
have swilled my wine!

He turned back into the house, reflecting that even she coul
scarcely have swilled more of it than his distinguished guests. I
their devotion to wine, as in their blood-lines, Egypt's nobleme
acknowledged no peer; and the changes it wrought in their dis
creet daytime personalities were interesting in the extreme. Ol
Thutiy had wept sentimentally into his cup about the days of hi
boyhood. Nehsi had grown progressively more somber as th
evening wore on and Hapuseneb more acidly cynical. Strange
Senmut told himself blandly—Nehsi the incorruptible, Hapuse
neb the repeatedly corrupted, had ended by gazing at each othe
as if at mirrored reflections of themselves. And Ineny—

Senmut smiled, not without a certain grudging admiration
Ineny had borne up rather well, considering that the often-en
larged model of the temple—altered now to include the northeas
colonnade, the great forecourt with its ramp, and part of th
sphinx-lined causeway—had stood on a prominently place
table at one end of the room throughout the evening. Ineny's fac
had been a study in control when he looked at it, but he had ten
dered the same elegantly worded praise as the others, and hi
great poet's eyes, still limpid in his wrinkled face, looked no mor
mournful than they always did. Well, Ineny had had his day o
building under the first Thutmose; he would have to be satisfie
with the few pylons and restorations that had come his wa
since. When a bright star rose, Senmut reflected complacently
the lesser ones must decline. There was nothing like an evenin
spent drinking the health of a man you hated, for driving suc
facts home.

He crossed the torchlit entry hall and entered his spaciou
main room, noticing as he did so that its earlier festive air ha
worn thin along with the self-possession of his guests. The flow
ers that twined the columns were bedraggled, the chairs wer
in disorder and every cushion awry; somebody had overturne

428

a cup of wine in a corner. A few servants moved about dispirit- edly, watching the juggler and the yawning dancing girls gather their cloaks and depart. After the fresh night air outside, the place smelled overpoweringly of flowers, heavily scented oint- ments, and wine.

Senmut walked to the long refreshment table and filled a goblet from one of the sweating wine jugs. Beckoning his chief man- servant with a jerk of his head, he made a gesture that included the whole disordered room.

"Clear all this away, I want to see no sign of it in the morn- ing. And carry the temple model into my study with your own hand."

He stepped out of the heat of the torchlit room into the cool quiet of the garden which opened off it. His brother Senmen was sitting on the bench beside the pool in an attitude of exhaustion visible even in the starlight. Senmut crossed the garden and stood looking down at him with amusement.

"Well, brother—I am fifty," he remarked cheerfully. "A sol- emn occasion, this birthday. A landmark in a man's life."

"You do not know if you are fifty, any more than I do," Sen- men grunted. "You are ignorant as an alley cat of the date of your birth."

"All the better. I was able to choose one in fine weather, at a beneficent time of year. Now poor Thutiy was born in the month of the winds."

"I think you were too. Aye, I know it. I remember the grit in my mouth when I first looked at you." Senmen glanced at him balefully. "I've no doubt Their Excellencies tasted some of it tonight."

Laughing silently, Senmut sat down beside him and began to sip his wine. "Fifty years," he mused. "Fifty years and still no noose. You turned out to be a poor prophet, didn't you, brother?"

"What ailed Nehsi?" asked Senmen bluntly.

Senmut looked at him and then back at the pool. "The same thing that has ailed him since Ma-ke-Re put on the crown," he answered. "Nehsi is haunted by a document."

Senmen's eyes narrowed in surprise; he leaned forward, drop- ping his voice. "But he condoned her action—he assisted in it."

"That is what haunts him." Senmut finished his wine and tossed the goblet to the grass.

"Bah, I've seen no sign of it. He captained her ships to Punt, he has served her well and faithfully for years."

"My dear brother, Nehsi has served but one Pharaoh in all his life—that is the first Thutmose. He thought he had found her father again in her, and beside that discovery no document mattered. Now comes this affair of foreign unrest and she shows him with every action that she is not her father at all, but someone quite different. So of course, the spectre rises." Senmut shrugged. "If men will lie to themselves . . ."

"And you can shrug about this?"

"Why not?" Senmut smiled at him. "Nehsi is no longer vizier."

"But think of his influence over the other Kinsmen! What if he decided to act? For example—to sponsor the Pretender's claims?"

"He will not do that."

"Why would he not?"

"Because he is not the fool you are, my cherished brother. He knows, if you do not, that power exerts the only real influence in this world—and *I* have that. While Her Royal Highness Neferu-Re lives, Nehsi is harmless as a week-old babe." Senmut grinned at his brother. "Be at ease, you are safe. Life is a birthday feast! It is almost as if the Pretender did not exist."

"It is, is it?" retorted the other. "What if Her Royal Highness were to die?"

Senmut shrugged again. "I said 'almost.'"

Senmen leaned back and contemplated him bitterly. "The blade's edge, as usual. You love it for a footpath."

"Not particularly—but I've grown skilled at balancing, since I had to. Is that a wine jug on the table yonder? Fetch it to me."

Senmen got up, grumbling. "You've had more than enough already."

"Aye, and I never show it, do I? It is another of my power over these sensitive nobles. I never weep about my boyhood or count my sins."

"That would be too great a task even for you!" Senmen returned with a jug still wreathed with wilting flowers, which he tossed into Senmut's lap. As the latter retrieved his goblet and filled it, Senmen said uneasily, "What do *you* think of these foreign troubles?"

"I do not think of them at all. As Nehsi has discovered, Ma

430

ke-Re is not her father. The border garrisons will simply have to do as well as they can when the time comes."

"Then you think it certain? Invaders will really be in Egypt?"

"My dear Senmen, not for years yet. They are still fighting each other. With any luck, we will be in our tombs by then. . . . Come, you depress me. I am going to bed."

Senmen followed him gloomily across the garden. "Speaking of your tomb, that sculptor was here today. The basalt statue is ready. He asks whether you want it in the chapel or below, in the burial chamber."

"Let him put it where he likes. It doesn't matter."

"Doesn't matter?" Senmen echoed. "Who's to care if you do not? It is your tomb."

Senmut stopped and faced him. "That tomb is for the public eye. Do you think I mean to lie where the Pretender could get at me? My eternity would last five years at most. Nay, I've another place—one he'll never find."

"Then"—Senmen looked at him, stupefied—"you wish to leave the first tomb unfinished?"

"Nay, let them finish it. But let him find it empty, later."

"Where is the second one?" Senmen whispered.

Senmut smiled. "In a place you would never think to look, my cherished brother. Nor do I intend to tell you."

"I see," Senmen said angrily. "And may I ask how you intend to get there, if no one knows where it is?"

"Someone will know, but not you. I have been grit in your mouth too long—some day it would unseal your lips."

He had started for his bedchamber again, with Senmen staring bitterly after him, when a subdued commotion at the other end of the garden made them both turn. A palace runner, accompanied by the manservant with a torch, had burst out of the door of the banquet hall and was hurrying toward them.

Senmut felt a cold inner breeze dispel the comforting warmth of the wine. In the moment he stood waiting, every detail of the runner's size and shape and gait and bearing, from his close-fitting cap to the lumbering way he swung his arms, was indelibly inscribed upon Senmut's memory. He felt he had known the man forever. He had pictured his coming many times—yet he had never pictured it quite like this, in the middle of the night, in his own peaceful garden, no warning or fanfare of any kind, merely four men standing in the torchlight and the runner handing a note. . . .

He unrolled it with fingers suddenly grown stiff and clumsy. It was too soon. Much too soon. He had always pictured it far in the future, on some reassuringly distant day. . . . *Come in haste, Nefer is very ill.*

It was dawn when Senmut stepped wearily out of the palace doors and walked across the columned porch to signal for his chariot to be brought. Behind him the ritual wailing echoed dimly from the corridors, proclaiming a royal death. Before him in the Great Court, which looked bleak and cheerless in the early light, Ineny and Thutiy were already climbing into their litters, their faces gray with exhaustion. Senmut stifled a yawn as he watched their bearers start across the dusty pavement, and controlled an almost irresistible desire to lean against the column beside him. He was stiff with fatigue, and with the aftermath of the wine he had drunk last night; all its glow had faded hours ago, leaving him only a desert of a mouth, a splitting head, and a face that felt as if mud had coated it and dried into a rigid mask. He winced as the tall copper gates swung open for the two Kinsmen's litters, reflecting a bright beam of sunlight into his eyes.

The royal physician came out of the palace with two of his magicians, and hurried nervously down the broad steps of the porch and into the courtyard. Senmut turned his back. He had seen enough of that man tonight—he knew his gestures and his bow-legs and that amulet on his wrist as well as he knew his own face in the mirror. There had been nothing else to watch, unless one wanted to look again at the still figure on the bed, or Hatshepsut's carven profile in the shadows, or the gray smoke curling upward from the censers, or the humped forms of the other Kinsmen sitting about the obscurity of the room's edge, motionless and silent. There had been nothing to do but force one's eyelids to stay open, endure the headache and the thick smells of myrrh and burning oil and approaching death, and wait for the final moment, which had come no sooner and no later for the physician's exertions.

The moment had been long arriving. In dying, as in living, Nefer had been tediously stubborn.

The palace doors opened again, emitting a swelling sound

wailing. Senmut found Nehsi beside him when the sound receded again, as if he had been washed out and deposited there by a wave of lamentation. They bowed to each other mechanically, but said nothing. Nehsi signaled for his litter. His eyebrows were quite grizzled, Senmut observed; they showed queerly against his black skin, like streaks of ash on ebony. In the merciless morning light he looked older than Senmut had ever seen him.

Well, he is old, reflected Senmut as he walked down the steps to his chariot, which had at last arrived. He is much older than I, and I am fifty, or somewhere near it—and by the gods, fifty is old too.

On a morning like this, needing wine the way he did and faced with two spiteful stallions to bully through the streets, he felt it impossible that anyone could be young.

He drove out of the palace grounds, cursing the horses under his breath, almost ready to admit that Senmen had been right about them. Thinking of Senmen reminded him of his new tomb. Instantly he knew that the sight of it would do more for him than the strongest wine. He turned west through the City of the Dead and followed the desert road to Djeser-Djeseru.

It was too early for workmen to be about; the great temple stood deserted in the morning sun. That was as he wanted it. He tied his stallions to a stone-hauling sledge that stood near the causeway and proceeded on foot along the uneven ground below the first great terrace toward the now-unused quarry near its northeast corner, where the shale for the causeway's embankment had been dug. Before scrambling down into the quarry he paused to glance cautiously around, and found his gaze lingering on one of the huge sculptured heads of Hatshepsut, whose serenely smiling countenance was repeated on every sphinx that lined the causeway.

In spite of himself a little warmth glowed through the chill of his depression as he studied her features. She had been magnificent—as always. Not by one word or glance had she conceded that anything was different, in Egypt or the palace, now that Nefer no longer lived. Senmut felt it likely that she had ceased to regard Nefer as a bolster for her kingship. And why should she not? He had never yet known a power in heaven or earth that could wrest from her a thing she really wanted.

The moment he took his eyes from her sculptured features

the little glow departed, and instead of the proud temple and causeway he seemed to see his own banquet room, disordered with the aftermath of the feast, the flowers wilted, the goblet holding only the dregs of wine.

He started down into the quarry. Three minutes later he stood before a carefully haphazard pile of boulders stacked near the quarry wall at its far west end. Reassurance stole through him as he looked at it. No one would dream a tomb was there; no one—except himself—would have dared to put a tomb there.

Stepping behind the boulders, he walked into the dark opening they concealed, picked up a torch from a heap lying amidst the rubble, and lighted it at a small wick burning in a bowl of oil. The torch's brighter flame illumined a long flight of steps leading down. Stumbling on the stone-chips underfoot, he descended. As the glow of daylight at the entrance dimmed and receded behind him, he felt the strain of the morning ease, and with every step that led him farther into dark security, his satisfaction deepened. At the first room that opened at the left of the stairs he paused, flashed his torch into it for a brief inspection, then went on. It was still rough and unfinished; he had not yet decided what decoration he wanted there. A few steps more, and he stopped with a sigh of pleasure, and thrust his torch into a bracket. This second room was his pride and his delight—it carried the spirit of his birthday party to its highest degree; it was the ultimate snap of his fingers under the nose of a pompous world.

Hands on hips, he pivoted slowly, savoring each detail. The sculptor had nearly finished; already three walls were minutely carved with vertical columns of hieroglyphs. He meant to lack no spell or magic charm needed for entrance into the Heavenly Fields, when he laid his urchin's bones here. The location of the tomb itself was as good as a passport to eternal bliss—he stood this moment beneath the northeast corner of the temple wall; his actual burial chamber would lie underneath the forecourt, inside the sacred area itself. He had never been a man to set limits on ambition; he saw no reason why Hatshepsut's favor should not provide him a princedom in the next world as well as this.

There, as here, he would make no bones about who he was: part of the stela carved on the wall opposite the door showed him with his brothers and his long-divorced wife Nofret-Hor, another part in pious converse with his parents, who were blatantly

434

labeled "The Honorable Remose, the lady Hat-nufer." On the ceiling above—Senmut threw back his head to relish the glory of his impudence—on the ceiling was an exact copy of the star-map in Hatshepsut's sleeping alcove, mute proclamation of his frequent presence in her couch. To drive the point home, down the ceiling's middle from wall to wall ran a bold inscription: *Long live the Horus, Mighty of Souls, Favorite of the Two Goddesses, Divine of Diadems, king of Upper and Lower Egypt Ma-ke-Re, Beloved of Amon, and the Chancelor, the steward of Amon Senmut, begotten by Remose and born of Hat-nufer*—linking his name with hers in brashest intimacy.

Oh, he loved this room; he was gloriously satisfied with his Precious Habitation. Now if he could only be positive he would really lie here . . .

He found a bit of crayon among the stone-chips and scrawled the date beside the last completed hieroglyph on the wall; it would keep his sculptor hurrying to know that he had been here. He retrieved his torch, shone it briefly down the unfinished flight of stairs that would soon lead to two more chambers, then started up.

Not for the first time, he was cursing Nofret-Hor for not giving him a son. A son would make sure his father lay where he wished to lie; it was a son's duty before the gods. But a brother . . . Senmut would have felt easier if he could have avoided the necessity for placing trust in any of his brothers. After considerable thought, he had chosen Amenemhet, who was still a priest on the bark of Amon, a pale, sanctimonious sort who Senmut felt sure would never neglect his duty if by performing it he could get his hands on a pile of gold. Senmut had seen to it he would do just that—*after* the duty was performed.

Aye, Ameni will follow orders, he told himself as he stepped out of the tomb. Nothing could be more trustworthy than his greed.

But what if Ameni were prevented? There should be some way in which a man could outwit everyone, forestall every possible revenge. . . .

Passing his stallions by, Senmut walked up the ramp from the causeway and stood alone in the great forecourt, gazing at his temple. The brilliant sunlight sent arrows of pain into his aching head, but they could not distort the beauty and dignity of what he had created. He stood drinking it in, remembering the parts he could not see directly—the chapels of Anubis and Hathor, the central Holy-of-Holies driven deep into the rock of the cliff's face, the score of little votive shrines opening off the columned court before it. He knew it all as a mother knows her child, and loved it better. A man who could build such things, he told himself, should have a place reserved for him on Osiris' footstool, and not have to wonder where he would lie. The temple itself should admit him to the company of kings and gods. The temple itself. . . .

The temple itself. His mind was suddenly filled with those many little shrines, scarcely larger than closets, which opened off every court and chapel. The next moment his plan was formed —a plan so outrageously bold that it dazzled even Senmut for an instant. Still, why not? The way those little shrines were arranged was perfect. No one would ever know—except one sculptor, and he could be disposed of when the work was done.

The more Senmut thought, the less he could find wrong with his plan. It was entirely feasible. It was brilliant.

When he turned and walked with springy step down the ramp to his chariot, his depression had vanished. He was remembering, with astonishment, the day of the temple dedication, when he thought he had reached the pinnacle of his ambition.

9.

The basketmaker burst into a cackle of laughter, slapping his thigh and delightedly catching the eye of the potter in the next stall. The young newcomer was really very clever, he reflected as he turned back to study the stocky, clean-muscled figure lounging against the corner of his stall talking to Ranofer, the old physician. An odd young fellow—the basketmaker couldn't quite make him out. Been ambling about the streets half the morning talking to this one and that one—seemed to have nothing to do. It wasn't just laziness, though. Nothing lazy about those eyes of his, and he had shoulders fit for a dockhand. The basketmaker ruminated a moment and decided the young man could not be a dockhand. Too quick-witted. Perhaps a scribe, though he carried no pallet— What had he said his name was? Thoth. From some

436

where up the river. Maybe only student to a scribe—but he seemed too old for that. How old was he?

Following the direction of the young man's glance, the basket-maker grinned and broke into the conversation. "Aye, she's pretty one, the baker's daughter! Looking your way, too— What, not interested—at your age? Why, you can't be more than eight-and-twenty." The basketmaker glowed with satisfaction at his own cleverness.

"Four-and-twenty," the young man said.

"Oh. You look a bit older."

"No doubt I do," the other said with a peculiar smile.

The basketmaker cleared his throat carelessly. "Your wife must rival Hathor herself, if you've no eyes for the baker's maid. I presume you are married?"

"Aye."

"Ah, and two or three young ones, I suppose."

"Nay, none."

"How, now! What's this?" said the old physician, Ranofer, as the basketmaker stared in surprise. "A young, vigorous man like you—and no children?" He leaned closer to the young man, lowering his voice. "Your wife is barren? My friend, be not troubled. I know a powerful remedy, a spell written on papyrus and dissolved in a bit of wine—"

"She is not barren!" the young man said. The quick anger in his eyes gave way at once to a more tolerant expression. "The truth is, my wife was a child when we wed. She is nineteen now —but I wasted much time, thinking of her as still a child." His glance moved across the street, and while the basketmaker was still trying to phrase another question he said suddenly, "Look you, at that beggar yonder. Are those not soldiers' sandals he is wearing?"

The basketmaker straightened uncomfortably and reached for his reeds. "Aye—that is young Up-wet. He was once of the Beautiful God's bodyguard, I believe."

"And now a tatterdemalion," the young man mused. "One almost forgets how it was, to have the barracks full, and soldiers clad in something besides rags."

There was an uneasy silence.

"Well," old Ranofer said briskly, "I suppose I must be off. No time to stand and gossip all day—"

"Stay, Old One," called the potter from the next stall. "Yonder comes your kinsman, the weaver."

"Ahhh!" breathed the physician, turning to peer anxiously in the direction the potter pointed. "Now we shall find out."

He hurried into the street and intercepted a middle-aged man with a dejected face and sagging belly, who was threading his way among the crowd with a bundle slung over his shoulder.

"That is Minemhab, the weaver," the basketmaker explained in answer to the young man's inquiring glance. "He has journeyed to Hermonthis, to try to collect a debt from the great lord Kautef."

"From the look of him, he had no success," Thoth remarked.

"Nay, I knew it. Poor fellow! Come, let us hear what he says."

A group had already gathered about the weaver, who had dropped his bundle at his feet and was talking sadly to Ranofer.

". . . knew it was little use," he was saying. "But my wife insisted I could be no poorer for trying. Well, I am poorer. Two deben for my passage, and now I have lost five days from my weaving while I waited to see the great one—"

"He would not see you?" the potter asked.

"Not he. His steward would not let me inside the gates. . . Five bolts of fine linen—lost—I've not seen a copper for it these seven months."

The young man had been listening intently; now he spoke. "Why do you not take your grievance to the Vizier's Courts?"

"The Courts!" The basketmaker turned to stare at him, as did everyone else.

"My friend, I am a poor man," the weaver told him. "The debt has ruined me. Where would I find means to go to the Courts?"

"Is not justice for the poor as well as the rich?"

There was a general exchange of smiles. "It is easy to see," the basketmaker said, "you have no experience of such matters."

The young man's eyes had become very alert as he scanned one face after another. "Nay, I do not."

"When a man goes to the Courts," the physician explained, "he must have gold or grain or hides to give to the scribe who writes his brief. The scribe extracts his little fee, then passes the rest on to the clerk of the Court, who extracts a much larger one

438

in return for giving the remainder to the inspector of the Clerks—"

"But the inspector's whole duty is to prevent such corruption!"

"Aye—well—that is how things go. The inspector then consents to give the brief to the Master of Records, from whose hand alone the judge may receive it. You can see plainly, my friend, that it is impossible to place a complaint before any judge unless one is a man of means."

"And that I am not," the weaver said bitterly. "Well, I must go home, I suppose . . ."

He made off down the noisy street with the physician beside him. The arrogant passage of a curtained litter borne by six Nubians scattered the remainder of the crowd, most of whom drifted back to their bargaining or their work. A few followed the young man and the basketmaker back to the latter's stall.

"It is the same story with the tax collectors," the potter remarked. "They seize for themselves almost as much as they collect for Her Majesty."

"Aye, true enough," the basketmaker agreed, ducking under a festoon of his wares to pick up his work again. "They come like locusts and gobble up everything in sight, and must be bribed merely to go away. What is more, the inspectors who are sent about from the vizier's office to discover such things—"

"*Hai!* The inspectors!" a wine merchant put in. "They come with their hands out—so"—he extended his hand craftily, rubbing the fingers together—"and when they return they are rich, but they've nothing to report, not they!"

"Just so, just so," the basketmaker said, glancing at the young man, whose expression had grown thoughtful, almost absent.

"I say they should be punished!" the wine merchant announced. "Forty lashes on the soles of their feet—the same as for any other criminal."

The basketmaker shrugged. "They would only bribe their punishers, and continue in the old ways. It is futile to punish them."

"They should be better paid, that is what should happen," the young man said suddenly.

Once more everyone turned to stare at him. He glanced around

439

the circle of uncomprehending faces, then leaned forward, restin
an elbow on the corner of the stall.

"Look you. Each one of those officials you have mentioned—
judges, tax collectors, clerks, inspectors—each one must pay
levy every year in order to retain his post. Did you know tha
A levy to the palace—to Ma-ke-Re, that she may erect anoth
statue of herself before her temple." He paused, his dark ey
moving from face to face, but no one cared to comment. "Wh
would happen if the levies were remitted—if every official we
allowed to keep the entire income of his office? Then he wou
not need the bribes. He could regain his dignity and rememb
the loftiness of justice." Again the peculiar expression cross
his face. "He would be well-fed enough to become an honoral
man. Come, is it not so?"

Clever. He is really *very* clever, thought the basketmaker
his fingers went on mechanically weaving the reeds. A most u
usual young man. Now how did he work that out so quickl
when none of us had ever thought of such a thing?

"My friend," the wine Merchant said, "do you think th
is true? That no man is honest if he is hungry?"

"It is not pretty, is it, Old One?" The young man shrugge
"Perhaps it is not quite like that."

"But is that what you think?"

"I merely think that there are two ways to do everything, ar
one works better than the other. You may beat a fallen horse
death for stubbornness, or you may expend the same energ
helping him to his feet. The first may be justice—but the secor
gets the cart to the market place." The young man smiled. "T
me it seems foolish to ignore man's nature, when you are tryir
to govern men. As well put it to work for you."

"There is much truth in that," murmured the wine merchan
blinking.

The potter, who had been leaning from his stall to listen, sa
suddenly, "What did you say your trade is, friend? A scrib
was it?"

The young man glanced at him amiably enough, but mere
answered, "I did not say." Before anyone could press the matte
he was talking about taxes again. "The inspectors do only wh
they must, I think. We groan loudly about it, but we pay. Th
is, we paid last year—and several years before. The harvests we
excellent. *This* year . . ." He raised eyebrows and shoulders i

440

shrug that reminded one inescapably of this year's inundation.
had been far lower than usual—uncomfortably close to poor.
his year we may groan in earnest. And next year, unless
a-ke-Re brings back the Nile . . . Add two poor harvests to
ese taxes—the sum is famine." The young man's black eyes
oved from face to face; then he straightened and glanced up at
e sun. "Which reminds me of my present condition. Is there a
ker's stall in this street? Or an onion seller's?"

"Stay and share my meal, friend Thoth!" the basketmaker
id quickly. "It is poor enough food, but—"
The young man flashed a glance into his face, and there was
thing peculiar about his smile this time. "Gladly!" he said
th a little bow.
The basketmaker stood up, warmed by the smile and feeling
extraordinary pleasure, almost elation. It was odd, he told
mself as he motioned his guest into the dark interior of his
all. Food was scarce and he had little. But he felt a remarkable
luctance to have this young man leave.

The garden gate clicked. Mayet looked up from her reflection
the pool to find Thoth walking toward her, flinging off an in-
edibly dusty cloak. Under it he wore a coarse white *shenti,*
ove it an ordinary square-cut black wig. That was all—no
wels or gold, not even an armband—no collar on his chest nor
adem on his head. His feet were bare and brown and very dirty.
Leaving the cloak where it fell, he stopped before her, smil-
g. "Well? What do I look like, little one?"
"Like yourself. Only dustier."
"Ma-ke-Re always said I had the build of a peasant," he re-
arked wryly.
"What have you been doing, Thoth?"
"Something *she's* never done—I've been walking in the city.
nding a Thebes she doesn't know exists." He dropped to the
ass and leaned back on his elbows, looking up at her. In a dif-
rent tone, he said, "Come here, beloved."
She sank down beside him and moved willingly into his arms.
hey closed hard about her. He was seldom gentle; his love-
aking was always rough and powerful, demanding complete
rrender, which she gave with all her heart. His lips were as
gent now as if he meant to take her right here on the grass—
perhaps he did. Mayet neither knew nor cared; she was

441

totally absorbed. A moment later, lying slack with the grass tickling her cheek, she opened dreamy eyes to find him frowning down at her sternly.

"Mayet, where is your diadem?"

Guilt streaked through her. She lay very still in the crook of his arm, trying to remember. "I must have put it somewhere . . . I know! On a limb of the tamarisk tree yonder. It looked so pretty hanging there— Thoth, I only meant to leave it for a moment."

"You child." He smiled a little, running his free hand through her hair, but his eyes remained serious. "I want you to wear it, Mayet, not hang it on trees. I want the cobra on your brow— every moment. It is important. I told you that."

"I know. I will, Thoth." She started to move and was instantly checked by the hard pressure of his arm. "Let me up and I'll go get it."

"I don't want to let you up," he whispered. "I want to kiss you again . . ."

Some minutes later he sat up, sighing. "Go fetch your diadem. Quickly—before I change my mind."

When she emerged from the shadows under the tree, he was strolling to meet her, the shabby cloak over his arm. "Have you been waiting to lunch with me?"

"Aye." She waved toward the pavilion. "It is all spread for us there. You said—"

"I know. Beloved"—he took her arm affectionately and started up the slope toward the gate—"forgive me and lunch by your self today. I will dine with you instead. As you see, I must bathe and change into fresh garments—"

"And put on your diadem," she added with a disapproving glance at his forehead. Her own was now properly adorned with the fiery-eyed serpent.

He laughed under his breath.

"Thoth, I am not hungry. I will wait until you have changed."

"Nay, I've had my meal—barley and stewed lotus roots, with a piece of dried fish that took me straight back to Babylon. I shared a basketmaker's lunch, cooked in his stall in the market place, over a charcoal blaze no bigger than my thumb. We drank Nile water."

"Poor man! Could you not have brought him some beer from the palace?"

442

"My little one, to him I was a poor commoner like himself— merely a friendly young fellow who stopped to admire his baskets. If he had known who I was he would never have talked to me. Nor would any of the others—the potter and the fish seller and an old physician, and the weaver who cannot collect his debt from my lord Kautef of Hermonthis . . ."

Thoth had stopped on the path and was gazing ahead of him, his mind far away from her again, back in the streets of the city with all those other people. She waited beside him, memorizing the bold curve of his nose, the subtle modeling about his temples, the little muscle at the corner of his mouth which always jumped when he was thinking.

"Mayet," he said presently. "Have you ever seen a vizier installed in his office?"

"Nay."

"It is a grand ceremony, solemn as a funeral. He is given the forty rolls of the law, which must always be spread open on his table for all to read. Pharaoh himself instructs him. He tells him the ways of justice, and he says, 'It is an abomination of the god to show partiality . . . Thou shalt regard him who is known to thee like him who is unknown, and him who is near like him who is far . . .' It is a fine instruction—above reproach. But, Mayet, it is all words. The law wears one face to the poor man and another to the rich. I discovered that today, in Thebes. By Amon, when the law is in *my* hands—if ever it is—" He broke off, his nostrils flaring as he drew one of those long, deep breaths with which he forced his emotions under control.

She watched him uneasily; it was as if he looked into a mist of trouble she could not see. "Has something bad happened?" she asked, trying to edge her way into the mist with him.

"Nay—nay—it is just that my patience runs out, I forget sometimes that I have to wait."

"Wait for what, Thoth?" she said, though she knew.

"As long as is necessary," he said, not really answering her question but an inner one of his own. "As long as it takes. My whole lifetime, if I must. I can do it. I will do it."

"Of course," she whispered.

He turned to her abruptly, smiling. "Go, beloved. Eat your luncheon. I promise we'll dine together."

He cupped her chin in his hand and kissed her, then pulled her

443

against him with a sudden passion that took her breath. An instant later the gate clicked behind him.

Mayet stood a moment, looking wistfully at its weather-silvered wood. Well, night would come. Smiling as she followed with her eyes the gay, flashing flight of an emerald-green bee-eater, she walked toward the pavilion to eat her luncheon.

Thoth's mood darkened as he strode across the Great Court, through the door in the opposite wall and along the arbored path toward his private stairway. *Be not enraged toward a man unjustly,* Pharaoh always instructed the vizier. *Show forth the fear of thee; let one be afraid of thee, for a prince is a prince, of whom one is afraid. Lo, the true dread of a prince is to do justice . . . Be not known to the people and they shall not say, "He is only a man."* Good advice, Thoth told himself. Old King Amenenhet's advice—as profound for a Pharaoh as for a vizier. It is good that I have time to ponder such things. . . .

There was no need to be impatient. He was learning every day, storing wisdom in himself against the time that was coming. Look what the weaver had taught him this morning, and those others in the market place. He was not wasting his time, all this was good, needful. There were many years before him, he was only twenty-four, he had fought impatience before and he could fight it again, cram it under discipline, make it stay down . . . and if there were times like this when it all seemed to be rising up violently in him like yesterday's dinner, forcing his throat open—

He broke into a run, took the stairs in a series of savage bounds, and stopped, panting, on the balcony.

"Tjesu! What is the matter?"

Rekhmi-re was standing in the doorway. Thoth eyed his startled face, but did not answer. He took one of his long, punishing breaths and pushed past into the bedchamber. He had been thinking that it was now nine years since he had thought six weeks an eternity to wait for his crown—but he did not say so. He never said such things any more.

He tossed the cloak on a chair, yanked off his commoner's wig, and began working at the knots of his *shenti*. "I want a bath," he said in ordinary tones. "Summon Unas, will you?"

"Aye, of course, Tjesu." Rekhmi-re crossed the room and struck the little silver gong.

444

"Where is Amenu?"

Rekhmi-re shrugged. "A message came for him, and he left. Not quite an hour ago."

Thoth looked at him curiously, then went on loosening the knots. "Odd," he said. "Who brought it? A runner?"

The slave Unas entered the room. Before answering, Rekhmi-re turned to the man and gave orders—rather unnecessarily in detail, Thoth thought—for the preparation of the bath. When he turned back he still seemed reluctant to answer the question.

"Well?" Thoth prompted. "Was it a runner that came?"

"Nay . . . as a matter of fact, Tjesu, it was—Sekheti."

"Sekheti?" Thoth looked up in amazement. He knew only one Sekheti—a youth who had been Amenu's horse boy in the old days on the drill field.

"Aye, the same one." Rekhmi-re studied his face a moment, then added carelessly, "I suppose he wants a few coppers—he looked ragged enough."

"Aye, every soldier is ragged these days. Even those who were captains and generals. . . . Rekhmi-re—why did you not tell me at once that it was Sekheti?"

"I thought it might disturb you. By the gods, it did me! That's a bitter memory."

"I have few that are not." Thoth paused, then added coldly, "But I do not need to be protected from them, as if I were a child. My troops turned against me. Very well. It happened. It's past and done."

"Aye—traitors, every one of them!"

"Don't be a fool. They could not help themselves. I saw that long ago." Thoth jerked off the *shenti* and walked naked into the bathchamber. Rekhmi-re followed after a moment.

"What did you learn in the city?"

"Much. There's something to be said for looking like a herdsman. They talked freely to me. But no matter how freely—" Thoth paused, perforce, as a jar of cold water, then one of warm, cascaded over him. "No matter how freely they talked," he went on as Unas began scrubbing him with natron-and-clay, "I did not hear one word against the queen. Against tax collectors, aye, and judges, and corruption—but not against the Divine Ma-ke-Re. They do not even connect her with these abuses—yet."

445

"Wait until harvest! The inundation was low this year, wer
none of them aware of that?"

"Naturally they were aware of it. They did not want to spea]
of it."

"What of the empty barracks?"

"Or of that, either. *I* spoke of it—they changed the subject."

The two eyed each other a moment. "They know," Rekhmi-r
said. "It is just that they have not faced it yet."

"Aye, I think you are right. But when they face it, what ca»
they do even then? She is Pharaoh—they are nothing. Th
people do not rebel."

"They did once."

"Aye, once!" Thoth smiled. "Egypt has been Egypt for thre
thousand years—and *once* the people rebelled." Water drenche
him again, all cold this time. He shivered, then felt the bloo
course through him invigoratingly as he wrapped the linen bath
sheet about him and walked to the rubbing table. "And tha
once," he added, "was so terrible it lives still in their great-great
great grandchildren's minds. Four hundred years of chaos, tha
is what the old ones brought on the land. I would not have i
happen again, Rekhmi-re, not for me, not for any reason. In
vasion is preferable. The Hyksos endured here for only two hun
dred years—men can conquer invaders, but not themselves."

"But with you to lead them—"

"I? They would not follow *me*—not yet. Gods! I scarcely exis
for them. Ma-ke-Re is all." Thoth lay silent a moment, his chi»
on his fists, while the scent ofmyrrh and oil rose thick in th
room from Unas' vigorous pummeling. "Did the runner arriv
from Tharu?"

"Aye, but he had found out nothing."

"As I thought."

One could never find out anything since old Tuaa had bee»
recalled. The young priest who had replaced him sent no scout
into the desert, questioned no roaming Sand-dwellers, paid n
heed to rumors drifting in from the east and north. Thotl
cursed him inwardly, trying to guess what must be happening i»
those lands beyond Tharu, where the king of Kadesh was stirring
revolt against the Egyptian garrisons in city after city, chipping
away the empire bit by bit, and making the bits his allies. His
progress had been checked in southern Palestine—Sharuhen anc
some of the cities around it still remembered Thoth's grand-

446

ather too vividly to dare seek freedom from Egypt. Others in he same area were eager to join the Kadesh hordes. The disagreement had erupted into civil war. That had been the situation when Tuaa left, but what it was now, no one knew and no one could find out.

We will know in a few years, Thoth reflected bitterly, when we see Asiatics pouring into the streets of Thebes. Gods, if I had an army! If I had *something* to work with, some weapon in my hand!

Not even an army would get him back his crown. What Egyptian would raise his sword against Ma-ke-Re, the Good God who was every man's breath of life?

"They must turn away from her," he said, "before they will turn to me. Everyone must drop away from her—the people, the nobles, the Kinsmen—she must stand alone, as I stood alone. That is the way a crown is lost. There is no way to hasten it. There is nothing to do but wait, wait—and hope to the gods Sharuhen will resist."

"Tjesu—the waiting will end. By Amon, it must! It cannot go on much longer."

"It can go on—and Amon has nothing to do with it. When was it he named me Pharaoh, by the power of his oracle? Thirteen years ago, Rekhmi-re. It would seem the god is in no hurry." Thoth laughed shortly, then raised himself on his elbows. "But when the time comes—I promise you, when the time comes—!"

"Aye—you will be your grandfather all over again. You need not assure me of that. I know."

Thoth looked at him thoughtfully a moment, then lay back on the table. "Nay, I shall not be my grandfather. His way was not good enough."

"Not good enough! He raised his boundary monument on the banks of that river you used to live beside—the one that flows the wrong way, and marks the end of the world. In all the lands between there and here he left not one city and not one rebel. All were ashes—and his slaves."

"Aye," Thoth said. "And twenty-four years after he has gone to the gods the ashes are cities again and the slaves revolt."

"That is Ma-ke-Re's fault!"

"Perhaps." Thoth sat up, waving Unas into the background with a sweep of his arm. "But perhaps it was his own."

"Tjesu, no nation stays conquered, of itself. Without a heavy

447

hand over it, and frequent punitive campaigns, you cannot really expect—"

"Exactly. A city that falls in ashes rises in hate. Every place my grandfather's torches touched, they dropped a seed of this present rebellion. Is that wise? To level a city and slaughter its people *after* it is conquered?"

"It has always been done," Rekhmi-re said blankly. "One must punish the barbarians—teach them they must not resist."

"Rekhmi-re, that teaches them only that they *must* resist—to the death, since surrender will only bring a worse death anyway. Look you—why not grant amnesty? The moment a city has surrendered, spare it—let the houses stand and the people live. Will not the next city fight less fiercely? Will not every barbarian be saying to himself, 'If I fight I die; if I surrender I live and keep my house and flocks, like the people of such-and-such'? Then will they not surrender quickly, to save what is left? Aye—and will not these kings be able to send me tribute all the sooner if I leave them with flocks and goods instead of ashes?"

"Aye," Rekhmi-re said drily. "And will they not be able to revolt all the sooner, the moment you are back in Egypt?"

"Not if I take their children with me."

Rekhmi-re's coarse-lashed eyes narrowed. He walked across the wet stones of the floor and stood close beside the rubbing-table, peering curiously into Thoth's face. "I see," he said, but Thoth knew he did not see. "You will reward surrender with amnesty—spare the conquered kings—then take hostages back to Thebes to insure their loyalty. But Tjesu—they will hate you more than ever, if you make prisoners of their sons."

"I will not make prisoners of them!" Thoth said triumphantly. "I will make Egyptians of them—and then I will send them home to put on their fathers' crowns."

Eagerly he studied Rekhmi-re's blue-jawed face, watching the full import of his plan slowly dawn there. He sprang down from the table, glistening with oil, tingling in every limb from the vigorous rubbing and the consciousness of his own strength. At that moment, as in countless other moments when youth and energy welled up inside him with the power of a rising Nile, he felt he could bring ten barbarian kings to their knees singlehanded.

He led the way into the bed chamber, talking rapidly as Unas brought out clean garments and began to dress him. "Do you see what will happen then? Rear these barbarian princes in Thebes, in luxury and civilized ways, and they'll ever afterward look to Thebes as the center of the world. They'll turn their cities into Egyptian cities. They'll call their tribute 'taxes' and their conqueror 'Your Majesty.' They'll send their sons—naturally—to be educated in Thebes as they were. Rekhmi-re, in two generations the cities of Syria and Palestine—perhaps even Mitanni—will no more think of rebelling against Pharaoh than Menfe and Abydos do today. There will *be* no Syria, no Mitanni—it will all be Egypt!" Thoth drew his belly in flat as Unas knotted a fresh-starched *shenti* about him. "There are two ways to do everything, by Amon! This was not my grandfather's way, it is my own. But it is better!"

"It is magnificent!" whispered Rekhmi-re.

"Aye—it is. I *know* it is, Rekhmi-re." For a moment every muscle in Thoth's body knotted with the force of his knowing. Suddenly realizing that the slave was fumbling clumsily with the latch of his sandal, he looked down to see the man's eyes fixed on his face, shining with awe and worship. "I believe even Unas knows it."

"Aye, Master!" breathed Unas. Abruptly he prostrated himself and stretched out his hands before Thoth.

"It seems I have gained another subject, Rekhmi-re," Thoth remarked. Bitterness flooded into his mouth as he added, "That makes four, with you and Mayet and Amenu. I need only a million more, then I can do what I have planned."

The words brought a wave of discouragement that blotted out Rekhmi-re's face, blackened the room's sunshine and turned his own vigor and strength into a mocking jeer. He coped with his fury as best he could; for some moments it required all the power of his will to cram it back into himself and make the doors fast against it. By the time he had obliterated the last image of Hatshepsut's smiling face, Unas had finished his task and gone, and he found himself pacing monotonously up and down the sitting room, with Rekhmi-re nursing a cup of beer and watching him uneasily.

"Tjesu," came a voice from the bedroom doorway.

Both of them looked around as Amenu came slowly toward Thoth.

"Tjesu, there is someone outside—on the balcony—who would speak to you."

" 'Someone!' " Thoth said irritably. "You pad about me like

cats, you two! It is Sekheti outside—why not say so at once?"

Amenu hesitated; Rekhmi-re strode up to him suddenly and stared into his face. "Because it is not Sekheti! Is that it? Whom have you brought, out there?"

Amenu shoved past him and spoke rapidly to Thoth. "Tjesu, it is not Sekheti. But I beg you to admit him anyway, hear what he says . . . he has news for you. He has been to Tharu."

"Tharu! Then in Amon's name, bring him in at once! Why did you—" Thoth glimpsed a movement in the bedchamber and looked up. Tjah was standing in the doorway.

For a moment Thoth had to fight the impulse to turn his back and order both Tjah and Amenu out of his sight forever. In spite of the cool common sense he had spoken to Rekhmi-re a few minutes ago, to look at Tjah was to see the silent throng in the Great Hall, with Hatshepsut sitting incredibly on his throne, and behind her a row of traitors he had known as comrades— with this well-loved face among them, staring as careless as a wooden image past his head. It was not staring past him now, it was bent toward the floor, eyebrows knotted.

"I thought as much!" Rekhmi-re burst out. "I suspected as much!"

Thoth silenced him with a gesture. He took a few steps toward Tjah, noting the soiled and ragged *shenti,* the callused feet, the strong warrior's body now gaunt and at the moment painfully tense. The picture of the Great Hall dissolved; he saw only an old friend wracked by circumstances beyond any man's control. He stood a moment struggling with his voice, and finally said, "Well, Tjah?"

Tjah's body seemed to wilt; he sank to his knees and stretched his hands out. "Tjesu—may Your Majesty live forever!"

"You still call me by these names? I have been neither your commander nor your king for years."

"I still call you by those names."

"Stand up," Thoth said. Tjah obeyed, raising his head slowly and reluctantly. It became clear to Thoth why his voice had sounded strange; his face was flushed, his mouth set stiffly, and he had to force himself to lift his eyes. The man was consumed with shame; this meeting with the king he had deserted was a torture for him.

"Why did you come?" Thoth asked him.

"To serve you."

"You have done that already, if you have been to Tharu."

Tjah's glance flashed to Amenu, then dropped. "We went months ago, Sekheti and I. We found out nothing Your Majesty did not already know."

"Call me Tjesu, as before," said Thoth shortly. He had caught the glance at Amenu and interpreted it. "You spoke to Amenu at that time? Why did you not come to me then?"

Tjah forced his eyes up again, and fixed them resolutely on Thoth's. "Because the news was no news, as His Excellency Amenu told you. After all that has happened, do you think I would come to you empty-handed?"

"Then you have some other news for me now?"

"Aye." Tjah's face began to come to life. "Tjesu, do you remember one called Uah, a great lord, a Kinsman? He was Master of the Armory when you first put on the crown."

Thoth shook his head blankly, but Rekhmi-re, who had been glowering at Tjah from a corner, now came to life too. "Uah? *I* remember him—my father knew him. But he has not been in Thebes for years. He is Prince of Nekheb."

"Just so, Excellency," Tjah said. "He is Prince of Nekheb. He is also an old opponent of the queen, and scarce can be called her subject. His fathers have been warrior-nobles for a thousand years, masters of that land which is Gate to the Nine-Bows, and princes of such power that they kneel to Pharaoh only because they wish to kneel. Tjesu, I have just come from Nekheb. Do you know how I gained an audience with Uah? I sent him this."

Tjah plunged a hand into his sash and held out a small clay scarab inscribed with the royal titles of Menkheper-Re Thutmose III. Thoth recognized it as one of a thousand that had been struck off to commemorate his coronation.

"Look at me!" Tjah said. "A ragged nobody without so much as a helmet or bow to show what I once was. But your name admitted me to his presence at once—aye, and alone! We talked for an hour." Tjah's eyes had begun to gleam, his wide mouth to curve with excitement in the old way. "Tjesu, he says I can train your army for you, *there*, in Nekheb."

"I have no army!" Thoth said. His heart was beating wildly.

"You have gold. Give me only a few deben to provide them with food and transport to the south, and I will find all the ragged ones like myself who *were* your army and send them to Nekheb.

They have lost flesh, but not their skills, Tjesu. Uah will feed them, build a barracks next his own—"

"What of arms?" put in Amenu. "That will take more than a few deben! Can Uah arm them?"

"I will arm them!" Thoth said.

"Tjesu, it will take gold by the heap, by the heket—"

"No matter. I will find it somehow. It will have to be little by little—gods, it will take months, years maybe, but—"

Rekhmi-re suddenly stepped forward, stripped off four gold armbands, two rings, and a broad gold collar, and dropped them on the floor at Thoth's feet. "Here is a beginning," he said briefly.

Amenu looked at him, and his nostrils flared. He stepped forward and did the same. Thoth added his own ornaments to the pile, strode to his bedchamber and came back with two vials of myrrh, a silver mirror, and a casket of bracelets and collars which he poured in a glittering stream upon the others. When the clash of gold on gold had stopped, all four looked silently at the shining heap before them, seeing shields and bows, swords and chariots and horses rise and melt the gold away.

It was not enough, not the hundredth part of enough—but it was a beginning.

10.

The following year, the fifteenth (by Hatshepsut's reckoning) of the reign of the Beautiful God Ma-ke-Re, was not a comfortable one for her worshipers dwelling in their thousands beside the long green ribbon of the Nile. The previous harvest had been no more than fair, and many a farmer annd weaver and sandalmaker grew thinner, while his taxes waxed as fat as ever. This year the inundation had not even been fair, it had been poor. From the Delta to the cataracts, anxious eyes had watched it rise sluggishly, cover half the fields, and inexorably retreat; anxious hands had labored at the creaking water-lifts day and night in a straining effort to make up the deficiency. When the crops were cut at last and the yield was in the storehouses, it was no use pretending there would not be hunger in the land. The harvest was the worst in years.

The people were given no chance to brood about it. Within

a week after harvest, on a burning morning when both the river and the people's spirits were at their lowest, the royal herald led his procession of scribes out of the palace gates. Shortly afterward, the familiar cry was ringing over the streets of Thebes:

"Silence—silence—silence—silence—"

"*Now* what can she find to tell them?" Thoth said, pausing on the water-stained steps of the royal docks, below which his bark rocked lazily in barely enough water to keep it afloat.

"Shall I go back and listen?" Rekhmi-re asked him.

"We will all go."

The three climbed onto the dock and crossed it to a point from which they could see the street beyond. It was full of people hurrying to gather around the platform on which one of the scribes was standing.

"His Majesty Ma-ke-Re speaks through my mouth . . ." The familiar words floated to them across the intervening space. "A command was heard from the throne, an oracle of the god himself . . . My father, Amon, spoke to My Majesty, saying, 'Welcome, sweet daughter, my favorite! Thou art the king, Hatshepsut. I have caused thy glory to be celebrated in all lands, by all people. I will cause thy anointment to be celebrated likewise in thy Festival of Eternity, which I command thee to make at the time of the next rising of the Nile . . .' "

A murmur of excitement rose from the crowd in the street. "Heb-Sed—she means to hold a Heb-Sed!" At the scribe's stentorian bellow, "Silence—silence—" the murmur subsided to an expectant hush.

" '. . . which I command thee to make at the time of the next rising of the Nile, to mark and glorify that day of thy anointment, when thou wast named Successor to the throne of Re, in the twenty-first year of the reign of thy father, Thutmose . . .' "

The three on the dock turned to stare at each other.

"In his twenty-first year?" Amenu burst out. *"Thirty years ago?"*

"In Mut's sweet name!" Rekhmi-re said in a stupefied voice. "Can she be asking them to believe she was anointed crown prince *then*—while Amenmose was still alive?"

Thoth did not answer. He, too, was astounded by the magnitude of Hatshepsut's newest departure from the truth; but it did not stupefy him. On the contrary, it set his mind to working furiously.

". . . I sat in the palace," the distant voice was shouting. "I remembered him who fashioned me, my heart led me to make for him two obelisks of electrum, whose points shall mingle with heaven . . ."

The scribe launched into a long and glowing description, in the queen's own words, of the gift she planned to present on the last day of Heb-Sed to her father the god. The obelisks were already taking shape, it appeared, in the granite quarries to the south, under the supervision of that greatest of excellencies, Count Senmut. There followed further praises of Senmut, of Hatshepsut, of Amon, which the three on the dock did not wait to hear.

"Thirty years ago!" Amenu said as they started back toward the steps and the waiting bark. "Not even she could expect them to believe that!"

"They will believe it, though," Thoth told him. "They believed my father was never named Successor, and that she was so named. They've been convinced of it for years, and why not? She told them so herself. Now she is telling them that it all happened much longer ago than they had realized—in fact when she was eleven years old. They will believe that too." He added thoughtfully, "My friends, it doesn't matter."

"Doesn't *matter?*" Rekhmi-re echoed.

"Nay." Thoth stopped and faced them, savoring the almost-forgotten taste of hope. "What matters is that her confidence has begun to crack. Two poor harvests—she must fear the gods are turning from her, or she would not have ordered a Heb-Sed. And because she cannot bear to face her fear, she must make up ever more elaborate fancies to cover it—to justify her actions and her crown. What is more, she is beginning to believe these fancies herself."

"Fancies! They are outright lies."

"Aye, they are. But this lie is different from the others. Can you not see that? This one stretches past the bounds of possibility. Something is forcing her beyond self-delusion, clean into unreality. Several somethings, in all probability. I'll wager I could name one."

"What?" Amenu said.

Thoth smiled. "Mayet. The little Forgotten-One-of-the-Gods. Egypt is about to be reminded of her in a way it cannot forget."

"So it is!" Amenu looked at him with his long, slit-like eyes gleaming. *"Ast!* Tjesu, I told you. This is my plan of years ago!"

454

"I know." Thoth's smile twisted as he started again for the teps. "But do not delude yourself, Amenu. In Amon's name, let us leave the delusions to Hatshepsut! Mayet is not the whole answer."

"At least she may provide an answer to Ma-ke-Re's obelisks," Rekhmi-re observed cheerfully. "Meanwhile, we have found out where Senmut has been journeying so often. I feared he might be calling on Count Uah."

"Gods, I wish Uah had the electrum she plans to use on those obelisks!" Thoth said.

"Gold, gold, gold," Amenu said with an exasperated sigh. "When I had plenty, I never dreamed it could be hard to come by. If I had only one of the herds I once owned, only one of the villages or vineyards— Did you order the new chariot, Tjesu?"

"I ordered two—as elaborate as possible. Even the planks underfoot are gold-plated." Thoth laughed shortly. "The wheelwright was much upset—he argued that such a contraption would never run properly. I told him I wanted it for my tomb."

"It will run well enough when Uah strips that plating off," Amenu said.

"Aye—I only wish I dared order a dozen at a time."

"Your tomb," Rekhmi-re mused as they started across the gangplank to the bark. "Now there is an idea—why can we not all begin furnishing our tombs? Jeweled weapons, gold and silver collars, ivory boxes—"

He broke off suddenly. Thoth turned to see him standing in the middle of the gangplank, staring up at the great curving prow above him.

"Sweet Hathor's breasts!" he was muttering. "How is it one can look at a thing day after day and never see it! Tjesu, come here, I beg you!"

When Thoth stood beside him, he pointed with a grin toward the prow. It was covered with gold leaf.

All three stood gazing at it silently, picturing the bows, helmets, maces, battle chariots into which it could be transformed. "I'll make you vizier for this, Rekhmi-re," Thoth said. He clapped his friend upon the shoulder and led the way onto the deck. "Someday," he added.

The word threw a grim shadow over all three faces. As the bark moved slowly into midstream Rekhmi-re, leaning with both muscular brown arms on the rail, squinted balefully through his lashes toward the glinting flagstaffs of the Temple of Amon.

"I will be happy to step into Hapuseneb's sandals someday—any day," he said through his teeth. "I would be even happier to empty them for you tomorrow. You have only to say the word, Tjesu."

"Nay, nay, it is too early for that—too early." Thoth, too, gazed toward the temple. "We must let time work for us a little longer. Time and Hatshepsut. The old sages spoke the truth sometimes," he added with a smile. " 'He who sails with false-hood for a cargo does not reach land.' Let her pile the lies a little higher, let the ship begin to founder. Then we shall start ramming holes into its sides."

As the bark with the gold prow crossed the river, the scribes rolled up their scrolls, and the people, elated and talkative, dispersed to their tasks, dismissing all forebodings about the harvest. Even a certain basketmaker, who had shared his lunch some months ago with a likable young fellow and had ever since caught his mind working in the most unusual ways, felt that all would be well now that the Heb-Sed was to be enacted. Hunger was nothing new to the likes of him, he remarked to the potter in the next stall as he picked up his reeds again. Neither were taxes, though it was going to take a Pharaoh of a tax collector to find any coppers in *his* sash next month—he could scarce find bread in his cupboard this minute. It had all turned out the way that young fellow said, one had to admit it. . . .

Oh well, they could eat next year. The Heb-Sed's magic would bring the Nile back, and the farmers would come to the market-place to buy baskets again instead of making poor lopsided things themselves out of whatever stalks and weeds they could find. *This* year it was enough to watch the Great Ones journey to Thebes in their golden barges. He meant to take his wife and children to the temple gates every day of the Heb-Sed, did the basketmaker. Sometimes, if one could find a good place to stand, one could catch glimpses of the riches heaped before the shrines, and smell the fragrance as loaves and great meat haunches burned to ashes upon the altars.

Summer came; the sun blazed down on Egypt with a powerful and unremitting heat, aggravated by the sandy, burning winds

456

that came each year out of the Nubian wastelands. Far south of Thebes, in the granite quarry near the first cataract of the Nile, a horde of men toiled from dawn to darkness with sand gritting between their teeth, torturing their inflamed eyelids, and stinging against sweating backs and arms already welted by the overseer's whip. With incredible speed, though still not speedily enough to suit the overseer, their mallets and wedges and tiny copper chisels were freeing two vast forms from the bed of granite. Rising higher than a tall man's head at their broader ends, the great shafts lay on their sides, still part of the rock from which they were being wrested, and they stretched so far across the sunbaked quarry that eighty men could work along their length, from the bases to their sharply tapered points, without getting in each other's way.

In the lee of an outcrop above the quarry, a noble in a wovengold headcloth and exquisitely crisp linen stood under a canopy held by four slaves, inspecting the obelisks with a critical and practiced eye. The overseer stood near him—not, of course, actually sharing the canopy, but much closer to it than his head foreman, who waited nervously at a little distance. Both were examining Count Senmut's face as expertly as Count Senmut was examining the shafts.

"Four months they have been working," mused the count, without moving his glance from the quarry.

"And the great shafts are nearly released from the womb of their mother rock!" exclaimed the overseer in a burst of poetic enthusiasm.

"Released! I would say the birth pains had scarce begun." Senmut gave him a chilly glance. "The queen is in a hurry, as I think I told you. I think I have told you several times."

"But Excellency!—I beg Your Excellency to consider the difficulties! I assure you, I am doing my utmost—I have spared not one blow of the lash that might urge one of these wretches to chip a little faster, pound a little harder—"

"You had best conscript another hundred men. The work goes too slowly."

"Amon help me, there is no room for more men to work! Unless"—the overseer washed his hands together—"unless I could divide the shafts? Into just two sections each, perhaps?"

"Unthinkable. The shafts must be single stones, unbroken by so much as a crack the width of a hair. These are not ordinary obelisks. These are Ma-ke-Re's." Senmut shifted his jeweled staff to the other hand and made ready to depart. "Therefore, you will have to do better. After the obelisks are rowed to Thebes, there are still the inscriptions to be carved and the points to be covered with electrum. They must be loaded onto the barge by the end of Mesori, at the latest. That gives you a month and a half."

"A month and a half!" the overseer whispered. "By all the gods in Egypt, it cannot be done! I am only human! I—"

"Surely," Senmut said, "you would not care to be the cause of my breaking a promise to the queen? . . . Nay, I thought not." He smiled, and the deep grooves that slashed from nose to mouth bore a striking resemblance, for a moment, to the crevices in the granite outcrop behind his head. "I will return in a month and a half to supervise the loading," he said crisply as he turned to leave.

The overseer stood motionless, watching the linen-draped litter vanish in the direction of the Nile; then with a convulsive effort he straightened and turned toward his foreman.

"All right," he said hoarsely. "You heard. You heard! Now, then, be off with you and get that whip of yours to work, you excrement of a pig! I want speed, speed, speed, speed—"

The foreman was already on his way. Snatching up his own whip, the overseer hurried desperately after him into the quarry.

On the last day of Mesori, exactly seven months after their quarrying had begun, the two obelisks were loaded onto an over-sized towboat under Senmut's calmly approving eye. The following day, tugged by three rows of oared barges—nine in a row, with a pilot boat preceeding each row—they started toward Thebes upon the rising waters of the Nile. At every village they passed, the people gathered on the banks to marvel and stare after them; for these were no ordinary obelisks. They were without seam or joint from their bulky bases to their delicately pointed tips—solid blocks of granite, perfectly shaped and far longer than any shafts in Egypt. Their like had never before been seen.

If the obelisks were unusual, the site that was being prepared for them in Thebes was extraordinary. Ineny, who had been entrusted with ordering the huge inscribed bases and placing them in readiness to receive the shafts, could not at first believe the orders his queen was giving him. Stumbling from Hatshepsut's sitting room, he all but collided with Thutiy, who was passing in the corridor. The latter glanced in astonishment at his old friend's dazed and incredulous face.

"Re give you life, Ineny! Are you ill?"

"Nay . . . nay, I am not ill . . ."

"Then what is the matter?"

Ineny glanced up and down the corridor, then drew Thutiy into an alcove at some distance from the queen's door. "I have been talking with Her Majesty. My friend, do you know where she means to raise those obelisks at Heb-Sed?"

"Why, before the temple, I suppose . . . Nay? Ah, I have it . . . she will raise them before Djeser-Djeseru! Perhaps on the first terrace . . . Well? Where, then?"

"In the Hall of Praise."

Thutiy stared blankly at him. "What do you mean, *in* the Hall of Praise?"

"I mean exactly what I say!" Ineny seemed about to burst into agitated tears. "I asked her and that is what she told me! At the Temple of Amon in Thebes, in the Hall of Praise!"

"But that is impossible! There is no door wide enough to admit them—there is not even room among the columns. Why, the obelisks are far taller than the roof!"

"She means to tear the roof off," whispered Ineny. He peered, wide-eyed, into Thutiy's face, while the other stared back in growing consternation. "She means to demolish the whole south wall in order to drag them in, take out all the columns in that end of the hall to give them room—that will not be enough, I shall have to tear down some in the northern end as well." Ineny wrung his hands and burst out, "*I* am to do this, I who planned that hall and built it, who sent to the mountains beyond the Great Green for the cedar of those columns and supervised every inch of carving on them, I who planned it all as a perfect whole for my beloved Pharaoh must now make a wasteland of it. What would her father say if he knew what she means to do to his work? It was his gift to Amon, the finest of many gifts, the Good God's own favorite . . ."

Ineny's voice trailed into incoherent mourning.

"Does she—realise that?" Thutiy said numbly. "Did you—mention—?"

459

"I did. I felt it my duty. She said—she almost shouted, Thutiy —'I and my father are one. He approves of all I do, all I ever did! We are as one heart and as one king. This will prove it!'"

The two old men gazed at each other, baffled and in despair.

"Then you must obey," said Thutiy finally.

"Aye. I must obey."

Ineny turned and walked slowly down the corridor and out into the Great Court, to find his litter and begin the terrible task which had been assigned to him. Next day his crews were at their work of destruction. Great stones on slings battered at the southern wall, spreading cracks in every direction through the beautifully carved inner surface and finally bringing great sections crashing down in a cloud of dust. Before long other crews were prying and tearing at the roof; the sun glared down upon the cedar columns which for a generation had dwelt in muted shade like that in the forests from which they came. At last the columns themselves were set upon with ropes and levers, fell one by one and were dragged away from the hall—the hall in which Amon had once named Hatshepsut's nephew king.

Some weeks later the obelisks arrived, towed by their fleet of barges. Already preparations for the Heb-Sed were far advanced; there was no time to be lost. Thutiy, who was charged with the decoration of the obelisks, set his sculptors to work on the carving at once, then hurried to the palace to ask audience of the queen. To his surprise, he found himself ushered ceremoniously into the Hall of State, instead of into the King's Apartments as he had expected. The entire court was assembled, and on the throne Hatshepsut sat smiling at him.

"Your Majesty—my petition is a brief one. I merely wish to inform Your Majesty that I have selected a crew of goldsmiths to perform the task of adorning the tips of Your Majesty's obelisks. I further wish instruction as to how much gold and silver Your Majesty wishes me to withdraw from the treasury for this work."

Hatshepsut's smile broadened; her voice quivered with anticipation. "I expected your petition, Excellency. I wish to show you my answer, not tell it. I have summoned all Egypt's nobles to bear witness to it. . . . Come here; stand beside my throne."

As Thutiy took the place she designated, she nodded quickly to Senmut, who signaled a chamberlain. Instantly a door at the side of the Great Hall flew open; two servants hurried in with a huge sheet of linen, which they spread on the floor before the dais. After them came a procession of slaves, each bearing a leather-lined basket upon his shoulder. The baskets were grain measures; but it was not grain that poured from them onto the sheet—it was gold and silver circlets from the treasury.

"Behold!" Hatshepsut's voice rang out over the ringing of the metal. "Let all behold how My Majesty's hand opens when it gives gifts to my father the god! Never has any king since the days of Re given such a goft—never will it be equaled in the Two Lands!"

Slave after slave came into the Hall, emptied a glittering stream upon the sheet and departed for another load, while even the richest courtier's jaw sagged, and Hatshepsut sat trembling on her throne, her hands gripping its golden arms, her eyes luminous with excitement, and the serene smile on her mouth occasionally jerking out of control. Not until twelve bushels of treasure were heaped before her did she order the priceless flow to cease. Even Thutiy was awed to speechlessness by the splendor of Ma-ke-Re. Clearly, when these obelisks were finally raised upon the ruins of the fallen columns, Egypt would see a spectacle like no other in the world.

Ineny did not see them raised. The swinging stones that had battered against the carven walls of his life's masterpiece had broken him too; all his years of hoping to build and create for Hatshepsut had ended in an order to destroy. Some days before the obelisks at last tilted ponderously over their ramps of sand onto the bases he had prepared for them, he had taken to his couch. By the time the seven trumpeters stood in the dawn atop the temple pylon, blaring their proclamation that the Heb-Sed had begun, Ineny had been dead a week.

After the Dedication of the Field on the last day of Heb-Sed, Hatshepsut walked into the House of Reeds, still breathing rapidly from her vigorous circuit of the Field. She was conscious of a flush of heat in her cheeks, a curious quivering in her legs, and most of all, the strange, irregular surges of emotion that kept gushing up inside her like a crowd of tiny bursting bubbles.

"My Majesty will rest now," she heard herself say in a high, unnatural voice.

The priests backed away and vanished; other figures material-
ized from the shadows and followed after her as she moved down
the right-hand corridor to the Chambers of the King. Senmut
was waiting there; he bowed formally, in silence, and as she
passed him and stood motionless in the center of the room he
spoke to the three noblewomen in attendance behind her. "You
may remove the Good God's ceremonial garments."

He turned his back and walked away to a table at the side of
the room, where wine and cakes were arranged on a refreshment
tray.

Hatshepsut was scarcely more aware of him than she was of
the three countesses who moved about her. She was entirely occupied with the mystic spell she had just enacted, and with
thoughts of her father, Thutmose. All through the five days of
the Heb-Sed memories of him had been accumulating, and today,
this moment, the sense of his presence was overwhelming.
Twenty-five years ago it was he who had made that running circuit of the Field, who had walked to a room like this afterward
and stood as she was standing now while the Red Crown was
lifted from his head, the heavy collar from his neck, the ceremonial bull's tail from about his waist. When the hands were
withdrawn, as these were withdrawing now, he had turned—
master of all the earth, god and Horus like herself—and sat in
that chair as she would sit presently, and lifted his gaze to Nehsi,
who was standing where Senmut was standing now, and had
spoken to him—

In a treacherous flash her mind was showing her a picture of
herself, a maiden of sixteen, standing with her back pressed flat
against the wall of another chamber in the House of Reeds, listening to Nehsi announcing her father's will that she should be
wed to Nenni in three days' time.

"You may go," she said loudly to the three women. Her voice
shattered the picture; by blinking rapidly an instant, and con-
centrating fiercely, she pieced together the scene that had preceded
it—her father sitting in the armchair, Nehsi standing where Senmut was standing now. . . .

Aye, and then her father had spoken to Nehsi, and had reminded him that years ago, in accordance with the desire of his
heart and the command of Amon's will, the princess Hatshep-

462

sut had been anointed his Successor, and that she must rule as Horus after him on the throne of the Two Lands. And it had come to pass.

She let out her breath carefully, so as not to disturb the shining outlines of the new picture, the true one, the right one, the one she had held before her like a standard all the years of her kingship. Then she turned to Senmut.

He was standing beside the table in profile to her, his hand still on the wine jar, his eyes fixed on space and a secret, exultant smile curling his full lips.

With a sickening tremor of fear that of late had become hatefully familiar to her, she stepped closer to him. He did not move; he gave no sign that he was aware of her existence.

"Senmut!" she said. "What are you thinking of?"

For an instant his face went blank; then the mask she had learned in the past few months to know—and dread—slipped into place.

"What am I thinking of?" he said easily. Picking up the two goblets he had filled, he turned to extend one to her, and no one but herself could have distinguished between this smile and the real one of a moment ago. "What could I be thinking of today save the glory of Hatshepsut?"

"That is not true," she whispered. "It is a lie, a lie! You are keeping something from me!"

"My beloved!"

"It is so! I know—I have seen. You have been hiding something for months, a year, perhaps ever since Nefer died! What is it, what is it?"

"You wrong me. I pray you, listen to reason. I have never—"

"Lies, more lies!" She backed away from him, her hands clenched by her sides. "Nay, do not argue, do not speak to me! I know what I know. Leave my presence!" Her voice rose to a shriek. "Leave my presence!"

"As you wish, my lotus. I know you are fatigued." He bowed and turned away.

I am not fatigued, she thought as the door closed behind him. *I am not fatigued. A god is never tired!*

Her knees felt as if they were crumbling away beneath her; she was suddenly aching in every limb. For an instant she wanted to

463

rush after him, call him back to her, surrender her weary body to his arms and forget his secret, whatever it was—forget that he had ever turned a mask to her instead of his harsh, beloved face.

She did not call him back. Nor did she drink the wine or sit down in the chair, because she was not tired, a god was never tired—particularly one who had just regained the full glory of youth and strength at the culmination of the Heb-Sed. Instead she began to walk about the room with a vigorous, springy step, holding her head rigidly erect. Forcing her lips into a smile, and blinking rapidly, she allowed the picture of Senmut to form gradually in her mind—the old picture, the true one, without the mask. For a moment the bubbles gushed up in shimmering crowds, and she shivered, as if her *ka* recoiled within her at their stealthy, *kheft*-like touch. Then her will brought them under control, and the smile set firmly on her lips.

He is not really keeping something from me, she thought. Not really. Nothing important. If it were important I should know. Probably I was a little hasty, to send him from me, but he must be disciplined for his little secret, he must learn that I do not need him as he thinks I do. I do not need anyone, not anyone.

There was a frightening gush of bubbles streaming up through her suddenly; she felt they were bursting in her head, behind her eyes. Through their silvery confusion she saw Senmut's smiling mask, Ineny dying on his couch, Nehsi standing haggard and incorruptible before her the other night—arguing, arguing.

No matter, let them all go, I do not need anyone! she thought, rapidly blinking the bubbles away. I am Ma-ke-Re. I am *Ma-ke-Re.*

Her knees buckled; she stiffened them with a jerk and walked to her dressing table. She would sit down for a moment, here on this stool. Not that she needed to rest, far from it—but one could not apply *kohl* to the eyes while standing up. That would be absurd. It was also absurd, she thought as she eased herself, trembling, onto the stool, to say "Let them all go." No one was going, no one was turning from her—poor old Ineny had died, and of course she missed him, but aside from that nothing had changed at all. The poor harvests were behind her now, the gods were with her again, Senmut's secret was some inconsequential trifle which he would presently confess to her, and as for Nehsi—

464

There was a tap on the door. As if her thought had summoned him, Nehsi entered the room.

"Your Majesty—"

His voice seemed to desert him. He stood silent just inside the door, his lips working, his eyebrows streaks of white against his dark, drawn face, his eyes sick with dread as he looked at her.

Her fingers closed with cramping tightness on the *kohl*-stick. "Well, Nehsi?"

"I have come for—Your Majesty's command."

"I have no further commands. I have already given all that are necessary pertaining to the dedication of the obelisks."

"I know that, Your Majesty." Nehsi paused, obviously gathering himself inwardly for some painful effort. "I have come for those pertaining to the life and safety of the Two Lands—to the naming of the Successor."

There was an instant's silence. Then Hatshepsut flung down the *kohl*-stick and stood up, blinking, fixing her lips in a smile and holding her shoulders very straight.

"Nehsi, I can find no excuse for this. I found little enough last week, when you came to me as you did, on the very eve of the Heb-Sed, arguing, contending with me, insisting over and over on this foolish idea of yours that I should name a Successor—I, Ma-ke-Re, still in the radiant prime of my life!—and talking on and on about some document in the Archives about which I know nothing, care nothing . . ." She hurried on, raising her voice to drown out whatever he might be intending to say, ignoring the look on his face. ". . . and worst of all, most inexcusable of all, actually daring to mention Thoth's name to me—Thoth's—and Meryet's—those despised ones of my father the god—" She broke off, fought the shrillness out of her voice. "I have been patient with you, Nehsi. But I will not hear those names again!"

Nehsi stood watching her. His whole body seemed to have shrunk, his cheeks to have fallen in; his face was an old man's. "That is your final answer to me—to Egypt?" he said.

"It is. There is no reason and no need to name a Successor. I am Pharaoh. The crown is mine, not another's! My father Amon gave Egypt and all its peoples into my hand."

"Nay, Amon did not do it," Nehsi whispered. "I did it. *I did it.*"

He turned like one blind and groped for the doorway.

465

I will not think of him, Hatshepsut told herself as the door closed. He is growing old and stubborn, but he will see presently that I am right, he always has. I will not think of Thoth—

There flashed unwanted into her mind the picture of Thoth leading Meryet gently across the Great Court into the garden. For a moment she could see nothing through the rush of bubbles but Meryet's face, her ominously altered figure.

Quickly Hatshepsut picked up one of the wine goblets Senmut had filled.

It is foolish of me, she thought, to worry about Thoth and his many follies on such a glorious day as this. If he wishes to strip the gold from the prow of his bark, from his chariots, from his own neck, even from the latches of his sandals, for some strange reason of his own, it is certainly nothing I need concern myself with. Let him be as shabby and eccentric as he likes, it is probably the beginning of madness. That is to be expected; he is like his father. Even this attachment to Meryet is to be expected—both are scorned and ignored by everyone else in the world— Aye, quite natural. But I must not allow it to dim my pleasure today, of all days. I will not think of them. I will think about my obelisks, and my beautiful temple.

A new crowd of bubbles gushed through her, but this time their effervescence was exhilarating; she felt a warm glow spread through her body. The bubbles were nothing but excitement, why had she let them frighten her? Of course she was excited, perhaps even a little overwrought. What Pharaoh would not be, at this culmination of everything glorious and splendid? Her thoughts flashed to Djeser-Djeseru, which stood almost complete now in the bay of the western cliffs. It was all there, carved in enduring stone—the glory of Hatshepsut; on the walls of the lower right-hand porch the full story of her miraculous conception ("Then came the glorious god to Aahmes the queen, when he had taken the form of her husband . . . She awoke at the perfume of the god . . . Enflamed with love, he hastened toward her, the majesty of this god did all that he desired with her . . . His love entered into all her limbs . . .") and the exact words of Amon's pronouncement as he rose from the queen's couch ("Khnemet-Amon-Hatshepsut shall be the name of this my daughter, whom I have placed in thy body . . . she shall exercise the excellent kingship in this whole land . . .") and the forming of the infant prince, Hatshepsut, and her *ka* by Khnum the Divine Potter (". . . I have given to thee all health, all lands, all countries, all people . . . I have given thee to appear upon the throne like Re, forever . . .") and after them the carved depictions of her god-attended birth, her suckling by Hathor the Divine, her anointment as Successor in her very cradle.

Hatshepsut drew a long, tremulous breath, finished her cup of wine and picked up Senmut's. *It was all true, all true. It had happened just so.* As she drank, the whole world seemed bathed in a golden glow, the reflection of her glory.

Scenes from the other porches of her temple moved in majestic procession across her mind—the scenes of her coronation; of her triumphal journey through the kingdom; of her ships sailing to Punt and returning laden with riches and myrrh trees; sculptured depictions of her own serenely smiling face ("Her Majesty's form was like a god . . . she was a maiden, beautiful and blooming, to look on her was more beautiful than anything . . .") and already the sculptors were at work depicting the transportation of her obelisks to Thebes, for generation after generation to see and marvel at.

All true, all glorious; everything she had done was right, right, *right*.

"Senmut!" she cried. Flinging the cup away, she snatched the mallet of her little gong and set it clamoring. "Senmut, Senmut!"

The door burst open; Senmut's big frame and startled face filled it. Swiftly she held out her hands; he was beside her in an instant, pressing his lips to them. *It was all my imagination,* she told herself through a wild gush of bubbles. *He is my love, my favorite. Nothing will ever come between us.*

"My beloved—are you quite well?"

"Of course I am well, I am radiantly well!" She heard herself laughing too loudly, and quickly controlled the sound. She could scarcely see him through the golden haze that clothed everything.

"You look feverish."

"Nonsense, I am only excited. Quickly—have them bring the Goddess of the Double Crown. I am ready to dedicate the obelisks."

I must be careful, she was thinking as she walked into the sun-

467

shine five minutes later. I am almost too excited—why, I am trembling. With joy. Not with nervousness. What have I, Ma-ke-Re, to be disturbed about? Meryet is nothing, less than nothing, the whole thing is beneath my notice.

"This way, Your Majesty." Hapuseneb's whisper rose to booming oratory. "Live, the female Horus, daughter of Amon-Re, his favorite, his only one . . ."

The massive bases of the two shafts half filled the unroofed hall; their tapered sides rose up and up, dwindling against the blue to pinnacles of pale gold which caught the sun in flashing, dazzling splendor. They dwarfed the crowd below them, dwarfed the remains of the hall, dwarfed everything that had ever been seen or known.

Her eyes followed them to the top, then lowered to gaze about in pride at the awed and worshiping faces. Ineny's was not there —of course. Nehsi's was not there either.

The smoke of myrrh rose fragrant into the sunlit air, she could hear the wine of the libations splashing against the granite bases, but suddenly the place seemed empty, frighteningly empty. Nehsi was not there—he had not come.

No matter, no matter, she thought, catching her breath and making her eyes wider, brighter with excitement. I need no one, I am Ma-ke-Re, I need no one at all. I need no one at all.

"Now, Your Majesty—"

She stepped forward, raised her head to its usual imperious angle. "I have done this from a loving heart for my father Amon, I have entered upon his project . . ." She drew a quick, trembling breath, and the words began to pour out. "O ye people who shall see my monument in after years, do not say 'I know not, I know not why this was made, and a mountain fashioned entirely from gold as if it were an ordinary task.' I swear, as Re loves me, that these obelisks which My Majesty has made are of one block of enduring granite without seam or joining. Hear ye! I gave for them the finest electrum, which I had measured by the heket like sacks of grain, and the quantity was more than the Two Lands had ever seen!" Her bright smile was jerking convulsively; her voice rose high and shrill. "Let not him who shall hear this say it is a lie which I have said! Let him rather say, 'How like her this is! *How like her this is.* Worthy of her glorious father, Amon . . .' "

*   *   *

The dedication was the climax of the festival. Within the hour, the four golden arrows burst into the air, proclaiming the majesty of Hatshepsut to the four quarters of the earth. The Heb-Sed was over, and no Successor had been named.

Three days later, as if the gods stirred uneasily to correct the oversight, an old and yet always new miracle took place in one wing of the palace. Late in the evening, on the couch that had once belonged to royal Aahmes, the all-but-forgotten Princess Meryet-Re was delivered of her first child—a girl—in whose tiny body already waited the promise of future kings. Her father named her Meryet-Amon.

II.

Three years went by. On the surface all was as it had always been in Egypt; the Nile rose and fell, the winds blew for their fifty days and then departed, the seasons passed in slow procession over the long black land. But underneath the surface, a new unease was working, unseen but powerful. The gods were not the only ones who had noticed the queen's oversight in failing to name a Successor. The people noticed it too.

They were not used to thinking, the basketmaker and his like, they were used to accepting what their betters told them; but this time they had not been told enough. Here was the Heb-Sed over and done with, and not one mention had been made of who would next provide them with the breath of life. It gave one an indescribably lonely, unprotected feeling. When did Ma-ke-Re mean to name a Successor, if not at Heb-Sed? Such delay was dangerous—something might happen.

Immediately something did happen—something dreadful enough to frighten the *ka* out of a man's body, and keep on frightening him over and over for years, whenever he thought about it. A scant week after Heb-Sed, for some dark reason no one was ever able to discover, Count Nehsi, friend and favorite of Pharaoh, went into his bedchamber one evening, bolted the door, and stabbed himself through the heart.

Egypt was terrified by the very incomprehensibility of his action, news of which had spread from his servants to their cousins and thence to every market stall in Thebes before the horror

469

was a full day old. Most fearful of omens! Why would such a grand, respected, honored, wealthy noble kill himself? And when he did, what disaster did it portend? No one could imagine—but dread of the day, surely coming, that they would find out, trebled their burden of uneasiness. Egypt could never be secure, they told each other, without a Horus-in-the-Nest. Ma-ke-Re must name one, she must name one soon . . . still, even if she named one tomorrow, who would it be? When one thought about it, she had repudiated long ago the sole person in Egypt who could logically be called her heir.

Deep in their hearts, though they dared not put it into words even to themselves, the people began to wonder whether this had been altogether wise.

As the years went by the strange new questioning in their minds spread to other matters—signs and portents formerly ignored, which now seemed all related in some complex way. A man might stop on his way across the market place and stare thoughtfully, for moments together, at the corner where the old Sand-dweller merchant used to sell his wares—and now came no more. Another man, trudging along the causeway to Djeser-Djeseru with an offering, would study with the same dubious, thoughtful eye the frieze of barbarians carved on the bases of the sphinxes. A third, delivering his jars of honey to the palace kitchens, would stumble repeatedly because his gaze was on the empty barracks, not the road. All would be speculating about those rumors which used to flit about the market place, and all would be wishing they had paid more heed. Was all the world beyond Egypt actually roiling like new wine in the fermenting vats? If so, why did they not see soldiers in the barracks, in the streets rounding up recruits?

"But even if there were soldiers, who would lead them?" someone always said when these things were discussed in lowered voices. "Not Ma-ke-Re, not the female Horus."

Each pair of dark, painted eyes would meet the others anxiously, and after a long pause someone else was sure to whisper what all were thinking: *"He* could lead them—the other king—"

At once all the eyes would shift away, and no tongue would actually form the name of Men-kheper-Re. There was no *other* king, they would tell themselves nervously. Ma-ke-Re was Pharaoh—Ma-ke-Re the divine.

But they were vividly aware, these days, of the boy who had once been Pharaoh. After years of seclusion during which they had all but forgotten his existence, he had begun showing himself again upon the streets of Thebes. The jingling of harness would sound above the squabbling voices in the market place; then suddenly a war chariot—such as they had not seen since the days of the first Thutmose—would sweep around a curve of the street, drawn by two ebony-black stallions. The voices would fall silent as every eye fixed on the lone figure of the driver. One thing was certain—he was a boy no longer. Here was a man—stocky, lean-hipped, in the full vigor of his late twenties, with a look of suppressed but fiery energy in his set, bronzed face. He wore the Blue Helmet of Battle on his head, and a bow the equal of his grandfather's slung from one powerful shoulder; the very look of the old king was stamped upon his hawklike profile.

Deliberately, holding his rebellious stallions to an even pace, he would move down the attentive, silent street. He looked neither right nor left; he simply showed himself, and went his way. A few days later he would appear again—perhaps in an open litter this time, with his graceful young queen beside him and his three-year-old daughter crowing and laughing on his lap. Always, riding or driving, he wore the Blue Helmet, with the cobra jutting conspicuously over his brow and matching his nose for fierceness. Scarcely a week went by that he did not remind the people of his existence.

It was impossible not to be aware of him, not to notice the radiant health of his wife and the chubby vigor of his child—impossible not to think long and wistfully about that helmet and remember, with sinking heart, the frieze of captives carved in stone which was all Ma-ke-Re offered in its place.

Well, no matter, no matter, Ma-ke-Re was divine, was she not? the people asked each other loudly. That frieze was powerful magic, wasn't it? No invader had entered Egypt so far, had he? The thing for basketmakers and onion sellers to do was to spend less time thinking and more—much more—at the wineshop, watching the golden globes bounce and sway at the ends of the dancing-girls' braids, and sitting on the bank of drunkenness. A man should enjoy life and forget tomorrow; that was the advice every harper in Thebes was singing nowadays:

"The gods that were aforetime rest in their pyramids,
They that built them palaces, their places are no more.
Their walls are destroyed,
Their habitations are destroyed as if they had never been . . .
Rejoice, and let thy heart forget that day when they shall lay thee to rest!
Cast all sorrow behind thee, and bethink only of joy
Until there comes that day of mooring in the land that loveth silence;
Follow thy desire, put myrrh on thy head, clothe thee in fine linen,
Set singing and music before thy face.
Lo, none may take his goods with him, and none that hath gone may ever come again!"

In the palace, too, the harper's song was heard. The hearts of nobles as well as onion sellers were weighted with riddles, and the heavier the burden grew, the more urgently they craved the harper and the more gaily they followed his advice—encouraged and abetted by the queen herself, who lately seemed determined to turn the royal banquet hall into a scene of never-ending festival. Night after night wine flowed like the Nile, inundating yesterday and tomorrow beneath its cheerful flood. Jugglers, wrestlers, dancers, musicians, followed one another across the polished floor, while lotuses wilted in luxurious profusion on every column and cones of priceless ointment melted opulently atop every wig to run in fragrant streams down faces flushed with laughter. Expense meant nothing; Hatshepsut measured gold for the diversion of her court with the same lavish hand that had measured it for her obelisks.

Her courtiers blessed her for it. When everyone was behaving eccentrically from too much wine, it was easy not to notice her eccentricities—her repeated blinking, the exaggerated stiffness of her carriage, her strange new habit of wearing one crown and keeping the other two beside her in the chair. When everyone's laughter was shrill, hers did not shock; when everyone's eyes were bright and hard, hers did not remind one of a person with a fever. In the morning, at the Audience—well, one must simply set one's teeth and endure it if one could. But if one drank enough wine while it was flowing, one could arrange a morning headache of such proportions that Audience and throne alike receded into a haze; in fact, sometimes one could avoid appearing at the palace at all.

One small group of the courtiers did not—because they dared not—avail themselves of the protection of drunkenness. These were the younger Kinsmen, scions of noble families who had stepped into vacancies in the Council during the past few years and were too new to their responsibilities and too inexperienced in their duties not to need all their wits about them. It was difficult enough, as young Lord Anpu, Master of the Royal Storehouses, often had occasion to reflect, to oversee a hundred scribes and the many hundred varieties of wealth for which he was accountable; it was thrice difficult when one was continually being confronted with two sets of conflicting orders, neither of which one dared disobey. Scarcely a week went by that His Highness Men-kheper-Re—wearing the cobra—did not walk into Anpu's offices and demand linen, leather, copper, everything one could imagine, in staggering amounts. And then what did one do?

"But—but Your Highness!" Anpu, appalled, had stammered the first time this happened. "I have no authority for such—such wholesale disbursements, the queen would—" He broke off, turning a little pale, and inquired respectfully what His Highness wanted the stores for.

His Highness declined to say.

"Well, I—naturally, Your Highness understands that I must consult Her Majesty before issuing such quantities of the royal stores."

"Very well, consult her," Men-kheper-Re ordered. As Anpu stared at him in utter disbelief, he added impatiently, "Go at once! I am in haste."

"Your Highness—I beg Your Highness' indulgence, but I —I do not believe Her Majesty's attitude will be favorable to your request."

"I did not ask for your opinion, I asked for stores!" Men-kheper-Re said. "Go, consult the queen. Ask her"—a faint smile twisted the corners of his hard, flat-planed mouth—"ask her if it is not her gracious command that His Highness should have everything he desires."

"But, Your Highness—"

"Name of Amon, man! I said go!"

Anpu went. The curves of His Highness' mouth had set hard

indeed, and the black eyes above bored into a man in a way that left no thought but to obey. Before Anpu had recovered from their influence he found himself facing just such another pair.

"Well?" the queen said. "You have a petition?"

"If Your Majesty please—I am sent by—by His Highness Men-kheper-Re, who wishes to draw certain stores from the—"

He stopped abruptly. The queen's face had turned white as linen; the eyes looked like burning chunks of ebony.

"He is to have nothing!" she screamed at Anpu. "Nothing, nothing, not a scrap of leather, not a length of cloth!"

"Aye, Your Majesty," Anpu whispered. He was half bent in his obeisance when his eagerness to leave the room was suddenly tempered by the strong suspicion that he would be sent straight back to it if he did not say what he had been told to say. Swallowing hard, he slowly straightened. "Your Majesty's indulgence— but I—is it not Your Majesty's gracious command that His Highness is to have everything he desires?"

Ma-ke-Re stared straight through him for a moment; he had never seen so motionless a countenance. Then, slowly, she settled back in her chair. "Aye, that is My Majesty's gracious command," she said in an entirely different voice. She smiled, blinking very rapidly. "It has always been so. His Highness has had every comfort, every honor. My Majesty even included scarabs inscribed with his name in the foundations of holy Djeser-Djeseru, and caused his image to be carved on one of the porches Those who look upon My Majesty's monuments in later years will say, 'How like her this was! How kind, how good . . .'"

Anpu, able to breathe again, was recovering some of his composure and all of his eagerness to be gone. However, there was now the problem that the queen seemed to have forgotten all about him. He waited for a pause in her flow of words, and quickly leaped into it.

"Then it is Your Majesty's command that I issue these store to His Highness?"

"My command?" She turned on him, eyes blazing again. "You heard my command, he is to have nothing! Nothing, nothing By the Beard of Ptah, why can I not find able ministers to serve me! You new ones—all dolts, all strangers—new faces, that is all I see about me, new strange faces! Leave me, leave me!"

Anpu left; indeed, he fled—but only to return to his office

and the other pair of eyes. With the hopeless calm of a man with his back to the wall, he told Men-kheper-Re all the queen had said.

A strange expression passed over His Highness' face. After a moment he said in a harsh, peculiar voice, "Poor Lady Shesu! Reality is closing in."

"I beg Your Highness' pardon?" Anpu said blankly. Since he got no answer, he forced himself on to the inevitable conclusion of his tale. "Therefore—as Your Highness can see—I must refuse to issue you the stores."

Men-kheper-Re drew a long breath and straightened. "Aye, so you must," he said briskly. "No matter; I will fetch them myself."

He started past Anpu, into the storerooms. Trembling but desperate, the young man stepped in front of him. "Your Highness—it is not permitted."

The eyes were only inches from his own. "I wear the cobra," said Men-kheper-Re. "Will *you* lay hands on me to stop me?"

It was a moment Anpu never forgot; it was, perhaps, the most important moment of his life. Some months later, when sheer agitation prevented him from keeping it any longer to himself, he described it in all its harrowing detail to his two closest friends—young Count Puemre, Ineny's successor as Overseer of Works, and Intef, Prince of Thinis and Master of the Western Oases—both newcomers to the Council, like himself.

"Mother of mighty Amon! What a predicament," Puemre murmured fearfully, when he had finished.

Intef said nothing, but his eyes were bright with interest.

"What is more," Anpu told them, "that was only the first time. Amon help me, it has been happening ever since."

"Well?" Intef said. "Go on, go on! What do you do about it?"

"My friend, what can I do?" Anpu spread his hands helplessly. "I issue him the stores—and beg him not to tell the queen."

"Haaaah! Naturally!" Intef breathed, with an air of triumph.

The other two studied him guardedly. "Is it so natural, then," Anpu whispered with the beginning of hope in his voice, "to do as he commands?"

"I think it is." Intef teetered on his toes a moment, casually glancing about the garden where they were standing. Finding it empty, he went on, very softly. "I had a similar experience—three years ago. In my case it did not need to be repeated." He leaned closer, dropping his voice to a whisper. "Do you know what crop we are raising on the Western Oases—by His Highness' order—and have been raising for three years? Horses. War stallions. The queen does not yet know."

That year, on a bright, breezy morning a week after the Festival of the High Nile, news of another terrible omen shook Thebes. On the previous evening the Vizier and High Priest of Amon, Hapuseneb, had received a folded message as he sat at dinner, had risen and gone into his garden, and had been found there in the moonlight half an hour later with a dagger protruding from his throat.

When questioned, the servant who had delivered the folded message insisted hysterically that the note had been given him by a Captain of Archers—he had distinctly seen the insigne on the stranger's leather wrist guard when he showed him into the garden to wait. They could get nothing else out of him; and since there had been no such thing as a Captain of Archers in Egypt since Ma-ke-Re disbanded the bodyguard, his testimony was useless.

The concensus in Thebes was that the murder had been committed by a *kheft*—for the strangest aspect of the whole occurrence was that there was no indication whatsoever of a struggle. When they found Hapuseneb, he was lying quietly beside his lotus pool, his garments still immaculate, his jewels still intact, and his features still calm—as imperturbable in death as he had been throughout his lifetime.

Hatshepsut received the news from Senmut early in the morning. Two hours later, she was sitting before the great golden shield in the council chamber, with the Double Crown pressing upon her forehead and the other two, Red and White, close beside her in the chair. She knew why she was here—a new vizier must be appointed; the Kinsmen had been suggesting, advising, arguing among themselves about it for an hour. She made no effort to listen to what they were saying. One voice spoke, then another, then another, and she could think of nothing but that all were strangers to her. New voices, new faces, all around her. Where had the old ones gone, so quickly, in a few short years, like a puff of smoke vanishing before one knew it? When she planned her obelisks all had been as it had always been. Now Ineny was gone, Nehsi was gone, Hapuseneb was gone; Thutiy was an old, old man with wandering thoughts, always talking of his childhood, no longer strong enough to leave his couch. And Senmut—

She turned her head slowly and looked at Senmut. He was standing against the golden hanging, silent, watching the others as she had been doing, his face a dark, derisive mask. He was wearing a silver headcloth that reminded her of the first time she had ever seen him.

For an instant the room faded into desert sand, and she was sitting on a stone bench in a little desert chapel, looking up at a sinewy young man with mocking, bold, black eyes, who reeked of cheap wine and filled her with a curious excitement. They had talked about the temple. Even that first day, they had talked about the temple.

The memory dissolved in a fragile rush, as if her sigh had blown it away. She stirred herself, sitting up a little straighter yet, trying to listen to the Kinsmen. He is not keeping anything from me, she thought. It is impossible, what would it be? He does nothing save by my wish, he lives only to serve me. Besides, he loves me. He loves me.

"If Your Majesty would consider a moment the qualities of His Excellency Ramose of Menfe—a young man, vigorous and brilliant of mind, descended from all the princes of Menfe and already experienced in the governorship of his nome . . ."

Hatshepsut stared at young Puemre scornfully and let him talk. She had already decided who would be her next vizier— old Nibamon, who had been Overseer of the Hall of the King when Nenni was Pharaoh. He would not know much about a vizier's duties, but at least his face was known to her, known and familiar. Senmut would instruct him anyway, as he had always instructed Hapuseneb. In actual fact, Senmut had been vizier for years.

She glanced at him again, and this time caught his eye—the same black, bold eye, gleaming with mockery, though his body had grown heavy and slack, and his face as creviced as granite. The look they exchanged reviewed the decision they had agreed upon before they came to the Council chamber—all the decisions they had privately agreed upon for years—and suddenly a warm, clear rush of confidence filled Hatshepsut. She raised her hand abruptly, silenced the jabbering strangers who imagined they could advise her.

"My Majesty," she announced, "will appoint His Excellency Nibamon to the office of vizier three days from now, at the monthly Festival of the Sun."

She smiled, blinking rapidly to fight down the rush of bubbles that suddenly engulfed her. She did not look into the Kinsmen's faces, but serenely over their heads. They were silent, and their silence was aghast. No matter. She had not expected them to approve her choice, she expected them to obey her. And they would, they would obey her. She was Ma-ke-Re, and she wore the crown.

Close by her side, her hand moved as if of its own accord, closed over the edge of the White Crown and gripped it tight, while the other hand found the Red. At the edge of her mind, like a *kheft* whispering from the shadows, Nenni's long-stilled voice echoed: *"They must obey that, do you see? It is their own invention."*

"The council is dismissed," she said loudly, to drown it out. She rose, watched the stiffly expressionless faces before her bow once more in submission to her will. Then she left the chamber, safe inside her Circle, with a crown hugged in either arm. Let all the faces be new, it did not matter. She was ruler of all the world —and she still had Senmut.

The people were given a feast at the appointment of the new vizier, to help them forget the strange death of the old one. The entertainments were resumed at the palace, on a more lavish scale than before, and in the market place the talk at last died down, though the uneasiness did not. Only the peasant, in his faceless thousands, was able to submerge his fears in the monotony of work. The flood was receding off the fields, and he had his planting to attend to—and after that the endless lifting of water in earthen jars, at which he had been laboring ceaselessly for two thousand years and would still be laboring two thousand years hence, no matter how many Great Ones came and went. His high priest and strictest taskmaster was the Nile; and his days moved slowly by, whether toward disaster or joy he did not know, to the wailing music of the water wheel, the buzzing of flies, and the changeless glare of the sun.

478

Early one morning toward the end of the Season of Coming Forth, Senmut drove alone to Djeser-Djeseru. The atmosphere at the palace was beginning to get badly on his nerves, which had seldom been shaken by anything. Ever since Hapuseneb's death six months ago he had felt like a man moving alone and conspicuous in a glare of light through a dark and dangerous street, and he needed reassurance.

Tying his horses to a boulder at the edge of the deserted quarry, he mounted the ramp to the temple's lower court and paused in spite of his preoccupation to check with an architect's eye the unfinished colonnade on the northeast. Part of the inner wall and a few columns were still lacking; as he walked toward it he automatically completed it in his mind's eye, and felt the familiar thrill of pleasure at the result.

Passing between the columns, he stopped before one of the little closetlike shrines that had been carved out of the cliff behind the colonnade. He glanced behind him quickly, then stepped into the tiny room. He had to wait a moment for his vision to adjust to the deep gloom within, but gradually he began to make out, on the wall against which the wooden door would open, the carved outlines of a kneeling figure. Its hands shielded its eyes in worship, and it faced toward the west end of the shrine, where the image of a god would stand. Close in front of the figure—though without a torch no one could read the hieroglyphs—was inscribed a short prayer and a name. Senmut stepped close to the wall and traced the carved symbols with his fingers, his heart beating fast. The name carved here was his—and the figure was his. So far as he knew, no mortal on earth had ever before presumed to invade the premises sacred to his monarch. Here only Hatshepsut might inscribe her name—yet here his was, nevertheless—and not only here but in each one of dozens of such sanctuaries opening off every court and chapel in the temple. For untold centuries to come, as long as the temple itself stood, he, Senmut of the fish wharves, would kneel here behind the door in the presence of the gods, enjoying the prerogatives of an anointed Pharaoh, sharing the offerings, breathing the incense, living forever.

He drew a long, satisfied breath and stepped out into the early sunshine, making a mental note to rush the hanging of these last few doors. Once the doors were hung, his monstrous audacity

479

was safe from discovery. He smiled as he walked down the ramp and headed for the quarry. He could imagine, only too vividly, Hatshepsut's reaction should she ever discover his secret. But once she was safely installed as Osiris in the Land of the West, he did not think she would really be angry to find him standing as usual beside her throne. Angry or not, that was where he intended to be.

The first squealing of the water wheels rang through the early-morning air as he started over the brink of the quarry; the day was beginning. He hurried down the quarry's side and across its rocky bottom. In the dusk of his tomb's entrance he paused, uncertain whether or not he had glimpsed a flash of movement just as he slipped behind the masking boulders.

Some workman arriving early, he thought. Or more likely a mongrel—or nothing at all.

He lighted one of the torches from the lamp flickering on the first step, and descended the stair.

The first room was still rough and unfinished; he had decided to have painted scenes here instead of carved inscriptions, and that would be the last work done. On either side of the stair outside, however, a change had occurred—on one side a round-topped niche had been carved into the wall, and opposite, the rock had been smoothed in preparation for another. Two stelae setting forth his accomplishments would be let into these niches; already they were in progress, at a sculptor's shop in the City of the Dead. Meanwhile, Senmut noticed to his amusement, one of his draughtsmen had found the smoothly prepared surface of the far wall irresistible. Holding the torch closer, Senmut studied his own unmistakable profile, sketched in rapidly but expertly with a reed pen. "The Steward of Amon, Senmut," it was labeled, and it was he to the life, crinkled wig, harsh lines about the mouth, derisive smile and all; there was even his own *ankh*-amulet about the throat. It was an excellent sketch, and the man's impudence appealed to Senmut. As he moved on down the stairs, he resolved to locate the artist and set him to doing bigger things; this little effort would be destroyed as soon as the stoneworkers began on that second niche today. For an instant his mind went back to the flash of movement he had seen—or thought he had seen—in the quarry. A workman would have been down here by now. Probably it had been a dog—or his imagination.

480

Senmut dismissed the matter, but he was frowning a little as he entered the second room. He had never seen a mongrel in the quarry—and he was not in the habit of imagining things.

The carvings in the second room were complete now, and the room itself half filled with stonecutters' chips from the passages beyond. Senmut climbed over the pile of chips and descended the next flight of stairs into a third room. More steps led down from it, but these were so choked with rubble that he would have had to crawl to reach the bottom. He knew what was there—the small, vaulted chamber in which he would rest throughout eternity. He stood a moment, gazing down into the darkness, feeling an odd sensation along his spine. His jaw clenched as he went over in his mind every inch of the completed room above, assuring himself that every spell was inscribed there, every trick of magic, every declaration that his *ka* must know to cross the Lily Lake and enter the world of the dead.

Of course they are, he thought, shrugging his shoulders to relax them. They are all there, I have forgotten nothing. I doubt if I will even need them, considering those shrines up yonder. . . .

He turned briskly, flashed his torch once around the still-unfinished third room, and climbed the rubble-strewn stairs to the second. Before he left it he checked the spells on the walls once more, then climbed on, smiling with grim satisfaction.

He had forgotten nothing, there was no eventuality he had not foreseen and provided for. Once the last shrine doors were hung, all would go exactly as he planned. He was as good as sitting on the footstool of Osiris this minute. And considering how indispensable he was to Hatshepsut in this life—

His thoughts stopped short, his eyes flew to the square of daylight at the top of the stairs. A shadow had crossed it. A workman, he thought mechanically. A dog. My imagination. He knew it was none of these.

He dropped his torch and beat out its flame with his sandal. The dark swooped in around him; for a moment he could see nothing but the bright, blurred square above. Slowly, as his eyes adjusted, the walls of the stairway grew dimly visible to him —most visible near the top. He could make out a low mound on one side of the doorway which he recognized as the pile of torch-sticks, but he looked in vain for the wick burning in the bowl of oil. It had been extinguished. On the opposite side of the doorway was a shadow blacker than the rest—the motionless, waiting figure that had extinguished it.

He stood for some moments, trying to make out a face, the outlines of a form, but the gloom was too deep there in the corner. Nothing was really visible except the rough-hewn, slanting tunnel of the stairwell that led straight up to it from where he stood. From where he stood— The full import of his situation stole over him, filled him to his fingertips. Behind him lay a tomb; ahead an unused quarry, empty and echoing in the early sunlight. The tomb door was perfectly concealed behind its boulders—that was how he had planned it.

The workmen. Hope leaped in him and instantly sank like a stone. The workmen would not be coming today—obviously the waiting figure would have seen to that.

He moistened his lips, gazing ahead at that solid shadow. Half seen though it was, it had an unmistakable air of patience. It had planned well; he could not restrain a certain bitter admiration. It had left him but one course to follow—one, precisely one. It was quite clear that he must walk straight up those stairs and find out what stood beside the door.

He drew a long breath and started. Two steps up, he remembered that the last doors to the shrines were not yet hung. His foot faltered, almost missed the next tread. It was not fair, he too had planned well, and he had wanted to be sure, *sure*—now he was being rushed. With security almost within his grasp he was being forced to gamble his Three Thousand Years in paradise on a few wooden doors. . . .

His foot steadied and found the step; he forced his nerves to steady as well. Why, after all, should he balk at one last gamble? He had been gambling all his life. His mouth twisted in a smile as he placed a silent wager with the gods.

He was more than halfway up now. Slowly, but without pausing any more, he climbed the remaining stairs. He felt no real surprise to find a Captain of Archers waiting for him at the top.

12.

The sound of the chisels had started up again in Hatshepsut's head. She sat still and erect on her electrum throne, trying to listen to old Nibamon and young Intef, now Royal Herald, who between them were conducting the Weekly Audience, but their voices were blurred and strange. They seemed to come from a thousand leagues away. All she could hear were the chisels, and someone weeping so piteously that all sadness, all despair seemed to be wrapped up in the sound. It was herself who was weeping, she knew that—but only deep inside; she never let it show. In all this long and terrible year since Senmut's death she had never by one tear, one sound, betrayed to her enemies that Ma-ke-Re was a woman, who was suffering like any mortal. Every hour she had to pay the price—eyes forever burning with all those unshed tears, ears ringing with the echo of chisels whose actual clatter had faded months ago from Djeser-Djeseru, mind filling with pictures of the little piles of chips that had accumulated outside the doors of the shrines. . . .

I will not remember, she thought. *I will not remember.* She opened her eyes wide and strained to hear, above the desolate sound of the chisels, what was going on in the Great Hall. The Kinsmen were grouped around the dais, in their proper positions; one of them would step forward with the long, gliding step of the courtier, and his mouth would move, and his hand would gesture; then some other would respond, or the royal scribe would bring forth his leather roll, or a petitioner would be brought in or sent away. It was like an elegant dance, but it had no meaning for her because she could hear no voices. She could only see their faces—young, smooth, untried—Puemre's instead of old Ineny's, Intef's instead of Thutiy's; there at the left, instead of Nehsi's grave and dusky features, Nibamon's foolish, vapid ones, and here close beside her, where Senmut used to stand, nobody, nothing, emptiness.

For a moment Senmut's face hung in the air before her, dark, slashed with the harsh lines of his smile, set with his mocking eyes that she knew now had been mocking her, too.

I will not remember! she told herself.

It was no use, the old sick sensation squeezed about her heart, and she was remembering. The carpenter's face, and his mouth whispering—something about the hanging of some doors—she had not comprehended at first what he was saying, and when she did, she did not believe, could not believe. Even when she stood inside the little shrine, with the torch mercilessly revealing the shape of treachery, she could not believe what her eyes had proved. When she stepped outside again the world was black and ugly, the fields ashes, the sun an evil cinder. She heard her voice giving orders, remembered her leaden feet moving into every shrine and the torch lighting the same horror in endless repetition, remembered a stoneworker cringing before her, whispering, pointing toward the quarry, the leaden feet moving again, the torch shining cruelly on the sly, secret walls of the stairway which burrowed under her holy temple, on the copied star-map which boasted coarsely of her truly-given love, on the insolent inscription blazoned across it. When she walked out again into the dark and terrible day she was staring, unprotected, at the face of truth.

She had rewarded the carpenter; hating him, longing to beat him to dust with her own hands, she had rewarded him. It was Senmut she had beaten to dust. She had ordered his body snatched from the hands of the embalmers and thrown into the desert, forbidden it to lie in any tomb. She had set the chisels to ringing across the quiet terraces of Djeser-Djeseru, and in the quarry tomb, and in the other tomb on the hill, and on every statue and inscription throughout the length of Egypt which had borne his name or image. She had obliterated him from the land, and she had torn him from her heart, but the wound that was left would not heal, and the chisels would not stop sounding in her head, and she could not hear what was happening in the Audience. . . .

She shifted a little on her throne and tried with a straining effort to shift her attention too, to make her ears hear outward noises instead of the weeping and the lonely inward clatter. Puemre was saying something about the works of Her Majesty. With a chill she realized he was talking about the new gold mine in Sinai, proposing to stop the work there and call the gangs and their overseers back to Egypt.

"What nonsense is this?" she cut in sharply. "What are you doing behind my back? My Majesty has given no orders concerning the recall of these men, and will give none."

"Then Your Majesty must be prepared to lose them, and the future treasure of the mines as well," Puemre said. "A deserted mine may be concealed. The camp of a thousand workers cannot.

484

If the location of this rich new vein should fall into the hands of Sand-dwellers—"

A wall went up in her mind; she held it there desperately, propping it with whatever came to hand. "Nonsense! There is no more danger from Sand-dwellers than from a few buzzing flies."

"It is so no longer, Majesty. There is violent unrest. Raids, uprisings—"

"Nonsense!" She was leaning forward, gripping the arms of the throne, frantically stuffing the chinks of her wall, which kept crumbling here, trembling there. Senmut had always been her wall, but he was not beside her now, she had it all to do alone and she strained with the effort of it until even the flesh of her face seemed to be stretching taut as a mask against its bones. "The work in the mines will continue!"

Puemre's eyes, veiled and unreadable, met hers a moment, then flashed to Intef's under cover of a slight, hostile bow. "I fear it is not nonsense, Your Majesty. War spreads like an inundation through all the tribes of the Sand-dwellers, for a dam has broken—Sharuhen has fallen to the king of Kadesh."

Her wall crumbled and fell with a roar into scattered rubble. Inwardly whirling from it, she snatched at the battered remnants of an old, familiar shield to hold between herself and the truth's terrible visage. "Let them squabble. I am more interested in the insolence of my Overseer of Works, who presumes to have more wisdom than his Pharaoh." She paused, glaring into Puemre's eyes. "I am Horus! It is my command that the mine continue to give forth its treasure. Not one foreman, not one slave, shall be recalled."

There was silence in the Great Hall, but it was suddenly filled with menace, as a dozen pairs of eyes stared back at her as inscrutably as Puemre's, as near rebellion. At her sides, her hands felt for the crowns, closed over them in terror. "I am Horus!" she repeated. *"I am Pharaoh."*

Puemre's eyes wavered. After an endless moment they dropped. "It shall be as Your Majesty commands," he muttered.

Hatshepsut sank back slowly, let her fingers go slack on the hard edges of the crowns. *They must obey that, do you see? It is their own invention.* "Let the Audience continue," she said in a dull, low voice.

485

Intef cleared his throat and announced the next petitioner, while the chisels and the weeping took up their monotonous antiphony again in Hatshepsut's mind.

So Nenni was right, she thought. Perhaps he was always right.

A memory, long barred from her mind, crept back to haunt her—a familiar tall, stooped figure with weary eyes and a heavy crown upon its head.

Has it come to that, then? she thought. Have I nothing left but the crown?

Fear stole into her heart as she thought of Thoth. He had been gone from Thebes almost a month now, on one of his mysterious voyages to the south. When he came back, would these hostile ones obey even the crown? They had almost refused to obey it today.

I could name him Successor, she told herself. I could place him beside me on the throne, let him ride just behind me in processions. . . .

Ah, yes. The compromise. The solution which solves everything but the problem.

She stiffened, trying to push Nenni's long-silent voice from her mind. I will not compromise! she answered it passionately. I am Pharaoh, and I shall be Pharaoh until I die, or else my life is meaningless, meaningless!

Aye, no doubt all lives are meaningless.

They are not, they are not! she cried, while the chisels clattered in her ears and the sound of weeping rose to a wailing of despair.

Let me speak to you of facts, of which you know little, my Shesu, despite all your efforts . . .

Her passion collapsed like a punctured wineskin, leaving only a void, and no wall to shield her from it. Truth had many faces, she was beginning to realize. All were terrible. And one of them wore this fever-wasted countenance with the ironic mouth and the unutterably weary eyes.

"Your Majesty. Your Majesty! Ah. I crave Your Majesty's pardon, but does it please Your Majesty to grant this petitioner's request, or—"

"The request is granted," she said. She had not even seen the petitioner, had not heard a word he said.

"The god has heard your plea. You may go."

486

Intef cleared his throat. "The next petitioner—"

"There will be no next," Hatshepsut said. "I will hear no more today. I am—"

Tired? She was only forty-seven years old, and she had never been tired in all her life, she had never known illness, she had walked in strength and radiance, like a god. But today—though she did not finish her sentence aloud—she felt a weakness and a heaviness throughout her limbs that made her look upon the journey to the door as endless.

"But, Your Majesty—today is the awarding of the gold of favor to His Excellency Anpu."

She paused in the act of getting to her feet. How many times had she stood on that balcony, proudly, joyously throwing down gold and honor upon Senmut, until his servants were heavy-laden with the tokens of her love? There was not one memory that was not bitter now. This favoring of Anpu would hold no love, no joy—not even pride. It was a political expedient.

She straightened, feeling old as the Nile. "I will confer the gold," she told old Nibamon.

Black wigs and white headcloths dipped before her, leaving a path of shining floor between their ranks. The Circle formed around her, attendants at either side reverently lifted the White and Red crowns. She walked slowly down the steps of the dais and started the long journey toward the big double doors, with the courtiers falling in behind her to witness the ceremony of the gold.

Nenni, she thought. Nenni, I am tired, like you.

There was some other clatter in her ears besides the chisels— she realized it was coming from outside, approaching up the avenue from the river. Chariot wheels, running feet, a confused, exultant shouting. . . . She stopped, turning cold. "What is that noise?" she asked Nibamon.

"I think—if Your Majesty please—I think it is Men-kheper-Re returning."

If Her Majesty pleased. What a fool the man was. (Men-kheper-Re. It was always Men-kheper-Re now, never just "His Highness.")

She walked on, stiff with dread, passed from the Great Hall into the transverse corridor, and stopped again. The noise had suddenly become a din; obviously the palace gates had been thrown open. She could hear chariots, horses, men, pouring into the great court against a background of shouting that seemed to extend far down the avenue toward the river. Worse, she could make out, now, what they were shouting: "Men-kheper-Re! Men-kheper-Re!"

Behind her, the courtiers were crowding out of the Audience Chamber and into the hall where she stood, transfixed. I must move, I must go on, I must ignore it! she told herself. She did not have time. The outer doors burst open, and Thoth walked into the hall.

He halted at sight of her, and a look of fierce satisfaction came over his face. He was burned black as a Nubian from the southern sun; his features were hard, his eyes so hard and bitter she had the sensation of bruising herself against a rock. How different, how frighteningly different from Iset's little boy, or from the bewildered Babylonian child who had been so easy to manage. . . .

"We have returned," he said.

After a tiny pause, during which she forcibly restrained herself from moistening her lips, she answered. "We?"

He stepped aside, out of the doorway, and her glance flew past him. The Great Court was a confusion of horses, chariots—and soldiers.

Soldiers. Officers. It was as if they had sprung out of the ground, fully armed, fully uniformed. They were in battle dress—helmets, coarse kilts, cuirasses of quilted leather marked with the insignia of their rank, scarlet belts with daggers or battle hatchets thrust through them. There was a Foot Captain piling shields and javelins on the pavement near the palace steps, a Captain of Archers standing at the outer gates, watching a double line of bowmen pass down the avenue toward the old barracks. Her eyes jerked back. *A Captain of Archers.* He half turned toward her, speaking to someone over his shoulder, and she saw his face—a dark, alert face with a wide, curving mouth.

The scene wavered and blurred, and the inner sound of chisels rose to a din. She was intensely aware of the throng of courtiers behind her. She said, in a voice she did not recognize, "Who are these men?"

"The troops of Egypt!" Thoth flung the words at her, and she flung hers back.

488

"Egypt has no troops! My Majesty needs none and desires none."

"Nevertheless, you see them before you. Others—ten thousand others—are on the river, coming from Nekheb."

Nekheb, she thought. *Uah*. Gods, after all these years . . . all my friends dead, my enemy living.

"I see," she said. "They are coming from Nekheb." She strained to raise her voice above a whisper, to make it even and natural. "Very well, they must return to Nekheb. Command them to re-embark at once."

"Nay, I will not. I am moving them to Thebes, where they belong. I need this barracks now, and the drill field."

"I will not permit these hordes to occupy My Majesty's barracks!" she cried.

"It makes no difference," he said quietly, "whether you permit it or not." He started to turn away.

"Thoth!" she screamed.

He turned back and looked at her with the hardest eyes she had ever seen. *Oh gods, oh gods!* she thought. *Nenni, help me! You always loved me, help me, help me!* "I gave you a command, did you not hear me?" she said, again in that hoarse, strained whisper.

"I heard."

"Then you must obey. I am Ma-ke-Re. I am Pharaoh! *Disperse those troops!*"

A change came over Thoth's face. His eyes lifted to the crowd of silent courtiers behind her, moved slowly over their faces, and returned to hers.

"If you are Pharaoh," he said bluntly, "*you* disperse them."

Outside, on the avenue, the shouting rose in volume as some new regiment marched by. "Men-kheper-Re! Men-kheper-Re! . . ." Inside, there was no sound at all. She saw herself walking angrily to the Great Court, heard herself arrogantly, clearly, giving the command—but she could not see what would happen then. Her silence, and its agony, stretched on and on until it seemed a lifetime must have passed.

At last she whispered, "You must obey me—you must obey me."

"I am done with obeying you," Thoth said. "Now. Forever."

He turned and walked away. This time she did not call him back. She stood gazing straight ahead, listening to the hard, vigorous sound of his footsteps die away in the direction of his apartments, where Mayet, heavy with his second child, awaited him. There was still no sound from the courtiers crowded motionless behind her; but they were there. They had seen, they had heard. "If you are Pharaoh, *you* disperse them." And the answer? Silence.

In Hatshepsut's mind a picture rose as vividly as if it were taking place before her. She saw the pavilion in the little garden, the children playing on the steps with their baskets of colored eggs, Nenni silent in the gold-and-cedar chair, and her mother, Aahmes, head proudly erect on her withered neck, face set in a mask of queenly serenity, listening to another hard and confident young voice. *"It is not necessary that you understand it, my lady mother. Nenni, I will join you at the Council, as I planned."*

So she had spoken, on that long-ago sunny day—in the same ruthless tones Thoth had used just now, walking away with the same self-sufficient step, leaving her mother standing motionless in this same lonely dignity, all her authority departed.

I will be Pharaoh until I die, she thought.

She did not allow herself to moisten her lips, though they moved stiffly, as if they were made of stone. "Bid my court gather beneath the window," she said to Nibamon. "My Majesty will award the gold now."

She walked stiffly to one side of the double stairway, mounted to the Window of Royal Appearances, willed her eyes to be blind when it was thrown open to the milling soldiers in the Great Court. Methodically she threw down necklaces and golden chains to Anpu and his servants, until the baskets beside her were empty. When it was done she turned and walked stiffly down again, across the transverse hall and along the corridor to the Apartments of the King. There she dismissed the Circle and walked alone into her yellow-walled sitting room. The door closed behind her.

For a moment she stood motionless, as the sound of the door closing repeated itself in diminishing echoes in her ears. Then she forced herself on, across the room, to her dressing table. Picking up her silver mirror, she looked long and silently at the face of Pharaoh. *Her Majesty was a maiden, beautiful and blooming* . . . Her Majesty was only forty-seven years old, but no one was watching now, and the chisels were sounding in her ears.

490

The face began to change. Before she put the mirror down, it was the face of an old woman that looked out at her.

Her Majesty was a maiden . . . Her Majesty was a *maiden*.

She turned slowly away, moved on her leaden feet across the sitting room and into the alcove off her bedchamber where the golden image of Amon stood in its niche at the foot of her couch. Overhead, the star-map on the ceiling had been obliterated; the room no longer seemed familiar. But the image stood where it had always stood. She dropped to her knees before it and stared up into the golden face.

Moments passed in silence.

"Why do they deny me?" she whispered at last. "Have I done anything that was not by your bidding, and to your glory? Have I? Have I? Have I left anything undone that a king should do?"

The tears she had not shed all these months suddenly came in a torrent. She buried her face in her hands, and her body bent with the racking force of her sobs. I have not, I have not! she thought. My works are good, they are great. I have no fault, save that I was born a maid, and not a man.

At last her sobbing quieted. She raised her head slowly, feeling exhausted but somehow cleansed by the tears and by the knowledge that she had spoken truth. Reaching into the little box beside the brazier she found a pellet of myrrh and tossed it into the fire.

"Hear me," she whispered. "Hear your beloved daughter. Change my form when death takes my *ka*. I pray you—let me mount the throne of Osiris as a *man*."

After a moment she rose and walked to the table beside her couch. *I will be Pharaoh until I die. . . .*

A carafe stood on the table. She poured wine into a goblet, took a sandalwood box from the shelf above it. Inside the box was a smaller box of alabaster; inside that, a tiny ebony casket containing a pellet that was not myrrh. She dropped the pellet into the goblet.

Clasping her hands tightly in front of her, she began to whisper the Declaration of Innocence.

"I have committed no wrong against people. I have not done evil in the place of truth. I allowed no one to hunger, I caused no one to weep. I did not murder, *I did not command to murder* . . ." Tears sprang again to her eyes at the bitter truth of those

491

words. If she had been only a little less merciful, a little less opposed to bloodshed—if she had let Senmut do the ruthless thing he had always thought best—Egypt might still be hers this minute.

Senmut . . .

"I did not load the weight of the balance," she whispered hurriedly. "I did not deflect the index of the scales or snare the fowl of the gods. I caused no man misery! I am pure! I am pure! I am pure! I am pure!"

Senmut . . .

Her mouth twisted uncontrollably; the sound of the chisels had begun again, faintly, in her ears. Quickly she raised the goblet to her lips and drank. The potion was bitter; but not so bitter as the cup she had already drunk.

She sank down onto her couch. Stretching herself flat upon it, the Double Crown still upon her head, she crossed her hands on her breast.

13.

Thoth stood high on the cliff above Hatshepsut's temple, watching the scene he himself had set in motion. A few paces behind him, Rekhmi-re leaned against a boulder, watching too. All Thebes was watching. Thoth had only to lift his eyes in any direction to see figures on every rooftop, on the palace walls, rimming the far curve of the cliff, blackening the desert road and the western fringes of the City of the Dead. The bay in the cliffs had become a vast ampitheatre, and the temple was its stage. For five days all work had been forgotten, and every eye had fastened in awe on what was happening at Djeser-Djeseru.

Let them watch, Thoth thought grimly. Let them note well.

His eyes came back to the carnival of destruction taking place below him. A shifting cloud of dust hung over the once-peaceful terraces; workmen swarmed everywhere, and the sound of chisels echoed over the valley. On the highest terrace, six of the huge limestone statues of Ma-ke-Re as Osiris had been toppled from their places between the columns and lay in fragments in the upper court. Gangs of workmen were hauling the larger pieces

492

away, while other gangs stumbled amid the rubble, tugging with ropes upon the next one. The great kneeling statue of black granite from the sanctuary court was moving slowly on rollers across the lowest terrace, headed for the rim of the old quarry—where its mate in red granite already stood, headless and wreathed in smoke from the charcoal blazing in its lap.

Smoke rose from a dozen other places along the quarry's edge, where fires burned on stone figures and huge pieces of figures. As Thoth watched, a white fog of steam rolled up from one, accompanied by a mighty hiss and the crack of stone. The men around it put down their water jars and began hoisting into the quarry the fragments of what had been Ma-ke-Re's gigantic, white-crowned head.

Elsewhere, scattered over the vast forecourt, men were working with hammers at countless smaller statues—battering the royal cobras off the foreheads first of all, next gouging out the wide, painted eyes and hacking away the nose and mouth so that the statue could neither see nor breathe, then breaking up the body. Along the causeway, five of the great sphinxes were gone from their bases. Thoth could see the head of one, here, staring at the sky; the leonine hindquarters of another, there, at the foot of the embankment; huge fragments of others jumbled together at the bottom of the quarry. A sweating crew was moving on down the causeway to attack the next one.

Inside every porch and chapel the same was happening to the figures of Ma-ke-Re carved on the walls; it was happening to the hieroglyphs of her name wherever they appeared—not only in Djeser-Djeseru but across the river in Thebes and up and down the length of Egypt from the Delta to Elephant Island, even in the Western Oases and in the farthest mines of the eastern desert.

The seventh giant Osiride statue toppled with a crash amid a cloud of dust and scattering men. The noise vibrated through every nerve in Thoth's taut body. He sensed Rekhmi-re's glance at him, and stiffened the set of his jaw until his face felt like the stone of those broken faces below him in the quarry. One huge face, wearing a fragment of the Double Crown, stared up at him from its sightless eyes, as she had stared up at him in death from the couch where they had found her. It sent the same convulsive shudder through his flesh.

It was unbelievable that she was dead. Unbelievable. Unbelievable. Not until he had hacked every trace of her from every stone in Egypt could he be sure of it.

He tore his eyes from the sightless painted ones and swept a glance eastward, where beyond the emerald fields and the sail-dotted silver of the Nile the buildings of Thebes rose roof on roof, dominated at the north by the Temple of Amon, which was in turn dominated by two towering spikes of stone capped with flashing electrum. Men swarmed on these too. Already a sheathing of blank masonry covered the obelisks to the height of the roof she had torn from her father's columned hall. It would creep higher yet—too high for any inscription to be read, too thick and muffling for her high, hysterically self-justifying voice to penetrate to his ears as he walked by . . . *"O ye people who shall see my monuments in after years . . . do not say this is a lie which I have said; say rather, 'How like her this is! Worthy of her father, Amon . . .'"*

He turned back swiftly to the destruction below him, but suddenly her voice was coming from all directions, sounding through the din of mallets and chisels, through the bursts of hissing steam and the crack of stone—not the shrill hysterical voice now, but the clear, confident one of earlier years. *"You are being wildly fanciful. No harm could come to Egypt from that tiny, wretched village of barbarians . . ." "Postpone the reburial? Of course not. My father must not remain in this place another hour . . ."*

That voice faded too, and despite all he could do another took its place. This one was faint and far-off, from the distant past, and it was accompanied by the vision of a face framed in loose, silken hair—a face both beautiful and gay, yet unknowingly, terribly the same in feature as those set, stony faces in the quarry. The sweet, faint voice was saying gaily, *"Ast! What a sorry state you get your clean* shentis *into by the end of a day . . . Of course I am not angry, little one! Come, I suppose you wish a story too . . ."*

Thoth's muscles were drawing into knots, his throat contracted until he could not swallow. He stared blindly into the dust clouds of destruction, trying not to see a beautiful, soft, beloved face bending over him and laughing.

"My father, I have beaten for thee those who have beaten

494

thee!" he whispered. *"I have beaten for thee those who have beaten thee!"*

"Tjesu, did you speak?"

"Nay," Thoth said harshly. After a moment he added, "Go down there, Rekhmi-re. Keep them working."

Rekhmi-re's footsteps moved quickly down the hillside and faded from hearing. At last the voice of Lady Shesu faded too, and the beautiful, laughing face was replaced by a tired old woman, lying dead in the Double Crown.

Below, the steam clouds continued to rise, the clamor of revenge to sound—and Thoth's hand was wielding every mallet, the force of his whole soul was behind every blow.

But his mind had become a vast, lonely plain, with dust blowing sadly and the wind moaning from one end of the earth to the other, crying, "Oh, a pity, a pity . . ." With an abrupt movement he turned and followed Rekhmi-re down the hill, as the plain widened and widened until the whole world was full of pain and blowing dust and crying wind.

One week after harvest, while destruction still sounded at Djeser-Djeseru, a war galley, built in Nekheb and christened *The Wild Bull,* set out from Thebes and started swiftly northward. After it trailed vessels of every description—merchant ships, Nile boats, barks and barges—carrying ten thousand warriors and seven thousand hastily trained recruits. At Tharu, in the Delta, the army disembarked, assembled into its ranks, and set out by foot and chariot across the borders of Egypt and into the desert.

Nine days afterward—though no one but Men-kheper-Re had believed it could be done—the desert was behind them. They encamped that night at the city of Gaza, on the shore of the Great Green. The day was the 4th of Pakhons, a memorable one for Men-kheper-Re. It had been exactly twenty-two years since Amon had named him Pharaoh in his grandfather's Hall of Praise.

He did not linger to celebrate the anniversary. Early the next morning his troops were on the march again, heading northeast this time—toward Kadesh, and a fortress called Megiddo in the plain of Jezreel.

Epilogue

It was the tenth day of Paophi in the forty-second year of the reign of the Good God Men-kheper-Re. (Really the twentieth year, the people added to themselves—the twentieth year since the Nameless One died—but naturally one took no notice of the period of the Usurper; in the eyes of the gods it had never occurred. When the Tired One had put aside the crown forty-two years ago, Men-hkeper-Re had put it on; Horus had succeeded Osiris, as always. That was all one needed to remember. In truth, who could remember when Men-kheper-Re had not been Pharaoh? Who wanted to remember? It seemed like another world, that far-off time. . . .

It was the tenth day of Paophi, and the flood was over the land, and it was time for Men-kheper-Re to come home. Not for twenty years had the Good God failed to come back to Egypt for the Festival of the High Nile. In the summer he was far away, fighting, conquering, disciplining the Rebellious Ones (not that there were many of those left now) and pushing out the boundaries of the empire until it spread to the earth's very edges; but when the Nile rose and the Dead God returned to Egypt, Men-kheper-Re returned too, and Horus dwelt again among the people.

He will come today or tomorrow, they assured each other. We know he is on the river, the runner said so. The lookout will sight the *Wild Bull* soon. . . .

Their eyes turned for the hundredth time to the top of the highest pylon of the temple, where a figure stood outlined against the sky.

Many eyes watched the lookout—the eyes of slaves and servants who were decorating the royal landing with pennants and lotuses and golden ribbons, the eyes of the Divine Consort Meryet-Re who waited with the princess Meryet-Amon and Crown Prince Amenhotep on the palace roof, and the eyes of a chamberlain posted atop the palace wall, whose responsibility it was to notify Their Excellencies Count Rekhmi-re, Vizier of Egypt, and Amenuser, Prince of Thebes and Steward of the Red

Crown Palace, exactly when the welcoming procession should start.

At last, two hours past midday, the lookout stiffened, peered northward for a long moment, then raised his brazen trumpet to his mouth. Its first notes pealed across the valley; its last ones were drowned in a hubbub of shouting, cheering, and pounding feet as all Thebes poured out of houses, market stalls and workshops, and headed for the riverbanks. At the landing, great plumed fans were lifted into position over the flower-strewn steps; in the Great Court, Rekhmi-re and Amenu exchanged triumphant glances and hurried through the confusion of bearers, chariots, and glittering nobles to their waiting litters—Rekhmi-re limping on the foot nearly severed fifteen years ago in a battle at Arvad. On the palace roof, Mayet stood up eagerly and beckoned to her son and daughter. "Come, hasten!" she said. "He will expect to find us in the garden."

A few moments later all Thebes saw what the lookout had seen—the familiar worn sail and thrusting prow of Pharaoh's warship, the *Wild Bull,* rounding a bend of the river north of Thebes. Amidships they saw the glitter of a golden canopy; under it, they knew from countless other such returns, sat a stocky figure with a fierce, arching nose and granite features, wearing a scarred leather cuirass and the Blue Helmet of Battle on his head.

"Men-kheper-Re! Men-kheper-Re!" they cried, and though they could not see him yet, they held their children up, whispering, "Look well, little one! It is he, it is the god himself—see him sitting there in his divinity! He is thinking of his glory."

Men-kheper-Re was not thinking of his glory. He was watching his inundated land slowly unwind like a scroll before him —saffron desert, glistening fields, turquoise sky—and thinking of a day some forty years ago when a frightened Babylonian boy had first sailed up this river to Thebes. Then, too, crowds had gathered at the water's edge to watch his passing—but for reasons as different from these of today as the Babylonian boy was different from the man who sat here now. Everything was different—Thebes, the river traffic, the very shape and size of Egypt, which he had enlarged until it stretched from the southern Nile

497

to the northern Euphrates. One might almost say the scroll was written in another language.

In many languages, Thoth reflected, ignoring a faint, familiar twinge of uneasiness as he watched a long-necked Phoenician galley on the far side of the river contend for passageway with a Mycenaean trireme and a bark with fantastically embroidered sails from the Islands of the Sea. Forty years ago—indeed, twenty years ago—Egypt had known only Egyptian vessels and Egyptian faces. Now every third ship that sailed up the Nile was of a foreign shape and brought a load of foreign riches; the temple, the palace and the market places overflowed with tapestries and Syrian chariots, with the spices of Punt and the dark beer of Kede, with damascened bronzes and Cretan pottery. One could even see the fringed fabrics of Babylon hanging from a merchant's stall, and knives from faraway Mitanni. The faces on the streets ranged from ebony-black to ivory-white, and spoke a multitude of tongues.

Once and for all, Egypt was entangled with the lands beyond her borders; the old days were as lost as an old man's childhood.

Men-kheper-Re sighed—he did not know why. To avoid asking himself, he brought both his thoughts and his eyes back to the *Wild Bull*. Intef, the royal herald, moved at once to the pavilion's steps.

"Your Majesty has some desire?"

"Nay, nay, I was only thinking . . ." Or perhaps trying not to think, something within Men-kheper-Re added. Walking cautiously, like a man in the dark, sensing the presence of a door he does not wish to open, a destination he does not wish to reach. . . . He went on quickly, "I was thinking that the old ship has probably made her last voyage, Intef."

"*Hai!* She is good for a dozen more."

"Aye—perhaps." Pharaoh smiled briefly. "But I doubt she will have to prove it. I cannot say I am sorry. By Amon, I am fifty-two years old, and in the last twenty years I have fought seventeen campaigns. It is enough. It is enough for anyone."

"It was more than enough for the enemy, I think," Intef remarked.

"Aye. However, just in case—" Men-kheper-Re exchanged a glance with his royal herald. Just in case, he had instructed Intef to see to it that the Phoenician coast towns—long Egypt's possessions—were fully stocked with every necessity of war and ready at any moment for his return. If the occasion arose, they both knew there would be an eighteenth campaign, and it would be as efficient as all the rest.

He did not think the occasion would arise—not now. Kadesh was finally his.

Kadesh was his. Men-kheper-Re drew a long breath, savoring the almost incredible truth. "Go, Intef," he said. "Find one of those musicians and tell him to sing of Egypt—of home. I think we can all stay home at last."

At last—after two long decades of war and foreign lands. Thoth let his mind wander back, glad to find a path of thought down which he could walk without need of caution. Seventeen campaigns—and both the first and the last of them had been fought for Kadesh. It was bitter to remember that he might have crushed it in the first battle, the first hour of fighting, had it not been for his own soldiers. He had surprised the enemy that long-ago day at Megiddo, coming down through the narrow Aruna Pass where they had never dreamed he would dare expose his troops. The result was that the hordes allied against him had scattered at the first charge, and fled across the plain of Jezreel to the fortress-city in its midst, where their terrified people pulled them up over the walls by ropes of clothing hastily knotted together. If it had not been so crucial a moment it would have been comical—he could still see those walls, alive with frantically kicking heels, strung with ropes of knotted cloaks and undergarments. However, his own soldiers had been blind to all but the riches abandoned on the plain—chariots, horses, rich armor and weapons. They had stopped to loot, in spite of all he could do.

"Had you afterwards captured this city," he had raged at them later, "I would have given a rich offering to the gods this day, because every chief of every country that has revolted is within it; it is the capture of a thousand cities, this capture of Megiddo!"

After that, of course, they had come to their senses and captured it—surrounded it, snared it in a wooden enclosure and starved it into submission. Many of the rebel chieftains filed out of it at last and gave him all their possessions and pled for mercy, which they received. But the king of Kadesh had already escaped to the north. In the course of that first campaign and the fifteen that followed it, Men-kheper-Re had conquered everything else between the Nile and the Euphrates; but even a conquered Asia continued to wriggle like a basketful of snakes as long as the king of Kadesh was alive to poke them. In the end he had been forced to come back and crush Kadesh, too, or go on campaigning until he died.

On what little things did great things depend! Twenty years of warfare might have been avoided that day at Megiddo, and the chance was missed because his soldiers could not resist the gold. They could resist it now, he reflected grimly. His own hand struck down those who did not. His—or Tjah's.

He glanced toward the starboard gunwale, where Tjah stood talking to one of the standard bearers. Twenty years of battle had transformed his lithe young Captain of Archers into a gnarled old General of All the Armies. Tjah was tough as rawhide, and about as beautiful, and his curving mouth had set flat and hard; but his loyalty to Men-kheper-Re and his hatred of the king of Kadesh had only deepened with the years. Certainly he was as alert as ever. In plain truth, if it had not been for Tjah, Kadesh might still be free today.

Thoth's eyes moved upward to a rippling black horse-tail that hung from one corner of the canopy—another small thing on which great things had depended. Twenty years of warfare had again hung in the balance just four weeks ago, when the gates of hard-pressed Kadesh had suddenly opened and that black mare had come galloping out, straight for the chariotry of Pharaoh. A mare in season—among all his stallions! Thoth turned cold again at the thought of what might have happened, but at the same time he could not restrain the smile that tugged at the corners of his mouth. The strategy was as simple as it was devastating. A worthy adversary, the king of Kadesh; in twenty years one could not help learning to admire him. That last stroke of brilliance might have saved his neck and his city for another year—but for Tjah. How Tjah had managed to catch that frightened mare—on foot!—was a miracle nobody could explain. But somehow he had intercepted her and killed her. Kadesh had fallen two days later—and now, thanks to that black horse-tail swaying from the canopy, Pharaoh could come home, out of the desert and the jagged mountains and all foreign places, into Egypt.

There was a stir beyond the edge of the pavilion, and presently the sound of lute and harp, and a clear male voice:

> *"Praise to thee, O Nile,*
> *Lord of fish, that maketh the waterfowl to go upstream!*
> *When he riseth, the land is in exultation,*
> *Every jaw laughs and every tooth is revealed . . ."*

The musicians had come to sing of home. Thoth listened, and his eye moved gratefully over the green land, crosshatched with its silver canals. Home. Egypt.

Suddenly his mind was full of Babylon, instead, and of the old man he had seen last night who had brought it into his head. Or was it sailing up to Thebes again that had brought it back so clearly? One could not journey from those lands to this one without feeling the contrast, as he had felt it first as a boy of eleven. In those other lands life was as intemperate as the landscape—anxious, raw, rent always by the conviction of disaster. Here it was serene as the flat green fields and the rhythm of the Nile.

On the surface, anyway, Thoth reflected.

He ran his eye over the joyful faces on the riverbanks, over the assured and proud ones on the deck around him, and—as always—he found himself wondering. How deep did the serenity go?

> *"Bringer of nourishment,"*

sang the clear untroubled voice.

> *"Plenteous of sustenance,*
> *Thou art verdant, thou art verdant!*
> *O Nile, thou art verdant . . ."*

Aye, Pharaoh thought, the river is verdant. Food is plentiful. The sun is unchanging. Ma'at has never been put to confusion. Every man journeys to a paradise just lik eEgypt when life is done. Aye, aye, aye. Look at these confident ones around me— it is all on their faces. Then why do they fill their tombs with magic, scratch spells on every rock, swear long oaths on the sides of their coffins listing all the things they have not done? Why do they make up poems quite different from this one?

In silent antiphony to the singer's confident refrain, the Song of the Harper began to whisper in Thoth's mind.

"I have heard all that happened to my forefathers—
Their houses have fallen to ruins, their market places are no more.
Lo! what the priests in panther's skin strew on the ground,
What they place on the table of sacrifice,
To what purpose is it?
No man who has gone away
Has ever returned to tell of how he fares there . . ."

That was a song of Egypt too, though a despair that seemed pure Babylonian breathed from every line. There, Thoth mused, speaks the trembling mortal man beneath the confident face. Like my father—who was feared and hated for saying it aloud—even the Egyptian does not *know*. His mouth smiles with assurance, his heart trembles with questions; he produces spells and tales to give meaning to the world. But at bottom he suspects there is no meaning, no final answer, no gods and no life beyond here and now.

Thoth stared straight ahead of him for a moment, fingering the ivory hawk's heads on the arms of his chair. And I? he asked himself presently. Do I know? Any more than I did twenty or even forty years ago? Fifty years ago—ah, then I knew; I was a child, in the garden. But since I left it I have found out nothing, except that there is a mystery in the sky and one in my wrist, both beyond my understanding. I am as ignorant as all the rest, I have never found my answer. Men simply lift up their ignorance and their need to worship, and mold a golden image around the two, and call the image by a multitude of names. I call it Amon, since I am Pharaoh and must call it something.

Men-kheper-Re sighed once more, caught himself at it, and shifted impatiently in his chair, scowling because the old wound in his left leg had given a nasty twinge.

I think too much, he thought. The Good God is like his father.

His own sourness made him smile. Crochety old man you've become, he told himself. Aye, you're getting old, that's why you moon about past times, and remember Babylon as clear as Egypt. Today is today; look around you, think about your victories, and the crowd cheering. . . .

The crowds had increased now, along the edge of the river;

n the deck, the soldiers of the Personal Guard were beginning
o shift into their formal array. Thoth straightened and looked
round him. The *Wild Bull* had left the outskirts behind and was
n the city proper; there was the Temple of Amon, moving slowly
ast on the left.

Instantly his eyes flew, as though captured and drawn there,
o the twin points of electrum coruscating against the sky. He
glanced sharply at the shafts of the obelisks, then turned away,
mollified. The workmen had replaced that piece of masonry
sheathing which had fallen away last year. He could not see a
single inscription, or a foot of carving. He would not be reminded
of her this time—he need not even think of his oldest enemy.

Enemy? he thought. She helped to make you what you are.
She was the hottest of the fires that forged you, the heaviest of
the hammers that beat you into shape. Who were you, what
were you, before you hated her? In his mind sounded the echo
of a childish voice: *I am Mayet.* Aye, he told himself, you were
Thoth. But—admit it—you were not yet Men-kheper-Re.

"Intef!" he grunted, suddenly irascible.

"Aye, Your Majesty." Intef came hurrying to the pavilion.

"Bring beer. I've the dust of Kadesh in my throat yet. And
have them adjust those fans."

"At once, Your Majesty."

Men-kheper-Re turned away from the Temple of Amon, being
careful of the leg, and examined the river in the other direction.
But his thoughts refused to change.

For that matter, who and what is Men-kheper-Re? he asked
himself. Do you know yet?

A wry smile dragged down the corners of his mouth as he remembered himself, at seventeen or eighteen, suffering because he
did not know who he was. What a young fool he had been, to
think he could know, at that age. *Who am I?* It was a thing men
spent their lives defining. That was what you did with your life
—discovered who you were . . . and many people never did
find out. He wondered if *she* had—at the very end, when she put
down the goblet and crossed her hands on her breast. No doubt
she thought she had known all along: *I am a great woman; a
great king* . . . Thoth felt tired suddenly. No doubt, in essence,
she was right. Though she had had to steal her crown, usurp
her throne, turn her face forever from the face of truth—*a great*

503

woman, a great king. After twenty years, with his anger burned to ashes, he could admit it.

He removed his eyes from what he had left of her desert temple and tried hard to think of something else—the measure of the inundation, the state of the empire.

Ah, the state of the empire. Now that was something to think about, something of the present, not the past. In the past—even the recent past of his own youth—there had been no such thing as an empire. There had been only conquered cities, held by force for the sake of their tribute. Incredible shortsightedness! His way was better. All his plans were beginning to mature and prove themselves now: amnesty to the conquered—Egyptianization of the foreign princes—aye, the plan was working, just as he had outlined it to Rekhmi-re years ago. Today everything was Egypt, from southern Nubia to northern Naharin, a single empire under Pharaoh's protection as well as his command. Never had Egypt—or Amon—been so rich. Why, the priesthoods were like assemblages of kings.

The thought was like a sudden, foot-bruising rock heaving up in the smooth path of his reflections. He backed away hastily. Not kings, of course, he thought. But they are rich . .

They were almost too rich. And there were almost too many of them—had to be, to manage the expanding temples, to cope with the swollen floods of revenue.

"Your Majesty—?"

Thoth turned in relief. It was Intef with the beer, dark Kede beer in a turquoise goblet made in the new way, in two sections —a bowl and a little stand into which it fitted. Thoth welcomed the interruption and searched his mind for some way to prolong it. There was, he remembered, something he must mention before the fleet reached the docks and the captives scattered far and wide into their new lives of servitude.

"Intef—stay a moment. Do you recall the old man we saw last night when My Majesty inspected the prison ships?"

"The one you spoke to, Majesty? The man of Tunip?"

"Aye, that one."

"I remember him. He is on the fifth ship, *Shield of the Good God,* among the captives of Naharin."

"Good. Take him off that ship as soon as we moor, and bring him to the palace."

504

"Aye, Your Majesty." Intef hesitated, then presumed on his twenty years' standing as royal friend and ventured a question. "The prisoner has displeased Your Majesty in some way?"

"Nay, he has not displeased me," Thoth said. He waited a moment, then relented. Curiosity was Intef's only fault, as far as he had been able to discover. He smiled at his royal herald, who through seventeen long campaigns had never failed to have the royal tent pitched or a captured palace prepared for occupancy and stocked with every luxury of home, when his Pharaoh arrived at the end of a long day's march. "I want to make certain his master is a good one, Intef," Thoth said. "He is a wise old man."

And he reminded me a little of Ahmose, he added to himself as Intef left him. Or perhaps only of all wise old men.

He lifted the bowl of his goblet and sipped the cold beer, thinking of the brief and curious conversation with the old Tunipian. He had reminded him of Inatsil, too—that was why he had been thinking of Babylon all day. He would never have noticed one prisoner sitting there in his fetters among the others if this one had not had that drooping, houndlike cast to his features which brought back the Scribe's School and the smell of clay as if he had left it only yesterday. He had stopped, gazing at the old man through a haze of memories, and on an impulse spoke to him in Babylonian.

"What is your name, old one?"

The old man lifted his head and smiled slowly at hearing a familiar tongue, but when he answered, it was with an Egyptian word.

"*Seqer-ankh,* Master."

Captive.

"Your father gave you another name," Thoth said.

"Aye, since men cannot read the future. He called me Ilishmiani."

My-god-has-heard-my-prayer. It was a Babylonian name.

"Your father was a man of Babylon, then, not of Tunip."

The old man shrugged. "Of this place, of that place—of no place. Am I of Tunip now? He was a man. It is all one can say."

His eyes were ancient and accepting, and his words caused Kadesh and the recent victories and forty years to dissolve from

505

Pharaoh's mind as if they had never been. Thoth could see only a lonely child sailing up to Thebes in his foreign fringes.

"I know it is hard, old one," he said quietly. "To begin life anew, among strangers in a strange land. I am sorry for you."

"All men are strangers to each other, Master, is it not so?" The old man gave another of his accepting shrugs, and smiled as if he would comfort Pharaoh, not himself. "I shall feel no lonelier in Egypt than I did in Tunip, among my sons."

So he knew that too. Perhaps, thought Men-kheper-Re as he set his goblet on its stand, all men came to know it, in the end.

His eyes strayed back to the receding columns of Djeser-Djeseru, and his thoughts to the broken images of a face he had not forgotten in twenty years, though he had wiped all trace of it from Egypt. They had been strangers to each other too, she and he, from beginning to end—two hard, unyielding shapes like chisel and stone, striking sparks and chips from each other without ceasing. The chisel had proved harder; and now the old, simple days were gone forever, and the priests were too rich and too many, and Egypt was filled with foreign faces and foreign ways—as if a dam had been torn down and the sea and the Nile were washing back and forth, mingling their waters past all separating.

But this is good, Men-kheper-Re told himself uneasily. At least, inevitable. The world is there—once we know that, we cannot go back to ignorance and the old, simple days, however peaceful, however good they were.

He wished he knew, precisely, what the new days would be like, for he had brought them upon Egypt. Nay—not I alone, he thought. His hand had torn the dam down, but she had helped to shape that hand, to shape his nature. No doubt the Tired One had shaped hers before that, by the same constant friction. It was all inevitable . . . For a moment Thoth wondered what form events would have taken if the three of them had been other than they were, had moved in different ways; then he gave it up. No man could solve that riddle. Mortals were mortals, they rubbed and chafed and struck against each other willy-nilly. . . .

A picture came into his mind of the barrel of gems revolving in Murashu's little workshop, long ago in Babylon.

It is like that, he thought. The friction against each other, that is what shapes us, and we cannot help it. Some come round and

rilliant from the barrel, and some take fantastic, crippled forms,
nd some are ground to powder and are lost. It depends on how
ard a core there is inside.

And how hard a core had Egypt?

He was suddenly facing that door he had not wanted to open;
watching it swing wide, trying to draw back.

The priests. . . .

There was no drawing back now. He had seen the flaw in the
core, and cruel logic forced him on. The more foreign revenue
streamed into Egypt, the more swollen the priesthoods and their
temples would become. And the larger and more powerful they
became, the more vital the foreign revenue would be to their support. . . . And what if someday a weak or careless Pharaoh
should come to rule his empire—one who did not know how hard
it had been won, who did not remember the bearded Hyksos, or
the king of Kadesh? If there should be two such Pharaohs in a
row—perhaps three or four? If the stream of foreign tribute into
the temples should dwindle—and then cease? He tried to imagine the priesthoods, fat with a century of living like kings,
consenting to live like priests again; but he could not. Riches to
keep them fat and their storerooms overflowing would have to
come from somewhere—if not from the empire, then from
Egypt's own lifeblood. . . .

The tribute must not cease! he thought. It will not. I have
made it safe forever.

Forever? Nothing lasted forever. Remember the garden,
the face of Ahmose, the ziggurat, the pattern of three white
sails—all had vanished, one by one. When he was no more than
twelve years old he had known already that all things pass away,
that nothing is permanent except impermanence and change.

Gods, what have I done to Egypt? he thought. I meant only
to do good—I have done good. Have I somehow done evil, too?

Do not think about it, he told himself, unable to think of
anything else. You have done what you had to do, you could
not do otherwise. It was all inevitable.

Inevitable. Aye, no doubt. Friction—mortals chafing against
each other—Kadesh rebelling—the old, lost days and ways impossible to regain—all true. Perhaps since the hour the first
Hyksos chariot rolled into Egypt every event, every act of
every Pharaoh, had been pointing toward this day, and toward a

future unforeseeable, unpreventable. They, as much as he, had done it. . . .

But whose hand had torn away the dam? Whose hand, meaning only to bring life, had come down, loving, unwitting, fatal, upon the breast of Egypt? Men-kheper-Re's.

Nonsense, he thought swiftly. Men cannot read the future. I cannot know, I may be wrong.

But if he were right?

He finished his beer and set the goblet on its stand with a crash, and tried again to think of Kadesh, and his victory. But an old and well-known picture was forming in his mind, of a vast lonely plain, filled with blowing dust and a crying wind.

The *Wild Bull* bumped gently against the royal landing. The crowd yelled and leaped, gold-decked dignitaries stepped forward, great plumed fans were lifted over the gangplank. Across it, presently, walked a stocky, indomitable figure with a fierce nose and a battle-worn blue helmet—to half the world, the very shape and form of kingship.

"Look, little one!" whispered a mother as she held her little girl high to see the king. "Look at the Strong Bull! See him there —it is the Good God, it is Men-kheper-Re!"

"Aye, I see him!" said the child. After a moment she added softly, "He looks tired."

AUTHOR'S NOTE

Hatshepsut never lay in her fine tomb. Her body has never been discovered; but one of her obelisks still stands near the temple of Karnak. The masonry with which the vengeful Thutmose sought to hide it has long since fallen away, revealing its beauty and her greatness. Her broken statues have been painstakingly dug out of the old quarry by Egyptologists, laboriously fitted together and restored. Her temple, even in ruins, remains the most beautiful building in Egypt, showing a remarkably Greek feeling for proportions and the use of the column, many centuries before there was a Greece.

As for Senmut, he won his last wager with the gods. Archaeologists, after puzzling over dozens of chiseled-out patches on the walls of those dark little shrines at Djeser-Djeseru, discovered four carvings which the ancient workmen had overlooked. All were obviously identical with those which had been erased. In those four shrines Senmut still kneels, triumphantly undisturbed throughout thirty-five centuries, paying homage to his gods and reveling in the prerogatives of a king.